Penguin Books
Girl, 20

Kingsley Amis, who was born in Clapham in 1922,
was educated at the City of London School and St
John's College, Oxford. At the age of eleven he
embarked on a blank-verse miniature epic at the
instigation of a preparatory school master, and he has
been writing verse ever since. Until the age of
twenty-four, however, he remarks: 'I was in all
departments of writing *abnormally unpromising*.' With
James Michie he edited *Oxford Poetry 1949*. Until 1963
he was a university teacher of English; he is a keen
science-fiction addict, an admirer of 'white jazz' of
the thirties, and the author of frequent articles and
reviews in most of the leading papers and periodicals.
His novels include *Lucky Jim* (1954), *That Uncertain
Feeling* (1955), *I Like It Here* (1958), *Take a Girl Like
You* (1960), *One Fat Englishman* (1963), *The Anti-Death
League* (1966) and *I Want It Now* (1968). Of his other
fiction, *My Enemy's Enemy* (1962) was a book of short
stories, he wrote *The Egyptologists* (1965) with Robert
Conquest, and *Colonel Sun* (1968) was published under
a pseudonym. *A Frame of Mind* (1953), *A Case of
Samples* (1956) and *A Look Around the Estate* (1967)
are the titles of his books of poetry, and he is also
the author of *New Maps of Hell* (1960 – a survey of
science fiction) and *The James Bond Dossier* (1965),
which he terms 'belles lettres'. Later publications
include *The Green Man* (1969), *Girl, 20* (1971), *On
Drink* (1972), *The Riverside Villas Murder* (1973),
Ending Up (1974), *Rudyard Kipling and his World* (1975),
The Alteration (1976, Winner of the John W.
Campbell Memorial Award), *The Faber Popular
Reciter* (edited; 1978), *The New Oxford Book of Light
Verse* (edited; 1978), *Jake's Thing* (1978) and *Collected
Poems* (1979). Kingsley Amis has two sons and a
daughter.

Kingsley Amis

Girl, 20

Penguin Books

Penguin Books Ltd, Harmondsworth, Middlesex, England
Penguin Books, 625 Madison Avenue, New York, New York 10022,
U.S.A.
Penguin Books Australia Ltd, Ringwood, Victoria, Australia
Penguin Books Canada Ltd, 2801 John Street, Markham, Ontario, Canada
L3R 1B4
Penguin Books (N.Z.) Ltd, 182-190 Wairau Road, Auckland 10,
New Zealand

First published by Jonathan Cape 1971
Published in Penguin Books 1980

Set, printed and bound in Great Britain by
Cox & Wyman Ltd, Reading
Set in Monotype Garamond

To Mary and Mike Keeley

Contents

'Is this chap really as good as you say?' asked Harold Meers.

'Well yes. He may be even better. In the sense that it's a bit early to tell. At his stage you can't be sure whether –'

'You mean technique and that sort of thing.'

'More than that,' I said. 'It's . . . He understands the music he plays. You'll see there that I've –'

'I should have thought they all did that.'

'They all don't, believe me.'

'By definition.' Harold added suddenly, as if in simple wonderment, 'He's from East Germany.'

'That's it.'

'One of the most backward and corrupt and tyrannical regimes in the world. Outside black Africa, of course.'

'No doubt. It hasn't stopped Kohler being a cracking good pianist. Perhaps it should have done, but it hasn't.'

'As you know, I had reservations about running a music column in the first place. People don't go to concerts any more, they buy records. All part of the stay-at-home culture. We deal with them already. And the whole thing goes on here, anyway. Manchester. Birmingham. Once in a blue moon. You've heard me say this isn't a London newspaper, it's a national newspaper. Is he a Jew?'

Harold said all this at his usual regular pace and level pitch, his small hands (joined on to small arms and by way of them to small shoulders) loose and palm upwards on his desk, the weak sunshine gleaming tranquilly on his nearly bald head. His style of discourse, with the mild strain it laid on his hearer's attention and powers of recall, was as usual too. One item, indeed, had strained my lot to breaking-point. I had not known that he had had reservations about my having become, a few months previously, the paper's music critic, or rather musical-events reporter. He had told me then that this innovation, dreamed up by him alone as the first blow in a campaign to raise cultural standards in journalism generally, had been fought through by him alone in the teeth of opposition from his proprietor, his features editor and perhaps the liftman. Facing him now in his large, modern and shabby office, I answered his question truthfully.

'I don't know,' I said.

'Do we need to advertise these bastards? What about the do where there was that dust-up, you know, that Bolivian song-and-dance lot last Friday? People read about the hooligans busting in and being arrested and so on, but what about the actual stuff? A bit less esoteric than Telemann and Prokofiev and who's this other chap?'

'There was Beethoven too. I heard the Bolivians rehearsing, and I didn't think they really –'

'A critic ought to go easy with his superlatives.' Harold dropped his lustrous brown eyes to my copy that lay before him, and for a moment I thought he was reading it. 'We didn't put politics into art,' he went on very soon. 'They did. You do realize, don't you, that this chap's only allowed abroad because he's a loyal and trusted servant of that bloody awful regime? A walking advertisement for it?'

'Whether I do or I don't doesn't come into what I'm supposed to be at. The job you hired me for was to cover the most important musical events, and important judged by musical standards, not by any . . .'

One of Harold's telephones had started an enfeebled rattling, and he picked it up with one small hand while waving me down with the other.

'Yes,' he said on a high note. 'Yes. Who? Get her number.' He replaced the telephone and said to me, 'All right, what do you feel about just scrubbing where he comes from?'

'Just saying he's German, you mean?'

'Not saying he's anything. We're not handing out publicity material.'

'But Harold, if you're against the Eastern lot, then surely you –'

'All right,' he said again, neither impatiently nor coaxingly, in fact in not much of a way at all, 'all right. We'll leave it. But, as I say, you must let up a little on these technical terms. Remember, you're not writing for the profession.'

'Apart from one reference to a slow movement and another to a theme and variations, which ought to be elementary enough even for –'

'Fine. Give Features a ring about five thirty as usual, would you, in case we have to lose an inch or so? Right. That call was for you.'

'Who was it?'

'Kitty Vandersomething. Not Mrs Sir Roy Vandervane?'

'Sounds like it.'

'He must be worse than ever with that knighthood. Services to music, Services to the Prime Minister's backside more like.'

'He's better than that, Harold.'

'Yes, you used to work for him, didn't you?'

'For his orchestra.'

'Fine. See you.'

Along the corridor in Features I got the switchboard to put me through to the number Kitty had left there, realizing or remembering now that the Vandervanes had moved some miles north of Hampstead, where I had last visited them a year or more earlier, to a reputedly rather grand establishment on the fringes of the Hertfordshire countryside. After half a minute of ringing tone the distant receiver was lifted, but at first nobody addressed me. Instead, I heard a wordless yelling, loud but some way from the instrument, and a man's muffled voice saying he would go mad if that noise were not stopped. When the yelling had a little receded, I got my turn.

'Hallo, yes, who is it, please?' asked the same man's voice crossly. It sounded coloured.

'This is Douglas Yandell. Lady Vandervane wanted to speak to me.'

There followed no indication whether these facts had been absorbed, but at the end of another interval, during which the yelling changed to a vague shouting that faded out, Kitty came on the line.

'Is that you, Douglas?'

'Yes, Kitty.'

'Oh, thank God, thank *God* you're safe, my darling, my love, and I can start to live my life again' would not really have been an excessively emotional follow-up to the tone of heroically controlled hysteria in her opening question. But I knew Kitty always talked at that level, and all she actually said, with a mixture of dignified reprobation and a sorrow too deep for any mere words to be adequate, was, 'It seems ages since we saw you.'

I agreed, and in no time at all, without any formalistic nonsense about how I might have been intending to spend the rest of my day, I was listening to a fully researched account of how to get from where I was to where she was. She said she absolutely did most desperately need to see me, meaning she wanted to see me and took it for granted that I would come belting up to be seen by her as soon as so informed. Well, presumably there was the chance of seeing Roy as well.

'Is Roy round the place?' I asked as soon as I could.

'No, he's not, not at the moment. Actually, it was . . .' – I had no trouble visualizing the dignified furtiveness of her glance over her shoulder – 'it's him I so terribly urgently have to see you about. He's getting ready for another of his goes, Douglas. He may even have started.'

'Has he told you?'

'I just know.'

'Not the pants again?'

'*Yes.* How incredible of you to remember.'

'I've never forgotten.'

Who could? Though no stinker, Roy had never been one of the most fanatically cleanly of men except when building up to, or embarked on at any rate the pristine stage of, one of his 'goes', as Kitty called his affairs. Over the period since their marriage in 1961, she had learnt to recognize this situation by the stockpiling of pants in his underclothes drawer. Sudden rapid diminution of the pile, accompanied by an equally sudden flurry of oddly timed off-the-premises interviews with foreign journalists, abortive get-togethers with recording-company executives, etc., was the signal that the go was off the ground. Kitty had told me this years before, when I was still working as secretary of the orchestra of which Roy was then resident conductor. On ordinary male-trade-union grounds, I had promptly warned him about this dead give-away, but it seemed that he, unlike myself, had forgotten. Or had he? How could he have?

I had been considering matters while I listened and talked. It was exactly midday. What I had planned was a walk up Fleet Street for a couple of smoked-salmon sandwiches and glasses of hock at El Vino, a nice noisy afternoon in the flat going through some of the new discs I had to review in *The Record-Player*, an early dinner at Biagi's and a trip to the South Bank for a rather routine Bach-Handel concert. And there was always, or rather never, my book on Weber to be hauled past the Early Years phase. But I experienced no real inner struggle. Curiosity, always a powerful motive in matters Vandervanean, won hands down, though I had the sense not to indulge it for the moment. Asking Kitty over the telephone how I could help would have earned me twenty minutes of impassioned and impermeable hints. I said I would come straight away and added, out of more curiosity,

'How did you know where to find me?'

'Oh, that was Gilbert. He's marvellous at things like that.'

'Who's Gilbert?'

'You'll see.'

I was turning to go when the features editor, a fat man called Coates with a terrible cough, said to me,

'How was the great man?'

'Don't you know?'

'Sure I know. I was just wondering how you found him.'

I thought for a moment. 'What word would you use to describe being very decent about not paying attention to anything and not caring about nobody being any good?'

'I'd settle for shitty, but then I've got a simple mind. Did he cut you?'

'Not yet. He turned political again.'

Coates drew at his cigarette and coughed terribly. He seemed unaware of any link between these two actions. When he had finished coughing he said,

'Can't you get the Greek colonels to form a symphony orchestra and come over? It'd kill him. See you next week, if I'm spared.'

I took an 11 bus along the Strand and got on to the North-Western Line. As the train clattered out of the tunnel beyond Golders Green, and the April sunshine, stronger now, lit up an arbitrary mixture of cut-back greenery and what looked like emergency housing, I pondered Roy's goes.

The current crop of them must have started about four years after his marriage, itself product of an ancient go, for it had followed upon his divorce by a first wife. On my last meeting with Kitty, she had said that they were getting worse, in the sense that the girls seemed younger and more awful each time and Roy's involvement became successively deeper, and I had felt she was right. At that stage he had just come back from an actual week-end – the first such since their marriage – spent with somebody who called herself an actress and singer, but had never been seen or heard performing in either capacity. Kitty had said that she lived in acute hourly dread of some sort of final walk-out, and that she was plunged in despair, and I would have believed her easily if all her worries were not represented as acute dreads, and the tardy arrival of her cleaning lady did not regularly plunge her into despair. Anyway, I felt I could understand how Kitty, at forty-six or seven, must feel, and could not understand why Roy, at nearly fifty-four (twenty years my senior to within a week), should have to grow sillier as he grew older, except that his growing wiser would have been unbelievable.

The train stopped at the end of the line, and I and not many other people got out. Following instructions, I telephoned from a box near the station entrance and gave some either female or effeminate person the news that I had arrived. I was told to start walking and to expect to be picked up by a car. Asked what I looked like, I said – quite truthfully – that I was six foot three with red hair and glasses. I started walking, first up a stiff slope and then down a suburban road, past a garden with an artificial pond and a lot of painted plaster ducks in it.

Presently a large, new-looking car approached and pulled up rather violently alongside me. I saw that its driver was a young black man, conventionally dressed in dark jacket, white shirt and striped tie, and knew at once that this was Gilbert, as well as being the owner of the voice I had first heard over the telephone. I climbed in beside him. Without looking at me or answering my greeting, he turned the car round and drove off, accelerating fiercely.

'What a nice car,' I said. 'Is it yours?'

'You think a stupid nigger could never make the bread to buy himself a status symbol like this.'

'Well, since you mention it, it would be remarkable, certainly.'

'It's Roy's car, if you've got to know.'

'He is doing nicely for himself.'

We turned off, climbed a long hill and emerged into an impressive thoroughfare with a wood and then a common on one side and infrequent large houses on the other.

'Where do you come from?' I asked.

'London.'

'Oh, I see.'

'You don't care anyway.'

A pond, a real one this time, came into view on the common, and the car pulled off the road at one end of a considerable dwelling with plaster urns and large rhododendron bushes in front of it. I remembered Roy telling me he had got the place for a song: yes, a song with mixed choir, double orchestra, brass band and organ. Then I realized that the car had stopped in front of some blue-painted wooden gates, and that my companion was sitting motionless beside me.

'Would you like me to open those?'

'If you think it won't soil your fine hands.'

'I'll risk it.'

I opened the gates and walked into a paved courtyard adorned with small trees in a sickly or dead condition. As I did so, a ferocious barking, diversified at times with a kind of slipping-ratchet effect, broke out within the house. I recognized the voice of the Furry Barrel, the Vandervanes' red cavalier-spaniel bitch. I had always thought it slightly odd that someone with Roy's political views should tolerate, let alone adore, as he did, such a reactionary little dog: authoritarian, hierarchical, snobbish, with strong views on the primacy of the family, the maintenance of order, the avoidance of change, the sanctity of private property and, as I was soon to discover, the preservation of barriers between the races.

The immediate focus of this last prejudice had driven the car in at speed and stopped it as if he had noticed a crevasse a yard in front. He slammed his door, came up to me and said,

'You are an imperialist racist fascist.'

'But how on earth did you know?'

He referred to my job on the newspaper whose offices I had recently left.

'What about it?'

'It's a white supremacist colonialist organization.'

'Of course, but I'm not an employee of theirs, I just do regular pieces for them. And colonialist music is rather hard to –'

'While you're still working on behalf of such an organization, you must expect yourself to be called a fascist and so on.'

'Yes, I suppose I'll just have to.'

Despite what he had been saying, Gilbert's tone had so far been remarkably free of hostility. His last remark, in particular, seemed to have been intended as a piece of moral suasion. But his face, which I now noticed was of European rather than African cast, and his voice, pleasing in the abstract, turned quite angry when he said,

'Don't you think that's a bloody serious accusation, to call you a fascist?'

'No I don't. Nor a communist or a bourgeois or anything else. I just don't care about any of that, you see.'

He looked at me in pure amazement. 'But these are some of the great issues of our time.'

'Of your time, you mean. The great issue of my time is me

and my interests, chiefly musical. Can we go indoors now?'

With Gilbert following in defeated silence, I went through a glass porch of recent addition where there were a lot of very old coats on an old coat-stand and a lot of empty whisky - and wine-bottles. A further door gave on to a passage. I saw a near and a distant staircase and, fixed to the wall, an empty Perspex box labelled 'Anti-apartheid Fund'. Preceded, then accompanied, by tremendous barking and growling, the Furry Barrel pattered round a corner and danced about in our way. I bent over her, noting that she had grown still more like a furry barrel (with appendages) since our last meeting. She either recognized me or saw that I was admissible under her pass laws, for she moved on to Gilbert, showing a tooth or two. I could have told him that although her bark might be bad her bite was non-existent, but, no doubt still reeling under my revelations of a moment before, he seemed a good deal daunted by her. At this point Kitty appeared, greeted me and drove the dog away out of sight more or less simultaneously. We entered a drawing-room with a large bow-window at the farther end and Roy's splendid old Schwander-action concert Blüthner slightly off centre. A young man and a girl were sitting on a couch muttering together. He looked up at my entry, jerked his head and neck in salutation or suppression of a belch, and looked down again, but not before I had recognized him as Roy's twenty-or-so-year-old son Christopher. The girl, who was dressed like – rather than as, I suppose – a Victorian governess, kept her face lowered.

'Christopher, you remember Douglas Yandell,' said Kitty. 'Douglas, this is Ruth Ericson.'

This time there was no doubt about it: the lad distinctly nodded. The girl glanced at him, me and him again in what might have been sleepy consternation. Kitty's demeanour overflowed with mute appeal to me not to despise them utterly on such brief exposure.

'Hallo,' I said. 'How's Northampton?' I alluded to the university there, impressed at having performed the feat of recall needed.

'Oh, you know, usual crap. Nothing really gives.'

'What are you reading?'

'I'm doing sociology, politics, economics and sociology. I mean anthropology.'

'Ah. Sounds a pretty, uh, all-embracing course.' I battled to keep out of my voice the senile tremolo I imagined the pair were willing me to put into it. 'Are you there too?'

Christopher answered the question I had put to Ruth Ericson. 'No,' he said.

'I see.'

'Darling, if you're going to show Ruth the garden before lunch I really do think you ought to start soon,' said Kitty, smiling and blinking.

'Soon, yeah.'

The two resumed their muttering. Kitty drew me over to the window, from which there was a view of descending lawns, a sunlit wall with trees fastened to it, and some much bigger trees, cedars of different types, farther down. Much farther still were the roofs of the town, looking rather serious over the distant treetops, as if someone in particular had once been beheaded outside its church or unique glassware formerly made there. Nearby, some croquet debris was lying about.

'Where's Gilbert?' I asked idly.

'He doesn't really mean all that, you know,' said Kitty, illuminating the truth that not all types of egotist are unobservant. 'He feels he has to say things. His friends go on at him so if he doesn't. The white ones more than the black ones. He's terribly nice when you get to know him.'

'Oh, good.'

'He'll have gone back up to Penny and Ashley. They're absolutely marvellous with him, both of them.'

I retained a very clear picture of Penny, Roy's other and elder child by his first marriage; indeed, if possessed of the least graphic skill I could that moment have dashed off a rough scale-drawing of the outward semblance of her breasts, which I had once unsuccessfully tried to fondle in a taxi between a concert of Roy's and the subsequent party at Hampstead. Ashley Vandervane was an altogether different case, the comparatively recent joint issue of Roy and Kitty, whom I had barely seen at any time and had quite forgotten about. I tried to conceal this.

'He's what, he must be four now?'

'Just turned six.' She gazed at me with rather too rich a mixture of emotions, so that I hardly knew whether she regarded her only child with pride-plus-grateful-humility or with apologetic horror. Then she said very eagerly, 'Would you like to see the house?'

'Later on, perhaps,' I said, in the hope of avoiding such an ordeal. 'But it, uh, it looks jolly nice. Must cost a packet to run, though.'

'We're managing. You know, Douglas, it's quite frightening how much Roy earns now. He's really arrived. Oh, we know he's had the respect of the musical world for years and years, but these days he's a national figure, in the top bracket. And without lowering his artistic standards.'

At this opportune point, the couple on the couch, probably feeling that enough time had elapsed for them not to be thought to be leaving because they had been asked to leave, left. Kitty at once turned an overmasteringly urgent face on me, but switched it off again as fast and told me to have a drink. When I demurred, she pleaded that she must have a drink herself to talk to me properly and could not drink alone, or should not, or would not, or one of those. I mentioned beer and she went out.

I was glad to see and hear that Roy was doing well. He deserved to be, in a 'musical world' in which so few people deserved to earn literally as much as their daily bread. It was more doubtful whether that world had ever accorded him its highest respect, but he had always been more or less grudgingly admitted to be well trained and conscientious. He could get a better performance out of the average orchestra than some conductors who perhaps surpassed him in musicianship, by means of charm, or alternatively by means of doing a certain amount of comradely swearing at rehearsal, buying drinks for the section leaders, and similar stratagems. His career as a solo violinist, never very distinguished, had ended early, though not so long ago he had still been quite creditably taking on a

Vivaldi or a Mozart concerto at charity jamborees and the like. He had been, possibly still was, a composer too, of what I had heard unkindly described as a sub-Rachmaninov persuasion, to be sub-whom was not, to me, any sort of disgrace. His pieces were not often performed, apart from an early and sugary *Nocturne* for fiddle and strings, plus a xylophone and one or two other novelties of that period, or the one just before. This had been turned into a popular song about 1950, and had recently enjoyed a fresh lease of life, or somnambulism, as that sadly different thing from a popular song, a pop song. As the latter, it must have contributed not a little to the frightening amount he was alleged to be now earning.

It was as a composer, of the most serious sort, that Roy had tried to see himself in the days when I had known him better. But it was evident even then that he had come along a bit late in the day to make the best creative use of his taste and talent. Somebody called Vandervane would have fitted fairly neatly – by more than coincidence, I had always thought – into the era in which it had evidently been compulsory for English composers to be called something non-English: Delius, Holst, van Dieren, Moeran, Rubbra. But he had turned up a good half-generation after it ended, and, again somehow characteristically, would not have fitted into it with total neatness because of the anglicization of his surname, imposed by grandfather van der Veen upon arrival from Rotterdam a century ago. (Roy would sometimes warmly defend the change, at other times deplore and threaten to reverse it, depending simply on how he felt, not on how his countrymen seemed to be treating him.)

Before I could start speculating on the current level of his artistic standards, Kitty came back with some beer for me and almost as much of what looked like sketchily diluted gin for her. I thought on a second view that, while still attractive in a plump, florid, not-my-cup-of-tea way, she had aged since I had seen her. Or perhaps she was just tired and strung-up – strung-up higher and tighter than she habitually was. Certainly her torn, faded check shirt and stained jeans were indications – in one whose breakfast wear was likely to recall Mary Queen of Scots – of lowered morale. But the dry, scoured look of the skin at the outer corners of her eyes pointed to something more permanent.

We settled down side by side on the couch vacated by Christopher and the female mute. Turned towards me with arched back, and drink and cigarette held before her in a sort of low boxer's-guard position, Kitty started.

'I checked on the pants after you telephoned. There are definitely three fewer than there were last week-end. What's so utterly terrifying is the openness of it. He knows I deal with all the laundry and things. He must realize . . . It's not even that he doesn't mind if I know. He wants me to know. Flaunting it. Throwing it in my face. Using it to show how he hates me,' she shrieked quietly, giving her usual treatment to an earlier thought of mine.

'I doubt it. He's just careless.'

'Why can't he buy a pair and change somewhere? Just answer me that – if you can,' she challenged me challengingly. 'What's to stop him buying a brand-new pair at a shop and changing at his club, for instance? Come on, what's to stop him?'

'I don't know, Kitty. Well, he just doesn't think of it. He wouldn't.'

'I wish to God I knew who it was. Or rather I don't. Not after that one who designed jewellery.'

'Oh, there's been one who designed jewellery, has there?'

'Belts and bracelets and things. You must have heard about it. He took her to Glyndebourne and Covent Garden and Aldeburgh and everywhere. That was the only thing that saved me. It was all fixed up for them to go to Bayreuth and at the last moment she found out what it was.'

'What it was about what?'

'Bayreuth. Wagner. Opera. Music. Weeks of it. Really, Douglas.'

'Sorry. Where is he now?'

'You may well ask.' Showing all her command of oral italics, ditto inverted commas, black-letter and illuminated capitals, she said, 'Having a working lunch he's not sure where

21

because the chap hadn't made up his mind with a chap whose name he can't remember because it's so unpronounceable who's got some very vague ideas about fixing up a tour of Brazil which he thinks probably almost certainly would be a bad idea but he might as well find out more and anyway it's a free lunch and he's no idea how long it'll go on.'

'I see. It does rather sound like a — '

'I don't mind him just having a go occasionally. He probably needs it. Or he thinks he does. It isn't really him taking them to bed.'

'Isn't it?' I asked as required.

'Well yes of course it is. I mean I hate that like bloody poison, but I can put up with it. It's the going off altogether thing that petrifies me.'

'But there's no sign of that at the moment, surely. This Brazilian lunch. He's doing his best to cover up. Doing something towards it, anyway. Not like trying to take her to Bayreuth.'

'That'll come. I know the pattern, Douglas dear. I've been through it all myself, you see. I know it from the inside.'

'Did he take you to Bayreuth?'

'That kind of thing. Anyway, I went. That was how I scored. I was the best one he'd met at being told about music since his first wife. I can remember so clearly him playing the tunes over on the piano and then bits of the record, so I could follow the themes and recapitulations and things when he took me to the concert. Still, why shouldn't I be able to remember it clearly? It's only about ten years ago.'

There were tears in her eyes, but then there so often were. Had Roy really married her for her docility as an audience? I said, 'But you really do like it, don't you, Kitty? Music, I mean.'

'Oh yes, I like it all right,' she said, making her moderate statement of the month. 'I'm very fond of music. Always have been.'

'Well, then . . . Look, what do you know about this girl? How old is she?'

'I don't know anything at all about her, but they've been

running at about twenty to twenty-two over the last three years or so. Tending to go down. Getting younger at something like half the rate he gets older. When he's seventy-three they'll be ten.'

I checked the last bit mentally and found it to be correct, given the assumptions. It seemed to me extraordinary that anyone capable of making these in the first place, and then of following them through to their 'logical' conclusion, should (as Kitty clearly did) see the final picture presented as nothing but tragic or repulsive. 'And when he's eighty-three they'll be five,' I said experimentally.

'*Yes*,' she agreed, glad that I had followed her reasoning.

I gave it up. 'Well, I was going to say, if he wants a music pupil he's looking in the wrong place. Nobody in that sort of generation cares at all about any sort of music. Except very sober types with horses and lists of who to send Christmas cards to. Not Roy's speed at all.'

'At his age he may have decided the music-pupil thing isn't so important,' she said, and added incuriously, 'Isn't pop music music?'

'No. Anyway, what can I do to help? I do want to, but I can't see quite – '

'Dearest Douglas. First find out who she is . . .'

'But you said –'

'. . . and how far it's gone, and then we can sort of make a plan.'

'But that's spying. And what kind of plan?'

'I don't mind you telling him I've asked you to have a word with him about it. And surely you'd do anything to stop him from, that is surely you'd agree he mustn't throw himself away on some filthy little barbarian of a teenager? It would be such a crime, so awful for everybody, for me and the children, and for him too of course when he gets fed up with her, and for people like this young 'cellist boy he's encouraging, and there are so many people who depend on him, everybody he's got obligations to . . .'

Not to mention the chaps at the nuclear-disarmament talks. 'I suppose it would. I mean of course it would, I quite see that.

But I still don't see what you or I or anyone else can do to stop him if he's made up his mind.'

'But if you found out something about it, then at least we could . . .'

A distant but rapidly approaching disturbance had broken out on an upper floor, constituted of the wordless yelling I had heard over the wires, the Furry Barrel's tones with full slipping-ratchet effect, Gilbert sounding annoyed, traces of a fourth voice, and variegated footfalls. Kitty got up and behaved for a few seconds like somebody about to be machine-gunned from the air, then moved as if to a prearranged spot. Here a fearful small boy in a smart suit of bottle-green velvet, after blundering through the doorway and starting to yell louder and at a higher pitch, threw himself into her arms: Ashley Vandervane, I judged. Gilbert was not far behind, and an altercation ensued. It was soon clear that Ashley had not been fleeing from Gilbert so much as coming to enlist his mother's support in gaining possession of some object, like his eleventh chocolate bar of the day or a bottle of hydrochloric acid, which Gilbert had perversely denied him. But I paid little attention, because I was looking so closely at Penny Vandervane, now also of the company, and most closely of all at her breasts.

This was not difficult, in the sense that a good half of their total was directly visible in the wide V of a dark-brown Paisley-patterned blouse or shirt or, just as possibly, pyjama-top. They struck me as not so much large as tremendously prominent, that and high, yes, and somehow immovable, giving the impression that poking at them with a finger, say, would have no more effect than poking at somebody's knee-caps. That was it: they were like a pair of knee-caps carefully sculpted and re-covered in Grade A skin. I saw now that they were attached to a rather tall, long-limbed frame, and finally surmounted by a shapely shorn head that included a face remarkable for the width and blueness of its eyes.

These last turned towards me as I reached them with mine, and I got a very brief stare, with no recognition in it and slightly less curiosity than one passenger in a lift will normally show another. Never mind: I had realized that I was in the presence of the reason for my ready yielding to curiosity when Kitty had asked me to come up that day. But I was clearly going to have to wait quite a long time, if not for ever, before I would be in any position to start explaining to Penny Vandervane about her breasts.

Ashley, twisted round in his mother's arms, had one thumb in his mouth and the extended first two fingers of the other hand going up and down in the air, a manual combination I could not remember having seen before. He removed the thumb for a space in order to accuse Gilbert of having hit him. Gilbert denied it, and I believed him, but the Furry Barrel, growling near his ankles, took the other view. Kitty solved the matter by carrying her son from the room, the dog bustling officiously behind them.

'The way you bring up that boy is decadent,' said Gilbert.

'It's nothing to do with me how he's brought up,' said Penny in her classless accent, or one combining the ugliest features of at least two dialects.

'It seems nothing to do with anybody. Toys, presents, candies, ice-creams. Why isn't he at school today?'

'He didn't feel like it.'

'He should be forced to go. At six years of age he can't be blamed. What do you expect of a boy who's allowed to sleep in his parents' bed?'

Penny shrugged her shoulders, a movement which had good results lower down, and started to turn in my direction, but stopped and turned back again.

'I'm Douglas Yandell,' I said, thinking it safest to start from scratch.

She grinned slightly and said, 'I know.'

Gilbert frowned at her, holding it until she had noticed. Then he said to me, 'I'm Gilbert Alexander,' and held out his hand, which I shook.

After a moment's inner toil, I said, 'How's your father?'

'Blind drunk. Oh, don't be a sodding idiot, Gilbert, it's an old music-hall gag thing. He's no more blind drunk than he always is. Quite fit, actually. Going after the birds always tones him up.'

Gilbert made a disgusted noise and went out.

'Dead funny, aren't they?' Penny began giving me quite a lot of her attention. 'You know, Victorian. He's even a bit Victorian in bed. He was when I first met him, anyway. Speeded up a lot since. Well, he's got the equipment, you see. That's all true, all that.'

It interested me a little that she had taken the trouble to drive Gilbert from the room and then at once switched to what was, for someone like myself, an in-depth anti-pass move, though I quite saw that another might take it as a come-on. I wondered whether chance or a sure instinct had guided her. A look at the width of those blue eyes firmly decided me for instinct.

'Jolly good for you,' I said heartily. 'What sort of bird is it this time?'

'No idea. Young. She got you up here to, you know, get on to him about it?'

I took this to refer to Kitty. 'She's worried.'

'Listen, did you ever see her when she wasn't worried? It's her life. Her bloody life, mate. I think she had sodding Ashley to give herself something new to go on about. Crisis on tap. No wonder he does all this bird stuff,' she went on in her pronominal style. 'But then he lets her know about it and we're off again. You needn't think it's any different from today. This is pretty quiet, actually.'

'Do you live here?'

'It's free,' she said, answering my thought.

'What about Gilbert? Is he a resident, or just passing through?'

'Oh, he thinks he's a resident.'

'What do you think?'

She gave another shrug, saw my look, and came an inch or two nearer. 'Where do you live, then?'

'Maida Vale. I've got a flat there.'

'Anyone else in it?'

'Not at the moment, I'm sorry to say.'

'Oh.' She lowered her green-painted eyelids.

Even without taking into account her earlier praise of

Gilbert's physique, I knew what I was in for at this stage, but there are situations in which a lancer must charge an armoured car. I could hear somebody approaching the doorway across the uncarpeted wooden floor of the hall. 'Can I show you the place some time?' I asked.

'No,' she said, grinning and shaking her head. 'No,' she added.

Kitty came in with the face and carriage and then voice of one just released after a secret-police interrogation. She told us we might as well have lunch now, and we trooped off. I wondered why Penny should dislike me so much: not, surely, because of my breasts-fumble of a couple of years previously. She, or they, must long have been hardened to that kind of thing. And I sensed there was more to it than simple suspicion of any presumptive ally of her stepmother. Perhaps it was just the sight and sound of me she found unpleasant. Then I cheered myself up by reflecting that it was overridingly important to have renewed my assault, even verbally and vainly, on the tested principle that every minute a girl is allowed to spend in official ignorance of a man's intentions means two extra minutes of build-up when the time comes.

I followed the women through a small room full of boilers, tanks, pipes and associated machinery, and into another doorway. 'Mind your head, Douglas,' said Kitty as I gave myself a smart crack across the hairline with the edge of the lintel. It hurt like hell. I stumbled down two or three steps into what I came by degrees to see was a large, lofty kitchen looking on to the courtyard. Most of those present reacted to my misfortune, Kitty by repeatedly crying out and pressing a wet tea-towel against the place, Gilbert by sending me glances of satisfaction while he transferred a number of bottles of sauce and jars of chutney and pickles from a wall-cupboard to a laid dining-table, an elderly domestic with sympathetic concern, Ruth and Penny with smothered and open laughter respectively. Only Christopher was unmoved, going on rapidly and noisily loading a tray with materials for two. This, a minute later, he carried out of the room, followed by Ruth, and the domestic soon went too, urged on with some dismissive gratitude from Kitty. So it was only she and I and Gilbert and Penny who sat down at table.

Gilbert took charge, doling out bowls of soup, distributing cold meats and salad, fetching tinned beer from a larder that diffused an Arctic breath. He asked the women whether they wanted this or that by the use of words, me by raising his eyebrows or chin, sometimes both. Ordered by Kitty to tell me what he did, he conceded with what in the circumstances was quite good grace that he was connected with the stage (by moving pieces of scenery on to and off it, I guessed) and had nearly finished a book about West Indians in London.

'A novel?' I asked.

'No, no. The culture that produced it is dying. Something much freer from narrow traditions, more adventurous altogether in form. It bears analogies to music and the visual arts. I've got into the habit of thinking of it as my *London Suite* in three movements and three colours.'

This, if indeed an ingrained habit, was one I considered he should set about breaking while there was still time, but did not like to say so. 'Is it very autobiographical?'

'That question has no meaning. We can all only re-create what we have felt and experienced and suffered in our lives.'

While I tried, not very conscientiously, to apply his dictum to Suppé's *Poet and Peasant* overture, Kitty asked, 'But it's got a story?'

'Story. Rhythm. Characters. Plasticity. Shape. Melody. Frame. Plot,' said Gilbert, so oratorically that I could not tell whether he was ridiculing these concepts or claiming that the *London Suite* had as much of all of them as anybody could possibly want. Kitty seemed to be in a similar difficulty. At my other side, Penny showed no sign of ever having been in a difficulty in all her born days.

'And what are you doing these days,' I said heavily, 'Penny?'

'I wish you could see what you look like with that bloody great egg on your head.' Her laughter sounded quite unforced, even engagingly naïve. 'It's overdone. You know, like a false nose. As if you're not meant to believe it.'

Gilbert clicked his tongue and Kitty said, 'Penny,' in torpid reproof, going on to add, 'She's at a domestic science college in –'

'I am not at any sodding domestic science college. I've left it, see? I don't go there any more. I am eh drop out. Not that it's very far to drop. I am completely idle. I . . . don't . . . do . . . anything.'

Her tone could have been described without either trouble or inexactitude as one of cold anger. The eyes were working hard too, though they were not looking at anybody. I decided I was not whole-heartedly enjoying my lunch, always having preferred something quick and light midday, and started to plan my leave-taking. Then I saw someone finish passing the window and go in at the glass porch, but could not make out who it was. After a moment, a man's voice began loudly singing somewhere inside the house, the throat muscles tensed to produce the plummy effect often used in imitations of Welsh people, though this last was not evidently part of the singer's intention.

> Ah-ee last mah-ee hawrt een ahn Angleesh gawr-dan,
> Jost whahr thah rawzaz ahv Anglahnd graw ...'

Most musicians have a poor ear for linguistic or verbal nuances, and many for musical ones too, come to that, but it was like Roy, whom I had heard singing this song in this style more than once before, to take the trouble to substitute 'Angleesh' for the 'Eengleesh' that might have been expected, thus subtly hitting at persons who pronounce the name of our nationality as it is spelt. Indeed, the tone of the whole performance, which continued and drew nearer as we all listened at the table, was hostile, wounding, designed to humiliate, though Roy could hardly have supposed that some individual or group keen on the vocal manner he was caricaturing had stolen into the house while his back was turned. Rage at absent or largely imaginary foes, however, was a part of his life-style. A more obvious explanation of his behaviour was, of course, that he was trying to be funny, to which the objection was that he often did quite closely similar things that nobody, not even he, could have intended to be funny. Just the same cycle of reasoning applied to the notion that he was showing off. More likely, this was nothing more than a way of entertaining himself, something he might often have had to do in youth, as the child of middle-aged parents whose earlier progeny were well into their teens by the time he came on the scene. And why was he singing about Angleesh gawrdans at the present moment? To give the fact of his unexpectedly early return a chance to sink in before he actually appeared, rather as Jonas Chuzzlewit had once done after much more serious delinquency than anything Roy would have been up to.

The door into the kitchen opened and Roy came in, a bulky figure in a wide-lapelled double-breasted jacket that, after a then recent fashion, set up uneasiness in the beholder by looking very, very nearly as much like a short overcoat, a glistening two-tone shirt and hairy trousers with widely separated stripes on them. His face was unchanged, a unified whole, I had always thought, with prominent straight nose, full lips, and pointed, slightly receding chin, a physiognomy I had often come across in photographs of public figures of the 1930s, especially actresses – a resemblance now underlined, I noticed with some concern, by the rough bob in which his thick, dark, ungreying hair had been done. There could never be anything actressy about Roy, that sort of behaviour being heavily oversubscribed hereabouts as it was, and in general he was uneffeminate to a fault; but at the sight of him today I felt a twinge of a kind of discomfort that I would have sworn he could never arouse in me. In his hand was a large brown drink.

He, at least, seemed unreservedly glad to see me, and a moment later very, if briefly, concerned about the state of my head, though he might have been piling it on a bit as a diversion from his present moral disadvantage. Kitty and Penny heard out in staring silence his detailed account of the Brazilian's sudden indisposition owing to an attack, he said with a wondering laugh, of some tropical bug the chap had picked up on a trip up the Amazon, of all things and rivers. I asked myself sadly if he would ever learn that to think an explanation convincing because it sounded too obvious and uninventive to be invented was the sort of typically male error most males discarded before they left school. The reappearance of Ashley, now in pyjamas and escorted by the Furry Barrel, saved him from public rout. Father and son went into a reunion scene of Neapolitan warmth, on father's side at least; son soon started wriggling and asking about his present. This was quickly produced from one of the immense patch-pockets of the jacket-overcoat, a miniature fire-engine with, as we soon discovered, a hee-haw siren on it. The lad began playing with it on the floor under the table and round our feet. Gilbert, who had duly shown his disapproval of the fire-engine, asked Roy if he had had lunch.

'Of course not; I rushed back here as soon as I could,' he said seriously. 'But don't bother about me – anything'll do.'

'How did you get here from the station?' asked Kitty, speaking for the first time since his arrival. Her tone was distant, about ten yards more distant than where she sat.

'What?'

'*How* ... did you *get* ... *here* ... from the *station*.' This came out in chewy, easy-to-lip-read chunks, with churchyard-pigeon head-effects.

'I walked. Glorious day. Whatever's easiest, Gilbert, thank you. Spot of corm beef'll do me fine. And some tim pineapple or tim peaches to follow, if they're there. Great.'

When I first met him, Roy had had a sort of Northern accent that disappeared into public-school English at all his frequent moments of excitement. No doubt recognizing, at some intermediate level of self-consciousness, that the disparity was too obvious even to the uncritical ears of the other prosperous socialists he spent most of his time with, he must have decided on the new slurring policy as more adaptable, better politically and like young people talked, too. I thought I saw him wondering whether I had noticed the change.

Having said no more, the women left the room, followed, after he had laid in front of us a piece of board with cheeses on it, by Gilbert. Roy ate meat and salad with studied ferocity. Presently he said,

'Can you stick around for a bit? Something I want to talk

to you about. There's, uh, a favour I'd like you to do for me if you possibly could.'

'I'm already supposed to be starting on some sort of aid programme for Kitty.'

His chair juddered as the fire-engine crashed into it. 'Christ. Sharp,' he seemed to say, sounding a note of warning over the bray of the siren and the Furry Barrel's outraged barking.

I nodded. 'I don't want you to think I've sort of come up here behind your back.'

'Certainly not. Anyway, I heard you were going to be asked. Everybody knows what everybody else is doing around here, though they don't always admit it. That didn't go down too well, did it? That stuff about the Amazon and so on.'

'Not too well, no.'

'I thought it was bloody good myself. But I'm no judge. They never give you credit for anything, do they? You'd suppose that a chap who'd winged his way back to the nest for a late lunch of corm beef and the rest of the rubbish instead of stuffing himself with delicacies at his club or in Soho somewhere and rolling up pissed at half past five would thereby ingratiate himself slightly with the women. Not a bloody bit of it. I'd have been better off all round doing the other thing. You're looking well, Duggers. Apart from that head. Nasty. Anyway, how's your life?'

'Moderate. Pushed for cash as usual.'

'Someone told me you and Anne had broken up.'

'She went back to her husband. For the sake of the children.'

'Oh balls, I do wish people wouldn't behave like that. So stuffy. Boring beyond words. It's the books they read, and all these television series. Nobody would dream of "going back" if they hadn't been told for years that it's what you do – not even what you should do, just what you do. Most depressing. Still. Got anyone to replace her?'

'Only part-time.' I considered whether it would be in order to reach down and cuff or pinch Ashley, who was making a number of runs with his fire-engine on one of the front legs of my chair. 'A girl who lives on the other side of the river, so I do a fair amount of commuting.'

'Ashley, stop that.'

'Shut your trap, you fucking monkey-face.'

I heard this remark with hidden pleasure and anticipation. Roy was rightly famous for his way with every grade of defiance, whether offered by a world-renowned soloist with strong unacceptable ideas about *rubato* or by a surly waiter. But the shocking event was that he told Ashley in the mildest of tones to come and sit on his knee and be given some special chocolate he had brought for him. This order was obeyed. The Furry Barrel, now directing sultry looks at me from a nearby chair, yapped peremptorily.

'You are a silly old His Majesty King Charles the Second cavalier-spaniel dog,' said Roy, and added to me, 'You've got the cheese by you, you see. Could you give her some of that Cheddar? Not too much and cut up small and see that she sits when you give it to her. You ridiculous old hound.'

The dog ate with head nodding and eyes still fixed on mine, the child like a gluttonous ogre. After some suspiciously paraded rumination, Roy said,

'Of course, you and I have always differed fundamentally about, uh, well, people like Anne and so on. You never get invawved, do you?' (This is as near as I can get to representing the curious gliding sound he made, a valuable and popular accent-worsener of the period.)

'You mean you are involved.'

'He's always invawved with somebody,' said Ashley thickly. 'Mummy says she'd give a hundred quid to know who it is this time.'

'I was talking about Mr Yandell, darling.'

'Yeah.' The boy said it as his half-sister might have done.

'Perhaps we'd better –' I began.

'No no, it's all right. Anyway, you don't, do you? Get invawved.'

I wanted to say that, whether through natural virtue, constitutional prudence, coldness of heart, cowardice or luck, I felt I had so far managed to avoid some of the grosser symptoms, at any rate, of invawvement. But Roy was pushing on regardless, still ruminatively.

'I've never been able to make out what chaps like you are really looking for.'

'I'm not looking for anything. At least, nothing that can't be fairly easily found if you're a bachelor with a bit of energy and a place of your own.'

'You don't want to get married.'

'No. Not at the moment, anyway.'

'Perhaps not ever.'

'I don't know.'

'Don't want the responsibility.'

'If you like. It's expensive, too.'

'Perhaps it's just a matter of a physical type.'

'What is?'

'That you're looking for.'

Still talking, he grasped both of Ashley's wrists in one hand, just in time to prevent a lot of chocolate being wiped on to his clothing, and bore him off to the kitchen sink, where he set to work on him with the very tea-towel used earlier on my head. Doing all this, he was under no obligation to meet my eye.

'I mean, Duggers, it's always struck me that you do seem to cast about pretty bloody widely in your choice of, you know. Moce people –'

'You talk as if I collect them like butterflies. I just grab what's going past. It's all luck, availability . . .'

'I know, I know. I only meant what you'll admit is true if you'll just bring yourself to consider it for a moment, that *moce chaps* seem to *prefer* one particular *type* of . . .'

'*Bird*,' said Ashley, efficiently maintaining tempo and sound-quality.

'Belt up, you little bastard,' said Roy, restoring something of the respect he had lost. 'No, uh, you know perfectly well that some chaps go for tall ones or short-arsed ones or blondes or . . . you know. But you don't. I've never been able to see any consistency in your tastes at all.' He made it sound grave, and looked it himself. 'I don't even know what your sort of basic standard is, absolutely basic.' He finished polishing Ashley's mouth with a preoccupied flourish. 'For instance, how would you rate, say, well, young Penny? I mean, she's –'

'No, Roy. I've no idea what it is, but no. Whatever it is, no.'

'I don't know what you're talking about,' he said coldly. 'I asked you a simple question. However. Well, my little tough guy' – he swept his son up into his arms – 'my little bruiser, what are we going to do with you, eh? Let's go and find your mummy, shall we?'

Mummy was easily found in the drawing-room, listening to, or apparently keeping quiet during, a Miles Davis record. Gilbert presided at the gramophone, which faithfully rendered that tiny, elementary universe of despair and hatred. Penny was eating chocolates, a good antiquarian touch, and reading a paperback book of what looked like poems, or at least non-prose. Roy dumped Ashley, who seemed drugged with chocolate to the point at which he had forgotten about his fire-engine for the time being, and took me and the Furry Barrel out into the garden.

'Changing-huts,' he said, gesturing towards some loose-boxes.

'When you build the swimming-pool.'

'Right.'

'Roy, what's this favour?'

'Favour?'

'You said you wanted me to do you a favour.'

'Oh. Oh, just bearing with me when I maunder on. Sympathetic ear. There's nobody much round the place I can talk to.'

'I see. Not a very arduous favour.'

He led me into a barn full of empty cardboard boxes and pieces of wood shaped for some now superseded purpose. 'I was thinking of turning this shack into a music laboratory.'

'Before or after the swimming-pool?'

'Oh, Duggers, I do wish you'd try not to be such an ole square. Times are changing whether you like it or not. Weber's bloody good, I agree, but he's hardly as relevant as Webern. That chap might have produced something that would make even you sit up if the Yanks hadn't murdered him.'

'To hell with relevance, and it was an accident, and he was sixty-three, and sit up –'

'Verdi was over eighty when he –'

'And sit up and lean over slightly to one side in order to fart briefly. Don't let's go into all that again, Roy.'

'No, sorry.'

We came out of the gloom of the barn and walked down a modest avenue littered with fallen wood. Bars of soft shadow lay across it. The Furry Barrel, nose to the ground and tail wagging at half tempo but full stretch, hurried aside into some laurel bushes.

'How are you on the ivories these days?' asked Roy.

'Hardly concert standard, but I usually spend most of one day a week at the instrument.'

'I thought we might tackle a snarter together later on.'

'Tackle . . . Oh, yes. Yes, that would be fine.'

'Do you feel up to the Brahms D minor?'

'You'd have to be in a pretty tolerant mood.'

'In thack case we might be better advised to go for something a little less demanding. Any objection to Mozart?'

'On the contrary. While I remember, for God's sake let up on those pants of yours,' and I went on to explain at once and in full to save the time he would have wasted on very slowly dawning comprehension and the rest of it.

'Bloody Gestapo,' he said when I had finished.

'Kitty wonders why you don't buy a pair somewhere and I must say I agree with her. You could save yourself so much –'

'Yeah, and have the bloody shopman say, "And will there be anything further, Sir Roy? Some deodorant, or a packet of horn pills?" It's that bastard telly. Honestly, half my troubles come from never knowing when some bugger isn't going to recognize me. Only the other evening I was sneaking into a block of flats in, well, never mind where, and the bloody porter stuck his head out of his window and yelled, "The lift's not working, Sir Roy, I'm afraid you'll have to use the stairs." If you don't bleeding well mind. It was those concerts I did last year for L.C.M. Television. Them and that ballocking silly panel game. I wish I'd never let them talk me into it.'

I wished the same thing, though for different and perhaps priggish reasons, but I said, 'If you think buying one pair's such a give-away, and I can't see it matters, buy a dozen. Or are you afraid the bloke'd think you were taking on a dozen birds one after the other? What if he did? I can't understand why you're so sensitive about it.'

'I'm not going to carry a dozen pairs of pants with me everywhere I go.'

'No need to. Leave them at your club.'

'Out of the question.'

'But just by –'

'I don't want to discuss it any further.'

The avenue petered out at a five-barred gate, beyond which was a field with two inexpensive-looking horses in it. Roy seemed to think it would diminish him politically if I were allowed to take away the impression that the animals belonged to him. He explained at length that they did not and whose they were. I was wondering whether Kitty's flaunting theory about the pants might not have something in it after all. Guilty alarm lightly dusted with embarrassment was what anybody who knew him would have predicted as his response to my warning, the dead opposite of the evasive-defiant mixture I had been handed. The thought of the favour, too, was worrying me. Presumably I was not at the moment in a fit state of mind for its nature to be broached, and Roy was waiting for my wits to become impaired by lust, alcohol or fear of imminent extinction, especially lust: it must be here that the Penny thing fitted in. I decided to try to take him near enough to the favour for him not to be able to resist asking it, and pushed forward my first pawn.

'If buying a pair of underpants makes you want to wear a false beard, how do you manage when you take her out somewhere?'

'I don't. Take her out anywhere. Do you think I'm a bloody fool?'

'What do you do, then?' I asked, hoping he would not insist on an answer to his question.

'Stay under cover. Occasionally I go to her flat, though there's a lot of room-mate trouble there. On the up-grade, too. Or I borrow a flat off someone. But that's tricky in a different

37

way. I only know a few people with flats well enough to ask them, and most of those know Kitty too, and go British on me if I do ask them. And then the ones I can ask are always the ones who'd talk about it. It's odd how strictly that rule applies.'

With an air of philosophic gloom, he led off down an overgrown path that proved to be two or three inches deep in rotting leaves. My forebodings, however, had vanished.

'If that's all you – I mean, you're welcome to my place any time with a bit of warning. And I can keep my mouth shut, as you know.'

'Thanks a lot, Duggers, I'll take you up on that,' he said, making it as clear that this was not the favour as turning round and bawling the news in my face would have done, and feeding my forebodings back to me in mint condition.

'How old is she?'

'Nineteen.'

'Good God,' I said, largely out of respect for the accuracy of Kitty's observation.

'What's wrong with that?'

'Well, nothing at all really, I suppose, though it did strike me that it's somehow a bit young.'

'What's wrong with that? I do wish you'd make an effort to get out of this habit of thinking in categories all the time. The whole generation-gap idea's just an invention of the media and the Yanks. You obviously don't know the first thing about youth in the true sense. You've no conception what it's like, what it knows, what it can do.'

The path had turned a corner and begun to climb back towards the house. We moved on to the lowest of a series of lawns, rather squashy underfoot. I was enjoying the garden and the air and sun, but was clearly getting nowhere with the favour. I plunged on nevertheless.

'Is it just youth you're talking about, or this lot of youth?'

'The whole bit. She's shown me so much I'd never even suspected the existence of before.'

'Really? What sort of thing do you mean?'

'Oh, everything – ways of feeling, ways of seeing.'

'Not ways of hearing too, I hope.'

'Oh, bugger off, Douglas. Of course she likes pop; they all do. And if you look into it at all, I mean the good stuff, Led Zeppelin, say, not Herman's Hermits, you'll come across a surprising amount of real music. But I suppose you wouldn't accept that.'

'No.'

'School of thought!'

This phrase I recognized as one of Roy's obscenity-savers, or fuckettes, to which he was prone in moments of stress. His use of much greater amounts of genuine obscenities alongside them, whatever his company, inclined me to feel that here was no outcropping of prudery, more likely just the relic of a childish habit, originally taken up as a way of observing the letter of some law of home or institution. To qualify as a fuckette, a phrase had to have annoyed him at some stage of his life, and this in some cases could be fairly positively identified. School of thought itself, for instance, might spring from some middle-period academic experience; sporting spirit, another favourite, from a slightly earlier epoch. Christian gentleman, I had established through research, had been an admiring description of General Franco at the time of the Spanish Civil War, and I had often imagined Roy, baulked of any more active form of defiance, growling it out from the Barcelona hospital bed where he had lain with appendicitis and its aftermath during the autumn of 1937 – all but the first few and last few hours, in fact, of his stay in the country.

After a silence, Roy was going on, 'She likes jazz too. She hears different things in it from what we hear, but she likes it.'

'Good for her. Who is she?'

'Nobody you know,' he said, spelling out by his tone the fact that who she was was important.

'Anyway, I've got to give you one thing. It's good going for a man, uh, of your general –'

'An old shag like me to have it off and go on having it off with a kid of nineteen.'

'Yes. But I meant more than that. Not just the having it off, but keeping her happy with never going out with you, no parties or flash restaurants, none of the perks of being Sir

Roy Vandervane's bit of stuff. That's new with you, isn't it, by the way, Roy, keeping the whole thing dark, except from the family? Kitty was telling me –'

'There are special circumstances.'

'No doubt. But she must be an unusual kid of nineteen, especially by today's standards, to put up with being kept indoors like that. Or has she got another bloke who does take her about?'

We had reached the top lawn and were moving across it to the courtyard. Now, abruptly but abstractedly, Roy turned and began pacing back the way we had come. I joined him, certain that the favour was about to declare itself.

'She's not putting up with it. Every time I see her she spends longer complaining about being hidden away. Any moment now she'll refuse to come to bed with me unless we go out in public. And I can't have that. Not just the two of us on our own.'

'So it'll have to be the four of us, you and she and Penny and I disguised as you and your daughter's girl-friend and your daughter and her girl-friend's boy-friend who also by a happy coincidence turns out to be an old friend of yours. Very neat. Cosy, too.'

He showed no appreciation of my acumen. 'It's the only thing I can think of. I was at my wits' end until you happened to turn up today. Her putting me off this morning was all part of it, you see. Bloody war of nerves.'

'It strikes me that Gilbert would be far more your man. Penny likes him. Presumably. And then he's, uh, he's more the right age and everything.'

'I've already asked him.'

'And he turned you down.'

'Flat. These ... chaps can be very puritanical, you know. Result of all the bloody Nonconformist propaganda we pumped into them to keep them quiet while we were exploiting them.'

'There's quite a few it hasn't rubbed off on so's you'd notice, from what I hear.'

'Well, it's rubbed off on him. He won't do it.'

Roy kicked savagely at an already disintegrating croquet ball and waited for me to make a start on the huge list of objections to his proposal.

'It's grotesque.'

'It may sound a bit on the grotesque side to you at this stage. When you've thought about it, which I want you to do before you decide, then you'll see it won't look in the least grotesque when we do it, not even to people who know us, assuming there are any of those round the place.'

'It would feel grotesque.'

'You'll get into the way of it.'

'Gilbert wouldn't like me taking his girl out on expeditions he already thinks would be immoral.'

'One expedition. No, really, Duggers, I promise you that. Just to give me time. And what can he do? Go for you or Penny with a knife? He's not that type.'

'No. Yes, there is that. But what about her? She can't stand me.'

'Oh, balls, that's all juss the way they go on. You know, cool. I suppose you know about cool? Of course you do. She'll come like a shot if I . . . put it to her in the right way.'

'You're proposing to bribe your own daughter to do camouflage duty so that you and your mistress can have an evening out against her boy-friend's wishes and behind her stepmother's back.'

'Mistress, eh? By gad, sir. Not bribe. And it'll do Gilbert good to have a bit of opposition. And the stepmother part's just what she'll like about it.'

'She oughtn't to, and you oughtn't to put her in that situation.'

'I see we've got more than one puritan round the place. No, honestly, I didn't mean it like that. I don't care for how she feels about Kitty either, believe me. It's a fact, that's all. And she's exactly the type, Penny is, to be much nicer to her after something of that sort. Anyway. I know all this makes me look a right shit, and probably be a right shit, and I don't want to, but I am in love with this curious little creature, and perhaps that doesn't justify anything, but you can't imagine how it makes me look forward to each day, and really want tremen-

dously to work, which hasn't happened to me for years. I can
assure you. You know, it's true the young deserve a bit of special
tolerance and understanding, because they're young and in
conflict and have this different vision, but poor old sods at my
time of life deserve it too, or anyway we need it, just starting to
shape up to the idea of being dead or ole men. It's all right for
buggers like you. In the middle. That's the place to be, by
Christ. Now let's drop it. What do you say to K.481?'

'Is that the one in E flat?' I asked torpidly.

'Yeah. Come along.'

He led me away and to the drawing-room. Christopher and
Ruth got to their feet respectfully at the sight of us, and at
once left. Only Penny remained, having finished the chocolates but continuing to read her book, or so it seemed while
Roy and I tinkered about and finally got into our stride with
the Mozart. Then, during an undemanding bit of accompaniment, I saw that she had not turned a page since we began. Very
few women outside the profession take any kind of interest in
music at all, and the idea that a girl like Penny might be a
secret listener surprised me so much that I nearly muffed the
passage of modest bravura that then confronted me. After that
I played at my very best, and we rounded off the first movement
really quite creditably.

'Bloody good,' said Roy. 'Nicely done, old lad. You certainly have been doing a bit of work.'

'So have you.'

'Oh, glad it shows. I've been reasonably hard at it for the
last couple of months now. One of the results of, uh, feeling
pleased with life.'

'Are you building up to something public?'

This plainly scored a hit, but his damage-control unit
lumbered into action at once. 'Not really, no. More for the
satisfaction than anything else. I may have some sort of charity
do in the autumn, but it's all quite vague. I don't know where I
might be by then.'

Penny turned a page of her book and caught his attention.

'I say, Pen, do try listening to this next bit. First-rate stuff. I
can't think why it isn't better known. Quite short.'

As an eviction order, this could not have been surpassed. On her way to the door I heard Penny mutter something about having to help Kitty, which I thought was fulsome of her.

'Oh dear,' said Roy when she had gone. 'Touch me not, what? One simply can't reach thack girl.'

'Doesn't Gilbert reach her?'

'I suppose he must, here and there, but it doesn't seem to make her any easier to live with. Still, you can't blame her, can you?'

'Why can't I?'

'This bloody awful society. Simply doesn't offer anything to anybody with any kind of sensibility or creativity or . . . I know you think it's absolutely unimprovable, of course.'

'I don't think anything about it.'

'Precisely. Let's get on, shall we?'

The slow movement went rather less well, largely because, with Penny out of the room, I was free to think about the favour and whether to take it on. Curiosity, as always, said yes. What said no most loudly was the thought of what a fearful evening it would be. Penny's recent performance had amplified this objection. Halfway through the finale, the sight of Kitty coming into the room decided me. No.

Kitty was so good about not interrupting or distracting us, her mouth thinned and eyes narrowed with concentration as she fetched, opened, deployed and started on some sewing, that Roy and I had to work hard to prevent the closing pages from degenerating into chaos. We finished approximately together. Kitty hurled down her sewing and clapped in the childish mode, hands pointing the same way instead of across each other at right angles.

'I do wish I'd been able to be here for all of that,' she said in a faint voice designed to show something of what the frustration of this wish had cost her.

'What?' Roy cupped his hand behind his ear, either not having heard or countering the faint-voice tactic.

'I said I do wish I'd been able to be here for all of that,' shouted Kitty, no elaborate mouthing about it this time.

'Thanks.'

He put his Stradivarius back in its case. Kitty, her neck looking several inches longer than it had a moment before, picked up her sewing again. I got to my feet and looked round the room, which was furnished with a hi-fi set-up, a mahogany sideboard that had a marble top visible here and there among bottles, a science-fiction giant lily or two, some bloated china cats, and framed posters of Che Guevara, Ho Chi Minh, a nude couple making love and other key figures of the time.

Behind me, I (quite distinctly) heard Kitty say, 'Darling, I wonder if you'd have a word with Ashley about the bathroom.'

Roy answered, 'Have a word with him about what?'

'I wondered if you'd have a word with Ashley.'

'That was the bit I heard. Have a word with him about what? I heard the bit about having a word with him.'

'About the *bath . . . room.*'

'What about the bathroom?'

'Darling.' Kitty sounded relaxed to the point of imminent sleep. 'Would you have a word with Ashley about it?'

'I know! I know! I heard the bit about have a word with him about the bathroom. What about the bathroom? Christ – what is it about the bathroom that you want me to have a word with him, Ashley, about?'

'Really, darling. About *peeing* in the bathroom. That's what I want you to have a word with him about. If you would.'

He howled like a wolf, his usual method of indicating belated comprehension, and said, 'There at last. You want me to have a word with Ashley about peeing in the bathroom.'

'Yes,' said Kitty in a voice full of lines of strain and glazed eyes and skin stretched tightly over cheekbones.

There was a pause, during which Roy nodded his head a good deal and I began to wonder, for the first time in my life, whether the experience of listening to the whole of Bruckner's Eighth Symphony might not have something to be said for it after all. Then Roy asked,

'What about it?'

'*Oh!* Tell him *not* to!'

'I've done that and he goes on peeing.'

'Use your authority.'

'How? What authority? We agreed he's not to be punished and we can't go back on that. I'm not suggesting for a moment we go back on that. But what sort of word can I have with him? I'm not asking rhetorically, I can assure you. I really would like to know.'

'Could I make a telephone call?' I asked.

'Certainly, old lad.'

Roy took me across the hall to his study and departed. It was a small room on which some sound-proofing had been done, not enough to keep out the faint wails and solid thumps of pop from the floor above. Some thought, perhaps too much, had gone into the selection and arrangement of objects on view: photographs of Brahms and Castro, small busts of Beethoven and Mao, copies of Hutchings on Mozart's piano concertos and Marcuse on liberation, posters announcing a Nikisch concert in 1913 and an anti-American demonstration in 1969. I telephoned the airline office where somebody called Vivienne worked (where I had first met her, in fact) and arranged to pick her up at her flat for some supper after my concert, which was taking place conveniently close by. As I talked, I noticed a sheaf of music manuscript lying on a miniature upright piano across the room, and hurried to pick it up the moment I had rung off.

It was several pages long, unfinished, in Roy's hand: a quartet, or chamber concerto for violin, with parts for sitar, bass guitar and bongoes. Across the top of the first sheet *Elevations 9* was written, perhaps by way of title. I felt a particular loathing for that *9*: either there were eight other *Elevations* or the numeral was arbitrary, a piece of decor, which was nearly as bad. I studied the violin part for a few moments. As far as I could tell, which was probably far enough, it called for some virtuosity but not much – not too much, anyway, for a trendy old idiot of a fiddler who until quite recently would have had, not the sense, but the sense of style, to refrain from musical adventurisms like writing a sort of pop tune (as I now saw it to be) with a classical-type violin *obbligato* to be performed by himself – who else ? A first-rate example of the not-lowering-artistic-standards Kitty had talked about.

Then I thought I must be going too fast and far. There was no real reason to suppose that *Elevations 9* was anything more than an exercise, an experiment, or even a parody, designed to raise a laugh or so as part of some cod mélange at a charity do. But, to a Roy who went on as he now did, that would be in-admissibly square. And an exercise for its own sake, with no thought of performance? Hardly Roy. And the amount of practising he had so clearly been doing. Then why had he . . . ?

I went quietly out into the hall and at once caught sight of what I had been certain would be there: a perfectly good telephone, in working order, as it proved. I returned to the study and stared at the pages of manuscript. Yes. By God. I (representing the orthodox musical public) and they were the artistic equivalent of Kitty and the pants. Flaunting it. I went on staring, mostly into space.

After a couple of minutes I looked at my watch. Five thirty exactly. I dialled the newspaper and soon got Coates's cough, then his voice.

'We've had to lose half an inch, Doug.'

'The half-inch about where Kohler comes from and where he studied and the rest of it.'

'That's the one. Reasons of space, of course.'

'You or him?'

'Well, both, in a way. He was in here when we were making up. Sorry, I didn't realize.'

'Is he in his office now?'

'He wasn't five minutes ago. Look, we can put it back if you want. We'll have to lose a half-inch somewhere else, though. Have you got a carbon there? What about this bit near the end about this fellow whose name begins with J's early style?'

'Janáček. No, I need that.'

'Well then . . . You can't pop in, can you?'

'No. Leave it. Leave it as it is.'

I rang off. Over the past few days I had been telling myself now and then that if Harold cut me materially, as he had done twice before, I would do no more work for the paper. But I knew now without thinking about it that I was going to carry on. Why not? Nothing said I had to inform five million readers that Heinrich Kohler was an East German; their continuing ignorance of this fact could not damage him, only, by remote extension, his country, and *it* could blow itself up tomorrow for all I cared either way, on the understanding that it sent its good musicians and singers and instruments abroad first. My sole concern had always been to promote the people and the works I admired and to demote the other sort. I must positively hang on to my job with Harold, then, if only to keep out the sort of little mountebank likely to do a turn at it between a spell on the books page and the real prize spot, the restaurant column.

Across the hall a door slammed and someone – Kitty – ran upstairs at a great rate. Another, more distant door slammed. I scratched my backside. Nothing said (did it?) that I must never do anything that those who behaved like Kitty would probably not like. Doing my best to block *Elevations 9* was a higher obligation. So I was changing my mind about Roy's favour, with its opportunities for exploration of his immediate musical intentions. That still left a problem about Penny, but I pushed it out of sight.

On the desk, the telephone bell pinged. I thought briefly, then went back into the hall. Roy was at the telephone there. When he saw me, he gave a glance and a nod that invited me over beside him; I went; he jabbed his finger at a dog-eared directory lying before him. Its cover bore what I had always felt was a dispensable slogan about its being a great place to look up people's telephone numbers in.

'I've been meaning to do this for a long time,' said Roy. He had a serious, dedicated look about him. 'They shouldn't be allowed to get away with this kind of ... Inquiries? Good afternoon. I wonder if you can help me ... I'm sure you will. Now: the other evening, last Thursday to be precise, I met a very nice chap and his wife at a party in Chelsea somewhere. He was about forty, forty-five, running a bit to fat, dark, hair receding rather, said he worked in public relations. Uh, smoked a pipe. She was a few years younger, on the thin side

I think one would say . . . Do let me finish; there isn't much more. Yes, she was wearing a green dress with a wide belt, and earrings, they looked late eighteenth century to me, two children they had, a boy and a girl, both at school. That's about all I can remember. I do hope it's enough . . . For you to tell me their name, of course, so that I can look up their number in the directory. I want to telephone them, you see . . . But if I knew their *name*, I could look up their *number*, as the Post office so helpfully reminds me on the front of this foam book I have here. It's precisely because I don't know their name that I got on to you in the first place . . . You can't? What bloody use are you, then?'

He rang off with a triumphant crash. 'Pity in a way. She sounded quite a nice girl, actually. I should have got hold of the supervisor. I can do that tomorrow. Got to keep at them. What's the matter with you?'

'Nothing. I don't think that rubbish is on the latest directories.'

'That doesn't affect the principle. Like a drink?'

'No thanks. You have one.'

'I most assuredly will.'

He had walked me down the hall a few paces and now switched on a light (the house was generally rather dark), in an alcove where there was a squat refrigerator and a couple of shelves piled with glasses and bottles, most of them dirty and empty respectively. The ice compartment of the refrigerator looked like a small sample of a glacier, but Roy tugged an ice-tray out of it and put some of its contents into a presumably clean tumbler. After that he took me into the drawing-room, poured about a gill of Scotch on top of the ice, and drank a certain amount of it. He still had the intent air I had noticed at the telephone. We started speaking at the same time; he signed to me to go on.

'Sorry. Roy, I've changed my mind about that favour you wanted me to do for you. We can fix an evening whenever you say.'

He pointed his nose at me and did one of his rich, dependable-sounding laughs. 'I was just going to tell you I shan't be needing it now. The whole thing's off.'

'Off?'

'I'm giving her up. Cleam break. Best thing for everybody. You'd probably agree, wouldn't you? I had the whole thing out with Kitty just now.'

'It didn't sound as if it went down too well. I couldn't help hearing . . .'

'Oh, that was just a minor point. I think I rather over-stressed the attractions of, uh, what I've been up to. It'll blow over in no time. The great stroke is that I've told her the full story from the word go.'

'With what object?'

'Oh, Christian gentleman! What object would you expect? So that I can stop feeling guilty and she can stop feeling insecure. You know.'

'And clear the air and wipe the slate and square the account. Yes, I know. You must be off your head. I thought you were supposed to be in love with this girl. Or have you wiped that clean too?'

'Do you imagine I can't see how difficult it's going to be?'

'Indeed I do, despite your past experience, and when you find you're starting again, or trying to, you'll realize that all you've done is create fresh difficulties for yourself. Once you start making with the pants again, Kitty's bound to –'

'Bugger the pants! You and Kitty are obsessed with the bloody things. She even brought them up just now. It seems such a trivial point to me.' He was quietening down, preparing to pull out of the whole topic. 'Why don't you stay to dinner, Duggers? We're having a few locals in, nothing very spectacular . . .'

'Thanks, but I've got a concert. You've just erected a permanent obstacle in your own path without doing anybody else any good.'

'Oh, I don't know. What is your concert? I might come along.'

'But what about your . . . ? Oh, London Handel Players under

Matheson. To have heard all the details isn't going to make Kitty the slightest bit –'

'It's not a formal party. People just drop in. They've come on a lot since Matheson took over. What are they playing?'

'Even if you never touch another girl in your life you'll suffer because of it. Bach and Handel. The First Suite. A concerto grosso, one of the op. 6, I forget which. Some other stuff. Why can't you ever keep it to yourself? You –'

'I can get that kind of thing better performed on my hi-fi. No, I think I'll stay after all. Kitty would like me to be here.'

Having now to contend with Kitty herself, Ashley, the Furry Barrel, Gilbert and Penny, who had started infiltrating the room, as well as Roy in top evading trim, I gave up. A headache had spread out from the place I had hit on the door frame. The best part of an hour's journey by Tube lay ahead of me. I said my goodbyes, receiving from Penny a wordless grin and a glance at my forehead. Gilbert drove me to the station in unbroken silence. A train had just left. The one I took stopped for a quarter of an hour under the river. I hurried to the concert hall and arrived exactly on time. There was a ten-minute delay in starting. The concertino violin broke a string in the Handel. Afterwards I walked nearly a mile in a light drizzle before I reached shelter. Vivienne, at the best of times an undistinguished dresser, was wearing a fearful trouser-suit that looked as if it had been made out of the seat-covers of some excitingly new motor-coach. She was mildly sullen and preoccupied, but would not say about what. At the restaurant, her omelette was dry and too salt, and I spilled most of a glass of wine over the tablecloth. It was a little better in bed. Not much, not nearly as much as I had had solid grounds for expecting. I saw next morning that the paper had transposed two lines in my piece and misspelt Kohler's name. After such a promising plunge into the bush, life seemed to have returned to its old beaten path.

I heard nothing of Roy for five or six weeks. Nothing direct, that is. But his name remained before me and the rest of the public. With others, he signed a letter to *The Times* calling for an ultimatum to the Smith Government in Rhodesia to hand over all power to black leaders within forty-eight hours or face an airborne invasion. He gave an interview to a Sunday newspaper, in which he developed the ideas about youth he had dimly outlined to me in his garden, saying, in part, that it – youth – was in the process of discovering something as momentous as Christianity, and that those who resisted the free sale of hashish and other drugs did so out of guilt. He appeared in a television discussion on the future of the arts, no doubt forgetting the troubles that such exposure had allegedly brought him not so long before. I missed the programme, but heard that it was political in tendency, the views represented ranging from Roy's to those of an American sculptor who, it seemed, had demanded an end to all art not directly destructive of society. I was relieved to see a paragraph on some cultural chit-chat page saying that ebullient conductor Sir Roy Vander-vane was preparing with the New London Symphony Orchestra to give a series of concerts of the symphonies of Mahler. Trendy, true, I thought to myself, but far, far better that than such as *Elevations 9*.

Nothing much happened to me over this period. *The Record-Player*, having tried all the reviewers senior to me and been re-buffed, sent along a huge box with a couple of dozen early Haydn symphonies and a small library inside it: eight long-playing yards, or about ten hours, of perfunctory periwiggery, not to speak of all those words, which provided a frightening amount of information on the composer's life and times without descending to any particulars at all about the symphonies concerned. That week I had Haydn coming out of my ears, or rather out of the other ear than the one he went in at. Harold Meers behaved himself on the whole, vetoing only a passing reference to the successful tour a string quartet had had in Poland. I finally winkled Weber out of Salzburg and established him in Vienna. I got the laundry to render up a shirt of mine they had been sitting on, if not wearing, for a couple of months, and had my piano tuned. Vivienne's sullenness-cum-preoccupation, never so marked as to sour any occasion, continued to fluctuate in a regular pattern: deepening as the week-end approached, vanished by Saturday afternoon, when I usually drove her out somewhere in a hired car, beginning to stir faintly again by Sunday evening. It was one Sunday about eight o'clock that I decided to change my usual policy of sitting (or, in this case, lying) about and waiting for female moods to go away.

'Has this other bloke been acting up, or what?'

'No,' said Vivienne.

This reply illustrated one of the best things in her character. Although the other bloke had been on the scene since Christmas or so, and took up all her free time and half her bed every Tuesday and Friday, and although she knew I knew about him, he had not been made conversational flesh until now. It was a relief not to have to machete my way through a jungle of what-are-you-talking-aboutery before I could get at him. Admittedly, this readiness to concede facts went with a reluctance to volunteer them, so that the process of finding out from her what, for instance, her father did for a living (it transpired that he was the lay secretary of an ecclesiastical body) was too much like one of those yes-or-no guessing games. But one cannot, and in this sort of case probably should not, have everything.

'Is he rich?'

'No. About the same as you.'

'I see. Married?'

'No.' She spoke with some heat.

'Well, a lot of people are, you know. Is he nice?'

'I wouldn't go with him if he wasn't nice, would I? He's

fairly nice. No, a bit nicer than that. Say about halfway between fairly nice and really nice. He's rather small, you see, only about an inch taller than me. And then he's got this beard. Without a moustache. It goes all the way round his face without him having a moustache.'

'He doesn't sound anything like as nice as me.'

'He isn't. Not in that sort of way. But he's very kind and thoughtful. Oh, I mean you're kind when you think of it, but he always is. It's a big thing with him. And he's dependable. I can rely on him no matter what it is.'

'Don't mind me saying it, will you? but I think you're making him out to be rather dull.'

'There is a touch of that,' said Vivienne.

After a pause, I said, 'Does he know about me?'

'Oh yes.'

'How did he find out?'

'He asked me and I told him.'

'Yes. Does he mind sharing you?'

'He'd far sooner not, but he says it's better than not having me at all, and it's up to me, he says. He leaves all that side of things up to me.'

'Do you mind being shared? Have you done it before?'

'I'm usually shared, actually, and once I tried three for a bit, so I suppose I can't really mind. And I know you don't mind, in fact you'd sooner, wouldn't you? because it means I can't get serious. It sort of looks as though it ought to be wrong, doesn't it, sharing? I mean it's just exactly the kind of thing that is. I can't see why it isn't, but I went over it all in my mind before I started it, and I couldn't find anything that said I shouldn't, as long as I stuck to the rules, telling the truth and no married men.'

'Why no married men?'

'Making someone else unhappy. Same with a man who's got a girl he'd marry if he could, but his wife won't divorce him. You don't mind, do you? Me quite liking being shared?'

'Fine with me.'

'Because it's so enjoyable. Oh, darling,' she said, moving up against me and in other directions as well, and immediately, in fact simultaneously, breathing hard. It was easy for me to do something about that, since we were in bed together in my flat at the time. Doing something adequate about it was, as always, a matter of a good deal more than a couple of minutes. Vivienne was quick off the mark all right, but she was equally quick off a more or less indefinite successive series of marks. It was really very practical of her, quite liking being shared.

There was a different side of things that I, and in all probability the other bloke too, left up to her: the moment when the gentleman should come into his own. That evening, as always, she picked it admirably. Very soon afterwards she said, 'Good heavens, is that really the time?', jumped out of bed and ran into the bathroom. I lay on my back, put my glasses on to aid thought, and decided slowly that the sullenness-cum-preoccupation must be derived from the unflattering uninterest I had formerly shown in the question of the other bloke. I would have to remember to inquire about his welfare every so often, without at the same time letting it be known what hell I thought he sounded.

When Vivienne came out of the bathroom I went in there, returning to find her dressing. She kept her back to me, but this was standard; indeed, I had only recently, and after constant pressure, been able to stop her going into the bathroom to dress. Her underclothes had their familiar look of being both new and old, as if she had that afternoon come across a hermetically sealed unused set from her mother's trousseau behind a secret panel. On top of them went a variegated shiny silk shirt in lilac, flame, mustard and navy blue, a thick, rather long skirt with a black hound's tooth pattern on pinkish beige, pale green stockings and brown shoes. A chain belt, amber beads, a charm bracelet constructed for maximum noise-level, and earrings featuring little gold birdcages with painted parrots inside – these were added as I put my clothes on. Apart from intrinsic qualities, the ensemble abolished the substantial breasts, narrow waist and curving hips beneath it. She had brought her abundant and (literally) coal-black hair into disservice by piling it up into a roughly rectangular wedge across the top of her head, and now smeared mauve grease-paint over the firm outlines of her lips. But even she had not been able to muddy the brown of her eyes, pock her skin, skew her nose, unwhiten or snaggle her teeth. These failures were what had led me to her that first morning in the airline office, together with what the olive uniform she wore there had not concealed. (She had told me once, without making any evident deduction from it, that it was funny how only tried to pick her up in the office.)

'Would you like a drink?' I asked.

She looked at her watch, which had a spaceman's head depicted in pop-art style on its considerable face. 'We mustn't be too long, Doug. I don't want to be late back. Could I have a small bianco and soda?'

I prepared a couple of these, and we were drinking them in the sitting-room when the telephone rang. After the idiot periodic tweet, signalling a call from a public box, I heard Roy's voice.

'May I speak to Mr Yandell, please?' (He had not yet learnt to bring his telephone manners up to date by baldly naming the person he wanted.)

'Yes, Roy, speaking.'

'Duggers. Marvellous. How are you? Look, old lad, I'm clutching at straws. Have you got anybody with you?'

'Yes.'

'Oh, sporting spirit. Oh, that's it, then.' He sounded in some distress. 'Oh well, never –'

'We're going out soon to have dinner.'

'Oh. Oh, I see. Well, look, I've got somebody with me too. We've been sort of let down. I wonder if I could possibly –'

'Where are you now?'

High-pitched female giggling came from the other end, then some muffled words from Roy, remonstrative in tone. Soon he said, 'What? Just round the corner from you. Carlton Hill.'

'Come along straight away. I'll let you in and we'll disappear.'

'Are you sure?'

I convinced him I was, rang off, and did some explaining

to Vivienne. Without surprise or delay, as expected, she took in the situation and agreed that, should it prove necessary, I could later share her bed, which she insisted on occupying on Sunday nights anyway, so as to begin her working week on her own ground, as she put it – and incidentally, as I had discovered, at six a.m. Then I told her which Roy it was who was coming.

'You mean *Sir* Roy Vandervane. Doesn't he go on television?'

'Frequently. And conducts orchestras. He's an old music friend of mine. You won't tell anyone, will you, Viv?'

'Of course not. Isn't he married, though?'

'Yes. It's all a –'

'What about his wife? Doesn't she mind or anything?'

'I suppose so. It's hard to be sure. She must. Or she would. She probably doesn't know. Almost certainly.'

'People always know.'

She stared at me accusingly, and I could find nothing to say, but at that moment my doorbell rang and I hurried downstairs. Of the two waiting figures I got a brief look at through the glass panel, one, which I took to be Roy, was so much larger than the other that I wondered for a moment whether, Kitty's forecasts having fallen short, he might not have reached the child-abduction stage already. When they stepped into the hall, I saw that matters had not yet reached that pass, but, in the spirit of a bibliophile taking his time about polishing his glasses before starting to peruse some rare tome, deferred a comprehensive survey until we were all four gathered in the sitting-room.

'This is Sylvia,' said Roy, leaving us in no doubt that he would much rather have introduced her as Miss X.

Not to be outdone in pointless mystification, I introduced Vivenne as Vivienne. The matter of the pants recurred to me as something more to the point than any number of suppressed surnames, and I felt very much like letting Roy know that, if he ever happened to take up espionage, he would in no time at all find himself asking a policeman the way to the bacterial-missile launching site. But he would have considered that fanciful, and it might have interfered with my scrutiny of Sylvia, so I kept my mouth shut while Vivienne, curiosity and disapproval bursting out of her eyes, exchanged amiabilities with him.

Was this Roy's great love of a few weeks back, or just something he had picked up at a party an hour before? The latter, I fervently hoped, studying face (pale, round, thin-lipped), hair (waist-length, lank) clothes (jeans, midget-fisherman's jersey, long sleeveless leather jacket), figure (none perceptible: Vivienne's get-up was shamelessly provocative by comparison). She exuded a curious smell, not unlike that of damp hay. I watched her looking round at the rows of books, the hi-fi, the piano, the record-racks, the typewriter, as if these objects were not only mildly strange but also virtually indistinguishable from one another. Every few seconds she scooped aside the two long hanks of hair that fell from a centre parting across most of her face, which they as regularly repossessed; troublesome for her, no doubt, but infinitely preferable to the gross humiliation of haircut or ribbon. Through it all, she put me in mind of somebody, or perhaps she had just had her picture in the papers, like most people under twenty-five.

'What a terribly nice fluht,' she said, using the then fashionable throaty vowel. Her voice was thin and clear, with the sort of accent that Roy tried to suppress in his own speech. 'Do you live here all on your own?'

'Most of the time I do.'

'You seem to have an awful lot of books and records and things like thuht.'

'I've sort of got to. It's to do with my job.'

'Roy was telling me,' she said. Then, just as I was beginning to settle down to nothing worse than a couple of minutes of boredom, she gave a loud snigger and looked not so much at me as at my face, as one in search of imperfections there; I immediately thought of the way Penny had reacted to the lump on my forehead, though it was not she of whom Sylvia had reminded me a moment before.

Roy broke in abruptly. 'I'm really moce grateful to you two for doing this for us.'

'Not at all. Right, Viv, let's be on our way.'

'Oh, don't rush off.' Roy sent me a private scowl of emphasis. 'You can spare ten minutes. Stay and have a quick drink with us.'

'What can I get you?' I asked Sylvia.

The girl had perhaps been doing her best to hold her mirth in check, but this last hilarity proved too much for her. She hunched her narrow shoulders and made a tearing, sneeze-like sound at the back of her nose. Repeating my question in shaking tones, she rotated slowly and unsteadily, her eyes coming to each of us in turn, but not in any very directed way. Tears or sweat lay on her pale cheeks.

'She'll have something soft,' said Roy, who seemed a little embarrassed. 'I don't suppose you've got a Coke or a Pepsi? Never mind, tonic, bitter lemon, dry ginger, anything.'

'Nothing for me, Douglas.' Vivienne clearly thought that her censorious looks at Sylvia looked like nothing more than looks.

'She'll have something soft,' quavered Sylvia. 'She'll have something soft.'

'I'll have a whisky if I may, Duggers. Let me give you a hand.'

'Is she always like that?' I asked Roy in the kitchen.

'No, only sometimes. Not often, really. You know, when she's high.'

'High? Do you mean on filthy hash? Pot?'

'My dear ole lad, I do wish you wouldn't always come up with the middle-class reaction. So predictable.'

'Well, she's not going to smoke it here. And what class are you?'

'Sorry. All right, I'll see she doesn't.'

With a show of irrevocable decision, he drank off about half the Scotch I had given him. Even in the days when his hair had been shorter and he would speak up occasionally against rock 'n roll, Russia and the like, he had never diffused much confidence in any of his non-musical promises or decisions. It could do no good now to remind him that I would be breaking the law in my absence if he later failed to prevent his fearful little companion from lighting up a joint. I parenthetically wondered for a moment about the current state of his musical reliability.

'Is this the one, by the way?' I asked, pouring out a bottle of tonic water and wanting to top it up with dishwashing fluid.

'The one?'

'Roy. The one you said you were in love with up at your place.'

'Oh yes. Yes, this is the one. Of course, that was the day I decided to give her up, wasn't it? I remember now. Didn't last, as you see.'

'What changed your mind?'

'That I can't remember. Oh yes, Kitty put me in the wrong about something. Yes, it's all coming back to me now. I turned up sober for a dinner-party she was giving and she took it very well. Kitty did. Considering how pissed I'd been when one of the same chaps and his wife had come along the time before. Hungarian chap who settled here after the civil war there. Very reactionary. As a matter of fact I was very nice to them both, both times, as I recall. Couldn't have been sweeter.'

'What about the pants?'

'Oh, Puck-like theme! Have you been talking to Kitty again?'

'She rang me up the morning after that day and I told her I hadn't found out anything, which was true. Not a word since then.'

'I prefer to keep my underwear to myself, if you don't mind. No, actually I've been watching that. Laid in a whole stock of them, pants I mean, and vests and handkerchiefs as well. It would take a genius to keep track. Hang on for another few minutes if you can bear it, Duggers, to help me cool her down. Nice girl, that one of yours. What is she, twenty-eight? Do you mind if I top this up before we go back in?'

Back in, we found Vivienne not only still alive, but listening with apparently close attention to something being explained to her by Sylvia, who sat on the couch scooping her hair off her face with the regularity of a bodily exercise.

'We're not like that. We're different.' Without looking

anywhere near me, she put her hand up and out in my direction, fingers and thumb spread, so that I was able to fit her glass of tonic into it with the minimum of trouble and delay. 'Uhbsolutely different. We reject money and making your way in the world and setting yourself up in life and rules. All the things they want us to use up our energies on so they can stay in power.'

'The structure,' said Roy encouragingly, and with an air of relief, sitting down next to her on the couch.

'Do you reject the fire-brigade when your house is on fire?' asked Vivienne.

Roy smiled indulgently and shook his head, so that his back hair waggled to and fro. 'That's not the same thing. Of course you use all this stuff. You use houses and telephones and shops and television sets and schools and so on. That's quite different from being dominated by them.'

'Who does the fire-brigade dominate?'

Boredom again seemed entrenched, so firmly that I felt I could well do with another bout of sniggers from Sylvia, now quite impassive apart from blinking hard and biting at her thin lower lip. Roy told Vivienne that she had chosen a bad example, and that he was talking about what lay behind the fire-brigade. Vivienne asked who the we was that rejected money and the fire-brigade, and, on learning from him that it was broadly speaking youth, said she considered herself still part of broadly speaking that, or had done until quite recently. At this, Sylvia sniggered in a way that showed how wrong I had been a moment before, and whispered into Roy's ear, putting one arm round his shoulders and the other hand on his knee.

'No no,' said Roy. 'No.'

Vivienne pursued her point. 'And you won't catch me doing any rejecting.'

'Why not,' said Sylvia, giggling hard, 'why not make a start with that blouse? If that's what you call it.'

'I beg your pardon?'

'Why do you wear such awful clothes? And so many of them. Doesn't *he* tell you? And those earrings. Are those birds in them?'

'That's enough, Sylvia,' said Roy without emphasis.

'Really, the things some people think they can say.' There was only a little indignation in Vivienne's tone and her cheek remained its usual light pink, unexpectedly in a girl who blushed almost as readily as she breathed.

Roy turned expository. 'I suppose the real division comes between those who want to have and those who want to be. What the have ones want to have can be a lot of different things, not all of them bad in themselves. Some are, of course, like power in all its forms, which is what politicians obviously exiss for, and I don't just mean fascist dictators, I mean anybody who wages politics. Then there are, well, businessmen and priests and administrators and all that lot, but I'm talking about personal power too, by one person over another person, like in most marriages and so on. Or it can be possessions, cars and washing-machines and furniture and collections of china and things. The people who want to be can be a lot of different things too, like artists and mystics and philosophers and revolutionaries, some sorts anyway, and just people who live and feel and see. You've got to make up your mind whether you're a have person or a be person.'

Outside the concert hall, I had never admired Roy more than during the couple of minutes it took him to get through to the end of this speech. As early as 'real division' Sylvia had started stroking the back of his neck; by 'politicians' she was stroking his thigh fairly near the knee and nuzzling his ear; at 'personal power' she fell to stroking one cheek and kissing the other. Up to this point Roy had pretended, carrying what conviction he could, that she was not there, but then he had changed his policy to one of non-violent resistance, crossing his legs and canting his head over as near as possible to his farther shoulder. When 'collections of china' saw her moving round towards his front, trying to undo a shirt button and pushing her hand between his thighs, he caught her by the wrists, and immediately after 'philosophers' had cast her at his feet, trying energetically to uncross his legs, he crossed them tighter and bent forward until belly met upper thigh, intensifying his grasp on her wrists. So matters stood for the moment.

'We really must be going,' I said.

There was a testing interval while Vivienne looked for and found her cigarettes and lighter and put them in her handbag, but the two of us had gained the door only an instant after hearing, from the direction of the couch, a double thud which told that the heels of the shoes on the feet at the end of Roy's finally uncrossed legs had struck the floor. I called to him over my shoulder that I would telephone in the morning.

'What was she going to do?' asked Vivienne during dinner at Biagi's.

I allowed time for the waiter to finish pouring out Valpolicella and go away before indicating what I had seen as the choice before Sylvia and saying which alternative I thought the more likely.

Vivienne blushed. 'Not with you and me there. She wouldn't have done that with us there.'

'Oh, I think especially with us there. That was the whole point. Or most of it. Demonstrating her liberation from such-and-such and her contempt for this, that and the other.'

'For what? Why?'

'Oh, God. To go against what she thinks we think is decent. To show she's a be person. It's not worth finding out. That girl's a puzzle you'd have to be out of your mind with curiosity even to consider finding the answer to. Viv, why weren't you cross when she . . . had a go at you?'

'Well, I was a bit, of course, but I know what you mean. I could see she was annoyed at your nice place and us getting on all right together. And it being all right for us to get on. Was she stoned? you know.'

'I think she must have been.'

'Well, you can't really be cross with someone in that state, can you? They're not themselves. At least, they're . . .'

'Yeah.'

After efficiently throwing down some more of her *escaloppe di vitello alla Biagis* for a minute or two, Vivienne said, 'Doug, is this blouse awful? And the earrings? You've got to say.'

'You dress in your own style. What you've chosen yourself. That's just the sort of thing she'd resent. Somebody who won't conform.'

'Conform? She doesn't exactly dress like they tell you.'

'No, well I don't mean what the magazines say. Her own crowd. All rejecting everything. Including very much King's Road or wherever the hell it is now.'

'But you do like the blouse? And the earrings?'

'You know I do.'

'She could talk, the way she'd flung on any old dirty thing she'd happened to pick up. All tatty.'

'She was awful.'

'I just hope your flat's all right,' said Vivienne.

So did I, especially when I telephoned Roy there the next morning as promised and found him vague, uncommunicative. Sylvia had left; he would wait until I returned; we might have a chat if I could spare the time. I said I could, even though I had used up a good deal of it already that day, notably between five thirty, when Vivienne had woken me, and six o'clock, when, right on schedule, she had got out of bed. More time had elapsed while she bustled about putting clothes into and taking other clothes out of cupboards and drawers, and more yet while she vacuum-cleaned the flat in its entirety, paying special attention, I thought, to the area immediately round the bed in which I still lay, but out of which she turned me soon after seven so that she could pack up the sheets for the laundry. A lot of bacon and eggs and coffee, prepared by me according to custom, acted as a temporary reviver; indeed, she looked so appealing in her office uniform that I would have been tempted to get her to take it off again, if time had not gone into short supply at that stage. We left and parted to our respective buses, having confirmed our usual arrangement to get in touch on Wednesday; Monday evening was the one on which she went to see her father in Highgate, and Tuesday was the property of the other bloke. There was a tinge of sullenness-cum-preoccupation in her farewell, rather less than normal for this point in the week. I dismissed it from my mind without trouble.

Smells of a strange breakfast hung about the Maida Vale building, or at least its ground floor, where there lived a Pakistani (employed, so he said, in some radio service of the B.B.C.) and his fat Welsh wife. I climbed the stairs and con-

63

fronted Roy, who appeared unshaven, though patches of dried blood on his cheeks and chin testified to some sort of struggle with my razor.

'You look a bit shagged,' he said.

'So would you if you'd been awake as long as I have. And so you do, anyway.'

'I bet I do. A heavy night, one way and another.'

'I can well imagine.'

'I doubt it, old lad.'

My eye fell on a patch of bare floor in front of the sitting-room couch. 'What's happened to my rug?'

'I'm sorry about that, Duggers. It had an accident.'

'Which destroyed every fibre of it.'

'No, I got Sylvia to take it away with her. That was no mean achievement on my part, I can assure you.'

'I'm convinced. What happened to it?'

'It wouldn't have been any use to you after, uh, what happened to it. I'll find you another one and have it sent up to you today.'

Roy's practice in matters of this sort was such that I knew a rug would indeed arrive and that it would be better than the one I had had, without being absurdly better. The rest of the sitting-room appeared unchanged. I wondered what the other rooms were like, especially the bedroom.

'There's nothing else much,' said Roy, who had followed my glance. 'A couple of plates and a cup. Also I gave your Scotch a bit of a pasting. I'll see to all that as well, of course.'

'No, the Scotch is on me.'

'Thank you, that's very nice of you. Look, I'm sorry about, uh, the way she went on last night. She's not as bad as that as a rule.'

'Oh, good. Never mind, it was a laugh of a sort. I'm going to shave now, if you've left me any blades. You put some more coffee on.'

The bedroom was in no worse a state than usual, the bed even rather carefully made: a waste of Roy's labour, because this bed was another bed that was going to have its sheets changed, not on his account. I deferred the operation, out of returning fatigue and the thought that to catch me in the act might dash him slightly.

Over coffee in the sitting-room, he asked, 'What are you up to this morning?'

'Well, it was supposed to have been Weber, really, followed by a recording at Broadcasting House at twelve fifteen – Music Diary.'

'Weber can hang on for a bit, can't he? How long is it till his bicentenary? Ten years?'

'Sixteen. At the present rate of progress I'm going to need all of them. What had you got in mind?'

'Oh, nothing in particular. I thought we might idle about for a spell, ending up at my club, where I could shoot a couple of glasses of champagne into you and send you off in top form to your recording.'

'After which we meet Sylvia and Penny for lunch at the Mirabelle.'

'No, honestly, nothing like that.' Roy looked neither transparently honest nor pained at having his honesty thrown in doubt, which meant he was being honest, or very, very nearly. 'How do you feel about Gilbert Alexander?' he went on. 'You remember, the chap who –'

'Yes, the black chap. I feel fine about him. Why?'

'He's bringing the car in for me. I said I'd give him a drink and show him the club. You wouldn't mind if he joined us?'

'Not in the least, but isn't he going to find things rather on the fascist racist side at Craggs's?'

'I don't think so, much. I've explained to him about it.'

'You mean that although it may look fascist and racist it isn't really?'

'He won't make any trouble,' said Roy confidently.

Acting as the Vandervane all-purpose social diluent had been no uncommon experience during our former association. Today's usage seemed unlikely, in prospect, to take much out of me, differing in this regard from the favour to which I had alluded a minute before. While Roy put the new Oistrakh on the hi-fi and I carried the rubbish bucket down to the dustbin, the full complexity of my intended role in the favour dawned on me: not only diluent, not just camouflage, but whipping-boy, bodyguard, odium-sharer, listener to tales of the have people and the be people, and probably getaway man, fetcher of police, ambulance, or the rejected fire-brigade. I went over my recording-script and set about hardening my heart against all talk of the favour.

'Are you ready, Duggers?'

'Bit early, isn't it? I can't drink champagne for an hour and a half and then go and work.'

'It's a bloody marvellous day. I thought we might walk down as far as the flyover, or anyway the canal.'

It was dusty, windy and noisy in the Edgware Road, but so sunny that even the tower blocks on the western side looked inhabitable, gave the illusion of being places where the good life, whatever that might be, was possible to pursue. The buses seemed unusually red and solid, the articulated lorries to be clattering and bouncing to some purpose. I said,

'What's special about her? I mean I can see she's young and all that, and you say she knows a lot about whatever it is, and I've only met her for a few minutes, but what's special about her?'

'The chief special thing about her as far as I'm concerned, and I'm the only one who is concerned, is that there she is. I met her and I started going to bed with her. It's Sylvia and not anybody else that I met and started going to bed with. Oh, the being young thing and knowing things is important, sure, but a lot of other kids have got that. Only I haven't met and gone to bed with them. Another point about her is that she isn't my wife.'

'True. Very few people are Kitty.'

'It isn't Kitty she isn't, you bloody fool. What she isn't is my wife. Not the same thing at all. As you get older you'll find that absolutely straight-down-the-middle sex doesn't strike you in quite the same way as it did when you started off. It *is* the same when you get to it, in fact it may be rather better, because you'll probably have picked up a few tips over the years, got better control and so on, but it doesn't strike you as the same. And there's no whacking fucking as a side of life where how things strike you matters at least as much as what the things are really like. Whatever they are really like. Everybody spends much more time being struck by it all than actually on the job. Not juss stuff like looking at tit magazines and pulling your wire, though you can't leave that out, and not just all the ground you cover in your mind from first catching sight of a bird to throwing the definitive pass, though there's a lot of that, too. No, it's looking at your wife in the bath, seeing a bird for a few seconds in the street and wondering how it would be, reading a sex scene in a novel and putting yourself in the chap's place, or not, and why not, and running into an ex-girl-friend and wondering about that, and wondering how you'll be functioning in ten years' time if you still are. All that. Anything to do with sex that isn't any kind of actual sexual activity, and there's a hell of a lot of it. Ah, now here's a bit of luck, by Christ.'

We had halted on the kerb at the corner of St John's Wood Road, waiting for a green light or a gap in the traffic. Near us there also waited a man of about thirty, wearing a sober dark suit and a large pair of dark sunglasses. Roy went over to this person and abruptly linked arms with him.

'Don't you worry, old lad,' I heard him say. 'I'll get you across. Mind you, if I may say so, I think it's a bit silly of you not to carry a white stick. And you really ought to go into the guide-dog question. I'm told they're absolutely marvellous. Transform your life.'

The flow of vehicles stopped for a few seconds, and before the man had thrown off his bewilderment Roy had conducted him to the opposite pavement. Here he shook himself free.

'What the devil are you playing at?'

'That's no way to talk to somebody who's juss seen a blime man across the street. Talk about ingratitude.'

'You crazy or what? I'm not blind.'

'Then why are you wearing dark glasses on a day like this? Any reasonable person would certainly assume that you were blind. Wasting my time. Pure bloody affectation.'

'Roy,' I said when we were side by side again, 'it is quite a sunny day, you must admit.'

'Not that sunny. This is England in May, not Italy in August.'

'Agreed, but some people have weak eyes.'

'That's not why that little turd was wearing his blinkers. Pure showing off. You can't let them get away with it all along the line. Got to keep at them. No, I quite see it would have been better if the sun hadn't been shining. The trouble is it's so rarely one's going to get the chance, with the chum there actually waiting to cross. I've been wanting to do that for two or three years, and this is the first time it's come up. I couldn't let it go, could I?'

After we had walked in silence for a time, I said, 'Go on about how sex strikes you.'

'Oh yes. Well, what I was really building up to saying was, you remember the chap in that Joyce book who went round the streets at night yelling out "Naked women!" to give himself a thrill. And there was some other chap, in some book by a Frenchman I seem to remember, who said he couldn't read "Girl, 20" in a small-ad column without getting the horn. Well, that was all very bloody well for them. We all went through that stage in our youth. Nowadays, as far as I'm concerned it's got to be something more. For sex to really strike me. More detailed and off the beaten track. I suppose in one sense it doesn't matter what it is as long as it's something. Take the chaps who after three-quarters of a lifetime of the most boring marital respectability start trying to bugger Boy Scouts, or flashing their hamptons at little girls in trains – I think Aldous Huxley's got a bit on that somewhere. It's not that they'd really rather have been doing that right from the start and finely decide they'd better get it done if they're going to, not just that, anyway. It's much more that Girl, 20 won't work any more as a thing to strike them. As a slogan, sort of. Girl, 20 as a reality might be fine for them, but that's different. Look, I don't know about you, but I'm pretty well knackered with all this walking. Let's get a taxi, for Christ's sake.'

'How does your own case fit into this?' I asked when we had done so.

'Yes, well I was coming to that, as you may well surmise. Sometimes, you know, you find yourself thinking things over as if you were well, deciding which country to emigrate to, climate versus cost of living, exetra. What about turning queer? you say to yourself. Plenty of facilities, these days highly respectable, pleasant companions, comparatively inexpensive. And a prick is a splendid thing, and a splendid *idea* as well. It strikes you. The trouble is that in every case it's got a man on the end of it. Which I'm afraid puts paid to it as far as I'm concerned. Then there's flagellation. I never even seriously considered that. It strikes you, sure, but what's it got to do with anything? You might as well play tennis or knit a pair of socks as a way of working up to a screw. And the same goes for those other capers like necrophily and bestiality. No point in even discussing any of them. It would just be flogging a dead horse.'

I turned in my seat and stared hard at Roy, who twitched a hand and a knee and a shoulder, and muttered to himself.

'Well ... I mean, that's only a way of saying it's of no interest,' he said defensively. 'And flogging and dead and horse. Surely you got that?'

'Oh yes, I got it all right. I just wanted to make sure you had. Carry on.'

'Really, Christ ... Anyway, I was knocking Girl, 20 just now, but it gets about fifteen per cent better as an idea if you can expand it to Girl, 20 and man just old enough to be her grandfather if you assume a soupçon of juvenile delinquency in both generations. And, uh, didn't I tell you it was Girl, 19? Yes, that's what I tell most people. I mean the people I have to tell something. Well, between ourselves, Duggers, it's actually Girl, 17. That jacks it up no end, I can assure you.'

'Good God.'

'Ageing shag tries to stimulate jaded appetite by recreating situation of days of firse discovery of sex plus whiff of illegality, corruption of youth, dirty ole man luring child into disused plate-layer's hut and plying her with wine-gums and dandelion-and-burdock to induce her to remove knickers and slake his vile lusts. That's it exactly. No better description possible. Hit the thing right on the nose.'

I was still a little shaken. 'Aren't you taking rather a risk?'

'Yes, there's that too. You can see why I've been keeping her out of sight to some extent. Actually I haven't been breaking the law much, as far as I know. She doesn't drink, and anyhow she'll be eighteen soon, I'm sorry to say.'

'How do her parents feel about this?'

I could see him start to take evasive action as plainly as if he had been a merchantman and I a U-boat. 'Well, they . . . give her a lot of freedom . . .'

'They seem to, certainly. Do they know about you?'

'No.' He laughed at the absurdity of this idea. 'They know she has men, of course, but, uh . . .'

'It might be awkward if they found out, mightn't it? Where had you been last night before you turned up at my place?'

'Some party. Friends of hers. Quite safe.'

'Who are her parents?'

'Oh, he's a . . . banker,' said Roy, eliminating at a stroke one category of employment tenable by Sylvia's father, and adding with dissimulated relief, 'Here we are.'

We descended at Craggs's Club. Roy shouldered me aside in order to pay, crying out like a man in a film falling off a high building when a florin rolled over the edge of his hand. The driver put his vehicle in gear, revved up and said in a high monotone,

'You Sir Roy Vandervane?'

'That's me.'

'Why don't you bugger off to Moscow if it's so bloody awful here?'

The cab shot away. Roy sighed heavily as we turned towards the steps.

'No use telling a chap like that I spoke out against the invasion of Czechoslovakia.'

'Not the slightest use. He'd think you ought to go just the same.'

'He's got his ideas laid out in blocks.'

'That must be it.'

We entered a lofty, squarish hall where a ticker-tape ticked, or rather chattered. Roy went over to a porter who was glaring at us from within a glass-and-mahogany emplacement. Another man, doubtless a member, but resembling a pop singer attired as a City gent, swung past with hanging jaw towards the street.

I took in a small fraction of the scores of portraits and groups that covered the walls, feeling anew the shakiness of the whole concept of a population explosion, there having demonstrably been so many more people about a hundred years ago than now.

Roy rejoined me and we walked down a carpeted passage that crepitated very loudly underfoot. At its end there was an equally tall and much larger room with enough writing materials spread about to supply a hundred compulsive correspondents for the foreseeable future, and sheltering at the moment half a dozen solitary men in slightly different stages of torpor. Roy pushed a bell-push, a youthful white-jacketed waiter came and an order for champagne was given. I looked thoroughly round the room and then at Roy.

'It's convenient,' he said placatingly. 'Somewhere to be between appointments. Good food. It impresses Americans. And you can stay here.'

'With birds?'

'No, but you can cash cheques. And it's a good alibi spot. Of course I was here, dear. Asleep in the colour-television room. The porters are getting very slack. I'll have to have a word with the secretary. You know.'

'Speaking of alibis, where were you last night?'

'Here. Frugal, wholesome dinner and early bed. No phone calls; I checked.'

'That's all right, then. One thing you didn't go into was the business about you-know-who not being your wife. I can see that Girl, 20 or Girl, 17 don't come in as that anyway, but what about Girl, 28? I suppose she'd just be too –'

'Let's leave that until the drinks have come.'

When they had, we settled in a corner bounded by volumes of *Punch* and *Who Was Who*, and Roy began,

'There are two things really. The obvious one about anything up to about Girl, 45 being more striking than your wife, not better in fact, just –'

'I've got all that. Let's have the other thing.'

'Well, that's simply a matter of you wanting to get away from normal, decent, God-fearing sex and your wife being no good for that. The tone of the thing's all wrong, the whole context. It can't be done. Darling, here's a letter from the Toolboxes asking us down for Easter and you remember how you enjoyed it before when you, I don't know, uh, pissed in his rain-gauge so shall I accept? And would you give me my hambag off the dressing-table? And could you ring the bloody, oh, paraffin man as you promised and give him hell? And anything interesting in your post? Not really, dear, just the tickets for the Shit-shitski recital and the B.U.M. contract and a few clippings and have a look at this and what about going down?'

I sat on for a moment while a clock at the end of the room struck the half-hour. 'You mean it's all so routine, getting up and going down to breakfast and never getting the –'

'Oh, peace in our time, Duggers! Statesmanlike act! *Going . . . down.* Where have you been? She takes your –'

'Quiet. I know what she takes all right.'

'Allow me to present you with the information that these days it's called going down.'

'I know what it's called.'

'Well, you didn't seem to just now.'

'You threw the phrase at me without sufficient preparation.'

'Did I? Sorry. Let me top you up. Well, you get the point. Girl, anything will do that for you, and other things besides, whereas . . . It's not so much that she will as that you can ask her to. I suppose it is very much an age thing, too.' He turned judicial and wise, reminding me that a week or so previously I had read of his forthcoming contribution to a symposium, run by some churchman, on a sexual morality for our (or their) time. 'I think even somebody like you would admit that one solid, unarguably liberating gain from the new atmosphere of tolerance, among younger people at any rate, has been the admission of all that type of stuff to the, Christ, to the standard repertoire of what people get up to in bed.'

'So that everything becomes as natural as breathing.'

'Precisely. Where's Gilbert got to? Normally he's punctual to a fault. I hope nothing's wrong at home.'

'Might something be?'

'Something might always be.'

He looked at me assessingly, and I guessed he was trying

to make up his mind whether to present domestic going-wrongness as an inevitable effect of the bourgeois social structure or, alternatively, as a healthy sign of a larger, higher going-rightness just round the corner. But, before he could decide, Gilbert came into the room. I had not noticed his slimness before, nor the ease of his movements. His face, however, was at the moment troubled. He addressed himself immediately to Roy.

'Penny's here.'

'What! She can't be. Women aren't allowed in before five.'

My immediate thought had been that here was one of the little prearranged surprises that had brought Roy a modest fame in the past, but it was soon clear that his wonder and apprehension were every bit as genuine as his feelings of outrage at such infringement of Club protocol. This, it was next revealed, had not actually been infringed after all, or not yet: Penny had been left sitting in the car, which Gilbert had parked in St James's Square. In admitting as much, he went out of his way not to offer the smallest comment or suggestion or comfort. Roy gave a sweeping gesture of anger and hopelessness which blended into a jab at the bell.

'What's she playing at?' he asked. 'What did she say?'

'She barely announced her intention to make the trip,' said Gilbert.

'Perhaps she felt like a bit of a jaunt, a look round the shops and lunch out somewhere,' I said, drawing upon myself remarkably similar glances of pitying contempt for such imaginative poverty.

'Come on, Gilbert, what's she up to? How's she been behaving? You must have some idea, surely to God.'

'She's been perfectly silent. It appears to me that she's bent on some destruction, as usual.'

'Yes, I'm afraid you're right. All part of the pattern.'

'What can she destroy from inside a parked car?' I was beginning to feel like one of three ennobled surgeons called in at short notice to advise on the lancing of a royal boil. 'I suppose she could work on the upholstery a bit with her nail-scissors, if she's got any.'

Gilbert ignored me. 'She must suspect you're engaged in some activity that she could somehow spoil with her presence, or the threat of her presence.'

'Like having it off with me, you mean, in the colour-television room.'

'Cut out your pawky, perky little sallies for the moment, Douglas, if you would.' Roy moved aside to talk to the returning waiter.

'Miss Vandervane,' said Gilbert to me, 'is totally unaware of your existence.'

'I should have thought that, if anything, that rather strengthened my point.'

'This is the kind of elitist environment in which one might expect to find someone of your basic attitudes.'

'Yes, or Roy's. It's his club.'

'You are against life.'

'Oh, wrap up.'

'Cool it, Duggers,' said Roy. 'We've got to think what's best to do.'

'No doubt you have.' I looked at my watch. 'I must go or I'll be late.'

'You've got over twenty minutes.' Roy gave me one of his person-to-person scowls. 'Hang on just a second and we'll drop you. Have some more shampers.'

'All right. Thanks.'

'Then we can all go off together and you and I can take her to the Savoy, Gilbert. She said once she liked it there. That's the thing.'

'What's the age of this building?' Gilbert spoke with an anthropologist's detachment.

Roy told him that and other things. A champagne glass arrived for Gilbert and a tumbler of Scotch for Roy. Both drank, while I thought about the problems of being a jobbing diluent, more vaguely about Penny, and then more specifically about how late I was going to be at the B.B.C. We left the Club at the point in time at which a brisk trot along King Street, followed by a rally team's type of progress up Regent Street, would forestall any reproaches on my arrival.

'What have you got on this afternoon?' I asked Roy as we walked.

'Whole pack of stuff. Buggering around here and there. One thing that should be fun. Telling a shag why I won't do *Harold in Italy* for him.'

'I suppose the viola part would be rather on the –'

'No no, this would have been waving the stick. Because of Byron.'

'What's he got to do with it?'

'Duggers, the music by Hector Berlioz, ob or dee 1869 as we both have cause to know, is based on a –'

'God. I'm with you. God.'

'Sorry, but these days you do rather seem to need to have stuff spelt out.'

'What's Byron got to do with it?'

'Christ, he's a Greek national hero. They're always going on about him.'

'So we refuse to perform a piece of music by a Frenchman inspired by a poem by an Englishman who died a hundred and fifty years ago in case it might get blokes to turn soft on the present government in Greece. I see.'

'You can't let it slip, you know. Got to keep at them.'

'I'm surprised you thought it was all right for you and me to play K.481 the other week. Wasn't Hitler an Austrian too?'

'That's a dead issue now. And the idea's too far-fetched.'

'Too what?'

'Far-fetched,' said Roy loudly. 'No flag-waving sentiment in Mozart.'

Gilbert, on Roy's other side, had been showing a respectful impatience, clearly resenting my readiness to waste Roy's time while rather admiring his lenity. Now he settled my hash by chiming in scornfully, 'Hell, I should just about say not.'

The car came into view, singling itself out from others by its size and splendour. Not at first sight the obvious choice for a be person, I reflected uncharitably, then considered the notion that Roy did not so much own it as fulfil his personality by means of it. Anyone else might be said to *have* it; it was his distinction to *be* the person it belonged to. Or perhaps it was just that he had not yet finished changing over from having to being.

A bowed shape inside revealed itself as Penny under a cart-wheel-sized hat. She was in the back seat. Why? She had moved there after arrival so as to allow her father to take his place in front. Out of the question. She had spent the journey there so as to emphasize her disaffection from mankind, as personified by Gilbert. Much more like it. But it touched the edge of my mind that she might have wanted to diffuse the impression (among a limited audience, admittedly) that the flagrantly progressive Sir Roy Vandervane kept a coloured chauffeur: a part that Gilbert, with his dark-blue suit, pale-blue shirt and black-knitted-silk tie, could plausibly have filled. To have thought of this at all made me feel humiliated in some way.

'Right, into the car with you,' said Roy in grim, riot-squad tones. 'You in the back, Douglas.'

Penny moved a few inches away from me like somebody in a bus making room for a not necessarily very drunken stranger, a relatively effusive greeting. Roy half turned in the passenger's seat in front and was very bald about dropping me at the studios and going on to the Savoy, while she looked out of the window at some nearby railings. What with this and the hat I could not see much of her, but even so I caught a strong physical reminder of Sylvia. It was gone before I could do more than decide tentatively where it had not originated: face, hair, figure, clothes, smell. In the last-named department Penny was offering a good deal of, though nothing more than, the consequences of warm female flesh; perhaps she was a secret washer as well as a secret listener to music. Excellent, but if I had glimpsed a resemblance elsewhere between the two girls, it was likely, or possible, or conceivable, that Roy had too. Perhaps an incestuous fixation had been transformed into a . . .

Vowing weakly to dig out the popular-psychology paper-back I was nearly sure I still had in a cupboard at the flat, and to drop the volume unopened into the Regent's Canal at an early opportunity, I prepared for a closer look at Penny, but had to defer this for the time being when Gilbert drove out of the parking area like an international ace leaving the pits at Le

Mans (or somewhere) and snapped my head back against the cushions. More delay supervened while he took us into a tight fast semicircle that held me against the door on my side at a pressure of several Gs and sprawled Penny horizontally across my lap, which was all right.

'Steady, Gilbert,' said Roy in his richest tone.

'Poor me boy! Good me do and thank-ye me get!'

I understood this utterance as a protest, perhaps not unjustified if one cared to look far enough. No time for that now. Penny pulled herself upright before I could assist her, and resettled her hat. She was wearing a mulberry-coloured skirt apparently knocked together out of an old curtain and ample enough to cover another three or four legs besides her own, bicep-height crimson fish-net gloves and a kind of low-cut suede waistcoat above which her breasts showed like the tops of a couple of ostrich eggs. She looked at me and I took in the eyes and skin.

'Your head's better, I see,' she said.

'Yes, thank you. Cleared up in no time.'

'It's left a little mark, but I expect that'll fade away soon. It hardly notices now, as a matter of fact. It's really only because I know where to look that I can see it at all.'

'Oh, good.'

'I'm sorry if I was rude to you that day. I was very depressed about something, and I know I do get rude when I get depressed.'

'I see.'

'Anyway, I'm sorry.'

'That's all right.'

My eyes seemed to want to go on looking at her, but I switched them round until they were looking out of the window. Was she experiencing some fool kick or other, off on some pitiable good trip? Or was I in for a session of the sincerity-sarcasm game, in which A steps up her sincerity to the point where B must declare himself either a moron for going on taking it or a boor for telling her to stuff it? What told against this view was that the game is much better with an audience, and Penny was keeping her voice down, though admittedly she would have had to raise it a good deal to vie with the noise Gilbert was getting out of the engine as he took us hurtling up towards Piccadilly Circus. Perhaps she had simply been apologizing. Then, still quietly, and still in a face-value voice, she asked.

'What have you and him been talking about?'

'Oh, musical stuff. Gossip.'

'He didn't mention Saturday? This coming Saturday?'

'No? What's happening then?'

'Are you free that evening?'

'I can be.' I had a lieder recital and a date with Vivienne, but the one could be missed and the other deferred. 'Why?'

'He told me he was thinking of giving a sort of little dinner-party somewhere. In a restaurant. He wanted me to come, and you, and then this girl.'

The favour! So Gilbert's instincts had not been altogether wrong, and Penny had managed to prevent Roy from putting the proposition to me in his own time. How he had been going to do this with Gilbert within range I could not envisage, but Roy's resources had always been large and varied.

I asked mechanically, 'What girl?'

'She's called Sylvia. You must have met her. She's got long hair.'

'Yes. Indeed she has. When did you meet her?'

'Oh, I've never met her. He told me about her. What's she really like?'

'She's . . . not my kind of person,' I said with an effort.

'Yes, he said she was young. Is she pretty?'

'Not to me. But of course different people –'

'You are going to come to the dinner, though?'

'I don't think so.'

'Oh come on, it'll be fun. You said you were free.'

'*Fun*?' I tried not to sound too airy and gay. 'I can't really see it being much of that, given the . . . given her. But, uh, it would be fun for you, would it, to go out on the town with your dad and his bird and another bloke to make up the number?'

'What's wrong with that?'

I drew in my breath to tell her that if, on grounds of some

mouldering old thing like taste, she could see nothing wrong with the proposed outing, I would have to join in with my fellow deacons and churchwardens and not be able to answer her question. Then I held my breath for a moment, realizing, to my vexation or uneasiness or something, that I was no longer sure whether there was much wrong with it after all. Then I let all my breath out at once when the car stopped as dead as if it had run into a brick wall and I bounded forward and hit the top of my forehead against the edge of the back of the seat in which Roy was sitting. The car had not been going very fast, and the line of contact was not as sharp as the lintel of the Vandervane kitchen door had been; nevertheless, the effect felt remarkably similar, and must have looked similar too, at any rate to Penny, who broke out into similar laughter.

I took in facts. The car had run into not a brick wall but the back of a bus, and had dented it somewhat, while itself seeming unharmed. My three fellow-passengers were likewise whole, had no doubt seen the bump coming. Gilbert had his head out of his window, Roy had opened his door, Penny went on laughing without giving any impression of artificiality. Some crossing pedestrians stopped and stared and stayed stopped. We were at the corner of Conduit Street. It was exactly twelve fifteen. A policeman came into view on the far side of the road.

I told Roy I would be in touch, got out of the car and gained the pavement. Lines of stationary traffic stretched unbroken as far as Oxford Circus. I set off at light-infantry speed, opting for arrival at my destination twenty or so minutes late in fair condition rather than something less than a quarter of an hour in a pulp. I negotiated family groups moving at toddlers' pace, ladies with dogs on yard-long leads, arm-in-arm trios, suddenly becalmed old men, a phalanx of schoolchildren, two girls halted in serious conversation, an approaching Sikh with his eyes on an open street plan. What had been chiefly unwelcome about Penny's laughter was that I knew I would be able to see a very good case for it tomorrow without being able to see any particle of that case now. It was the obliteration of this time-lag, not, or not nearly so much, any revelling in others' misfortunes from a safe distance, that made funny stories enjoyable. After my recording I would go along to the George and have a pint of bitter and a round of cheese-and-pickle and a round of ham with too much mustard. Then, at the flat, the new Walter Klien of K.415 and K.467.

I had crossed Oxford Street when I heard my name being called from behind, and it was nobody else but Penny, carrying her hat in her hand. I stopped. Everybody she ran past turned to stare after her. I felt all at once that I had been awake for seven hours, that I had rather liked the rug that had had an accident, that a social diluent ought to have a clause written into his contract saying his duties did not include being put in the wrong about everything from his presence in a club to Mozart's lack of flag-waving sentiment, that I was hot and my head hurt.

She came up, showing less sign of exertion than might have been expected in such a committed idler, but quite enough to draw my eyes to the top of her waistcoat. She must have them propped up, I thought. On supports of some kind. Rolled-up tissue-paper, perhaps.

'Hang on a minute,' she said.

'I can't, I'm due at the B.B.C. Late already.'

'So? They'll wait.'

'Penny: I have to go.'

A man in overalls coming from behind me barged into her hard enough to swing her half round, but she showed no resentment, as Vivienne or I would have done. 'You coming to the dinner on Saturday?'

'I can't, sorry.'

'What do you mean you can't? You said you were free.'

'I can't, I won't, I'm not going to.'

'Listen, you sixty or something? You go on like you were older than him, twice his age. You're sodding dead, you are.'

I leaned over her. 'I'm not coming because one of the girls who are coming is an exact replica of you and the other one is you. I'd need a good half-hour to go into all the things I object to about you, so I'll just tell you that helping *him* on with this thing of his is being nasty to Kitty, and don't tell me she knows about it and doesn't mind. She's taken you on and she puts up with you, God help her, and I don't want anything to do with someone who thinks it's all right or funny or why-not or groovy or *wild* to behave in that way. Now clear off.'

The clock in the B.H. foyer stood at twelve thirty-nine when I pushed my way in through the swing door. The producer of the programme I was on, standing by the reception desk, saw me and hurried forward.

'Sorry, Philip. Got hung up.'

'And beaten up, it seems.' He looked at my forehead. 'Are you all right? Good, now not to worry, we've got the studio until one. If you can –'

He looked past my shoulder in muted consternation. It was Penny again.

'I'm sorry I laughed in the car.'

'That's all right. Now just –'

'Help me.'

There is no other injunction like this, in that you have to heed it but cannot, by the fact of its being put, hope to do what it says. I pressed my hand against my head.

'All right. I'll be back here in about twenty minutes, so . . . Or you can telephone me.'

We got through the recording without a single fluff. By the time I had hurried back to the foyer, Penny had gone.

Helping Penny became a less daunting prospect as the day advanced and as I considered the possibilities and ethics of stretching it, or confining it, to helping her off with her suede waistcoat, out of her pyjama-top, etc. I felt partly protected on my Vivienne flank by the open and tolerated existence of the other bloke – only partly, so to speak internally: that gnome about the transferability of sauce is far too obviously the result of a consensus of ganders to make any useful impression on the average goose. When it came to Penny herself, matters seemed less clear-cut. The kind of help she might have been asking for ranged presumably from adopting her as my daughter to saying I would come on Saturday after all, with agreeing to be prick-teased by her coming somewhere in the middle, or off to one side. I felt this last as a kind of moral counterpoise to the implications, if any, of throwing a pass at somebody in a state. Yes, and whatever sort of state it might or might not reveal itself to be, it was not that of innocence, in any sense of the term. All this was good self-justifying stuff, and available in fully sufficient quantity to be going on with.

Anyway, when Roy rang me up that same evening, ostensibly to ask if the new rug had arrived (which it had) and if I liked it (which I quite did), and then went on to say casually that he gathered Penny had mentioned to me a very vague sort of thought he had happened to have had about a possible minor jaunt on the approaching Saturday, I agreed that she had, and told him I thought it was rather a good idea.

'A good idea? You didn't say that the last time we discussed it.'

It was no use reminding him that on that occasion I had ended up by saying something to that very effect. I remembered that, although a great one for making other people do what he wanted them to do, he tended to turn suspicious if they showed signs of wanting to do it on their own account. I came back with something about approving only conditionally, in the abstract, and put in a vigilant request for details. This, carrying the bonus of giving him ample scope for mystification, went down a treat. Under pressure, he finally disclosed the name of the pub in Islington where we were to start the evening, and even threw in the time. After that, he said in the tone of a full and inflexible planner, we would see how things went.

'How's Penny?' I asked.

'Penny?' He sounded puzzled. '*Fine*. Why?'

'She didn't seem very fine the last I saw of her.'

He did his comprehending wolf howl. 'Oh-oo. That. That was nothing. You did get the point, I take it? That she thought she'd been rude by laughing when you hit your head and wanted to apologize? I mean you grasped that?'

'Well, yes. Rather drastic, wasn't she being?'

'Nop by her standards, I can assure you. How is the head?'

'Labouring. How's the car?'

'Try smice on it. Oh, it'll be in dock a few days. You seemed so terrified of being late for your bloody recording that Gilbert forgot what the brakes were for. Nobody's fault, really.'

'No. Tell me, how did you join up with Penny again?'

'Gilbert worked out, Gilbert stayed with the car and I just strolled up to the B.B.C. and collected her. We had quite a jolly lunch at the Savoy eventually. Pity you couldn't join us. She kept complaining that you hadn't, incidentally, which Gilbert didn't much care for.'

'What does he think is happening on Saturday evening?'

'Leave that to me. Yes, I don't know what you said to her, but you seem to have made something of an impression. Fine as far's I'm concerned. If you could, you know, reach her in some way it would be a splendid thing for all concerned.'

All concerned, I thought when I had put the telephone down. Like Gilbert, for instance. Like Vivienne. Like the other bloke. Like me. But most of all like Roy. Was what he had said – he had said more in the same strain before ringing off – just a prophylactic against Penny's probable conduct on Saturday, or had he a deeper scheme in train, of the sort I had glimpsed when, in his kitchen that afternoon, he had asked me what I thought of her looks? The real trouble with liars, I decided as I belatedly got Weber out of his drawer, was that there could never be any guarantee against their occasionally telling the truth.

Saturday afternoon found me in reasonably good heart. Earlier that week, Harold Meers had accepted without question, and allowed to appear in his newspaper, a half-sentence of mine in praise of a Bulgarian soprano. I had given Haydn the modified rounds-of-the-kitchen treatment, cunningly laying off by warm praise of the performance and recording, and had sent the review off to *The Record-Player*. The Nonpareil label had commissioned me to do the sleeve-notes for the complete Mozart piano sonatas executed by some Paraguayan newcomer. Vivienne was no problem, having gone more than halfway to meet me, in fact a little further than I really wanted, when I suggested cancelling, rather than putting back, our date for that day. She said it would give her a chance to catch up with her letter-writing, thereby injecting such an authentic note of humdrumness that I almost wished she had told me a lie.

Deciding what to wear took me longer than my usual three seconds. All things considered, the ideal outfit would have been a leather jacket that became the top half of a dinner-suit when turned inside out, a denim dickey over an evening bow, steel-tipped patent-leather pumps, and so on; but I did not possess any of these, and settled on dark everything from shirt to shoes, including a dark neck-scarf, with a little quick-change protective coloration up my sleeve, or rather stuffed into my hip pockets, in the form of two neckties, one psychedelic (a joke present from my sister), the other sane. At half past five I drank a pint of milk to protect my stomach from whatever Roy might have in store for it, transferred my wallet from my right to my left breast-pocket, and got on my way.

A nasty dog-leg journey by Tube, nasty both topologically and as regards the quality of the experience, delivered me at length outside the Angel station. It seemed to me that a newspaper-seller there flinched slightly when I mentioned the name of the pub I sought, but from a distance it looked harmless enough. I had been rather expecting to find the streets deserted, the buildings uninhabited, having been quite recently told by a left-wing bassoonist friend and his left-wing harpist wife that they were among the first people to have moved into the area. On the contrary, there was every sign of occupancy, and throngs of young and old passed to and fro, no doubt in transit or going out for the evening, since at this advanced hour – very nearly six o'clock – they could scarcely have still been coming home from work. I moved freely among them and gained the front of the building unmolested.

Close to, it looked less harmless. Its fabric suggested, though not seriously, only to a fleeting glance or to eyes like mine when unassisted by glasses, that it was made of variegated planks of wood and strips of galvanized iron. Here and there archaic war posters, or reproductions of such, were somehow incorporated into whatever material composed the exterior. None the less I went in, and found myself in a small vestibule lit only by a number of signs and arrows: Wipers Bar, Blighty Bar, Cookhouse, Dug-out. Roy had said something about below ground, so I chose the last of these. At the foot of a steep wooden stair with no risers and a rope hand-rail, I beat aside a clinging obstacle that, seen by what illumination there was on its farther side, proved to be a plastic curtain got up to look like sacking, though here again the pretence was half-hearted. Two dimly seen couples crouched in sham-concrete alcoves. Replicas of rifles, gas masks, grenades hung on the walls. I took in no more of this, but went to the bar, where I was confronted by a girl in service-dress with medal ribbons and sergeant's stripes. Just then a wordless yelling, recalling Ashley Vandervane's but rather lower in pitch and accompanied by clashes and soggy thumps, burst from several invisible sources. Nevertheless I managed to get myself a Guinness, and went and sat down on a padded ammunition-box in a corner.

After an hour or so of subjective time, in fact perhaps two minutes, I was preparing to go and wait in the street, but then

Roy and Penny fought their way past the curtain. Penny was hatless and had boots on; I could not know what else she might or might not have been wearing. She settled herself mutely beside me while Roy went to the bar, and I asked her how she was, cunningly keeping my voice well down to normal volume.

'What? I can't hear with this row.'

I moved much closer to her, close enough for a good noseful of the warm clean smell I had noticed in the car, and repeated my question.

'I'm all right. Why?'

'You didn't ring me up.'

'What about?'

'I don't know. What it was you didn't ring me up about. Because you didn't ring me up.'

'I didn't say I was going to, did I?'

'No, I said you could if you wanted to.'

'What for?'

Most of my brain seemed suddenly to have become unusable, cut off for ever by a massive haemorrhage. It occurred to me that these days, after so many precedents in film and TV drama, especially of the strong variety, people left questions unanswered whenever they felt like it, often shrugging their shoulders as well, so I silently shrugged mine. Then I realized that, in the gloom, Penny might mistake this gesture for an outsize nervous tremor, or even miss it altogether. Accordingly, I muttered for a few seconds. Penny did not pursue the topic. No doubt I had been inept, either in reminding her too early about the helping project, or in assuming she remembered having mentioned it in the first place. There was nothing like the society of youth for making one feel young: about fourteen, in fact, and an abnormally blush-prone, naïve and thick fourteen into the bargain. I found myself asking her if she liked this place.

'Sodding wicked,' she said, lighting a cigarette.

'I don't see why they have to have it so dark. And noisy.'

'What?'

Roy turned up at that point, carrying what I could only assume were drinks for himself and his daughter.

'We were just saying how much we hated this pub,' I said.

'Bloody awful, isn't it?' he agreed readily, drinking.

'Why have we come here, then?'

'Just that it's convenient.'

'How do you make that out?'

'For where we're going next.'

'Where's that?'

'Only round the corner.'

'No doubt, but what is it?'

'I think you'll both agree it's fun.'

I hoped very much that this brick wall had been thrown up out of habit, not so as to conceal a prospect so dreadful that any preview of it would send me, or Penny, or both of us haring down the City Road. I pondered the point intermittently while Roy took me more or less bar by bar through the rehearsal of the Mahler Fifth he and the N.L.S.O. had been engaged on earlier that day. The other sort of noise that still surrounded us would have made it difficult for him to address Penny as well without continuously shouting his head off, and her hunched-up silhouette told of withdrawal on her own part. After he had described for the second time a passage of arms he had had with the principal double-bass (was he, understandably enough, drunk already?), I broke in to say, not very ardently, but at least loudly.

'You know, I think old Gus must have written out programme notes first and then worked back from them to his score. Sort of, after the strings have failed to reach the moment of reconciliation they had seemed to promise three-quarters of an hour earlier, trumpets and trombones solemnly deliver a message of –'

'Here she is.'

Sylvia approached, wearing what my night vision, eked out by such knowledge as I had of her, suggested was the rig-out of our previous meeting. Roy had risen and seemingly kissed her, and now introduced bird to daughter, gesturing, even gesticulating, in a way that faintly recalled his manner on the rostrum at a moment of drama. Then he and Sylvia went over to the bar. I turned to Penny, feeling by now several decades older than fourteen, but she surprised me by shouting first.

'Where's he taking us, then?'

'No idea.'

'I don't want to go to it.'

'I said I'd no idea where he's taking us.'

'I heard you. I don't want to go to it. Wherever he's taking us. Got it?'

'You mean you'd rather stay here?'

'Don't talk like a bloody fool.'

I found I could whimper to myself really quite powerfully, at a volume that would have carried across, say, the aisle of an Underground train in motion, without seeming to reach Penny's ears. 'What would you like to do?'

She leaned forward to a point at which she could talk audibly at an almost normal pitch. 'I wouldn't like to do anything. There's nothing I'd like to do. Ever. I can't stand it up there with her' – Kitty, I assumed, rather than the domestic or the Furry Barrel – 'and there's nowhere I want to go outside. I can't stand being on my own, and I can't stand being with one person, and I can't stand being with a lot of people. Well, I can stand it, but I always feel I won't be able to another second. I can't think about anything, except about how I feel, and how I feel's always just me thinking about how I feel. I don't mind being asleep.'

She spoke without the flat hostility she had displayed a few moments before, nor was there the least trace of self-pity in her tone. She might have been a television story editor in conference, briskly outlining in the first person a substantial minor character she was proposing to have written into the script. In a brief glow from her cigarette, I saw her looking at me as if she simply felt it was my turn now. I said conversationally,

'Are you on drugs?'

'Not at the moment. You always think they're going to be good, but they're not, not really. Not for me, anyway. It gets like seeing everything in a lot of mirrors, or through funny glass like a migraine, or looking up from the floor, but it's the same thing really. Even when all the things look different, all covered with stuff or turned into lights and things, or even when you can't see or hear anything you're sort of used to, you know it's all there really. Not just it's going to be back when you're back, it's there all the time. Even when you can't just remember what it's like. Of course, I haven't had anything . . .'

I lost her voice under a short *feu de joie* of howitzers intended to lend emphasis to some crux in the performance that raged about us. 'What?'

'Heroin!' she bawled. 'What they call a hard drug, actually, where you –'

'But you haven't taken that.'

'Not so far I haven't.'

'But you're not going to.'

'Why not? Why shouldn't I?'

'Why not! Because it kills you. God almighty.'

'What's wrong with that?'

At this point, the ambient uproar stopped. I stared towards Penny under the momentary illusion that now I should be able to see her better. She broke into laughter as hearty as if I had hit myself on the head a third time.

'Don't you worry, mate,' she said with friendly contempt. 'I don't have any plans for the old needle just at present, thanks all the same. So you can afford to cool it. All safe and sound and wrapped up snug.'

I had still not thought of anything to say when Roy's shape loomed above us.

'All right, chaps? I thought we might move on, if you've no objection.'

At this I found speech. 'Let's go,' I said.

The illumination at the bar was slightly less minimal than elsewhere in the room. By it, as Sylvia took her time about drinking up, I saw a small, hairy young man turn his head and reveal himself to be wearing sunglasses. I moved on reflex, precipitating my frame between him and Roy's line of sight before I had really got started on wondering just how far, given that incident at the corner of St John's Wood Road, Roy would escalate his reaction to a sunglasses-wearer in these surroundings. In moving, I trod on Penny's foot and collided with Sylvia's elbow, not quite causing her glass to spill over.

'Christ, what's the *muhtter* with you?' she asked me, swinging round and spilling her drink without my assistance. 'You pissed already?'

'It wouldn't be that, darling,' said Roy authoritatively. 'Our Duggers is never pissed. Foreign to his whole nature.'

'Yeah, see him letting go.'

'Sorry,' I said. 'I sort of tripped. Sorry, Penny.'

'Easy enough to do in this bloody mausoleum, old lad. Come on, then – off.'

Roy watched me over his shoulder as I weaved behind him, duplicating or trying to anticipate his movements and keeping a mental bearing on the position of the sunglassed young man.

'You're sure you're all right?' He leaned across to push the curtain aside and studied my shift to the relevant flank. 'You seem a bit –'

'Rather stuffy in here.'

'I blame myself. I'd forgotten how crappy it was. No, actually I think they must have made it crappier since I was last here. But the food's nop bad, or wasn't. You used to be able to get quite a good sort of scampi, hamburger and salad kind of a lunch in the Cookhouse,' he said, outlining in a few swift strokes the sort of meal he must have forgotten I knew he hated most.

Hullabaloo was renewed behind us, and more of it came from all sides when we reached ground level. I had expected it to be at least fully dark out of doors, with perhaps even the eastern stars beginning to pale in presage of the dawn, but in fact the sun was still very much about. White-painted caffs and stores selling hooligans' attire were mingled with murky places calling themselves bistros and boutiques. The two girls walked ahead of Roy and me, Penny seemingly looking at passers-by, Sylvia with her eyes fixed on the shop windows.

'You were getting on a treat with young Penny, I saw,' said Roy.

'Yes, okay.' I could not start about Penny now.

'She'll come round in the end, you know. All this drop-out stuff is just a stage. All talk.'

'That sounds a bit authoritarian. What about her new ways of seeing things? Are they all talk?'

'She hasn't got them much. It's more Sylvia who's got them.'

'So Penny isn't really a part of youth?'

'Not in that sense, I'm afraid, no.'

'How can you be sure?'

'Bugger it, she is my daughter.'

'Yes, there is that.'

We had turned a corner and come up to a large black car parked at the kerb. I could see some of the back view of a man in the driving-seat, and caught Roy by the arm.

'That's not Gilbert, is it?'

'Christ no. Pull yourself together, Duggers. It's a car-hire driver and this is a car-hire car. Just for the evening. Makes us more mobile.'

He put me in the rear seat between the two girls and got in front. We moved off. Penny had turned her back on me as far as she could without kneeling up on the seat. I looked at Sylvia, who was smelling of carrots that evening, and said, neutrally I would have thought,

'Do you know where we're going?'

'Why does it bother you so much?'

'What do you mean, bother me?'

'So much. Listen to you. Everything you do, you've got to have done it before. Whatever it is, it's got to be part of a *pluhn*.'

'I simply asked you –'

'You can't, you know, get into things properly if you always know what's coming. You mustn't let it all be like it was the last time. You can't sort of get hold of it properly if that's what you do. It's all got to be something else. You know.'

Roy's head nodded once or twice, in approval or in response

to the motion of the car, which was not well sprung. I tried to imagine his private conversations with Sylvia, and then tried not to instead. For the second time in the last couple of months, the possible virtues of Bruckner's Eighth Symphony presented themselves to me. Sylvia went on,

'You're half out of your mind worrying you won't be able to fit everything in together. You call that living? Just making sure today's like yesterday and last week and last year? You're all frozen up. You can't feel. I'd hate to get myself tied up with you, I really would. You wouldn't go anywhere with anyone in case you had to do something you weren't used to.'

Her demonstration of new ways of seeing things closed at that point; after travelling perhaps as much as half a mile, we had apparently arrived. As with Penny in the Dug-out, Sylvia's manner had not matched the content of what she had said: in this case thoughtful, troubled, sympathetic, that of one really concerned to advertise dangers and propound remedies. The total effect, on me at least, was not much improved thereby. Operating at reduced efficiency, I became part of a small crowd or untidy queue moving towards and into the stone porch of a large red-brick building. Posters abounded, some of considerable age and depressive quality.

'Bingo?' I said wonderingly to Penny.

'Use your eyes, chum. Sodding wrestling.'

I wanted to tell her that she must be joking, but could not devise any non-fashionable way of suggesting this, so muttered to myself, not for the first or last time that evening. Our progress slowed, and I looked to see whether Roy would have us red-carpeted through or insist on our democratically standing in line for tickets. I rather predicted the former, since a programme of wrestling, however distinguished and exclusive, would surely not be thought momentous enough to need symbolical atonement in advance. A Tube-bus-and-on-foot journey to Covent Garden and seats in the middle of the grand tier for the first night of a new *Otello*, followed by a champagne supper at the Savoy Grill – that was more the usual scale. However, I was wrong: we shuffled up to the box office two by two. The two I was in consisted of a sulky Penny and me. At the moment when Roy pulled out his wallet, Sylvia announced that she would go no further.

'Load of old cruhp,' she said, pushing her fists into the pockets of the knee-length buttonless waistcoat she wore. 'Mums and dads stuff. A real hitch.'

This plainly disconcerted Roy. Just as plainly, what disconcerted him about it was far less the prospect of argument, change of plan, etc., than his having guessed so wrong about what Sylvia would like to do, in itself such a substantial proportion of her total outlook upon the world. Bearing just then, for some reason, an unfairly close resemblance to an overgrown Claudette Colbert or Jean Arthur in male rig, but with hair let down for the night, he told Sylvia it was great fun and a real gas and things like that, but did it badly. I chipped in on his side, realizing too late that I would have done far better to denounce the sport as immoral, vulgar, new-fangled, never like it was last time. Instead of simply walking away, Sylvia expanded her objections. Those in the queue behind us grew restive; I shared their feelings. A stout woman in a hat like a yellow fez called to us, not very provocatively, to get on or get out of the road. Sylvia took her hands out of her pockets and turned round quickly, her narrow eyes narrowed.

'Shut up, you,' she said through her teeth. 'Just shut up.'

She was asked who she thought she was talking to, who she thought she was, how she dared, and other knotty questions while Roy blathered disconnectedly.

'Let's go, for Christ's sake,' said Penny, 'or we'll have a sodding pitched battle. That stuff in there's all balls, anyway. I've seen them do it on television. Arm-locks and back-hammers and body-slams and the rest of it, with that maple-leafer bloke explaining. The whole thing's rigged beforehand, everybody knows that. Bloody childish. Come on, let's get out. I'm hungry.'

Having shut the yellow-fezzed woman up just by telling her to shut up, a marvel of economy, Sylvia turned back to us in time to catch Penny's last few remarks.

'Okay, okay, *okay*,' she said, sounding on the verge of impatience, but smiling slightly, 'if it means that much to you.

93

But I tell you I'm going to walk out the moment I feel like it.'

The hall carried traces, in bits of plaster moulding, a fretted frieze along the top of one wall and fragmentary, smudged-gilt electroliers nobody had bothered to rip out, of a previous history as variety theatre or archaic picture palace. It was three-quarters full of a sociologist's amalgam of ages, races and classes, with only the elder landed aristocracy perhaps under-represented. We took our seats at the ringside, Penny on my right, Sylvia on my left, Roy on her left. The first bout was announced as an international middleweight contest between a man from Swindon with a German name and a man from Bolton with a Polish name. I found it quite skilful, in that blows sounding like a sack of cement hit with a cricket bat, backhand chops at the windpipe that travelled a full semicircle before making contact, belly-first drops from head height on to an out-thrust knee – all these and more would see the sufferer on his feet, groggy but game, at the count of nine. In between, there was much paraded chivalry, instant desistance from atrocity in response to the bell, handshakes.

'Couple of blue-eyes,' said Roy at the end of the fourth round.

When neither girl stirred, I asked him what that meant.

'Good sports. Fair play,' he said vindictively. 'To get the crowd impatient for the dirty stuff that's coming.'

The girls snorted as one, glanced at each other and then away. I wondered where Roy had done his research, and half recollected a magazine article some Sundays previously. The bout continued. Eventually, German or Pole picked up Pole or German, held him extended across his shoulders, whirled round with him a number of times, laid him quite gently on the floor and knelt on him. The bell rang. A man in evening-dress, who had done a lot of talking at the outset, climbed into the ring with a hand-microphone and announced, with the slow pomp of a returning officer declaring the result of a constituency election, that, by an aeroplane-spin followed by a shoulder-press, somebody had gained the single fall necessary to decide the winner. There was moderate cheering, in which Roy joined with a judicious air, as when applauding a fellow-violinist accurate and agile enough, but deficient in warmth of tone. I joined in too, for appearance' sake, then fell to seeing if I could hum (to myself) the openings of all the movements of all the Beethoven string quartets in order before life moved on again.

I was just embarking on the scherzo of the Harp Quartet (op. 74) when what one would have to fight hard against calling an expectant hush descended on the hall. It was broken by yet another variety of wordless yelling coming from one corner. A moment later, accompanied by a rattling of chains and a mixture of growls and shouts, a rather tall and very broad figure was manhandled to the ringside by a knot of men in white T-shirts and cotton trousers, one of them with what looked like a pitchfork at the ready. This concourse was followed by a comparatively ordinary person, platinum-haired and wearing a silver cloak covered in sequins. Each principal climbed into the ring, the one after a lot more growling and chain-rattling and several flourishes of the pitchfork, the other quite readily. The M.C. appeared too with his microphone. He said, in part, and after declaring that famous scientists were unable to come to an agreement as to this strange creature, and between outbursts of largely ironical booing, and approximately,

'In-nuh the red-duh cornah, at eighteen-nuh stoh-oon-nuh five-vuh pounds ... the Thing-nguh ... from-muh Borneo-oo-uh!'

Amid more booing, the Thing's shackles were removed and, with spread arms and legs, he jumped up and down for a time in an unassuming way, but very high in the air. He wore a stylized loin-cloth, or breech-clout, and was certainly as hairy a man as I had ever seen, though the shaggy curtain that hid most of his face looked to me as if it also hid a largely bald pate. I had heard no less than Penny, or anyone else, about the dramaturgic tendency of professional wrestling, and had enjoyed the chains and pitchfork along with the rest of the audience, and yet somehow was pretty thoroughly glad not to be pitted against the Thing. There was a neglectful air about him, a suggestion that he might spontaneously decide to emend, or forget altogether, crucial passages in his assigned role. He was

95

much heavier than his opponent, now named as the Knight of St George and acknowledging cheers from what I took to be the blue corner; still, with his cape discarded he appeared muscular enough.

The bell clanged, the Thing gibbered, shambled over to the Knight and, with the side of his forearm, dealt him a buffet that made him not only start to fall down at once, but get the act of falling over and done with a good deal faster than I would have thought possible. This was followed up, no less promptly, with a head-foremost descent on to the prostrate one's stomach from a hand-stand position. The Knight gave a cry of pain and outrage, which the Thing cut short by stamping on his wind-pipe. This move was evidently felt to be unseemly, and after it had been repeated a dozen or so times to mounting protests from the audience, the referee took a double handful of the Thing's back hair and pulled, using a raised knee for added leverage. The Thing turned about with disquieting speed, but the referee had had to endure nothing worse than roars and a few of the yard-high jumps when the Knight, now recovered, came at his opponent from the rear, felled him with a kick behind the knee that would have made a tyrannosaurus lurch, and started doing something complicated and awful to his arm. But it seemed no time at all before the Thing hit the Knight very hard on the head with his head and then dropped him on his head.

So it went for the rest of the round and the next two or three: the Thing giving a good deal worse than he got and being generally unsportsmanlike, the referee intervening more rarely and tardily than, on the whole, I felt he should, though vigorously enough once roused to action. During this phase, Roy kept glancing sideways to see how the rest of us were taking it, Sylvia fidgeted grumpily but also seemed watchful, I sat there being glad I was no longer in the Dug-out and not yet in what fearful other environment lay in store, and Penny was immobile and expressionless. Then came the point when the Knight, whose retention of his left leg struck me as miraculous after what it had suffered over the previous few minutes, brought the Thing's head low with a chop to the back of the neck and drove his right knee up into the creature's chin with more force than either had used so far. The Thing left the ground and landed some feet away on the back of his head and one shoulder. The onlookers cheered with patent sincerity, but quietened down in seconds when the Thing, having taken a count of nine, got to his feet and advanced on his adversary without roars or jumps, with (to my eye) every sign of real, as opposed to manufactured, menace. I told myself that the fellow was a more accomplished mime than I had thought. Penny stirred in her seat, so that her shoulder touched my upper-arm.

After a very quick grab, the Thing had the Knight's head in the crook of his left arm and was working on his face with his right hand, elbow rising and falling in the motion of an impatient man using a screwdriver. Loud, prolonged screams came from the Knight; they sounded genuine, but of course they would have had to. I could not see what was going on. The Thing kept turning his man so as to hide his doings from the referee, who ineffectually circled and recircled the rotating pair. The Knight started screaming at a new pitch of realism. The crowd's boos and yells had lost all irony. Upon me there crept a strong and hideous sensation I had experienced to a minor degree once before, at a bullfight in Majorca, my first and last: a blend of physical fear, or dread, and a voluptuous, almost dizzy excitement: I wanted this to stop and to go on. I felt Penny's thigh press against mine and her long, cold hand grip mine in a grasp I knew was one of fear untainted by any excitement.

'It's all right,' I shouted to her. 'Just acting. They're putting it on.'

This view of events became harder to sustain when the Thing forestalled the referee's intervention by picking him up in one hand and throwing him violently on to the corner-post, and when the two seconds and a third man who might have been a wrestler in mufti jumped into the ring and began trying to break up the fight. One of the seconds hit the Thing repeatedly with a wooden stool he had brought with him. All round the hall, people were on their feet shouting in protest, and Sylvia at my left side was on hers shouting to the Thing to gouge the bastard's eyes out, which was when I saw that Roy had after all not entirely miscalculated in deciding to bring his party here. Gouging the Knight's eyes out was just what the Thing, apparently unscathed by the stool and all other efforts, seemed to be getting to work on, with both his outsize hands over the upper part of his opponent's face, though, among the half-dozen shifting bodies, it was still hard to make out what was going on. The excited half of my reactions had vanished; I caught hold of Penny's arm and squeezed it. Then, momentarily but unmistakably, I saw through the crisscross of arms and hands and trunks that the Thing's thumbs were not where I had feared they would be, but resting against the Knight's cheekbones. I said loudly into Penny's ear,

'It's all right. I just saw. He's not going for his eyes. He's only pretending to. It's all right.'

She turned towards me a face that had lost its colour, an excessively rare condition among the healthy. Her mouth was open and turned down at the corners, and her eyes were unfocused. I pulled her to her feet at exactly the moment at which a woman in the row behind hit Sylvia in the small of the back with the head of her umbrella, but I did not wait to see what would ensue. Instead, I kept hold of Penny's hand and, being bigger and heavier than anybody I encountered, quite easily shouldered a way for us both through the knots of bawling men and women that now occupied much of the aisles.

In the hallway, we found perhaps a dozen other people in varying states of distress. A middle-aged attendant greeted us with an upward nod.

'Fantastic,' he said morosely and amicably. 'Gets 'em every time. He does this once a month regular, and every time half of 'em think it's real. Half of 'em. All of 'em. Fantastic. Best actor I ever seen, that Thing chap. Beats me he isn't in Shakespeare. Eh? I mean he'd pull in ten times more at Stratford-upon-Avon than what he gets here. Ernie Adams. Comes from just up the road here, you know.'

Roy arrived a minute later accompanied by Sylvia, who objected with some violence to the idea of leaving, but quite soon after it must have become clear to her how clear it was to

Roy and me that her prime reason for wanting to stay was Penny's anxiety to go, she dropped these objections, following for once, I thought, a rather old way of seeing things in preference to any of the new ones at her disposal. I got back into the car between the two girls, aware of hunger, thirst, incipient weariness of mind and body, renewed general wonderment at the way Roy was running his life, barely perceptible self-contempt for having fallen victim to the Thing's histrionic talents, and Penny's shape beside me, which seemed at the moment to be more three-dimensional than most human shapes I could recall off-hand.

'What happened back there?' I asked when we were in motion.

'They got a sort of tourniquet on the hairy shag's wimpipe,' said Roy, 'and then disqualified him.'

'Really. I meant about the woman with the umbrella too.'

'I clobbered her,' said Sylvia.

Roy gave a laugh, not one of his rich ones, conveying roughly that girls would be girls, but leaving it uncertain whether he referred to Sylvia's readiness to exaggerate or to hit people. After a pause, Penny asked carelessly,

'Was the other chap all right?'

'Of course he was all right.' Sylvia, leaning forward so as to see Penny properly, spoke in the solicitous tone she had used on me earlier. 'Why shouldn't he have been all right?'

'He sounded as though, you know.'

'Darling, it was all an *uhct*. Surely you could see *thuht*? You said yourself when we went in. You mustn't let yourself get so drawn about everything. It's all different, you see? Let it go on . . .'

The three of us let Sylvia go on while the car hurried south, mainly along side streets. A creditable time after deciding I could stand no more of her on her chosen theme, or on any fresh one, I braved the risk of a second lecture about my having to have done everything before and asked Roy where we were going now.

'Club I belong to.'

'Not Craggs's?'

'Oh, Socialist Gestapo! Do you think I'm off my head?' Receiving no reply, he went on, 'One of those places where there's music and people dance if they want to. You needn't. We eat there too.'

'Oh, good. You mean pop racket.'

'Well, it wouldn't be Stockhausen, would it?'

'A discotheque, in fact.'

Sylvia laughed with incredulous awe, as if I had mentioned Vauxhall Gardens or a bear pit. Roy explained more kindly that it was always called a club now, and added, to forestall any fear of social mortification on my part, that there were much flashier joints than the one we were bound for.

I thought this might well be true when, somewhere north of the Fulham Road, Sylvia and I descended a staircase lined with green electric bulbs that fizzed and flickered or emitted no light at all. Roy, adopting his riot-squad manner, had taken Penny ahead and told me to follow in one minute – not less. During that minute, Sylvia had suggested that I loosen up and quit worrying, and I had promised to try.

At the foot of the stairs, we went through glass doors into a cubicle where there was nothing obvious to do except hand over money and be given tickets and change, which Roy was doing, or stand about, which Penny and a small dark man were doing. This man came up and kissed Sylvia warmly.

'Hallo,' he said, leaving a perceptible gap where her name might have fitted. 'Good evening, sir. It's nice to have you with us tonight.'

I was at a loss for an answer, but Roy made marshalling gestures and took us through further glass doors into another cubicle. Here there was a wider choice of activities: going out to one of the lavatories, or passing outdoor clothing over a counter, or standing about. Across much of the far wall there stretched an immense wardrobe with mirror doors and with, by the sound of it, a great many people crammed inside. One of two or three additional small dark men who had taken the standing-about option accepted Roy's tickets and opened the wardrobe. As I heard immediately and saw by degrees, it was not a wardrobe, but a large room or complex of rooms with a quantity of conversation therein that, spread out equally, would have been about right for a fair-sized town on a mid-week evening. Roy led the way into it all. My impressions included a semicircular bar off to one side, somebody's navel with a lot of bare skin surrounding it, a stage at the far end with velvet-clad persons moving about on it, two long-haired albinos holding hands on a black-leather sofa, a great many feet I mostly avoided treading on and tripping up over, dark-blue electric bulbs in better repair than the illumination on the staircase and diversified with flashing red and white lights, a dirty middle-aged man in a sort of tracksuit playing a fruit-machine, and what turned out to be a restaurant slightly shielded by glass screens. On arrival here, I felt the apparently bottomless plunge in my well-being start to decelerate, a moment before a fresh dose of wordless yelling, of such impact as to suggest to me momentarily that anything of the kind was altogether new in my experience, broke out from the direction of the stage. Various mechanical noises, chiefly metallic, were being made too. I was sorry for having too hastily rejected those musical works which consist of a stated period of silence under concert conditions. First Bruckner, I thought. Now John Cage. Who next? Nielsen? Busoni? Buxtehude? Yes, listening hard to the works of any or each would almost certainly prove less onerous than having a tooth drilled down to the gum without anaesthetic.

We were taken to a table in the corner farthest from the stage, where the pandemonium was lessened by about one per cent and there were coloured-glass hyacinths. Roy put Sylvia and me on a black-leather banquette against the wall with himself and Penny opposite, no doubt in further pursuance of the fiction that he was there just to be paternal to the rest of us in differing degrees. And yet, in the murk of that restaurant, which approached that of the Dug-out and was emphasized rather than relieved by the strings of fairy-lights on sweet- or liqueur-trolley, I could not believe that anyone beyond arm's length could have recognized him – and, given the noise-level, anyone who did would have forgotten all about it before he had had time even to cry out. And what about it? What about all of it?

Now that the favour was actually in progress, was (I trusted to God) a lot more than half over, it had quite lost any plausibility it might once have had. My surroundings encouraged this feeling of remoteness. Perhaps somebody had slipped a hallucinogen into that Guinness and I was having what current little slobberers called a bad trip.

Time went by as if an unlimited fund of it had suddenly been made available. A girl clad in a piece of silk measuring at least eighteen inches from top to bottom appeared through the gloaming and gave out sheets of vellum which I took to be menus. I peered hard at mine, polished my glasses on the paper napkin provided, peered again and made out phrases to do with garnishing and 4 persons and white wine sauce here and there. One day, I foresaw, eaters-out, if any, would need a more than nodding acquaintance with Braille as well as lip-reading. I took advantage of a lull in the yelling to order soup, steak and beer, my only utterance, as distinct from renewed mutters and whimpers, for quite some time. Roy and Sylvia, their foreheads almost touching across the table, were conversing in amorous roars and howls like creatures of legend, incomprehensibly to me for the most part, but still audibly; Penny was too far away, in all senses, for any sort of chat between us to be feasible: it would have been like trying to borrow money down an ear-trumpet. My steak came, and surprised me, or would have done had I still been open to surprise, by being excellent. While I was eating it, Roy broke off his tender thunderings to remonstrate with Penny for not having ordered anything and to try again to persuade her to do so. As he talked near her ear, he poured himself out some more Scotch from what had been the full bottle that had furnished his aperitifs and now, without a break, had become the source of his table wine. She shook her head and gestured to the titbits plate she had emptied of olives and radishes immediately on sitting down. Sylvia turned to me. I noticed how nearly circular her face was.

'I can't *stuhnd* all these put-ons. She made her point at the wrestling. So she's sensitive. She wants us to sign a paper?'

'Perhaps she's just not hungry.'

'Ah, bugger awff.' (This piece of accentual grandeur,

coupled with a large part of what she had said and done that evening, made me strongly suspect she was a peer's daughter.) 'If you're really not hungry you get a plateful and then you just don't eat it. That's what you do, you see?' She leaned diagonally across the table and hooted at Penny, 'We're sold, Snow White. You feel absolutely frightful. O-*kay*. Now let's get on to the next thing.'

Penny looked down at her lap and shook her head again. I moved up to Sylvia.

'What makes you such a howling bitch?'

'I expect it's the same thing as makes you a top-heavy red-haired four-eyes who's never had anything to come up to being tossed off by the Captain of Boats and impotent and likes bloody symphonies and fugues and the first variation comes before the statement of the theme and give me a decent glass of British beer and dash it all Carruthers I don't know what young people are coming to these days and a scrounger and an old woman and a failure and a hanger-on and a prig and terrified and a shower and a brisk rub-down every morning and you can't throw yourself away on a little trollop like that Roy you must think of your wife Roy old boy old boy and I'll come along but I don't say I approve and bloody dead. Please delete the items in the above that do not apply. If any.'

This was delivered at top speed and without solicitude of any kind. Her upper lip was thinned to vanishing point and remained so while she stared silently at me. I found myself much impressed by the width of her vocabulary and social grasp. Roy had probably missed much of her text, but he would have caught her tone, face and so on.

'Penny,' he called to her rebukingly – 'oh, balls, *Sylvia*. Cool it, now.'

Sylvia did two or three of her suppressed-sneeze laughs.

'I don't like fugues,' I said, and might have gone on to tell her I considered the fugue the most boring artistic innovation before the adult Western if I had not been nearly sure I had once said so to Roy, if her harangue had not cowed me a little, and other ifs.

When Penny stood up, I started thinking immediately about

how best to separate two girls in a combat that could have rivalled that between the Thing and the Knight, but she only told me to come and dance.

I shook my head. 'I can't.'

'Oh yes you can. Come on.'

Half a minute later we were on a small dance floor below the stage. This was now quite bare of velvet-suited performers, but noises of the same general character and equal volume were being provided by a gramophone record. Everybody in sight was five or ten years younger than I. The majority of couples were performing at rather than with each other, making rope-climbing or gunshot-dodging motions with an air of dedication, as if all this were only by way of prelude to some vaster ordeal they must ultimately share. Before I had fully grasped how much I wanted not to join in any of it, Penny took me into a corner, put my arms round her and hers round me, and began rubbing the whole of the front of herself against me. She moved roughly in the tempo of the prevailing noises, but made no other concession to circumstance. Within a short time, and in direct defiance of everything I was saying to myself, we were both aware of a concrete result. Penny released me and stepped aside.

'Right,' she said. 'Let's go.'

I turned my back on everybody except her. 'I'm not going anywhere until you've given me a short account of the habitat, diet and main domestic uses of the Bactrian camel. And how do you mean?'

'I wanted to thank you, and so I wanted to give you something, and there's only one thing I've got that you might want, but I had to make sure you wanted it. But what's this camel thing?'

'The dromedary will do just as well. In fact I'm not sure it isn't the same as the Bactrian camel. I asked you anyway before, that time up at your place.'

'I made you then. I was depressed that day. You mean you want to think about camels for a bit.'

'Thank me for what?'

'At the wrestling. And not liking her.'

The Bactrian camel (or dromedary), though selected very

much at random, was having its effect. I said, 'That's not much, not liking her. I can't imagine anybody who would.'

'He does. So he makes out.'

'He's special.'

'He's special all right. Can you go now?'

'Just about. But we'll have to see this through before we take off.'

See it through we did; take off I thought we never would. In the end, however, after a space of time sufficient for a performance of *Die Meistersinger*, uncut and with supper interval, all four of us stood on the pavement in Park Lane and looked out for taxis – the hired car had been dismissed, presumably to make Roy feel better about security. He worried me severely with his parade of initial incomprehension, dawning comprehension, careful consideration and final approbation when I said I thought I would take Penny off and deliver her wherever she wanted to go. Surely the whole concept of the favour could not have been evolved simply to get me off with her? The answer was that on theoretical grounds it most assuredly could, but that few people who were not canonization timber would have deliberately arranged such an evening just for another's benefit. A taxi came and he and Sylvia moved towards it. I thanked him and said good night, and he said good night and told me he would ring me in the morning. Neither girl spoke nor looked at anybody.

Penny's and my taxi ride took place, after a couple of unanswered remarks from me, in total silence; in fact I was given a booster shot of the back-turning stuff I had had earlier. I foresaw trouble at the flat, but when we reached the bedroom she started undressing with the speed and conviction of someone about to go to the rescue of a swimmer in difficulties. I still foresaw the untoward – request for oddities, indifference with simulated ecstasy or just plain, last-moment refusal – but, again, all went merrily. Although the breasts were rather less hard than they looked, not having been sprayed with quick-drying cement, they were hard, and in the other sense soft. Everything else was good, too, and went on being so. I made no attempt not to compare her with Vivienne, and thought I felt or saw a difference in bodily behaviour: Vivienne (memory told me from a long way off) was unrestrained and unselfconscious, and Penny was those too, but there was an added beauty in her movements that nobody could acquire or intend. I kissed her ear and her temple and started murmuring.

'Darling, you are the most – '

She moved away. 'Listen, I don't want any of that. Stuff that. I don't want any thanks, thanks.'

'Sorry. Think of it as just a habit. One a lot of people have. It wasn't just thanks. Not that there's much wrong with just thanks that I can see.'

'I can. Anyway, I don't want any of it. Letting you talk soft isn't in the contract. If you try and do it again, talk soft I mean, I'm sleeping on the sofa or whatever you've got. Oh, and by the way, mate, so's you won't go and get any wrong ideas, this is it. Until breakfast I'm at your disposal, and then not any more. No phone calls, no letters, no flowers by request. Nothing about you personally, just how it is. Would you like a cup of tea?'

'I'll get it. You don't know where the things are.'

'I'll find them. Have you got a bath-robe or something? Not a good one. I always spill things down me.'

Twenty minutes later I was in the sitting-room, playing the Weber bassoon concerto very quietly to myself on the hi-fi, when Penny came in wearing an old corduroy topcoat of mine (the best I had been able to do in the way of a bath-robe) and carrying a tray with a good deal more on it than tea for two.

'I should have thought you'd had enough row for one evening.'

'Row, yes. That's why I put this on. Do you mind?'

'As long as you don't tell me about it. I hope it's all right, I found some sardines and some other junk and I made some toast. I couldn't eat at that club place. You know, her. Would you like some?'

'No thanks. Just tea.'

'He used to take me to hear things at concerts and play me bits on the gramophone and tell me about them till I could scream. Now he does it to his birds. Perhaps he always has. I felt quite sorry for her. In a way. Get those trombones, aren't they thrilling? Get the way he brings back the first subject of the first movement. Get the fingering in this passage. Get him going into 6/8 time. Get stuffed.'

Having given me my tea, she settled down on the couch with the tray beside her and began eating; quietly, I thought. I pulled down my copy of *Music Ho!* and pretended to read it, so that if she wanted to listen to Weber she could do so without fear of being spotted in the act. I found myself sympathizing with Roy and his tendency to tell birds about trombones. It was faintly comic, and yet not undignified, that he still tried to share or give art, still had not arrived at the sad fact that to listen to a musical work can never be other than a solitary experience. Then, at the start of the middle section of the concerto's slow movement, I noticed that Penny's gentle chewing of her toast had stopped in mid-mouthful. A glance round the edge of my glasses showed her sitting quite still with a half-eaten slice in her hand. Something I took at first to be a tear, but which soon turned out to be a blob of marmalade, fell on to the corduroy coat. The bassoon returned to its opening melody and munching began again. Nothing being more strongly inherited than musical talent, I felt I knew that, if Roy and Penny's mother and Penny and everybody had been born twenty years earlier, Penny would now be near the front of the first violins in a decent orchestra, if not in a string quartet. Anyway, even the back desk of the seconds in some grimy provincial city would be a better place for her than anywhere she was likely to find herself in twenty years' time. These thoughts ruffled me.

The record ended. It was ten minutes to three. My eyelids felt like tattered canvas, but Penny sat on and looked at the floor. I said experimentally,

'Curious evening, one way and another.'

'Sodding grotesque.'

'Why did you come?'

'Why did you? I wanted not to be in the house. And I wanted to talk. To try and explain. I didn't but I wanted to then.'

'Explain now.'

'You can't. I can't. I couldn't.'

'Why don't you go and live with your mother for a bit?'

She lit a cigarette. 'I screwed it up with her. I thought it was her fault, the divorce. It was his really, of course, but I didn't know then. And anyway her husband won't have me in the house. He's an estate agent.'

'Why don't you and Gilbert go off somewhere?'

'No thanks. I'd be gone on at all the time. It's bad enough when there are other people around. And I'd worry if I wasn't there.'

'What about?'

'For instance you know he's talking of going off with this little slag for good, do you?'

'Oh, God. He can't.' I felt as if I had been told my dinner had been poisoned. Questions formed in my mind and disintegrated again. 'He's off his rocker,' I said finally. 'Does Kitty know?'

'I haven't seen her. He only mentioned it the other day. But he'll leak it, the way he always does, and then we'll be off. And when we've all had plenty of that, he'll move out, I reckon.'

'That's the time for you to go too, isn't it? Or earlier. Anywhere at all. Abroad. Drop out properly. You'd be mad to say around up there, with Kitty doing her stuff from morning to night.'

'She'd come and find me. And there's Ashley, and Chris. He'll go berserk when he finds out. Burn the place down. He hates him. He won't mind much really, the thing itself, but he'll have an excuse then, see. And I don't want to not know what's going on. That's what I didn't like about last time. Keeping it from the children. A bloody scream, that was.'

I said nothing. She moved on the couch so that everything about her was pointing directly at me.

'He takes a bit of notice of you. Will you try and stop him?'

If I had not still been disconcerted by her news, and had not perhaps been suffering from her ability to take any number of years off my emotional age, I might have prevented myself from saying, 'So that was the help you wanted.'

'You and me tonight was nothing to do with that,' she said angrily. 'That was separate. I told you it's not going to happen again. Not after I go. And that wasn't to show you it was separate. It all just is.'

'I'm sorry.' I took in what flushing had done for the whites and irises of her eyes. 'I'd like to help about everything. Take you on.'

'Nobody gets to take me on. Sorry. I told you it isn't you. I quite like you. You're a bit pompous, but you're all right really.' Her faint grin at this reminded me of our reintroduction six or seven weeks before. Then she went urgent again. 'Will you talk to him?'

'I don't know what good you think it'll do. You know what he's –'

'But will you?'

'Yes. Yes, I will. I'll have to. I was going to anyway. I'll tell him.'

'Thanks.'

Penny got up, turned her back, and looked down in the general direction of the tray. I could not think of anything to say that had not been vetoed in advance. After over a minute she shifted half round towards me.

'I'd like to be asleep now.'

'How can a Japanese write music?' asked Harold Meers. 'I mean real music, not bloody pots and pans.'

'No trouble. I mean, of course it's trouble, but not any –'

'Totally alien culture, food, drink, dress, art, ways of thought, the whole lot.'

'Originally, no doubt, but there's been a certain amount of Western music in Japan for quite some time now, and in any case he's –'

'You can't change a whole culture overnight.'

'Possibly not, but this chap went to the U.S.A. in 1950, when he was eight, so he must know quite a bit about the West these days. And this concerto of his just is very interesting. Not great, but interesting.'

Harold looked down at my copy. 'You say here he's spent most of his life in California.'

'Yes, I do, don't I?'

'But there must be traces of Nip stuff in his work. Bells and so on.'

'None that I could hear.'

'Perhaps you just weren't listening hard enough,' said Harold with his standard lack of inflection. 'There was something else, too . . . What was this a concerto for?'

'Orchestra, if you mean that sort of for.'

'Yes, yes, but what was the, damn it, the solo instrument?'

'There isn't one. It's a concerto in the sense of –'

'Look, a concerto means there's a soloist. Beethoven, Tchaikovsky, Schubert. Even I know that. Anyway, will you check it?'

'No, Harold,' I said. 'You check it if you want to, and then if

I'm wrong you can send my fee to the Musicians' Benevolent Fund.'

'All right, all right.'

Harold went on reading, or at any rate lowered his head again. This morning's going-over had been stern, even on current form. It must have been that he resented the absence of any point he felt he could validly let himself go on: praise of a Cuban viola d'amore virtuoso or North Korean bass-baritone. I began mentally composing my last piece for him, the one after he sacked me, all about the glories of a new Bolivian opera with a white Rhodesian conductor and a mixed cast of Brazilians, Haitians, Spaniards, white South Africans and members of the John Birch Society. I had not got very far with it when the telephone rattled.

'Yes,' said Harold into it. 'Get someone to bring her up, will you?' He rang off and looked in my direction. 'My daughter's collecting me, so we'll have to leave it there. Check with Coates about five thirty as usual. And remember to watch those technical terms.'

I went along to Features and was jostled at its doorway by a small man coming out, white-haired yet wearing a cerise corduroy suit, gamboge Paisley shirt and Goliath-size orange tie. Inside, Coates was talking to Terry Bolsover, the hairy hobbledehoy who wrote for the paper on pop noises: not a bad fellow for all that. I did not join them at once, but remained by the long inner window on to the corridor, intent on a glimpse of whatever sort of person Harold Meers might have for a daughter. And my inquisitiveness was repaid hand over fist, for in less than a minute one of the grey-clad attendants from the ground floor came round the corner from the lift with Sylvia at his side and took her along to Harold's office. She did not see me.

'Jesus Christ,' I said.

'I hear profanity,' said Coates. 'And from a normally restrained source.'

'He's remembered he got an opus number wrong,' said Bolsover.

'Worse than that. I've just seen Miss Meers.'

'It is a shaker,' conceded Coates.

'You want to watch it there,' said Bolsover. 'She's not as nice as she looks, from all you hear.'

'No, she's not. I mean I'm sure she's not.'

I had no trouble now in deciding who Sylvia had reminded me of, that first evening at my flat. My imagination boggled away prestissimo while the other two looked at me with mild curiosity. Then Bolsover said,

'Oh, while you're here, Doug . . . You are a great buddy of this conductor character, Sir Roy Vandervane, aren't you? I haven't got it wrong?'

'No. You haven't got it wrong. What about him?'

I probably looked appalled at this collocation. Coates turned up his curiosity-level for a second before raising a riot of coughing. Bolsover brought from inside his guerilla-style jacket a leaflet printed in white on purple.

'You've probably seen this about the Pigs Out concert on Tuesday,' he said – 'Well, there are these other –'

'Pigs what? – sorry.'

'What you'd call a pop group. They do protest stuff mostly, not really serious, just, you know, I want a girl just like the girl that murdered dear old Dad, all this. But then now and again they reckon they'll show they're proper musicians too, extending the frontiers of art. That's where your pal comes in. I'd have thought you'd be sure to get one. Here.'

I took the purple sheet and read (to put it in plain English) that part of the programme would consist of *Elevations 9*, written by Sir Roy Vandervane and performed by him with the assistance of members of Pigs Out. Every purported fact about Roy, except for his sex and his committal to the cause of youth, was wrong. I suffered an onrush of conscience about having altogether dismissed this work from my mind, an onrush mitigated by the calculation that Roy himself had probably taken my name off the distribution list of the document.

'Is this Pigs lot any good?' I asked, handing it back. 'By the standards of the trade?'

'Not really, no. The lead guitarist's not too bad. But they're in the charts all right. Manager and Press agent are okay.'

'I see. Where do I . . . ?'

'I thought you might, well, ask him if I could have a word with him some time between now and Tuesday. How he came to write it, what pop can learn from classical, where it's all going, this type of stuff. I'd really be grateful if you could just mention it. So if I rang him he'd know who I am.'

'Once you've told him what you do you'd get him for as long as you wanted. But I'll tell him.'

'Thanks, Doug. I really appreciate it.'

Bolsover left. Coates was telephoning. When he had finished, I said to him,

'Albert, could I have a quick word?'

'Any speed you want.'

'Old Vandervane. I don't know whether you knew, but Harold's got his knife in him. Just on general grounds.'

'I didn't know that, but I can guess about the grounds. So?'

'I'm . . . I can't quite think how to put this,' – indeed, I could barely think what I was about to put – 'but I suspect Harold may have got something up his sleeve for Vandervane. Some bit of no good he can do him, like a snide para in the Diary or a crack at the foot of the leader. If you see anything like that, or get to hear of it, do you think you could tip me off?'

'Sure, but I couldn't block it, Doug, you realize that.'

'Of course not, but I could warn him or . . . Anyway.'

'Right. You seem kind of jittery or something. If it was anyone else I'd put you down as hungover.'

'Just the sight of Miss Meers,' I said, telling a version of part of the truth. 'Who was that I ran into when I was coming in here?'

'New education correspondent.'

I now had two extra, or extra pressing, reasons for getting hold of Roy, which I had not succeeded in doing since the night of the favour. In the intervening four and a bit days I had not, admittedly, tried as hard as I perhaps might have done. I had telephoned his house three times, finding Kitty at the other end on each occasion, and getting twenty, forty and twenty-five minutes respectively of formless lamentation with a rebuke or two thrown in – why had I let things reach this pass, not let her know before that things had reached this pass? I explained, working under adverse conditions, that I had hoped to exert some influence on Roy and to have something concrete to tell her, but in vain. This was broadly accurate, in that just to report and be told that Sylvia was awful would not have been worth either of our whiles, but I was relieved when she resumed formless lamentation without having asked me just what pass I myself thought things had reached, and so forcing me to lie: nothing but trouble could come of that revelation. As regards what pass things seemed to Kitty to have reached, I was still in doubt, at the end of the combined eighty-five minutes, whether Roy was at the stage of ordering the drink for an elopement reception, starting to drop the occasional complaint that life at home left something to be desired, or in between. Anyway, where was he? Kitty promised, with maximum fervour, to get him to ring me; I left messages at Craggs's, at his agents', at the hall where he was rehearsing Gus Mahler and everywhere else I could think of, with no response. He was lying doggo, no doubt aware that our next meeting would entail my telling him something of how I felt about Sylvia and his invawvement with her.

After leaving the newspaper office, I got through some hock and smoked salmon at El Vino with my colleague on the *Custodian,* went back to my flat and spent the afternoon with my eyes on my Weber notes and typescript and my thoughts on the Roy question. By degrees, I decided that Penny must have been exaggerating, or else I had done so in my own mind. Just talking about going off with that thin-lipped savage might well have been just talk, even though what sounded like just Roy's talk had a way of quitting that state, as a piece of apparently very much just talk about writing a Vietnam demonstrators' marching-song had proved a couple of years earlier: mercifully, it had never caught on. I also decided that it was less important to stop him going off with Sylvia than to stop him performing *Elevations 9.* The latter project was also the more straightforward: breaking his arm on the way to the concert would wrap the whole thing up beyond argument.

At half past five I got through to Coates and found, much to my surprise, that my piece was going into the paper entire. Not only to my surprise: editorial toleration of my existence must indirectly imply, either that Sylvia had not yet said anything about her doings with my friend Vandervane, or that the news had been divulged and welcomed, or that the Martians had landed. I determined to put the whole thing from me until the morning. Vivienne was due at six or thereabouts, as soon after her office closed as transport conditions would allow. I was ready for her in more senses than the usual one or two.

At ten to six my doorbell rang. No head and shoulders were visible through the glass panel downstairs, but Vivienne often moved aside in this situation to look at the flowers and shrubs and such that some forgotten toiler had planted in the small front garden, and on opening the door I really quite narrowly missed embracing Gilbert on the front step.

'May I have a few words with you, please?'

'A few, by all means. I'm expecting someone shortly.'

'Then I can return at any convenient time.'

'No, it's all right. Come on up.'

In the sitting-room, Gilbert refused a drink but accepted a chair, leaving on the piano the two paperbacks he had been carrying; the top one, I saw, was called *Bringers of the Black Dawn*. He was frowning worriedly and his clothes, which had been in noticeably good order on our two previous meetings, had a second-hand look.

'What can I do for you?' I asked.

He shook his head very slowly at this dismayingly facile view of the present occasion. After that, he sighed. When he had quite finished doing so, he said, 'The situation of the Vandervane household has reached the brink of chaos.'

'That's where it's been as long as I can remember. Still . . .'

'In most ways, I must admit, it's none of my concern. Roy's private life is of course his own affair, and the lines on which the family behaves are not my business. However, what I must consider are Penny's interests. It's essential, absolutely essential, that she must leave the house as soon as humanly possible. The tension and the awful feelings there are destroying her.'

'I know what you mean. But I think you'll have a job getting her to go.'

'I've been having such a job for nearly two months now, without any success. At first she was saying there was no money and no place for us to go, which was true, but it was an excuse. Then last week I got the news that the Arts Council will give me a grant to finish my *London Suite*. With good management, it'll be enough for both of us until the book's published. And a friend will lend us his flat for a few weeks, at least. But Penny refuses point-blank to budge.'

'I see. But would you mind coming to the point? As I say, I'm –'

'I need your help.'

'Oh ...' Sporting spirit, I thought to myself. Christian gentleman. I wanted to dash out into the street before Gwyneth Iqbal from the flat underneath could add herself to the majority of people in the Home Counties currently needing my help. 'What the hell can I do?'

'Believe me, Mr Yandell, if there were any other person I could ask, any whatsoever, I'd ask him. There just isn't. You're the only person I know who might be able to persuade Penny to leave that household.'

'If you can't shift her yourself, I don't see what difference I could make.'

'You're white, Mr Yandell.' Gilbert stated this as a fact, with none of the resentment or scorn that might have been expected of him. 'You and she have grown up in the same culture. Therefore in some ways you know her and understand her better than I can ever hope to do. Perhaps you can think of arguments that I can't think of. You can make an appeal to your mutual heritage. You've known her family. Please try. The poor girl's in a quite desperate state. And I'm desperate myself, too.'

'I don't think she'd even talk to me.'

'I think she would. She enjoyed what took place here last Saturday night.'

'Did she, now? Had you given your permission for that?'

'Not as such. Not specifically. She's a free agent. My only

stipulation from her is to answer truthfully any questions I ask her. You see, except in this one admittedly vital matter of our departure I have considerable influence over her. Which ... I take it you do find her attractive?'

'Yes, I do.'

'I gathered from her that she told you that your association with her, such as it was, must not continue. I think I could influence her to change that decision, within limits. Let's say one or two times.'

'Good God,' I said listlessly. 'That doesn't sound a bit like you. What I know of you.'

'What you know of me isn't much. But up to a point I agree. But I said I was desperate, and desperate men do many strange things. I'm coming towards the end of my tether, Mr Yandell.'

'You've been living at the Vandervanes' too long, Mr Alexander.'

'It's a distressing environment.'

'I meant more than that. All right, I'll talk to Penny, but you'll have to fix everything up yourself. I'm not going to talk her into being talked to.'

'Agreed. Many thanks.'

'If I were you I'd clear out from up there right away, Penny or no Penny.'

The doorbell rang. So, a moment later, did the telephone. I asked Gilbert to let my visitor in as he left and to get in touch with me as soon as he liked. He picked up his books and went. I lifted the receiver. It was Roy.

'Hallo, Duggers, you old sod, how are you?' He spoke with the heartiness-in-depth to be met with in persons laying off at the start of the evening for being fighting-drunk later.

'Fine, thanks. How's Miss Meers?'

'Oh, she's ... Oh. Who told you?'

'Nobody. I saw her in the office, going along to see her dad.'

'Oh. You haven't – no of course you haven't. Well. Now you know, anyway. We'll talk about it. Duggers, I'm sorry I've been out of the picture, but I've been up to my neck, what with old Gus and the Royal Commission and, uh, Miss Meers herself. Haven't had a bloody minute.'

'What's this Royal Commission?'

'I thought I'd told you about it. Endless discussion, entirely about what'll be discussed at future discussions. You can imagine. The silly old bugger from the –'

'What's it on?'

'On? You mean the Commission. Oh, you know, it's supposed to be dealing with youth problems, crap like that. Load of old rubbish, but somebody's got to –'

'They ought to be able to get a lot of help from you, anyway.'

He gave a rich but rather brief laugh. 'Yes. Look, are you free at lunchtime tomorrow? I thought we might have something to eat and drink and a natter. One or two things on my mind.'

I decided against asking him if Penny was one of the things, on the grounds that to do so would only warn him that she was going to figure prominently on our agenda tomorrow, thus giving him time to prepare his smoke-screens and diversionary sallies. So I said simply that that would be fine and that I would, as requested, turn up at the Queen Alexandra Hall, where he was rehearsing the N.L.S.O., round about twelve fifteen the following day. Perhaps, I reflected as I rang off, it was Roy's system of total permissiveness towards himself that made him such agreeable company; how odd that permissiveness directed elsewhere should have such different results.

Where was Vivienne? Repudiating Gilbert's accusations of white supremacist colonialist fascism on the doorstep? No, here she was, severe and sexy together in her uniform, carrying a canvas bag of the same olive-green colour and with the same airline insignia. In it, I knew, were her overnight things and whatever wondrous clothes she intended to wear later. We exchanged the cousinly kiss that was as much as she allowed herself or me on reunion, even with bed dead ahead. It was a warm evening, but her cheek was cool.

'One of those Pakkies from down below let me in.'

'Actually he's not a Pakky, he's a West Indian, and he was from up here.'

She had taken off her fore-and-aft cap and now took off her jacket, so that I had to concentrate slightly when she said, 'I thought he was a bit black for a Pakky. Friend of yours, is he?'

'Not exactly. He's Roy Vandervane's daughter's boy-friend.'

'Oh, him. Doesn't he mind?'

'Why should he? In fact I'm sure he's all for it.'

'I meant him minding his daughter having a black boy-friend.'

'Yes, I know.' I realized now why I had not simply agreed that Gilbert was a Pakky from down below and left it: because of the pleasure to be got from hearing Vivienne expound her opinions on almost any topic or situation. 'He's very progressive about everything. In favour of racial integration and so on.'

'Why would a white girl want to have a black boy-friend?'

'Why not? But I see what you mean. In this case I think it's because she hoped her father would object.'

'Oh, nobody has a boy-friend because of a thing like that. And anyway, you just said he was all for it.'

'Yes, I know,' I said again, having decided in the interval that there was nothing to prevent my stopping her talking at this point and starting her up again at a later one. 'Would you like a cup of tea?'

Although she must have been expecting it, this made Vivienne blink, if not blush. The question was the first line in what had become a ritual, perhaps puzzling to an outsider, of which the object was to get the pair of us to the brink of bed without the risk of damaging her susceptibilities by some overt word or deed. Now, as laid down, she lifted her head consider-ingly, narrowed her eyes, said she thought she would wait a little, and walked towards the bedroom with an air of medium-strength curiosity that would have been just right for a home-page journalist on an evening off. This maintained itself, as usual, until I had shut the door after us, and, not as usual, for a moment or two after that. Then it changed out of all recognition. The problem now, if any, was holding her off until there ceased to be any point whatever in holding her off; I surmount-ed it successfully. What finally ensued went on some minutes over par. This was, by a narrow margin, at her instance rather than mine, as she acknowledged afterwards by apologizing to me. When she pleaded in mitigation that she had been enjoying herself so much that she had not wanted to stop, I forgave her.

Her going-out apparel, when she came to put it on, was something of a disappointment. Most of it consisted of a familiar dress in good taste – dowdy and featureless, in other words, and so forgettable that the eye slid glumly off it at once. As often before, I tried to define its colour, but got no further than locating it in some nameless region between brown and purple. She had tried to liven it up with a shiny green belt, a neck-scarf of a different green, a sort of headband in a third green, but it would have taken a necklace of shrunken skulls and a nose-ring to do the job effectively. I put on a suit. Over biancos and soda in the sitting-room, she said, in a chatty tone,

'You've got someone else, haven't you?'

'I've had someone else. Saturday night. How did you know?'

'You looked at me before we ... started. Usually, well, I suppose you must see me, but you don't look. Is she as pretty as me?'

'About the same. I mean she's not at all the same, but she is pretty.'

'Is she as reasonable as me?'

'My God, no.'

'Is she as good as me?' Her eyes flickered towards the bedroom in what was, for her, a flamboyantly lewd gesture.

'I don't think so.' (That felt like a lie, but perhaps I had not made allowance for the first-time excitement of that night.)

'What do you want her for, then?'

'Didn't I look at you on Sunday and yesterday?'

'You may have done; I didn't notice. Perhaps you made sure not to then. What do you want her for?'

'Well ... People can be no prettier than you and not as good and still be pretty and good. And it was late at night. And she sort of suggested it.'

'She sleeps around a lot, then, does she?'

'I don't know. A bit, I imagine.'

'When are you going to go with her again?'

'I doubt if I ever will,' I said with verbal truth, though I was not above implying a loftier reason for doubt than Penny's fairly certain rejection both of me as I stood, so to speak, and of Gilbert's influence in the matter.

'I suppose she's younger than me.'

'A few years, but it hadn't occurred to me until you mentioned it.'

'Who is she? What is she?'

'She's Roy Vandervane's daughter.'

'Him again. No, not again: still. Phew. Had that black chap come to knock your block off?'

'No, he wanted me to give him a hand with something he's working on.'

'Easy-going sort of type, isn't he?'

'Isn't that what we're all supposed to be round here? What about you and the other bloke? He doesn't sound anywhere near as pretty as me from what you told me about him, in fact you said so yourself, but I quite see he might be a hell of a lot reasonabler and gooder, but anyway whatever he's like you've got him, so it isn't fair for you to start minding what I get up to.'

'Yes it is, it's perfectly fair for me to mind. What wouldn't be fair would be me going on at you, doing things or saying things, anything at all to try to get you to stop going with her. And I haven't, have I? I've been reasonable.'

'Yes, I give you that straight away.'

'Thank you. The other bloke's a bit more reasonable than you and just about as good,' she said, volunteering information for the second time that evening.

'I see. I still can't make out why you mind.'

'If you can't, you can't. Now we're going to forget it. I won't bring it up again and I won't make you think I'm thinking about it even though I'm not bringing it up.'

Unsurprisingly, she kept her word, denying herself even her smallish mid-week ration of sullenness-cum-preoccupation throughout dinner at Bertorellis' in Charlotte Street, the showing of the nuclear-submarine thriller I had chosen instead of the Hungarian film about the life of Liszt she had thought I must want to see, and the remainder of the night's events. Nevertheless, I was betting myself I had not heard the end of her part in the Penny question, and put on an internal red alert when she said at breakfast,

'Oh, Doug, have you got anything fixed for Monday?'

I got my diary out. 'Well, half. But I can easily not go. But isn't that the night you go to see your dad?'

'Yes, but I was thinking you might like to come along too. He's often asked about you.'

'Just the three of us?'

'Yes. I was thinking I could come up here about six, and then', she said, looking out of the window, 'we could get on our way about quarter to seven.'

'Fine. I'll look forward to it.'

I won my usual battle to prevent Vivienne washing up the breakfast things, saw her off, washed up the breakfast things, wrote a letter and hung about until three short rings at the doorbell signalled the departure from below of Gwyneth Iqbal, who minded my piano-playing, for the accountants' office where she worked. Accordingly, I sat down at the keyboard at once, although I knew that Fazal Iqbal, who also minded, was still downstairs, and would be for the next hour or so, doing none knew what. But he was tolerant of the piano, because I minded – it seemed to me with better reason – the unsteady wailing, punctuated by explosive clicks, he was in the habit of producing from some apparatus he owned, and I was tolerant about that.

I took myself through the Beethoven op. 109, first piecemeal and then, after a cup of coffee, entire. At the end, I decided that there was something to be said for the Iqbals' point of view. Hands had followed brain with fair efficiency, but brain had been sluggish, lazy, allowing eyes to usurp too much of its function. I decided that my favourite excuse to myself for having failed to become a practising musician, my piano teacher's obstinacy in stopping me from switching to some wind instrument and going for a job in an orchestra, was an excuse and no more. Oh well, bashing piano keys kept one in touch, but in future I had better concentrate on bashing typewriter keys with more elegant and readable results.

By half past eleven I had had enough and left, in the expectation that some royal occasion or sporting event, or one of those mysterious lemming-like impulses that can urge ten thousand extra vehicles into trying to cross central London inside the same hour, would intervene to use up at least the forty-five minutes I had in hand. Not a bloody bit of it, as Roy would have said. As virtually always in this situation, half the people were using the ring road that morning and most of the others had already left for the Channel ports. The drivers of my successive buses performed with dash and intrepidity, scraping through lights in the last instant of the amber, swinging out into the fast lane and rampaging round Marble Arch and Hyde Park Corner as if under notice of dismissal. At two minutes to twelve I was climbing the steps of the Alexandra Hall. In the foyer, a small-headed fellow in uniform came over to bar my way with an air of undifferentiated hostility. Almost at once he recognized me and changed his air to one of differentiated hostility.

'A rehearsal is in progress,' he said.

'So I understood from Sir Roy.'

The man's head seemed to shrink a half hat-size or so. 'There's a round dozen of them in there already, sitting about.'

'I'll have company, then.'

'Name?'

After some Yandell-Randall? – Yandelling, he went through an inner conflict, decided against asking me to submit to a search, and let me pass. I took a seat about a third of the way down the auditorium, as indicated by the acoustics of the hall. Roy, on the rostrum with score and baton, was in shirt-sleeves, both shirt and sleeves flamingo-hued and ruffle-adorned in a mode that might have appealed strongly to Vivienne. The orchestra were giving him their close attention.

'First oboe,' he was saying, 'remember not to take that minim off till the next beat. In the passage in general, the wood-wind balance is much better now, excellent, in fact, but I'd like just a shade more from third and fourth clarinets and a touch less from first flute. Strings, overall, a little more warmth if you can. Try to sing. Oh, I know a lot of silly sods go on about singing, but I'm afraid they're right. I'd use another word if I could, but there ain't one. But don't feel you've got to give it absolutely every bloody ounce at this stage. In these long works you've got to pace yourselves, keep just that little bit in hand, or by the time you get to the finale you'll be drained dry. Right, we'll take the whole of the movement straight through now. Okay, everybody? Fine.'

He drank from a glass that his enemies would have said contained vodka, but which I knew, *Elevations 9* or no *Elevations 9*, Sylvia or no Sylvia, must hold nothing but water. Then he picked up his baton and started them off.

The movement turned out to be the first movement of the First Symphony: a considerable mercy, seeing that it might so easily have been something broad, full, ample, spacious, massive, leisurely and going on for over half an hour from the Second or the Third. Thanks to some paroxysm of curtailment on the composer's part, I was in for little more than fifteen minutes' worth. (It was true that, in a comparable situation, Weber would have gone on half as long and used an orchestra a quarter as big, but then he would have had eight times as much to say.) As the music got into its lubberly stride, I made some attempt to separate it in itself from how it was being interpreted and played, but I had never been very good at this with works on my private never-mind list. At first against my will, I listened to Mahler's enormous talentlessness being rendered by Roy and the N.L.S.O. As they went on, flecks of seeming talent began to insinuate themselves. Factitious fuss turned itself into a sort of gaiety; doodles in the horns and woodwind were almost transformed into rustic charm; blaring and banging acquired a note of near-menace; even that terrible little cuckoo-motif reflected something more than the great man's decision to let the world know how jolly preoccupied he had been in those days with the interval of the perfect fourth.

The ending went off poorly, but that was mostly Mahler, and

I could have faulted the 'cellos with a bit of raggedness near the beginning, but all in all it had been a very good performance, approaching the best second-rate, that rare and exalted level to which Roy could decisively lift the orchestra when the concert came and where, I was much relieved to have found, he himself still belonged as he always had. The other listeners – not the crew of rioters at which the microcephalic had seemed to hint, but various attachments of the players – agreed with me. At least, they applauded. So did I.

'Bloody good,' said Roy. 'Thank you, all of you. Very nearly absolutely what I want. Now, it's now getting on for twelve thirty, so we might as well scrub the last half-hour. And everybody's worked bloody hard this morning and the last couple of days, so unless there's a lot of opposition I propose scrubbing this afternoon's session as well. Okay? Ten o'clock Monday, then. Thank you again.'

A couple of minutes later he came up the aisle, buttoning one of his uneasiness-dispensing overcoatish jackets, and greeted me. I suppressed a qualm at his ready cancellation of the afternoon rehearsal, telling myself that I had just now been full of appreciation of the standard already achieved, and had better stop coming over all officious whenever anybody started derelicting my ideas of his duty. No, not anybody. Getting caught up in Roy's affairs meant turning into either his accomplice or his aunt, or both.

We came out on to the steps. The weather had changed in the last day or two, and was making up for lost time with moist grey skies and sudden squalls. Roy's hair rose and swung to and fro in one of these.

'Well, Duggers, I rather think somewhere near. Somewhere close by, if you follow me.'

'Somewhere quiet, too. We've got a lot to discuss.'

'Oh, bugger off,' he temporized. 'I'm not discussing anything until I've got a gill of Scotch inside me. If then.'

'I thought you had some things on your mind.'

'What gave you that idea?'

'You said so over the telephone.'

'Oh, did I? Oh yes. Oh, nothing very much. We've plenty of time. What sort of row did you think we were kicking up back there?'

I gave him my views on the run-through I had heard while we made our way round several corners to somebody's Hostelry and Eating Rooms. Here, the decor turned out to be Vicwardian, not approached in the lukewarm spirit that had shaped the representations at the Islington pub, but carried out with frightening devotion: a bare-plank floor uniformly scattered with a thin layer of sawdust, engraved-glass panels and mirrors at the bar, tables with (perhaps) marble tops and the rest of them made of (perhaps) ancient sewing-machine stands. A whiskered waiter in a plum-coloured velvet waistcoat and ticking trousers took our order: a lager for me and two large whiskies for Roy.

'Well, glad you approve, old lad,' he said, drinking. 'I thought they soundig good myself, but when you get to my age, you know, you keep wondering if you can still tell. I could do with a bit of encouragement.'

'Maybe. What you certainly need is a lot of discouragement. *Elevations 9* and Pigs Out and all that jazz. No, Roy, I've seen the programme and everything. What the hell are you playing at? A bloke like you. When you ought to be –'

'Oh, erosion of personal freedom! I do wish you'd try and fight your way out of this box you're in about everything stopping when Brahms died. You can't pretend –'

'No, it stopped with Schoenberg and serial technique, that's to say apart from the characters who've managed to –'

'Don't let's start that, Duggers.'

'All right, sorry. But look. What is the point, what do you think is the point, of you getting mixed up in all this pop . . . rubbish? Doing your own thing is a phrase I seem to have heard, or did it go out with wing collars and Frank Sinatra? Anyway, your thing is music. What their thing is I don't know and I don't want to know, but I do know it isn't music. Now. Why do you, of all people, how could you justify trying to mix them up? How are we all supposed to react to it? If we're supposed to think it's just a laugh, then we won't. Everybody you care about won't. Whose opinion you care about. Or ought to care about. I just can't . . .'

'Let strine put it this way. Life's changing, changing pretty fast, so fast you just can't say where things are going to go. All right, let's agree, just for the sake of argument, that the whole pop bit's pretty ropy musically. But what's musically? That's changing too. You've got to look beyond these bloody categories we've all been brought up with. Under late capitalism, there's bound to be –'

'To hell with late capitalism.' I felt we had reached an important point, one that had been slopping about in the recesses of my mind for some time – reached it a good deal earlier than was opportune, but reached it we had. 'All I think you're really trying to do is arse-creep youth.'

Roy gave a laugh of full, authentic richness; anybody could make any sort of personal attack on him, which had always been one of the nicest and most disastrous things in his nature. 'Arse-creep. By Jove, Mr Yandell, sir, you do show an uncommon gift for a racy phrase. Well yes, there is that, and it seems to me quite reasonable in a way, because there are things I can get from youth I can't get anywhere else.'

I felt my face turn very tired all over.

'No, I'm not only thinking of the stuff about new ways of seeing I told you about,' he said, showing what were, for him, stupendous powers of intuition and memory. 'If you work it just right, with a bit of luck they'll give you something you really start to want when you get to my time of life. Shut up, I'm talking about uncritical admiration. A very rewarding thing to have, I can assure you.'

'The Furry Barrel will give you plenty of that. I should have thought you'd prefer the critical kind. Or let's call it reasoned appreciation.'

'That's good too, and I know I get it from you and one or two other people, and I'm bloody grateful, believe me, and remembering it bucks me up no end whenever I start thinking I'm a failed composer and mediocre fiddler ending up as a hack conductor, but you see, Duggers, old lad, the point is, through no fault of your own you don't happen to be ten girls of nineteen or twenty and their boy-friends.'

'Eh? Where do the boy-friends come into it?'

'Well, they sort of eke the chicks out. A girl might give me a lot of bear-oil because she wants to screw me because I'm on the telly, or because I'm a sir, or because she thinks she can twist a platinum bracelet out of me, though there's not much of that around these days, as a matter of interest, now none of them can tell platinum from plastic. Christ . . . Oh yes, the boy-friends don't want to screw me, so that puts it on a broad impartial basis. Makes it look like hero-worship. I know it isn't that really, but I enjoy it all going on. That's why I arse-creep youth. Mind you, I go for their attitudes and the rest of it as well. Quite a bit, anyway.'

After a pause, I said, 'What about Sylvia? Does she give you uncritical admiration?'

'Much more than you might think from the way she behaves on occasions like the other night. No, actually she doesn't, not a lot. Hardly at all. I don't really know why she . . . I think she just likes old men. Some of them do, you know. Still, it's a good thing, her not making with the uncritical admiration. Does something to stop it all going to my head.'

'Roy, I must talk to you about her.'

'What about? What about her?'

At this very point, some unseen master of timing set in motion a record or tape of a piano playing, at top speed and chock-full volume, a dance song of the 'twenties, impeccably in period by prevailing standards, and not exhaustively offensive, but a distraction for one whose ears had hardly stopped ringing after their ordeal of a few evenings ago. Roy beat me to the door by a yard or two. So how did he manage to stand up to the assault of pop in full caterwaul? – which must be substantially grosser to his senses than to mine or to those of almost anybody else not yet adult when the first bawls began. New ways of hearing? No, such could not exist. Not on the scale required, anyway.

Outside, I said, 'Where are we off to now?' I could sense

that I said it rather pettishly. I was not sure I could stand another Roy-directed mystery tour, even a diurnal one.

'Pick up Sylvia in some boutique or other,' he replied briskly, 'and then a spot of lunch at the Bolognese. Joint off Knightsbridge.'

'Oh, God.'

'Pull yourself together, Duggers. Be a man. You can face it. Or if you find you can't, then you can scream and run away. Not that I can see why. She likes you. Thinks you're a great wag.'

'How can you tell?'

'I quite see you might say she's got a funny way of showing it, but then you don't know how she performs when she's really taken against a sod. And you were going on about wanting to talk to me.'

'So I was.' Curiosity had already overcome whatever opposition I might have been able to find grounds for. 'Fine.' I noticed we had started walking at some speed, and added, without much curiosity, 'Where's your car?'

'Laid up,' said Roy, briskly again, but with a different kind of briskness. This kind told me at once that his car was being used, or had been burnt down to the axles, by somebody he was not for the moment inclined to have me discuss with him: Gilbert, or Penny, or Chris, or Kitty, or Ashley. Somebody somewhere in his circle.

We picked up a taxi. Roy, instead of taking his place beside me in the back seat, thrust down one of the folding affairs in the partition that separated us from the driver and threw himself youthfully upon it, perhaps in the hope of suggesting a cultural frontiersman's indifference to comfort. I asked him,

'Are you inviting me out to a jolly lunch, or do you still feel you need me for camouflage? Because I thought you were just about ready to tear off the mask and stand in the full glare of publicity.'

'How did you come by that idea?'

'Penny. But we'll get on to her in a minute. Are you thinking of leaving Kitty and setting up with Sylvia?'

'Yes, old lad, between ourselves I rather am.'

'You're off your head.'

'Yes, so everybody seems to feel. I suppose there really might be something in the idea.'

'She's terrible.'

'I think I see what you mean. There are times when I almost feel it too. Things you couldn't know about. For instance, she won't do anything.'

'Anything? I thought there was very little she –'

'Like cooking or preparing food or tidying up, making beds, all that. The first day I spent with her in her flat, there wasn't any food in it, just some milk that had gone off and some very quiet biscuits. You could bend them to and fro like wax. Well, we couldn't go out, you understand, because of being seen, so it ended up with me having to – ended up? Started, with me going out and buying steak and vegetables and stuff. And a bottle of Scotch, I may add. When I brought it all back she wouldn't do anything to it. Any of it. I was going to have to start from scratch on the potatoes. Fuck that. So I went out again and bought some sandwiches and made-up potato salad and cole-slaw, and then I had to wash up plates and knives and forks for us to eat them with and take the lot to her in bed.'

'How does she manage when you're not there?'

'Her flat-mate does it or she goes out. She won't starve, in case you're worrying.'

'And you want to go and live with someone like that.'

'Oh yes. In all other, in most other respects it was a bloody marvellous day. I can get someone in to shop and cook and the rest of it when we're out in the open. In fact, it's the thought of that as much as anything that's weighed with me over going off with her.'

'I see.' I also saw that my line of attack up to now was effectively blocked. 'I suppose you've given some thought to the Harold Meers angle. He had it in for you before this ever came up. When he finds out you're proposing to live with his daughter – if he doesn't know already – he's going to hit the roof.'

'He can beat a timp-roll on it with his balls for all I care. What can he do? Get whoever does the John Evelyn column to put something in about which recently knighted veteran conductor is buggering about with which teenage daughter of which prominent Fleet Street figure? If he pisses on me he's pissing on her too, and himself. And going by the dog-doesn't-eat-dog principle, that'll keep the rest of the Press quiet too. I ought to have thought of that months ago.'

'He'll come up with something.'

'He can't touch my sex life, or my professional life unless he sacks you, and whoever he got instead would still only be the music chap writing in the ... Sorry, Duggers, I mean you count because you're you, but the paper doesn't in itself, do you follow? Harold bloody Meers doesn't scare me.'

'Well, he does me.' I was going to have to switch again. 'Anyway, Press or no Press, the news'll get round soon enough. Won't you mind everybody who knows you and millions who don't thinking you're rather a charlie? Undignified? A bit of a joke? Even youth?'

'Yes, I expect I will. Not much, though. Partly because I shan't look all that much of a charlie. Film stars and people are going off with much younger girls all the time and nobody gives a shit. Or hadn't you noticed that?'

'I didn't only mean the age thing. You're proposing to do something that's really awful. What about Kitty? And what about Penny? And what about Chris? And what about Ashley?'

'Ashley's a problem, I agree. There'll have to be some sharing arrangement worked out there. And don't think I haven't thought about the others, too.'

'That's exactly what I do think, seeing that you're intending to leave regardless of all of them. Why can't you just stay put officially and see a lot of Sylvia on the side?'

'No. I've had enough of that. So's she.'

The taxi was moving up Grosvenor Gardens, more and more slowly as the traffic thickened towards Hyde Park Corner. Ahead, rattlings and crashings came into earshot from where something was being pulled down or put up or excavated. I would soon, yet again, have to start shouting, but we were nearing boutique-land and my chance would be gone.

'If you've had enough of it, then pack it in. And how do you mean, had enough? You talk as if you've spent the last couple of years fighting in the jungle. What you've had getting on for enough of, no doubt, is making other people's lives a misery while you're watching. I'm sure Kitty goes on at you all the time about why don't you shoot her and have done with it and so on. There's a straightforward answer to that, of course, to do with her going on just the same when the butcher forgets to send the dog's meat. But now and then perhaps it crosses your mind that crying out before you're hurt doesn't actually guarantee permanent protection against being hurt, and that without you Kitty really would be done for – there'd be nobody left in the world for her apart from Ashley, who's a little monster, thanks largely to the insane way you let him do as he likes all the time, because if you tried to stop him you wouldn't be so popular with him, and you couldn't have that, could you? Penny and Chris both despise you for the way you go on in general, but that doesn't mean to say they don't love you, or couldn't be made to again, but if you go off with Sylvia they'll never forgive you. I mean that literally. Do you understand what I'm saying?'

I had had some trouble competing with the noise outside, but Roy had taken in every word, his eyes never leaving my face, his head nodding in thought at irregular intervals. Something struck me about his posture on the folding seat; it was uncomfortable, almost studiedly awkward, that of a man perched on a hard chair or a stool while the man talking to him leant back against padded upholstery. That was why he had chosen the seat in the first place, to advertise his humility, put himself physically in the position of somebody being lectured at by a superior, be seen to be paying close attention – none of it possible with him beside me. My job here, perhaps not only here, was to dish out his medicine and watch him taking it like a man. He had planned to be helped to feel how deeply he was affected by the case against what he wanted to do before going off and doing it anyway. And now, for the moment at least, I saw the basic motive of all the favour business: to see to it that I got a good, solid, continuous six or seven hours of Sylvia and so could act as a key prosecution witness in the show-trial of his integrity, with Penny thrown in not, or not simply, as a lure to me but as a reassurance to him that, even at a time of such crisis for himself, he was thinking of her, trying to get her off with dependable, concerned old Duggers.

I hardly listened at first when he said,

'I understand it all right. The whole thing's an agony, you must know that. I'll just have to live with the Kitty part of it. In a way I feel worse about the kids, Penny and Chris. But they've got their lives to live. There's not so much left of mine, so they won't have to go on never forgiving me indefinitely. With luck I'll make sixty. Fine with me. I'm not interested in living out my span in an odour of sanctity, beloved husband and father, approval of my own conscience – all of which it's a bloody sight too late for anyhow – and no girls or whisky or careering around in my own inimitable irresponsible way. I'll take criticism from chaps who've been in my situation and chosen differently. No one else.'

I was listening now, but could find nothing to say, except for a possible query about the role of late capitalism in the present quandary, and rejected that. The taxi had turned off at St George's Hospital. Roy lit a cigarette and said,

'Anyway, let's have a jolly lunch.'

'Yes, let's. Do you mind if I go up and see Kitty tomorrow?'

'Not a bit. I wish you would.'

'I will, then. When are you and Sylvia thinking of taking off?'

'Not for a couple of months. After I've done Gus and she's over eighteen. Uh, Duggers, could you do me a small favour? Only take a minute.'

'Sure.'

'Nearly opposite this place there's a man's shop.' His eye held mine in a pleading look. 'Could you just nip in there and buy me a pair of underpants? Medium size, sort of boxer's shorts pattern. Or anything they've got that'll do. Nothing fancy.'

Forewarned, I neither sermonized nor laughed, and a couple of minutes later was standing in the shop, which was filled with loud pop noises, of all things. The lad who had served me peered through his fringe out of the window as he gave me my change.

'That's Sir Roy Vandervane over there, isn't it?'

'Is it?'

'Yeah, he often hangs round here. After the birds, see. My sister was at a party once he was at. Five minutes' chat-up and then boof!'

'Boof?'

He gestured outwards and upwards at crotch height.

'I see. How extraordinary. Thanks. Goodbye.'

I crossed the street making faces at Roy, who glanced to and fro in alarm.

'What's the matter?'

'Which way?'

'Along here. What's up?'

'Come on. Bloke in the shop recognized you.'

'Did he really? What of it?'

The pants changed hands like missile blueprints between two secret agents of the meaner sort, such as get sprayed with napalm from a passing car in the pre-titles sequence. When this was done, I said,

'I don't know. I don't know what of it.'

'That's better. All part of the fun, old lad. It ought to tone you up.'

'What? I only went on like that because of the way you –'

'I agree that things like pancy-curity can get me down, but when they tone me up, they tone me up. No, you come in too. Do you good. Broaden your mind.'

Uncouth minstrelsy enveloped me again when I crossed the threshold of what I supposed was the boutique. A single room about the size of a squash court, but with a low ceiling, was illuminated by a faint daylight glow through thick curtains and by some objects that might have been electric-toaster elements fixed to the walls at head height. By their aid I was able to pick out a shirt-collar, a belt-buckle here, a leg, the back of a head there. Roy was going to have to find Sylvia by touch and smell, touch rather than smell, for a rehoboam of deodorant would hardly have been too much to neutralize the miasma of surrounding bodies. It was very hot, too. I stayed near the door, enduring virtually continuous jostling for the sake of not missing Roy on his way out. Time went by. I recognized my present state, a milder but authentic version of that attained over long stretches of the night of the favour, as what a child experiences when his elders take him round a museum or on a conducted tour of a great house: a fusion of boredom and discomfort into some third thing, a solipsistic despair, a progressive and apparently irreversible loss of belief in anything not here and not now, in tea, homework, television, school, cricket, holidays – this place is hell, in fact. To give myself something to do, I started concentrating on trying not to breathe.

Roy became distinguishable, with what must be Sylvia at his side. At the doorway, I saw against the daylight a figure confront Roy and apparently deliver a series of quick punches on the front and sides of his trunk; but he passed on unscathed. When my turn came, the exercise turned out to be a search, expertly and not uncivilly conducted. This precaution, which struck me as unusual in itself, could surely, I thought, have been rendered much easier, if not unnecessary, by switching on a light or two. Then I realized that potential new customers at a place like that would simply turn back at the threshold if their chances of stealing something were to be so visibly hampered.

'At least they didn't have pop in the Black Hole of Calcutta,' said Roy as we moved off.

'Oh, I thought you liked it,' I said.

'When it's a decent group. That wasn't.'

Sylvia, whose black jerkin, black thigh-boots and extended waistbelt of chains hung with padlock-sized pendants (or whatever) made her look like a gaoler in an advanced musical of the 'fifties, said nothing.

She went on saying nothing while we made our way to and established ourselves in the restaurant, and while Roy went away for a couple of minutes, presumably to switch pants. I looked round the room. Its layout and decor, its furniture, even what the waitresses were wearing, seemed indefinably original, strange, almost exotic. It was some moments before I saw that the place was got up as a restaurant, with tables and chairs, people ordering drinks and food and being served with them, others handing over money and receiving change. An odd environment for Roy, I thought. Perhaps he was making a trip in reverse, an expedition to the old world, as a white man gone native might travel into town to see if there were still such things as shops and buses.

The issue was never raised. Nor was much else. Roy asked what I was up to and I told him about the Haydn symphonies and the Mozart sonatas, then about Terry Bolsover's desire for an interview with him. The last interested him more than the other two combined. I asked him what he was up to, and he told me about having had to turn down a commission to write the music for a film about Richard II.

'Why?' I asked.

'Oh, you know, some right-wing shag had written the scream-play. Glorifying the monarchy and so on.'

'Oh, I see.'

Throughout this and such, Sylvia remained silent, vocally at least, though she clanked and rattled whenever she moved at a volume far outdoing Vivienne's charm bracelet. The waitress brought our main course and went away with an awkward, rolling gait. Sylvia watched her go and, speaking for the first time that day in my presence, said,

'Why does that girl walk in that bloody silly way?'

'She's got something wrong with her hip,' said Roy. 'T.B., I think. She's the proprietor's daughter. I know them here.'

Sylvia ate spaghetti and went on with her mouth full, 'Why doesn't he do something about it?'

'He has, but there's not a hell of a lot you can do in cases like that, apparently.'

'He must make a puhcket out of this dump. You can see it's had nothing spent on it for ten years.' She was chewing and swallowing like somebody on an eating marathon; perhaps the flat-mate had failed to furnish breakfast. 'Why doesn't he lay out a few quid on his daughter's hip or whatever it is?'

Roy said casually, 'He's laid out all he has on operations in this country, Switzerland and America and is still heavily in debt because of it.'

This might have seemed to settle the matter, but Sylvia did not think so. She ate some more and said, 'He's been done, then, hasn't he? Why couldn't he have the sense to find a proper doctor somewhere? He probably didn't try. Just wanted to fling the cuhsh around so as to feel good.'

I recognized a fully fledged case of that moral vandalism which, in slightly different spheres, could take the form of beating up old ladies because nobody beats up old ladies, shooting at firemen fighting a fire because nobody shoots at firemen fighting a fire. And something else besides. All the more clearly for its distance from the present topic, I saw the root of Sylvia's attraction for Roy, that of the agent for the spectator who would act likewise if he dared, the bomb-thrower for the liberal too decent and cowardly and fastidious and old and late-capitalistic to countenance the existence of bombs. And/or.

With no more said, Sylvia finished her spaghetti, got up and left. I looked at Roy.

'She's young,' he said.

'Roy, forget all this side of it. It's not really important. You can behave like a selfish idiot for the rest of your life and it won't really matter. What Roy Vandervane does as husband and father and screwer and the rest of it concerns Roy Vander-vane and a small circle and will be all over and done with in fifty years. What Roy Vandervane does as musician concerns music, and that'll go on much longer. For God's sake drop this *Elevations 9* rubbish and concentrate on Gus. That's your job. What you're meant to do.'

'So music's more important than sex. For Christ's sake, Duggers . . .'

'I think it may well be. I think I'd rather be a monk in a world with music than a full-time stallion in a world without it. I like sex too and I haven't gone into the whole thing enough to be sure about the monk and stallion business, but that's not the point. The point is that music's more important than Roy Vandervane's sex life.'

'Ole lad, with the best will in the world I can't see what's so cosmically disastrous about this little *Elevations 9* caper. You talk as if –'

'What's happened to the other eight elevations?'

'Oh, they're not real. I mean there aren't any. There's a Beatles track – well, that wouldn't interest you. Then it's a sort of pun. You know, elevation, and nine inches.'

'I take it you'll be explaining that to the audience on the night. Or demonstrating it, perhaps.'

'Of course. But I still don't see why it's so –'

'You're bringing – you, a well-known figure with a lot of prestige and rightly so, are helping to bring that very important stuff, music, into disrepute. It's having a hard enough time as it is, what with Cage and Boulex and the rest of them. You're coming at it from the rear. I'd say there's quite a good chance that the time and the mood are right for what you're doing to catch on in a way that the idea of music with jazz sauce never has after dozens of tries. And if your rubbish does catch on, you'll have harmed music.'

'Oh, priceless jewel of melody! It's just a stunt, a romp. I do wish you could see things from that angle once in a way.'

'A romp that'll harm music. All right, perhaps I am being a bit hysterical about it catching on. But you'll certainly be helping to make music look like just another fun thing and now thing, like these clothes they all wear and theatre in the nude and flower power and environmental art and First War stuff. And that's a disgraceful thing to do. On your part above all. Because you know better. You can say what you like about uncritical admiration, you'll get plenty of that out of it, I'm sure, but all your colleagues and all your real friends will despise you. Including me. Especially me.'

Grimly, Roy poured himself more wine and looked at me; I shook my head. Then he looked at me again, with a twisted smile I had not seen before but recognized without trouble. He was taking a second dose of his medicine, being helped to feel bad about what he had unalterably made up his mind to do.

'I think I will have some wine after all,' I said.

He poured it with renewed grimness.

'Has she just gone off?'

'Oh no,' he said. 'She never just goes off. Not without letting you know in full that that's what she's doing. Here she is now.'

'Let's go,' said Sylvia, arriving.

'Sit down and have some coffee,' said Roy.

'Let's go.' She sent him a grimace that spelt bed in an unattractive script.

He got up. I said this one was mine and pulled out my wallet, but he said it would be put on his account and I could do the next one. On our way out, Sylvia jogged the elbow of a man in a chair next to the aisle, spilling his coffee on to an open packet of cigarettes on the table, and Roy apologized to him. A light rain was falling as we walked up into Knightsbridge, Sylvia setting a brisk pace. The traffic was heavy.

'We'll never get a taxi in this,' said Sylvia.

'I'll be off and find a bus,' I said.

'There's one,' she said, pointing.

She meant not a bus, but a free taxi, and sure enough one could be intermittently seen approaching slowly on our side of the road. Roy waved to it. So, at the same moment, did a small brown man, perhaps an Indian, standing nearer to it than ourselves. Just then the traffic accelerated, and the taxi, ignoring the Indian (who gazed after it in astonishment), swept forward and stopped beside us. The driver was a young black man with long side-whiskers. Roy said to him,

'Why didn't you stop for that chap back there?'

'I don't know, guv,' the man said in cockney. 'Perhaps I liked the look of you better.'

'But he was coloured.'

'Well, you were here first, weren't you? I mean it's your island, mate.'

'Turn round and go back and pick him up.'

'Look, I can't turn here, mate. Do you want me or don't you?'

'Get in, you stupid bugger,' said Sylvia. 'I'm in a hurry if you're not.'

'I refuse –'

As if we had been carefully rehearsing half the morning,

Sylvia kicked Roy in the shins, I grabbed him, arms and all, round the middle, she opened the taxi door, I bundled him up and in, she followed and the taxi shot away.

'So long,' she called out of the window, waving. 'Thanks a lot. See you.'

Roy's car made a quick recovery from its bout of indisposition, as I found the next morning when I telephoned and spoke to Gilbert, who told me, with mild but unconcealed satisfaction, that its owner had taken it to London and that therefore I would have to walk from the Underground station. Asked if there were taxis, he told me in the same vein that there was a taxi office at the top of the station approach, but that in his experience it was always shut. His experience proved a true guide. I set out on foot through the town, expecting a cloudburst at any moment, but the heavens, though no less grey than before, kept their moisture to themselves. The people in the streets looked quite normal, even the younger ones. I found this disproportionately reassuring, and found further, on self-scrutiny, that my subconscious had been harbouring a panic-ridden fantasy in which the whole place had, since my last visit, become a sort of Roytown, with pavements and roadway full of youth smoking pot, twanging guitars, rejecting out-moded ways of thought and calling 'Christian gentleman, man!' to one another. But if any of this was happening, it was hidden from sight.

I turned off at a garage and car show-room full of Bentleys and Rolls-Royces, made my way along the side of a gloomy green with patches of standing water, and traversed an area where almshouses round the church gave place to establish-ments that had their names done in reflectors at headlight height and metal statuary on top of their gateposts. This was more like Roytown in fact. When I approached the Vandervane residence I thought I saw Gilbert standing at an upper window, but there was nobody there on a second glance. In the court-yard, as before, I heard from the kitchen the Furry Barrel's barks and growls; in the hall she appeared, recognized me and submitted to flattery, snorting a good deal in a well-born way. Kitty came out from somewhere and embraced me. After we had moved to the drawing-room she said, quite temperately by her standards,

'It was sweet of you to come, Douglas dear.'

'Oh, it's good to get out for a bit. How are you?'

She gave me a brave, jerky smile that irritated me and made me feel sorry for her. 'Oh ... you know,' she said with an affectation of affected lightness. 'One carries on. One has no alternative. Would you like a beer or something?'

'No thanks. You have something.'

'I've got something.'

She had and no mistake: a tall tumblerful of what was no doubt her favourite fearful gin and water, somehow giving the impression of not being the first of its line. Her clothes and general appearance, like the state of the room, indicated slovenliness, but a slovenliness done with tremendous artistic restraint: her dressing-gown, or dressing-gown dress, was old, moderately torn, and clean; her make-up, though ill applied, had at least been applied that day; used crockery, brimming ashtrays, vases of decaying flowers and naked gramophone records lay about, yet the clock, a vulnerable one with its glass dome, showed the right time and the carpet seemed free of gross or recent stains. She and the place had gone to rack and a piece or so, no further for the moment.

Kitty had followed my glance. 'The cleaning ladies have stopped coming and I can't seem to get any other ones. I seem to have used up all the ones round here. Gilbert's marvellous, but he can't do everything.'

'He and Penny are still here, then?' I asked experimentally.

'Oh yes. Here at this very minute. They're always here. I thought you knew that.'

'How's Ashley?'

'He's at school.'

'Really. How's he getting on there?'

'Getting on?' She seemed puzzled.

'Sorry, I just ...'

'He goes there most days now. Much better than he used to be. We've got a new system. Every day he goes, he gets a surprise when he comes home.'

'What sort of surprise?'

'Something nice, of course. Something it's fun for him to play with.'

'You mean like a trench mortar or a flame-thrower or a –'

'There are no militaristic toys in this house, Douglas.'

'Sorry, I should have known. Whose idea was the surprise thing?'

'His.'

I gave an understanding grunt instead of any of the several sorts of yell that suggested themselves to me. Apart from a faint show of indignation over the militaristic toys, she had stuck to her cinematic war-widow style, behaving with such wonderful control that nobody except everybody would have dreamt for a single moment, etc. I told myself we were going to have to start some time.

'What's the latest?'

She went light again. 'Oh, haven't you heard? I thought everybody knew. My husband is leaving me. He's decided to run away with a younger woman.'

'Mightn't it just be the Bayreuth stage? You know, a half-way kind of –'

'No, it's gone beyond that. It's a luxury he's learnt to do without.'

'He'll be back. He won't be able to stand her for long. Nobody could.'

'Then he'll move on. Find someone with the same ... attractions. He won't be back. It's not his way, my dear Douglas. Oh, don't think I'm bitter. I've moved beyond all that long ago. He's human, God knows, like the rest of us. And it's human to choose any sort of path into the future rather than face the long road back to what you've left behind. Do you mind if we go out of doors? I'm beginning to find the atmosphere of the place oppresses me.'

I was beginning to find the same thing in a smaller way, and myself lifted the sash of the central window, under which we ducked in turn. The day had lightened a little. As Kitty and I strolled on to the lawn, the Furry Barrel approached at a fast gallop from the corner by the ruins of the greenhouse, an old sandal in her jaws. This she dropped nearby and savaged briefly to the accompaniment of falsetto growls and snarls; after that, barking now, she went off at top speed towards a bank of rhododendrons, alerted by some creature or movement of foliage. I noticed that parts of the lawn were bald.

'It's the stuff off the cedars,' said Kitty. 'Needles or whatever they call them. Anyway, they kill the grass. Nothing you can do about it.'

'Do you manage to get anybody in to garden?'

'Not really. Christopher does a bit of mowing because he likes going on the motor-mower. And Roy got a gang of students in a couple of times, but they pulled up a lot of real plants as well as weeds. Still, it doesn't matter now, does it? It's the next owner's headache.'

'God, you're not selling the place already, are you? Supposing –'

'I've got to get out. Oh, because too much has happened here. Too many words said that can't be taken back or forgotten. Too many tears. No, it's my own decision. He'd let me stay for ever if I wanted to. As I say, he's human.'

I thought that last bit showed a sense of continuity of an altogether higher dramatic order than the general level of style being attained, and nodded soberly. Just then, a small group of people came out from behind a shaggy box hedge and moved off towards the lower lawn. I recognized Christopher Vandervane and Ruth Ericson. Of the other two, both young men unknown to me, one carried a camera and some kindred device slung over his shoulder. Kitty and I halted near an enormous display of roses and thistles very impartially mingled, like a cover illustration for a book on Anglo-Scotch relations.

'What's going to happen to him?' I nodded over at Christopher.

'I don't know. Same with Penny. One thing's certain: neither of them'll take a word of advice from anybody.'

'Or be told to do anything by anybody.'

'You can't tell them; it's just not on.' She laboriously fitted each hand into the opposite cuff of her dressing-gown, looked up at me, waited, and said, 'There's nothing left for me any more, Douglas, my dear. Nothing at all, anywhere.'

'You've got Ashley.'

'I can't do anything with Ashley. It's bad enough with Roy there. I shall have to try and find someone to live in and deal with him. That'll give me something to occupy my mind all right. But no more than that. I haven't a lover and I don't think I want one, after everything. There's nothing I know how to do, like playing music or writing or acting or even being a secretary or typing. All I had was Roy and Roy's world. And now ... that's all gone. I'm nothing. Nothing.'

'You mustn't talk like that.'

Perhaps my words came out in a rhythm I had not consciously intended. At any rate, her gaze, which had been appropriately wide and unfocused, suddenly sharpened. 'That's what Roy says. Do you believe me at all, Douglas? When I try and tell you how I feel?'

'Of course I do,' I said as stoutly as I could, with no idea whether or how much I meant it.

'Perhaps you do. Roy's the same. I think you both do in a way, but it's sort of how I say it you don't really believe. Or you don't like it, the way I say it. It's too much like how I say things when I'm only tired and cross or late for something. I know I do go on an awful lot. I ought to have always said just I feel bloody fed up and bugger it and what a bastard, and then I'd have been all right now with this when it came along, and you'd both have believed me. But it's too late for that. You see, Douglas, you can't ever allow for how bad things can really get until they do.'

'I understand,' I said, and kissed her cheek.

'Thank you.' She clung to me for a moment. 'You are good. You're so good.'

'I'm not good at all. I've done nothing to help you. I haven't been able to find out anything that's made any difference, and as for trying to stop him, or even slow him down, well, I have tried a bit, I suppose, but even –'

'There's nothing to be done. It's all over. Surely you feel that.'

'I don't know what I feel.'

'But I'll just have to accept it. Whatever sort of experience that may turn out to be. Anyway, it's something I'll be facing alone, I know that much. There's no other way. You've managed to make me feel it's possible, even for someone like me. You've reassured me that I exist.'

Perhaps (I thought without much rancour, but with disappointment) I would have done more good, on balance, by trying to erode her faith in her own existence. At the same time I felt ashamed of my connivings with Roy. 'I wish there were something practical I could do,' I said.

Immediately her expression changed again. 'Actually there is a tiny favour you could do me if you would.'

'A tiny what?'

'It won't take you two minutes. Just a little telephone call. To the flat where this girl is supposed to live, to make sure I've got the right place. Just to see if she's there. Only take you a second, Douglas. You did say you understood.'

She gazed at me with the first faint glimmerings of reproach, not so faint that they obscured the nearness of a vast army of reproach all ready to be swung into action. I realized that there were some people who could use painful insight into themselves as merely one more lever on others, along with abuse, threats, hysteria and God knew what else. Kitty and I turned simultaneously towards the house.

'How did you get hold of the number?' I asked, picking at random from the glutton's plateful of questions in front of me.

'I got Gilbert to get it out of Roy. In case there were emergencies was what he told him, I think.'

'What sort of emergencies?'

'I left all that to him.'

'Why can't he make this telephone call?'

'He wouldn't do it. That would be meddling.'

'Wasn't getting hold of the number meddling?'

'No, I had a right to know it. Him ringing it up would be him meddling.'

'What do you want me to say?'

'Oh, anything, it doesn't matter. Just so I know she lives there. You know her voice, don't you?'

'Yes.'

'That's another reason why Gilbert wouldn't do, you see.'

'Supposing she isn't there? I mean she could live there and still not be there at the moment, couldn't she?'

'Then you try later.'

'Supposing she is there?'

'Then I'll know she's there. That she lives there. Then I can do things like writing her a letter and telling her what I think of her.'

'So you know her name. So why can't you just ring up and ask her if it's her? And you can't write a letter to a telephone number. And she wouldn't read it, anyway.'

'Oh yes she would. That just shows how little you know about women. She'd read it until she knew it damn near by heart and then she'd throw it away and pretend she'd never heard of it. Or even keep it hidden somewhere. And she'd probably ring off straight away if she heard a woman's voice at this end, so I'd never be sure.'

'This one isn't like most women, and what's the good of a letter?'

'Don't you believe it, my dear. We're all like most women. Gilbert got hold of the address for me – don't ask me how.'

'Having access to a telephone directory and knowing the alphabet would be a help, I should imagine.'

'The number isn't listed, Douglas. But Gilbert managed to find out the address just the same; he is wonderful, you know. And you're not to be like that.'

'Sorry,' I said, giving the telephone itself an unfriendly glance, for we stood now in the hall. 'What's the number?'

She produced it with a gunman's speed and deftness from a pocket of her dressing-gown, rather abandoning any implication that our common progress towards this point had been roundabout or accidental.

'What shall I say?'

'I told you, anything. Just so you're sure it's her.'

'Yes, I see that, I've got that. I wondered if you had any suggestions.'

'Say anything you like.'

'Yes, that's it, that's what I'll do. Of course. I'll say anything I like.'

I reached for the instrument. She faced me with joined hands in a mannish posture, like a fairly undevout man at a burial service, in fact. Discarding any hope of her removal, indeed preferring to have her under my eye rather than at the end of another extension, I dialled. The chances against getting through were surely enormous, considering the odds-on likelihood of connection with the speaking clock or a kosher butcher in the Bronx, no connection at all, precipitation into a duologue between psychiatrist and patient, and so on, added to other hefty contingencies such as non-payment of bill at the far end, absence of Sylvia and flat-mate, absorption of Sylvia in new ways of doing something or other. Nevertheless, not much to my surprise after all, the distant receiver was lifted after a couple of rings and loutish tweedledee burst upon my eardrums. A female voice said something.

'Is Fred there?' I asked.

'What? For Christ's sake why don't you speak up, muhn?'

'Is Fred there?'

'Ah, piss awff.'

I put the handset back and said to Kitty, 'That's her.'

'Thank you, Douglas dear. Now I must get a move on. I'll go and get dressed. You find Gilbert and tell him to have a taxi waiting outside the Two Brewers in an hour's time. You and I can walk to it. You don't mind a pub lunch, do you? It's very good there, actually. They make all their own soups and things. We don't want Chris and Penny and the rest of them round our necks, do we? Then I've got one or two things I want to do in Town, and the chap can drop you wherever you want to be. I'll be quite quick.'

I felt like shaking my head as if I had just been thoroughly hit on it, but refrained. 'Gilbert said you could never get taxis round here.'

'He can get one if he wants one. Make sure you tell him it's for me.'

She went away and up the curve of the staircase before I could ask her how to set about finding Gilbert; however, he emerged from some doorway within seconds. Wearing a lumpy cardigan and trousers of a baroque sort of tweed, he still bore the rumpled appearance of a couple of days earlier. His manner was reserved. He agreed to summon the taxi as requested, showing a certain impatience here, as with a task hardly calling for his qualities of generalship. After a pause, he said,

'Perhaps you might be so kind and go and see Penny now. I've told her you're here. You'll find her upstairs, in the second room to the left. I can't say how grateful I'll be.'

'If she makes any move to throw me out I'll let myself be thrown out.'

'She won't.'

Nor did she. Looking, in her flowing crimson robes, pale yellow kerchief and plain sandals, really remarkably like an illustration in a Victorian bible, she stood with her back to a window that gave a view of the common and a distant line of trees. I had been half expecting to encounter her weltering on an unmade bed among reefer butts and empty Coke bottles, and the neatness of everything was a mild surprise, until I remembered that Gilbert lived in here too. Neatness, in fact, was scarcely the word: the place had the bare yet not underfurnished appearance of a vacant hotel bedroom, and Penny might have arrived in it moments before, a few yards ahead of her luggage.

'Hallo,' I said. 'How are you?'

'Fine.'

The eyes could hardly have been bluer than usual, but seemed wider than usual. They stayed on mine while, in a swirl of draperies, she moved across to the bed and began pulling the coverlet off it.

I spoke without weighing my words. 'What's the idea?'

'Oh, Christ, chum. This is eh bed and I am eh girl and you are eh man and we are eh-lone too-gether. What could be the idea?'

'Are we? Alone, I mean. With Gilbert and Kitty and God knows who round the house, I don't feel very alone.'

'There's a bolt on that door. But of course Regulation 82(c) of the By Jove and Great Scott Society states, No gentleman shall lay a finger on a lady if the lady should presume to have the effrontery to make the first move.'

'You made the first move the other night and I laid a bit more than a finger on you that time.'

'What is it, then? Why are we having an argument?'

'Gilbert put you up to this,' I said, marvelling idly at how petulant and unconvinced I sounded.

'So what do you care? If you don't want me you just say. Go on.'

She had let go of the coverlet the moment I asked her what the idea was, and was standing half turned away from me, apparently looking out of the window towards the trees. I reviewed the children-of-Israel get-up, especially its top half, which would have done as much or as little for the thorax of a ten-year-old, a stripper or a great-grandmother, and saw why she had chosen to wear it, and found the explanation for my strange failure to have already hauled it off her or bored my way through it. Again I spoke without thought.

'That makes two of us. Oh, God, what am I saying? Forget it if you can. God. I mean, just for the moment, you don't feel like it any more than I do, just for the moment. Tell Gilbert I said I was having conscience trouble about my girl. He'll understand that.'

'You know, I never really feel like it, not it on its own. But I don't sort of feel not like it all the time either, really. But it's not that I don't care one way or the other.'

'You like a proper reason.'

She stepped forward, kissed me and laid her head against my shoulder, leaning prudently forward to keep the rest of herself out of contact with the rest of me. Both of us sighed deeply. I felt as if I had just sat through a complete performance of *La Traviata* compressed into one and a half minutes. I heard a jet passing somewhere high overhead, and then the Furry Barrel protesting against the violation of her air space. Penny sighed again and turned away. Could I ask her whether Gilbert had actually said to her, 'Now, when he comes, you go to bed with him, you see,' and whether she had indeed said to him, 'Yes, Gilbert; well and good, Gilbert'? No. A pity. A pity that the more interesting a question became, the more absolutely one was assumed not to need to ask it. I tried answering this one in my mind. Of course that was what had happened. That sounded quite certain, obvious, solid as iron, plain as the nose on my face. Of course that was not what had happened. That sounded exactly the same. But how could it?

'Shall we get the talking done?' asked Penny. 'There's that as well, isn't there?'

'Oh, yes. I was supposed to try to get you to leave here and go into a flat somewhere.'

'Oh, that one. He put you up to that, didn't he?'

'No, he didn't. Gilbert did.'

'Never mind, I'm staying here.'

'You're mad. There's nothing but unhappiness in this house and it's just going to go on and on. No it isn't just going to go on and on, it's going to get worse. More violent and more . . . awful. Do what Gilbert says. He's the only one round here you can trust.'

'Don't you believe it, mate. Anyway, you're wasting your time. Like everyone else. I'm not leaving, not this side of next Christmas. He wants me to go.'

'He. People can be right for the wrong reasons.'

'Not him.'

'And they're not all wrong reasons, for God's sake. He really does want to spare you as much as he can of all this; you've got to give him that. He doesn't want to chuck you out.'

'I'd like to see him try.'

'Yes, I think you would.'

She looked hard at me and turned farther away. I said to her back,

'Penny, I wish you'd let me –'

'Like I told you, nobody takes me on. Did you talk to him? You know.'

'Yes, I tried to . . .'

'But you didn't get anywhere.'

'No.'

'I had to ask you to try, though, didn't I? I'll make out, don't you worry. The next time you come I'll be much better. Not so depressed. I'm going to take myself on.'

I had been outside in the courtyard for less than a minute when Gilbert, alerted perhaps by his own closed-circuit television system, came through the porch and joined me. The diffidence of his manner struck me afresh.

'So you made no headway. I'm deducing as much from the shortness of the time you spent with her.'

'I'm afraid you're right,' I said, hoping it would be an hour or two before I would have to issue yet another communiqué announcing breakdown of talks.

'I can see now that it was a shot in the dark. But one feels one must have tried everything. I'm sure you understand.'

'Of course.' As an understander of this and that, now, I reflected, there was a tremendous lot to be said for me. 'I'm sorry I couldn't do any good.'

'Don't reproach yourself. The whole thing's a classical Freudian case of a girl seeking her father. Roy's opted out of performing that role, and I'm unfitted for it by nature. Debarred from it, in fact. Each man can only fulfil one or at the most two of the aspects in which he's dealing with a woman, like a husband, a brother, a friend and so on and so forth. I can only be a lover and at times a friend.'

'Yes, I see.'

He seemed uninhibited enough by now. Almost companionably, we sauntered over to a corner of the yard from which the barn, surmounted by an archaic weather-vane, could be glimpsed. The current ill wind would at any rate blow clean away any chance of the structure's being turned into a music laboratory. I speculated whether Kitty, Ashley, Christopher, Ruth, Penny and Gilbert could continue to exist here, visualized the house physically collapsing from neglect, fire or the weight of encroaching vegetation. Not even Gilbert, I felt, could stave off something of the sort.

'What are you going to do?' I asked him.

His face flickered with distress or vexation. 'What can anyone do? I shall continue to try, I suppose. But there comes a time when the will to try begins to disappear. You can't make your whole life out of being unselfish.'

'No indeed. But I hope you'll hang on here long enough to see her through the next few weeks or however long it's going to take.'

He was about to reply when I heard the porch door shut. Kitty had appeared, all dolled up in a bottle-green trouser-suit with frilly damson-coloured shirt, long gloves and what might have been a slightly undersized beach-umbrella, not to speak of well-applied artifices above the neck. I took all this in, marvelling at the promptitude with which it had been assembled, while she instructed Gilbert about Ashley's homecoming, the Furry Barrel's tea and such matters. She did so briskly and without self-consciousness, or with only as much as was appropriate, and inevitable, in a woman being efficient to a male audience. Neither then, nor during our walk to the pub (past, among other buildings, an old people's home from which old people stared resentfully out at us), nor while we lunched among horse-brasses and shopkeepers, nor on the taxi journey through Hendon, Swiss Cottage and farther did she relapse into paraded bravery. She came out with sound forgettable stuff about Christopher's tribulations at his university, the Common Market, whether she ought to take up Ouspenskyism again and when was I going to bring this new girl of mine along for her to meet. I was tempted to regard the impeccable smoothness of this part as further evidence of earlier insincerity, until I saw that what I was really doing was refusing to give her credit or sympathy however she might behave: not a very nice response from a supposed friend. So I started trying harder, but had hardly done more than start when she started acting like somebody summoning up courage for something.

'What is it, Kitty?'

'Douglas dear, please don't think I've gone off my head, but could I possibly ask you to do me one more teeny favour?'

'What is it? I mean of course I will.'

'I know you're tremendously reliable and careful and dependable, but I would feel just that bit easier in my silly old mind if you could have the patience to ring that number again and make absolutely certain that it is, you know, her at the other end. So that I can be sure my letter gets to her, you see.'

'Oh. Yes. Yes, all right.'

Two minutes later, in a telephone box somewhere on the edge of Bayswater, I went through the Fred routine a second time, with the same results as before. Ringing off, I noticed that the call-box telephone and the distant telephone were on the same exchange, a feat of observation that would have been no feat at all in those primeval days when exchanges had had letters instead of figures and so immediately advertised their whereabouts. This, and other matters, set me thinking. Back in the taxi, I said to Kitty,

'She's there all right. And I'm coming with you.'

'Please yourself, my dear, but there's no more to do there than at any other dressmaker's.'

'She may not be on her own, and even if she is you could probably do with a bit of support.'

'At my dressmaker's?'

'You should have put in some work on your dressmaker earlier. A witness might come in handy. How far away is it?'

'Two streets down. You are brilliant to have worked it out.'

'What are you thinking of doing exactly?' I asked when she had spoken to the driver.

'Well, I want to have a look at her is the first thing. Find out what sort of creature it is that's doing this to us all. And then just try to tell her what she is doing, make her see – you know what Roy is, he could have told her I'm running about with a millionaire or anything. If I could make her see . . .'

'Having a look at her you'll probably manage, but I wouldn't bank on getting through much of the rest. But good luck, anyway.'

Ideas of Sylvia and of squalor had become so firmly linked in my mind that nothing about her immediate neighbourhood could have surprised me: a razor-fight in full swing in the street outside, children crapping and giving themselves fixes on the steps, recumbent meths-drinkers cluttering up the threshold. In the event the pair of us walked unhindered along a passage abounding in potted greenery and entered a lift.

'Flat 6,' said Kitty, consulting a scrap of paper and pressing a knob. 'Gilbert is marvellous, you know. He ought to be some colossally high-powered secretary kind of person, not fooling about with . . . Still, I'm sure he's good at that too and I expect he enjoys it.'

She looked charged up: pink-cheeked and square-shouldered, genuinely intent on whatever was to come. When we got out of the lift, she marched straight to the relevant doorway and pushed the bell-push with a flourish. Ruffianly ululation sounded faintly from within, then, after quite a short interval, sprang into grievous volume as the door opened. Sylvia looked dully out at us.

'Hallo, Sylvia,' I said briskly, moving forward with my hand on Kitty's elbow – 'I was just passing so I thought I'd drop up as they say and see how you were getting on and while I was about it I saw no reason why I shouldn't give you a chance to meet someone you must have heard a lot about. Lady Vandervane.'

First score to the goodies: I had driven both females before me into what could with some reason be called a sitting-room, in that evidence of its use for eating, sleeping, and other personal activities and states, though present, was on the whole minor, random. It might also have served as a music-room, if indeed the gramophone, loud enough at this range to drown out anything much short of a piercing scream, had not certainly been wired up to reject actual music. Rather to my surprise, Sylvia went and turned off the amplifier.

'What do you want?' she asked.

As Kitty, using what was for her a measured tone, began to go through the themes she had just outlined to me, Sylvia sat down on the arm of a couch. This, like much of the other furniture, looked new and battered at the same time, as if somebody wearing football boots had set about it immediately after its delivery. I also took in some posters (including a large and well-produced one of a bare bottom), a cardboard box holding perhaps a hundred light-bulbs, a pie-dish full of pennies and threepenny bits, and an overall version of the smell I had noticed the first time I met Sylvia. Nothing else, apart from the long, multi-buttoned house-coat kind of garment she was wearing. It looked fairly clean.

'I'm appealing to you.' Kitty had got into her stride by now. 'It's all I can do. I've nothing to fight with, no bribe to offer. I can only ask you to realize the unhappiness you'll be bringing four people who've never hurt you.'

'Which are they?'

'Roy's two children, our own child, and myself.'

'You aren't including him, then.'

'That's not for me to say.'

'No, that's right. Well, from the way he talks about his life at home, I can't see he gives a sod for any of you, so I don't see why I should.'

'That's not true,' I said. 'He –'

'Please, Douglas,' said Kitty, and Sylvia said, 'Belt up.' Both spoke absently and without turning their heads.

'And don't come on so strong, Lady Vandervane. Don't try and queen it over me. You're not on camera now, you know. Just talk ordinary, if you can. What else have you got?'

Kitty toned down the queening straight away. 'All right, I suppose there's no reason why you should care about me, but think of the children.'

'I am. I've met one of them, and you can put her through a mincing-machine for all I care. The others I've never even seen, so screw them too.'

'If you can't see it or feel it, I can't make you.'

'No, that's right. Actually I can see it fairly well, and I can even feel it a bit, but not enough to make any odds.'

'Not even about a child of six whose father's going off and leaving him?'

'Well, he'll still have you, of course. And he'll need you more after Roy's gone, so that'll help you use up some of your time, won't it?'

With a fully advertised but (I thought) laudable effort, Kitty kept her temper at this. 'Can't I even ask you to go on . . . being with Roy, see as much as you like of him, but not go off with him, not take him away?'

'Sure you can ask. Why not?'

'I beg you, I implore you to think about it. I shared Roy with his first wife for two years, and believe me it's not so bad. You could –'

'That was because you knew you were winning,' said Sylvia in a reasonable tone. 'If he doesn't come away with me now, that'd mean I'm losing, and I don't like doing that. I'm not having that.'

'*Please*.' Kitty was crying and clasping her hands on the crook of her umbrella, making me afraid she might go down on her knees. 'He could live with you and just come and see us at week-ends. Say every other week-end. Surely that's not much to ask. Could you ... could you think about it?'

'Yeah. I'll think about it.'

'Oh, thank you, thank you.'

'You're welcome, you're welcome. Right, I've thought about it. The answer's no.'

Sylvia laughed when she said this. As was easy enough for anybody who had met her for more than a few minutes, I had been expecting something of the sort, but the reality was quite enough to make me swear inwardly not to do any laughing in company for a bit without first thinking over how it would sound. Kitty started back as if struck, or like somebody well used to meeting the phrase in print.

'Do you love him?' she asked loudly.

'Yeah.' Sylvia considered. 'Yeah, I think so. I don't know much about loving people, never had a lot to do with it, but ... Yeah.'

'You're not ... capable of loving!'

'Maybe I'm not – you could have a point there. But then maybe I am too. But anyway, it doesn't matter, that side of it, does it? Whatever I'm like he prefers me to you, and that's why he's leaving you and going off with me, and that's all there is to it. He wants to and I want to, so that's what we'll do.'

The renewed reasonableness of Sylvia's behaviour looked and sounded real, just that touch more real than Kitty's style could ever have encompassed. An impartial witness of their exchanges would probably have been sympathizing with Sylvia most of the time, provided he was ignorant of English. This qualification dwindled slightly in importance when Kitty said, with maximum voice and face and body,

'It's all so unbelievable. Now that I know the sort of person you are, I'm quite frankly incredulous. What could any man of the remotest intelligence or taste or discrimination see in you?'

'Oh, for God's sake let's go,' I said.

'Oh, that's easy,' said Sylvia. 'I'll show you.'

She drew the house-coat over her head and dumped it on the couch. Underneath she was wearing a brassiere and short knickers, not quite as clean as the coat, and these too she quickly removed. Kitty showed genuine consternation. I have no idea what I showed. Only one thing about Sylvia's body was clear to me: I could have no views on its beauty or health or likeness or unlikeness to others, because it was surmounted by Sylvia's head and face and because it belonged to Sylvia, but I could see (perhaps simply was aware) that it was a young body. For all I knew, Kitty's might carry no signs of age and even be better at all points, properly considered; still, I was quite clear in my mind that nothing of that sort could be of the least help to her now. At the same time, I felt a kind of surge of theoretical homosexuality pass through me.

'That's what he sees in me,' said Sylvia. 'Now get out of here, you old *buhg*, before I go hard on you.'

She advanced on Kitty, who swung her umbrella; a mistake, for any umbrella, though a potentially dangerous lance, is an ineffective club. Sylvia easily fended off the blow, and the two closed with each other. I came out of my lethargy, or put away my distaste for the prospect of touching Sylvia, and moved to intervene. She brought her knee up into my crotch, upon which I retired from the conflict for perhaps half a minute, listening vaguely to sounds of struggle and to cries of outrage from Kitty. Then somebody fell over; I looked up by degrees to see Kitty mostly flat on her back with Sylvia kneeling on some of her. So matters rested for a few more seconds, until Sylvia, whose head had been moving this way and that, evidently caught sight of what I made out as a fat lump of abstract sculpture, about the size of a human skull and done in some veined stone, a yard or so away from her on a low table. She swayed about on her knees as she tried to reach it without allowing Kitty freedom to move. I straightened myself, stepped forward and grasped Sylvia's forearm in both hands. After a quick, vigorous pull and turn I released her, remembering even in that moment having noticed both the wrestler with the German name and the Thing from Borneo use this move with telling effect on the night of the favour. Sylvia did a brief sidelong dash across the room and hit the wall. She was starting to climb to her feet from where she had fallen when, having grabbed Kitty and her umbrella, I got the two of us out of the room and then the flat. The lift was waiting.

'Are you all right?'

'Yes.' I shut the inner gate and pressed the ground-floor button. 'Very nearly. What about you?'

'I don't know. How do I look?'

She spoke dreamily. Her clothes were disordered but apparently undamaged; her hair was in modified madwoman's style; there were shallow parallel grazes across her forehead with a little blood, already drying; a large red patch and a small red patch stood out on her left cheek. I put my hands on hers, which were gripping the umbrella.

'You look as though you've been in a bit of a fight. Nothing out of the way. What would you sort of like to happen now? Cup of tea? Do you want to go to a Ladies?'

'Just the car.'

We went to the car. Inside it, Kitty sat back and sighed repeatedly while I held her hand and reflected that, for the second time that day, I had experienced a good deal in a short space, more so than could be rendered by any mere operatic image: the best of Dracula, Frankenstein highlights were fair approximations. After a couple of minutes, Kitty started putting herself in order. Her movements were lethargic. Normally she would be off like a whippet at the first distant shimmers of a shiny nose.

'That girl's mad,' she muttered. 'Stark, staring raving mad.'

'She certainly behaved very oddly.'

'Imagine her . . . stripping off like that.'

'Yes, extraordinary.'

'What could she have thought she was doing?'

'I know.'

'You do realize she'd have killed me if you hadn't pulled her off, don't you, Douglas?'

'Oh, I doubt it.'

'I tell you she'd gone crazy. She was berserk. She'd have bashed my head in if she'd had the chance.'

I went on doubting it, but inwardly, and without great conviction or interest. Inwardly too, I assured myself that, however loathsome the episode in that flat and however boring Kitty's appraisals of it, I must endure until she had had the chance to talk herself back to normal (or somewhere near one of her norms) as she worked on her face and hair. This she finally began to do, her voice strengthening and hands recovering assurance until she was very largely the Kitty of half an hour earlier in both appearance and manner. The manner part of this impressed me as odd at first. To be in even moderately good spirits so soon after the failure (however predictable) of a last hope, with a whacking physical and emotional humiliation thrown in, surely showed abnormal powers of recovery, especially for a woman like Kitty. Then it occurred to me that she had at any rate done something, struck a blow, survived an encounter with a naked madwoman, given herself something to think about, taken action after a long spell of inaction: and before a longer one. It further occurred to me that very few men would take her on while that meant taking Ashley on as well, and that she would not be free of him until he was twenty or so (if ever), and that by then she would be nearly sixty. I wished that Ashley would meet with a fatal but painless, or not too painful, accident. Something of that sort, not necessarily on that scale, would do Roy no harm, either.

'Where can I drop you, Douglas dear?'

'I thought my flat, if it's not too far out of your way.'

'No, it's right on my way.' She again spoke to the driver.

'On your way where?'

'Home. Or rather to the house I live in.'

The buoying-up effect of the Sylvia exploit had passed, at any rate for the time being. I got the cinematic war-widow all the way to Maida Vale. Her last words to me were,

'Dearest Douglas, I wish I could thank you enough for being such a tower of strength, such an absolute rock. I know it's too ghastly for you, but do come up and see me again soon. Meanwhile, you're not to worry about me. I'll be . . . I'll be fine. Really and truly, I promise you. Strange, the way one finds strength in oneself one didn't know was there.'

I heard my telephone ringing as I climbed the stairs, and climbed faster, failing to find strength in myself that I could pretty well have sworn was there. I picked up the handset and said my name. A huge cough came down the wire.

'Albert,' I said. 'How are you?'

'Terrible,' replied Coates. 'Look, Doug, that business you asked me to keep an eye on.'

'The old maestro.'

'That's the one. Well, nothing definite as yet, but your and my favourite shit has asked for all the griff about him.'

'Griff?'

'Christ, the file, the clippings, the stuff from what you'd probably call the morgue. My guess would be that your chum's booked as the first and probably the last of a controversial new series of profiles, Half-Witted Cunts of Our Time. I can't see what else it could be.'

'Thanks, Albert. Would you let me know if you get anything more definite?'

'Delighted. Anyway, see you Thursday.'

'Yes, I suppose so.'

The next morning, Sunday, I telephoned the Vandervane house to see how Kitty was. Or so I would have put it if challenged. An unassessed portion of my motive was the same old irresistible (and averagely vulgar) curiosity. Very much as on an earlier occasion, I got Gilbert and wordless yelling at the same time, then Gilbert on his own.

'Kitty's in bed,' he told me. 'Sleeping.'

'Don't disturb her. Is she all right?'

'Naturally she's not all right. Would you seriously expect her to be all right?'

'I was just asking. I meant is she ill or anything.'

'That's tantamount to a meaningless query. Perhaps you'd care to give me a concise definition of illness.'

'I'll drop everything and work on it. Look, Mr Alexander, I simply don't care how righteous you are, or how learned and sophisticated either. If you can bring yourself to tell Kitty I telephoned, that's fine. If not –'

'I'm sorry, Mr Yandell, I'm being affected by the atmosphere of strain under which we're all living. Of course I'll deliver your message. Hold on, please.'

Sounds like an argument in a deep dungeon reached my ear; I assumed Gilbert had put his hand over the mouthpiece. Then Roy came on the line.

'Hi, you old bastard, how goes it? In particular, how are your balls? I hear they took a knock yesterday. Very nasty,' – a sound pre-emptive approach, this, treating the whole episode as worthy of nothing more than brotherly concern for me dressed up as jocularity.

'They seem to be holding up all right, thanks. How are yours?'

'Aching rather in a metaphorical way. Gus is beginning to shag me out. I've got the bloody choirs coming in next week to rehearse the Eighth. If you had any conception . . .'

He talked at some length about his involvement with Mahler, then asked for and perhaps listened to information about Terry Bolsover, whose interview with him must be impending. With this behind us, he said rapidly,

'Oh, by the way, Duggers . . .'

Thus forewarned of the approach of his reason for talking to me, I started getting my diary out.

'. . . I was wondering if you were doing anything tomorrow lunchtime.'

'What I am not doing is going anywhere with you and Sylvia.'

'Oh, nothing like that.' He laughed slightly. 'The point is, old lad, your pal Harold Meers wants to have a little chat with me. He seemed very keen to pim me down: rang me up last night and pressured me into this date tomorrow. Into agreeing to it provisionally, that is. So I could make sure you were free first. Anyway, are you? I was just going to ring when –'

'Yes, I am, but where do I come into this? He's not going to want me there. He'd sooner –'

'I know it's a lot to ask, but I would very much like to have someone along to bat for my side. Outnumber him. Christ knows what he's got up his sleeve.'

'Yes, Harold needs a bit of outnumbering. But I don't see why he should –'

'That fits in with what I hear of him. No, actually, when I said I'd probably be bringing a friend he said more or less the more the merrier. Funny sort of sod. I suppose he just saw he wanted to talk to me and I didn't want to talk to him, so being on a whichever it is market I imagine I could have insisted on bringing the World Cup soccer team along without him being able to –'

'He'd have drawn the line a long way short of that, however keen he is to see you. Unless you agreed in advance to pick up the bill.'

'Near bugger, eh? That's worth knowing. Be fun watching

him trying to buy me off with thirty quid and his stamp album.'

'I don't think that'll be his approach. And I was going to say he'll probably draw the line at me too. Still, if I just turn up . . .'

'Oh, I told him it was you and he sounded as pleased as Punch. Punch with a hangover, perhaps, but manful as hell. By all means and all that.'

'Strange. I thought he hated the sight of me. But then he probably doesn't care for the sight of anybody much.'

'There again his daughter goes along with you. It would do you good to hear her on the subject. Draw the two of you together.'

'Has she got any ideas on what he's up to?'

'I haven't been able to get her to discuss it seriously. At all, in fact. Anyway, I'm meeting him at the Retrenchment Club at one o'clock. If you pitch up at Craggs's about twelve thirty we can have a fortifying noggin of something and walk down. Okay?'

I said it would be, rang off, and did my best to dismiss from my mind the consideration that Roy ought not to cut tomorrow morning's rehearsal short by the fifty or so minutes necessary for him to be able to keep his rendezvous with me. Failing in the attempt, I went back to where Vivienne was sitting up in bed reading the *Observer*. She wore a white nightdress that would have done very well for Norma in Bellini's opera, granted a rather traditionally conceived production, and a woollen jacket in pink and green, with hanging bobbles, that would have done very well for nobody but her. As soon as I appeared, she picked up and drank from a cup of (by now, surely, no better than) lukewarm coffee. She meant by this to stress the fact that she was finishing a leisurely breakfast and studying the latest news in what merely happened to be a bedroom, just as her attire proclaimed that she was doing these things in what was quite incidentally a bed. So much was her standard practice. But then, with a preoccupied yet antagonistic air, her eyes making wide sweeps over the print, she said,

'Did you get hold of your friend?'

'No. And she isn't my friend.' Out of what had seemed prudence, wanting to get my story in before (say) the irruption of Sylvia in talkative mood, I had divulged something of the previous day's events and the run-up to them – a positively Royesque misjudgement that all my insistence on Kitty's age, not-my-cup-of-teaness and down-stagey goings-on had done little to retrieve. 'Well, she is a friend, of course, but not in the way you mean, as I keep telling you.'

'Who were you on to all that time, then?'

'Only old Roy.'

'What's he up to now?'

'Nothing in particular. He asked me to lunch with him tomorrow.'

'You're not going?'

'Of course I'm going. Why shouldn't I?'

'But you said you were coming with me to see my father in the evening.'

'I still am. That's in the evening.'

'H'm,' she very nearly literally said.

'What do you mean, h'm? I'll be on the spot when you turn up here, sober, undrugged, and unimpaired by any form of sexual indulgence.'

To this, she said nothing in a marked manner, but differently marked from the one she had been using for the last three-quarters of a minute. I picked up the *Sunday Times* magazine section and started reading about poverty and oppression in British Honduras. Vivienne was reading on with equal attention, for after a few moments she said,

'Doug, what's a . . .? I can't even pronounce it. Something about . . .'

I dropped Honduras and went over to her. My more direct route being blocked by her breakfast tray and the chair it rested on, I made my approach via my side of the bed. Our shoulders touched.

'Where?'

'Here.'

She was holding the paper in a rather awkward position, low down and close to her, so that I had to lean some way across to get a view of the paragraph she was pointing to. As I did so, I noticed at close range, but in adequate focus, that the front of the bed-jacket had fallen apart and that a nipple was protruding from inside the Norma-style nightdress.

'A psephologist is a man who knows about elections,' I said, stumbling a little over the last word and taking off my glasses.

'Oh, darling . . .'

The remainder of the day passed pleasantly enough. No further mention of my friend was made, a reticence I did my bit to sustain by not asking after the other bloke. We parted after confirming arrangements for the following evening. I began the week's work with Weber, with actual physical addition to the words I had already written about him. After two hours and not quite a page of that, I switched to filling in some of the background – some of its remoter, mistier sections – that I might need for my sleeve-notes on the Mozart sonatas. Midday came at last; I put my books back on the shelves and made off.

There was a lot of sun in Maida Vale and down Edgware Road. It shone on girls by the hundred, girls with prominent bosoms, prominent hips, prominent faces. A man like Coates would have said (I was nearly sure I had heard him say) that the fine weather brought them out, dismissing the knottier question of where they were the rest of the time. I knew better. Today's contingent, at any rate, had been brought out by Roy, and not just in the sense that the always close connection between the subject of Roy and the subject of girls had sharpened my eyes; perhaps not in that sense at all, for I had noticed no sudden corresponding increase in the number of anti-American demonstrations or advertisements for Scotch. Most likely what was at work on me was nothing more than the usual tonic effect of going to see Roy. How unfair, I reflected as I walked along Piccadilly, that that sort of effect should so often be absent, if not actually inverted, when it came to meeting far worthier persons. But surely divine mercy was in operation too: except where music was concerned, no one in quest of worth would ever go anywhere near Roy.

I reached Craggs's. While I waited for the porter to finish doing something to a telephone switchboard at the far side of his emplacement, my eye fell on a notice saying that the Wine Committee had acquired a number of bottles of Dom Perignon 1959 and was in a position to offer them to members at £4 each; limit, 1 doz. per member. Below was a column of signatures of those wishing to avail themselves of the opportunity, with the quantity desired, and Roy Vandervane's name – 1 doz. – led all the rest. I found something incongruous in this placing, but only until I realized that I was not, after all, looking at the correspondence page of a newspaper, where alphabetical arrangement saw to it that Roy seldom came higher than last but one of a number attacking exploitation of immigrant labour in California or proposed increases in the price of school meals.

In due time, I found Roy in the *Punch* and *Who Was Who* nook with an opened bottle of champagne (not the Dom Perignon) and two glasses in front of him. He was wearing what could have been called a suit if the jacket had had visible pockets, and the tendency of his hair to seem an inch longer every time I saw him had been checked, if not reversed. Was this show of conventionality put on to conciliate Harold? Full morning-dress, with grey topper, white spats and ebony walking-stick, would hardly be adequate for that job.

Roy looked ill at ease, though not gloomy. When we were drinking he asked me if I had any ideas on what Harold might have in store for him. I told him roughly what Coates had told me two days earlier (and had had nothing to add to when rung up an hour before).

'Does he really think I give a fart what a rag like that – sorry, Duggers – says about me? He must be losing his touch, if he ever had one.'

'He had and has one. What dirt can he dig up?'

'Well ... the previous divorce, and one or two episodes since, I suppose. But that's all water under the bloody bridge. The only bit that could embarrass me is the Sylvia bit, and as I said the other day that's the one thing he can't use. Unless he's gone off his head, of course.'

'That is a possibility, yes. We'll have to see.'

'All a load of ballocks. Come the first week in September she can vote – not a right I can see her exercising much, admittedly –

and she can marry who she likes,' he said, pouring me more champagne with a casual and yet intent air.

'You're the one who's off his head, talking of saying things the other day. She can't marry you whatever –'

'Because I'm married to someone else, remember? as the Yanks say. I do wish they wouldn't, don't you? Kitty's agreed to a divorce if I ask her for one, with full co-operation, naturally, because that makes me seem more of a shit. Q.C. buddy of mine tells me that means you can squeeze the whole thing into about four months. And there's a change in the law coming along that'll cut it down to half that. Anyway . . .'

'Yes, anyway. Say you do marry her, what about Girl, 20? What about wanting to get away from normal, decent, God-fearing sex? What about ringing up the paraffin man? What about going down?'

'Yes, I know. But it'll take –'

'It won't hold her to you – you realize that? If she wants to be off she'll be off whether she's married to you or not.'

'There I disagree. It'll take her some time to get browned off with being Lady Vandervane and wife of controversial musician and maverick political figure Roy Vandervane. Without knowing she's going to have that, she'd be away tomorrow. As it is, I think I can probably reckon on a couple of years and that's a bloody long time when you get to my age. Not after it's over; it'll seem like about six weeks then; but from here it looks a lot, I can assure you.'

'Oh, good. But what about Girl, 20?'

'There is that. You get that. But as regards the going-down side of life, it'll have to be Girl, 50 if the point comes up. I couldn't take Girl much under that. I love Sylvia, but one of her's enough.'

'Is it worth all the mess, for a couple of years?'

'How would I know?'

'She's terrible.'

'Yes, I know that. You should have been in the pub the other evening, one of these places where they keep a bloody great tower of pennies on the counter for the blind or something. About ten thousand of the buggers, I imagine, colossally heavy, but she managed to knock most of them off on to the floor. Ankle-deep, and over a surprisingly wide area, too.'

'You mean on purpose.'

'Well, it's hard to say. On purpose or not on purpose doesn't come in much when you're dealing with her. She did tell me afterwards that one of the chaps behind the bar said something about her to the other one.'

'What?'

'She couldn't hear what, but she could tell it was about her.'

'And uncomplimentary.'

'Or complimentary, as the case may be.'

'You're going about with her openly these days, then?'

'More or less. There doesn't seem much point in not. In a way there never was, I suppose, but a couple of months ago I didn't really know what turn things were going to take. Not really. Part of getting older, Duggers, old lad, is doing more and more of those things which we do not want to do, and leaving undum more and more of those things which we want to do. Because there are fewer and fewer people round the place to do them with.'

Roy poured the rest of the champagne. I visualized the wedding reception, to which he would invite me, and which I would attend, and at which he would be wearing either morning-dress (probably minus white spats) or a boiler-suit, according to mood, and in the course of which Lady Vandervane II would perform the ceremony of cutting the cake before pelting the guests with it and setting about them with the knife. The picture depressed me, to the point at which I could not find the energy to administer the supplementary verbal drubbing Roy probably felt he ought to have. After two or three minutes of silence we drained our glasses and left, still in silence.

Outside, I started to turn down the hill in the direction of the Retrenchment Club, but Roy prevented me.

'I've got the car here,' he said.

'Just as quick to walk, surely.'

'I don't like leaving it where it is. May need to make a quick getaway, too.'

The real reason for this trifling change of plan came into view (without for the moment defining itself) when I saw, pasted inside the rear window of the car, a printed strip saying SUPPORT RHODESIA and next to it a fairly efficiently hand-lettered one saying AND SOUTH AFRICAN APARTHEID. I decided immediately that it would be more rewarding to allow the explanation to emerge rather than to demand it on the spot; I could always ask later if necessary. While Roy was taking out his keys, I noticed the same exhortation on the windscreen. He got in, unlocked the nearside door and put on his head a bowler hat that had been lying on the passenger's seat. I still held my peace.

We left the alley in which the car had been parked at perhaps forty miles an hour, causing a van and a taxi to brake violently. Roy blew his horn and shouted and shook his fist at them. He did more of the same when we reached the corner of Piccadilly just as the amber light appeared under the red, and lowered his window to shout and shake his fist to better effect as we swept past a knot of pedestrians who, far from making any move to cross in front of him, showed every sign of being prepared to remain indefinitely where they were. Hooting steadily, he changed lanes several times, and with some risk, as we covered the short stretch along to Duke Street. Here he resumed his policy towards pedestrians, stepped it up, rather, while we negotiated the turn at a speed that gave him the opportunity of singling out individuals for abuse. None of them showed the least irritation or disquiet at these onslaughts, only incomprehension. Between times, I could sense Roy glancing at me as I sat beside him displaying lively interest in everything around me except what he was doing. When the Jermyn Street lights halted us, I studied the goods in the windows of Fortnum & Mason's and Roy blew his horn. He stopped doing that at the sight of a nearby policeman, who approached, ran his eye over the windscreen sticker (with a hint of distaste, I thought), and spoke in at Roy's open window.

'Would you pull into the kerb, please, sir?'

I foresaw a confrontation with the forces of repression being substituted for my lunch, but Roy did as he was told in silence.

'You seemed to be getting a little impatient, sir.'

'Yes, I'm sorry, officer, but I was in a great hurry for a most urgent appointment.'

'These signal lights, like all others that I know of, are operated by a combination of mechanical and electrical systems, and are unaffected by the sound of any horn. May I see your driving licence, sir?'

Roy handed it over without a word. The policeman inspected it at length, and also meditatively, as though he would remember this moment all his life, before passing it back.

'I thought I recognized you, Sir Roy. I've seen you several times on television. Now you realize you've been infringing police regulations?'

'Yes, officer, I do realize that, and I'm very sorry.'

'All right, you can get on your way now, but I'd recommend refraining from excessive use of the horn in future. After all, it's not what one would call good driving manners, is it, sir?'

'No, officer. Thank you.'

We drove off at a sedate speed. When we were coming down into St James's Square, Roy removed his bowler and said,

'Bloody fascist.'

'Why didn't you tell him so?'

'He only let me go because he approved of these bloody slogans.'

'Cock, and why didn't you tell him he was a bloody fascist?'

'Only this lunch. I would have at any other time. No, I suppose I wouldn't, would I? It's this respect for authority that's dinned into us until it becomes a reflex. Conditioned response.'

'And cowardice.'

'Yes, a bit of that, too. Anyway, it isn't time yet for challenging the system direct. This sort of tactic' – he gestured – 'pays off much better as things are.'

'Tactic?'

'Oh, socialist camp! The negative demonstration. You pretend to be one of the other side behaving crappily, or rather behaving as they actually would if they felt strong enough. Not a new idea, but I think I'm the first in the field with this particular application. I'm going to bring it up with the Anti-Racialiss

Solidarity Executive. Just having the thing parked here in the middle of Clubland, saying what it says, will make some people angry in a useful way.'

He had parked the thing within a few yards of the space it had occupied the last time we had met in Craggs's, the day Penny had asked to be helped. Helped. What an idea. As we walked towards Pall Mall, I said,

'I should have thought most of the people using this square would be more likely to be cheered up by seeing that somebody powerful enough to own that sort of car agrees with them.'

'People like that don't notice anything unless it's rammed in front of their noses. Often not even then.'

'Oh, I see.'

'And you probably wouldn't know, but you don't have to be all that powerful to own that sort of car.'

The uncharacteristic malice here showed that I had registered a hit. Good. Well, goodish. Was Roy going off his head in more than a manner of speaking? As if in answer to my thought (or rather, I was sure, actually and quite non-uncharacteristically and reassuringly in answer to it) he burst into one of his bursts of offensive song while we were crossing the road.

'Thah cawl shuh-eeds ahv eveneeng thahr mahn-tahl wahr uh-spraddeeng,
Ahnd Mayoree, ahl smoileeng, wahs uh-leestneeng tah me . . .'

This, being delivered *molto largamente*, lasted until we were well on to the far pavement, and excited the interest of an eminent Sovietologist who was coming down the steps of the Voyagers' Club. Roy waved to him, deriving added power by grasping the forearm of the waving hand with the free hand and shaking it violently.

'Another bloody fascist,' he said to me jocularly, or in some way that half explained song and wave, perhaps also negative demonstration, possibly much more, as exercises designed to work off anxiety, divert it, outface it. 'Think how many fascists and bastards in general', he added in similar vein on the threshold of the Retrenchment, 'have passed through these portals.'

'I thought fascists and bastards in general were interchangeable.'

'You did? You're coming on. Right. That champagne at Craggs's is bloody good stuff. Lead on to the fascist and bastard in general of the day.'

We had entered a room several times the size of the house I occupied half of, opulent, classical and also strongly ecclesiastical in feeling, like an early Christian emperor's orgy chamber. Soberly dressed men in twos and threes straggled across a marble floor to a battered tin cart from which drinks were unhurriedly being dispensed. Roy led the way to the rear of this queue.

'Hadn't we better inquire for him?' I asked.

'Bugger that. This was his idea. Let him find us.'

He did when we were about halfway to the drinks cart. First he and Roy, then he and I, nodded at each other. Harold's second nod led without a break into a glance at his watch.

'Time's getting on,' he said. 'This confounded insistence on ice in everything. A lot of stuff piled up. Do you mind if we have a drink at the table?'

'No, I'd like that,' said Roy. 'But I'd like one here first as well, if I may.'

Harold turned to me. 'What about you?'

He was mistaken if he thought Roy would bow to an adverse casting vote, as also if he expected me to declare against my principal in the smallest particular. 'I must say I'd rather like one, too.'

'You mean here as well as at the table?'

'Yes, if that's all right.'

After another, slower nod, Harold walked briskly away and out of one of the corners of the room.

'Well played, Duggers. First round to us.'

'Do you think it's a good idea to annoy him unnecessarily?'

'Yes. And anyway this is necessarily.'

We got our drinks, but it was a technical triumph only. Harold came back as they were handed us, declined one himself, paid, and stood in silence rather more than a yard off. Although

Roy defended stoutly by gossiping to me about musicians and others Harold would not have known even by name, the three of us were in the dining-room after a bare ten minutes. A good half of it was occupied by a central table covered from edge to edge with dishes of cold food that not only were clearly untouched but seemed also inviolable, as at some metropolitan form of harvest festival. We skirted all this and sat down in a corner under a full-length portrait of a duke or other nobleman who, whether or not he had been a fascist, certainly looked the nonpareil of a bastard in general. Menus were before us, and an order pad, complete with carbon paper and uncapped ballpoint pen, lay ready at Harold's side. He led off without hesitation, wrote minutely on the pad and muttered (for publication, so to speak, rather than to himself),

'Tomato salad. Steak and kidney pie. Marrow and French beans.'

I noticed that all these items appeared on the clipped-in sheet on which the set lunch, a remarkably cheap package as it appeared to me, was laid out. I said I would have the same, and Harold wrote accordingly. Roy was finding it more difficult to come to a decision, frowning and cocking his head in a style he might have learnt from his wife. Finally he said,

'Tomato salad . . . yes. Then . . . I think duckling and orange sauce. And a green salad.'

'Three tomato salads,' Harold made an emendation on the pad. 'Duckling and . . . Where do you see that?'

'Over here,' said Roy with some force, hitting his finger at the à la carte section of the menu.

'Oh. Oh, over there. Duckling,' said Harold, in the tone, abruptly assumed, of a fanatical vegetarian. He made no move to write.

Roy swept his hand across his front as if cutting off a final chord. 'Could I change my mind?'

'By all means.'

'I'd like a whole lobster, please, cold, and stuffed with, uh, a portion of caviare. And a green salad, as I said.'

'All I'm thinking of is the time. It wouldn't be lined up like uh, for instance, the steak and kidney pie.'

'They'll be lined up separately, the lobster and the caviare, and there's no need for the chaps in the kitchen to do the actual stuffing. Get the doings brought to me and I'll stuff it myself.'

Harold gave up at that point. He took Roy's request for a preludial double champagne cocktail without overt demur, and made only a token stand by recommending the carafe Chablis. Roy said he found cheap white wines gave him acidity, and chose something with a long name from the wine list. All this Harold received with continuing absence of both good and bad grace, in fact with his habitual lack of reaction to events, reinforced, I fancied, with an unpropitious confidence in whatever weapon he had devised against Roy. The food and drink arrived with a speed that told either of unusual efficiency or of a long history of browbeating on Harold's part. While Roy was ladling out his caviare, Harold gave him a look that answered for me the slightly difficult question why the parties were facing each other here rather than somewhere private. If Roy proved to be restrained by his surroundings from acting up, losing his temper, perhaps physically assaulting his much weaker adversary, well and good; if not, there were very few places where any such misbehaviour would damage Roy more severely than in the crowded dining-room of the Retrenchment Club. Against my inclination, my respect for Harold rose: he knew how false were Roy's claims to despise the kind of society represented by what lay around us. He poured wine; then, with his eyes still on Roy, he took from his breast pocket a folded sheaf of typescript he did not at once open.

'Let's come to the point. You're an unsuitable companion for my daughter and would be a more than unsuitable husband to her. I propose to end the one relationship and prevent the other. For reasons I won't go into, my daughter's beyond my control. As recently perhaps as ten years ago, before the final disintegration of family ties and the whole network of duties and obedience and so on that went with them, I could have stopped this nonsense by stopping her. But now, wherever I sent her she'd break out and go back to you. Thanks to what you and your kind have done. The only place she'd be safe, that's to say comparatively safe, though God knows what with all the nitwitted boohooing about society being to blame and we mustn't brutalize the poor dears they seem to be able to walk out whenever they . . .'

Harold pulled himself up. 'I did seriously consider prison for her. Possession of marijuana. Nothing to it. But even if she didn't get away with a ten-bob fine and being told not to do it again for a week or two, if it wouldn't inconvenience her too much . . . Anyway, she'd have involved you. Medium-sized scandal. That would have injured you, which was a bloody good idea, but then the whole thing would have been out in the open and I'd have lost any hold on either of you. Therefore –'

'I don't get all this about my unsuitability,' said Roy with his mouth full. 'I can support her a bloody sight better than any of the little – any of the youngsters she was running round with when I met her. The age business doesn't matter. You're letting your dislike of my politics interfere with Sylvia's happiness, and that's –'

'I detest your politics, or rather the half-baked mess you call your politics. In the swim and bugger the facts. Sell the country to the Russians. That's nothing to do with it. You're the exact opposite of what my daughter needs. Firmness, common-sense, stability, self-discipline, patience. You're –'

'Save it. What's this point you said you were coming to?'

'I have here a draft of a feature article about you which I shall publish in my newspaper if I ever hear of your having any dealings with my daughter after the lapse of forty-eight hours from this moment. Let me give you some idea of the contents.' Harold unfolded the typescript. 'The Generation Gap.'

'Oh, Christ on a bloody great bicycle,' said Roy, forking in lobster.

'Leading figures of today as seen by their sons.'

Roy stopped chewing.

'I Love Me is Father's Slogan, says Chris Vandervane, 20, son of, well, we know all about that. Brief run-through of your musical attainments and the political stuff. Deadpan. Nothing snide. No need for it in view of what comes later. We do rather stress your involvement with the cause of youth, understanding of it, sympathy with it. But so would you. Before we go on, the lawyers have been over it. They're a little unhappy with I think it's three phrases, but this is only a first draft. You can take it from me that the final version will be writ-proof. Well, then we go on to your house, and its present occupants, Penny Vandervane, 23, who shares a room with West Indian writer Godfrey Alexander, 24 . . .'

'Gilbert,' said Roy. 'Can I have a brandy?'

Harold made a correction on the typescript. 'Thank you. A brandy. Yes. Yes, certainly. Later, in the coffee-room. Don't you want cheese or a pudding?'

'No thanks. Just a brandy.'

At the door, Roy and I waited while Harold thoroughly counted his change at the pay-desk.

'It's a try-on, Duggers. He wouldn't have the nerve.'

'I hope you're right. I think he would have the nerve if it came to it.'

'Lot of bloody nonsense.'

'Which we've got to pay very close attention to.'

'Little shit.'

The coffee-room was not crowded, but there were quite enough people about to deter Roy from any kind of outburst: not that he seemed so inclined in the least. We found another corner, with, this time, the life-sized statue of a long-defunct prime minister towering over us. It was done in a kind of stone that made its subject seem not so much a man as a man coated from head to foot in whitewash. Coffee arrived, also a large glass holding perhaps a tablespoonful of brandy. Roy simply drained it.

'Now,' said Harold, lighting a knobbly cheroot and reopening the typescript. 'In a way, it's not surprising my father goes for youth, because that's what he's like himself. Not grown up. He's like a kid of ten or even less. I don't know what he's like with his music, I don't know anything about that and I don't want to know, but in everything else all he ever thinks about is getting his own way. He's like little Ashley, that's my half-brother, he's six and absolutely diabolical. If you don't give him what he wants straight away he screams the place down, because nobody's tried to bring him up. Nothing in it for my father, you see. He just gives him expensive toys all the time to keep him quiet.

'Interviewer: How does all this affect the other members of the household?

'My sister thinks the same way as I do. He's always let us do exactly as we like, and we liked that until we realized it was all just less trouble for him. We don't get on much with our step-mother, but you can't really blame her. She's half out of her – no, that bit's cut. He, my father hangs around young people to make himself feel young and feel he's up with the trends. He tries to talk like them and it's pathetic. He thinks they think he's one of them, but they're just waiting for him to go. He thinks they like having him around because he's famous, but they don't take any notice of that. And all these politics, it's just showing off. How can you care about peasants in Vietnam when you give parties with champagne and a couple of blokes in white coats going round pouring it? I don't see that makes you any better than the rich people in Spain and Greece and these places. I asked him about that once and he said it was different, it was the society we lived in and he had a position to keep up. It's always different when he does it. I think rich people ought to mind their own business and leave it to students and workers to get on with changing society and the rest of it.

'Interviewer: You're almost saying you'd have found a stern Victorian parent more to your taste.

'No, I'm not saying that. I'm not in favour of that either. Those sort of people did a lot of harm by building up capitalism and the power structure. But they were doing it for the Empire and the ruling class and their religion, not just for themselves. Not all of it.

'Well, that's the core of the thing. Not very coherent or well expressed, but I think that gives it a certain –'

'You can't print that, Harold,' I said. 'Your lawyers must be – '

'Nobody asked for your view.'

'How much are you paying him to put his name to that?' asked Roy.

'Oh, we haven't discussed a fee yet. Welcomed the chance of getting it off his chest was how he put it.'

'I'll take that along,' said Roy, putting out his hand. He noticed it was shaking and lowered it to the table.

Harold gave him the typescript. 'Yes, you'll want to think it over. I've plenty of copies at the office. Time's getting on. One warning. I was never more serious in my life. Good afternoon to you.'

'It's malicious,' I said to Roy outside.

'Yes, that struck me, too.'

'I mean in the legal sense. It is a try-on. He can't hit you with that.'

'He already has.'

I refrained from telling him he would get over it. Whether he would get over the actual publication of the article was perhaps another matter. Whether Harold would publish it as threatened was yet another. In one important sense he was free to do so: the proprietor of the paper, an elderly and ailing peer, had been living in Malta for five years and for the last two or more of these, according to Coates, had confined his daily reading to *The Times*. Harold was one of the very few men I had ever met with the outlook and temperament to face without hesitation the row, the publicity, the dismissal and the loss of prospects that surely must, or probably would, or easily might follow the performance of what he promised. In fact, the only other man of such a calibre I could think of for the moment was Roy.

Turning up towards the square, Roy glanced to his left, had a proper look and gave a harsh yell like a man in a film taking a spear through the chest. I saw Harold's slight figure, neatly clad in its fawn tweed suit, begin to cross the road in our direction. We hurried on.

'Why's that little shit following us?'

'I'm sure he's not,' I said. 'He's probably parked somewhere up here.'

'If I go ahead there'll be no point in him publishing it.'

'Yes there will. Revenge.'

'A moment ago you said it was a try-on.'

'I've had a bit of time to think. Newspapers don't mind libel actions unless they're going to be the people who lose face. This one would be quite a circulation-builder. And imagine the sort of stuff that would be dragged up in court. Assuming you won, you'd be twenty thousand quid or so in pocket, which you don't need anyway, and worse off in every other respect than if you'd just let it go by. As Harold knows very well. He might be positively hoping you would sue.'

'That boy saying all that. Oh, Christ. Old lad, could you come up to Craggs's for some more brandy? Or sit with me while I drink it?'

'Of course.'

A policeman was standing on the pavement by Roy's car. I soon saw that it was the same policeman as earlier. He was about my age, with springy tufts of whisker on each cheek. I also saw, or fancied I saw, that the car sat unnaturally close to the ground.

'I'm afraid you've had a bit of trouble in your absence, Sir Roy. Somebody's been ripping your tyres. With a knife, it looks like.'

He indicated an inch-long slit in the rubber. Over his bowed back Harold came into view, moving on a course that would bring him within fifty feet of where we stood. Roy leaned forward, bent his knees slightly and came up on his toes in the attitude of a man about to spring at another.

'Little bastards!' he roared. 'Scum of the bloody earth! What a lark, eh? What a romp! Ear we are, Sid, ear's a fuyyin grake car blongin to some fuyyin toff – gish your fuyyin knife an ow fuyyin show im! Gawf! Beezh! Hoogh! Oh, how unimprovably witty and trenchant!'

A youthful couple in a peripatetic semi-embrace, the lad wearing one of his auntie's floppy black velours hats with one of her floral silk scarves looped round the crown, the girl in a sort of lead-foil top and patchwork trousers, had come to a halt within earshot. Harold approached the car next but one to Roy's and took out his keys. The policeman nodded sympathetically.

'Most annoying, Sir Roy. But these window stickers of yours, they would constitute what they call a provocation, don't you think? Not that that's any excuse, of course.'

Roy now noticed and glared at Harold, who was having some difficulty with the lock of his car door, wheeled round on the youngsters with a snarl and a yard-long sweep of the arm that (to my relief) got them moving again, and turned back to the policeman.

'And where were you while this little outbreak of high spirits was going on? Checking on meters and illegal parking, no doubt.'

'These days that kind of thing falls within the province of traffic wardens, Sir Roy. I was on my normal rounds, which brought me here only about a minute before you arrived on the scene. It's unfortunate that I came along too late to do anything about this deplorable act of vandalism.'

As he said this, he caught my eye for the first and only time. His demeanour throughout, and his expression now, were not quite incompatible with full understanding of the negative demonstration, nor with a desire to tease Roy by suggesting that the law had looked impassively on while a well-known foe of authority was having his tyres slashed. In a slightly more wooden tone than before, the policeman added,

'Mind you, this is a rather special area. London Library, Junior Carlton Club. You can never be quite certain of the sort of people you're going to get.'

Harold's car started. At no stage had he paid the least visible attention to our group. Roy looked up and his frame seemed to sag; I knew what he was remembering. Then he said to the policeman,

'Do you want anything? Like a statement in triplicate or a look at my medical history or . . .'

'No, sir. I was only wondering if I could be of some –'

'Well, you can't. Not of any.'

The policeman touched his helmet respectfully, and went. 'What do we do now?' I asked.

'Christ. What do we do. Well, we go back up to Craggs's and get the porter to sort out this bloody shambles. Then we have some brandy, as advertised. Or I do. Though you're very welcome if you feel like it. Actually, if you look at it in the right way, this business with the tyres is very encouraging. I said it would make chaps angry, didn't I? It just shows that even in the most ruling-class areas there's a real spirit of . . . Taxi!'

'How old is he, for instance?' I asked Vivienne that evening.

'You know, it's funny, but he'll never say. Never has. But I suppose he must be sixtyish, something like that.'

'And he lives alone.'

'Ever since my mother died, that's nine years ago now. But my brothers and I, we all go and see him every week. Separately, to spread it out for him. He has lunch at the pub and a woman comes in every week-morning and cooks things for him to warm up at night. She cleans the place as well.'

'What does he so to speak do all the time?'

'Well, this job he has with the religious people takes up the mornings and the odd afternoon. Then he likes music. At least he likes Gilbert and Sullivan and Viennese waltzes and the man who wrote *The Merry Widow* and things. Though I suppose that isn't music according to you.'

'Of course it is. A lot of it's very good.'

'On its level. Isn't that what you say?'

I found this an uncharacteristic remark. 'All right, if you like. But why shouldn't it be music at all according to me?'

'Just the way almost everything everybody else thinks is music you don't think is.'

Except in the bedroom of my flat an hour and more earlier, Vivienne had been allowing rather more sullenness-cum-preoccupation to show than was normal for a Monday. I sensed, however, that she had been genuinely trying to reduce its intensity, instead of having it there and letting me take it or leave it. This was new. But the bus we were on, the third in a fearful series, stopped at the stop we wanted before I could take up the point, and I forgot it altogether at the familiar (but always enlivening) sight of her vigorous march along the pavement and the unfamiliar sight of the attractive tobacco-silk trouser-suit she was wearing.

'It's only a couple of minutes' walk from here.'

'What a nice suit that is, Viv. New, isn't it?'

'Yes, I got it today. Do you realize that's the very first time you've ever said you liked any of my clothes?'

'Sorry. I just . . .'

'That's all right.' She took my arm. 'I always feel a bit, you know, hoping everything's going to go off smoothly the first time I bring somebody along. It always does, but you always think it might not.'

Here it would have been natural for me to ask her reason for bringing me along, but, as on all the previous occasions when the problem had come up in my mind, I could think of no way of putting the question that would not seem to carry a why-the-hell initial flavour and a for-God's-sake aftertaste. So I just said, 'Have you ever brought the other bloke along?'

'Who?'

'The other bloke. You know.'

'Oh, not for a long time.'

'A long time before you decided to bring me along, in fact.'

'Yes. He was more – he was keener on the idea than I thought you'd be.'

'I think I see.'

We were walking past a terrace of small houses with thickly hedged front gardens and stained-glass panels in the front doors. Vivienne led me up to one of them and rang the bell.

'I take it he knows we sleep together?' I suddenly asked.

'Oh, I should think so.'

'You should think so?'

'He's never asked, so I haven't told him. About anybody, not just you, But I should think he knows. He must do.'

'Oh, good.'

The door opened and a short, stocky man let us in. He was bald and had a closely cropped beard that (in a phrase that sprang complete and unabridged into my mind) went all the way round his face without him having a moustache. This, coupled with Vivienne's and my exchange of a minute earlier, made me think for an instant that what she had really brought about was a confrontation between me and the other bloke. Then I reproached myself for associating her with such a typically, even grossly, Vandervanean concept. Nevertheless, there turned out to be more than one point during the evening when I was to wonder momentarily whether I was dealing with an actor hired by Roy to coax or bluff me into some new machination of his.

'How do you do, Mr Copes.'

'It's very nice to see you again. But haven't you . . .? Wasn't there a . . .?'

He made passes at his chin and jaws, uninformative to the average outsider, but conveying clearly enough to me that it was now in his mind that the image of the other bloke had surfaced, and setting me to wonder in some discomfort how far I really resembled that unknown. Then I remembered Vivienne telling me he was only an inch taller than she, which made him eight inches shorter than me, and cheered up again. Unless there was another bloke . . .

'No, Dad, this is Mr Ee-andell, Douglas Ee-andell,' she was saying in her usual attempt to block off any Randalling on the part of people she introduced me to.

'That's all right, Vivvy, don't you worry, dear. Come on, what are we hanging about here for? Let's find ourselves a glass of something.'

We entered what was clearly a study, with an open roll-top desk, typewriter, postal scales, rows of reference works – or fairly clearly so; the walls were thickly hung with pictures and such of a devotional tendency. I noticed a reproduction of Holman Hunt's *Light of the World*, photographs of the Archbishop of Canterbury, a well-known American evangelist, a Negro divine and somebody who could perhaps have been Samuel Wesley, a lithograph or whatever of Haydn (presumably in his role as composer of *The Creation*), and representations of scrolls, inscriptions and illuminated texts.

Mr Copes waved his hand at parts of this. 'Something for everybody,' he said, making for a card table topped with pink baize on which there stood a silver tray bearing a decanter and three glasses. Briskly, he poured and handed out drinks.

'Not very nice, is it?' he said (to my silent agreement) when we had tasted. 'Cyprus sherry, they call it. A more exact description would be Cyprus raisin tea with some spirits in it. They soak the raisins in a water tank in the sun and either it ferments on its own or they make it ferment – I'm not quite clear which – and then they strain it and put the spirits in it. But perfectly wholesome. You saw what they've been up to today, did you? It was in the paper.'

He soon made it apparent that he was referring, not to the Cyprus sherry-makers, but to the government then in office. Some price-increase or wage-claim had been allowed or met. Mr Copes explained that he took no interest in politics and never had, but that what the country obviously needed was a dictator, a benevolent one, of course, or a reasonably benevolent one, who would surrender his powers the moment the necessary period of martial law came to an end. Asked what that period would have accomplished if all went well, Mr Copes said that unity and decency would have been restored by the fairest possible methods, without the singling-out of any class or group: profiteering tradesmen would be gaoled as readily as strikers and agitators, coloured landlords deported along with coloured tenants, rioting students and rampaging football-supporters shot down side by side in the streets. In the climate of opinion thus engendered, other problems, like abortion and homosexuality, would probably be found to have cleared up of their own accord.

After some minutes of this, Vivienne went out to the kitchen. Mr Copes recharged my glass and said, in the gentle tone he had maintained throughout,

'I must be right in thinking, Mr Yandell, mustn't I, that you and young Vivvy go to bed with each other?'

This query took me off balance. With as much as a throat-clearing by way of prelude, later in the evening, alleviated by Vivienne's presence, if ideas about the imposition of decency by martial law had been less fresh in my mind, it (the query)

might have been more manageable. As it was, I found myself saying, if not blurting,

'Oh no. Nothing like that. Not at all.'

'Not at all. In that case there must surely be some other girl, or even girls, among your acquaintance with whom you do go to bed, mustn't there?'

'Oh no. Of course not. No.'

'No. Perhaps you prefer your own sex? I must say, to look at you, I shouldn't have thought –'

'Oh no. Really.'

'Well, then you must without question find relief in the kind of solitary practices they used to warn us against at school, mustn't you?'

'No, I . . . don't go in for any of that.'

'I see. And you've been keeping company with Vivvy for how long?'

'About four months.'

Mr Copes twitched abruptly, as from a small bolt of electricity. 'And you're how old?'

'Thirty-three.'

'Yes. You know, Mr Yandell, I may be very old-fashioned, but I can't help feeling that, as a companion for a healthy, vigorous girl like Vivvy, an apparently equally healthy and vigorous young man who can totally suppress his physical desires over a period of about four months, uh, leaves something to be desired.'

'I can see that,' I said, doing some wistful, tender speculation about how Sylvia might be spending her evening.

'I call it Copes's Fork.' He gave the low, affectionate laugh of somebody watching the antics of a favourite animal. 'Like chess, in a way. Once you've said no to the first question – and the skill, such as it is, all lies in manoeuvring you into saying no at that stage – then your only possible chance of drawing the game is to say yes to the second question and play out time talking about the high plane your feelings for Vivvy are on. There was a fellow once who did that. He worked for a publisher, I think he said. But it's most exceptional. I must grant you, Mr Yandell, you went to your doom with dignity. Evidently you're an easy-going sort of chap. That must be one of the things Vivvy likes about you. She likes easy-going chaps. Do smoke if you want to.

'Over the years, Vivvy must have brought I don't know how many young men along to see me. There was one who was middle-aged, I suppose you'd have called him. Unmarried, naturally. Not divorced, either. Vivvy couldn't have been more than twenty-one or -two at the time. I put my foot down about him. In the first place there was too much of a gap in age, and in the second place I never trust a man who isn't married and a father before he's forty. I had a word with Vivvy and that was that.'

'She just stopped seeing him?'

'She stopped bringing him along to see me, and that means something. I don't think she'd have a great deal of time to see anyone she didn't bring along occasionally. She likes men, doesn't she? We don't discuss these matters, but it didn't take me much thought to work out how she runs her life. There were three possibilities. Either she wasn't going to bed with any of the fellows she brought along, or she was going to bed with some of them and not with others, or she was going to bed with all of them. Now, there've been some fellows she's brought along over periods of a year or more, and most of them have lasted a few months. So if she wasn't going to bed with any of them, she was rustling up an entire string of fellows who were going on going round with her because they were so keen on her conversation. Well, to be able to keep it up for ten years and more, continuously rustling up fellows like that, in quantity, these days, would take a very extraordinary sort of girl. And Vivvy's hardly extraordinary at all. That took me to possibility number two. There, it was harder to be absolutely certain in one's mind, but I noticed that she talked about all the fellows in just the same sort of way and treated them in just the same sort of way when she brought them along. That was pretty well good enough for me. Vivvy tells me your job's to do with music. I'm pretty keen on music myself.'

I had almost stopped feeling uncomfortable since the promulgation of Copes's Fork, thanks to its author's friendly manner, but was relieved on the whole when he started telling me about a performance of *Iolanthe* that he (and I) had recently seen on television. There followed a discussion of the propriety of modernizing the librettos of light operas intended to be topical in their day. Vivienne came back in the middle of it. She gave me a how's-it-going? look, and I gave her an all-right one in return.

'I can't help feeling Gilbert's wit has been rather overrated,' I said to Mr Copes, took a further look from his daughter that suggested I had chosen an unpropitious line, and added quickly, 'but at his best he can be very ingenious and inventive.'

'I'm glad to hear you say that. I know it's fashionable to decry him, but I am rather fond of the old chap. Perhaps it's simply that I'm used to him and know most of him by heart. I should certainly agree that Sullivan is the senior partner, as it were. Well, Vivvy, how's it going? Have your efforts been crowned with success?'

Vivienne seemed to think he was talking about dinner, which did in fact turn out to be ready in the next room. This was a kitchen in the old-fashioned sense, but not in the old-fashioned style: no wall-clock, rocking-chair or cat, nothing much at all, really, and I guessed that Mr Copes ate off a tray in his study when alone. He saw me hesitating to sit down as soon as it occurred to me that I was doing so, and waved his hand.

'Let's get on with it. Unless you'd positively like me to say grace ... I only say it when some sort of man of God is of the company, and as often as not I don't even say it then. I worked out a sort of rule of thumb years ago. Under about thirty, or these days let's say more like thirty-five, they're not keen on it. Outmoded ritual. I should have thought that a modish ritual or an up-to-date ritual was a contradiction in terms, but that's by the way. Then the middle lot, going up to fifty or so, they rather care for a touch of benedictus benedicat. Above that, it tends to be outmoded ritual again. You've no idea how much I've sometimes wanted to find out why chaps who feel like that feel like that, the older ones, I mean, but I can't help thinking it would be unkind to ask them. I don't know whether I'm making any sense to you.'

189

'Oh yes,' I said truthfully. 'Perfect sense.'

The soup was out of an opulent packet or authentic tin, the fish pie had been prepared by an expert and warmed up competently enough. Mr Copes poured stout of a brand unfamiliar to me and began to talk about the American and Russian space programmes. It seemed that development of these was altogether too slow and unambitious for his liking, and that our country's failure to have put up a decent orbiting satellite approached a national scandal. He said he realized that such projects cost a lot of money, but, by his reckoning, the outlay necessary to get a manned ship off to Mars and a new drive evolved, whereby the outer planets became reachable in a matter of weeks, could be met by stopping public expenditure on everything else whatever – far more than met: the abolition of income tax, sufficiently urgent on moral grounds, could be carried through at the same time.

'I don't quite see in that case where all the cash would come from,' I said.

'Oh. Taxation. Cars, television, tobacco, drink, all these domestic machines. Anything at all to do with cars. Anything people spend their money on, in fact. Food. That way you'd catch everybody.'

'You'd certainly need a dictator to run a system like that.'

'A dictator. Yes, come to think of it you probably would. As you imply, it isn't a particularly realistic scheme. But what a splendid thing for everybody if it could somehow be put into effect.'

'You mean the advances in knowledge that might be made?'

'Oh no. I don't in the least hold with advances in knowledge. No, it's the idea, the wonder of it all. Tell me, Doug – do you read any of this science-fiction stuff?'

'I know it sounds silly, but I have so much listening to do I hardly get time to read what I've got to read for my work.'

'No, I quite understand, but with respect I think you should make some time to read a few of these stories. They'd show you, much more clearly than I could explain, what I'm trying to get at about wonder and so forth. It's necessary, that sort of feeling, more and more so every year, as people bother less and less with religion. How much do you bother with it?'

Twice might have been coincidence: sex via (or hurtling out of the blue after) dictatorship, religion behind the snatched-off mask of space travel. To be certain I was faced with a full-grown policy, I was going to have to wait until nursery schools had led instantaneously to my income, its sources and amount, or an exchange of views about the fabled lost portion of Atahualpa's ransom had, in the twinkling of an eye, become an inquiry into the incidence of madness in my family. Meanwhile, I must answer the current question, doubly so, for Vivienne, instead of sending her father the now-then-Dad look I had been banking on, had turned in her chair and was sending me a look of genuine, amiable expectation.

'Well, I'm sorry, but I'm afraid I don't bother with it much.'

'Never be sorry or afraid to speak your mind. Don't bother with it much. You mean you don't bother with it at all,' said Mr Copes, almost more gently than I could bear.

'Yes, I'm . . . I suppose I do.'

'But you must think there's something more than just this world,' said Vivienne. 'I know you can have a lot of argument about what. But something. You must.'

'I can't see why.'

'Have you ever tried? To see why?'

Mr Copes frowned for the first time, in puzzlement, not disapproval. 'But surely the two of you must have gone into these matters together, mustn't you! Having known each other all these months?'

'No, Dad. Never.'

'Never. What an extraordinary state of affairs.'

'It just hasn't happened to come up,' I said, feeling slightly hedged in. 'And I don't think that's all that extraordinary. Not statistically extraordinary, anyhow.'

'Oh, I should have said statistically very extraordinary,' said Mr Copes, 'if you took a conspectus of the last couple of hundred years as opposed to the last couple of dozen. And even over the shorter term my considered guess would be that numbers would tell against you if one were to survey the country as a whole, rather than merely the south-eastern corner of it. I needn't speculate about the rest of the world. But do go on.'

I had no idea how I had come to seem to have started something, let alone what it might be; however, I went on. 'I just lead my life from day to day, like most people, whatever they may say to themselves or one another about it – in fact like everybody I've ever met or heard of, apart from a few prophets and such. Which suggests to me that what you say to yourself and your friends about what you're doing can't be very important.'

'I don't see why not. At all events, it's natural to think and talk about one's life in the whole. I should like to call it human in the most literal sense. It would take a funny sort of soldier never to think or talk about war, wouldn't it? I wonder how many sailors there are who've never thought or talked about the sea.'

'You've got to believe in something.' Vivienne did not look or sound very amiable now. 'Everybody has to.'

Trying to sound light and airy, I said, 'You'll be telling me in a minute it doesn't so much matter what it is as long as it's something.'

'Suppose I did, then? I'm not, but suppose I did?'

'Well, good God, it matters all right if it's fascism or communism or any of those. Or flower power or love-ins or any of –'

'I didn't mean anything soft or anything nasty. I meant something reasonable. I thought you'd have seen that.'

'Okay, sorry, but I still feel –'

Mr Copes broke in. 'Very, very nearly everybody who's ever done anything has believed in something, and by anything I don't mean anything important, I mean anything whatever. Rather in the same way as very, very nearly everybody who's ever done anything whatever has had two arms and two legs. But I seem to have interrupted you again.'

'No you haven't, Mr Copes. I've pretty well run out of things to say about all this. Not that I had very many in the first place.'

One still in stock concerned belief in belief in something reasonable, and just how reasonable the something had to be in order to count as reasonable, but I kept quiet. So, for a short time, did the other two. Then Vivienne said she would see about some coffee, and Mr Copes took me back into his study, where he poured out two glasses of port.

'I know you're not a drinking man, Doug, but that's no excuse for not giving you anything nice at all. This isn't in the least out of the way, but it is port and not port type or port character. Not too bad, is it? Now, while I've got you on your own for a few moments, I wonder if I could intrude on you a little, as it were, and ask you to put my mind at rest about something, if you would.'

He sat down facing me across the hearth, where a green paper fan partly hid the emptiness of the grate, and stared, for quite a few of the few moments he had me on my own, at a point on the opposite wall where there was a fearful reproduction of Guido Reni's sufficiently fearful *Ecce Homo*. When he had accumulated enough spiritual afflatus from this, he said,

'How shall I put it? Is this country heading for a state of complete moral anarchy?'

'Oh, I doubt it,' I said, trying not to fall out of my chair with relief. 'It's not a question I bother about much, quite frankly, but I would have said there's about enough respect for tradition still going, family life, discipline and that kind of thing, to see us all out. Perhaps you've been taking too much notice of the way some people behave in the south-east of England.'

'Well taken. Perhaps I was looking at it in the rather longer term. Have you ever thought of marrying Vivvy? I don't mean have you any sort of intention to – I've no right to ask that and it's none of my business – but simply and literally if you've ever thought of it.'

I had no trouble staying in my chair now. 'Oh. No. I can't honestly say I have. But that's nothing to do with Vivienne, it's to do with me. I just feel – when I look at the mess so many people –'

'With respect, Doug, what an extraordinary number of things you don't think about and haven't got time for. Science fiction. Religion. Whether the country's heading for moral anarchy. Marrying Vivvy or evidently anybody else either. I expect you must find a great deal to occupy you in other ways.

Your music and all that. Some men have made music the only really important thing in their lives, I suppose. Bach, Mozart, Mendelssohn. But then they were all . . . Ah, here we are. Well done, Vivvy.'

Vivienne came in and handed round coffee without any kind of look at me. While we drank it, Mr Copes talked about the doings of his sons, politely seeing to it that I could follow the main drift without being encumbered with detail. He passed over some photographs of the senior son and his family, for me to look at while he himself described to Vivienne his visit to them over at Ealing the previous day. I turned through the series of holiday snaps, amusing myself at first by trying to pick out bits of Vivienne and her father from her brother and two small nephews, but finding nothing recognizable. The maternal strains must have predominated there. Well, why not?

Finally, Mr Copes said he had an archdeacon coming to see him at crack of dawn, and would take the liberty of chucking us out, if he might. This proved within his powers, once I had rejected a return bus-journey in favour of some sort of cab and he had successfully telephoned for one on my behalf. We parted cordially. The sort of cab concerned had no lateral partition, and was also the sort with a driver lacking in geographical knowledge or aptitude, so that what with one thing and another Vivienne and I exchanged no more than a dozen words until we were back in the flat. It was five past eleven. She said she would make some tea. I followed her out into the kitchen.

'Are you cross with me?'

'Yes, a bit. Or I was. I'm getting over it.'

'What about?'

'You didn't think much of my father, did you?'

'Viv, what are you saying? It's quite true he disconcerted me once or twice, but that was just his way. I thought he was a marvellous old character. Most entertaining.'

'Character. Entertaining.' She put the lid back on the electric kettle and slammed the plug into its base. 'That's about it, isn't it?'

'I really don't know what you mean.'

'Where you're concerned. That's as far as it goes. You wouldn't discuss anything with him.'

'Now that is just not true. We covered a hell of a lot of ground and whatever he wanted to discuss I discussed back at him. Except your brothers, admittedly, but there wasn't much in the way of a side for me to take in the discussion about them.'

'You weren't really talking to him, you were getting him to go on saying more things for you to go on thinking what a wonderful old character and incredible old codger and fabulous old buffer and fantastic old gaffer he was. You do the same with me: that's how I noticed.'

'Me think you're an old gaffer? You must be –'

'Not a gaffer, but funny. Zany, screwy, dotty, kooky. Not on purpose, but because I can't help myself, because I was made that way. An oddball, a card, a caution. I've seen you watching me as if I was television. Comic.'

I took the lid off the teapot. 'I do sometimes think you're funny when perhaps you aren't really intending to be, yes. But I never think you're silly or absurd or undignified. And it's part of being fond of somebody: you must know that, surely. Anyone who was never funny except on purpose would be a freak, and a repulsive sort of freak at that, especially if it was a woman. From my point of view. And what about men, from your point of view? You're not going to tell me you've never thought I was funny not on purpose.'

'No.'

I was less whole-heartedly relieved to hear this reply than I had expected, but at once thrust aside the temptation to ask in what circumstances, and to what degree, I was funny not on purpose. 'There you are then.'

'But I don't go round thinking it's the main thing about you.'

'I don't think it's the main thing about you, for God's sake. You know what I think the main thing about you is. Not the only thing, but the main thing.'

'What is it?' She sounded considerably mollified.

I was in the middle of telling her when the kettle boiled. She turned it off with an absent-minded gesture and said conversationally,

'You know, Doug, I sometimes find a cup of tea this time of night keeps me awake. Do you ever find that?'

'Yes, I do sometimes.'

Without looking at me, she started to walk out of the kitchen. 'After all, tea's supposed to perk you up, not sort of slow you down.'

'Yes, quite,' I said, intrigued at this variation on our established cup-of-tea ritual. 'It's the caffeine, you know.'

'Really?'

'Yes, apparently there's more caffeine in a cup of tea than in a cup of coffee. Isn't that interesting?'

'Oh, darling . . .'

Afterwards I went and made some tea, and we both managed to fall asleep before the caffeine had had time to hit us.

It was the next evening, that of *Elevations 9*. I had arranged to meet Roy for a drink in Craggs's at half past eight and escort him to the concert hall, or rather to the converted tramway depot south of the river which, over the past couple of years, had served as the venue for many an exciting transmedial break-through, anti-Establishment manifestation and punch-up. His pre-performance routine, always strict, normally led off with a light early dinner attended by Kitty, two or three of the or-chestra with their wives, husbands, etc., and a close friend or so. For more than one reason, this custom was not going to be ob-served tonight. Nor, as I saw when I arrived and went to join him in his corner, were other familiar prescriptions: a caramel-coloured helping of what I took to be whisky stood at his elbow, replacing, probably as one of a group rather than solo, the single glass of wine to which the routine restricted him. I was relieved (taking one possible view of the matter) to see his violin case within his reach. Here, at any rate, tradition had held: no cloakroom attendant, waiter or functionary of any kind would be allowed to take the thing out of his sight for a mo-ment. At my approach, he got up and pressed a bell-button.

'Hi, Duggers. I suggest champagne. For you, that is. You do like it, don't you. In so far as you like anything one could properly call a drink. What was that about a bite to eat you said you were going to have eaten? Have a sandwich or something.'

'No thanks, I had a sort of high tea at the flat.'

'High tea, Christ. Ham and Russian salad and sweep pickle and tim peaches and plung cake and lots of cups of char. Each to his taste is what I always say.'

He seemed to me fairly drunk already. While he spoke to the

waiter, I dallied with the thought of plying him with his own drink to the point at which he would be unable to leave the club, or at least mount the concert platform, then put it aside. We must take off in half an hour or less, and ten times that time of continuous soaking would hardly have been enough to put him under any table I had ever seen in his vicinity.

'How's life?' I asked him when the waiter had gone.

'That's the silliest bloody question I've heard for longer than I care to remember. Life gets lived. That's how life is.'

'How's Sylvia?'

'That's more like it. A bit more like it. She's fine as far as I know, which is virtually no distance at all. I haven't seen her or been in touch with her for . . . But don't exult prematurely, old lad. Temporary arrangement. While we, or more accurately while I go to work on devising some counter-measure to your friend Harold Meers's little stratagem.'

'Any progress?'

'No. None whatever. Very nearly none whatever. To anticipate your next question, everybody else is in very much the condition you might expect them to be. Oh, I've been to work on young Christopher. Offered him anything he cared to name to refuse to let the interview be published. Can you do that, by the way? Stop a chap printing something you've already given him? Buggered if I know. Anyway, we didn't get to that stage. He and I aren't on very good terms these days, to tell you the truth. The others are all okay. Well . . . except Gilbert. Rock of stability normally. He's taken to going off for hours at a time, wandering round those woods that lead off from the common apparently. Nothing there apart from trees and sexual maniacs. You know, I sometimes wonder whether I might not end up as one of those, when Girl, 20 and going down and all the rest of it are as if they'd never been. You could easily find yourself stuck with flashing what was left of your hampton at Girl, 8. Or I suppose by that stage it might even be Boy, 8. No sign of it at the moment, I can assure you, but you never know. I expect it's quite an agreeable sort of life when you get used to it: plenty of fresh air and exercise, and Mother Nature on every hand, and a spot of spying on courting couples thrown in to rekindle memories of long ago. Quite romantic. Not much fun in January, though, I grant you.'

He went on like this until, indeed until after, some champagne, a plate of smoked-salmon sandwiches and another brunette whisky had been delivered to us. I refrained as studiously as I could from studiously refraining from any flicker of reaction when Roy poured the new whisky into the substantial remains of the old, but I must have over- or underdone it, because he stared coldly at me and said,

'Liberation from the tyranny of the bar-line! If I'm not good and pissed when I stand up in front of that lot I'll never get through it.'

'Fair enough. After all, it isn't as if this were a musical occasion.'

'Oh, random noise considered as art!' he half roared, incidentally providing me with further evidence that he was much more hostile to recent offshoots from music when he was off guard or stirred, as now, than when he was soberly lecturing me and others on our duty to keep abreast of new developments. 'I do wish you'd try to ... Well, it's a totally different sort of audience. Not one of those little ... Their ears aren't attuned to the kind of nuances in performance you're in the habit of looking for. Or I'm in the habit of looking for. Under other conditions. What does this bugger want, do you suppose?'

This bugger was the glaring hall porter, who came up and told Roy that a Mr Harold Meers wished to speak with him on the telephone. Roy asked me to watch his violin, I said I would, and he hurried out. When he came back, five or six minutes later, I was measurably better informed about who had been who in 1935 than on arrival. He looked puzzled, also drunk.

'What did he want?'

'I never got to him. Somebody took a lot of trouble, when he wasn't coughing his head off, to establish that I really was Sir Roy Vandervane and not his grandmother, and then took a lot more trouble to explain that he was speaking from Mr Meers's private house. He really let that sink in. Then whoever it was said Mr Meers had been called away but would be back in a moment.' Still on his feet, Roy began eating sandwiches at top speed, with gulps of whisky to eke out salivation, and continued to talk. 'Then I got a detailed account of how they'd found out where I was. What did Mr Meers want? He didn't know, but Mr Meers would be along directly to expound in person. I hung on a bit longer and then got fed up and rang off. I suppose it was his way of cheering me up for the concert. Though I can't understand why the bastard didn't speak to me himself. Very odd.'

'Call him back in a few minutes. I've got his private number on me somewhere.'

'Bugger that. I've got a little job to do that nobody else can do for me, and then we ought to be moving. I just hope Sylvia's all right.'

'If it were anything serious there wouldn't have been this mucking about. He was just trying to worry you. Don't let him.'

'I'll try not to.'

The tramway depot might, to all appearance, have seen the back of its last tram no earlier than noon on the day in question, in time for the rails to be ripped up and two inspection pits filled (to all appearance) with tins and broken bottles, but not for even a token assault on the layer of grime that clung to every visible square inch of the roof, its network of supporting girders and the otherwise bare brick walls. These last were partly hidden by broad strips of hessian or sacking hung so as to form a series of curtains along all four sides of the building, whether to mitigate draughts or for acoustic reasons or in the interests of decoration I could not tell, nor did I at any time inquire. The stage, a low wooden platform looking at once unfinished and not far from collapse, was occupied by jerking anthropoid figures with musical instruments or microphones in their grasp, and surrounded in depth by enough electronic equipment to mount a limited thermonuclear strike. Nobody who still retains his sense of hearing, I suppose, can properly claim to have experienced a deafening noise, but that was how I immediately felt like describing what was coming out of the loudspeakers, and was to continue feeling, too, with remarkable persistence, every time it started up again after an interval and now and then while it was simply going on. The element I was trying to breathe seemed not so much gaseous as fluid, or even some rarefied form of gelatin that shuddered constantly under the swipes of immense invisible ping-pong bats. It smelt of tennis shoes, hair and melting insulation, and was fearfully hot.

If the place itself had the look of the hastiest possible adaptation to human occupancy, the audience – five hundred strong? a thousand? – might have been making it their home for weeks. They were not exactly all lying about, standing, strolling, chatting, making mild love, beginning to dance, buying and selling, preparing food, but neither were they all sitting in the rows of unfolded folding seats attending to what they, or some number of them, must have paid money in order to witness. Every few feet were plastic carrier bags, radios, footwear and clothing discarded momentarily or for good, coloured newspapers of strange format, textiles that might have been blankets or stoles or things intermediate, and the already substantial foundations of piles of general litter. Here and there I could make out an ordinary human being: journalist, performer's parent or ill-instructed queer.

A degenerate descendant of Charles II came and took Roy away. My own guide, a girl (so I provisionally decided), escorted me to the end of a row, or lateral straggle, in which I recognized Terry Bolsover, a tremendous visual achievement amid the prevailing hairiness. Near him was a vacant chair.

The person with me articulated quite clearly, and yet without seeming to shout much, 'You can go closer if you like.'

'No thanks,' I bawled, 'I think I can get everything I want from here.'

'Sorry?'

'This'll do.'

Those sitting, sprawling, lying between the aisle and Bolsover made no attempt to move themselves or their belongings out of my path, but showed no vexation when I kicked, trod on, fell over booted foot or bulging string-bag. Bolsover looked up at my approach and made quite a show of checking what would have been an inaudible roar of laughter. I pulled my chair up to his and began wiping steam off my glasses.

'You here for the paper or just giving your pal moral support?' he asked in the same style of utterance as that I had heard a moment earlier: an occupational skill, no doubt, such as foundry workers and warship deck-hands must have to develop. I tried to imitate it when I answered,

'Moral support, yes. I don't know about the paper yet.'

'Eh? Look, hold it until this lot's over. There can't be much more.'

I mimed a question.

'Because he's already pretended to be going to stop and been carried away into going on twice. Three times is the usual limit for that one. Here, it's just coming up now.'

I looked at the stage. Sure enough, the young man who had been making most of the vocal noise, and whose body had so far merely been making stylized copulatory movements, plainly began to suffer the effects of some convulsant poison, perhaps conveyed into his bloodstream by blow-pipe dart: in its way an impressive sight.

'Yeah, this'll be it,' said Bolsover.

It was. What followed it surprised me mildly: hardly a scream, not a single whistle that I could hear, a small amount of ordinary yelling, nothing to compare with the pervading loud but fairly steady hubbub, like that of a cocktail-party on its second drink, that might well have been going on at much the same level underneath the din from the stage. I reasoned that no one turns enthusiastic about the maintenance of his natural environment; as well cheer when water comes out of a turned tap, give the milkman a standing ovation. When I tried it, I found I could converse with Bolsover as easily as if we had been in a record-breaking train.

'Are there any more acts before Roy comes on?'

'Acts? Oh, I get you. No, this bunch do one more, then it's Pigs Out with their ... like their latest hit number, you see, Doug. Then your bloke comes on and does his stuff with them. Did you say you were writing it up for the paper?'

'Harold wants me to. He says people would think it was interesting to have two different points of view on the same event. I don't think I shall want to.'

'There can't be more than about eleven people in England who read you and read me.'

'There can, I'm afraid. Anyway, I told him something of the sort, and he said that didn't matter: people would still think it was interesting.'

'I sort of get it. Could I pick your brains a bit on the classical side later? I won't go into it, that's your style, but just so's I don't say pizzicato when I mean 7/4 time. I'll do the same for you.'

'Thanks.'

'Nice fellow, old Sir Roy, I thought when I went up to see him. Makes you feel brilliant, doesn't he? There wasn't anything came up he didn't go on as if I knew ten times more about it than he did.'

'Including music?'

'You mean classical? In a kind of way. Like of course he *knew* more, but what would a bloody great genius like me care? Sort of, me witch-doctor, you heap big American scientist with computers and all. Does he always go on like that?'

'No. Only sometimes.'

'There was a parson down the youth club I used to go to . . . Here we go again. Full of piss they are, actually. Not much in them for me, never mind you.'

The ensuing stretch of time recalled to me a night I had once passed in the grip of a fairly severe throat infection. I had had a series of vivid, realistic dreams that each appeared to cover the events of an hour, an afternoon, a whole day, and had awoken again and again in a sweat, frightened or just bewildered, but with the thought that anyhow morning must now be appreciably nearer, to find something like two minutes had elapsed since my last awakening. So, there in the dirty vastness of the tram shed, my mind seemed to be plunging and skidding towards and through everything I could remember or imagine, seemed to be when measured against the all but stationary hands of my watch. When I put my fingers in my ears it was worse. I was very relieved when it came to me from somewhere or other that I had felt like this, though less intensely, in the Dug-out at the start of the night of the favour. It had been Penny's arrival that had put an end to that phase.

I had just decided to try to think about her when those on the stage stopped doing what they were doing and began to go away. Hubbub was restored, somewhat louder than before. Next to me, Bolsover had turned preoccupied, once or twice scribbling a couple of lines in a notebook of incongruously neat appearance. What were presumably Pigs Out appeared before us one by one. I registered a strong impression that, should the choice arise, I would reject them in favour of a joint Nazi-Soviet tribunal as arbiters of my destiny, then heeded them no more. A man aged between twenty and sixty, wearing a shoulder-length wig that might or might not have been made of fine silver wire and clothes that glittered fiercely all over, spoke over the loudspeakers in tones of clangorous wheedling. Then the noise was back.

Penny. When I tried to think consecutively about her, I found that my mental traction had slipped out of overdrive into bottom gear. It was hard even to remember what she looked like. I worked at it, but every time her image showed signs of clearing and steadying, my surroundings shook it out of focus again. In the end I clutched at a single idea and held on to it: that I would telephone her and try to get her to come down to the flat while Gilbert was on one of his nature rambles. Another thought swam up alongside, to do with something having happened or been said to me recently that had engendered the first thought, but a drum solo put paid to that.

After several false stops, the noise came to an end. The silver-wigged man stepped up and delivered a mixture of misstatements and (to me) unpalatable half- and three-quarter-truths about Roy, who presently came into view carrying his violin case. The ambient hubbub grew, became mildly enthusiastic, but I fancied that some of the enthusiasm had an ironical edge to it. So, it seemed, did Bolsover.

'I don't know why some people come,' he said. 'The bunch who went on first tonight have got a couple of queers on guitars, it's well known. That lot up the front gave them the hell of a time. I don't know why they come.'

'Roy's not queer.'

'No.'

'What is he, then, from their point of view? Old?'

'Yeah,' said Bolsover, implying in the monosyllable that that was only about half the story and that he was not going to tell the other half.

'I see.'

By now, with a grinning jauntiness that made me want to turn my eyes away, Roy had taken his fiddle and bow out of their case, disposed of the case, and shaped up to begin playing without further ado. I had never before known him to reach this stage without careful, even fussy, preparatory tuning. My heart fell. He had stopped caring. Or perhaps – my heart rose again a notch – he had reasoned that, apart from himself, me and any other professional critics who might be present, nobody would notice a disparity of pitch smaller than about a semitone. The hubbub sank to the level one might expect from a soccer crowd just before the appearance of the teams – a solemn hush by the standards prevailing.

Pigs Out squared themselves and played a short series of what they probably thought of as chords, during which the bongoes rattled and thumped. Roy lifted his bow – giving it, I thought, an inquisitive glance – and, as Pigs Out fell silent, brought it down across the violin strings. A faint slithering and squeaking, not altogether unlike that of rats in a cellar, was all that resulted. On the stage, general bafflement followed; elsewhere, heightened hubbub.

'Bum mike,' said Bolsover. 'Bloody bad luck. Still, they can –'

'I don't think it's that. It sounds to me as if someone's doctored his bow. Grease or oil of some sort. Anybody could –'

'Fuck me!' thundered Roy's amplified voice, refuting Bolsover's diagnosis.

The audience loved that. They also loved Roy's hurried production of his spare bow, his equally speedy discovery that it too was unusable, the intervention of the silver-wigged man, and the whole thing. The lot up the front identified by Bolsover loved it most. I could see Roy thinking, and could guess at least one of his thoughts: that it would take much too long to find by telephone some fellow-violinist who was not out at a concert, or just out, and have a bow of his or hers brought to this comparatively remote spot. Then he was struck by a thought I could not guess. Turning away from his microphone as he spoke, he said,

'I wonder if there's a doogher-boogh boogh aboogh.'

The silver-wigged man left the platform at a run. In the ensuing minute or two, the hubbub grew further and became less generally amiable. At one point, Roy turned towards his microphone again, and I was very much afraid he was about to harangue the audience on the repressive tolerance of bourgeois society, or perhaps lead them in some revolutionary community singing, but he changed his mind, followed a style more deeply rooted in him, and stood gazing over everybody's head with admirable impassivity. In the end, the silver-wigged man returned bearing what I recognized as a double-bass bow. Roy took it from him and nodded authoritatively at Pigs Out.

'But Christ,' said Bolsover, 'that thing's only about half the size.'

'He can make a fair shot at it. He's a professional, you see. And anyway, it's not as if –'

Elevations 9 began again, and this time continued. I devoted myself to the horrible task of listening to everything that was being played: the popping of the bongoes, the wailing of the sitar and the sticky thudding of the bass guitar as well as Roy's *obbligato*. This started off with some passage-work that, while probably exacting enough even for a performer equipped with the right kind of bow, made no demands on the listener – indeed, a contemporary of Brahms could quite safely have gone out for a pee during it. About the time that such a one would have been returning to his seat, however, Pigs Out took on a more subordinate role and the character of the violin part changed. Having calculated (I guessed) that by now, if ever, the audience would be reconciled to the fact and sound of a violin, Roy was going to show off his paces as a transmedial innovator. Or so he might have put it to himself. What he proceeded to play, still cleanly enough to an untrained ear, was a set of variations on his theme in, or not far from, a jazz style that even I knew had faded out thirty years before, round about the end of his student career. I remembered once having had to let him play me half a dozen thoroughly scratched records of some jazz fiddler of that epoch, an American with an Italian name, and thought now that I recognized one or two of the man's turns of phrase. I could have had no better proof, had I wanted one or known any use to put it to, of the total failure of recent or contemporary products of the pop industry to impress themselves on Roy's musical consciousness. Well, that was something.

Perhaps, in their unimaginably cruder way, those about me had come to a roughly similar judgement on what Roy was offering them, perhaps it was just too unfamiliar to be borne. At any rate, a momentary increase in the nearby hubbub distracted my attention from the stage sufficiently to bring it home to me that the central aisle, in which earlier there had been about as much movement to and fro as in a village street on a fairly busy morning, was now more than half full of people shuffling unhurriedly but steadily in one direction: towards the door. I drove my mind back to its business. Some sort of climax evidently approached: the fiddle mounted to a high note and held it, Pigs Out did another series of as it were chords and sustained one that quite closely resembled that of the 6/4 on the dominant – the signal, in the true classical style, that the accompanying forces are about to shut up while the soloist displays his technical skill in a cadenza.

I felt my cheeks burn. Absurdity amounting to outrage – how many of those still inside this abode of muck would recognize the 'wit' and 'piquancy' of this last transmedial stroke, or would fail to jeer at it in the rare event that they did? And what followed was worse: a passage of fast double-stopping into which Roy was putting everything he had, making what must have been troublesome enough with a violin bow, and quite fiendishly difficult with the short and clumsy double-bass bow, sound natural, effortless, easy. Oh God, I thought, how could he not know that this lot positively disliked the idea of the difficult being made to seem easy, seem anything at all, exist in any form – that what they liked was the easy seeming easy?

Without sparing me the trill on the supertonic that classically heralds the return of the accompaniment, Roy was briefly reunited with Pigs Out and brought his composition to a close in something like silence. Distant hubbub marked the departure of the last of the audience, except for a few individuals like Bolsover and myself. *Elevations 9* had been a complete flop. I had devoutly hoped it would be, and yet I found myself overwhelmed with feelings of anticlimax and defeat.

Bolsover lit a cigarette. 'Was it any good from your point of view?'

'No. It was . . . No. Was it any good from yours?'

'No. I'll have to put something about it in my piece, but not much. I might ring you, if that's all right. See you in the office, anyway.'

We got up and began to move along the row of empty seats.

'Right. All the best, Terry.'

'Look, Doug, I should get the maestro away a bit smart if I were you. There's some rather gaunt lads here tonight. I've seen a couple of them round the festivals, turning messy. The maestro's enough out of the ordinary to take their eye.'

'I'd better go and find him, then. Thanks.'

Lights were already being switched off and equipment dismantled when I came upon Roy on the far side of the stage. He, the silver-wigged one and a Pigs Out or so were standing in reflective silence near a low doorway through which (imagination suggested without trouble) overalled men carrying toolkits had once been accustomed to arrive on errands of repair and maintenance. Roy, violin case in hand, looked round at me with a fixed grin.

'There you are, old lad. I was just saying, it might have been as well if I'd accepted defeat when I had the chance.'

'I suppose it might.'

'Don't worry: I'm not going to ask you what you thought of it. That can keep, among other things. Anyway, the majority view was clear enough.'

'Dead ignorant,' said somebody.

'Lot of sheep,' said somebody else. 'One goes, next thing they've all gone.'

'Let's be off,' I said to Roy.

'Indeed let's. A drink and a chat somewhere or other, I think. Good night, everybody. My sincere thanks and apologies.'

After some handshakes, protests that no apologies were called for, and general Roying, the two of us made our way in near-darkness along the side of the building towards the main entrance, opposite which Roy had parked his car.

'Roy, I want to say I'm sorry about –'

'Don't say anything for now, Duggers, if you don't mind. Not another word until we're clear of this remarkably unwholesome spot.'

We reached the area round the entrance, which was crowded with chatting and dispersing groups. My eye fell immediately on a tall young man in a suede-and-leather jacket who turned briefly to the half-dozen others standing near him and led them across to bar our path.

'Hey, it's Sir Roy Vandervane,' said the leader. 'With his awful old violin. I say, fellows, let's be frightful rotters and take it off him.'

He made a token, indeed balletic, grab in the direction of the case; token or not, I took off my glasses and put them in the top pocket of my coat. Roy did a wriggling shrug.

'Yeah, well I know it ding go,' he said in his worst accent and a matey tone. 'Can't win 'em aw, you know.'

'Let's go, Roy.'

'Still, I thought Pigs Out did okay, din you?'

'Piss off,' said the boy in the jacket. 'Right, let's have it.'

This time he made a real grab for the case, while two of his mates seized Roy by the arms. Two others converged on me. As the leader swung away with the case in his hand, I hit him behind the ear and dropped him to his knees, which caused him inadvertently to slam the case down on the pavement. Somebody's head butted me in the stomach and brought my own head down. A knee came up, missing my face but connecting with my collar-bone hard enough to knock me over. As I fell, I was conscious of a silence spreading outwards round us. Before I could get up, somebody's foot swung at me; I caught it and twisted it and it slipped from my grasp. Another foot struck me in the back, not hard: whoever it was, I reflected, was merely going through the motions of inflicting damage. Now I did get to my feet, and began an inconclusive struggle with probably two people. I could hear panting and scuffling, and the splintering of wood, and then the dreadful sound of what I knew was a human head striking the pavement, and then running feet. I took a kick in the shin and was free. An arm came round my shoulders.

'Are you all right?' asked a frightened voice, that of a young man in a bluish corduroy suit.

'Yes. Thanks.'

Some way off, figures were fast receding into the darkness; at least one of them was a policeman. Nearer at hand were the violin case, its lid half ripped off, and Roy's Stradivarius in half a dozen pieces, held together here and there by its strings. Two girls were bending over Roy himself, who lay still. Voices called in the distance. More people began to arrive.

'Now are you sure you're all right?'

'Yes, honestly, Viv, absolutely. Just a couple of bruises.'

'It didn't sound like that in the paper.' Vivienne's voice over the telephone was distrustful, as if she suspected me of covering up a broken back for motives of vanity or financial betterment.

'Well, you know what they're like. All I really am is tired. I had to talk to the police, and then it took them God knows how long at the hospital before they were sure Roy hadn't fractured his skull and I could come home.'

'So he's all right after all, then.' This time, the implication was very roughly that Roy's cranium was of that special hardness commonly found among show-offs, adulterers, etc.

'Well, up to a point. A bang on the head can have all sorts of odd effects. They haven't given him a clean bill of health yet. Comfortable, was all they'd say when I rang them just now. I'm going along there later.'

'When will that be, about?'

'When I've summoned the energy. Probably about eleven. Why?'

'I thought we could have lunch together.'

'Fine. Shall I pick you up at the office?'

It was arranged that I should do so at twelve fifteen, returning her at one fifteen. The less than ideal time and duration of her regular lunch-break had meant that we rarely met in the middle of the day, and I would be seeing her that evening as usual, but I relished the thought of an earlier chance of telling her all about what had happened last night, plus whatever was going to happen at the hospital. Before I went there I had a couple of hours to fill in. This I managed without any trouble at all, shaving at *adagio sostenuto* pace instead of my usual *allegro con brio*, playing the gramophone (only records I had already reviewed, and nothing by Weber or any of his contemporaries, so that the remotest possible suggestion of work was rigorously excluded), falling asleep, and trying to wonder effectively what was going to happen about Roy's Mahler concerts.

The day was hot and hazy. I was sweating while, in the gloomy vestibule of the hospital, I tried to find someone who could tell me who to ask where Roy was. Eventually, after provoking much bafflement and a couple of rebukes, I was confronted by a middle-aged woman in grey who wanted to know if I was a reporter. I said I was not, gave my name, was asked if I were not the one who had been with Sir Roy when he was admitted, agreed that that was the one I was, received directions and climbed a great many stairs.

Roy was in a private room, sitting up in bed with newspapers and wearing what amounted to a lopsided white skull-cap. Otherwise he looked quite normal.

'Good old Duggers.'

'How are you, Roy?'

'Fit as a fiddle, old lad. They . . .' His face went loose. 'Though that's hardly the . . .'

He stopped speaking and drew in his breath. I was afraid he was going to cry, and that, if he did, I would do the same.

'There are others,' I said.

'Not enough others. You probably know four hundred odd were destroyed in the last war. But even if they hadn't been, there still wouldn't be enough. Oh, I'll find one all right, but it won't be the same one. Do you know, I'd had the bloody old thing for nearly twenty-nine years? Played my first concert on it. The Max Bruch war-horse. Anyway, in answer to your kind inquiry, I have five stitches, they say no concussion to speak of, and I should be out some time tomorrow, with a couple of days' rest afterwards. Balls to the last bit – there's Gus to think of. George' – the leader of the N.L.S.O. – 'is keeping them at it today and tomorrow, but I'll have to be back waving the stick the morning after that.'

I nodded. Roy grinned at me and shook his head slowly.

'A very neat job, Duggers. What did you use?'

'Butter. Finest New Zealand. I didn't mean it to happen as it did. I thought you'd find out as soon as you started tuning, or earlier. I'm sorry you had –'

'Not at all, it was highly dramatic. A bit of a surprise, though. On reflection, I mean. I hadn't realized you'd follow up your principles quite that far into practice.'

'I felt I had to do something.'

'Most laudable. Did you just sit there in the writing-room and smear away?'

'The Gents.'

'One likes to have the full picture. Well, it seems you were wasting your time.'

'So I saw and heard.'

'No, I mean the critical reception, so to call it. Have you seen the *Orb* this morning? Very quick off the mark.'

I took the folded sheets. 'Violinist-composer Roy Vandervane Blazes New Trail,' announced Barry somebody, and went on to declare that, despite a technical hold-up and an unappreciative audience and never mind about the deplorable scene that followed (see page 3), he considered himself privileged to have been present at the birth of a new this, that and the other which would surely lead to further exciting what-have-you. Before he ended, Barry drew a staggeringly learned comparison with the hostile reception given leading nineteenth-century German composer Ludwig van Beethoven's pioneering First Symphony.

'Terrified of being caught out being square,' I said. 'Like all of them.'

'Except you. Yes, there's a slightly shorter piece in the *Flyer*. Care for a flip-through?'

'No thanks.'

'Your piece comes out on Friday, doesn't it?'

'Yes.'

'So you'll be able to give it mature consideration.'

'Yes.'

'You thought it was piss, didn't you?'

'Yes. Everything about it except your own performance.'

'Thanks.' Roy settled himself back against his pillows. 'So you see it wasn't quite such a flop as we all thought. Mind you, last night taught me quite a bit. The sort of chamber concerto approach was a mistake. The kids got too much of me and not enough of Pigs Out. I'll give them a lot more to do next time. Quartet style, or quintet with a lead guitar added.'

A weary incredulity possessed me. 'Next time?'

'Oh, Spiro Agnew! You don't suppose I'm going to let myself be choked off by one adverse reaction like that, do you? Nobody would ever –'

'I've given up supposing where you're concerned,' I said, advancing on him. 'I can just see you next time, or after next time, when one of them's broken all the bones in your left hand, explaining that the time after that it might be a good idea to introduce a vibraphone and a tenor sax. You learnt a lot last night, did you? You didn't learn the most obvious lesson anybody could possibly have in his whole life. You're just incapable of . . .'

I stopped speaking because somebody else had come into the room. From the flash of white I caught at the corner of my eye, I momentarily took the newcomer for a nurse or other hospital person, but it was Sylvia, wearing a long coat that might once have belonged to an undersized cricket umpire or professional house-painter, though not undersized enough, in the sense that it was still too big for her, or would have been considered so by the vanishing minority of which I suddenly felt myself a member. Her hair had been sprayed with glue while she stood in a wind-tunnel – at that stage I could think of no other explanation for its appearance; her eyelids were dark green. She went straight across to Roy and started what gave every promise of being a long bout of embraces, interspersed with whispers. I moved to the window and saw a block of flats, red brick and stucco with little balconies, on one of which a large white dog hurried to and fro like a tiger in a cage.

'Why's he here?' asked Sylvia behind me.

'Now, Sylvia. Duggers came to see how I am.'

'He's seen, hasn't he?'

'Why's she here?' I asked, turning. 'If you don't mind my

putting it like that. I mean I thought Harold had put a stop to things.'

Roy gave a rich laugh and looked up at Sylvia with admiring affection. 'We think we've rather put a stop to him putting a stop, don't we, darling? That ole counter-measure we've been working on, Duggers, there's a better than even chance it's going to pay off, from what I've just heard. Fix everything.'

'Everything?'

'Yes, everything,' said Sylvia. 'Like him and me going off together and there's nothing you can do to stop it, or anybody else.'

'I see.'

With a show of great seriousness and strength of mind, Roy said, 'Go on with what you were saying, Duggers. About last night.'

'There's no point. Not now.'

'Yes there is. I want to hear.'

'You want to be able to tell yourself you listened to every word and you had to admit in fairness I was right in a way but it's just something you'll have to live with, and then you'll forget all about it.'

'Get out,' said Sylvia, who had evidently appreciated my tone, if nothing more. 'Get out of here and out of our lives. You're nothing but a big *druhg*. Nobody wants you around.'

'Shut up,' I said.

She started to move round the bed towards me with something of the same demeanour as when she had been about to grapple with Kitty. I picked up the water-jug from the bedside table.

'If you come near enough I'll pour this all over your head.'

'Ah now, be a *good* darling.'

One appeal or the other took its effect: she sat down on the bed with her back to me. Roy reached out and held her hand.

'Fire away, Duggers.'

'All right. I cannot understand, I will never understand, how you can even consider going on with this youth thing of yours after what happened last night. They didn't want you there; they felt you were out of place. And by God they showed it . . .'

'Oh, for Christ's sake, that was just a gang of bloody hoods. A tiny minority. You get them everywhere. You're not going to tell me they were representative of the whole –'

'Yes I am. In a way. Nobody tried to intervene, did they? They just stood by, because they –'

'People don't intervene. That happens everywhere too.'

'Oh yes they do intervene, at that kind of do. Punch-ups galore. Rival bands of youths, as they say.'

'Duggers, you'll really have to show me your birth certificate to prove you're not sixty-five. Young people don't consist exclusively of rival bands of youths. If there had been a rival band of youths there it had gone home. And Jesus, even if there had been one around it wouldn't have had time to do anything. You're talking complete ballocks.'

'All right, perhaps I am, on that. But the fact remains that that bunch were putting into action what the others were feeling. Partly – I mean not all of them can have felt aggressive towards you, but I bet the vast majority were out of sympathy with you. Last night, I thought they got up and left because they were bored. That too, no doubt, but now I realize the chief thing was that they were embarrassed. At the sight of somebody quite old enough, easily and demonstrably old enough to know better, making an exhibition of himself. Like seeing your auntie doing a strip. It wasn't your scene, dad, and it never will be.'

Sylvia began to speak, but Roy silenced her, perhaps by twisting her wrist. He kept his eyes on me as he had for the last minute, with the artless, total concentration of a man who is thinking about something else. I saw that I had been talking, and was going to go on talking, so that I could tell myself afterwards I had said everything, just as he was going to tell himself he had heard everything, but I went on all the same.

'You know what I honestly expected, after last night? After your piece had failed and you'd been beaten up and had your Strad smashed – which is like having your child maimed. Isn't it, Roy? After that I honestly expected you to swear to have nothing more to do with any of it, no more pop, no more youth, no more new ways of this and that – and then to sneak back to it bit by bit after a month or two. But here you are, twelve hours later, full of horrible plans for more of the same. That's frightening. You're going downhill faster and faster. I only hope you hold up long enough not to disgrace yourself and humiliate the orchestra over the Mahler. After that's over I advise you to retire to one of those places in California where nobody knows anything or notices anything. I'll be off now. Oh . . .'

Remembering, I brought out the half-bottle of Scotch I had been carrying in my coat pocket, and put it on the bedside table.

'Christ, Duggers, that's a handsome gesture, I must say. Thanks a lot.'

'I should hide it if I were you. Well, goodbye. You bloody fool. And good luck. To both of you.'

'Be in touch, old lad.'

Outside, I came to an unfrequented stretch of corridor, stopped, and kicked the wall several times, also hitting it once or twice with my fists. 'Fuck,' I said. 'Shit. Oh, God.' Then I saw and heard a trolley being pushed round a nearby corner, so I made for the stairs, and was soon outside the building in the same hot haze.

I still had nearly three-quarters of an hour in hand before meeting Vivienne, but there was nothing I wanted to do except in the world of theory, like getting drunk or rushing off to a brothel. I walked up through Hyde Park thinking of things I wished I had said to Roy, to do with Kitty and Penny and Ashley and such, and deciding that none of it would have done any good. At Marble Arch I got on a bus, then got off it again on finding there was nothing to distract me from the same cycle of thoughts. Making my way on foot along densely crowded pavements was better from that point of view, if from no other. I reached the airline office at eighteen minutes past twelve, collected Vivienne and took her across the road to a chain eatery of the sort that serves wine by the glass and beer to those devil-may-care few of its customers who want them.

We ate scampi and spinach and I told Vivienne my story, to the later sections of which she responded with what I took to be sullenness-cum-preoccupation, low intensity, preoccupation the more marked of the two. I told myself she had never approved of Roy. Then, over apple pie and cream, she said,

'Doug, I've got something to tell you. I might be going to marry Gilbert.'

A piece of apple fell out of my mouth. I said, 'Who?'

'Gilbert Alexander. That West Indian chap. You know him.'

'Yes, I know him, but I don't know you know him. I mean I didn't know you knew him. How do you know him?'

'I met him on your doorstep.'

'But that was only for a minute.'

'Just long enough for him to say good evening, and would I like to have a drink with him some time, and I said I couldn't then, and he said of course not, but would I write my name and telephone number on a blank page of a book he had with him, and he had his ballpoint out all ready and he just didn't give me time to think why to say no.'

'But this was only last week, last –'

'We're not getting married anything like yet. We're getting engaged.'

'But nobody gets engaged these days.'

'He says where he comes from they do. When they get married at all, that is. And they used to where I came from. I don't suppose they've stopped, either.'

'Does your father know?'

'Yes, I took Gilbert up for a drink yesterday evening. And the opposite to what you might think, he doesn't mind him being black at all.'

'I wasn't thinking anything about that.'

'Oh, Doug, don't be silly, of course you were. If you want to know what I think, the trouble with most black people isn't that they're black. Who could possibly mind that? – unless they were all prejudiced and horrible. It's a lovely colour. Anyway, it's never really black, not jet black. Even if it was, it would probably still be nice. No, what's wrong with a lot of black people is that they're Negroid, with great big lips and spread-out noses and the rest of it. But Gilbert's different: he looks like a dark-brown Englishman. Great.'

'I shouldn't have thought that was enough to get married on the score of.'

'Of course it isn't. What it is, he's my type. The sort of thing I mean, he interferes with my life. He makes me do some things and stops me doing others.'

'The masterful male.'

'Yes, that's right.'

'I thought we'd all managed to get beyond that stage.'

'Well, we all haven't.'

Coffee arrived at that point, and I extracted the bill at the same time. A memory from last night returned, bringing with it an explanation: I had thought about Penny with new resolve because I had unknowingly sensed a basic and (to me) adverse change in Vivienne's life. But I still hardly believed in it.

'It isn't just me wanting to be dominated the whole time,' resumed Vivienne. 'But when you care about someone, you've got to interfere with their life now and then. It's all part of it. I interfere with his over some things. For instance, he's a bit silly about being black, and I don't let him get away with any of that.'

'You sound as if you and he have spent about six months together.'

'It feels rather like that. We did spend the whole of yesterday together.'

'You took the day off? You've never done that before.'

'Not to be with you, no. You never asked me to. And here's more of what I mean. I've got bad taste in clothes and everything, haven't I? Give me an honest answer, Doug. You can now.'

'Yes, you have.'

'But you never told me, because you were being the unmasterful male. Not interfering. Gilbert told me straight away. He went through the whole of my wardrobe and picked out about five things and said I could keep them, but I was never to wear any of the others again. Same with my jewellery and stuff.'

After a moment, I said, 'What does you being engaged mean exactly?'

'Well, I got rid of that chap with the beard right off.'

'And now you're getting rid of me.'

'I hope so. No, Doug, the point is, you know about me liking being shared, because I like a lot of, you know, because I'm a bit . . .'

'Highly sexed.'

'I suppose so. Anyway, Gilbert doesn't approve of that, me being shared, I mean. Decadent, he calls it. He says he'd think the same whether I was having anything to do with him or not, and I believe him. And I agree with him, really. So, we're going to be engaged for three months and if I haven't had to be shared or missed being shared too much in that time, then we'll get married.'

'I see.' I paused again, then said as genially as possible, 'Of course, these blokes are supposed to be greatly gifted, aren't they? That would make up to some extent for . . .'

During our association, Vivienne had done her fair share of laughing, but mostly, I realized, out of high spirits or in response to a full-grown external joke, at the cinema and so on, not as now. 'Fancy someone like you thinking there's something in that. Oh, I know a lot of people do. Girls. Gilbert says quite a lot of stuff's come his way because they think – you know. If you're interested,' – she blushed and looked down at her coffee-cup, but with a silent snigger – 'it's just like yours, only black.'

I counted out money. 'So as far as that's concerned, you could have got engaged to me instead.'

'Yes, I could, except you never asked me, and I always knew really you were never going to. I suppose I took you along to see my father just in case it might make you think of it. Anyway, there's Penny, isn't there? Gilbert told me all about that. Now he's gone, you can move in. Or she can with you.'

I considered in silence. Actual moving-in either way round was surely out of the question; the general prospect of some sort of affair with Penny struck me as attractive but irrelevant, like the free offer of a new and prodigious set of hi-fi equipment.

'Gilbert thinks it would be a good idea. He doesn't want her to be left on her own. He's quite worried about her.'

'But not worried enough to stay with her.'

'Not now, no, but he thinks you might be able to tide her over for a bit. I must go, Doug.'

In the street, her manner, which had cooled rather in the last minute, warmed up again. She took my arm.

'Dad's having a few friends and neighbours in for drinks tomorrow about six, sort of a very informal unofficial engagement-party. I mean the engagement's unofficial as well as the party. Can you come?'

'Oh, you won't want me there, will you, you and Gilbert?'

'Yes we will. I will, because of you and me, and he will, because he thinks he owes you an apology, he says.'

'What for?'

'Well, he has taken your girl-friend off you, hasn't he?'

I looked into her clear brown eyes and at her firm mouth. 'Yes, he has, hasn't he? But tell him there are no hard feelings.'

We halted on the kerb opposite her office, between pedestrians and hurrying traffic.

'Can you come tomorrow?'

'I'll have to see,' I said. (What I would have to see was whether Penny would be at home and available later the following evening, when attendance at the informal-etc. party would have brought me nearly three-quarters of the way to her on the good old North-Western Line.) 'I'll make it if I possibly can.'

'Mind you do. Don't bother to come across the road with me: let's say goodbye here. I don't mean completely, of course, but – you know.'

'Yes, of course.'

'Thank you for being so sweet about everything.'

'I haven't been sweet at all.'

'Yes you have. Because of what you haven't said and haven't made me feel. You should have heard the way the bloke with the beard went on. Letting him down and letting myself down. I expect you can imagine.'

'Yes, I think I can.'

We embraced and kissed briefly. I could not see her eyes when she turned away, but her mouth had lost its firmness. Her figure, trim in the olive uniform, and strong-looking in a sense that had not struck me before, moved confidently across to the far pavement and, after a final hasty wave at her office doorway, disappeared.

I went back to the flat and wrote my piece for the paper, half of it about a new opera just then going into rehearsal, the other and slightly longer half about *Elevations 9*.

'Was it really as bad as you say?' asked Harold.

'Well yes. Even worse, if anything. I haven't gone into the way he used classical conventions to –'

'I hear all the other notices so far have been wildly favourable.'

'Not all. The *Custodian* this morning was very stuffy.'

Harold shifted his gaze from my copy to what appeared to be another sheet of typescript beside it on his desk. 'On this piece of . . . popsical music the kids voted with their feet, and only that noted sense of duty kept me from going along . . . mixture never got to the boil . . . somewhere between three stools. That's young Bolsover.'

'I know; he was –'

'The point of sending the two of you to cover the same event was to get two quite different points of view, and here you are both taking the same line.'

'It isn't the same line. From our quite different points of view, we each decided independently and for our own reasons that there was nothing in it for either of us.'

'A line which runs directly counter to the general verdict. We've talked before about the dangers of eccentricity for its own sake. Independence is one thing, but can't you find a redeeming feature or so? The technique of it, or something like that?'

'You can't talk about technique as if it were . . . No, Harold, and I don't think you'll get Terry to shift either.'

'All right, all right.'

'And you hate him. Roy, I mean.'

'I'm running a newspaper. How is he?'

'He'll be out of hospital some time today.'

'I'm sorry to hear that. They ought to have kicked his head in while they were about it. Still, in general they showed him up for the oaf he is.'

Perhaps for the first time since I had known him, warmth had entered Harold's voice, and, certainly for the first time, he looked me straight in the face. One more mini-mystery seemed cleared up: I had been included in the Retrenchment Club lunch-party not out of indifference but by design, so that I might witness my friend's discomfiture.

'You don't know him,' I said. 'You wouldn't –'

'One thing you can do for me.' Already he was back in his poky little shell. 'I want no further dealings with him, so you tell him he's won. I'll make no further move to interfere.'

I stood and waited, in the substantial hope that Harold's style of oral free-association would see to it that my curiosity was satisfied.

'It was much more damaging than the piece I was threatening to print. The two of them must have got together on it. No newspaper would take it, but *Peeping Tom* isn't a newspaper. You remember what they did to that actor chap last year, and he didn't get a bean out of them. Even if you win, they've nothing to pay you with. And you're fired.'

'Yes, I imagine you are,' I said, taking the last remark as a mildly fanciful description of what happened to you, or how you felt, when you tried to sue *Peeping Tom*.

'No no. *You're . . . fired.*'

'Oh, I see.'

'I'll make out a cheque for four weeks' worth and send it along to you.'

'Thanks. This is the next best thing to getting at Roy himself. Not a very good next best.'

'Better than nothing, and that's only part of it. Just the timing. I don't care for what you write. I was against hiring you in the first place, as you know.'

'No, Harold, I don't know. You told me it was all your idea.'

'Rubbish, you're dreaming. Good morning to you.'

Along in Features, I told Coates and Bolsover my news.

'It's the way he keeps thinking up new ways of being a shit

that you can't help taking your hat off to him for,' said Coates.

'So perhaps sacking me as well'd seem a bit tame,' said Bolsover. 'How much actual difference will it make to you?'

'Not an enormous amount. I can more or less walk into a small spot with *Discs and Listening*. And I've got a contact in Brandenburg Records. But it's a bit unsettling.'

'Come over to the Fleece and I'll buy you a beer,' said Coates.

'I owe you one. Several, in fact.'

'I'll join you when I've got my okay,' said Bolsover.

'Did I do all right the other night?' asked Coates in the saloon of the Fleece.

'First-class. You gave me all the time I needed.'

'I kept being afraid he'd think balls to it and hang up. How did your end of it go? – whatever it was.'

'As well as could be expected.'

'That's bloody well, isn't it, as well as that?'

'Looked at in one way, I suppose it is, yes.'

I arrived back at the flat about three, with a good deal of beer and some sausages under my belt, and settled down to play the Brahms-Handel Variations. I performed the piece, after a false start or two, with great dash and depth of feeling, but also with an unusually high proportion of wrong notes. Never mind, I thought to myself as I started to fall asleep on the couch – Schnabel had played plenty of wrong notes in his time. Tea, toast, a bath and change saw me through until five, and a long brisk walk, a ride in the Tube, and a shorter, less brisk walk brought me to the Copes doorstep just after six.

Mr Copes himself, wearing a pink-and-white striped jacket that recalled bygone musical comedies with a campus setting, let me in and took me into his study. Here, a couple of dozen people of high average age and rather crude type-casting stood about with curious-looking drinks in their hands. I caught sight of Gilbert face to face with a gesticulating cleric; then Vivienne came out from behind someone, gave me a cousinly kiss, and introduced me to her (elder) brother and sister-in-law, whom I recognized from having seen their photographs, together with a fat and silent aunt-like figure. Vivienne went away again at once, to be replaced by Mr Copes, who handed me a small tumbler containing what I tried, with some success, not to think of as a urine sample drawn from one gravely ill. He was accompanied by a man who could there and then have sat for a left-wing cartoonist assigned to portray a retired major, and who turned out to be called Major somebody.

'See what you think of it, Doug. It's by way of being a little invention of my own.'

Under the silent gaze of five persons, I forestalled, perhaps by the briefest of margins, actual spotlight and/or side-drum roll, and drank. The fluid was both sweet and bitter without blending or reconciling these qualities to any degree, held a powerful tang of something far removed from any liquor I knew – something like roast chestnuts or camphor – had a bubble or two in it and was slightly warm.

'Interesting,' I said.

'Interesting. That's a terrific postcard word, isn't it? Today we saw all round the folk museum; it was very interesting. Spanish champagne, Angostura, and something else I keep very dark. Yes, I think interesting is just about right. You saw what that fellow from Zambia was saying the other day, did you? Or was it Malawi?'

Since Mr Copes was looking at me, it was I who answered, 'No, I don't think so.'

'Oh yes, I promise you. Our Prime Minister was worse than Mr Hitler. I swear to you. Our Prime Minister.'

'Oh, but he's got to say that,' said the younger Copes. 'Home consumption. You don't want to take it too seriously.'

'And we and the South Africans were plotting to massacre the entire black population of Africa.'

'I only wish it was true,' said the major in a cockney whine so exaggerated as to make even me want to ask the name of his regiment.

'Oh, you're joking,' said the younger Copes.

'I bloody am not joking, mate. They're monkeys, that lot, all of 'em.'

'You're not to mind the major,' said Mr Copes. 'He's a bit of a reactionary. I don't feel we should go any further than just invading them all and turning them back into colonies. They'd thank us for it, you know. I'm thinking entirely of them. Unlike the major here. Would you let your daughter marry a black man, Doug?'

'Yes, if she really wanted to.'

'Ah, now that's the point exactly.'

'I'd have forced mine to if I'd had half a chance,' said the major. 'Teach the cow.'

'There, there, Major.' Mr Copes lifted his glass towards his mouth, then quickly lowered it again. 'Of course, it's a silly question, isn't it? One can't prevent them these days. Still, one can exert various sorts of pressure. I'm not going to. I positively wish my daughter to marry a black man – that black man over there, anyway – and I'll tell you why.'

'Don't you think, Dad, perhaps another time . . . ?'

'As many times as you like. I've told Gilbert all about it already. The whole thing is this. She really wants to, because she's bright enough to have foreseen the difficulties, and because she's always got on very well with me and her brothers and everybody and she's never hankered after any different sort of life and background from the ones she's got. And that means she hasn't decided to do this so as to show me or what the major would call teach me or get her own back on anything. She isn't doing it on purpose, if I make myself clear. That's good enough for me. Now you must excuse me while I go round and top up the beakers.'

Given that every glass in sight was at least three-quarters full, this move seemed unnecessary, but Mr Copes took hold of an earthenware jug and set off. The major's suitably bloodshot eyes flickered at mine. After some slow-motion twitches involving his head and shoulders, he whined,

'Not that I wouldn't rather die than make that fellow feel uncomfortable, you understand. Trouble is, I've had some unfortunate experiences of those people. I remember when I was in –'

With the sense of timing that was better developed in her than in any other girl I had ever known, Vivienne came up at this precise point and took me off to talk to two additional girls who worked in her office. That was all right, but their and her sudden withdrawal in favour of three further aunt-types was less welcome, and the later arrival of the gesticulating cleric, who turned out to gesticulate when listening (or not talking) as well as when talking, did little to mend matters. After some minutes of him, I disengaged myself, said goodbye to Mr Copes, and cornered Vivienne under the portrait of Haydn.

'Viv, I'm off.'

'But you've only just come, and we haven't had a chance . . . All right. I'll see you out. Hang on a second.'

By the time we reached the doorstep, Gilbert had joined us. He showed no traces of the scruffiness I had noticed on our recent encounters: this was the Gilbert of our first meeting, smartly and soberly clad. What with Vivienne beside him in her new trouser-suit, the pair of them looked ready for the taking of a commemorative photograph.

'Vivienne tells me you don't need an apology from me,' he said, 'but also I've good reason to be grateful to you. I wanted to tell you that.'

'Thank you, but there's really no . . .'

'But for you I should never have met her, you see. In addition, you've been kind to my friends the Vandervanes.'

'Not to much effect, I'm afraid.'

'You've been of some comfort to them at various times. If you can help Penny in the least, I'd be still more grateful. Perhaps you could let me know how she is.'

'Yes, of course.'

'You must be sure to come and visit us when we're settled. Goodbye for the present, Douglas.'

'Yes. Goodbye, Gilbert.'

We shook hands; then, without either hurry or hesitation, he turned and went back into the house. Vivienne looked at me in silence, rubbing between finger and thumb a head of lavender she had picked from a clump that grew by the wall.

'Why didn't he bring any of his, uh, pals along this evening?' I asked incuriously.

'Said he couldn't get hold of any of them he could be sure they'd behave themselves in time.' Her tone was as flat as mine had been. 'You know, wouldn't start going on about the colour bar and things. He's changed a lot about all that.'

'Really.'

'Doug . . . when I told you about him yesterday and you didn't make a scene or act up or anything, and I said it was sweet of you . . . Well, it still was sweet of you, but it was because you sort of didn't care all that terrifically, wasn't it? Oh, of course you liked me and everything, and you can see I'm not cross or upset, but I'd just like to know. You weren't so off your head about me that you'd try and stop me going, isn't that right?'

'I was very sorry we were packing up and I still am . . .'

'But.'

'All right, but I don't think people should try to stop people doing what they want to do.'

'Because people always know what they want to do without anyone else saying what they want, the other ones. I thought so.' She broke off another head of lavender. 'You're going off to see Penny now, are you?'

'Yes.'

'Do you think you'll be able to help her like Gilbert said?'

'I don't know.'

'Because you mustn't mind me saying this, Doug, but if you're really going to help somebody in the state she's supposed to be in, or actually if you're really going to help anybody at all, then you've got to really do something about it, take it on, do nothing else for a bit, well, not nothing else, but make it your number one priority until it's cleared up or you realize it absolutely can't be, whatever it is.'

'Gilbert tried to really do something about Penny, and he doesn't seem to have got anywhere.'

'I know, I'm not saying you'll always get somewhere if you really try, I'm saying you won't get anywhere if you don't. And at least he really tried.'

'I'm sure he did.'

'Sorry, but I've been thinking about you a lot, these last few days. Isn't it awful? – I was so relieved you didn't make a scene, and I was disappointed too. That's women for you, isn't it? Off you go now – I must get back to those people. I'll give you a ring, probably in a couple of weeks.'

We performed another cousinly embrace and parted. That point about helping others, or not helping others, had been well taken. At various times, Roy, Kitty, Penny and Gilbert had asked me for help. Amount of help actually given: nil. The sort of help I actually gave was assuring Terry Bolsover by telephone that his piece on *Elevations 9* contained no musical solecisms. On the other hand, or more likely the same hand, I had certainly adhered to my self-proclaimed rule about not stopping blokes doing what they wanted to do. Exception: delaying by two minutes Roy's professional and public degradation.

These and similarly disagreeable reflections occupied me until, alighting at the end of the North-Western Line into a still, clear evening, I started feeling apprehensive, and also mildly excited, at the prospect of seeing Penny. By the time I was passing the pond, over which a hawk hovered, a less mild excitement had driven out apprehension. I made my way past some Yandell-high nettles into the courtyard. A moment later, the Furry Barrel's voice rang out from inside the kitchen.

I entered the house through the glass porch and found Penny hurrying towards me. She wore a plain scarlet cotton dress that negated any concept of style or fashion, and looked both desirable and pleased to see me, though tired. I kissed her, hearing as I did so a curious sound from the direction of the kitchen. It proved to herald the approach of the Furry Barrel, not at her usual canter, but laboriously and on three legs. One hind leg, with what looked like a rubber bandage on it, stuck out at an angle, and there was an arrangement of straps over her rump. She hobbled up, smelt me and wagged her abundant tail.

'What's the matter with her?'

'She's broken something, or dislocated something. I'm not quite clear what it is.'

'But she'll be all right?'

'That leg won't, the vet said. She'll always be more or less on three legs.'

'How did it happen?'

'It was Ashley, apparently. I wasn't here, but he must have given her a kicking. He said she tried to bite him.'

'She'd never bite anybody.'

I stooped down and stroked the dog's silky head, feeling as if something dismal had happened right in the middle of my own life and concerns, something major, something irretrievable, as if I had taken a fatally wrong decision years before and only now seen how much I had lost by it.

'She's quite old,' said Penny consolingly.

'Oh, good.'

'You can't blame Ashley.'

'Oh yes you can. And you can blame his parents even more. Where is he, anyway? He's not here, is he?'

'No: Kitty's taken him away for a few days.'

'With a couple of ex-Royal Marine commandos in attendance.'

'A nurse, and she's gone to stay with a friend who's got a little girl of eight and another nurse. Near Brighton.'

'Four against two. They ought to be able to hold the number of animals crippled at a reasonable level. One a day, perhaps.'

'Calm down. Would you like a drink?'

'Yes. Yes, please. Does Roy know about this?'

'Scotch and water?'

'Yes. Does Roy know?'

'Yes, and he was terrifically upset and gave Ashley a frightful bawling-out.'

'And that was that.'

'Well, you know Daddy and Kitty are dead against hitting kids and so on.'

'So they are. Is there anybody else here? Christopher and his girl?'

'They've gone back to Northampton.'

We had moved along the passage, which was lined with piles of empty cardboard cartons, across the hall, where there was a mound of old newspapers and a much bigger one of apparently discarded toys, and into the drawing-room. Here, surprisingly, everything was in order, though there was no look of disuse. I said something about this to Penny when she came up with my drink.

'I live in here, really,' she said. 'Here and in my bedroom. The rest of the place I've pretty well had to let go. Oh, except for the kitchen. I can just about manage, with only me to look after.'

'Don't you get lonely, on your own in the house?'

'No, not a bit. I love it. I never want to go out: there's so much to do here. I know I should have gone down to see Daddy in hospital, but when I telephoned they said he was doing well, and I suppose it was ghastly of me, but he seemed to be coming out more or less straight away, and I was so busy I just didn't go. You'll have been, I expect?'

'Yes. He's all right, physically at least. Busy doing what?'

'Oh, nothing much.' She gave me an embarrassed half-glance. 'Reading and . . . all that kind of thing.'

I noticed, on a table beside a clean ashtray and a bowl of freshly cut roses, a thin paperback in a format I thought I recognized. I soon saw it was the B.B.C. publication by Denis Matthews on Beethoven's piano sonatas. And, I further saw, the first volume of these sonatas lay on the music-rest of the piano, open at the minuet of No. 1. Immediately – though belatedly enough – I said,

'What's happened?'

'Happened about what?'

'Even the way you talk. And your accent. And the way you stand. Have you fallen in love, or what?'

She laughed: a different laugh, with no edge of sarcasm to it. 'Oh no, nothing like that. That wouldn't be me at all.'

'What is it, then? You seem so self-contained. Happy.'

'Yes, both of those. It's very simple. I've gone on to the hard stuff.'

'You mean the booze.'

'No, Douglas. Hard drugs.'

'Heroin?'

'Don't sound so terrified. Yes, well, that kind of thing. It's not a bit what you think it's like. Surely you can see that just by talking to me.'

'The expectation of life of a heroin addict is about two years. A doctor friend of mine was telling me.'

'That's one of the things that's so nice about it. Nothing's going to last. None of that awful business of getting married and having children and being responsible. Nobody expecting anything of you.'

'What about Beethoven? He lasts.'

'He won't last me. I'll never be good enough. You've got to find out what your limitations are. I've found out mine, and I can arrange my life to fit in with them exactly. Not many people can do that.'

'Penny, go up and pack a suitcase and come down to my flat and let me look after you.'

She laughed again. 'Do you remember me telling you, nobody takes me on? Anyway, I do. That's one thing that hasn't changed. And you couldn't do it. Thank you for asking me, but you wouldn't stick at it, would you? Do you think you could do what Gilbert couldn't do?'

I looked down at the newly swept carpet. 'Does your father know about this?'

'I don't think so. I suppose he'll find out eventually. He won't do anything about it either. Why should he? He's got his own life to lead. You know, Douglas, going off with that girl is going to be the best thing he'll ever have done. For everybody, not just him. We're all free now.'

Kingsley Amis

JAKE'S THING

'*The funniest thing he has done since Lucky Jim*' – *Daily Mail*

In his hilarious, *outrageous* and wickedly funny story of Jake and his lost libido, Kingsley Amis does not pull any punches, but takes some well-aimed, unerring swipes at the crankier fringes of psychotherapy and at sex – seventies-style.

'Makes you sick laughing . . . all good, unfair, vicious stuff' – *Sunday Telegraph*

'I enjoyed it tremendously' – Auberon Waugh

'Very funny' – *Daily Telegraph*

'Vintage Amis . . . he has probably given as much pleasure as any novelist of his generation' – *Scotsman*

LUCKY JIM

The hilarious send-up of academic life which helped to set the style of post-war fiction and placed one of today's most popular novelists firmly on the course for fame.

'*Lucky Jim* deserves all the recognition it has won. It is highly intelligent and very funny' – C. P. Snow in the *Sunday Times*

MY ENEMY'S ENEMY

A consumate clutch of Amis characters, from soldiers to social workers, deftly drawn by a master of comic invention.
'Three-star Amis' – *Guardian*

'I found all these stories brilliant' – Edna O'Brien in the *Daily Express*

'The eye for revealing detail, the ear for exact speech, the pace and skill of the narrative, are as delightfully developed as ever' – *Observer*

Kingsley Amis

TAKE A GIRL LIKE YOU

When attractive little Jenny Bunn comes South to teach, she falls
in with Patrick Standish, a schoolmaster, and all the rakes and
rogues of a provincial Hell Fire Club. Her Virgin's Progress, amid
orgy and seduction, makes an uproarious comedy.

'Incendiary stuff . . . a really formidable blaze. This is his most
interesting so far . . . and no less funny than the first' – Karl Miller in
the *Observer*

'Mr Amis's best novel. This must be one of the most variously
funny novels in the language' – *Punch*

ONE FAT ENGLISHMAN

Introducing Roger Micheldene Esq. – one fat Englishman let loose
in America . . . Roger Micheldene, brimful of gluttony, sloth and
lust; bounding with anger; affronted by everything on the American
scene . . . An English gentleman who fails to see how his presence
might adversely affect Anglo-American relations.
From bed to bottle to nightly brawl, Kingsley Amis records the
picaresque antics of one fat Englishman.

THE ANTI-DEATH LEAGUE

Lieutenant James Churchill had been reasonably pro-death before
he made love to Catherine, and before he realized what the appalling
nature of Operation Apollo was. Officially, he and his fellow-
officers had a seventy-five per cent chance of survival. Unofficially,
he discovered, they had none. Then someone started the Anti-
Death League and there suddenly seemed to be a way out of the
horrors to come.

Hervey Allen

ANTHONY ADVERSE

'DAZZLING . . . HUGE AND BRILLIANT' – *Observer*

When it was first published *Anthony Adverse* took America by storm, outselling every other book ever published except the Bible. It is a truly classical swashbuckler of a historical romance, combining superb narrative and panoramic sweep with excitement, passion and a rich feeling for period.

Anthony, an orphan, grows up in a Europe dominated by Talleyrand, Pitt and Napoleon. As the nations succumb to the tramp of the First Consul's armies, he is propelled into intrigue and adventure that take him to tropical Africa, France, Spain, England and America. And, for each of the delicious and voluptuous women he loved and wooed life was never the same . . .

Gloria Nagy

VIRGIN KISSES

'My name is Arthur Freedman. I make fifty thousand dollars in a good year (more in a bad one). I am respected for my sanity, calm, cool and control. I am also a snob, a prick, a sadist, tense, anxious, alienated, a bad doctor and now a murderer.

'I am, in sum, the American wet dream.'

Dr Freedman has built himself a house of cards. He has a successful practice. He's got a charming wife. Friends too. And he's also got Rosie – ageing, cheap, stupid Rosie, framed in her nylon flounces and plastic feathers.

Rosie loves Arthur Freedman. She loves him when he drugs her and strips her and gets her to do whatever he wants. Dr Freedman is building a very shaky structure indeed. One day it's going to fall down.

'A lacerating, literate, funny, obscene exposé' – *Vogue*

Books by Michael Hiebert

DREAM WITH LITTLE ANGELS

CLOSE TO THE BROKEN HEARTED

A THORN AMONG THE LILIES

STICKS AND STONES

Published by Kensington Publishing Corporation

CLOSE
TO THE
BROKEN
HEARTED

MICHAEL HIEBERT

PINNACLE BOOKS
Kensington Publishing Corp.
www.kensingtonbooks.com

PINNACLE BOOKS are published by

Kensington Publishing Corp.
119 West 40th Street
New York, NY 10018

All Kensington titles, imprints, and distributed lines are available at special quantity discounts for bulk purchases for sales promotions, premiums, fund-raising, educational, or institutional use. Special book excerpts or customized printings can also be created to fit specific needs. For details, write or phone the office of the Kensington sales manager: Kensington Publishing Corp., 119 West 40th Street, New York, NY 10018, attn: Sales Department; phone 1-800-221-2647.

This book is a work of fiction. Names, characters, businesses, organizations, places, events, and incidents either are the product of the author's imagination or are used fictitiously. Any resemblance to actual persons, living or dead, events, or locales is entirely coincidental.

PINNACLE BOOKS and the Pinnacle logo are Reg. U.S. Pat. & TM Off.

ISBN-13: 978-0-7860-3955-5
ISBN-10: 0-7860-3955-8

First mass market paperback printing: January 2017

10 9 8 7 6 5 4 3 2 1

Printed in the United States of America

First electronic edition: January 2017

ISBN-13: 978-0-7860-3973-9
ISBN-10: 0-7860-397306

For Sagan

with the heart of a warrior . . .

ACKNOWLEDGMENTS

A debt of gratitude to my agent, Adrienne Rosado, for selling this book and its predecessor, *Dream with Little Angels*.

To my incomparable editor, John Scognamiglio, along with the rest of my friends at Kensington for their ongoing support and ability to surprise me with how much they really do stand behind their authors.

To Vida Engstrand, publicity director extraordinaire, for knowing when to give me a kick in the pants and knowing when to let me try the tightrope without a net.

To my girlfriend, Shannon Mairs, for putting up with my late-night write-a-thons and hardly ever complaining about it.

To my dearest friend, Julianna Hinckley, for providing me with answers to my infinite questions about life in the South.

To Yvonne Rupert for giving me a shoulder to cry on and an endless fountain of encouragement when things got overwhelming.

To Ken Loomes for reading a very rough draft of *Close to the Broken Hearted* and pointing out all my discrepancies, especially in the area of weaponry. Sometimes you scare me, Ken.

To the Chilliwack Writers' Group: Garth Pettersen, Mary Keane, Fran Brown, Lori Christine, and Terri

McKee, for giving me an audience for parts of this book and providing fantastic feedback and critique.

To my three children, Valentine, Sagan, and Legend. They continue to be my ongoing inspiration for the relationship between Abe and Carry.

And to my parents, Abe and Ann Hiebert, for providing me with everything I needed to finish this book, including the very roof over my head, not including everything else in my life. I doubt the scales will ever be balanced again.

Thanks to Mark Leland for taking time to help me find answers to all my questions regarding police work that I couldn't find anywhere else.

And to Pastor Badwell of the Parkway Baptist Church in Alabama for giving me guidance involving the Baptist faith.

Thanks also to the Mobile, Alabama, Police Department and their openness to answering my questions about Southern police work.

Finally, a shout-out to Writers' Village University (www.writersvillage.com); National Public Radio; Joshua Graham and his online radio show, *Between the Lines*; the Chilliwack Book Man; and the Chilliwack Library.

PROLOGUE

Alvin, Alabama—1971

The spring sun is low in the sky outside the single-paned windows of the kitchen in the small farmhouse where the family has gathered to eat. Upon the table sits a roast chicken ready to be carved, a plate of mashed potatoes, and a bowl of peas and corn, both harvested last year but kept frozen through the winter months. The light falling in through the windows is a deep orange, almost red, as the father, Tom Carson, stands to say grace. His hat sits on the top newel of the short run of stairs that separates this room from the living room below.

The table, like the house, was built by his father. The chicken and the vegetables came from the farm. Unlike the house, the rest of the farm had once all belonged to his father's father. Tom Carson is a proud man even though he lives a modest life. He is proud of his work in the fields that starts at daybreak and ends at supper. He is proud of his two children: Caleb, barely three, with black hair and fair skin like his father, and

Sylvie, five and a half, with blond hair like her mother used to have. They are good kids. Respectful kids. Long ago they learned not to make noise or fuss about while their father says grace. Soon Caleb will start working with his father little by little out on the farm. Sylvie already does some jobs with her mother around the home.

Each of the kids clutches their mother's hands. Mother closes her eyes. She is a good woman. Tom is lucky to have all he has. There're wrinkles around his wife's eyes he hasn't noticed before, and he wonders how hard this life has been on her. It's a thought that hasn't occurred to him until now.

In his cracked voice, he delivers the blessing, thanking the Lord Jesus for this wonderful bounty He has bestowed upon their family. The Lord Jesus has been good to Tom Carson.

Tom finishes and takes his chair at the table, folding his napkin onto his lap. Mother's fingers let go of the children's hands. Her gray eyes open and she smiles across the table at Tom. Tom reaches for the platter of chicken so that he may start to carve.

Across the room, there's a loud knock at the door.

Mother jumps. "Who would be knockin' aroun' here at suppertime?" she asks.

"Dunno," Tom Carson says gruffly. He gently lifts the napkin from his lap and begins to rise from the table when the door swings open with a squeak. It wasn't locked. Tom and his family never lock their doors. Nobody around these parts ever locks their doors.

Tom freezes, half out of his chair, as Preacher Eli Brown steps into his home. The preacher man is dressed in a white shirt with black trousers and vest.

Muddy boots cover his feet. His thin face is fixed and stern, but what's caught Tom's attention is the gun the preacher holds in his right hand. It is pointed at the floor, being held as though it wasn't there at all.

"Preacher Eli," Tom says, trying to keep his voice calm. "What brings you round here? We's just 'bout to sit down to supper, as you can see." He sits back down.

The preacher says nothing, just stomps across Tom's living room leaving a trail of dried mud on the wooden floor. He comes up the few stairs toward the small kitchen where the family squeezes around the table. With each of the man's footsteps, Caleb wiggles out of his chair and crawls under the table where he seeks out the safety of his father's legs.

Preacher Eli dangles over the rail along the top of the stairs, the gun hand waving conspicuously in the air as he speaks with a low, slow drawl. "Tom, you and I have quite a land dispute goin' on. This thing oughta be worked out soon or there could be some trouble comin'."

Tom Carson looks down at his empty plate. "There ain't no dispute, Eli. The land's mine. It belonged to my father, just as it belonged to his father. Been in my family at least three generations. Maybe even more."

"The church disagrees with you."

Tom turned back to the preacher, his face red. "The church has no jurisdiction here, Preacher. If the land belonged to you, you'd have a title to it. If you got a title, produce it. But you can't do that cuz you ain't got one, and since you ain't got no title, you ain't got no land."

"The title is *missing*. You can't produce one either."

"Yes, well, the title seems to have *gone* missing."

Tom clears his throat. "I'd say you had somethin' to do with that. Doesn't matter, Eli. Everyone knows the land belongs to me."

"You wanna start asking folk?"

"No. Folk is 'fraid of you."

Preacher Eli Brown's teeth form a thin V of a smile. They are more brown than white and less than straight.

"That how the church doin' things these days, Eli? Bit of a step backward ain't it?" Tom nods at the gun. "That why you here? To scare me into giving you my land so you can build your new 'facility' on it? I got news for you, Eli. I ain't afraid of you or your 'church.' "

This time it's Preacher Eli who reddens. "Well, you oughta be. You oughta be very 'fraid. It is a spiteful and vengeful God you forsake. One does not just turn his back on the will of the Lord Jesus without severe repercussions." His bony voice grows in anger and volume. From under the table, Caleb climbs up onto his father's lap.

For a minute, Tom Carson says nothing, just stares pathetically back at the tall preacher who looks somehow scarecrowlike bathed in the red-orange light of dusk. "You are a fool, Eli. Who said anything about forsakin' God? I ain't turned my back on the Lord Jesus. Your church has nothing to do with neither God nor Jesus. Least if it does, it sure ain't my Jesus. If it were, heaven help us all. There is absolutely nothing holy about your affairs, Eli. You oughta be ashamed of callin' yourself a man of the cloth. You've made a mockery of everything folk hold sacred."

Tom turns back to the chicken. He's done talking to the preacher. He's given this man too much time in his house already. But as soon as he picks up the knife to begin carving the bird, a strange feeling comes over him, and he hesitates, glancing back at the man with the gun.

Preacher Eli's eye twitches. His facial muscles tighten. When he talks again, it's with the same commanding voice he uses from the pulpit. "How dare you speak to me with such irreverence? It is *you . . .*" His hand holding the gun shakes. "*You,* Tom Carson. You who must . . . who *will* answer for your sins."

Something flashes in the preacher man's eyes: a flicker of insanity.

Tom Carson has never been much of a gambler, but in that instant when he sees that look in Preacher Eli's eyes, he knows he's made a grave mistake. Until now, Tom had thought Eli Brown was many things, but a killer was definitely not one of them. Sure, the man had brought a gun into his home, but Tom had never really been scared. At no time did he think he or his family were in jeopardy of being hurt. Tom had chalked up the weapon to being part of the preacher's game—part of his ploy to scare him into giving up what was rightfully his. Tom had decided almost immediately after the man entered that he wouldn't let himself be so easily duped.

Only now, in this split second, Tom knows he's played his cards all wrong. Everything is over. It's all about to come to an end at the hands of a madman he grossly underestimated.

That thought's the last thing to go through Tom's mind as Eli raises the gun and pulls the trigger.

The small room, suddenly gone dark, fills with the smell and the sound of a gunshot. It echoes off the wooden walls and floor like a thunderous death knell.

Tom hears nothing else, only that deadly explosion. It seems to last an eternity and fills everything, even his mind.

In fact, Tom has been so focused on Preacher Eli, he hadn't noticed when Caleb made his way up his pant legs onto his lap minutes ago.

Now, as the sound dies away, leaving only the smell of gunpowder in its wake, Tom looks down, expecting to see his own stomach blown open, expecting to see himself dying.

What he sees is far, far worse.

There in his lap lies what remains of his little boy.

His perfect little man who just turned three years old barely two weeks ago lies with half his head on Tom's leg and one arm wrapped around his papa's waist.

Tom's eyes fill with tears as he takes in the blood splattered across the table, the floor, the counters, and most of this side of the kitchen. Tom himself is covered in it. He begins to shake. He rubs his son's arm as the world grows very small, and he looks back up to the preacher. It takes a minute for the words to come. When they do, they barely escape his lips. "What . . . what have you done?" he asks quietly.

The preacher's eyes widen in surprise as he steps slowly back down the stairs. His hand holding the gun falls to his side, the weapon slipping off his fingers and falling to the floor. His head shakes. "No . . ." he says. "No."

Across the table, Mother begins screaming, "My baby! My baby!" She comes around to where Caleb lies dead in a bundle in his father's lap. "My poor sweet baby."

Their daughter, Sylvie, remains quiet. She just pulls

her feet up onto her chair and, wrapping her arms around her knees, tries to make herself as small as possible. She watches her mother and father cry over their dead son. She sees the preacher man who came in right before supper and killed her baby brother in the name of Jesus leave by the same door he came in through. She watches it all like a movie, unable to really comprehend what it means. It's so emotionally confusing, she feels almost nothing.

Just an emptiness inside. All empty and hollow.

She begins rocking back and forth on the wooden chair, her long blond pigtails swinging against her face. In her mind, a voice screams, "No! No! No!" over and over, but it's only in her head. On the outside, she's quiet. In fact, she doesn't even hear her parents crying anymore. She sees them, but she doesn't really process what she's looking at.

Nothing makes any sense.

When she woke up this morning, she had been a happy five-year-old girl with a good family and a good life. For the last year, she always told her mom her biggest wish was to raise horses and have babies when she grew up. Three babies.

Those had been her dreams. Horses and babies.

Now, sitting in that kitchen of death, Sylvie Carson no longer cares about the horses or the babies. She no longer cares about life. Preacher Eli killed her baby brother and he also killed her dreams. And none of it made any sense.

What Sylvie doesn't know is that this is only the beginning.

Because for her, the world will never make sense ever again.

CHAPTER 1

Seventeen Years Later

"Dewey," I said, "if I say it was blue, it was blue. Why the heck would I say it was blue if it was some other color? It's not like the important part of the story has anything to do with it bein' blue."

"I just ain't never seen one that's blue," Dewey said. "That's all, Abe."

"You ever seen one any other color?" I asked.

"What do you mean?"

"I mean, have you ever even seen one at all, blue or not? This one was the first one *I'd* ever seen. I mean other than in movies and on TV an' all that. It's not like you see 'em every day."

This question seemed to stump Dewey for a bit as he thought it over. Least, I think he was thinking about it. He may have been pondering the aluminum foil he was unrolling around my mother's living room floor. "Not sure," he said. "Not that I can remember."

"I think that's enough aluminum foil, don't you?" I asked. "How much is in a roll?"

He read the side of the box. "Fifty feet."

"And you had four boxes? That's two hundred feet, Dewey."

"I know, but when I paced off your livin' room, it was ten by twelve. Right there we have a hundred and twenty feet. And it ain't like the foil's gonna be laid down flat. And I reckon for this to work, Abe, we're gonna need to go into your dinin' room, too."

"Well, there ain't no more foil," I said. "My mom's already gonna be mad we used up two brand-new rolls."

"I took two from my house, too," he said. "At least we're sharin' responsibility."

"But the difference is that you reckon this is gonna work. I don't."

"It'll work."

I sighed.

"We need two more rolls," he said.

"We ain't got two more rolls, Dewey. I reckon if two hundred feet don't do it, two thousand feet ain't gonna make no difference."

He thought this over. "You might have a point. At the very least we should see some indication of it workin'. Then we can show your mom and she'll gladly buy us two more rolls."

"My mom ain't gonna want aluminum foil runnin' around the inside of her house, Dewey."

"She is when she sees what it does for her television reception," he said. "Think of how much money we're savin' her."

"How do you figure?" I asked.

"On a satellite dish."

"She ain't buyin' no satellite dish."

"Exactly."

"*Why* aren't we doing this at your place?" I asked him.

"Abe, my mom's *home*. It's hard enough to do anythin' at my place when my mom *ain't* home," he said. "You're lucky your mom works all day shootin' people."

"She don't shoot people all day," I said. "I don't reckon she's ever actually shot *anyone*." My mother was the only detective the Alvin Police Department had, and, if she had shot anyone, she certainly hadn't told me about it. And it seemed like the sort of thing she'd probably mention.

"I reckon she has."

"She hasn't," I assured him.

"I bet she thinks about it, though," Dewey said. "A lot."

"Can we just get this finished so I can have it cleaned up 'fore she gets home?" I asked him.

Dewey was taking the aluminum foil and rolling it into a sort of shiny rope. He made sure all the new pieces fit tightly against the old ones, making one solid snake that ran around the inside of my living room, starting and ending at the back of the television set.

"So why was they *all* blue?" Dewey asked. "The knights, I mean. Or was there other colors, too? They can't *all* be on the same side. Be awful confusin' if they was all blue."

"The other ones were red. I saw one of them later."

"Which ones were the good guys?" Dewey asked.

"How do you mean?"

"There's always a good side and a bad side, Abe. Were the blue ones the good ones or the bad ones? These colors make it hard to know. Usually they use somethin' obvious like black and white. Then you know who you should be rootin' for."

"Do you root for the good guys or the bad guys?" I asked.

Dewey stopped laying down his aluminum foil pipeline and considered this. "That depends on when in my life you had asked me. When I was little I always wanted the good guys to win. Then I went through a phase where I secretly hoped for the bad guys."

"And?" I asked. "What about now?"

"Now I guess I just want to see a fair fight," he said. "Did the blues and the reds both have swords?"

I started to get excited. The swords had been the best part. "You shoulda seen the swords," I said. "The red blades actually glowed the same color as the knights, and they were huge. They looked so big I doubt I coulda lifted one off the ground. And each sword had a different gem in its pommel and smaller ones all over its hilt. They actually had *real* swords for sale in Sleeping Beauty's Castle, but Mom refused to buy me one. She told me I'd wind up takin' somebody's eye out with it or somethin'."

"Wow," Dewey said, looking off into the distance and seemingly speaking to himself. "A *real* sword. That would be somethin'." His attention came back to the living room and all the foil. He looked me straight in the eyes. "Especially if we *both* had one. We could have sword fights."

"Are you even listenin' to a word I'm sayin'?" I asked him. "These were *real* swords, Dewey. We couldn't have sword fights with 'em. We'd wind up killin' each other."

"Still, it's fun to think about."

I hesitated. "You're right. It *is* fun to think about."

Dewey's aluminum foil rope ran along the walls of the entire living room, running behind the big stuffed chair and coming right up to the back of the TV. We'd even pushed the sofa away from the wall so that we could make sure it was as long as possible.

"Okay," I said, just in case Dewey had other ideas, "I think we've done as much as we're doin' with the foil. Now what?"

"Now I unhook the cable from your TV and attach the foil antenna with these alligator clips," he said.

"Can I ask where you got this idea?"

He shrugged. "While you was at Disney World I started an inventor's notebook. Turns out I'm pretty smart. I got lots of great ideas. They're probably worth a million dollars."

I glanced around the room. My mother was going to have a conniption when she saw what we'd done to it, and especially when she found out we'd used up two brand-new rolls of her aluminum foil. "Probably," I said. "You give off a glow of genius, that's for certain."

The light falling in through the window above the sofa was starting to turn purple and orange, which meant it was getting late. This further meant my mother would probably be home soon—unless she wound up working late like she sometimes did. I took another look at Dewey's tinfoil snake and hoped this was going to be a late night for her.

Dewey hooked up the alligator clips to the screws attached to the electronic box where the Cable Vision wire normally attached to the television. "That should do it," he said.

"So now what?"

"Now we turn on the TV and enjoy havin' all the stations folks get with satellite dishes without payin' a cent. All it cost us was the price of four rolls of aluminum foil."

"It didn't cost us nothin'," I reminded him. "We *stole* the foil from our moms, remember?"

"Even better," he said, rubbing his hands together. He pulled the button on the television that turned the set on. For a minute the screen stayed dark, then it slowly grew into a picture of white static.

"Works well," I said sarcastically. I snuck another glance out the window. The weather had cleared up considerably from this morning. It had been four days since we'd gotten back from Disney World, and every day since we'd returned had been full of pouring rain, including the beginning of this one. This afternoon, though, the sun had finally broken through the clouds and cleaned up the sky.

Dewey changed the channel to more static. "Somethin's wrong. We didn't hook somethin' up properly."

"You know what's wrong?" I asked. "You're tryin' to get satellite TV with aluminum foil."

"Wait, this *has* to work. I had it all figured out." He started rapidly switching channels. Then he came to a channel that was clear as Mount Bell on a brisk autumn morning, as my mother would say. "Look!" he said, nearly screaming it. "It works! Look how clear it is!"

I had to admit it was clear.

"Told you it would work!" He went around the dial the entire way and found three more channels we could get. All tremendously clear. This seemed to satisfy him immensely.

"So you're happy with your invention?" I asked.

"I'll say."

I looked at him and blinked. "I'm a little confused."

"About what?"

"Who exactly you'll be marketin' this to."

"What do you mean?"

"I mean, is this for folk who can't afford Cable Vision but happen to have a surplus of aluminum foil and one or two favorite channels they simply cannot live without?" I once again looked at the foil running along the edge of the floor everywhere. "Or will you try and make it some sort of home décor product? Not to mention the fact that you can't really charge more than the price of four rolls of aluminum foil for it or people will just go out and buy their own and set everythin' up for themselves."

Dewey frowned, perplexed by my complex questions. "It's a start, okay? I have many inventions. I've already filled half a notebook," he said. "You may have been wastin' time in Disney World with blue and red knights, but at least *I* was doing somethin' productive."

Nodding, I said, "Okay. Now, do you mind if we try to get all this put away and see if we can make the television work properly again 'fore my mom gets home from work?"

Dewey glared at me. "You just don't know genius when you see it."

"You're probably right. I don't. I've never really been much of a noticer of brilliance."

He unhooked the alligator clips. I began to roll up the two hundred feet of foil.

Just then my sister, Carry, came into the living room. She'd been out with some friends all day and I hadn't even heard her come home. "Abe?" she asked quietly. I looked up into her blue eyes. Her blond curls swayed on either side of her face. "What the hell are you two doin'?" she asked.

"Preparin' ourselves for the future," I said. "It's comin'. And it's full of aluminum foil."

"And other inventions!" Dewey said. "Wanna see my notebook?"

"Mom's gonna kill you," Carry said.

"I know," I said.

CHAPTER 2

Leah Teal pulled her squad car into the driveway of the home of Sylvie Carson. She was attending because of a call Sylvie made to the station saying something about somebody illegally trespassing on her property. Leah wasn't entirely sure of the report that was taken because she hadn't taken it. Her partner, Officer Christopher Jackson, had. Like most times when Sylvie Carson called, Officer Jackson laughed after hanging up the phone.

"Guess who that was . . . *again,*" he had said.

It bothered Leah when Sylvie was made fun of, especially when it was by Chris. She had a pretty good hunch as to why it irked her so much, too.

"You know," she had told Chris, "it wasn't so long ago that I can remember folks makin' all sorts of a ruckus 'bout you bein' hired by the department."

"Yeah, well, those folks were wrong. They just like to hate people," Chris said. "Especially black people. This is different. The woman is nuts. She calls the station every week."

"This *isn't* much different, Chris. Sylvie can't help

the way she is no more than you can help the color you is."

"What's wrong with the color I am?"

"That's not what I meant and you know it." Leah looked back at Police Chief Ethan Montgomery's office for a little backup but his door was closed. She could see through the partially opened blinds hanging down over the window in his door that the chief was sitting back in his chair with his hands behind his head watching the television that hung from the ceiling in the corner of the room. The chief loved to watch his sports.

Chris wouldn't let things go. "Leah, most people get better over time. But Sylvie's gotten worse, far as I can tell. Her calls are coming in at an all-time high." That was likely true. Leah had at least noticed them more, and she was the one who usually ended up attending to them.

"And every single one turns out to be some sort of false alarm," Chris said. "I don't know why you even bother showin' up. I stopped takin' her seriously a long time ago."

"Because it's our job to show up, Chris. Because for every hundred or so false alarms, there might actually be one real emergency and it's for *that* real emergency I attend to the ninety-nine others. Besides, what else do I have to do? We live in a town of barely two thousand people; it's not like our phone's ringin' off the desk."

"I'd rather do the crossword than deal with Sylvie," he said. Leah couldn't believe how heartless he was being. She was about to tell him that when he started talking again. "I'm sorry," he said, "but I've just reached the end of my wits with her. I think it's on account of the baby. I think she must be all hormonal or somethin'."

Okay, Leah knew then it was time to end her conversation with Officer Christopher Jackson, or she would say something she definitely would regret.

Grabbing her pistol from her desk, she headed for the door. "Well, I'm gonna go see what she needs. At least one of us is gonna represent this department."

Chris laughed behind her. "Have fun."

It was the part about the baby that had almost pushed Leah over the edge. Even now, sitting in her car in front of Sylvie's house, thinking about that baby kept Leah worked up to a degree that wasn't healthy for nobody.

Generally, Leah tried not to think about Sylvie's baby, especially when she was off shift. It was the sort of thing that would lodge itself into her head and wouldn't get unstuck for hours while she lay in bed trying to fall asleep. To make matters worse, she couldn't even refer to it as anything but "The Baby" because Sylvie Carson hadn't given it a name yet. It had been three months now, and the girl still called her daughter "The Baby." Whenever Leah asked her why she hadn't named her, Sylvie told her, "It's so much responsibility. I get too overwhelmed thinkin' that whatever I come up with is gonna be with this girl for the rest of her life. It's a huge decision that's gonna affect everything. Nothin' I think of is good enough. Not for my daughter. Not for her whole life."

Leah couldn't argue with her. It was pointless telling Sylvie that anything was better than "The Baby." So Leah just let it lie as best she could. But her brain wouldn't let go of it quite so easily. It hung on to things like the baby not having a name and how *that* might affect the rest of her life. Or what effect having a mother who could barely manage to keep herself together an entire day might have.

Some babies come into the world with better chances

than others right from the start. This one seemed to come in with a pretty bad poker hand, at least in Leah's eyes, which was probably one of the big reasons Leah felt compelled to take Sylvie's calls seriously.

Leah also suspected she had a soft spot for Sylvie because deep down she felt they weren't so different. If fate had changed up some of the pitches Leah had been thrown, her life might have turned out very similar to Sylvie's. In some ways it had.

They were both single mothers. Sylvie had The Baby and Leah had two children: a fifteen-year-old daughter named Carry, and a twelve-year-old boy named Abe.

Both Leah and Sylvie had lost the fathers to their children unexpectedly. Sylvie's was named Orwin Thomas and he had been barely an adult when Sylvie got pregnant. He just up and disappeared one night without even leaving so much as a note. There was no indication the day before that anything was wrong. He took Sylvie's car, a few dollars cash they'd kept in a jar, and some clothing. He left her three months along in a pregnancy she then had to face all alone.

Leah's husband, Billy, coming home from work after pulling an overnight shift, had accidentally run his car—headlights first—into an oncoming car while passing an eighteen-wheeler. Abe had only been two. Those had been very hard times for Leah. She didn't like to think about them, even now.

Neither Leah nor Sylvie had living parents. Sylvie's had died tragically when she was in her teens; her mother was murdered and her pa took his own life shortly thereafter. Leah had lost her parents when they were older; her ma from a stroke a year after Leah had lost her husband, and her pa to cancer three years later.

But that was where the similarities ended, because

at least Leah could cope with life. Sylvie was a different story. Sure, she had emotional problems (yet another reason for Leah being upset at Chris. Although, comparing her disorder to him being black would probably not be a good idea on Leah's part). Possibly it was post-traumatic stress disorder brought on from what happened when Sylvie was a kid. She'd actually seen her baby brother get murdered just a few feet away from her. It happened long before Leah became detective, back when she was only fourteen. But Leah's father had been on the force then, and he had handled the case, so Leah knew a lot about it.

After Leah's husband, Billy, died, there were times Leah didn't think she would make it. And she hadn't had to deal with any of the psychological trauma Sylvie faced. Leah tried not to forget that. No matter what it looked like from the outside, this girl was rising above herself—or at least trying to—and that was something to be applauded, not laughed at.

Leah couldn't imagine what her own life would've been like had she been in the same shoes Sylvie was during her childhood. Leah tried to picture what it would be like watching her own uncle, Hank, get shot to death right in front of her when, not ten minutes earlier, she had been ready to enjoy a happy supper with her family.

She shivered. It was so horrific, she couldn't even think about it.

Yet it was something Sylvie had to live with every single day of her life. And everyone seemed so surprised the girl was a little messed up. Something like that had to do strange things to your mind. It had to haunt you in unimaginable ways.

Sylvie was a lost soul trying to navigate in a world she always seemed to be trying to catch up with.

Leah got out of her squad car and headed for the few wooden steps that rose to the landing in front of Sylvie's front door.

Sylvie's house was small and old. It would be considered a shotgun shack if it weren't for the hallway and bedroom someone had added on some time ago. Shotgun shacks were normally fewer than twelve feet wide with no more than three to five rooms, all arranged one behind the other.

The outside had once been painted white, but most of the paint was flaking off the siding, leaving the bare wood showing underneath. The picture window that looked out of the living room beside the front door had the drapes pulled shut, but Leah could see the yellow light of a lamp through the crack between them. Leah had been inside enough times to know that was the only light in that room. At times like this, after the sun was down, that light cast everything inside with an amber glow that threw long, eerie shadows.

It certainly didn't help the atmosphere any.

Leah stepped up and knocked on the wooden door. Like the siding, the paint on the door was also starting to peel. "Sylvie?" she called out. "Sylvie, it's Detective Teal. Alvin Police."

It didn't take long before she heard the chain slide and the dead bolt shoot. Like always, Leah waited while Sylvie opened the door a few inches and made sure Leah was who she said she was. Leah didn't really mind this behavior. She would rather see somebody overly protective than the other way around, although Sylvie's protectiveness crossed the line well into paranoia.

"Hi," Sylvie said. Her dirty blond hair hung straight down over her eyes. For a brief moment, those eyes caught the moon, and Leah saw its reflection in their speckled blue pools.

Sylvie Carson looked and dressed like a homeless person. She'd gotten worse since Orwin took off. It was funny, because Leah could tell if the girl dressed in nice clothes and wore proper makeup she could be really pretty. Maybe she looked this way intentionally. Like a victim.

Yet the baby seemed clean enough. That had been a huge worry of Leah's when Sylvie first brought her home from the hospital. Leah really hadn't wanted to involve the state with the child's care, but part of her suspected she would eventually have to step in given the way Sylvie was.

So Leah had kept a close eye on the baby for the past three months. Sylvie had given her many opportunities to do so with all her calls. Every time Sylvie called into the station, Leah just chalked it up as another chance to check on the welfare of the baby.

Leah heard Sylvie slide the chain again. Then the door opened completely. "Thanks for comin' out," Sylvie said.

"Not a problem," Leah said stepping inside. "Glad to see you're okay."

Sylvie immediately locked the door again behind Leah. "Yeah," she mumbled. She was always very quiet when she talked. Quiet, pensive, and uncertain. It was very much like dealing with a child.

Which, Leah assumed, Sylvie probably still was. Chronologically, she wasn't much older than a teenager. What had she turned on her last birthday? Twenty-two? And hadn't Leah read somewhere that when something traumatic happens in childhood the person emotionally stays at whatever age they were at when the event took place?

Leah was pretty sure wherever she had read that fact they'd gotten it right because Sylvie had been five when she lost her brother and, in many ways, Sylvie still seemed like a five-year-old trapped in a twenty-two-year-old girl's body.

Surprisingly, given her appearance, Sylvie's home always had that just-tidied-up-in-a-rush look when Leah showed up. That might be because she just had tidied it after calling the station—Leah had no way of knowing. But at least she kept it fairly neat. Each of these little things—the clean house, the clean baby, and other little changes—gave Leah some hope that Sylvie might have it together enough to actually be a proper mother. God knew she appeared to love the child enough. If love was all you needed (like that Beatles song said) then Sylvie was like a billionaire.

Unfortunately, Leah didn't think John Lennon had taken everything into account when he wrote that song. He'd probably never met anyone like Sylvie Carson.

"So what's the problem?" Leah asked.

"Someone's been in the yard," Sylvie said.

Leah sighed. This wasn't a surprise. The girl always thought someone was in her yard, or spying on her, or something.

"Place looks nice," Leah said, for now tabling the "someone's been in the yard" discussion.

"Thanks."

"Baby okay?"

"Yeah, she's fine. A bit colicky, I reckon."

"That'll go away," Leah said.

"I think so," Sylvie said.

"You okay? You look pale," Leah said.

"I'm fine."

"So," Leah asked, "what exactly makes you think someone's been trespassing on your property? Who's been where?"

"The yard," Sylvie said. "Someone's been in the backyard." She was wearing an old oversized LSU Tigers T-shirt that hung untucked over gray sweatpants. Her hands trembled as she wrung them together while speaking. Leah could tell she was scared. She was hoping her little conversation diversion might settle Sylvie down.

Leah knew enough about Sylvie and her calls to know this would undoubtedly turn out to be another false alarm.

The living room had a dark hardwood floor that creaked when you walked across it. The drapes in the window were missing some hooks, and that made them hang awkwardly from the inside. They were once white, but now they looked a more pale washed-out yellow than anything else. Dark stains covered one.

Tattered magazines were stacked on the oval glass coffee table in the room's center. An old TV with wood panel trim sat on some plastic crates on one side of the table. Two paintings of clowns hung crookedly on the chestnut-paneled wall behind the TV.

"Been cleanin', I see," Leah said.

"I like it clean for The Baby."

"That's good. Babies need things clean. You should clean yourself up, too."

"What do you mean?"

Leah pointed to the oversized LSU shirt with the ripped holes in it. "Don't you have any clothes of your own? Orwin's stuff's gettin' a mite old."

"These are comfortable. Besides, my money goes to The Baby."

The Baby. It made Leah cringe every time Sylvie said it.

A small white cat came in and brushed up against Leah's leg, purring.

"Snowflake," Sylvie said. "Get outta here. Leave Officer Teal alone."

"Oh, she's all right," Leah said, bending down and lifting up the cat. She'd come here enough times that she knew the animal well. It was an indoor/outdoor cat that had surprised Leah by lasting as long as it had. Sylvie had gotten the cat as a kitten after Orwin left her. Normally, cats allowed to go outdoors in these parts became prey to other animals pretty quickly.

There were two small unmatched sofas in the room: one was green and threadbare, the other was taupe, with silver duct tape covering up tears in the upholstery. The only light in the room—a black metal floor lamp—stood beside the sofa. Its bulb shined a circular pattern on the white textured ceiling.

"You know, this place would look a lot better if you had more light," Leah said.

"I only have one lamp."

"I'll see if I can dig up somethin' for you."

"That would be nice."

"This one makes the room too dark."

"I don't mind it," Sylvie said.

The baby was asleep on a small blanket on the green sofa. She was wearing pink pajamas that appeared to be as clean as she was. So clean, they didn't even look like they'd ever been washed. The baby's brown skin shone in contrast to those pajamas. She'd inherited that skin color from her daddy.

Leah walked over with Snowflake in her arms and looked down on her. She appeared healthy. Leah hoped to God she was doing the right thing leaving this baby with this girl. "New PJs?" she asked Sylvie.

"Salvation Army," Sylvie said.

The living room looked into the kitchen. The kitchen lights were off, making it appear creepy by the light of this single lamp with the yellowish bulb. An old kitchen table with a brown Formica top stood in the darkness with three chairs around it in various states of disrepair. Behind it, the kitchen window allowed a view into the backyard, but from where she stood, Leah could only make out shadows. Living here alone with just a baby and this creepy lamp, it was no wonder Sylvie was seeing things in the backyard. Even if it *was* clean, this house was old and ghostly. It felt off, somehow.

Leah rubbed the cat under its neck, listening to it purr louder. She wondered how Sylvie ever managed to give *it* a name. She just hoped her daughter didn't end up with a name like Snowflake. But then, she figured even Snowflake would be better than growing up with no name at all. "What makes you think someone's been in your backyard?"

"Things have been moved," Sylvie said. "An' there's footprints."

Leah sighed. This was obviously turning out to be another false alarm. She wanted to take Sylvie's mind off the immediate problem. Deciding to try to put it somewhere else, she asked a different question: "Found a name for your daughter yet?"

A pause followed. Then, "Not yet."

"You gotta name her soon, Sylvie. It's not good for a baby not to have a name."

Another pause. "I know. I will."

They stood there in silence a minute or two, then Leah said, "Why don't you show me what's been moved?"

She followed Sylvie through the kitchen to the back door, noticing the dishes in the sink had been recently washed but not dried. Sylvie didn't turn on any lights, but Leah could tell the house was cleaner than ever. Every time she came to Sylvie's there appeared to be some improvement in some way. The only thing that didn't seem to improve were the number of calls into the station.

A shotgun stood beside the back door, propped up against the wall. Leah knew the answer to the question she was about to ask before even asking it.

"That thing loaded?"

"You betcha. No point in keepin' an unloaded shotgun around now, is there?" Sylvie said.

"You do realize how dangerous it is, right?"

"You guys tell me that every time you come in here and every time I tell you the same thing. You won't take me seriously, so that shotgun's the only recourse I have. I ain't livin' with my baby and bein' unable to defend myself. Not when someone's after me."

Leah let out a big breath. There was no point in arguing with her. Not while she was like this.

Sylvie fumbled with the dead bolt on the back door until she finally opened it.

"You got a light out here?" Leah asked.

"Burned out a few weeks ago."

"Should replace it."

"I will," Sylvie said. "Haven't had time."

Leah pulled out her pocket flashlight. She wasn't in uniform because she didn't wear one, but she had a pack snapped around her waist containing small items she commonly used. Her major gear was in her car, packed in her "go bag."

"You see that you do. Not safe having no light back here," Leah said, coming down the steps that led to the backyard. Sylvie followed behind her in shoes that had holes bigger than golf balls. "Those the only shoes you have, girl?" Leah asked.

"Yeah."

"Get some new shoes, too."

"Can't afford new shoes. The Baby takes all my money."

Once again, Leah felt something pull inside her. She liked this girl. Deep inside, she was rooting for her to win a war she never should have been involved in to begin with. A war that enlisted her without any permission.

What Sylvie had improved upon inside the house was more than compensated for by the state of the backyard. It looked like it hadn't seen any attention for a long time. Car engine parts littered the long grass and wildflowers that fought to choke each other back from existence. It had rained the past few days. That morning there were spotty showers, but the sky had started to completely clear just as the sun began to set. Still, everything had that wet smell to it. Even though it was a bright night (now that Leah's eyes had adjusted to being outside and seeing by the stars and moon), it still *felt* wet. Rainwater pooled in everything around her. There were jars, stacks of old newspapers, tires, even an old, broken kitchen sink. The yard was maybe a quarter acre before the surrounding forest choked it in, yet somehow it held a treasure trove of junk so well hidden that, until now, Leah hadn't even realized Sylvie had so much crap out here.

She followed as Sylvie walked slowly over to some small flowerpots that stood on top of a wooden box laid on its side against the back of the house. "Here," she said, gesturing to the pots. "These."

"The flowerpots?" Leah asked. She had pulled out a notepad and had her pen poised over it, ready to start a report.

"Yeah."

"What about them?" Leah asked.

"They was moved," Sylvie said. "They used to be inside the box. Now they're on top."

"When were they inside?"

"Yesterday."

"How do you know?" Leah wondered what kind of person notices something like clay flowerpots. She never would. She doubted many other people would, either.

"I saw 'em," Sylvie said.

"How can you remember somethin' like that?"

"I just do. I noticed 'em."

"I'm sure they were where they are now and you just reckon you saw 'em inside," Leah said, trying to placate the girl.

"No," Sylvie said. Leah heard the frustration in her voice. She'd heard it many times before. "They were *inside*. I'm *sure*. Somebody moved 'em last night. Or during the day today."

"Why would somebody move your flowerpots?" This was the rational question that Sylvie Carson's mind seemed incapable of asking itself.

"I don't know."

"What else was moved?" Leah asked.

Sylvie hesitated. "Nothin'. Just the pots."

Now it was Leah's turn to pause. "That's it?" She

realized she hadn't written anything down and was probably making the girl feel bad. She quickly wrote on her pad: *Flowerpots moved. From inside to top of wooden box.* "You say you have footprints?" Leah asked, glancing up.

"In the vegetable garden."

"Show me."

Sylvie led her to a patch of dirt that could only be a vegetable garden by mere designation. If it ever had been such a thing, many years had passed since then. Now it was a patch of ground with spotty grass and weeds that had grown in not quite as dense as the rest of the yard. Some of it was bare of any growth. Those areas were a gray color, and Leah suspected the ground was clay there. The clay looked moist and soft on account of all the rain.

Sylvie brought Leah's attention to one of these patches of clay. "Here. There's one here," she said. She moved over about two feet, straining to see in the night's light. "And here."

Leah shined her flashlight on the spots. Sure enough, the imprints in the clay could've very well been footprints. They might also just have been natural indentations made by the weather. They were pretty formless. Any detail they had—*if* they ever had any—had been washed away by the rain. "They don't necessarily look like footprints to me," Leah said. "I can't make out any details."

"They were detailed earlier," Sylvie said. "I *saw* them. They *were* footprints."

"Maybe you made them?" Leah asked.

Sylvie looked at her. "They're this big," she said, holding her hands almost a foot apart. "I'm a seven. They ain't mine."

"They don't look like anythin' to me," Leah said.

"Not anymore. But they did."

"I believe you."

"No you don't."

No I don't, Leah thought. "Okay," she said. "Let's say they *are* footprints. So somebody came into your backyard and moved your pots up to the top of your box and left footprints. So what?"

"I don't like strangers near my home. I have a baby."

Good girl. Too bad her worries were so misplaced. "I understand that," Leah said. "But I don't reckon this would be the kind of person you'd have to worry much 'bout, do you?"

"I would be worried 'bout anyone comin' into my yard," Sylvie said.

Leah thought about this. She didn't know what to say to the girl. All she could really do was tell her the truth. "I'm sorry, Sylvie. There ain't nothin' I can do with what you showed me. I'm afraid I need more to go on than some pots that may or may not have been moved and some spots in the clay that might possibly be footprints."

"They *was* footprints," Sylvie said. Leah could tell she was almost angry now, she was getting so frustrated.

"Okay, they was footprints. Listen, Sylvie. Think about this: Say they still was *perfect* footprints. And say the pots were obviously moved. Even then, *what would you expect me to do?*"

"Figure out who moved 'em?" Sylvie replied, forming it more like a question than an answer.

"And do what then?" Leah asked. "Nobody's really broken any laws now, have they? *Maybe* trespassin'.

But it ain't like I'm 'bout to arrest someone for movin' a few pots."

Sylvie took a deep breath. Leah could tell the girl was shaky. "So what're you sayin'?" Sylvie asked, her voice quivering. "I'm supposed to just stay here with my baby while people come into my backyard just as merrily as they please?"

Leah held up her hand. "I can tell you're upset and worried. How about this?" Everything in Leah's head was telling her not to do what she was about to do, but she didn't listen. She already knew she was going to do it. It was the only way she could come up with of getting out of here and still making Sylvie happy in the process. "I'll give you my home number. You have any problems, you can call me. *Any* time, day or night." The quarter moon rose in the night sky like a tipped grin. "Try the station first, of course. If I'm not there, try me at home. How does that sound?"

Sylvie thought this over. "Okay, I suppose. I guess it might help if somethin' else happens. You're the only one whoever comes right away anymore."

Ouch. That last one stung. Leah immediately tried to cover with an excuse. "Things get really busy sometimes, Sylvie," she said. But as soon as it came out, she realized both of them knew it was a lie.

They went back inside and Leah wrote her home phone number on a blank page of her report pad. Ripping out the page, she handed it to Sylvie, regretting the action the moment she felt the paper leave her fingertips. "Remember," she said. "This is only for emergencies, and *only* after tryin' the station first. Deal?"

"Deal," Sylvie said. She seemed a lot better. Being inside probably took the edge off. Leah couldn't imagine what it was like to be as paranoid as Sylvie, but being paranoid like that *and* being outside at night had to be even worse.

"Thanks for comin' out," Sylvie mumbled.

"You don't have to thank me," Leah said. "It's my duty to come out. It's my job. Just like your job's to look after your daughter. You just do me a big ol' favor, okay? Find her a name nice and quick?"

"I'm tryin'," Sylvie said. "I really am tryin' hard."

"Try a little harder. I don't think it matters as much as you go on about it matterin'."

"Wish I thought same as you," Sylvie said.

Leah walked to the front door. "Just take care of yourself, all right? And look after your girl." She unlocked the door, opened it, and stepped out onto the porch. "Don't forget to lock up behind me."

Leah walked down the stairs, hearing the door shut and the dead bolt shoot in her wake. She thought she probably didn't need to add that last bit. She doubted locking up her doors was something Sylvie Carson ever forgot to do.

CHAPTER 3

My mother actually did turn out to work late the afternoon Dewey talked me into wrapping aluminum foil all around our living room. I doubt I would have gotten into much trouble for it anyway—my mother knew a Dewey scheme when she saw one. But it definitely saved me from having to come up with a whole bunch of explaining about why I didn't think for myself before I did stupid things conjured up by other people. It was a conversation I'd had enough times that I didn't really relish the thought of having to go through it yet again.

When she finally did get home, it was late enough that I had already gone to bed. Carry was up watching something on television, but I was exhausted. I guess running tinfoil in a big circle around your house was a harder job than I thought.

I managed to still be awake when my mother came in to check on me.

"How was your day, Abe?" she asked.

"Not bad," I said, sitting up in my bed. "How 'bout you?"

She let out a little sigh. "Oh, I suppose it was all right. Had to go see Miss Sylvie again."

I knew all about Miss Sylvie. My mother was called to her home at least every other week it seemed for one thing or another. I didn't really understand why Miss Sylvie couldn't get along without always calling the police. Everyone else in town seemed to manage to do all right.

"Again?" I asked. "What's wrong with her, anyway?"

My mother shot me a look and I immediately knew I'd said something wrong. She had a way of just glancing at you that made you wish you could go back in time thirty seconds and completely change what you just said.

"There's nothin' *wrong* with her, Abe. She's just . . . *different*. She's got problems."

"Aren't problems something that's wrong?" I asked. I figured I already got the look, I might as well keep going and see where my line of reasoning took me.

"Well, yes and no, I suppose. You know what happened when she was little, right?"

"You mean 'bout her brother bein' shot by that preacher man and it happenin' right in front of her?" I asked. I looked down at my comforter. "Yeah, I know."

"Just imagine if you was her and that had happened to Caroline. How would you feel?"

I thought it over and realized I didn't rightly know exactly how I'd feel. "Probably sad?" I asked.

"Probably," she agreed.

"But I don't think that would make me keep callin' the police all the time when I grew up, would it?"

"You don't know what it would do, Abe. When things happen in your childhood, they change you. They affect you emotionally in unpredictable ways. Miss Sylvie can't help how she is. Do you think she likes bein' this way?"

"I ain't never thought 'bout it 'fore," I said. "I guess not. I guess you're right. I don't reckon anybody'd want to be callin' the police all the time."

"Anyway," my mother said, "you get back to sleep. Oh, and she might be callin' the house. I gave her our number to set her mind at ease."

"You gave her our *home* number?" Even to me, a twelve-year-old, this seemed like a ridiculous thing for my mother to have done.

"She needs to know she has access to someone she can count on, Abe."

"Will she be callin' all night?"

"What does it matter to you? You won't be answerin' it."

"I'm just askin'."

"I don't know if she'll call."

I hesitated, then asked, "Do you know what you're doin'?"

"Just go to sleep."

She got up off the edge of my bed where she'd been sitting and walked to my door as I lay back down. She stopped in the doorway and turned. "Oh," she said, "and in the mornin' we can talk about the oodles of aluminum foil I found spillin' outta the trash can outside."

I swallowed. "It was—"

"I know, Abe," she said. "It was Dewey's idea. That's what I want to talk about. The blind leading the stupid."

She walked out of the room, leaving me staring up at my ceiling wondering what Dewey was doing right now. Most likely he was lying in his own bed, dreaming up some ridiculous new invention that made no sense other than as a tool to show off my ability to be led by an moron.

The more I hung out with Dewey, the more my mother thought I was an idiot.

Dewey came over the next morning and asked if I wanted to ride my bike down to the grocery store to get his mom some more aluminum foil.

"I bet you got in some serious trouble when she saw you'd taken it all," I said.

"She never suspected a thing," Dewey said smugly. "She just told me, 'You know, I coulda swore I bought some last time I went grocery shoppin'.' " Dewey smiled. "Took all I had not to laugh." The way he said it made him sound just like her.

Sometimes I think some of Dewey's traits run through his family.

It was pretty early in the morning, having just gone on seven thirty. My own mother was still asleep, but I woke her to ask if it was okay if I went along with Dewey. Experience had taught me that my mother's sleep wasn't as valuable as me getting permission to do stuff, especially where Dewey was concerned.

She told me it was okay if I went, so I threw on my sneakers, grabbed my bike, and we headed off into what felt like a fine summer morning. The sun had already started beating down something fierce, making the world extremely bright. Sunlight bounced off the windows of the houses and stores along the sides of the street, and it reflected off the chrome of the cars parked along it, but there was a slight breeze that would pick itself up every so often and blow over us, keeping things tolerable.

Normally, for something like a couple rolls of aluminum foil, we'd just go to the Mercantile or what my mother referred to as Mr. Harrison's five and dime. But, it being so early on a Saturday, I was pretty sure the Mercantile wasn't going to be open. "I think we're gonna have to go all the way to Applesmart's," I told Dewey. Applesmart's Grocery was halfway up Main Street. Almost twice as far as Mr. Harrison's place.

"You don't think the Mercantile will be open?"

"I doubt Mr. Harrison gets up as early as Mr. Wyatt Edward Farrow," I said, referring to my neighbor across the street, who I knew liked to go on early-morning walks every Saturday. I also knew the grocery store opened at seven in the morning every day on account of my mother sometimes took me shopping early in the mornings. "Besides, it will be cheaper at Applesmart's," I said.

Dewey looked at me strangely. "Now you sound like my ma."

"Yeah, I don't know why I said that, to be right honest. Must be my own mom comin' out in me." I felt a little shiver run up my legs and through my arms.

We rode down Hunter Road and passed the Mercantile, which was indeed closed. "It doesn't open until eleven!" Dewey yelled out, riding up on the sidewalk so he could get a close look at the sign in the door. "Mr. Harrison must really like his sleep."

"Oh, well," I said. "It's a nice day for a ride."

And it was. It was an enjoyable ride all the way to Main Street.

Then things changed.

Because that's when I noticed something strange happening while we were on that bike ride.

A car was following me and Dewey. I'm not sure where it started, but at some point I noticed somebody was driving slowly behind us. Even though we kept going to the side of the road to let the car pass, it wouldn't. It was like whoever was driving wanted to keep on our tail and see where we were headed.

I didn't like it one bit. It gave me a sick feeling in my stomach.

At first I kept the fact about the car to myself, but after a while I figured it was only fair to let Dewey in on it. After all, he was being followed, too.

So I told him. I couldn't tell if he got the same sick feeling as me. It's hard to tell things like that with Dewey sometimes.

"This is creepy," Dewey said, sounding oddly excited.

"Just ignore it. It's probably one of the high school kids bein' a goof." I think I was trying to make myself feel better about the whole thing by saying that.

I kept trying to glance back and get a look at the car, but I couldn't see who was driving on account of the sun reflecting off the windshield. I hoped my guess was going to turn out to be pretty close. I tried to tell myself to relax. Who else would be following us on a bright and sunny Saturday morning in Alvin? It's not like me and Dewey were fugitives or anything. But then, what kind of teenager woke up before noon during the summer holidays? Sometimes Carry didn't roll out of bed before three.

From what I could tell, the car was a dark gray sedan that looked quite new. It may have even been black—it was hard to tell in all this sunlight. It looked pretty nice, and probably expensive. This didn't help the feeling in my stomach one bit. High school kids didn't drive nice, expensive cars. They drove old broken-down beaters they used to get them to and from school in Satsuma because they were lucky enough to not have to take the bus.

The car continued following us all the way to Applesmart's. We leaned our bikes up against the front window that said APPLESMART'S GROCERY in big arched lettering. I was considerably relieved when the car picked up speed and headed right past us. If it had been following us, it obviously decided we weren't worth stopping for. Thank goodness for that. Because, as I said before, it certainly didn't look like a car that belonged to one of the high school kids.

The town of Alvin was too small to have its own high school. All we had was an elementary school, so for anything above seventh grade you had to go all the way to Satsuma for school.

Even me and Dewey would be going to Satsuma after summer break was over, but we wouldn't have the luxury of driving. For one thing, we were still too young to get our licenses and for another thing, neither of us could ever afford to buy a car. Not even one of those lousy ones you always saw the high school kids pulled over in on the side of the road with their hoods up, trying to pretend they knew anything about fixing cars. Besides, there was no way my mother was about to put out that kind of money.

My sister, Carry, had been going to school in Satsuma for three years and she *still* had to take the bus back and forth. It took more than two hours total if you counted both ways. It seemed like a colossal waste of time to me. Especially compared to how good we had it here in Alvin for elementary school. Just a fifteen-minute walk, sixteen if there was a headwind.

No, I certainly wasn't looking forward to the end of this summer. Me and Dewey had better make the best of this one, that was for certain. It was almost like this summer marked the end of something special, like these days were a countdown of our final days of childhood before we moved on to a new part of our lives.

It turned out Dewey's mom had given him a bit of extra money for candy (which was increased by the fact that we probably saved an extra twenty cents coming to Applesmart's instead of going to the Mercantile), so that was a nice surprise. He hadn't told me until we got to the store. So we managed to get a grab bag each from old man Eakins, the guy who owned the store. I remembered his name on account of my mother tried to make me remember the names of adults I met so that I could be polite and say hello next time I saw them. She liked to say, "If you remember someone's name it impresses upon them that you're worth listening to." I wasn't quite sure what that meant, as I really didn't have much to say to anyone that was worth listening to, but I tried to do as she told me. So I remembered as many names as I could.

The part I couldn't believe is that Mr. Eakins remembered *my* name. Or at least he remembered me. As soon as he saw me and Dewey, he said, "You're the boy with the mother who's a detective, that right?"

"I sure am, Mr. Eakins, sir!" I said with a big smile. I'd always found big smiles worked in your favor at times like this. And I used his name so he'd know I was someone worth listening to.

It turned out, using his name got me more than that. With a grin, he quickly threw some extra gummies into my and Dewey's grab bags after asking us what our favorite candies were. Of course we said gummies were our favorites. I didn't understand why gummies weren't everybody's favorites.

I had forgotten all about the car that had been tailing us on our way here.

We were laughing and joking with Mr. Eakins about all sorts of stuff—nothing in particular, just the kind of mindless stuff you talk to guys who own stores about, you know.

That's when I happened to look outside.

Well, let me tell you, I stopped talking immediately. My mouth hung open, and my eyes grew wide. The car that had been following us, the nice black one (and it *was* black, I could tell now) was parked across the street from the general store and the driver was watching us through the window. The car was parked in the shade of a line of maple trees, so the sunlight was blocked from reflecting off the glass and the chrome, allowing me to see the driver. It was a woman, not a high school kid—a woman who must've been at least as old as my mom. Or maybe not quite that old, I don't know. I wasn't a very good judge of age when it came to anyone over twenty.

I heard Dewey and Mr. Eakins still jabbering away behind me. "Dewey?" I said quietly. But he didn't hear, he just kept laughing and filling his face with gummies.

"Dewey," I said louder.

"What?" he asked. "What's wrong with you?" He was near on impossible to understand since his mouth was stuffed with gummies.

I continued staring out the window. "Look. It's . . ."

"The car," he said, astonished, as he came up beside

me. "She really *was* followin' us." Only he didn't sound scared like I was. He sounded . . . *excited*.

I looked at him. "What the hell's the matter with you?"

He swallowed. "What?"

"Aren't you pissin'-your-pants scared right now?"

He shrugged. "Not really. I think it's like a movie."

"You're so weird." Then, quietly, I added, "I'm really worried. What do we do?" Behind us, Mr. Eakins hadn't even noticed we'd moved on from our conversation with him. He was busy now helping some old lady find a bag of biscuits for her dog.

"I dunno," Dewey said. "Nobody ever wanted to follow me before." Then it was like all the shutter blinds opened up in his head. I heard him gasp and his hand came to his mouth.

"What is it?" I asked, looking at him again.

"What if," he said, "she's after my inventions?"

Oh my God, this guy lived in a fantasy world. "Are you serious?"

"I think it's a strange coincidence that she shows up right when I've decided to start puttin' them in a book, is all."

"I think you have mental problems."

"What are we gonna do?" he asked.

"Not much choice," I said. "I guess we get back on our bikes and head home."

"And what if she follows us?"

"Then I get my mom."

"And what if she *doesn't* follow us?"

I stopped and thought about this. "Then . . . then there's no problem."

"Oh." Dewey sounded disappointed. "What if she does somethin' else?"

"Like what?"

"I dunno," he said. "Shoots us?"

I let out a big sigh. "I don't think she's gonna shoot us. Besides, she had the whole ride here to do somethin' and she didn't. That's the weird part. It's almost like she wanted to see where we was headed."

"I know!" Dewey said. "Maybe she's after our candy."

"Or our aluminum foil!" I offered sarcastically.

"You think maybe?" Dewey asked, not getting the sarcasm.

"No," I said. "I don't. Come on."

We went outside and I kept glancing over at her as we got back on our bikes. The driver's side window of her car was rolled down, so it was easy to see her. She had blondy-brown hair that was tied up, and she wore a lot of makeup. She was probably older than she looked, I guess. Her face was thin. She had big blue earrings on.

We began riding back the way we had come. At first it looked like she was just going to sit in her car, but then I heard it start up. I looked back to see her slowly start moving and go back to following us down Main Street.

"So much for there not bein' a problem," Dewey said.

I didn't reply. Instead, I just tried not to notice the stone turning over inside my stomach.

A couple blocks later, I heard her car getting closer. Then closer.

Then closer still.

Then I realized she was pulling up beside us.

Part of my brain remembered what Dewey had said in the store. I hoped she wasn't about to shoot us.

"Hey!" she called out through the open passenger

window. Her voice had a strange kind of nasally accent.

I ignored her and kept riding. My mother always said never talk to strangers and all that. I was sure it included stalkers.

"Hey," she said again. "Is your name Abe?" she asked.

That caught me off guard. Now I wasn't sure what to do. Was she a stranger if she knew my name?

"She knows who you are," Dewey said from the other side.

I decided to answer her. I looked up. "Yes."

"I need to talk to you," she said.

What? Why did this strange woman need to talk to me? I didn't know what to do. I had no idea who she was. "I don't know who you are," I said honestly.

"I'm . . . I'm your aunt."

I paused. Then I said, "I don't have an aunt."

"Yes you do. On your dad's side. I'm your daddy's sister."

Suddenly, it was as if a burst of sparrows sprang into my mind like they were flying from the treetops after a gunshot. I had never known my pa. He died when I was two. I didn't know very much about him. My mother never wanted to talk about him, and whenever I asked anything, she always kept her answers as short and to the point as possible. I certainly had no idea he had a sister.

Wouldn't my mother have told me if he had? Did she even know if he had?

I decided this was too important not to find out.

I hit my brakes.

"What are you doin'?" Dewey asked.

"I need to talk to this woman," I said.

"You don't know her from Adam," Dewey said, then stumbled. "—er, or Eve. She could be makin' this all up. She could be one of those child abductors or somethin'."

"You don't have to hang round here," I said to him. "You're free to go home and tell my mom where I am, if you like."

"Hell no," he said. "If you're stayin', I'm stayin'."

"Where's a good place to talk?" the woman in the car asked.

We wound up sitting with her on the outside steps of the library, the same steps Robert Lee Garner had stood on last fall when Mary Ann Dailey went missing—a time of my life I will probably never forget.

That day, it had been pouring rain, and Dewey had been wearing galoshes ten times too big for him. Today it was so hot I didn't know how long I could survive out here before I fainted. The wind that had been making the ride tolerable on our way into town seemed to have given in to the pounding sun as the day continued into the early morning.

"How come I ain't never heard of you?" I asked the woman as we took our seats.

"I don't know. I guess nobody ever thought to tell you . . ." She sort of drifted off. "I'm sure they had their reasons."

I kept waiting for reasons that never came. Instead, she held out her hand and said, "My name's Addison, by the way."

"I'm Abe," I said, shaking her hand, "which you already seem to know. This here's Dewey."

Dewey shook her hand, too. "Mighty pleased," he said.

"I would've just come straight to your house," she said, "but I'm worried about your mom's reaction to me just showing up like that. I was hoping you might tell her you met me and give her my phone number. I have some important things I need to talk with her about. You know what I mean?"

I had no idea what she meant. I thought this over. It was weird that this woman seemed to know so much about me and my family. "You *do* know my pa died, right?" I asked.

She smiled sadly. "Yes, Abe. I do. I'm really sorry about your loss."

The steps were white marble and had recently been cleaned. They looked extremely bright today. "I didn't really know him much," I said. "Carry knew him better than me." Then something occurred to me. This woman—Addison—had mentioned my mother and followed me, but hadn't said a thing about my sister. "You know about Carry?"

"Yes, I know quite a bit about you and your sister, actually. My mom and dad have pictures of both of you growing up. Lots of pictures."

"Your ma and pa?" I asked, trying to figure out how that fit. "You mean—"

"Your grandma and grandpa," she said.

"I have a granddaddy and grandma?" I asked.

She laughed. "Of course. You think the stork brought your dad? How old are you, again?"

"They still alive?" asked Dewey.

I elbowed him. "Don't be so rude," I said. Then I looked at Addison and quietly asked, "Is they?"

She nodded. "Sure are. That's kind of what brought me here to meet you."

"What do you mean?"

She sat there as though thinking about whether or not she should answer my question. I suppose she decided not to because the next thing she said was, "I really should be talking to your mother about all of this."

"How come you know so much about 'em all?" Dewey asked suspiciously, his eyes squinting at her on account of the sun.

She looked over at the other side of the street as if once again contemplating whether she should give out some important information or not. Her eyes came back to mine. "Just get your mom to call me. Then we can figure this whole thing out. I promise it will all become clear soon enough. Okay?"

"Okay," I said, disappointed in her answer.

She pulled a piece of paper and a pen from her purse and wrote a telephone number on it. Folding the paper once, she handed it to me.

I unfolded it, and read the number. "You don't live in Alvin?"

She laughed. "No, I'm from up in Boston. Can't you tell? Most people know immediately by the way I talk."

"I just thought you talked strange," Dewey said. "Some kind of weird accent."

I shushed him. "Don't be so rude."

She laughed again. "It's okay. Lots of people think I talk strange. Lots of people where I live would think *you* talk strange." A starling caught her attention. "A whole bunch of people . . ." she said, trailing off.

"You came all the way from Boston to give me this number?" I asked.

She paused again. "Yes and no. There were a few reasons I came down here. Again, I need to talk to your mom about this. Please get her to call me. But make sure you explain that I won't be back in Boston until the day after tomorrow, so she should wait at least two days before calling. You know what I mean?" She sounded especially funny when she said words like *again* and *about*. I almost expected Dewey to say something. I was glad when he didn't.

"I'll give it to her," I said, blocking the sunlight with the back of my hand as Addison stood up.

"Thanks, Abe, and let me tell you what a nice experience it's been to finally meet you. You too, Dewey. You seem like very nice boys."

She walked back down the street to her car and got inside. A moment later she drove off. We watched her go in silence until she was out of sight.

"She seems like a psycho to me," Dewey said.

"I thought she seemed nice enough."

"She hunted you down from Boston."

"Yeah, somethin' weird's going on."

"Think she's really your aunt?" Dewey asked.

"Dunno."

"She looks nothin' like you."

I didn't respond. I just wondered about all the questions she kept refusing to answer. And what did she mean by it's been nice to *finally* meet me? One thing was for sure: She did seem a little bit creepy.

Something was definitely not right.

CHAPTER 4

My mother was just getting out of bed when me and Dewey made it back home from the grocery store. We didn't even bother going to Dewey's first to drop off the aluminum foil before heading straight to my place so I could tell my mother about this strange woman who called herself my "aunt."

My mother met us in the kitchen.

Quickly, I told my mother everything that had happened, the words fighting their way out of my mouth.

"And she wanted me to give you this," I said when I had finished relaying the story. I handed my mother the piece of paper with the telephone number written on it.

"Abe, what have I told you 'bout talkin' to strangers?" my mother asked.

I looked down at my sneakers, which I had forgotten to take off at the door in my mad rush to come inside and tell the story. "I know," I said, "but this woman seemed to know who I was. She told me I was her blood."

"People can tell you a lot of things, Abe."

My eyes turned up to hers. "So she's not my aunt?" I felt strangely disappointed.

"To the best of my knowledge, your pa never had no siblings," she said. "Would've been strange for him not to have mentioned 'em to me. We were married five years 'fore he . . ." She trailed off and I knew bad memories had started swooping in like hawks going after field mice.

My pa had married my mother when my mother was just a kid, not much older than Carry. I think the reason they even got married in the first place was all on account of my mother getting pregnant with Carry, but from what I've come to understand they *were* in love. But then, when I was two years old, my pa died.

I never really got to know him. It made me sad that I barely remembered him. When I was older, I found a picture of him in my mother's closet that I kept. I still carried it around with me all the time. I don't think my mother knew that I had it. I found it in a box in her closet with a whole bunch of other pictures of my pa and my mother. They were the only pictures of my pa I'd ever remembered seeing on account of my mother getting rid of all the ones around the house after him dying.

She didn't like to talk about my pa much. Even now, she still seemed very uncomfortable when topics spilled over into anything regarding him. I didn't think she'd dealt with his death properly.

That was something I got from watching the TV, that you had to go through a certain grieving process. And, until you got through it, you couldn't get over the person you lost.

I think my mother was stuck somewhere in the middle, just going round and round.

"Well, how did this woman know so much about Abe and Carry if she's not their aunt?" Dewey asked.

"I don't know," my mother answered after thinking about it, "but if she tries to talk to you again, you come and find me or go to the station and get Chief Montgomery to talk to her, you understand?" It was funny how Dewey had asked the question, but her answer had been directed straight at me.

"Yes, ma'am," I said, watching the toe of my sneaker outline one of the checkered squares of our kitchen floor.

My mother seemed upset by our news, and I hadn't wanted to upset her. I thought she'd be happy, or at least interested in knowing more about what was going on, the same way me and Dewey were. Instead, she seemed almost angry, or maybe it was scared I was looking at. I couldn't tell.

"I think she's a nice lady," I said. "I don't think she means to hurt anyone."

"She seemed like a psycho to me," Dewey said. "She hunted Abe down from Boston."

"You don't know nothin'," I said to Dewey.

"You're too young to know if someone's nice or not," my mother told me.

"What do you mean?" I asked. I thought this was a ridiculous statement.

"I mean you're naïve, Abe. Anyone can make you think they're nice when really they have ulterior motives."

"That's not true," I said. "If anythin' it's the opposite. I tend to think people ain't nice when they really are. Remember what happened with Mr. Wyatt Edward Farrow?"

Mr. Wyatt Edward Farrow had moved in across the

street near on a year ago and, at the time, Dewey and I thought for sure he had been up to no good. Little girls were disappearing around Alvin and my mother was trying to figure out who was nabbing them and I thought with all my heart that Mr. Wyatt Edward Farrow had something to do with it. He just seemed so suspicious. Dewey and me even followed him one morning all the way into town to see what he was up to.

In the end, he turned out to be one of the nicest fellers I'd ever met. He was a carpenter, and he made Dewey and me biplanes—real big ones—that we played with all through the winter. We were *still* playing with them. When we weren't, mine hung from fishing line right above my bed. I loved it.

My mother still hadn't answered my question. Maybe she was thinking about something else and hadn't heard me ask it. At any rate, I decided to drop it. It didn't matter what she said, I *knew* I was able to tell bad people from nice ones. It was something I was good at. Like I said, it was the other way around I sometimes had problems with.

"You gonna call the number?" Dewey asked her.

She let out a long sigh. "I dunno."

What I didn't know was why Dewey's questions were getting answered and mine weren't. "Why wouldn't you call?" I asked. "What's the worst thing that could happen? And even if he didn't talk 'bout them, surely Pa must've had a mom and a pa. So that part's probably true, don't you think?"

Another sigh came to her lips. "Your pa never spoke of his folks," she said. "I don't *know* why. But—" She stopped as if in deep thought about all this.

"I don't see what callin' the number can possibly hurt," I said.

"I don't know who this person is, Abe," she said. "I don't want to call someone I don't know."

"You gave Miss Sylvie your home number and you're afraid of talkin' to a stranger?" I laughed. "Whoever this number belongs to, she's gotta be more normal than Miss Sylvie." I regretted saying it as soon as it came out.

Then Dewey followed with, "You *really* gave Miss Sylvie your home number? Are you *crazy*?" And then *he* laughed, and everything got even worse. A *lot* worse.

My mother's eyes narrowed, and if laser beams could've shot right out of them, we'd both have been fried all over the fridge and stove. "I'll hear none of that from either of you!" she said. "Miss Sylvie is *not* to be made fun of. Especially not by *you* two. Especially not in *this* house. Am I clear?"

Dewey's hands went into his pockets. "Yes, ma'am," he said quietly.

I hung my head and just nodded.

"Good. Now, Dewey, I reckon you oughta get home with that aluminum foil 'fore your ma starts figurin' out she didn't go through two rolls on her own in a single day, don't you?"

Dewey had set the foil, which was sticking out of the top of a brown paper bag, on the counter when he came into the kitchen. "Yes, ma'am," he said again.

I was about to tag along with him when my mother said. "And, Abe . . ."

I stopped and turned.

"I want your room cleaned."

"But—" It wasn't even messy.

"No buts. You're stayin' in today. Go take off your shoes."

"Yes, ma'am," I said. She was in one of her moods. I knew there was no point in even trying to post a disagreement.

Dewey was barely out the door and my sneakers had just been kicked off my feet when the phone rang. I raced from the back door through the dining room back toward the kitchen to grab it when my mother picked up the receiver right in front of me. I could tell she was still upset; I just wasn't sure what she was upset about. I think it was a number of different things, some of which made sense to me, some of which did not. My giving her the phone number of this woman who called herself my aunt seemed to really have knocked her for a loop.

I stood in the kitchen beside the sink listening to my mother's side of the telephone conversation. The sun was higher in the sky now and just edged the top of the window looking outside over the backyard where the cherries hung from the two trees, just waiting to be picked. Their dark red skin glistened under the hot sun.

"Hello?" she answered. "Oh, hi, Ethan. How are you this mornin'?"

Ethan was Ethan Montgomery, the police chief of the Alvin Police Department, my mother's boss.

"What do you mean?" she asked, suddenly on the defensive.

"No, I didn't do it so she could threaten you. I—" Whatever Chief Montgomery was saying to her was making her even more agitated than before. This was definitely not a good day to be stuck inside with my mother. I wished more than ever I had been able to escape with Dewey.

"No, Ethan, listen. I told her she could call me if she *needed* to, but only for emergencies. And I emphasized that she had to call the station *first*."

I was guessing this had to do with my mother giving Miss Sylvie her home phone number. I don't think anybody would think that was a good idea. I still wasn't quite sure why *she* did.

"Well, I certainly didn't mean for her to use it as leverage." There was a brief pause and then, "Yes, I'll talk to her. I'll let her know."

Another pause and, "Ethan, before you go, do you mind if I ask you something about an unrelated issue? It concerns an encounter Abe had with a woman on Main Street this morning."

And my mother told Chief Montgomery the whole story about the woman claiming to be my aunt. She got most of the details surprisingly accurate. I guessed that's what made her a good detective. When I had told her about it, I hadn't thought she'd been paying that much attention, but I suppose she actually had been.

When she was finished, she fell silent while Chief Montgomery spoke. Then my mother said, "Well, I guess I just wanted your opinion. Do you think it's *possible* this woman might actually be Billy's sister? Could Billy have had siblings and not mentioned them the entire six years we were together?"

Billy was the name of my pa.

Another pause and then, "I don't know. Do you think I should? That seems a bit like using the system for my own personal agenda. And I feel somehow like I'm being disloyal to Billy's memory. Like I'm spyin' on him or somethin'." She turned a thing over in her mind and then said, "Okay, go ahead and do a background check on Billy." She let out a deep breath "I don't know how I feel about this, but at least I'll know whether or not to trust this woman. Oh, and she says she's from Boston. Abe said she sounded funny, so she's probably got the accent to go with the claim. Thanks, Ethan. I owe you one. And don't worry 'bout Sylvie; I'll talk to her right away. It won't happen again."

My mother hung up the phone.

"Why you doin' a background check on Pa?" I asked.

"To see if it turns up any brothers or sisters."

"Why don't you just call the number?" I asked. "Wouldn't that be easier?"

"Because I don't trust people I don't know, Abe. I'd rather not go into this blind. It's too strange, her showin' up after all this time. It just strikes me odd."

"Everythin' 'bout Pa strikes you odd."

"Now what's that supposed to mean?"

"I dunno."

She searched my face, as though trying to decide if I had insulted her and deserved a good talking-to. "I reckon you think too much."

I had no idea what she meant by that. "What did Chief Montgomery say 'bout Miss Sylvie?" I asked, figuring she'd answer my question by telling me to mind my business.

She surprised me. "Oh, apparently she called the station again with another problem and asked Chris to put her through to Ethan. When Ethan took the call, she immediately threatened him by sayin' if he didn't take her seriously, she would just call me at home. So now I got Ethan thinkin' I'm in cahoots with Miss Sylvie, givin' her ammunition to blackmail the department into attendin' to her."

"Why would they think that?"

She took another deep breath. "Because apparently you're not the only one who reckons givin' out my home number to Miss Sylvie was a bad idea. And they all know how I feel about the way her calls are treated at the station. I don't keep it a big secret. I think the girl is treated unfairly. I hate injustice, Abe. You, of all people, should know that."

I thought about it. I reckoned I did know it and it was something I admired about my mother very much. "I hate injustice, too," I said.

She held out her arms and I moved in close. Pulling me into her chest with a warm hug, she said, "Now you're just tryin' to suck up."

"Mom?" I asked, while her arms were still wrapped tightly around me. "Did I really do something wrong today by talking to that woman?"

"You did what you thought was right," she said. "I just wish you hadn't talked to a stranger. At least you did it in a public place. This time it turned out okay. You got home safe. But next time you might not be so lucky. I just don't want anythin' bad to ever happen to you."

"I don't want anythin' bad to ever happen to you, either," I said.

She let go of me. I could see a tear standing in her eye. "All right. I reckon it's time for you to go start cleanin' up your bedroom."

"Okay," I said reluctantly, and slunk down the hall, wondering what all might show up in that background check Chief Montgomery was doing on my pa. There were sure a lot of things about him that *I* didn't know. I would *love* to find out more.

* * *

That night, Leah Teal went to bed with a lot on her mind. She left the drapes of her bedroom window open, and outside heavy clouds had started moving in. Somehow, the moonlight still managed to find gaps between them to shine through and, once Leah turned off the lamp on her nightstand, a pale gray light fell into the room. It was enough to cast small shadows on her sprayed white ceiling. She stared up at that ceiling, unable to stop thinking about poor Sylvie Carson all holed up in that little house with that newborn. The times Leah managed to release those thoughts, her brain just switched over to ciphering about this woman who had suddenly appeared into her little Abe's life claiming to be his aunt.

Could Billy have had a sister? Was it *possible* he kept that sort of information private all those years? Do you keep that sort of thing hidden from your wife? Then she started second-guessing herself—wondering if it's really a lie if you just don't mention it. Because deep down, Leah didn't want to believe Billy was capable of ever lying to her.

But *could* it all be true? And *parents*. New grandparents for Abe. That idea both excited and scared Leah. The last thing she wanted to do was see her boy get attached to someone only to lose them. The first time that had happened was almost too tragic to survive. She doubted she could manage it a second time around.

But Billy certainly *did* have a ma and a pa; he just rarely mentioned them. Not that he was one for being too outspoken. She used to tell him he could keep the devil's secrets in a poker game with Jesus if he'd wanted to.

Did he lie to her?

She couldn't figure it out.

One thing was for sure. She wasn't getting any sleep tonight. It didn't help that she went to bed so early. The room grew darker. The cherrywood of the dresser across the room became lost in the shadows of the waning light, but she could still make out the bright white face of the clock set on its top. It was barely ten. She'd only tucked Abe in a half hour ago. From the living room, she heard the sound of canned laughter coming from the television. Caroline was still up, no doubt cuddled in a blanket on the sofa. That girl was a night owl during the summer, and she always had that damn television set so loud it was a wonder Leah ever managed any sleep.

That's when the phone rang and Leah nearly jumped out of her pajama bottoms. Her head and pillow had been right beside the nightstand where the phone sat between the bed and the lamp.

Figuring it was likely Sylvie, she quickly answered it. The last thing she needed was a reason for Abe to give her any more back talk about handing out her home phone number than he already had.

She was surprised, though, when the voice on the other end didn't belong to Sylvie Carson at all, but to Police Chief Ethan Montgomery, whom she'd just spoken to barely four hours earlier.

"Ethan, what is it?" She hoped it wasn't Sylvie blackmailing him at the station again. She hadn't had a chance to talk to the girl about it yet. She figured that was a conversation best done in person when it came to someone like Sylvie Carson.

"Leah, we got ourselves a problem."

"I figured that. Otherwise, why else would you be callin' me at all hours of the night?"

"Since when is ten all hours of the night?"

"Since I got a boy comin' home tellin' me he met his auntie in the street today. Can we just move past this part of the conversation?"

"You know what tomorrow is, don't you?" Ethan asked.

"Sunday."

"I know it's goddamn Sunday. You know what *else* it is?"

"Why don't you just assume I don't and tell me and save a whole bunch of time?"

"Tomorrow is the day our old preacher man gets released."

Oh dear Lord Jesus, how did Leah forget *that*? She'd marked it on her calendar at work barely two weeks ago. Eli Brown finished his sentence tomorrow after spending over seventeen years in jail. Twelve of them in the Federal Correctional Institution in Talladega, the rest up in Birmingham at the Work Release Center. He was being let out just under three years of the full twenty he got handed down for manslaughter after killing little three-year-old Caleb Carson.

After a period of silenced panic while Leah's mind raced over ideas about how to handle damage control on this event, she finally came to a realization. "Sylvie doesn't know," she said. "Does she?"

"Well, she's not *supposed* to," Ethan said.

That was an odd thing to say, Leah thought. "I don't see this as bein' a huge problem, to be right honest, Ethan," she said. "Sylvie doesn't know, and the man's done his time. In the eyes of the law, he's no longer a criminal. Besides, she might never find out. He probably won't ever return to Alvin. After all that happened it's the last place I'd think of headin' back to if I were him."

There was a slight chuckle in Ethan Montgomery's voice when he responded that Leah didn't like one bit. "Go turn your television set on," he said.

"What?"

"Turn on your TV, Leah. Channel six. The ten o'clock news."

"Caroline's watching the goddamn TV," she said. "Just tell me."

"Go turn the channel," he said and hung up.

"Oh dear Christ." She set down the receiver. Pulling back the covers of her bed, she swung her legs over her mattress and slid her feet into her slippers. Even though it was July, the hardwood floors of the bedrooms still managed to somehow get cold at night.

She padded down the hallway, through the kitchen and dining room, and into the living room where Caroline sat curled up on the sofa just as Leah had expected, wrapped in the yellow blanket she'd had since she was about ten years old. The thing was ridiculously worn, with tattered corners and even holes in some places, but Caroline refused to give it up, even when Leah offered to replace it with a new one.

She was watching some situational comedy Leah hadn't ever seen. Before Caroline even had a chance to complain, Leah walked over to the television and started turning the dial.

"Hey!" Caroline yelled. "What are you doin'? I was watchin' that!"

"Police business," Leah said. "Now shush."

Leah got to channel six and stopped turning the dial. On the screen, a reporter was at the Birmingham Penitentiary interviewing a very old-looking Eli Brown.

His face was even more creased than it had been the last time Leah had seen the man, when he was transferred up to Birmingham. He had less hair and what little he had was pure white.

"Mother," Caroline whined from the sofa. "Please turn it back to my show?"

Leah shushed her again and turned up the volume. "So," the reporter asked the old preacher man, "after seventeen years, how do you go about stepping back into your life?" The reporter was a young dark-haired kid in a gray blazer.

Eli Brown was wearing an orange prison outfit. Leah couldn't help but think it kind of suited him. "Just the way I left it, I s'pose," Eli said, his voice more hollow and broken than ever. "I'll find my way back to God and back home to Alvin. For me it's really about picking up the thread right where it started to unwind."

The phone immediately rang again. And this time, Leah had no doubt when she picked it up whose voice she was going to hear at the other end. It certainly wouldn't be Police Chief Montgomery. Not *this* time.

Staring at the screen, she let the phone ring once more as two words came out of her mouth. One was "Oh." The other was "Shit."

CHAPTER 5

As Leah had imagined, the telephone call was a disaster. It was Sylvie, of course, and she'd been watching the same channel six news program. Until now, nobody had told her that Eli Brown's parole was coming up two and a half years early. Far as Leah knew, the girl didn't even know the man had been moved from Talladega into the work release program in Birmingham. Apparently, old Preacher Eli was as good as gold behind bars. Nobody wanted to see him spend any more time there than he had to.

Obviously, Sylvie Carson didn't feel the same way about the man.

"What are you gonna do 'bout this?" she asked Leah, although it was more like she screamed it into her phone than so much as asked a question. Leah could barely understand a word the girl was saying she was talking so loud and fast.

"What do you mean, what am I gonna do?" Leah asked back. She tried to keep her own voice as quiet and slow as possible, hoping to calm Sylvie down, but she knew in her mind there was no calming this girl down. She'd been jumping at boogeymen hiding in corners too many years. Now, suddenly, she felt she had a real boogeyman to jump at and seeing him on the television screen made the danger more real than ever.

"I mean you *can't* just let him walk out free! You *know* what he did to little Caleb!" Leah heard Sylvie begin to wail. "He don't deserve to ever be free. He don't deserve to be alive. He shoulda been sentenced to die!"

Leah stayed quiet. It was the only thing she could think of to do. Nothing she could say would placate Sylvie when she was this upset. Preacher Eli Brown had been convicted of manslaughter in the first degree, a class B felony in the state of Alabama. "He got the maximum prison time the judge could sentence him to, Sylvie," Leah said. "The minimum was ten years. Eli got twenty. You should be happy 'bout that. Justice was served."

Sylvie's voice suddenly grew eerily quiet as the sobbing stopped. It almost sounded scary from Leah's end of the phone. "Justice was served?" Sylvie asked, now speaking slowly. "Justice was served?" Her voice slowly rose in volume. "You didn't see your little brother get blown apart four feet in front of you at the supper table when you was five. Don't *you* tell *me* that justice was served when the murderin' son of a bitch who done it is about to walk out of prison a free man tomorrow."

"You're right," Leah said, remaining calm. "I can't possibly know how it feels to be you. It must be horrible. But Eli Brown has done his time. By the laws of this state, he's no longer a criminal."

"Yeah? Well, by the laws of me, he's still a murderin' son of a bitch who better not show his face anywhere near round here on account of I got a loaded shotgun with his name on it just waitin' for a chance to have its trigger pulled."

Leah sighed. "Now don't you go doin' nothin' stupid. You just go on pretendin' things are the same as al—"

"I will *not* pretend things are the same as anythin'," Sylvie said. "If I have to, I will hunt that man down, but he will get what he has comin'. Because the law might not think he deserves to serve his full sentence, but I'm gonna make certain he is fully punished for the crime he committed. I don't think the *law* completely understands real life. Things might look good to all them fancy lawyers, but all them fancy lawyers ain't livin' with pictures in their heads of their baby brother bein' blown to bits. They're just sittin' round big tables makin' chitchat and decidin' on things they have no right decidin' on." She kept talking and Leah wondered if she was even going to stop to take a breath. "But I'm gonna make the decisions regardin' what's adequate punishment for Preacher Eli from now on because I'm someone who *does* live with those pictures in my mind. I'm someone *affected* by all this. I can make the *right* decision."

Leah heard something in Sylvie's voice she didn't like. Maybe it was on account of the fact that the panic seemed to have gone. It was replaced with something more like determination. Sylvie meant what she was saying, and that scared Leah. The last thing she wanted was Sylvie becoming a vigilante and going on a manhunt, trying to kill someone who had just finished serving his time.

Leah decided this was something too important to just shrug off or even to leave until tomorrow to deal with. By tomorrow, Sylvie could have disappeared and be fully engaged in some or other creative plan.

Leah had to change Sylvie's mind. And she had to do it tonight.

"I'm comin' to your house," she said.

"Why's that?" Sylvie asked. She sounded genuinely surprised.

"To talk."

"We's talkin' now."

"I want to talk face-to-face."

"Ain't gonna make no difference," Sylvie said. In the background, Leah heard the baby crying. "Oh, damn it, The Baby just woke up."

"Well, you go put her back down and listen to me, Sylvie. I want you to be there when I arrive, you understand? And you'll let me in. And you're gonna talk to me."

There was a long pause and Leah thought Sylvie might have gone to get the baby, but then she heard her breathing on the other end. Finally, Sylvie said, "Okay, but I might not listen too close."

"That's okay," Leah said. "I can't control how much you listen. Just do me a favor and put the kettle on? It's been a long day already. You *do* have coffee, right? If not, I can bring some."

"I got coffee," Sylvie said. "But I ain't got no milk. Well," she laughed, " 'cept for my breast milk. You better bring some of your own milk."

"I'll take it black," Leah said. "Just make sure it's strong." Leah dug her forefinger and thumb into her temples. The day had given her a headache. Now, instead of letting her go to bed early, it was continuing on into the night, giving Leah a second act.

"How long will you be?" Sylvie asked. "I wanna know it's you when you come to the door. I don't like people comin' to the door after dark."

Leah already knew that. "I'll leave in ten minutes. Probably be there in twenty-five. Don't worry, I'll call out from the other side of the door and let you know it's me. Don't ever open the door for anyone you don't know. Understand?"

"What you think I am? Stupid?"

"No, Sylvie. Just young."

"I ain't so young."

Leah's fingers dug harder into the side of her head. "Maybe not. But you're a lot younger than me."

Sylvie Carson lived up on Old Mill Road in the north-east part of town. The road should have been called Old Mill River Road, as it almost exactly followed the Old Mill River, although the river ran all the way down to the Anikawa and the road started where the old rail-road tracks crossed Main Street at Finley's Crossing.

It was one of the oldest roads in town, and most of the houses along it were spaced far apart, giving it a very desolate feeling as you drove along, especially at night. In a way, it was much like the area on the exact other side of town called Cloverdale where a lot of the black people lived. Both Cloverdale and Old Mill Road were probably built around the same time.

Alvin had the distinct look and feel of a town that was originally built from the outside in. Leah hadn't noticed this in other small Alabama towns. When you came into Alvin from the west side by Highway Seventeen or from the east side through Finley's Crossing, you came through the oldest farms and ranches first. Once you got off the main highways, the roads on the outskirts were all gravel. It wasn't until you started getting past the perimeter that things became paved and houses started looking newer.

This was opposite to how she thought it should be. In her mind she thought a town would start with a single building, maybe a Town Hall, and then grow around that building. Start with a central street, such as Main Street, and grow around that street. Alvin had a Town Hall and a Main Street, but it all seemed in much better repair than the buildings and streets on the outskirts.

This was a question she would one day ask her uncle Hank about. Hank knew lots about everything, and even if he didn't have the right answer, he'd give her an answer that she would be satisfied with. That was the way Hank worked.

Earlier, when the sun had gone down, the sky had only been partially cloudy with a waxing moon. Before going to bed, the sunset had been quite pretty, even with the clouds stretched across it. It was one of those late afternoons when the sun and the moon were in the sky at the same time, something Leah had once thought impossible when she was a kid. It wasn't until she was well into her teens that she realized the moon didn't only come out at night.

But since sunset, a layer of thick clouds had rolled in, and now there was no moon and no stars whatsoever. To make matters worse, the few streetlights along Old Mill Road were sparsely strung while it curved and twisted its way along the edge of the river. The road felt even

more desolate, cold, and lonely as it began to climb upward into thicker forest. And, as she came up on
Sylvie's old house with the peeling paint, things felt
more desolate, colder, and lonelier still. Even though it
wasn't actually cold at all, this road just brought with it
a chill Leah didn't like at all.

Leah parked in the drive and walked the few steps to
the door, hoping Sylvie had that coffee ready. Leah's
eyes were barely staying open on their own. She knocked
on the door and called out, "Sylvie? It's Leah." Then
she caught herself. She was being much too friendly
and informal. Normally, she would never act so casual.
Quickly, she knocked again and corrected the mistake.
"Sylvie? It's Detective Teal, Alvin Police Department."

Surprisingly, Sylvie didn't go through her usual
routine of sliding the chain over and peering through
the crack to verify Leah was who she said she was before opening the door. She just shot the dead bolts,
opened the door, and welcomed her in. This was so unprecedented that, for a moment, Leah just stood there,
stunned.

"Well, you comin' in or what?" Sylvie asked. "You
said you wanted to talk, let's talk. I've had your coffee
ready for ten minutes. It's probably not even hot no
more."

Blinking her eyes wider open, Leah stepped across
the threshold into Sylvie's place. Once again, the ugly
living room lamp was on, but this time the light over
the kitchen table was on too, so things didn't look quite
so much like death.

The living room wasn't as tidy as it had been on
Leah's last visit. The magazines were no longer neatly

stacked, and there were a few plates with leftover food sitting on the old coffee table. But Leah had come unexpectedly. She had to remind herself that there were times her place looked like a hurricane had hit it. *Having kids will do that. Kids of any age. Speaking of which—*

"Did you get the baby down again?"

Sylvie smiled. One of her front teeth was crooked. Leah hadn't noticed this before and wondered if maybe that was on account of this possibly being the first time she'd ever actually seen the girl's teeth. Could she really have never seen Sylvie smile before?

"Yeah," Sylvie said, "she fell right back to sleep after I fed her for a bit. Come on in. Never mind the mess. Coffee's in the kitchen."

As soon as they walked into the kitchen, Leah's eyes locked on the shotgun still leaning against the wall beside the back door. She knew it would be loaded. There was no point in even asking anymore. She'd asked so many times she'd lost count, and the answer never changed. There was no way it would be any different *now,* of *all* times.

They sat at the table. Leah instinctively took the chair facing out into the room.

"So what brings you here so late?" Sylvie asked. Her voice was pleasant. She even smiled again. It felt so strange to Leah. It was as if she was talking to somebody normal. And, really, she should be very happy about that, but something inside her wouldn't let it settle right, because she knew very well that Sylvie wasn't normal. Sylvie shouldn't be acting normal. She shouldn't be happy. A half hour ago, she was yelling on the phone that she was going to hunt down and kill a man tomorrow, and now it was as though she had turned into Miss Congeniality.

Leah took a sip of her coffee. Sylvie was right, it had gotten a bit cold, but at least the girl had listened to her and made it strong. It tasted like the old campfire coffee she used to make when she and Billy would drive up into Mississippi for the weekends. That was before their marriage. She'd been seven years younger than Sylvie. "I wanna talk about Eli, Sylvie," Leah said. "I wanna finish what we was talkin' 'bout on the phone."

"Oh." Sylvie looked away and, for a moment, her face fell. Leah watched it very closely. The girl was being very guarded with her emotions, and that scared Leah, because it meant she really did have a plan. This wasn't just some displaced reaction; this was something cold and calculated.

The smile came back, as though by magic. "Would you like to try some oatmeal raisin cookies I made? They aren't too good. I'm not much of a baker, but I thought I'd give 'em a try. I watched this woman on the TV make 'em? And she said they was easy as pie. So I tried to follow step by step, only she started going too fast, and I think maybe I—"

"Sylvie," Leah said, reaching out and touching the girl's hand, which was grasping the side of her coffee cup. "I didn't come here for cookies. I came to talk about Preacher Eli. He's bein' released tomorrow and he says he's movin' back to Alvin. Now, that probably bothers you a mite. I know if I were you, I'd probably be bothered a mite by it, too."

Concern fell over Sylvie's face. "You think I should be worried?"

"That's not what I said. I said I think it bothers you. Which means I think *I* maybe should be worried. Tell me how it makes you feel."

Sylvie looked at her cup. "Mad. Sad. I dunno. Kinda like it hurts and I can't do nothin' 'bout it." Turning her face back up, Sylvie revealed tears pooling in her eyes. "How do you think it makes me feel? I want the man dead, Miss Teal. I can't rest without him bein' dead."

"Please call me *Officer* Teal, Sylvie. And him bein' dead won't help your rest any. I agree you need closure, but not the kind of closure you think you need. That kind of closure never actually closes anythin'. You'd wind up with his ghost hauntin' you the rest of your life."

"What do I do then?"

"I reckon you need to find a way to forgive him for what happened all them years ago."

Anger flashed in Sylvie's eyes, and for a brief second Leah thought things were going to blow out of control. But the anger was washed away by more tears. They still just stood there, tiny pools reflecting the light overhead like small blue moons.

"I can never forgive him for what he did. Not to Caleb. Or to me. He took away everything I ever had." As she said this, her voice broke, betraying the control she'd been exhibiting since Leah had arrived.

Leah sighed. She remembered what she'd heard about Sylvie still being emotionally five years old. She had to talk to her like she was a five-year-old and this was a concept far beyond a five-year-old's understanding.

"No, Sylvie, he didn't. He accidentally shot your brother. Caleb wasn't meant to die. What happened to him happened because the Lord saw fit for it to happen. For whatever reason, it makes sense in some way or another. That's why Eli only got sentenced to manslaughter. To be honest, I don't think he meant to pull that trigger at all. I don't think he even meant to shoot your daddy."

Sylvie just sat there quietly as Leah took a long sip of her coffee before continuing. The girl actually seemed to be listening.

"My own daddy was the police officer assigned to that case," Leah said, "and he would come home at night and tell me 'bout it. I was only a kid then, but I remember him sayin' how remorseful Eli was about what happened, and my daddy felt sorry for him on account of him feelin' so bad. What happened to your brother was terrible, don't ever get me wrong."

With another gulp, three quarters of Leah's coffee was done. She was trying to time it so she'd be done just in time to leave.

She continued talking, grateful Sylvie hadn't tried stepping into the conversation. Instead, she just sat there with her hands folded in her lap like a little girl. Occasionally, she would lift one hand to the table to take a small sip of her coffee, but then her hand would go right back to her lap.

"But all the hate you're carryin' for Eli?" Leah said. "It ain't hurtin' Eli none, Sylvie. It's hurtin' you. You're carryin' it round with you like a bucket o' poison. And every time you think 'bout how much you hate him, you drink a little bit more of that poison. Eli don't drink any of it, you do. And that poison eats away at you from the inside. It makes you see the world as a dark, scary place where people are out to get you."

Sylvie looked down at the table.

"And the only way you can heal the wounds you've got from drinkin' all that poison is by learnin' how to forgive," Leah continued on. "And when you forgive, you're not givin' anything to Eli either. He ain't the one gettin' the forgiveness, *you* are. If someone gives you a gift and you don't take it, who does it belong to?"

Leah wasn't sure if Sylvie was even listening to her anymore. She was just staring at a spot on the table directly in front of her. The light above the table began to flicker and buzz for several seconds before settling back to normal. Leah sat there, waiting for a response. Finally, Sylvie looked up and answered her question. "I guess it still belongs to the person givin' it?" she offered.

Leah was happy to hear her sounding like her old self again, even if that old self was the scared, paranoid Sylvie who called the police every time a car so much as backfired in the neighborhood. The way Sylvie had been acting when Leah got here had scared Leah into thinking Sylvie was well on her way to making some really bad decisions. Now Leah thought that just maybe she might have turned things around.

"Exactly," Leah said. "Eli's not acceptin' your gift of hate, and he ain't gonna accept your gift of forgiveness, neither. Besides, these gifts ain't *for* him. Both of these things belong to you. One of them tears you up and hurts you inside, and one of them will heal you. Do you understand any of what I'm sayin' to you?"

Sylvie sniffled. "A little, I guess."

"Can you do some thinkin' on it?"

Sylvie blinked away some tears. "Guess so."

"Can you stop talkin' 'bout killin' Eli? Because all that's gonna do is put you in prison, and you won't even get manslaughter. You'll get murder one. And then there really *will* be no justice in the world. And who would raise that little girl of yours? Who would be left to give her a name?"

Sylvie wiped her eyes with the back of her sleeve. When she spoke, there were tears in her voice. "No one."

With a drink of her coffee, Leah nodded. "No one. That baby needs you more than you need to drink any more poison from that bucket you's carryin' round with you. So I want you to just relax for the next few days and let things settle. If you need me, or get anxious at all, you call me. You don't even need to call the station first. Do we have a deal?"

Sylvie was crying. "Okay."

Leah rose from her chair. "Now stand up and give me a hug."

She did. And Leah felt the girl tremble in her arms.

With a look back at the shotgun, Leah asked, "I don't suppose there's any chance I can convince you to take the shells out of that 'fore I leave, is there?"

Still crying, Sylvie shook her head.

"Didn't think so. Just be careful. And call me if *anything* happens, you understand? Do not pick up that shotgun. Pick up the phone. Am I clear?"

Sylvie nodded.

Leah kissed her forehead. "You'll be okay. Just take care of that baby. And get some sleep." Reaching down, she lifted her cup to her lips and finished her coffee. "Tell you what I'll do. Once Eli Brown's moved back here, I'll pay him a little visit and just get a feel for the man—make sure he's as safe as I believe he is. Then I'll come back here and tell you everything me and him talked about. Does that sound like a good plan to you?"

Sylvie nodded. "I'd appreciate that." Her words were broken.

"Okay. I've gotta leave now." Leah stepped into the living room. "Don't forget to lock the door behind me."

Once again, it was probably something that didn't need saying.

CHAPTER 6

On Monday afternoon I came up with a brilliant plan.

It was too late to get a real sword; they were back at Disney World, and my mother wasn't about to buy me one anyway, but she couldn't stop me from making my own. Sure, it wouldn't look as impressive as the ones I saw while on vacation, with the steel blades and the hilts full of gems, but at least I'd have a sword. And if I made it out of wood, I could use it to play fight with Dewey, which would mean I'd have to make two of them.

Problem was, I wasn't so good with building stuff when it came to wood. Not that I was all that bad; I just didn't have any experience. But I knew somebody who did. My sister, Carry. And Carry was home right now, in the living room, watching television. And my mother was at work, so the timing was pretty near perfect.

All that remained to my plan was to come up with another plan on how to get Carry to help me.

I decided the direct approach was the best. So I

walked into the living room where she was sprawled all over the sofa and just asked her straight-out if she'd do me a favor,

"Well, I guess that depends now, don't it?" she said smugly.

"On what?"

"On what the favor is, dork."

I didn't feel we were off to a great start with her calling me a dork already, but I decided to press on. "Will you help me build a couple swords from some of the wood Pa left in the garage?"

She didn't even look at me. Her eyes were glued to that television screen. "What are you talking 'bout?"

"I wanna make two swords so me an' Dewey can pretend sword fight with 'em, but I need your help on account of I ain't no good at woodwork and stuff."

She laughed. "And you think I *am*? You *do* remember the non-tree tree fort we made when you was little, don't you? That thing didn't last through the night."

The drapes above the sofa were open and sunlight was pouring into the room, casting my sister in the shadow of the sofa cushions. It made it hard for me to see her properly. "Yeah, but we was just kids then. You're almost an adult now."

"Tell Mom that. She still thinks I'm twelve." She hesitated and added, "No offense."

"None taken," I said honestly.

"Anyway," I said, "I'm thinkin' swords might be easier to make than forts. They don't seem to me like they'd be all that complicated."

I stood there, waiting for her to reply, but a response never came. She just kept watching her television show. After what felt like at least five whole minutes of waiting, I asked again. "So?"

"So, what?" she asked back.

"So will you help me?"

"I'm watching *The Facts of Life* right now. Maybe later."

I looked at the television. "This is a rerun. You've seen this one at least a hundred times. I think I've seen it more than half a dozen, and I can't even stand this show."

"So what? They're all reruns. The show ended in May. I wanna watch it again, ass face."

"Hey! Mom told you to stop callin' me that!"

"Oh, you gonna tattle on me?"

I kicked at the gold shag carpet with the toe of my sock. "No. I just really want you to help me make a couple swords so me and Dewey can pretend sword fight. Please? It'll only take an hour."

She turned her head and stared at me. "An *hour*? You think I have an hour to stand around and make stupid swords with you? *Please*."

I sighed. "Okay, then a *half* hour. It won't take long, I promise. They can be real simple."

Lying there with her head on the rise of the sofa's arm and one leg thrown over the top and the other askew along the cushions, I could tell she was considering it. Finally, she pushed herself into a sitting position. The sunlight from the window lit her blond hair from behind, making her look almost like an angel. "Fine! I'll help you make simple swords," she snapped. "But they're gonna be *real* simple. And you're gonna owe me somethin' for this. Don't you forget it."

My heart flipped over in my chest. "I won't," I said, smiling. "I promise. Cross my heart."

* * *

Crossing your heart and promising your sister you owe her one is like signing a pact with the devil. Especially if your sister is Caroline Josephine Teal. Oh, she helped me make the swords, all right, and they turned out not half bad. We made them from two pieces of narrow pine. One piece was about two feet long and it made the handle and blade. The other was maybe six inches and we nailed it across the other maybe six inches from the bottom to form the cross guard of the hilt. Carry figured out how to use my pa's old belt sander to taper the long piece down into a point. When we were done, they looked pretty good. Even better than I'd hoped.

"There," Carry said, as I inspected our handiwork, one sword in each of my hands. "You happy with 'em?"

I beamed back at her. "I sure am. Dewey's gonna love 'em." The garage smelled like old car oil, which was strange because there hadn't been a car parked in here for as long as I could remember. It was too full of wood and tools and other junk left over from my pa after he died that my mother had never bothered cleaning up or getting rid of. We had the garage door open for light and the sun picked out specks of dust scattering through the air.

"How long we been out here?" Carry asked.

I checked my watch. Uncle Henry had bought it for me last fall—it was a Timex, just like his. Except for when I had baths, I always wore it. "Just over half an hour."

"That's a lot of my time. You remember our deal?"

I fell silent, trying to figure out what she was talking about. I didn't rightly have any idea what she meant.

"We had a deal, ass face. You promised if I made you your swords that you'd owe me one."

"Oh, yeah," I said. "What do I owe you exactly?" I realized now that I'd been so excited at the prospect of getting my swords made that I never confirmed what the "one" was that I owed her and that the whole deal was probably a mistake.

"That's for me to decide. But when the time comes, I'll let you know."

"Okay," I said hesitantly. The way she said it made me wonder if she was going to get me to kill someone for her or something.

Oh, well, there was no point in worrying about my deal with Carry until the time came for me to fulfill whatever she came up with. I decided to just ignore it for now and be happy I had swords.

I was just about to rush inside and call Dewey when my mother drove into the driveway. Unsure of how she'd feel about us being in the garage and playing with Pa's tools, I nearly raced over to close the door, but realized she'd see me do it, and that would just make me look guiltier. Besides, way back when Carry helped me build the non-tree tree fort, my mother hadn't been upset at all. She'd been right happy about it, in fact.

As I mostly do—at least more times than not—I decided honesty was the best policy and walked out of the garage into the afternoon sun with my swords in my hands to show her my and Carry's handiwork.

"What're you kids doin' in the garage?" she asked, getting out of her car.

"Carry helped me make some swords so me and Dewey can pretend sword fight." I held up the one in my right hand, pretending the sunlight was glinting off its hardened steel blade. It actually looked more like sun shining on dull wood with rounded corners that

Carry had sanded so we wouldn't hurt ourselves, but I had a pretty good imagination.

"Did I say you're allowed to play in the garage?"

"I—" I started, but changed to "You didn't say we *wasn't* allowed to."

"Don't be smart with me, Abe."

"Should we not have made them?" I asked, wondering why this was different than the fort had been.

For a moment she seemed at a loss for words. I think her mind was somewhere else and she wasn't really sure what she was angry about. "You just should've asked first. Did you clean up after yourselves?"

I nearly laughed. That garage was such a mess, you couldn't find an elephant in there with a magnifying glass. We *had* to clean up just to be able to get at things. So, "Yes," I said, quite honestly.

"Good." She still hadn't really looked at my and Carry's woodworking projects as she closed her car door and started toward the house. In her hand was a file folder.

"You never said if you liked my swords," I said from behind her, still raising the one majestically. A slight breeze picked up, swirling leaves around my feet. They had fallen from the shrubs planted around the driveway.

"They're fine. Just don't play with 'em in the house."

She walked up the front steps and was just about to open the door when I asked, "Somethin' wrong?"

Stopping, she rested her forehead against the door. After a minute she said, "Listen, Abe, I'm sorry. It's not you. Here, let me see your swords."

I walked over and showed them to her.

"Oh, these are nice. Did Carry help you make them come to a point like this?"

I nodded. I decided not to tell her that I had to sign a pact with my sister in order to engage her services. "I think Dewey will like 'em," I said with a grin. "We can pretend sword fight."

"Just be careful. Just because they're not metal doesn't make them not dangerous. You could still poke out an eye with one of these."

"I'll be careful. We rounded the corners and made the ends blunt, see?" Then I nodded to the file folder in her hand. "What's that?"

She looked at it and her expression fell. "Oh." She took a breath. "It's the background check Chief Montgomery ran on your pa."

Suddenly, my swords were no longer important to me. Excitement frizzled through my body. It was like an electric bolt of lightning had erupted at my heart and quickly spread throughout my entire insides. "What's it say? Can I read it?"

Looking down at me standing there expectantly, she exhaled so hard her shoulders heaved. "Come in the house. We'll sit at the kitchen table and go through it together."

I couldn't get inside the house fast enough. Leaning my swords up against the wall beside the door outside on the porch, I went in and took off my shoes. It seemed to take her forever to get to the kitchen table where I was already anxiously seated and waiting. I could tell there was something inside that folder that my mother obviously didn't like. Still, I was filled with anticipation. I never really got to know my pa. I barely even remembered him. Mostly I remembered the picture I carried around in my pocket that I found in my mother's closet. And it seemed nobody would ever give me any details about him when I asked anything either. But now, here was a file folder, full of real information concerning my pa. And it was only a few feet from my hands.

We sat there, our chairs almost touching, and my mother laid the folder in front of her. "There's not a lot of information here," she told me. "Your pa never got in trouble with the law or nothin' like that, thank the Lord"—she said "thank the Lord" in a way that made it sound like that was a potential possibility, given something else she found—"so it's really limited to things like employment, family history, stuff like that. It's really quite boring."

"Then why are you so worked up over it?" I asked.

"I'm not worked up."

"Seems like it to me."

"Okay, maybe a little. But it's for something dumb."

"What?" I figured if she was worked up about it, it couldn't rightly be so dumb.

"Well, in a way, I think your daddy lied to me, and that don't sit very well is all."

"Pa was a liar?" I didn't know much about him, but this was the last thing I thought about my pa.

"Now I didn't call him a liar. I said *in a way* he sorta lied to me."

"What do you mean by sorta?"

"I mean he didn't rightly tell me the truth."

I couldn't figure out the difference between that being just a "sorta lie" and a real lie, so I asked her.

With yet another sigh, she flipped open the folder. Inside was a document on blue paper with a staple in the corner. It turned out to have three pages to it.

"He didn't *not* tell me the truth, I suppose, better explains it," she said.

I scrunched up my forehead. "Huh?" I asked. "What does that mean? I don't get it."

"Your pa had a family he never told me 'bout. In fact, he had an entire past he seemed to have neglected mentionin'."

"Doesn't everyone have a past?"

"Yeah, but usually bits and pieces of it come up from time to time in casual conversation. Your pa kept things all to himself. He didn't so much as even hint at any of this." She was flipping through the pages. I still hadn't heard a word of what any of "this" was.

"So he lied to you by not tellin' you what he was lyin' 'bout?" That question didn't even make sense to me.

""Why did I expect anythin' different from him? But for some reason, I never thought of his life before we met, and since he never mentioned it, it was like it never existed. And that life led into the life we spent together. So, in a way, to me, he had no life before our marriage. Our marriage was his life. Now I find out about all this stuff and that he really did have a life that led into our life together, and so it changes our marriage in a way. It's sort of like our whole life together was a lie."

She was sounding crazy, but I wasn't sure I should tell her that. "Maybe Pa just didn't think the stuff that happened to him 'fore he met you was important. Maybe in a way he liked pretendin' his life didn't really start until he met you."

Her head jerked up and her eyes met mine. There were tears in hers, but they looked surprised.

"Did I say somethin' wrong?" I asked, worried I was about to get in trouble.

She took me in her arms. "No, Abe. You just said possibly the single most right thing you've ever said."

"I did?" I asked, my voice muffled by her shirt. I wasn't even sure what I'd said. This conversation had stopped making total sense to me a while back.

When she let go, I asked, "Will you tell me what it says about Pa now?"

"Well, for one thing, the woman you met? Addison? She probably really is your aunt."

I couldn't help but smile. I'd met family. "Really? Is her last name Teal like mine?"

"Yup. Least it was last time these records were updated. Unless she got married since. And you do have two grandparents livin' in Georgia. I *knew* he had parents. He *had* mentioned them from time to time, but only in passing. He told me he didn't get along with them and sort of left it at that. From what little information I gathered from your pa, your grandpa ran the house like some sort of military sergeant. I never dreamed they was livin' barely three hours away the whole time. The way your pa talked, it was like they was clear across the country or somethin'."

"I have another granddaddy!" I said.

"And a grandma," my mother said.

"Wow! This is really great! I can't wait to tell Dewey! Are we gonna meet 'em?"

She looked at me sternly. "I dunno yet. That waits to be seen."

"Waits for what?"

"For me to decide."

I looked down at the table. "Oh."

My mother flipped to the last page. I could tell there was something on that page she really didn't like.

"What else does it say?" I asked.

"Nothin' that concerns you."

"Please? He was my pa and I don't know nothin' 'bout him."

She looked into my eyes for a second.

"Please?" I asked again.

"Fine, I guess." I watched her swallow hard before she continued. When she did, her voice was much quieter than before and it sounded like she might be holding back tears. "Says here your pa was married once before. Can you believe it? You know how young he was when he married me? He'd barely turned twenty. Well, he was even younger when he married her. He was only eighteen. They lasted two months."

"That makes you mad?"

"He shoulda told me."

"So you could get mad at him?"

"So I would know."

"What would you have done?"

"Gotten mad at him."

"I'm bettin' that's likely why he never told you," I said. Why did this all seem so easy for me to understand and yet my mother seemed to be having such a hard time with it?

"He *still* shoulda told me. For better or worse. We vowed that. I'm supposed to know all the 'for worse' parts."

"But this was before your weddin'."

She glared at me. "Why don't you run along and play with your swords? I want to be angry some more and you're just makin' it tough."

"There anythin' else in there about Pa?"

"Nothin' interestin'."

"You sure? You said that 'fore and then you tol' me he was married once before."

She lifted the papers off the table and snapped them in the air. "Well, let's see. You wanna know his fishing license number? His driver's license number? How about his Social Security information? I can give you some of his tax records if you'd like. Any of this sound like somethin' you'd like to be let in on, Abe?"

I pushed myself off the chair. I could tell she was done showing me the file. "No," I said. "Thanks for letting me know 'bout the family stuff."

"You're welcome."

"I'd really like to meet 'em," I said.

"I know you would."

"And I know you're scared to," I told her.

"I know you know. Now take off. You're too old for your own good."

"I know," I said, and left the kitchen.

Leah watched her little Abe leave, wondering how in the world she'd managed to raise him all by herself and still have him turn out so well.

Then she thought of Miss Sylvie and realized she was going to turn out okay, too. It was just going to take some time, was all. Eli Brown had moved back to Alvin already and, even though Leah hadn't yet paid him her little visit that she promised Sylvie she would, Sylvie seemed to be handling the situation just fine. Leah would go see Eli sometime in the coming week. She wasn't worried. The man was harmless. She'd seen him when he'd been moved from Talladega to the Birmingham Work Release Center and the man she'd seen was a kind and gentle man, not a man worth being a mite scared of.

Sylvie was just afraid of her memories. And they were memories being amplified because they were coming from a five-year-old girl.

No, Leah wasn't worried one bit about Eli Brown. That's why she hadn't *bothered* going to see him yet.

Despite Sylvie's fears, nothing bad was about to happen.

Or so Leah thought.

Then, four days later, Sylvie found her cat, Snowflake, lying dead on her back porch.

CHAPTER 7

Leah was at the station when the call came in. Chris had picked up the phone and immediately Leah knew it was Sylvie by the way he rolled his eyes. "Yes, Miss Carson," he said in that condescending voice that made Leah want to pistol-whip him. "And what can we do for you today?"

Sitting at her desk, Leah tried to keep looking busy, as though she wasn't interested in listening to Chris's side of the conversation, but the truth was that she was eavesdropping because if she didn't take an interest she knew nobody else would. So, while she pretended to be going through files and looking things up on her computer terminal, she was actually on autopilot, eavesdropping on Chris sitting at the desk beside her.

It was probably pretty obvious to Chris. The station had only switched over to computers in the last year and Leah still wasn't really sure how to use hers properly. Chief Montgomery liked to go on about how one day all the computers in all the police departments across the country would be connected and share a central repository of information, but that all sounded like science fiction to Leah. Right now, any data they wanted in the system, they had to put there and store on floppy discs that they kept in a cabinet. They had probably five hundred such discs and, once the data was inputted, it was easier to work with. But inputting it was a big job. This was why the only data Leah had access to was recent events that happened in and around Alvin. For anything else, they still had to order background checks or reports, usually from places like Mobile.

She knew just enough about her computer to get by. She wished she knew as much about it as her son did. Sometimes, after hours, when it was just her and Abe (and occasionally his friend Dewey), she'd let them go on the terminal. They were much better at it than her and even discovered a game they liked playing on it called *Super Slither*. Leah had no idea the computer even had games. She still didn't understand why it does.

But for now, while she listened, she pretended she knew what she was doing. Even if what she was doing was only scrolling the bright green text of her contact list of other stations and emergency numbers up and down the dark green screen.

"Is that so?" Chris asked. "And how long do you figure he's been dead?"

Dead? Who's dead? This immediately grabbed Leah's attention. She no longer pretended to be playing with her contact list or shuffling around papers. Now she was just in her seat, obviously paying attention to what Chris was saying to Sylvie.

"I'm sorry," he said. "*She.* How long do you figure *she's* been dead?" He wrote something down on the pad in front of him. "And what was the cause of death?" He wrote a bit more and said, "I see."

She? Well, for someone being dead, Chris was remaining awfully calm. It better not be the baby, or there'd be hell to pay. In fact, she couldn't think of anyone it could be that would allow for his demeanor to be so inappropriate at such news.

"Yes," he said finally, still remaining calm as a salamander sunning himself atop a rock in mid-July, "of course we'll send an officer out right away." He sat back in his chair, half turned, and gave Leah a smile and a wink. "Yes, I'm aware of the severity of the situation. You just sit tight now, all right? Okay. Bye, Miss Sylvie."

Reaching over, Chris dropped the receiver onto the telephone and said, "And now the community tax dollars shall once again be spent on yet another crazy quest for that woman."

Leah didn't share Chris's lackadaisical attitude. She was anxious to find out about the details of the call. "What was that about? Who's dead?"

Chris laughed. "You're not gonna believe it. It's her damn cat. She found it dead on her back porch. Now she wants to file a police report. I guess she suspects murder?" He made a gun out of his forefinger and thumb and pointed it at the floor. "Pow!" he said, lifting the barrel of his finger-weapon. "That'll show *you,* you mangy cat. Next time you'll know better than to mess with us." He laughed even louder this time.

Still Leah felt anxious. "What did she say happened to it? What killed her?"

With a shrug, Chris said, "Damned if she knows. She said she can't see no reason why the cat should be dead. It isn't like it's very old or nothin'. She sounded a bit loopy, if you ask me. I think she was pretty messed up about it."

"You think?" Leah asked, standing from her seat.

"Where you goin' so fast?" Chris asked.

"To Sylvie's. To check out what happened to her damn cat. Some of us have to take our jobs a little more seriously." Grabbing the keys to her car, Leah headed straight for the doors.

"It's just a goddamn cat!" Chris yelled in her wake, his sentence getting cut off by the sound of the door slamming shut behind her.

Leah had been getting more and more annoyed with Chris's attitude at work lately. It had gotten progressively worse since he single-handedly made what could've been called "Alvin's biggest bust" (and *was* in some papers even as far up as Birmingham).

Chris had brought down a cocaine deal that went bad for the people involved, and he did it pretty near all by himself (although a lot of it happened by utter good fortune) and seized over one and a half million dollars' worth of coke off the street, according to the values the feds in Mobile came back with.

Stories of exactly what happened that night tended to vary. Some said the deal was in progress, some said Chris caught them by surprise as they were leaving their hotel room with the drugs to make the deal. Some said both they and Chris caught each other by surprise. There were stories involving civilian passersby getting involved and helping Chris take down the gang. Some reports said Chris was responsible for two of the men. Chris said that he nabbed all four men, and had planned his entire takedown well ahead of time. At any rate, four men did go into custody. Ethan was just happy Chris was still alive.

What that amount of drugs had been doing passing through Alvin was anybody's guess. Chris only got

wind of it from a last-minute tip. Then he did a one-
man stakeout, which Leah thought was incredibly irresponsible of him, not bringing her into the loop. He
could've easily been killed. Drug dealers don't carry
around product worth millions of dollars without also
carrying around weapons.

But it all worked out in the end. Chris rounded up
the two or four men (depending on who you listened
to) and got the coke. He even made all the papers right
across the state and, for five or six days, Alvin was actually put on the map, so to speak.

Leah found it funny that she could solve crimes of
girls going missing and turning up murdered and raped
and that didn't make nothing but the local news, but
when cocaine was involved, everyone was suddenly
interested.

Anyway, the bust happened, oh, must be going on
nine or ten months or so ago now, and Chris seemed to
have been resting on his laurels ever since. It wasn't
that he didn't do *anything*; it was just that his work
lacked its usual dedication, commitment, and luster. If
it stayed like this much longer, Leah was going to have
to say something to Ethan about it. She hoped Chris
would figure it out and work things through on his
own, though. She hated going above people's heads, or
behind their backs, or around any other body part. It all
just sounded so sneaky.

Chris did know his stuff, and he was dead on with a
bull's-eye when Leah arrived at Sylvie's. Miss Sylvie
was truly messed up by what had happened to her cat.
"Thank God you got here so fast," she said, opening
the door before Leah was even fully out of her car. "I
didn't know what to do. The cat—she's . . ."

Leah tried to calm her down. "It's okay, honey. I'll take care of it."

Sylvie let Leah into the house. She had the baby on her shoulder. The baby was awake but quiet. The moment Leah was inside with the door closed and locked behind her, Sylvie started pacing the floor, rubbing the baby's back. Leah got the impression she'd been doing this ever since calling the station.

"Where's the cat?" Leah asked.

"Right outside the back door."

Opening the door, Leah found the animal lying lifeless right on the back step. It looked as though it just fell over and died. Putting on blue latex gloves, she squatted down and, touching the body as little as possible, turned it different ways looking for any sort of mark that might indicate a cause of death. She expected to find some blood somewhere. Maybe the cat caught itself on some barbed wire or a piece of sharp metal. God knew there was enough garbage lying around this backyard for anything to kill itself on if it tried hard enough.

But there was nothing. No puncture wounds. No blood. Not a mark on its body. Rigor mortis had begun setting in, so the body was stiff. Leah didn't have the background needed to discern any time frame as to when death might have occurred.

But the lack of obvious means of death niggled at the back of her mind. *Something* killed this cat. Normally, the first thing Leah would suspect would be a coyote. But if it had been a coyote, there'd be no body left here for Leah to be examining. Whatever it was that took this animal's life did so without leaving a single mark. Not even a scar. And, like Sylvie told Chris on the phone, it wasn't like Snowflake was old. She wasn't even a year yet, by Leah's calculations.

Something wasn't right. Leah could feel it. She hated that feeling, that gut feeling she got all the time when something "wasn't right." Her own daddy and Police Chief Montgomery always said it separated the good detectives from the bad ones. She hated it because it meant she had to follow it, even though, rationally, she knew it was crazy.

But she wouldn't be a good detective if she didn't. So, turning around, she started back for her car.

"What're you doin'?" Sylvie asked, a slight panic in her voice. Leah suspected she thought Leah might just be leaving her alone again to have to deal with the dead cat by herself.

"I left my radio in the car. I'm going to call Chris. I want him to come out here, too."

"So you suspect somethin's up?"

Leah looked into Sylvie's eyes, searching them for any emotion. It was uncanny how much she could feel that five-year-old girl staring back at her. "I don't know what I suspect, Sylvie. I just don't want to leave any stone unturned is all."

Leah got into her car and radioed Chris back at the station, telling him to come by Sylvie's and bring the cruiser with the CSI kit in the trunk. Even though she could tell he was trying to contain it, Chris couldn't help cracking up. "Backup?" he asked, his laughter breaking up a bit over the radio. "For a dead cat?"

She steeled her voice and said loudly, "Chris. Get your ass over here, now."

That got rid of his giggles but fast. "I'm comin'," was his only reply.

When Leah returned to the backyard, Sylvie was standing in the frame of the back door, purposely looking anywhere but down where the cat was lying basically at her feet. She still held the baby in her arms, but Leah was quite sure the baby had fallen asleep.

"You think same as I do, don't ya?" Sylvie said, whispering now, so as not to wake her daughter. "That someone killed Snowflake? That someone came into my yard and killed my poor kitty?" The poor girl was on the brink of breaking down. Leah didn't need that right now.

"I don't reckon I know *what* I think right now, Sylvie. I just reckon we gotta check this out as thoroughly as possible. Now I promised you I'd take your calls seriously, so I'm takin' this one as seriously as I can. That's why I called for Chris, understand? That's the *only* reason. Don't go readin' anythin' into this that ain't there."

"You talk to Preacher Eli yet?"

That was a question Leah had hoped Sylvie wouldn't ask. "Not yet."

"How come? You promised me that you would do that, too. He's been back in town over a week now, and here my cat winds up dead on my back porch. I'd say that's a mite coincidental, wouldn't you?"

"Now, Sylvie, I don't think Eli killed your cat."

"Why not?"

"Because what would his motive be?"

"Just that he likes killin' things smaller than him. He killed my baby brother."

Leah rubbed her eyes in exhaustion. She hoped Chris wasn't taking his time getting here. The last thing she wanted was to keep up this line of conversation with Sylvie any longer than she had to. "I will go talk to Eli Brown tomorrow. Hell, I'll go do it today if we get done here in time. You have my word."

"I've had your word before. It's suddenly not meanin' so much no more."

Wow. The girl knew how to make things sting, that was for certain. But guilt trips were something Leah was used to. She had two kids at home and one was a fifteen-year-old daughter who made Sylvie look like a rank amateur when it came to laying on the guilt.

"My word is my word, Sylvie. You take it any way you like. Folks around town know what it's worth. Main thing is that *I* know what it's worth."

Fifteen minutes later Chris showed up, but the time seemed to go by so slowly that it could've been hours. He took one look at Snowflake on the porch out back and said, "Hmm. Dead cat. Yep. Dead." Then he saw the look in Leah's eyes and his demeanor instantly changed. For the rest of the time he spent there, he was very professional and polite to Miss Sylvie, which made Leah quite happy. If he hadn't gotten rid of the attitude, she was ready to tear a side off him something fierce when they got back to the station. Leah could shout louder than Chris could. Besides, she had seniority. And her pa and Ethan Montgomery went way back. When it came right down to it, it was exactly like they said: Blood was thicker than water. And Ethan and her pa had been close enough to consider each other blood. You didn't turn your back on blood.

And technically, Leah outranked Chris, although it was only a formality. Ethan Montgomery had made her detective as a favor to her pa before he died, so that the station would be able to pay Leah more money in order to help raise her family. Then it became doubly important when she lost Billy.

Leah was just happy none of this mattered, as Chris seemed to come around now that he had arrived on the scene.

He searched the cat's body more closely than Leah had by using the various tools in the CSI kit and eventually gave up establishing a cause of death. It definitely wasn't anything external. It seemed like the cat had just simply dropped dead. "Maybe it had a heart attack?" he speculated.

"The cat was barely a year old," Leah said. "Seems a bit far-fetched to me."

"Well, somethin' might of scared it to death," Chris said. "But then, it's s'posed to have nine lives." He smiled at Leah, who didn't smile back. Chris's smile disappeared immediately. "Sorry, that was just a little joke to lighten the mood."

"We can use a little less lightenin', thanks," Leah replied.

Pulling the camera from the CSI kit, Chris took pictures of the body from all the different angles, exactly as he would a real human body at a real crime scene. *Good,* thought Leah. *Now he at least looks like he's taking this seriously.*

When he was finished taking pictures, he put the camera back in the case. "Well," he asked, "what do you want me to do with the cat now? I've pretty much done all I can."

"Bag it, I guess," Leah said. "Give it to Norm in the morning. He can probably tell us how it died and give us a rough time of death."

Chris looked up at her. "Seriously? You want me to get the coroner to give your dead cat an autopsy?"

Leah came in close and lowered her voice so Sylvie wouldn't hear. "I want to set this girl's mind at ease, Chris, and if that takes pulling some strings and getting Norman Crabtree to take a few minutes out of his day to examine this here body? Then, yes. That's exactly what I'm sayin'."

Chris just shook his head. "I think you're almost as crazy as she is."

"Chris, what if someone *did* do somethin' to this cat? I mean it didn't die of old age. There's no indication a coon or a coyote got it. *Somethin'* killed it, and we can't tell what after an hour of examinin' it? And *you* don't find that odd?"

"I reckon you've been readin' too many detective novels."

"I reckon you've been spendin' too much time behind your desk doin' too many crosswords."

With a huge sigh, Chris reached his gloved hand into the CSI kit and pulled out a bag big enough for the cat's body to go into. "Bagging the cat," he announced. "But I'm gonna have one problem."

"What's that?" Leah asked.

"I'm not really sure how I'm gonna attach the toe tag."

CHAPTER 8

Most nights when Sylvie suffered "incidents" she had trouble sleeping.

Tonight, she lay in bed with thoughts circling like a kaleidoscope inside her head. This happened often. Usually, it was always the same thoughts; she'd go through different parts of the past, trying to make sense of them. But making sense of some things was impossible. Sylvie knew that, but she couldn't do anything to stop the endless spinning. Sleep would come eventually, but before it did, she would have to succumb to the pain of reliving the memories of her childhood.

For a long while, she'd known she wasn't completely normal. When she saw her baby brother murdered that day something broke inside of her. Sylvie remembered it all so clearly: like a photograph, only one that went forward and backward in time with different pictures developing on it.

She'd known something inside her wasn't right back then, but she managed to hide a lot of it. After the initial shock wore off, and everyone grieved for Caleb, her folks appeared to somehow move on with their lives. It seemed they thought Sylvie had, too. The first indication her pa got that something was truly wrong with his daughter didn't actually happen until she was twelve. Until then, she'd done a good job of hiding her depression and her paranoia from the world. Sylvie would hear her folks refer to her as "a kid who likes to spend a lot of time in her room" and "someone who likes to go on long walks, alone."

That was back when she would still leave the house by herself. Now she couldn't imagine going on even a short walk alone.

But in her childhood, Sylvie helped around the house the way she was expected to, lending Mother a hand with cleaning, and making supper while her pa worked out on the farm.

"Can you wipe the dishes, hon?" Mother asked one particular night when Sylvie had been brooding. She brooded a lot, although much of the time she had no idea what she brooded over.

"Yes, Mother," Sylvie said.

With each wipe of a dish, she felt the thoughts of Caleb grow slightly more distant. Doing anything had a way of pushing the bad thoughts a little farther back.

"Is there anything else for me to do?" Sylvie asked when she was finished, hoping the answer would be yes.

"No, that's fine. Thank you. You really are a good little girl," Mother had said.

But Sylvie's motives weren't as selfless as Mother believed. She would have done anything to take even a tiny bit of those bad feelings away.

After the initial incident, it had taken Sylvie's pa a lot longer than her ma to get over Caleb's death. Sylvie would hear him crying some nights after everyone had gone to bed. She knew he was in his own bed being rocked gently by Mother, who was telling him that everything was going to be all right, and that Caleb was with the angels now.

"God called him early," she heard her tell him once. "He had plans for our little boy. We just don't understand them."

Sylvie would never understand plans from God that involved a three-year-old being shot all over her kitchen during supper. Especially such a happy three-year-old like her baby brother.

And that was how Sylvie remembered Caleb: happy. Maybe time had painted her memories, but Sylvie could not remember a time when little Caleb wasn't the perfect little brother.

Then Preacher Eli killed him.

Time is peculiar. It does change things.

Sylvie had come to understand this.

But she had hated Preacher Eli since that day. That thing hadn't changed. Time had left that one all alone.

And Sylvie had never been happy since that day. That was another thing that hadn't changed.

Not even when the baby was born. She *should've* been happy. It was *her* baby. But, somehow, Preacher Eli stole that, too.

Yet, before she was twelve, nobody really knew how much of a mess the inside of Sylvie Carson's head truly was.

Then came the day she saw her pa butcher the hog.

It was just before Easter, and Sylvie was coming back from one of her walks. She'd been out through their fields, past the horses and cattle, and well into the woods, which were full of mostly oak and birch. She remembered it like it was yesterday, but then she remembered every day of any importance in her life like it happened yesterday. It was that damn time-traveling photograph capable of developing a picture of anything in her past. The pictures were almost always ones she didn't want to see. But she couldn't control them. They just popped into her mind.

The morning had been wet and the grass full of dew. She had left for her walk around ten o'clock, just as the sky was beginning to clear. As usual, she walked to get away from everything. Mainly the farmhouse. Because getting away from the farmhouse was like getting away from the source of all the badness. It was like walking away from the tangled mess of nerves that her mind had become.

As she walked, she tried desperately to keep her thoughts clear—to just be in the moment with nature. She had found *that* was the key to feeling normal: to have no thoughts. Because without thoughts, you could have no feelings. Some days were less successful than others. Some days she got completely lost in her walks, and ended up deep in the forest when she realized the sun was falling and she'd better head for home.

This particular day, her thoughts refused to stop circling like sharks around a rowboat and, after an hour or so of plodding through the wet spring woods, she decided to head back and see if Mother might have some work for her to do that might take her mind to other places. Lately, Sylvie had started to realize just how much Caleb's death had and continued to affect her, and she was beginning to see how much different it made her from other kids.

Sometimes the difference scared her. Sometimes it

made her think thoughts that scared her even more. Thoughts of joining Caleb and his angels.

Looking back now, she wondered how she ever managed to make it through all that time without something like that ever happening. Especially given the years she would soon face alone. With absolutely nobody.

The sun was out when she made it clear of the tree line and she slipped through the fence into the cattle field. The day had grown warm, and the dew no longer clung to the grass. She climbed over the horse fences, giving Willow, her favorite of the six horses they kept, a quick pat down before continuing to the other side of the field to the barn where her pa was.

That's when she stumbled on him slaughtering the hog.

She saw the whole thing. And although she didn't want to see it, she couldn't look away.

First, her pa shot it in the head. And the moment that shot rang out, all Sylvie could see in her brain was Preacher Eli's handgun raised, and the trigger being pulled, and her little brother, Caleb, being blown apart.

Then, taking a knife, her pa cut the hog's throat. Blood gushed.

The kitchen full of Caleb's blood gushed into Sylvie's mind.

She stood there, ten feet away, staring. But what Sylvie didn't know was that she was also screaming. Screaming exactly like she was that day Caleb was shot. Only, on that day, she had just screamed in her mind. Today, she was screaming out loud.

Her pa raced over and tried desperately to calm her down. But Sylvie kept shouting, "Caleb! Caleb!" Pointing frantically, her arm trembled.

Picking her up, Tom Carson took her inside the house. Mother raced from the bedroom. Pa gestured for her to keep quiet.

They lay Sylvie down in her bed and put a damp cloth on her head. The screaming stopped, but she kept shaking uncontrollably. Visions of her baby brother, as fresh as the dead hog outside, continued playing around and around her mind.

She got very little sleep that night. The next day, Sylvie's parents called for the doctor, who gave them a prescription for sleeping pills. If her folks had known how close Sylvie came to swallowing that entire bottle, they wouldn't have left it on her bed stand. But for some reason, she resisted.

But she never was the same again after that.

No longer did she leave the house to go for walks by herself. Her folks never again referred to her as "a kid who likes to spend a lot of time in her room," even though she rarely left it.

Now it wasn't just Sylvie who knew she was broken, but her whole family. At first Sylvie thought it might make things easier, but it didn't. It only seemed to affect Sylvie's pa, who relapsed into his nightly sobbing about his dead son. Sylvie would hear Mother telling him everything was going to be okay while she waited for the sleeping pills to kick in and take her to that one place where nothing ever hurt. That place she always hated waking up from.

Then, two years later, they lost Mother.

Her pa found the body, but Sylvie heard when he told the police how he came upon it. They must've made him tell the story at least three different times.

"I was walkin' into the barn and there were a bunch of flies buzzin' behind one of the horse stalls," he said.

It had been less than an hour since he found her, and he could barely speak through his tears. He was seated on the chair in the living room. Three policemen were at the house. Well, two policemen and one woman. One of the men was taking his report. The woman wasn't wearing a uniform. She was out in the barn looking over the scene. The other man seemed to be interested in the inside of the house. Sylvie couldn't figure out why the house would be interesting to anybody when everything had happened in the barn.

Sylvie was sitting in the parlor just around the corner from the living room with her back to the wall so she could hear. She was crying, but not as much as she reckoned she should be, and it made her feel ashamed. Mainly, she just felt numb.

"I ain't never seen so many flies," her pa continued, " 'cept when somethin' like a dead coon or somethin' shows up on the property, so I looked round the stall expectin' to see somethin' like that." Sylvie heard her pa break down then and start sobbing.

"It's okay, sir. Take your time," one of the officers (probably the one taking the notes) said.

When her pa spoke again, it was hard to understand him. His nose was stuffed and his voice was full of tears. "And she was lyin' there. Covered in flies. I don't know how long she'd been there. I've been in town most of the day."

"What were you doin' in town?"

Sylvie's pa sniffled. "Buyin' feed and tack."

"You have receipts? People can verify you were there?"

There was a hesitation. Then, "What? Yeah, o' course. I was at Arnold's. And I talked to Pete for musta been twenty minutes. That's Pete at the tack shop."

"Where was the last place you was 'fore coming home?"

Another pause before Sylvie's pa answered. "Jim's," he said. "You know. The feed store. Why? You don't think I—"

"We just need to ask these questions. Standard procedure."

Then the other police officer asked, "Was anyone else home?"

"Yeah," Sylvie's pa answered. "My daughter. She was probably in her room." *Because she ain't been right since her brother died, and so that's the only place she ever is,* Sylvie thought, finishing his sentence in her head.

"We'll need to talk to her, too."

They asked Sylvie a bunch of questions she really didn't have very good answers to. She started feeling very accused, like they thought she killed her own mother. The fact was, there was no obvious cause of death, so a case file was opened and an autopsy was performed.

Turned out Mother had somehow ingested rat poison. After an investigation, the police arrested James Richard Cobbler, a radical member of Eli Brown's congregation. There was no evidence linking Eli Brown to the murder. Cobbler had acted alone and was, in his own words, "Acting in God's and Preacher Eli's best interest." He wound up being given the death penalty and died by electrocution.

Sylvie's pa never did get over it.

Now, no longer did Tom Carson have anyone to console him at night as he cried for the death of his three-year-old son. And he sobbed for the loss of his wife, too. The weight of having lost them both turned out to be too much for him. Ironically, in the end, he wasn't as strong as his daughter. Luckily, Sylvie hadn't been the one to find him. While she was at school one day, he'd gone out past the cattle fields, strung a rope over the bough of one of the oaks close to the outer edge of the woods, and hanged himself.

Once again, there was a police investigation and an autopsy. Tom Carson's death was determined to be a suicide.

Mother would've said, "God called them all early. He has plans for every one of us. You just don't understand them."

Sylvie would never understand plans from God that involved taking everyone in her family away from her before she even turned fifteen years old.

Besides, Sylvie had always wondered about the deaths of her folks. It had always nagged at her the way they both went: so close together, and so strangely. Why would her pa leave Sylvie all alone? Especially knowing she was the way she was? If Preacher Eli hadn't been in prison, her suspicions would have gone directly to him over her pa's "suicide."

Then part of her thought maybe *she* was the reason her pa did it. Because he couldn't deal with her without anybody else helping him. Part of her thought maybe it was her fault.

Sylvie not only suffered from what the doctors refer to as post-traumatic stress disorder (something Sylvie didn't really understand), but she had been extraordinarily lonely pretty near her whole life. Foster care didn't do anything but make her lonelier than ever. Even after meeting Orwin Thomas, she'd still felt lonely most of the time.

She wondered if this was how most other people felt.

All of these thoughts continued bouncing through Sylvie's head as she lay in bed staring at her ceiling until, finally, sleep took mercy on her. She either didn't dream or, thankfully, didn't remember what she dreamed after she awoke the next morning.

CHAPTER 9

The first thing Dewey had done once I showed him the swords was pull out his notebook and start jotting down a new invention. "What is it?" I asked, looking on.

He sketched a big circle with a smaller circle attached to the side. Then he wrote the word *rope* with an arrow pointing to the big circle and the words *wire tie* with an arrow pointing to the smaller circle. Then he said, "I'm a genius."

I still didn't know what it was. "How does this make you a genius?" His notebook was over half full of inventions. He'd been pretty busy considering summer wasn't even half finished yet.

He held out the pad for me to see more clearly, although I'd already seen pretty well what he'd drawn. "This will allow us to wear our swords on our hips like real knights. Like they is in, you know, scabbards."

I studied his diagram. "I'm assumin' the wire tie isn't pulled all the way tight?"

"No, we gotta keep 'em loose so the sword hangs down a bit. The cross guard will stop it from fallin' through."

So we went into my garage and started rummaging through my pa's stuff. Sure enough, we found some nice yellow rope that was flexible and perfect for wrapping around our waists and tying at the front. I thought we were going to have a problem coming up with wire ties, but Dewey even managed to find those in all that mess, too. I realized my pa sure did have a lot of garbage in that garage.

Within another ten minutes, both of us had our swords at our sides. Dewey's invention worked perfectly. I thought it was a much better idea than his satellite television reception with aluminum foil.

Me and Dewey had spent the last five days in my backyard playing with the swords me and Carry made in the garage on Monday, and I think they turned out pretty good. They didn't look as nice as the ones at Disney World, but after a minute or two of thrusting and parrying, our imaginations took over. After that, they may as well have been the real things. It was apparent very early on that I was a much better swordsman than Dewey, although he showed signs of improvement each time we fought.

Every day had been nice and sunny with just the odd cloud overhead to give us a slip of shade. Today there was a slight wind, which was a welcome break from the heat beaming down on us while our blades continued crashing. When they hit, they made a knocking sound like wooden blocks being banged together, but in my head I heard the clanging of solid steel forged by the finest of blacksmiths.

"Take that!" I said, with a thrust after blocking Dewey's slash. We were in my backyard, fighting between the two cherry trees. The sun was dancing in and out of the clouds that hung throughout the sky. Currently it was between them, beating straight down on us. I wiped sweat off my forehead with my left arm. It was getting hot.

Dewey stepped back. "Missed me!" he said and took another step back.

I kept coming forward, slicing as I approached.

"Hey, watch it!" Dewey's back came up against the narrow trunk of one of the cherries.

"You can't tell me to watch it," I said. "We're sword fighting. This is how you sword fight." I took another jab. He tried to block it with his sword but missed. The point of my weapon slid right down the edge of his and hit him square on the knuckles.

"Ow!" he yelled.

He dropped his sword to the grass and stuck his knuckle in his mouth. "That's the fourth time you've hit me there! Can you watch what you're doin'?" It was hard to understand what he was saying with his knuckle in his mouth.

"Dewey. We're sword fightin'. Fightin' sometimes involves gettin' hurt. Just be happy these aren't *real* swords. *You* wanted to use *real* ones, *remember*?"

"I never said I wanted you to scrape my fingers."

"No, just cut 'em off."

Dewey said nothing. Just stood there with his hand in his mouth.

"Pick up your sword," I said.

"No, I'm done playin'."

"C'mon," I said. "Don't be a baby. I hardly hit you."

"Abe, it hurt."

"You're a baby."

"Let me hit you."

"Go ahead. All you gotta do is get past my expert blocking technique."

"No, I mean just let me hit you so you can see what it feels like."

I put my hands on my hips, holding my sword at my waist with its tip facing the ground. "Do I look like an idiot?"

"Do *I*? Why would I keep playin' when all you do is whack my fingers?"

"Cuz it's fun?" I offered.

He just glared at me. I got the feeling it was less fun for him.

Just then my mother called me from the back door.

"What?" I called back.

"We're goin' out. Dewey has to go home. He can come back later."

"Where are we goin'?"

"Shoppin'."

"Where's Carry?"

"What does that have to do with anythin'?" she asked. The sun went behind a cloud. It was amazing how fast the temperature dropped.

"Can't I stay home with her?" I hated shopping. Especially the way my mother shopped. It was like she had to look at every single item in the store before making a decision about buying anything. You'd think my mother would let me stay home by myself, me being twelve and all. She sometimes did, but only on special occasions like when she didn't have any choice. But maybe because she worked as a police officer, she worried more than other parents about me being alone. Like she just expected someone to come to the house and snatch me away or something.

"No, she's goin' out," she said. "Besides, I wanna buy you a new pair of sneakers."

My head fell. I hung my arms from my sides. My sword went limp. "Do we have to go today?"

"Abe. Do as you're told. Do we need to have a talk about listenin'?"

I'd had enough talks with my mother about listening to last me the rest of my life. That wasn't the problem. I knew her point of view when it came to listening. "No."

"Good. Let's go. Dewey, thanks for comin' over."

"You're welcome, Miss Leah." He stood there, his hand still in his mouth. His words came out half mumbled.

Slowly, I wandered toward the back door. "What's wrong with his hand?" my mother asked.

"Abe tried to cut off my fingers with his sword," Dewey said, his mouth continuing to make the words near on impossible to understand.

"Abe," my mother said as I walked by her into the house, "do I need to take your new swords away?"

I stopped and looked up at her. "I barely scraped the edge of his hand. He's just being a baby. Look at this." I held up my sword, displaying both sides of it. "Carry even dulled the edges. I doubt I could kill a beetle with it."

"Just be more careful,"

"Thanks, Miss Leah," Dewey said. He was still standing in the backyard with his back against the cherry tree.

"Dewey?" my mother said. "Take your sword and go home now. I think your hand's gonna be fine."

"Yes, ma'am." He picked up his sword with the hand not in his mouth and headed around the house to the front where his bicycle was waiting.

"I'm not gonna get a call from his ma, am I?" my mother asked me.

"No," I said. "I barely touched him. Honest."

"Okay, cuz if I do, I'm tellin' her I had nothin' to do with it, and you were the mastermind behind the whole thing."

I searched her eyes to see what she meant by that and saw a sparkle there. She was kidding around. She knew Dewey was just as big a baby as I did.

Next thing I knew, me and my mother were in the car and going through town. About fifteen minutes into the drive, I realized we weren't headed anywhere we might be able to buy me a pair of sneakers. We were rumbling up Hunter Road, toward Blackberry Springs—away from downtown or anything even closely resembling a store of any sort. "Where are we goin'?" I asked. "There's nowhere to buy sneakers up here."

"I have an errand to run before we go shoppin'."

I had no idea what we could be doing going up in this part of town. There was nothing here except lonely houses spaced very far apart and a lot of forest. It was actually a rather pretty part of Alvin, with densely packed elm, hickory, oak, maple, and other trees lining the edges of the road. If you went up far enough, you came to the springs that ran between Cornflower Lake and Willet Lake. I had heard the springs were popular with teenagers who liked to drive up and park along the side of Hunter Road with their girlfriends.

Thinking of that brought back memories of me and my mother sneaking up on Carry and her boyfriend. That was last year when they were in his red car on the outskirts of town parked at the side of one of the old ranch roads. My mother actually pulled her gun on Carry's boyfriend and threatened to shoot him in his private parts. That memory brought a smile to my face. "What sort of errand is we goin' on?"

"I need to talk to someone. It won't take long."

I had no recollection of anyone we knew living up near Willet Lake. "Who do you need to talk to?" I narrowed my eyes. "Is this police work?" My mother had developed a habit of taking me with her on police-related matters.

She looked at me with a raised eyebrow. "Yes, it's police work. Why is it important to you *who* I need to talk to?"

I shrugged. "Just askin'. Since I'm comin', figured I should know."

A minute went by while it seemed like she was considering whether to tell me any more about it. Finally, she did. "I'm goin' to talk with Eli Brown. I promised Miss Sylvie I'd pay him a visit."

"Preacher Eli?" I asked, astonished. "Isn't he in jail?"

My mother took a deep breath. "He's done his prison time."

"And he's back *here*?" I asked. "In *Alvin*?" I found this exceptionally discomforting that a killer lived in my town.

"Yes, Abe. He's done his time. He's no longer a felon. He's a free man. He can live wherever he chooses."

"But he's a killer, Mom. He killed a kid!"

She sighed. It sounded like it came out through gritted teeth. "You don't understand the legal system, Abe. He killed a boy by accident. Eli Brown was committed to prison for doin' it and did all the time he was supposed to do. From the law's point of view, he's no longer a criminal."

"But he did kill Sylvie's brother."

She paused. "He did. But that was a long time ago. Time has forgiven him of his sin. So should *you,* Abe."

I didn't rightly understand what she meant. All I knew was that she was taking me to the house of a man who killed the last kid he ever got close to, and this didn't sit well with me. "Do you think bringin' me with you is the best idea, Mom? He *likes* killin' kids."

My mother hit the brakes, bringing the car to a stop on the side of Hunter Road. She turned and looked directly into my eyes. "Abe! I want to make sure we're perfectly clear on this subject. First, Preacher Eli Brown doesn't *like* killin' kids. He killed Caleb Carson by accident. According to the court, he never meant to kill *anyone* that day, especially not poor little Caleb. Second, I would *never* put you in harm's way. If I thought there was even a hint of a chance that you comin' to his house was puttin' you in danger, I would *not* be bringin' you. Do you understand?"

I just watched her, not knowing if she actually wanted a response from me at this point.

"*Do* you understand?" she asked again.

I nodded.

"Good. Third, Eli Brown is *no longer* a criminal. *Do not* treat him like one. He is a member of society with the same rights as you and me. He is no better or worse in any way. Is that clear?"

Quickly, I nodded again.

"Good. Cuz you're comin' to the door with me, so you better be comfortable."

I swallowed. "Why? Why am I comin' to the door?" This made *no* sense to me.

"Cuz I want to see his reaction when I show up with you on the doorstep. I'm paying him a visit as an *assessment,* but I don't want him to know that's what I'm doin'. Please, Abe. Trust me. The man is old now. He was old when he went to prison. That was almost twenty years ago."

I thought all this over. After what I considered the proper length of time to consider it, I answered, "Okay, I trust you."

"Good." My mother started the car and pulled back out onto Hunter Road. She drove onto the small wooden bridge over the springs until we came to a small run-down house on the left side of the road about another quarter mile up. It was painted brown with a black roof and nestled in a small clearing surrounded by pine and fir trees. The ground around it was mostly dirt. There was a rusted truck trailer beside the house and a dented station wagon parked on an angle out front. Farther back in the woods, I could make out a small barn or maybe a garage that was stained a deep red. The siding, like the boards on the house, was aged and in need of refinishing.

"Come on," my mother said, opening her door.

I got out of my side. The air was thick with the smell of the pines, but a hint of an oil smell came along with it. I followed my mother's lead up to the door and watched a monarch butterfly float across the hard-packed ground beside the steps while she knocked.

Preacher Eli answered. A tall man, he was wearing a red-and-black-checkered shirt with sleeves that came down to his wrists. The sleeves were unbuttoned, but the shirt was done up to his neck and tucked into gray pants. He wore a black belt with a silver buckle. His pants went down into boots that looked remarkably similar to cowboy boots. He certainly didn't look much like a preacher to me.

His eyes went from my mother's to mine. It was obvious he had no idea who we were.

"Preacher Eli?" my mother asked.

Eli Brown rubbed his nose. "Now there's a name I haven't gone by in quite some time. Who might you two be?" His voice sounded like someone had taken a chisel to it. He asked the question in what I considered to be a most suspicious manner.

"My name's Leah Teal. This here's my son, Abe. I'm with the Alvin Police Department."

"You don't look like no police I've ever seen." His teeth were brown and crooked. There was a scar under his right eye as though he'd been slashed with a knife. It somehow reminded me of Dewey's hand being hit by my sword.

My mother pulled out her badge and flashed it. "I'm a detective."

Preacher Eli's eyes narrowed. He gave me a long look that made me very uncomfortable. "That so," he said, his eyes still lingering on me. "And what is it you is detectin', Detective Teal?" I was happy his gaze drifted back up to my mother.

My mother held up her palm. "I'm just here to ask you some routine questions, is all. Nothin' for you to worry 'bout."

"I think I'll decide what I should or shouldn't be worryin' 'bout if it's all the same to you." His eyes cut to my waist. I realized I was still wearing my sword on my hip. I'd grown so used to it, I hadn't even noticed it in the car. My hand automatically went to its handle.

He looked back up to my mother.

"Fine," she said. "I understand you was just released from the Birmingham Work Release Center a couple weeks ago."

The preacher's eyes narrowed again. "I don't hear a question in there. And what makes all this routine?"

"Just not very often we have someone like yourself return to the town where all their trouble started, is all. Just wanna make sure I understand your motivations."

Preacher Eli rubbed his chin. "I'm not so sure I'm obliged to discuss my motivations with the 'town detective,' to be right honest."

My mother swallowed. "No, you probably aren't obliged, but in the nature of goodwill, I think it might be a good idea. Especially since Sylvie Carson still lives in this very town."

Preacher Eli stared off between my mother and me at something distant and far away, as if lost in memories. "Sylvie . . ." he said, more to himself than either of us. Then he glanced at me again. "That was the daughter, right?"

"That's right," my mother said.

"And how's she after all these years?"

"She's holdin' up."

"Good." He looked at my mother expectantly. "Is this what you came to talk to me 'bout? Sylvie Carson?"

"Have you been near her property since you got out of Birmingham, Mr. Brown?"

I tensed up. I figured if any question was going to set Preacher Eli off, it was going to be one like this. It almost sounded like an accusation to me. I wasn't all the way wrong, either. Only he didn't set off with quite the fireworks I anticipated. Something flashed in the man's eyes. I wondered if my mother saw it, too. "Hell no! Why would you ask me somethin' like that?"

Again, my mother's palm came up. "Just an honest question." She had her pad out and was taking notes. "Now you're absolutely certain? You didn't even happen to drive by one day?"

"I don't even know where the hell the girl lives!" Preacher Eli said. "What do you think? I got outta the joint just to finish a job I never meant to start in the first place? Have you even *read* the court records? I didn't *know* that boy was sittin' there. I'd . . . I'd . . ." He stopped, and for a second, I thought he was actually going to start crying, although I got the feeling they weren't real tears. They were them crocodile ones my mother was always keepin' on about. "I don't need to talk to you about this."

He began closing the door, but my mother reached out and held it open. "Preacher Eli?" she said softly. "Listen. I'm sorry I've upset you. I just came here to make certain you're not a threat to anyone."

His eyes were wet. He looked like a lamb the way he gazed back at her. "A threat? Is *that* what you think? I have just spent almost eighteen years repentin' every single day for the sins I have done. If I could go back in time, don't you think I would give that boy back his life? I have thought 'bout him constantly. 'Bout birthdays missed. 'Bout graduations. 'Bout girlfriends. 'Bout him not gettin' to have kids of his own. All missed. All cuz of me. And you think I'm a *threat*?"

My mother looked down. "I'm sorry, Mr. Brown. I don't know what I was thinkin'."

"The only thing I am a threat to is not bein' able to live my life long enough to make up for the sins I committed eighteen years ago." Now tears really did come to his eyes. I still didn't trust those tears.

"Look," my mother said, "I really am sorry. I didn't come all the way up here to upset you. How 'bout your family? How's that boy of yours?"

Even through the tears, Preacher Eli managed a chuckle. "Boy. He ain't no boy no more. He's forty-one. While I was gone, time kept goin' and he went ahead and grew on me. I got some catchin' up to do with him."

"He came and saw you while you were . . . inside, though?" my mother asked.

"Yeah, he did. Even more so after my Louise passed."

"I'm so sorry to hear about the loss of your wife."

"She'd stopped comin' by so much anyway, after what happened on that ranch."

"What do you mean?"

"After they found them Carson folks dead. Especially when Tom showed up swingin' from that tree . . ." He looked away and fell silent a moment. "She just stopped comin' by so much."

"How come?" my mother asked. I had no idea what either of them were talking about. I'd never heard of either of the Carson folks swinging from a tree. It sounded funny for someone to be described that way.

Eli shrugged. "Dunno. You'd have to ask her. But that won't be happenin' anytime soon."

My mother let this information digest. I didn't rightly know what it was that had her so lost in thought. "And . . . you have a grandson now, too, isn't that right?"

Another chuckle came through Eli's tears. I knew I shouldn't be trusting those tears. "What did you do, check up on everything you could about me 'fore comin' out?" he asked.

"Just bein' polite is all."

"Yeah, I got a grandson. Lives up north in Alabaster, 'bout twenty miles this side of Birmingham. Haven't seen him for a long time. I hope that changes soon."

"I hope so too, for your sake."

"Well," Preacher Eli said, "I'm gonna go now. I trust I've answered all your questions and you won't be back botherin' me no more?"

"Wait," my mother said as he was closing the door. "Can I ask you one more thing?"

"What?" he asked through the narrow space left between the door and the edge of the frame.

"Why did you return to Alvin?"

He didn't even think about that one. His answer came right away. "Because Alvin's where this all started and Alvin's where it has to be finished. I need to preach again and I need to preach from here. The only way I will ever find peace is through redemption and it's only here that I can find that. You can tell Sylvie Carson she is safe from the crazy preacher man. In fact, you can tell her he is so sorry for what he did to her brother and her life and that he knows he can never make up for it and for that reason he will not be in contact with her. Because any contact would just belittle such a thing. It would make it all seem too . . . what's the word? Trite, I guess. Now, please leave me alone."

With that, Preacher Eli clicked his front door closed. I felt relieved to have the conversation over. Something about the man didn't sit right in my soul. Whenever he had looked at me, I felt like a chicken on its way to the chopping block. I was very happy to be on our way back to my mother's car.

"Well, that settles that," my mother said as she backed her vehicle out of Preacher Eli's driveway and headed back south down Hunter Road.

"What settles what?"

"I can safely say Eli Brown is not a risk to Miss Sylvie or anyone else."

I didn't say a word, even though I wondered how my mother had arrived at that conclusion. To me, the whole encounter had been unsettling and, if anything, put Preacher Eli right on my radar of crazy people to watch out for. I couldn't believe this convicted killer was in my hometown, living right here in Blackberry Springs. Now, after meeting him, not only did I think Miss Sylvie might be unsafe, even *I* felt more unsafe on account of him knowing about *me*.

But then, my mother and I had a history of disagreeing over such things.

CHAPTER 10

One Saturday morning, once my mother had finished with breakfast and had all the pots and pans put away and the kitchen cleaned up, I finally asked her the question that had been bothering me for weeks. Well, actually, there were a number of questions nagging at me, but this one was especially bad, because to me it seemed like it shouldn't be a question at all.

"Aren't you gonna call that number?" I was still in my pajamas and my bare feet were cold on the kitchen floor, even though the rest of the room was hot—not only from breakfast but on account of the weather. It had been pounding down sunshine for well over a week now. And anyone can tell you, when the sun wants to fry up Alvin in late July, it can do a pretty darn good job of it. That's something Officer Jackson liked to say, although the way he said it was slightly different and contained a cuss word I wasn't allowed to use.

"What number?" my mother asked.

I couldn't believe she didn't know what I was talking about. "The number on the paper I gave you that belongs to my aunt." I turned my palms up in exasperation. "She told me to tell you to phone it. That was weeks ago."

My mother sat at the kitchen table, relaxing and enjoying a cup of coffee while reading the newest issue of *Cosmopolitan,* which I was almost sure belonged to Carry. When she heard my response, she hardly even looked up. She just slowly turned to the next page of her magazine and said, "We have no idea that woman is your aunt, Abe. I thought we've been through this."

From the living room, I could hear the television set. Carry had run in there as soon as breakfast was over and planted herself in front of it. If this was like most Saturday mornings, she wouldn't be moving until my mother demanded she go and get dressed and do something with the day. I think that girl could watch TV forever if nobody stopped her.

"I thought we got a background check spyin' on Pa that said she was my aunt," I told my mother.

Now she looked up. "First, we wasn't spyin' on nobody. And second, the background check simply said he had a sister. It doesn't necessarily mean the woman you met is her."

I raised one of my eyebrows. "You're scared of callin' her." I knew I was on shaky ground with this, but I felt it was the truth and my mother always told me I'd never get in trouble for telling the truth.

She laughed. "What would I possibly be scared of?"

"I dunno, but there's a reason you ain't callin', and it ain't because you don't think she's tellin' the truth. If that was all it was, you'd call just to check and see. You're scared she *is* tellin' the truth. You don't want to meet Pa's sister."

I saw her bite her lower lip and I wasn't sure if she

was holding back yelling at me for something I said or if it was something else she was doing. But something I had told her made her go quiet. She didn't say anything for a long while. When she finally did, she actually surprised me.

"You know what?" she asked, closing the magazine and looking straight into my eyes. "I think you might be right. I think maybe I *am* scared. Maybe I *don't* want to meet your pa's family."

"Why?" I asked softly. This made no sense to me. I was overjoyed at having suddenly discovered new members of my family. I couldn't see why anyone wouldn't be.

"Because, Abe . . ." She started and then stopped. "It's . . . you wouldn't understand. There's just so many memories. Things I don't want to . . . things I would rather have stay in the past."

I frowned. "You're afraid of the past."

"What does that mean?"

"You never want to talk about Pa. You never want to think about him."

"Why would I want to think about what happened? It was horrible."

"Not about what happened. I mean about *anythin'*. It's like you would rather pretend he didn't exist than have to think about what happened to him. Well, that's not what *I* want. I want to know who my pa was." I realized I was starting to get loud and sounding like a baby. My mother was probably on the verge of sending me to my room.

"You don't even remember him," she said, almost as though she were talking to the walls. "You were so young. You can't possibly even remember what he looked like."

"I remember," I said, looking at the floor. "I have a picture of him I carry round with me."

Both our heads rose and our eyes met. It was the first time I'd told anyone about the picture, and the last person I thought I'd ever tell was my mother. After all, I sort of stole it from her. I searched her eyes. They were wet. Tears were coming to them. "Where did you—"

"Your closet," I said. "I found it in a shoe box. I hope you're not mad. I was lookin' for some wrappin' paper for somethin' I made you at school."

"My closet . . ." she mouthed.

"Are you mad?"

"Where do you keep it?"

"The picture?" I asked. "In the drawer beside my bed. That's when it's not in my pocket. Usually it's in my pocket. It brings me good luck." Then, I repeated myself. "Are you mad?"

"Oh, no, Abe, I'm not mad. Come here." She opened her arms and I walked over and let her wrap me in a big hug. I felt her tears on the side of my cheek. "I've been so selfish," she said.

I didn't quite understand how she thought she'd been selfish, but I was sure glad she wasn't angry I took the picture from her closet. I was even gladder she wasn't going to make me give it back.

When she finally let go of me, she wiped her eyes and said, "Tell you what. I'll make that call. How does that sound?"

I beamed. "Really?"

"Really. But I'm not promisin' anythin' else will come of it."

"That's okay. I just want you to talk to her."

I saw my mother's chest heave as she took a deep

breath and let out a big sigh. "Okay, well, I may as well get this over with."

I stood right beside my mother as she made the call from the kitchen telephone. Luckily for me, the woman I met on the street, Addison? She had one of those voices you could hear from the other end of the phone without even having your ear near it. I figured it probably had something to do with her being from Boston and all.

"Hi," my mother said after the call was answered. "I'm looking for Addison?"

"This is Addison." Right away, I recognized the accent. It was strange how people from different places talked in different ways. Even people from the same country.

"Hi, Addison, my name's Leah Teal. I got your number a while ago from my boy, Abe. Apparently—"

She didn't have to go any further, because Addison picked up the conversation right there. "Leah! I was wondering when you were gonna call. I was startin' to think you weren't, after all this time. I'm so glad that you did. I have so much to tell you. There's so much you and I have to talk about. I assume Abe has told you who I am?"

"Well," my mother said slowly, "he's told me who you *say* you are."

"Ah yes, you're a police detective. I mustn't forget that." I heard her laugh. "Trust me, I promise you I am exactly who I say I am. I have no reason to deceive you. I did not go all that way to just pretend to be Billy's sister."

"Yes," my mother said, ". . . about that. And I'd also like to know why you were followin' my little Abe round in your car. Seems a mite creepy to me."

"Let me guess," Addison said. "Billy never told you he had a sister?"

"Well, that would be a correct guess."

"Figured as much. I was sort of the black sheep of the family. Hard to believe, hey? Knowing Billy? But trust me, take all Billy's faults and multiply them by a hundred and you have a version of me back in those days. At least in my parents' eyes."

"I didn't really find too many faults in Billy," my mother said, a bit perturbed. I was getting the distinct impression she didn't rightly like this woman and it bothered me that they might be getting off on the wrong foot.

"Well, that's something!" Addison said. "Good for Billy. Maybe my memories are all mixed up. Wouldn't be the first time I got something wrong. Anyway, I did not call you to find fault with your poor dead husband, God rest his soul. And I am so sorry for your loss. Even though my condolences come at such a late date."

"Thank you," my mother said. "It was a very hard time for me and the kids."

"I can imagine," Addison said. Then she stopped and reevaluated. "Actually, I can't. I don't have children. But I can only hope that things have gotten better since Billy's passing."

"They get better. You know what they say," my mother said, "that time is the great healer. Why don't you tell me why it is you did contact my little boy, Miss Addison? And again, why were you followin' him like some sort of stalker?"

There was a hesitation on the other end of the phone as Addison took a breath so loud I had no problem hearing it from where I stood. My mother even pulled the receiver away from her ear.

"Well, first off, I was worried if I came straight to you, you might not believe me, or worse, you might just throw me out of your house. I had no idea what Billy had said to you 'bout me."

"He said nothin'," my mother said. "I already told you that."

"I didn't know that at the time. Anyway, I needed to give you some important news, and going through your boy seemed like the best way to go about it. You have to admit, it *worked*. We *are* talking on the phone. Maybe I made the wrong approach, I don't know."

"What news brought you round these parts then?" I could tell my mother was starting to get impatient.

"I wish I could say it was the good kind," Addison said. "But unfortunately, it is not. You see, my mother has been diagnosed with early-onset Alzheimer's and I would really like her to see her grandchildren while she is still in a state that she'll remember them. You know what I mean?"

"Grandchildren? You mean Abe and Carry?"

"Yes, of course. She still remembers seein' Abe."

"Where would she possibly remember him from? She's never met him."

There was a pause on the other end and then Addison said, "Actually, that's not true. Not exactly. She's met Abe. Once."

Now my mother was on full alert. I could tell her whole body went tense at this news. Even I wasn't quite sure what the heck Addison was talking about. I'd never met this grandmother. I'd surely remember something like that. But the idea of meeting them now made my skin tingle all over.

"I think you need to come back to Alvin and come on down to the station," my mother said. "Answer a few questions there for me."

"Wait," Addison said. "Let me explain before you freak out, okay? Your father brought Abe over to my parents' place once when Abe was a lot younger. He didn't stay long, but long enough that my parents got to meet him. They simply adored him. And they will love Carry too, although they've never met her. They've only watched her grow up through photographs."

"Photographs? What photographs?" My mother was trembling now, she was so panicked. None of this was making any sense to me and I was sure it was making no sense to her either.

"Leah, listen, please calm down. I can hear it in your voice that you are stressing about this. It's not so complicated. Your father met my parents at Billy's funeral, and ever since that day, until he became too sick to do it anymore, your dad had been sending my parents pictures of their grandchildren on a regular basis. And boy, did they ever love him for it. You know what I mean?"

My mother just stood there in silence, saying nothing in return. Behind her eyes it was like the gears of a clock were spinning. "But . . . but why? I don't understand. Why didn't he tell me?"

"For the answer to that, you would have had to have asked your father. And again, I am so sorry for your loss. He was a good man."

"You . . . you knew my pa?"

"I met him once, but my parents spoke very highly of him. They still do."

"Your folks, they was at Billy's funeral?" my mother asked.

"Yeah. Only they stayed out of sight because they didn't think you'd want them there. They assumed Billy would've told you nothing but bad things about them, given his past and everything."

"I . . . I don't understand," my mother said. "What past? Were you at the funeral, too?"

There was a hesitation and then Addison replied, "No, unfortunately, I had a more *pressing* engagement up in Boston. But that's another story and not one I want to get into right now over the phone. You know what I mean?"

"So your pa," my mother asked, "is *he* still alive then, too?"

"Yes, my father is alive and well, thank goodness. He looks after my mother. If he weren't here to do it, I don't know what would happen. Right now, my mother's not so bad, but she's going to get worse, you know what I mean, right? Anyway, they would both really appreciate it if you could find it in your heart to allow them to see Abe and Carry just once before my mother's condition worsens. Right now, most days, she's still pretty much normal. Lucid. You know what I mean."

"I . . ." My mother stumbled. "Listen, Addison, I appreciate that your ma is sick and I am sorry for that. But you have to understand, this is a lot comin' at me all at once. I need some time to come to terms with it. I gotta sort through it and make heads or tails out of it. I gotta figure out if I even *believe* it."

"I understand."

"Where are your folks now?"

"They live about twenty miles your side of Columbus up in Georgia. It's about a three-hour drive from Alvin. Of course, it would be much easier for my mother's sake if you could go see them, but if you would rather, I am sure they would make the trip out to you if it meant seeing Abe and Carry."

My mother took a deep breath and let it out slowly, trying to calm herself. "I'm gonna go now, Addison. I'll call you back when I've had a chance to digest this."

"Thank you, Leah. I appreciate you even considering it. You're a very nice person."

My mother put the receiver back in its cradle. She was white as a cotton sheet hung out to dry on a spring day. Her hands were still trembling. Turning, she slid her back down the cupboards until she was sitting on the floor staring straight ahead, looking way off into the distance the same way Preacher Eli had done that day we'd shown up at his house in Blackberry Springs.

"You okay?" I asked quietly.

"I'm not sure," she said. "You have grandparents alive on your pa's side. They want to see you."

I'd already heard, but hearing it again sent lightning bolts from the bottom of my feet surging up through my body. I had *new family*. Family I hadn't even *known* about.

"We gonna go?" I asked, trying to keep my excitement contained, although I'm certain my mother saw it in my eyes and heard it in my voice. It's hard to wrestle back that kind of energy.

"I dunno yet."

"Oh," I said.

Two houseflies were buzzing around the room, zigging and zagging, making complex patterns through the air. I stood and watched them. My mother kept staring at something way past that kitchen wall.

"Anythin' I can do for you?" I asked.

"Nothin'." Whatever she was fixated on was far, far away. "If this is all true, my daddy lied to me the last four years of his life." She turned toward me with the weirdest look in her eyes. "First I find out *your* pa lied to me, now I find out *my* pa lied to me. Has *anyone* told me the truth my entire life? Nothing makes any sense anymore, Abe."

"I tell you the truth," I said.

"I certainly hope you do."

"I do. I always do."

"Let's try to always keep it that way, okay?"

"Okay," I said. "How 'bout we pinky swear on it?"

But it turned out she didn't feel much like pinky swearing on anything.

CHAPTER 11

Leah showed up at work and gave a light rap on the office door of Police Chief Ethan Montgomery. She had already said hello to Chris and made a pit stop at the coffee machine to fill up her mug.

"Come in!" Ethan called out.

She opened the door and popped her head inside. "Got a sec?"

Ethan was sitting, as usual, in his large padded chair behind his big oak desk. He had his own cup of coffee, freshly poured, on the desktop in front of him. He motioned to the chair on the other side of his desk. "Sure. Come on in. What's on your mind?"

Leah closed the office door and took a seat.

"Well, as you know, that woman showed up and told Abe she was his 'aunt' and all." She took a sip of her coffee.

"I thought we straightened all that out with the background check on Billy. He had a sister. Her story's good." Ethan didn't touch his mug. It just sat there, pretty much dead center between his hands, steam rising from the top.

"Well . . . just cuz Billy had a sister don't mean this woman is her. This woman could be anyone."

Ethan Montgomery rolled his eyes, or came as close to it as Leah figured he dared do in front of her. He knew she had a temper. "Come on, Leah, you aren't that dumb. Now why would this woman show up on your doorstep claimin' to be Billy's sister? 'Specially after all this time? Ain't like there's any sort of inheritance or nothin' to be had. Least none that I know of."

Leah laughed. "None that I know of either." She held her mug in her lap with both hands. It was hot and she kept having to shift it from one hand to the other.

"Well . . . there ya go."

"It's just that—"

"It's just that you don't like anything drumming up memories of the past. I know. I've known you since you were just a bean sprout. You've always been the same way. Got that from your momma." Now Ethan grabbed his coffee and drank some. He put his mug right back down where it had been.

Leah took a few deep breaths. Suddenly, she wasn't sure why she was even in Ethan's office. She felt stupid for coming to him, like a little kid coming to her father for advice on something he couldn't possibly help her with, like when she first started liking boys in school. She glanced nervously around the room: at the law books stuffed along the shelves on the walls, at Ethan's big oak desk that barely fit width-wise in the room, at the floor, at the blinds hanging down the windows that looked out into the large room (they were always closed)—anywhere and everywhere but at him.

"What's really on your mind?" he finally asked, his chair squeaking as he leaned back, coffee cup in hand.

That chair had squeaked for as long as Leah could remember. Now it annoyed her that he hadn't bothered to fix it, or oil it, or do anything about it. Then she realized it was just her mind finding something to fill itself with other than answering the question he had just directed her way.

"Abe wants to meet this new family of his that's suddenly popped up out of nowhere." The windows behind Leah looked out on to the street. Through those windows, the sun peeked out from behind a cloud, its light breaking through the boughs of the fig tree that stood outside.

"You mean the aunt? I thought they met already?"

"There's more than just the aunt. There's grandparents, too. Billy's ma and pa. They live just outside of Columbus in Georgia."

Ethan leaned forward, putting his big forearms on his desk, bringing his hands almost as far forward as the pictures standing along the front. "Now how do you know that?"

Leah looked away again. Above her head, the large wooden ceiling fan slowly turned. "Cuz I called her. The aunt, I mean. Abe made me do it."

Ethan laughed. "Abe 'made you' do it? What did he do? Pull out your gun and hold it to your head?"

"No, he played a guilt card I wasn't ready for. Turns out he found a picture of Billy in my closet years ago and has been carryin' it around with him ever since. Never told a soul. Told me it's his good luck charm. Told me since nobody ever wanted to talk about his pa he had to just look at the picture and imagine what he was like."

Ethan turned sideways in his big chair and crossed

one leg over the opposite knee. He looked out the long rectangular window beside the large bookcase. "Wow," he said. "That kid's good. Gotta give him credit."

"Made me feel horrible. Like I've hidden his father away from him all these years on purpose."

Ethan paused, then turned to her. He waited until she looked up and their eyes met. "Well, haven't you, Leah? Isn't that *exactly* what you done?"

Leah felt tears coming. "Oh, don't you go tellin' me stuff like that. I already feel bad enough." She took another sip of coffee, but barely tasted it. Her senses were all focused on her guilt.

"Well, if you came in here lookin' for sympathy, I think you picked the wrong guy."

"Actually, I came in here lookin' to make some sense outta things. See, turns out I got a few problems to reconcile."

Ethan's eyes narrowed. He was interested now. "What sorta problems?"

"Well, for starters, Billy lied to me throughout our entire relationship. Never once mentioned his sister and barely said a word 'bout his ma and pa. You'd think they'd all come up at least in passing."

"You didn't just assume he had a ma and a pa?"

"Oh, you know what I mean. And when I spoke to Miss Addison—that's the sister—she told me the reason he never talked 'bout her was on account of her bein' the black sheep of the family. But then she said something strange. That it was funny, her bein' the black sheep in a family with someone like Billy in it. She was tryin' to say Billy had to be pretty bad or somethin', I guess." Leah looked into Ethan's dark eyes. "What do you think she meant by that?"

Ethan took a big gulp of coffee. When he set his

mug back down, it seemed almost empty. He slid it across the desk from one hand to the other. "I don't rightly know, to be perfectly honest. I didn't know the boy that well, but from what I did know, he seemed like a fine gentleman to me. Did well by you and those kids. And if there had been anything too bad, it'd shown up on that background check we done."

"That's what I keep thinkin'. But she made it sound like he was a bona fide hell-raiser. I tried to get something specific out of her, but she wouldn't give me any details. In fact, most of what she told me was vague. Especially when it came to her life and Billy's. She was more open about her folks."

"Some people are like that. You know that better than anyone."

"I know."

"So, what else?" Ethan asked her.

"What do you mean?"

"You said Billy lied to you, for starters. What's the rest?" Another big drink of coffee and this time Leah thought Ethan's mug was completely empty. His hands played with it on his desk, spinning it one way then the other.

She hesitated. This was the part she wasn't sure she wanted to talk about, especially with Ethan Montgomery, because of all the people she knew in Alvin, he might be able to actually tell her the truth. And she wasn't sure she really wanted to know the truth.

Above her that big fan continued to turn, always so slowly.

She let out a sigh.

"You're gonna tell me eventually," Ethan said. "May as well just get through it." He gave his mug another spin.

"All right then," Leah said. "According to this Addison woman, my pa knew her folks for the last four years of his life. She says they was at Billy's funeral, but stayed out of my way on account of they thought Billy would've told me things about them that would've made me not want them there. But they met Pa and he struck up a relationship with them."

She watched Ethan carefully while she said this, with the eyes she had developed during her dozen or so years working as a detective for the Alvin Police Department. And she was pretty sure in those eyes she saw something. Ethan had shifted in his seat uncomfortably during her little talk. He'd stopped playing with his mug, but he'd covered any other reaction well. Still, she thought she definitely saw something underneath his calm demeanor; she was certain he knew something and was weighing whether or not he was gonna tell her.

"You know anythin' 'bout this?" she asked him straight-out.

"Your pa was a good man, Leah," he said flatly. He moved his chair back slightly from his desk, pushing himself away from her in the process, she noticed.

"My question was one with a 'yes' or 'no' answer, Ethan. I gotta know if my pa lied to me the entire four years before he died."

Ethan held up his hand. "You're startin' to get all riled up. Don't. And 'fore I answer your question— and I *will* answer it, I promise—I want to discuss your interpretation of the word *lying*. You have already convicted Billy of lying to you when really all he did was avoid tellin' you somethin'. Those are two different things." He pointed a thick forefinger at her.

"Ethan, come on. Failure to disclose is lyin'. You know that better than anyone, probably more so, to use your words right back at you." She was getting upset now. "Don't you read any of these law books you have on these shelves? If Billy didn't tell me 'bout his sister after five years of marriage, he *lied* to me. I don't care what you say. And if my pa was carryin' on a relationship with Billy's folks knowin' damn well I didn't know they even existed or anythin' 'bout 'em then he lied to me, too. And if you're gonna try to defend that position in any way then you're a goddamn liar yourself!" Her hands were trembling as she lifted her mug to her lips and finished her own coffee. It wasn't nearly so hot anymore.

Both Ethan's palms came up now. "Whoa, Leah, slow down. Seriously. Relax."

"Answer the question, Ethan!" she said, nearly shouting. Her mug swung down at her side. There was no question Chris sitting at his desk in the room outside the office could hear her yelling.

"Okay, okay," Ethan said. "Yes, your pa knew Billy's folks. He did meet them at Billy's funeral." He went back to sliding his mug from one hand to the other across the top of his desk.

"And *you* knew this, too? And you didn't tell me either?"

"Go ahead. Call me a liar. Might as well. Everyone's a liar. There's a reason you weren't told, Leah."

"Oh, yeah? And what's that?"

"Because," Ethan said. "Because you had enough on your plate with Billy's death. You had two kids to look after and you was refusin' to let anyone help you. You was still reeling from the Ruby Mae case, which nearly cost you your sanity. The last thing we all thought you needed was to have Billy's folks pop into your life."

Once again, he raised his forearm and pointed at her.

"Within a week of him dyin'," he said, "you took every picture of Billy down from the walls of your house. You basically packed your memories of him away. You didn't want anythin' to do with him no more. We was worried havin' his folks in your life would push you too far. As it was, we were all worried you was close to the edge." He picked up his mug and set it down hard on his desk with a thump. "And that's the God's honest truth."

Leah fell silent. Had she been that crazy after Billy's death? It was true, every photograph of him had been taken down and put away. To this day, she still hadn't looked at any of them. They were all in her closet. Her wedding ring came off the day after the funeral and was still in the shoe box with all the pictures Abe found. Every present and little gift Billy had ever given her she had taken out of sight and tucked away inside her closet. Some things she even threw away.

"Oh my God," she said quietly. "You're right. I packed Billy right up and tossed him out of my life the moment he died."

Ethan nodded. "Only you didn't really. You've never let him go inside of you. You've never gotten over his death. Part of you even hates him for what you think he did: You think he purposely left you to raise two young children on your own."

Her hand came to her mouth. "I'm . . . I'm an awful person. No wonder his folks didn't want to meet me."

"Oh, they wanted to meet you. They wanted to be

part of your life so bad they was crazy 'bout it. They offered to support you and the kids. They wanted to be real grandparents to Abe and Carry, but Joe knew that couldn't happen, so he made them a deal and told them they had to settle for letters and photos that he'd send them on a regular basis."

"Apparently, he took Abe to visit them once."

"Is that so? Joe never told me about that. Good on him, I reckon. Does Abe remember?"

Leah shook her head. "No. He was too young."

"But at least they got to meet their grandson. What about Carry?"

"They only know her from pictures."

Putting his hands behind his head, Ethan interlaced his fingers and leaned back in his chair. It made another loud creak. "So I guess you got a decision to make."

"What's that?"

"Whether or not you try to make up for some lost time now and let these fine folks get a chance to play Grandma and Grandpa after all these years."

"I don't think I have much choice in the matter."

"Oh, it's entirely your choice."

Leah smiled. "You *have* met my son, right? He has his heart set on meeting them. When Abe sets his heart on somethin', it usually happens, one way or 'nother."

"Yes, I've had some experience with that myself," Ethan said. "I know his momma. Anyway, if it's any consolation, I think it's the right decision. As long as you can handle it."

Leah looked down at the floor. " 'Bout time I stopped runnin' away from ghosts."

"I think you'll find they ain't so much ghosts as imaginary monsters that are hauntin' you," Ethan said.

"Same thing."

"Not really."

Leah started to get up out of her chair. "Sorry for yellin' at you."

"It's okay," Ethan said. "Wouldn't feel like work if you didn't yell at me from time to time. But don't go so fast. Sit down for another minute or two." Pushing his mug out of the way, he pulled a file folder from a stack of papers he had on the top of his desk while Leah settled back into her chair.

Opening the folder, Ethan pulled out a few pages that were stapled together and flipped through them. "Am I to understand you asked for an autopsy for a *cat* last week?"

Oh Christ, Leah thought. *Here we go. Now I'm gonna get in trouble for wasting the department's resources.* "Yeah, I did, but I can explain. It was because Miss Sylvie was so—"

Ethan held up his palm again and Leah went quiet. "I'm not askin' you to explain. I just wanted to tell you the results are in. Thought you might like to know what caused the demise of your little kitty."

Leah tried not to look too surprised at this response. "Okay," she said. "What was it?"

"Well, first off let me read the note Norman attached to the front of his results here. It says, 'Thank you for giving me something other than heart attack victims to work on. This was quite refreshing.' " Ethan looked up at Leah. "I think that man needs to get out more."

Leah laughed.

Ethan flipped to the next page. "There was no physical signs of death, as you and Chris discerned at the crime scene, so our Mr. Crabtree did a pump of the animal's stomach as well as a toxicology analysis. It turns out your cat ingested common off-the-shelf brodifacoum. In other words, rat poison. What's surprising is the amount of poison Norm found in the animal's system. According to our coroner, there was enough to kill an elephant, or so it says here, although I reckon he may be exaggeratin' a mite." Ethan looked back up. "Norm figures there should be evidence of the cat bein' sick around the area. Find anythin' like that?"

Leah shook her head. "We searched the property pretty well, too."

"Any idea where that cat would find that amount of poison around Miss Sylvie's house? He couldn't have gone too far after consumin' it. Norm figures thirty minutes to an hour at most before he'd be dead. Probably sooner."

Again Leah shook her head. All she could think of was how dangerous it would be for the baby to have rat poison lying around. She hoped Sylvie wasn't that stupid. As far as Leah knew, Sylvie didn't have a rat problem, so why would she have brodifacoum lying around?

"Something about this is ringin' familiar to me," Leah said.

Ethan leaned forward and started playing with his mug again. "What's that?"

"Remember when Sylvie's ma was found in the barn?"

"Yeah, you investigated her death. Ruled it accidental."

"I did. With the help of some experts out of Mobile. It wasn't just my call."

"Right. What's your point?"

"She died from ingestin' brodifacoum, too," Leah said.

Ethan hesitated. "You're sayin' you reckon this cat's death and the death of Miss Sylvie's ma seven years ago are linked? Please tell me that's not what you're thinkin', because that's crazy talk. Besides, we caught the person behind Mrs. Carson's death. I should say *you* caught him. James Richard Cobbler. Crazier than a shit-house rat, that one. And I know *he's* gone. I watched him die. Up at Holman, in Atmore."

Leah remembered the look in Cobbler's eyes the last time she saw him on death row before his execution and shivered. That man had no emotion, just a cold, icy stare that pricked the bottom of her backbone and caused an electric shock to wind its way up. "I'm just sayin'," she said, "the whole thing has a familiar ring to it. Coincidence is all." Leah found herself lost in thought for a moment.

Ethan narrowed his eyes at her. "Coincidence *is* all. And don't you forget that. *Do not* try to link the death of a cat with the murder of someone seven years ago by one of Eli Brown's radical congregation members and turn them both into open murder cases. You'll have this entire department laughed out of town."

"What do I look like to you, Ethan?"

"It's not what you look like that's got me concerned," he said. "It's the way your mind works that *I'm* worried 'bout."

CHAPTER 12

The weird coincidence of Sylvie's cat dying from ingesting rat poison and Sylvie's ma going the same way settled itself into Leah's mind in a manner that wouldn't let itself go as Leah got into her car and headed for home. Only Police Chief Montgomery didn't have to worry, she wasn't thinking the cases were linked, but she did start thinking back about the investigation all them years ago when Sylvie's ma died. The court had decided James Richard Cobbler acted on his own volition and Eli Brown had no link to Mrs. Carson's murder. But what if that wasn't true? What if Preacher Eli's role in his land dispute hadn't ended with him going to jail? Everyone just assumed that had put an end to the whole contentious situation, but what if he kept connections with people on the outside and the whole thing had kept going? How much did the police and the courts really know about the land dispute, anyway?

Back when Eli Brown shot little Caleb, Leah's pa, Joe Fowler, had still been on the Alvin police force and he had been the lead on the case. Leah hadn't ever looked over her pa's files, so she didn't really know much about it other than what had been in the news since and local gossip. She had been the investigator for the death of both of Sylvie's parents ten years later, so she knew all about *those* cases, but she'd never pushed the idea that the murder of Sylvie's ma might be linked to the earlier case her pa had handled involving Preacher Eli.

Now she couldn't help but wonder if it was.

So it turned out Ethan Montgomery did know Leah all too well. Her mind liked to make connections, only it wasn't the cat he had to worry about, but the digging up of old bones from the far-flung past. That's where Leah's brain was making links.

She decided it was time to review the old case files her pa had worked on and maybe pay a visit to the records office that was part of the Alvin Courthouse. Between the two of them, she might be able to come up with something pointing its way toward Sylvie Carson maybe not being quite so crazy after all. Because, like it or not, part of Leah was starting to believe the girl's calls weren't all false alarms. There were just too many things going on. Sure, some—probably even most—of her calls into the station were just cases of shadow jumping, but something in Leah's gut told her not to write Sylvie off as fast as everyone else had. Like she'd told herself a hundred times before, her daddy and Ethan had drilled it into Leah's head that she should listen to her gut. It was her biggest asset. And if she was perfectly honest with herself, she actually wasn't that comfortable calling the death of Snowflake accidental. It just seemed so odd that the cat would show up poisoned after all this time when she'd been going in and out of that house since the day Sylvie brought her home. And Ethan had raised a perfectly good question to which Leah didn't have an answer: Where did that cat find so much rat poison, anyway?

One thing being a detective had taught Leah was to not like unanswered questions. They never sat well in her stomach or any other part of her, for that matter.

Checking the clock on her dash, she realized she wouldn't be able to go to the records office until tomorrow. They likely closed at five and it was already half past. She would try to drop by work first thing in the morning even though she wasn't supposed to be on duty tomorrow. After looking through her daddy's old files about Preacher Eli and the Carson family (which she figured would make for some pretty interesting reading), she'd head on over to the courthouse and pay a visit to the records office.

But tonight she was going straight home for a nice relaxing bubble bath.

Or so she thought.

All too often, such thoughts turn out to be too good to be true. This turned out to be one of those times because, right at that instant, she got a call on her radio from the station. It was Chris telling her Miss Sylvie had just called in again with another disturbance. This time, he said, she'd seemed almost as frantic on the phone as she had when she'd found her cat lying dead on her back porch.

"What was she callin' 'bout now?" Leah asked.

"Hell if I know," Chris said uselessly. "She was so upset, I could barely understand a word that girl was sayin'. I finally just told her you'd be by as soon as you could get there."

Leah ground her teeth. She hated the fact that she'd become part of the protocol when it came to handling

Sylvie. It pissed her off that nobody else would pick up the ball. She even found herself somewhat hoping it *did* turn out that her calls weren't completely benign just so everyone else would feel stupid. But that was a horrible way of thinking. She really didn't want it to turn out that Sylvie was in any actual danger.

"She said somethin' 'bout some door bein' open or somethin', I reckon," Chris said, after much prodding. "I'm not sure what door, or why it was open."

"You do know I was on my way home for the night, right?" Leah asked him. "I was off duty a half hour ago."

There was a long pause, then Chris said, "So you're not gonna show up?"

She wondered if Chris would go if she didn't. If he did, he wouldn't take anything Sylvie said seriously, so there'd be no point in him being there. He'd be as useless as udders on a Brahman bull. "No, Chris, I'll go. My kids can go hungry a little while longer. They're pretty well getting used to it."

This was a little white lie. Leah had started getting the kids to make their own meals on her workdays almost a year ago. She just figured that was fair. The last thing she ever felt like doing when she got home was cooking. On the odd day, she would break the rule by taking them out for a burger or something when she got home, but, for the most part, on workdays it was everyone for themselves. The rule hadn't worked out quite so bad, other than the fact that Abe seemed to eat a lot more macaroni and cheese than was probably healthy for a twelve-year-old boy to consume.

Leah could almost hear Chris sigh with relief on the other end of the phone. It just annoyed her. For the past month, there'd been really nothing else crime-wise going on in Alvin except Sylvie Carson's calls, and so he'd just sat behind his desk doing nothing while she worked unpaid overtime covering for his inability to be sympathetic.

"Okay, that's great," he said. "I appreciate ya doin' that. Montgomery said you would."

Oh, Leah thought. *That figures. He probably thinks I want to go investigate more of the cat murder scene, too.* "Yeah, yeah," she said. "Y'all better get me somethin' nice at the office Christmas party this year."

"We always do, don't we?"

"Chris, last year you got me nothin' and Ethan gave me a bottle of eight-dollar wine. I know hobos who drink better than that."

"Oh. Well, we'll try to do better this year."

"You got five months to think 'bout it."

"So, you're goin' to Miss Sylvie's now?"

"Yes, Chris," Leah said. "I've already turned my car round and I'm headin' back up Main Street. I'll be passin' the shop in 'bout two minutes. If she calls back, tell her I'll be there in less than ten."

"You're the best."

"I know it."

She hung up her radio, not bothering with the siren. She'd get to Sylvie's quick enough following traffic. Main Street cut an angle to Old Mill Road, making it less than a couple miles to her place.

On either side of Leah's vehicle, the shops along Main Street went by. Some were closing up for the night; others, like the restaurants, were just getting ready for the dinner crowd. Not that anything ever got that crowded in Alvin. Except maybe church.

She'd already gone back past the station. Now she came to a stop behind a Honda that was trying to parallel park in front of PJ Party Pizza. Outside her window were the two most popular stores with local farmers, Superfeed and K's Bait & Tack—both of which were owned by rancher Jacob Tyne. Superfeed was already closed and Pete was taking the sign for K's in from the sidewalk, so it was shutting its doors for the night, too. A broad sassafras tree stood between them, its canopy of gray-green leaves extending from thick brown boughs that touched the sides of either building.

The Honda managed to make it to the curb and Leah continued driving, hoping Sylvie wouldn't be too agitated when she arrived.

She made it up past the courthouse, which pretty much marked the east end of Main Street. Most of the buildings and shops were flanked by the courthouse at this end and the library at the other, although the city had been doing recent development down past the library: mainly a small strip mall called Brookside that Carry and her friends hung out at. It was convenient because before it went in, Leah had to drive all the way into Satsuma to do most of her shopping.

Main Street didn't officially end until you continued past the courthouse and came to Hawk Tail Crossing where the road transformed into an iron bridge that went over the Old Mill River. After the bridge, Main Street became a highway that took you out of Alvin.

Leah drove over the bridge, hearing it rattle beneath her wheels. Under the bridge, the river ran low and slow. There hadn't been much rain lately. Some days, that river could be high and so fast you'd think it was going to wipe out everything in its path.

Right after Hawk Tail Crossing was the turn for Old Mill Road that led the short distance north up to Sylvie's place. Nobody lived between the turnoff and Sylvie's house—the area was just filled with forest on either side of the road. Mostly it was tall old oaks that cast the road in shadow. But among the oaks were lots of birch and maple, plus the odd elm and cedar. The woods broke tightly against the road, and if you stared into that dense forest you saw the trees quickly constricted and became closed very fast. They became full of thick, dark trunks wrapped with lichen. The boughs of most of the trees were covered in Spanish moss that hung like wild demon hair. Strangler fig and ivy wrapped around the bases of trees, and, in places, climbed up near the tops, choking everything off.

Leah didn't think the state of the woods probably helped much with Sylvie's mind—the way she was— living way out here by herself with just the baby to keep her company. Those woods conjured up all sorts of nightmarish images in Leah's mind even in the afternoon daylight. Once the sun went down, if you weren't careful, your brain could get away on you about it, Leah was sure.

The baby was lying in its bassinet, sound asleep when Leah arrived. She was glad to see that. She figured whatever emotional state Sylvie was in had to rub off on the child in some way, so if that baby was sleeping, things couldn't be that bad.

But she soon reassessed this idea. Sylvie seemed awfully upset as she escorted Leah outside to the backyard to show her what she found.

"Someone's been out here again," Sylvie said.

"Now what's happened?"

"Look."

Beneath Sylvie's house was a cellar, although to call it a cellar was really giving it more credit than it deserved. It was more like a crawl space. There couldn't have been more than two feet of room between the ground and the floor of the house.

It was enclosed, and to access it you had to enter through two tiny wooden doors that were made of what looked like tongue-and-groove cedar boards. They were constructed at an angle set between concrete sides. The doors weren't very large, maybe a little more than three-feet square each. A wooden block was attached to the center front of one door that swiveled through a notch built into the frame of the other to keep them closed. There was no other lock.

The left one was wide open. The right one (the one with the swivel-block attached to it) was closed.

"This is how I found 'em," Sylvie said shakily.

"Open, like this?" Leah asked.

Sylvie just nodded her head.

"Sylvie," Leah said. "This little piece of wood ain't much holdin' these shut. The wind could've blown this open, or even an animal could've swiveled that block of wood loose." Leah scanned the backyard, wondering where the brodifacoum that killed Snowflake might have come from. She also had her eyes out for any indication of where the cat may have gotten sick that she and Chris might've missed. "It's been pretty windy lately. I don't think this is any indication that anyone's been in your backyard."

Leah could hear the panic rise in Sylvie's voice. "They ain't never blown open before. Besides, that little piece of wood would've had to blow around off the other door. I don't think that's possible, do you? I think someone's been here."

Squatting down, Leah closed the open door and swiveled the block back into place. It was a pretty tight fit, she had to admit to herself. She wasn't about to say that to Sylvie. "Anythin's possible," she said instead. "I don't think anyone's been in your backyard. It's either the wind or some other simple explanation. Maybe you left it not quite closed all the way and all it took was a bit of wind to do the rest?"

"I ain't never been in that cellar in my life," Sylvie said adamantly. "I'm scared to death of what might be down there."

Leah looked up at her. "What you mean?"

"I dunno. It's just so . . . dark."

"Sylvie, there ain't nothin' in your crawl space 'cept maybe some mud." She opened the door back up again, took her pocket flashlight from her small-item pack, and shined it around inside the immediate area. It had a dirt floor that was pretty much level. She couldn't see anything other than dirt going back as far as her flashlight would allow her to see. "There's nothin' in here." She really should've probably gone under the house and taken a proper look, but truth be told, Leah had two fears in this life that she didn't tell nobody about. One of 'em happened to involve being stuck in tight, enclosed, dark spaces and the other was an irrational fear of spiders. Looking into this crawl space, even from outside, Leah was quite sure it fit both criteria all too well. It was dark and confining and probably the home of more than one spider. She didn't even like the view from the cellar doors. It gave her the creeps. She thought about Sylvie. *We all have our own monsters. Some of us just hide them better than others.*

She shined the light around a bit more. "There's nothin' here. It's clear."

"I still ain't ever goin' in there."

Leah stood up. "Nobody's askin' you to."

"Well, somebody went in there," Sylvie said.

Leah let out a long breath. "If there ain't nothin' in your crawl space, then why would someone want to go in there? It don't look like the most comfortable place in the world to me. I wouldn't go outta my way to be crawlin' round underneath your house in the muck." The dirt Leah could see from where she stood did show what could be scuff marks, but they really weren't indicative of anything positive, so Leah just wrote them off. They could've been made anytime. Orwin could have stored things under the house back before he left and they could still be from then.

"I think it was Preacher Eli," Sylvie said. "He's probably tryin' to figure out some way to kill me. Maybe he's gonna put a bomb under there."

Leah closed her eyes and thought happy thoughts. This was going to take all the patience she could muster. "Now, Sylvie, I went and saw Eli Brown just like I promised I would."

This got the girl's attention. Her eyes went wide and she moved closer to Leah. "What did he say? What happened? Did you mention me?"

"Slow down there, girl. Yes, I mentioned you. He told me in no uncertain terms that it would be a cold day in hell before he stepped anywhere near you. He said he deeply regrets what he done and that he can't possibly make amends to you so there's no point in even tryin' to apologize. So he won't be botherin' you. And he certainly ain't puttin' no bombs under your house."

Sylvie looked disappointed and dubious at the same time.

"Sylvie," Leah said, "the man is old. He's not the

same as he used to be. He's done his time. He just wants to make peace with himself."

"He's foolin' you."

"No, he's foolin' *you*," Leah said. "And that's sad, cuz he ain't even doin' anythin', and you're lettin' him control your life. He's harmless."

"Then who opened my cellar door?"

"Nobody opened your goddamn door. The wind blew it open!" Leah stopped. She couldn't let herself get angry. "Listen," she said, much more quietly and calmly, "I'm sorry, but I can't let you go on thinkin' Eli Brown's out to get you. It ain't healthy for anybody. It definitely ain't helpin' you get on with your life. Now I went and talked to the man. I don't know what else I can possibly do to make you believe me."

"You honestly think the wind blew this door open? Even though it ain't ever blown open before?"

"I do," Leah said, although she wasn't quite certain she really did. "And there's no real discernable footprints or scuff marks that I can make out anywhere around here in the dirt."

"The dirt's hard packed here."

"You'd still think I'd see somethin'. All I see is your shoe prints goin' back and forth toward this area from the back door. They've made a track. Even if there had been footprints, they're lost now. I really think it was the wind, Sylvie."

"It hasn't been *that* windy. We've had windier times. It didn't blow open then."

Leah shrugged. "I can't explain that. All I can say is that it makes no sense that someone would come and open your cellar door. Ask yourself why would they do it, Sylvie? To go into your crawl space and get all dirty? And why would they leave it open? Why not close it if they're gonna do something sneaky? Why leave evidence?"

This one seemed to stump Sylvie. She looked deep in thought.

"You really have to start askin' yourself questions like these," Leah said. "Or you'll drive yourself crazy."

"What if someone's tryin' to *make* me crazy?"

Leah didn't think that would be much of a challenge. But then she chided herself for having a thought like that gallop around her mind. "Nobody's trying to make you crazy, Sylvie. Again, ask yourself: Why? Why would someone want to make you crazy?"

Again Sylvie looked deep in thought.

"Exactly," Leah said after a few seconds of silence. "There is no reason."

Sylvie let out a deep breath. "I guess . . ."

"You gonna be okay?"

"I guess so."

"How's the baby?"

"She's fine. Sleeps a lot."

"I noticed she was sleepin' when I came in. That's better than cryin', ain't it?"

Sylvie shrugged. "I dunno. I like it when she's awake. I like the company."

At that, Leah felt a twinge of pain in her heart for the girl. "Well, you just wait. Before you know it, she'll be fifteen and you'll wish she just kept quiet all the time. Trust me, I know." Leah smiled.

Sylvie smiled back, but it was a smile that didn't quite reach her eyes.

"Well, speakin' of which, I best be goin'. I have to get home and make sure my kids don't starve themselves."

Sylvie looked at the door still open where Leah had left it. "Okay."

"You want me to close that 'fore I go?"

"No, I can do it."

"Okay." Leah took one more look around the yard. Then, right before heading toward the back door, she turned and asked Sylvie, "By the way, have you ever had a problem with rats?"

Sylvie looked confused. "Rats? What do you mean?"

"You know, rats. Have you ever had them in your house or anythin' and had to get rid of 'em somehow?"

"No, why?"

Leah shook her head. "Just wonderin'. I'll talk to you soon. In the meantime, you take care of yourself and that baby. And find her a name, goddamn it."

Sylvie gave her a hint of a grin. "I'm tryin'."

"Well, try harder."

"Bye," Sylvie said. "Thanks for comin' out."

Leah walked into Sylvie's kitchen, hearing Sylvie swing the cellar door closed outside. Along with everything else, Leah now had a new unsettling feeling in her stomach because she really didn't like how tightly that wooden lock clasped between those two doors. Sylvie was right. It *was* very unlikely that the wind blew that door open.

CHAPTER 13

Just like when she found Snowflake dead on her back doorstep, Sylvie couldn't get to sleep after finding the cellar door open outside. She hated the fact that the police wouldn't believe her. She didn't blame Officer Leah. If she was honest with herself, Sylvie doubted she'd believe her stories either. And she had called the police so *much,* she was almost like that boy in that story about the wolf.

But she felt so vulnerable, especially it just being her and the baby way up here all by themselves out amid all the woods like they were. But then, Sylvie never really had felt like she had anyone. Not since Caleb died, anyway. It always felt like people could just be taken out of her life so easily. And they had been. First Caleb, then Mother, then Pa. One by one, they was gone.

That's partly why she jumped at dating Orwin Thomas when she had the chance. He was the first boy to show interest in her. Sylvie had a difficult time with relationships of any sort. She had no friends at school. So when Orwin Thomas, the number-one tight end for the Satsuma Westland Eagles, asked her out, she felt compelled to say yes.

Unfortunately, it was only a month after they started dating that Orwin tore out his anterior cruciate ligament.

It was during a rivalry game between Satsuma Westland High and Mobile Evercrest High. At the half, the score was tied at seventeen. It was right at the top of the third quarter that it happened. The Mobile Evercrest Panthers kicked off to the Westland Eagles.

Terrance Williams caught the ball on the fifteen-yard line and managed to run it to the thirty-five. The offensive team took the field, led by quarterback Barrett Mosley. Orwin Thomas had played tight end for Mosley for a year and a half and Mosley trusted him as much or more than any other player on the team. That's how good Orwin Thomas was. He would tell Sylvie all the time about how much he had *college* written all over him. There was even talk that he'd be able to write his own ticket, that he could go wherever he wanted after he graduated: Ole Miss, LSU, or Alabama. Football was the one thing in this whole big world that Orwin Thomas was good at.

Then came the next huddle. The call was a pass to Orwin, who would run out and down the edge of the field ten yards before cutting back in to make the catch. Mosley made the count and Orwin started his run. In the stands, as she pretty near always was, Sylvie sat watching her man. She was damn proud of him.

Orwin made his run down the field and cut in behind the Panthers' defenders just as the football was sailing straight into his open hands. The throw was slightly high, so he had to jump for it.

That's when it happened.

Two hits at near on the exact same time.

One came from the front, the other from the side. Both came low, both caught his knee. The side hit may have come slightly ahead of the one from the front. They tore his ACL completely to shreds, ripping apart his knee.

Remarkably, Orwin made the catch. But it would be the last catch he'd ever make. The doctors told him he'd never play organized football again. Certainly, all thoughts of college flew out the window with that catch, because a football scholarship was the only way Orwin was going to college. He didn't have the smarts to do it any other way.

It turned out, other than football, he didn't have much ambition either. He dropped out of twelfth grade less than two months later. Sylvie knew then that things were taking a turn for the worse, but in the back of her mind she wanted to stay hopeful. After all, Orwin was all she had.

Even though he had been in the twelfth grade, she was only in the eleventh. Yet, she was two years older than him on account of her missing school due to what had happened to her when she was younger. She had been set back three years of schooling. After her pa died, Sylvie had spent a couple of years in foster care, but was on her own when she met Orwin. She reckoned now that was half the attraction for him: that she lived on her own and was pretty easy pickings—something she now hated herself for.

Orwin Thomas was eighteen when Sylvie let him move into her place in Alvin. Everything about their relationship was like fireworks. When the romance clicked, it went off like hand grenades. Except, usually, it wasn't so much the romance but Orwin's temper going off like firecrackers on the Fourth of July.

"Where's the goddamn beer?" Orwin liked to yell when he came home from work. He did a lot of odd jobs around town, but mostly he pulled late-night shifts at Emmett's garage. One particular evening he seemed downright ornery.

"Maybe you drank it?" Sylvie offered.

"I didn't goddamn drink it! Have you been drinking my beer, bitch?"

Sylvie tried to laugh off his anger. "No. I don't like beer."

"Well, there was beer here last night, damn it!" He slammed the refrigerator door.

"Maybe we can go get some more?" Sylvie asked softly. She was always trying to keep his temper in check.

"With what? You think I'm goddamn made of money? I work and work and work my ass off and come home to this goddamn house and it's always a fucking pigsty."

Sylvie looked around the house. She had spent the day cleaning it because she knew Orwin liked it clean. There was nothing she could do when he was like this. But she did feel bad for him. She knew he was hurting about losing his football scholarship and he *was* the one bringing home the money.

"Is dinner at least ready?" he asked.

"It will be in ten minutes."

"What are we having?"

"Pork chops."

She knew he wouldn't argue with that. Orwin loved pork chops.

"How 'bout I go get you some more beer?" Sylvie asked.

This is the way it usually went. She tried to keep him appeased because, many nights, neighbors would call the police after hearing him yelling at her through the thin-paned glass of their small house, calling her all sorts of things before sometimes stomping out into the dead of night, occasionally not to be heard from for a day or two.

Even with all this, if truth be told, Sylvie was still upset when he disappeared that night, especially with him leaving her three months pregnant and all when it happened. She didn't much like being yelled at, but she took it. It was part of her lot in life. And she *did* love him. When he wasn't yelling and things were good, she was almost happy. As happy as she could be, given all that was going on inside that head of hers. She knew, deep in his heart, Orwin Thomas was a good man. He may have yelled a lot, but he did treat her well. In her heart back then, she figured he'd never hit her. And if any man ever had, she would pity him, for Orwin Thomas would hunt that man down and kill him to his last breath.

That, Sylvie Carson was certain of.

She suffered through these thoughts late into the night until the light outside her window began to grow to a light pink. Then she managed to fall asleep for a little bit until the baby woke her up just a short while later, wanting to be fed.

CHAPTER 14

My memory of visiting Preacher Eli that day with my mother continued to dig a great big hole in my stomach through the days that followed. I did not trust that man, nor did I like him living in my town. I decided something had to be done about it and, if my mother wasn't going to do anything, it was up to me and Dewey to.

I called Dewey on the phone and told him all about the meeting we had on the preacher man's doorstep and how he was crying those crocodile tears and all.

"I ain't never seen no croc cry," Dewey said.

"That's what I mean," I said. "I mean they wasn't real tears. He was just makin' 'em up to make my mom think he was sorry for everythin' he done."

"Then why don't you just say that?"

"It's an expression."

"I ain't never heard it before."

"You ain't never heard a lot of stuff before," I said.

"So you think he's up to no good?"

"No, I *know* he's up to no good."

There was silence for a second or two and then

Dewey said something dumb. "You know, this reminds me of somethin'."

"What's that?"

"Your neighbor. Remember? You was sure he was up to no good. Turned out he wasn't."

"Dewey, you was sure too, remember? And this is completely different. Preacher Eli was in prison for near on twenty years for killin' a little kid. Mr. Wyatt Edward Farrow is just a carpenter."

"Still, parts of it feel the same to me."

"Well, it's different enough to me." I was getting frustrated, wrapping the telephone cord around my finger, wishing he'd let me get to the part where I told him my plan.

"So, what do you want to do?" he asked finally.

"I say we go watch his house."

"Again—" Dewey started, "this is soundin' like—"

"Dewey. The man was in *prison*."

"So you want to go spy on a man who killed a kid? What if he catches us?"

"He ain't gonna catch us," I said, now wrapping the telephone cord the other way.

"Why's that?"

"Cuz I'll have you with me."

"What's that supposed to mean?"

"Well, you're the great inventor," I said. "You're gonna invent a way for us not to be seen."

There was another pause on the other end of the phone until Dewey came back with, "Okay, give me a few minutes to think of somethin'. Then I'll ride my bike over to your place."

* * *

Dewey showed up about twenty minutes later on his bike with his inventor's notebook tucked in his pocket and a pair of garden shears and a roll of kite string in a small box in his carrier. "What are them for?" I asked. He had his rope scabbard tied around his waist and his wooden sword hung down his side from the wire tie.

He flipped open the notebook. "My brilliant design for hiding out. You told me there ain't nothin' but woods round where Preacher Eli lives."

"Yeah. So?"

"So, we're gonna become part of the woods."

In the notebook he'd drawn pictures of people with what looked like wings. Actually, to call them people was giving them far too much credit. They looked more like stick figures. "I don't get it. Are they angels?"

"No, they ain't angels. Those are branches of leaves tied to their arms. And down their bodies."

"What's that on this one's head?"

"A branch."

I stared at him, my eyes wide with disbelief. "You really are brilliant," I said flatly.

He closed the book proudly and stuck out his chin. "I know. Let's go."

We took our bikes and rode the route down Cottonwood Lane, which was the road we both lived on. Then we turned up Hunter Road, which was the road Preacher Eli lived on. Cottonwood Lane is a nice ride. Before we left, I decided to bring my sword along, too. You never knew when a weapon might come in handy on a job like this, and we'd basically started taking our swords with us everywhere we went. Dewey's design actually worked out really well—it didn't even interfere with bike riding.

Cottonwood Lane was fairly flat, and on either side, pretty little houses were nestled among gardens and a wide assortment of trees that were planted on purpose, so they looked good. We rode past cherry trees, tulip trees, and magnolias. Near the end of the road, we even passed an orange tree in the front yard of a small blue house.

The ride up Hunter Road was a different story completely. There were very few houses along the way, and the ones we did pass were spaced very far apart and surrounded by thick, quiet forest that seemed to close in on the road the farther up we went. Most of the ride was uphill, which was exhausting. There were a few flowering trees in the front of the woods that I didn't know the names of, but mostly the trees were tall and dense, filling the edges of the street with oak, fir, birch, and pine. It seemed the higher we got, the darker the forest appeared, until we finally made the wooden bridge that passed over Blackberry Springs.

We pulled our bikes to a stop on the bridge. The water gurgled and sputtered beneath us. It ran a curved path splashing over and around rocks and stones, some of which looked almost as big as me. The smell of the water filled the air where I stood, leaning over the bridge. It tasted like nickels and pennies in my mouth.

"Preacher Eli's place is only another block up," I told Dewey. "It's a shotgun shack on the left. There's no other houses around it."

"Then we'll have to be extra careful when we get close. We can dump our bikes in there right before we reach it." He indicated the deep ditch running along the right side of the road. "Then we'll dip into the woods and make the rest of the way on foot just behind the tree line."

Looking at the blackness of the forest made me

swallow hard. The woods appeared ancient to me, like some evil thing out of a storybook filled with monstrous trees of every shape and size. I didn't really want to go traipsing through those towering giants.

But I followed Dewey's lead and, just before coming in sight of Preacher Eli's house, we threw our bikes into the ditch as he suggested (but not before he removed the kite string and shears from his carrier), and began our trek into the woods. At first, I jumped at every creak and crack of leaf and branch breaking beneath my or Dewey's feet, but soon I relaxed a little. After a while, it became not so bad. It really was just another forest, although this one hadn't been walked through in some time, if ever. We had to cut our own path through vines, strangler fig, brambles, and briar as we went. It took quite a while to make the short distance from our bikes to where we could see Preacher Eli's house peeking through the space between the massive tree trunks.

"Okay," Dewey said. "Now you have to climb one of the fir trees and start cutting off branches."

"I ain't climbin' no tree," I said. I was a terrible tree climber, for one thing. Even though I wasn't about to admit that.

"You have to. We need the branches."

"*You* climb the tree. I'll hold the string."

With a deep exhale, Dewey gave into the inevitable. "Fine. I'll need you to help me up to the first branch."

It took us a while to get him into the tree, but once he was there, Dewey turned out to be not a bad tree climber at all. Over the years I had noticed this about Dewey. He had strange abilities at some things and then at other, normal things, a complete lack of ability.

At any rate, he was doing a fine job of scaling the

tree and shearing off big branches of fir with lots of leaves along the way. Up he went, his sword dangling from his side with its tip pointing straight down at me. As each bough fell, it brought with it the fresh smell of sap. I collected them as they came down, inhaling the deep aroma of the leaves. All my senses were alive to the woods. Now that my eyes had grown accustomed to the darkness, things no longer seemed so bleak and black. It all just looked very green. I placed all the boughs into a pile. Some did look like wings, much like the picture Dewey drew in his notebook. I wasn't about to tell *him* that, though.

"I think that's enough," he whispered.

"Okay."

He looked around beneath his feet. I immediately saw his problem. He'd cut off most of the branches he'd used to climb up the tree and now didn't have them to use to get down with. "Um, I'm kinda stuck."

"Can you slide down?" I asked.

He looked at me like I'd lost my mind. Somewhere off in the distance the sound of a woodpecker echoed through the trees. It sounded like someone knocking two blocks of wood together.

"No," he said. "Have you ever climbed a tree?"

"Not a lot. But I doubt if I did that I'd cut off my only way down as I went up. I think you'll have to jump."

"I'm way too high up to jump." I had to agree, he was quite high up.

"There are knots in the trunk sticking out along the way for a while below you. Can you use those to step on?"

Dewey kept looking around below him, as if some magical branches were about to appear. His lower lip

twisted between his teeth. "You know, I have an invention in my book for just this very thing, but we don't
have none of the stuff to build it."

"Ain't that always the way," I said.

Finally, he gave into the inevitable and used my
idea. Slowly and deliberately, he came down, putting
his feet on the knobs extending from the trunk. A few
times his foot slipped off and my breath caught in my
throat. I thought for sure he was going to fall and wind
up stabbing himself in the side with his own sword,
but somehow he managed to hang on. Then he got low
enough that it wasn't so scary anymore.

"Okay, I think I can jump now. Can you catch me?"

"No."

"You have to."

"Okay," I lied.

He jumped and I stepped back out of the way. He
landed on the soft forest floor, right on his rear end.
Looking up at me, he asked, "What happened to catching me?"

"I told you I wasn't going to."

"Then you said you would."

"The second one's always a lie," I said.

He shook his head, wiping dirt from his shorts and
his legs. "Whatever. Let's just get these branches tied
on so we can start our stakeout. I'll tie yours on, then
you tie mine."

It took another twenty minutes or so to dress up as
fir trees. When we were done, Dewey looked remarkably like the stick man he'd drawn and I kind of felt
bad about laughing at his sketches earlier. We both had
big branches of fir leaves on our arms like wings, one
coming down the front of our body, and one drooping
over our head like some weird bird. I had to say, we

did blend in much better with the green of the tree leaves and bushes around us than we had before we tied all the branches on.

Quietly, we crept to the front of the tree line right along the roadside that looked directly across at Preacher Eli's house. Both of us lay on the ground and propped up our heads with our hands on our elbows. We knew we were going to be here a long time, so we might as well get comfortable.

Well, as comfortable as we could be covered in itchy tree branches.

Leah felt odd pulling the Brown/Carson file from the archive drawer. She figured she must've been the first person to touch it since her pa put it there seventeen years or so ago. It made her remember her original days on the force, joining not because she wanted to, but because she *had* to. It was a year before she became pregnant with Abe and, with Billy's work being so sporadic, they needed the extra income.

She had been at her pa's house when he talked her into coming on board. It was right before his cancer got so bad. They had only gotten to spend barely two months working together before he had to quit.

"You'll come work for the department," he had said, but she'd only laughed.

"I ain't no cop," she'd said. "Remember that time you took me huntin'? It was the one and only time I ever shot a gun." She was sitting on the flowered sofa that was more the size of a loveseat. Like everything in her folks' home, it looked and felt brand-new. It was the way her ma had kept things, back while she was still here.

"You were bound to hit something. You were shakin' so bad you were aimin' at the entire forest," he said, and smiled. "But bein' a cop is different. We'll train you. This ain't a question, by the way." Pa sat at an angle across the small coffee table from her in the Queen Anne chair. He had his large elbows resting on the curled armrests, but they barely stayed there. He was a man who liked to conduct while he spoke.

"What makes you think Chief Montgomery would even *want* me?" she asked. "It would be complete favoritism."

"He's big on favoritism."

She rolled her eyes.

Her pa pointed at her. "I'll tell you one thing. He's big on you. And you can say this 'bout that man. If ever there was anyone whose heart was bigger than his brains, he's the one."

She threw a tasseled pillow at him. "You're not very nice. I happen to like Chief Montgomery."

"You won't. He's a son of a bitch when you work for him."

"I'm *not* comin' to work for the department. I ain't no cop."

Pa suddenly grew all concerned. He leaned forward, but before he could talk, Caroline went toddling down the hallway chasing her pa's Irish setter, Putter, with a squeal. Leah's pa waited for the noise to die down. "Leah, you have to start thinkin' 'bout your next move. You can't feed that kid on dreams, wishes, and stardust. I wish you could. Please. Take my offer."

"Don't you need to discuss this with Chief Montgomery?"

"Hang on."

Picking up the phone beside him, he made a call into

the station and right then and there told (not asked)
Ethan Montgomery that his daughter was coming on
board to work as an officer at the Alvin Police Department. The call barely lasted a moment.

He hung up and smiled. "Done. You start tomorrow
at eight."

"You're serious."

"Oh, honey, you're gonna find police work is *very*
serious business." Six months later, she got her first
big case when Ruby Mae Vickers disappeared from
town and she discovered he hadn't lied. You couldn't
get any more serious than that.

Shaking the memory from her mind, Leah laid the
file folder on her desk. It was rather thick, thicker than
most of the files she worked on. That usually meant the
case wasn't as clear-cut as everyone would've liked. It
meant there was lots of information that had to be kept.
Extra information. Complications.

She wondered what kind of complications she was
about to uncover about Preacher Eli Brown and Tom
Carson's family.

Flipping the file open, the first thing she came to
were the statements taken at the scene of the crime.
They were in her pa's handwriting and, once again, she
had to fight off old memories. If this didn't stop, she was
never going to get anywhere with this case. She decided
she had better strengthen her resolve and stop being so
emotional. "Quit bein' such a goddamn girl," she said
softly to herself.

"You? Bein' a girl?" said Chris from behind her,
making her nearly jump clear out of the county. He had
been in the restroom when she came inside.

"What you doin' sneakin' round?" she snapped.

"I wasn't sneakin' round . . . I was . . . well . . . that

ain't no business of yours. What are *you* doin' is a better question. Ain't this supposed to be your day off?"

She sighed. "I came in to check on somethin'. Sort of a personal project for the time bein'."

Chris looked over her shoulder. "Preacher Eli Brown shootin' Caleb Carson has become your 'personal project'? I think you need to get out more. Miss Sylvie's really gettin' to you, huh?"

"I just want to check some things out."

"Suit yourself."

Grabbing a cup of coffee, Chris took his seat at his desk, picked up the newspaper, and began reading as though she wasn't there. She half expected his feet to come up on his desktop he looked so relaxed and at home.

"Oh, I'm sorry," Chris said, noticing her staring. "Did you want a cup?"

"No, I'm good."

"Okay."

She went back to the statements in the file. Tom Carson's account of the incident was this:

Eli Brown entered Carson house armed. He mentioned his and Tom's ongoing "land dispute" as to which Mr. Carson replied, "There is no dispute, the land is mine." Mr. Carson said Mr. Brown wanted the land to build some kind of "institution." To this, Eli Brown asked Mr. Carson to produce a deed. Mr. Carson said production of said deed was impossible as Mr. Brown had made sure the deed was disposed of. Unsure at this point what is meant by "disposed of" and why Mr. Carson cannot just get the government document

*reissued. Mr. Carson seemed unable to answer
this when questioned. Mr. Carson went on to say
his boy, Caleb Carson, had crawled under the
supper table and into his lap before Eli Brown
took a shot at Mr. Carson and because of that
the shot hit the child and not Mr. Carson, as Mr.
Carson believes Mr. Brown intended. It is noted
that Mr. Carson's report is sketchy at best due
to his understandable duress at the crime scene.*

What her pa had written for Preacher Eli was somewhat different from Tom Carson's take on things:

*Eli Brown was found in his church next door to
the property assumed to belong to Tom Carson
kneeling in front of his altar praying. It took a
long while to calm him down, and, once we did,
he would not talk about the murder right away.
His initial concern was about the land Tom
Carson lives on. Mr. Brown claims that Tom
Carson stole it from him eight years ago. When
questioned about how he stole it, Mr. Brown
said he didn't know, but that the land belonged
to his daddy and became his after his daddy
passed. When questioned if he had documentation confirming this, Mr. Brown vaguely said
there was no written will but a verbal agreement
and everyone knew the land was church land.
He further stated that for eight years he let Mr.
Carson live on his land unmolested and only
now wants it back in order to use it for a project.
He claims to have told Mr. Carson he's willing
to pay Mr. Carson the same price Mr. Carson*

*paid for the land when he purchased it back in
1963, a sum he remembers as being nine
thousand dollars.*

*(Mr. Carson later corroborated this sum, but
stated that the land was worth at least ten times
this much in today's market. When told this,
Mr. Brown went on to state that the thievery
committed by Mr. Carson didn't happen in
today's market and therefore should not be
held to its prices.)*

*When he finally talked about the murder, Mr.
Brown confessed right away to the shooting of
Caleb Carson so Officer Cody read him his
rights. Mr. Brown apparently waived his right to
remain silent (Officer Cody had to ask him three
times if he understood that he was doing so)
because he kept talking anyway, saying that
what happened was such a terrible shame and
that he did not mean to pull the trigger and
never planned on killing no one. Not Tom
Carson, he said, and especially not that little
boy. After that, he fell into tears and it was
impossible to get any more from him. So we
cuffed him and brought him into the station.*

Leah had known the whole "Carson affair" was
over some sort of land dispute; she just hadn't known
the details until now. There was one more report, taken
from Caleb's mother, but it didn't differ much from
that of Tom Carson. Strangely, Sylvie was never interviewed. Leah wondered why. There was hardly even
any mention of her in the notes, just that she was there

and had blood on her from the gunshot on account of where she'd been sitting. When that bullet got Caleb at such short range, it splattered pretty near the whole side of the kitchen.

Details of the land dispute were now high on Leah's list of things she wanted to know more about. Farther on in the file, she found an appraisal of the land. Tom Carson had estimated a bit high. The appraisal was dated June 15, 1971, and put the value of the land at forty-two thousand dollars. That was still a pretty nice gain from what he had purchased it for only eight years earlier. Still, back then land hadn't skyrocketed yet the way it did in the eighties. Leah couldn't even imagine what that ranch would be worth today. Probably over a quarter-million dollars.

Where had that money gone? Even if the ranch had been sold as part of Tom Carson's estate after his death, which Leah suspected it had, Sylvie should've gotten the money, but if she did, where was it? The girl showed no sign of having a pot to piss in.

There was only one way to find out what had happened, other than asking Sylvie directly, which might not really help at all. Lifting her phone, Leah put a call in for financial records to be delivered to the station for Tom Carson's ranch dating from the time of Caleb Carson's death up to the time Tom Carson was found hanging from the oak tree in his back field. She also made a call to order a copy of Tom Carson's tax returns during that time so she could get an idea of the ranch's profit and losses.

Meanwhile, Chris just went on reading his paper from his desk beside her.

Continuing with the file, Leah found the property

deed that Tom Carson had apparently complained didn't exist. It was, in fact, his land, he owned it entirely, his being the only name on the certificate.

What was missing was any clarification as to what this "institution" or project was that the notes taken at the crime scene referred to. Leah found that strange, too.

"Chris?" Leah said, looking up at him. He actually *had* put his feet up on his desk. She could barely believe it.

Chris looked at her over the top of his paper. "Mm?"

"I need you to do me a favor."

"What's that?"

"I need you to go pay Preacher Eli a visit and ask him a question for me."

"Can't we just call 'im up on the phone?"

"I want you to look into his eyes and make sure he ain't lyin'."

"And you're askin' *me* because this is *your* pet project and . . . why?"

"Because last time *I* went, the man nearly threw me off his property, that's why. Come on, please? I think I found somethin' important."

"What do you want me to ask him?"

"Ask him what he planned to do with the land he wanted from Tom Carson eighteen years ago. It says in the report that he planned on buildin' some sorta 'institution.' I wanna know what it was."

"Now why would Preacher Eli tell me anythin'?" Chris asked.

"Cuz you're a police officer, goddamn it. Now get off your ass and go. And get your feet off your desk. You ain't at home."

Chris just laughed at her. He could tell she wasn't actually mad. "You really think Preacher Eli's up to no good?"

"I dunno. I didn't after I went and saw him, but now that I've read his file, I dunno. I just have a funny feelin' there's a lot more to the man than shows on the surface. Apparently, he has superpowers. He knows how to make things like property deeds disappear. At least until the police or the bank comes lookin' for 'em, that is."

Chris stared at her a long minute. "You're serious 'bout this."

"Somethin's up, Chris. Maybe it's all in the past, but there was definitely somethin' dirty 'bout him. I just wanna make sure the past stays in the past. As for the magic powers, I'm guessin' he had some inside help."

Chris laughed. "You mean like maybe God?"

"I don't think God would be the side I'd be choosin'," she said.

Chris might give the indication of not doing much at work, but the truth was he was a damn good cop. He noticed things most people missed and as he pulled into Eli Brown's yard, he noticed a new car parked on the right side of Eli's shack. Eli's station wagon was parked on the left.

Chris knew the car didn't belong to Eli for a number of reasons. First, it was too new. Eli had been in prison seventeen years and this Toyota was barely four years old. Second, the tire tracks leading through the dirt in front of Eli's house behind the car were fresh, so whoever drove it in did so recently. From what Leah told Chris about Preacher Eli, he wasn't getting out much these days. And lastly, what the hell would Eli Brown need two vehicles for? He wouldn't. His wife had been dead for four years. He lived alone.

So this meant he had company, which just complicated things for Chris. Chris hated complications. With a huff, he got out of his cruiser, put on his hat, and closed the car's door. He walked up the porch steps and knocked, expecting to see the aged face of the preacher man answer.

Instead, a young kid, probably in his late teens, swung the door open.

"Hey," he said.

"Hi," Chris said, trying not to appear too taken aback. "Is Eli Brown home?"

"Yeah, sure. Hang on."

The kid left the door open and walked off into the house. A minute later Eli Brown appeared in the doorway and things became much more the way Chris expected them to be.

"I already talked to you guys," Eli said, his voice thin and reedy.

"You haven't talked to me," Chris said. "I'm Officer Jackson." He held out his hand for Eli to shake. Eli studied it a moment before taking it in his own.

"What can I do for you, Officer? And is this gonna be a regular occurrence, the police showin' up on my porch like this?"

Chris laughed. "I hope not. It's a long drive and not a lot to look at but trees."

The preacher didn't return his laugh.

Growing serious, since the laughing didn't break

the ice, Chris said, "I hope you don't mind me askin' you a few questions."

"I'm havin' a game of rummy with my grandson, who drove all the way down here from Alabaster just to see me. I'd really rather not waste his time answerin' your questions."

"They won't take but a few moments, I assure you."

"What are they 'bout?"

"Well, there's only one, really. And it concerns something we found in the report taken at the crime scene during the whole Carson incident."

Preacher Eli looked back into a room, presumably the room where his grandson was sitting waiting for him to return and play cards. Then he opened the door fully and stepped out onto the porch. Chris had to take a step back to accommodate him.

"Let me tell you somethin'," Eli Brown said in a clipped whisper. "I don't want any of that past bein' dredged up, you hear me? I done my time. I don't *need* this, and I certainly don't deserve it."

Chris held up a hand. "I assure you, you've got it all wrong. It's actually a question 'bout your intent."

Preacher Eli's eyes narrowed. He studied Chris's face. "My intent? What you mean?"

"Well . . . the report says you was gonna use the land to build some sorta 'institution,' but nowhere in the file does it explain what you meant by 'institution.' We was all just wonderin' if you could tell us what you had planned. We're all just interested, is all."

The preacher continued analyzing Chris, as if unsure as to whether to take him seriously or not. Finally, he said, "Okay, I'll play. I planned on buildin' an education complex."

"Education complex?"

"Yeah. You know, like a private school. Baptist. Alvin doesn't have a proper school that runs from kindergarten all the way to the twelfth grade so I was gonna give it one. I had the business plan, the blueprints, everythin'. I even had people ready to work on it. I was basically set to start diggin'. Then that whole fiasco happened."

Chris couldn't believe he'd just referred to killing a three-year-old boy as a "fiasco."

"I see," Chris said.

"That answer your question?" Eli Brown said, his eyes once again narrowing. He tilted back his head and looked down his nose at Chris.

"Yeah. That was it. Just the one."

"Good." With that Preacher Eli walked back into his house and closed the door behind him.

Chris angled into his squad car and backed out of Preacher Eli's yard onto Hunter Road. Just before he got to the bridge, he radioed Leah back at the office. "Well," he said, "his idea wasn't half bad. He wanted to build an education complex. Basically provide a private school for Alvin that went from kindergarten to twelfth grade. Save kids having to take the bus all the way to Satsuma for high school."

They talked a bit more about it. He told Leah about the grandson.

"What's the grandson's name?"

"No idea. You told me to ask about the institution he was buildin'. That's what I did. I ain't goin' back. The man gives me the willies."

"Fair enough."

When they were done talking, Chris added, "Oh, just before you go? There's somethin' you probably ought to know. Your son and his little friend are sittin' across the street in the woods from Eli's place with fir tree branches tied all over 'em with kite string. I think they're havin' a little stakeout."

Leah didn't say anything for a good couple of seconds. "You sure it's my son?"

"Oh, I'm sure."

"Dear God. Does Eli know they're there?"

"I don't think so. They actually did a pretty good job camouflagin' themselves."

He heard her frustration right through the radio. "Okay, I'm on it."

Chris set the radio back in its cradle and smiled. No, not much got past him.

CHAPTER 15

The most exciting thing me and Dewey had spotted so far on our watch of Preacher Eli's place was Officer Chris Jackson stopping by for some reason. We had no idea why he was there, but we did see Preacher Eli whisper something to Officer Jackson and then make a point of coming out on the porch to talk to him.

We figured this was on account of the fact that someone else was over at the preacher's house. Some guy who looked like a teenager who happened to answer the door when Officer Jackson knocked. I didn't have any idea who the guy was. Now that I knew he was there, I was guessing the silver car parked out front of the house might belong to him since I didn't remember seeing it when me and my mother came here. I figured this way of thinking was how detectives did their work. I was probably a natural detective.

Luckily, me and Dewey were dressed as trees and hiding in the forest, because if Officer Jackson had seen us he'd probably have told my mother and she would likely have not thought my idea of spying on Preacher Eli was a good one. We didn't see eye to eye on some things. I figured spying on people fell into the category of being one of those things.

But Officer Jackson had left maybe fifteen or twenty minutes ago (I'd forgotten to check my watch) and, of course, hadn't seen us. So we were in no danger of my mother finding out we were here. And Preacher Eli obviously didn't know either, or he'd have undoubtedly told Officer Jackson about us. That made me feel quite a bit better.

Since then, we hadn't seen any sign of Preacher Eli or the other guy in the house. Wherever they were or whatever they were doing they were doing it in a room away from the front windows.

"They're probably makin' plans," I told Dewey.

"What sorta plans?"

"Not good ones."

But still, it would've been better if we actually got to *see* them from time to time.

In fact, I was starting to get the feeling this whole idea might not have been my best idea. Worse yet, the only good part of it might turn out to have been Dewey's invention of creating a method of making us invisible to anyone who happened by.

That's when a car stopped on the road right in front of where we were lying. I didn't recognize the car right away because I wasn't really bothering to look at it. After all, we couldn't be seen, so the car must be doing its own business and was of no concern to us.

At least that's what I thought.

Then I studied the car a little more closely as I heard the driver's side door open. I actually *did* recognize this vehicle.

It was my mother.

I gulped. Had she come to see Preacher Eli again?

What was *she* doing here? Why hadn't she parked in his driveway?

Then, as she came around the front of the car, I found out.

"Abraham Teal! Get out of those woods right this instant!" She was nearly screaming. I wanted to shush her. Tell her to keep it down on account of she was going to attract the attention of Preacher Eli, but there was no shushing her. "How dare you do something like this?"

I looked at Dewey. He looked at me. I still wasn't sure she could see us, even though she seemed to be staring right at us. "You too, Dewey, get up! Come on! Now!"

Slowly, we stood from where we were lying, both of us covered in fir tree branches tied to our body with kite string. "Oh my God! You look ridiculous! What the *hell* are you doin'?"

"Watchin' Preacher Eli," I said quietly, still hoping not to be overheard across the street.

"Chris was right. You *are* on a stakeout. Well, guess what? Your stakeout just ended. Where's your bikes?"

Dewey pointed to the ditch, down a little ways.

"Nice," my mother said. "You threw your bikes in the ditch. Go get 'em!"

I started walking toward the ditch on the outside of the woods, but she stopped me.

"Take those things off you first," she said. "You look absolutely ridiculous."

I couldn't undo Dewey's knots. He had to take my branches off and then, using the garden shears, I had to take off his. Then we went and got our bikes. Dewey carried the shears. Halfway there, he turned around.

"What are you doin'?" my mother asked him.

"I left the roll of string in the woods," Dewey said. "I need to put it back in my dad's shed."

My mother let out a deep breath. "Go get it. But do it fast. You're ridin' home. I want you on your bike and down that hill in the next five minutes. Abe, you're comin' with me. Bring your bike up to the car. I'm throwin' it in the trunk."

"Why can't I go with Dewey?" I asked, climbing into the ditch. It was a very wide and deep ditch and getting my bike out wasn't easy. Luckily, there was no water in it on account of all the sun we'd had lately.

"Because I said so. Why do you have to spy on people?"

I thought this over, but before I could answer she told me it was a rhetorical question. Then she clarified: "That means I don't expect you to answer it. I expect you to *think* about it." I didn't really understand, but I knew when to keep my mouth shut.

After four or five attempts, Dewey got his bike out of the ditch. By then, mine was already in the trunk. "Bye, Abe," Dewey said with a wave. "Bye, Miss Leah." And with that, he kicked off and headed down the hill toward the Blackberry Springs Bridge and his home.

"Get in the car!" my mother snapped.

I got in the car. She got in her side and slammed her door. Turning the key to start the ignition, she told me, "If I ever catch you doin' somethin' like this again . . . so help me. Didn't we go through all this once before?"

I knew what she was talkin' 'bout. She was talkin' 'bout Mr. Wyatt Edward Farrow, just like Dewey had been on the phone this morning. But just like I'd told him, this was all different on account of Preacher Eli actually having shot a kid and gone to prison for it. I was about to tell her just that when she turned her face to me and I saw that look in her eyes that meant it was best to just keep my thoughts to myself. I'd learned that over the years you didn't mess around when she gave you that look.

So instead, I asked, "Where're we goin'? This isn't the way home." We'd just driven by the turnoff to Cottonwood Lane.

"I'm still workin'. Now you're stuck comin' with me."

"Comin' with you where?"

"Just mind your business."

She kept driving down Hunter Road, heading toward Main Street. Soon, the silence seemed to become too much for her because she broke it. "So. I decided to call that Addison woman back and tell her we'd drive into Georgia next time I had a day off. Meet these grandparents of yours. How do you feel about that?"

It was like dozens of lightning bugs suddenly swarmed up into my chest. "That's great!" I said.

We turned left onto Main Street and drove right past the library where me and Dewey had sat with my aunt Addison that morning it was so hot. The marble steps still looked bright white this afternoon, but a scattering of green leaves covered some. They'd blown from the maple trees planted beside them. "I'm hopin' your sister thinks it's great, too," my mother said with a slight worry in her voice.

I frowned. "You don't think Carry'll wanna meet her grandparents?" I found this a very odd thing to be figuring on. Surely, everyone wanted to meet their kin.

"It's tough to call how Carry will react to things sometimes. Your sister can be"—she searched for the word—"complicated."

"How do you mean—complicated?"

"She's just . . . never mind. She's a *girl*. You can't expect to understand 'em. Especially at your age."

I didn't say nothing, just watched the businesses sail by on either side of the road, while trying to guess what our destination was. Finally, I asked again. "Where are we goin', anyway? Seems like we're headin' all the way to the other end of Main Street."

"I *told* you," my mother said. "Mind your business."

I figured since I now seemed to be working with her it *was* my business to know where we were going, but I found out soon enough. It actually *did* turn out to be pretty near all the way down at the end of Main Street. She pulled her car to a stop right in front of the Alvin Courthouse. At first, I figured that was our destination, but it turned out we were headed to the public records office right beside the courthouse. I think the records office actually was part of the courthouse, but we entered through the front from the outside, so it seemed like a separate building. Compared to the courthouse it was small and squat.

Inside, it wasn't even as big as it looked from the outside. The room was filled with a musty smell, like the pages of old books. Sunlight shined through the three main windows along the front wall. The rest of the room was lit with fluorescent lights.

Bookshelves separated the room into sections, making it almost like a maze. Most were floor-to-ceiling shelves packed with spines of all sorts of books. There were also catalogs and files like we have in our school library explaining which books had what information in 'em so you could find what you were looking for. Maps and old photographs hung on the walls.

"I'm Detective Leah Teal from the Alvin Police Department," my mother told the clerk working behind the small pine desk tucked away in the back corner. "I'd like to check out your property records, if I may." The clerk's desk was stacked with papers, making it appear even smaller than it was, so it suited the room. The stacks were so high, some of them rose taller than the woman, who was a brunette with short, curly hair and large round glasses. The stacks made her appear even smaller than she turned out to be once she stood up.

"Oh, absolutely," she said, seemingly impressed with the fact that my mother was a detective. Her eyes fell to the sword at my side. Then they went back to my mother.

"This is my son, Abe," my mother said, explaining. "I reckon he believes he's Peter Pan."

The clerk laughed. I didn't find it very funny. My mother had just made a joke at my expense.

The clerk escorted us through the maze of shelves right across the room to the other side, where the thickest of the white-covered books packed a series of shelves on the back wall. I had never seen books so tall. Each one had to be nearly two feet in height. "You'll find all of the properties in Alvin and the outlying areas listed here. Each volume is categorized by location. You can refer to this map." She pointed out a map on the back wall that was broken out into squares.

My mother thanked her and set about tracing her finger up the map, northward. At first, I thought she was heading toward Eli Brown's new place, but she wasn't. She was following Fairview Drive, but instead of veering left like Fairview did, she let her finger curve off right and continue around the bend where it turned into Bogpine Way.

"Goin' frog huntin'?" I asked, with a laugh.

"Mind your business," my mother told me again, not taking her eyes off the map.

I thought I was being funny. Bogpine Way wraps around a dense forest that opens onto Beemer's Bog, a place known to get overrun with toads in late spring. Nobody goes near it on account of the smell and all the noise.

She stopped her finger about a third of the way up the Bogpine bend and tapped. "What street number do you reckon this is?"

I looked behind me to see if the lady clerk was still standing with us, but she wasn't, so I figured my mother must be talking to me. I didn't have a clue what she meant. "I don't know. How would you ever tell?"

"I guess you just estimate. This says one hundred down here and three hundred up here. That's about two inches between them. Would you say this is around another inch and a little bit? I'm looking for four-oh-five."

"I guess." I didn't rightly know an inch from an inchworm, to be quite honest. But I didn't want to sound dumb.

"Okay, that puts us in square zero-seven-C," she said, reading the numbers from the side and top of the map. "See if you can find that volume."

I started looking at the white books on the shelves. It took me a moment to realize they had numbers and letters on their spines. Unfortunately, it appeared the only ones low enough for me to see were from the letters E to T. "I reckon it's in one of the top rows," I said.

"I reckon you're right." My mother scanned the top three shelves. It took her a minute before she pulled one of the books from where it sat. It turned out to be even larger than I expected, at least half as wide as it was tall. These books were massive and thick with pages full of information.

My mother laid the book on a table under the map and carefully opened it to the back where an index listed the addresses by street number and page. She quickly flopped the pages back to the page she wanted. I found myself looking at a detailed map of a bit of road with some forest on the right of it. She flipped ahead the next five pages; every one showed a bit more of the road and the trees as it went farther up and curved right into the forest. I realized I was looking at one big parcel of land.

In the bottom right corner of each page was a square with writing inside it:

> 405 Bogpine Way, Alvin, AL 36573
> $120,000.00
> 320 Acre Property (Cattle Ranch)
> Owner: Unlisted.
> Mon. 2 Mar. 1981 08:00:00

My mother stared at that square a long while.

"What is it?" I asked.

"I dunno," she said. "It don't make no sense to me."

"What don't?"

"The land's sat there this whole time untouched. Nobody's developed it. The old farmhouse and barn are just rotting away. I don't understand why there ain't no owner listed. I thought the state would be listed as owner, or at least the county."

"Owner of what?"

"The land Miss Sylvie's pa owned 'fore he died."

"Wouldn't Miss Sylvie own it? I thought kids got whatever their folks had when their folks died." That was my understanding of the whole thing.

"Miss Sylvie couldn't afford it."

"What do you mean?"

"Ranches cost money to upkeep, and Sylvie was only fourteen when her folks died. She was in no shape to look after the ranch alone, let alone worry about making the costs. She went into foster care."

"What's foster care?"

"Nothing you don't ever need to worry 'bout."

"Why would anyone want to live so close to Beemer's Bog?" I asked her, but she completely ignored me. She picked up the book and, leaving it open at one of the pages of the ranch Miss Sylvie's pa used to own, lugged it back to the desk where the clerk sat. "Mind if I bother you with somethin'?" my mother asked her.

The clerk smiled. "Of course not. That's why I'm here."

My mother came around to her side of the desk and bent down, showing her the page and the square with the writing in it. "Right here," she said, "where it lists 'Owner.' Can you tell me what 'Unlisted' means?"

The clerk looked confused. "I ain't never seen that 'fore."

"Could it mean it's owned by the county? Because that's how I figure it *should* be. And the date of the record would be pretty near right."

The clerk continued to look at it in confusion. "No . . . if it's owned by the county, it always says 'Vacant,' not 'Unlisted.' Don't ask me why. 'County' would make more sense. But I don't know what 'Unlisted' means. It's almost as though the owner wasn't put in the records, but I don't see how that's possible. It's public information."

"That's what I thought," my mother said. "Would there be somewhere else I might be able to find out who this property belongs to?"

"We can run a title search on it. That will involve sending off a form to the Mobile County public records office, but it usually doesn't take long to get a response."

"And that will definitely have the owner listed?"

"It should. If *that* doesn't, something funny's goin' on. The next step would be to request a copy of the deed. That would list ownership for sure."

"What's this dollar amount?" my mother asked.

"That's the amount the land was appraised at when this survey map was made. We keep the actual assessment records separate, so if you wanted a recent assessment record, I could get you that. But it shows here that, on March 2, 1981, this property was worth one hundred and twenty thousand dollars."

My mother thought this over. "Is there any way we can tell if there is a lien on the property?"

"We can request that information as part of the title search. I'm sorry, Officer—"

"Detective," my mother corrected her. "Detective Teal."

"I'm sorry, Detective Teal, Alvin's just too small to have a records office that keeps much more than just basic records. Would you like me to help you fill out the request for the title search? We can do it right now and save you a lot of time."

"Sure."

And so my mother did that while I went back and looked at the big map of Alvin hanging on the wall. As I did, my eyes were constantly being drawn upward and westward to that little spot of land in Blackberry Springs where I knew, right at this very moment, Preacher Eli was planning his next move.

And I was willing to bet dollars to dingbats it had something to do with that teenager who drove that strange silver car me and Dewey had seen parked beside the house.

CHAPTER 16

The next day, me and Dewey rode our bikes down to Main Street just for something to do. We often did this—went for bike rides while we talked about this and that. It was nice having the wind on our faces and the sun on the tops of our heads, especially in the summer when it got so hot. We were in the middle of an especially hot spell, and sweat clung to my hair and occasionally ran down the sides of my face while we went along. Of course, both of us had our swords dangling from our hips. They'd become pretty much part of our standard wardrobe.

Today, Dewey had been doing most of the talking, going on about one of the inventions from his book. It was for an outboard motor he had developed (so far on paper only) that should work with the rubber dinghy he had in his dad's shed. "We can take the dinghy up to Willet Lake and I'll show you how it will work. That is, once we build it."

I wondered why he chose Willet Lake. It was a nice enough lake and all, but the only way to get there was by walking through a narrow path in the woods that opened on Hunter Road pretty near a half block up from Preacher Eli's place. Alvin had two other lakes to choose from, Cornflower Lake and Painted Lake, but Dewey had to pick the one that sat on the doorstep of a convicted murderer. Somehow it just figured.

"I don't really like boats," I said. What I really meant was that I didn't really like being shot to death in the middle of a lake by a crazy old preacher man.

"You'll like 'em when they have motors attached. Especially my motor. It'll go really fast. Did I tell you it uses a car battery and an electric eggbeater?"

"No," I said. At that point, I started tuning him out as he went on about the intricacies of motor building using household appliances and common garden supplies.

Finally, I couldn't listen to him go on about ridiculous ideas for motors anymore so I casually changed the subject.

"Guess what my mom told me yesterday."

"Now how could I possibly guess something like that?" he asked.

"I didn't mean for you to really guess."

"Then why did you say it?"

I rolled my eyes. "It's just somethin' people say. Like 'Betcha don't know what I've been up to lately.' "

"I wouldn't know that either."

"I suspect you would have a better idea than anyone else would, though." We were getting off topic.

"Well, if I had to guess what you'd been up to," Dewey said, "I'd guess it would have somethin' to do with your ma bein' upset with you for catchin' you spyin' on Preacher Eli yesterday. She sure seemed mad."

"Aw, she wasn't so bad," I said. "I've had her much

madder at me than that. Heck, all she did was force me to go to the records office with her."

"The records office? What the heck for?"

I pedaled backward slightly and slowed down my pace. We were coming up on Vera's Old West Grill on our left and the air was full of the smell of burgers sizzling on the grill. My mouth watered and my stomach gave a little rumble.

Dewey saw that I was braking and matched my speed. He knew what I was about to say was important. "Now you can't tell nobody," I said, trying to keep my voice to a whisper, even though it's impossible to hear somebody whispering when you're riding a bike. So I ended up just talking as quietly as possible.

A group of three men came out of Vera's, laughing. They were all wearing golf shirts and dress pants. I figured they probably worked together—maybe at one of the office spaces that would soon be coming up on our right. Likely, they were on their lunch break.

Dewey knew I was serious. He waited until we were well past hearing distance of the men before he spoke. "I won't. You know you can trust me." Boy, did I have his interest now.

"My mom was checking out the land owned by Sylvie Carson's folks 'fore they died. I didn't know exactly what she was lookin' for, but from what I could catch, she seemed to think somethin' sneaky's goin' on. And all I could think of was that if there is anythin' weird, the obvious person behind it is Preacher Eli."

"Of course," Dewey said. "Did your ma agree?"

"I didn't ask her. But she did find out somethin' strange. Apparently, whoever owns the land isn't listed at the records office and the woman workin' there said that was quite unusual. She appeared rather concerned 'bout it, actually."

We came to a stop at the intersection where Sweetwater Drive runs through Main Street. On the corner across the street, Fast Gas looked deserted. There were no cars at the pumps and I didn't even see an attendant working there. Looking at the gas station made me think of my pa and how he used to work at a gas station farther down Main Street during nights and how, if he'd worked days, he'd probably still be alive. I was glad that gas station he worked at wasn't around no more and that they'd built the Brookside Mall where it used to be. Judging by Fast Gas, it certainly seemed like working the day shift was a much easier job than nights. You didn't even have to be out front. You could just hide somewhere inside if you wanted.

"So what did your ma do?" Dewey asked as we started riding again.

"She sent off for more records from the Mobile office that's a lot bigger and has more information. The woman said they'd know for sure who owns the land. My mom was really suspicious 'bout the whole thing and didn't seem to like it one bit that there wasn't no one listed. I really got the feelin' Preacher Eli's gonna turn out to be somehow involved."

"Wow," Dewey said. "That's somethin'. I can't wait to hear 'bout those records when they come."

The row of business centers came up on our right. There were three of them; each was a three-story cement building named after a hawk. There was Hawk Ridge, Hawk Point, and Hawk Landing. I didn't rightly know what hawks had to do with business. Each business center squatted back from the road surrounded by poplars and gardens full of rhododendrons and wild roses. The light wind picked up the sweet smell of the roses as we passed.

All three buildings had a sign saying OFFICE SPACE FOR LEASE out front. Ever since those structures went up over six years ago, they'd all had those signs in front of them. I doubted they'd ever find enough business folks in Alvin to lease three entire three-story buildings.

"Oh, and guess what else," I said to Dewey.

Dewey started to speak but I cut him off. "Again, I wasn't really askin' you to guess. Anyway, my mom told me she's gonna take me and Carry to Georgia to meet my new grandma and granddaddy that my aunt Addison told us 'bout."

I could see cogs spinning in Dewey's brain; he was thinking about something. "What?" I asked.

He brought his bike to a complete stop.

I stopped too, but had to walk it back to get alongside him. "What?" I asked again.

"It's just . . . I thought your ma was worried that Addison might not really be your aunt?"

"Oh, she doesn't think that no more. We got a background check on my pa and it showed he has a sister."

"Yeah, but you said she was still thinkin' this might not be *the* sister but someone else pretendin' to be her."

"That was 'fore she talked to her on the phone. Now she believes her."

"But . . . what if she *isn't* your aunt? And what if these other folks ain't really your grandparents? What if they ain't related at all?"

"Now why would anyone go and pretend they're my relations?"

"I dunno. What if they're after some sorta inheritance?"

I laughed. "Dewey, we ain't got nothin' to inherit."

"You got some things."

"Like what?"

"Access to information pertainin' to all the inventions I told you 'bout."

Laughing, I just shook my head. "You're 'bout as smart as a can of dew worms on a spring mornin' sometimes, you know that?"

Dewey got all indignant. "I'm only lookin' out for your best interests."

"Don't worry, my interests are all fine." I started pedaling again.

We were halfway up Main Street, just a little ways past the police department where my mother worked, when Dewey came up beside me again. "You know what? I got an idea."

"Yeah? What's that?"

"Why don't you and me go to the records office and check what kind of information they have about your grandparents? I bet they at least have their names. Maybe even their pictures."

I thought this over. It wasn't a bad idea. Not because I thought the people my mother wanted to take me to see weren't my grandparents, but because I would love to know as much about my family history as possible. It was the one thing I never really had in my life. Dewey now had me wondering exactly what kind of information they *did* keep at that records office about family stuff.

"Okay," I said. "That sounds like as good a way as any of spendin' the afternoon."

* * *

The same clerk was sitting behind the desk when we arrived at the records office. Neither her nor the desk looked so small today, as the piles of books and papers that had covered the top were gone. She had her hair the same and wore the same big glasses. Today she had on a blue shirt with frills around the collar. She recognized me right away. "You're that policewoman's son. Where's your momma?"

"At home." Once again I was overwhelmed by the odor of musty books. They actually tasted like old dust on your tongue, although the room was clean enough. It looked like it had just been washed up. The windows sparkled with the afternoon sun pouring in.

The woman looked a bit confused. "Oh, is there somethin' I can help *you* with, then?"

"I, um, want to find out 'bout my family. You know, my past family and all."

A wide smile spread across her face. "You mean your *genealogy*. Isn't that great! Is this something you're doin' for school?"

"No, ma'am," Dewey said. "School's out for the year. It's the summer."

Concern fell over her face. "Oh, that's right. So, this is just somethin' you're doin' on your own, then?"

I nodded. "Yep. Is that okay?"

"Absolutely. Although the only information you can get here is *public* information. Anything private, of course, isn't available from any of our records offices."

I didn't rightly know what she was talking about, but I just nodded anyway. "That's fine. I just wanna know about my . . . I can't think of the word."

"Ancestors?" she asked.

"That's right," I said, smiling. "About my ancestors. Find out who they were!"

"Or *are*," Dewey corrected. "That is, for the ones that are still livin'."

"Okay, let's see what we can pull out for you." She stood from the desk and it turned out she was wearing a black skirt as she came around. Once again she saw my and Dewey's swords.

"So are you *both* Peter Pan today? Or are *you* a Lost Boy?" she asked, turning her attention to Dewey.

Dewey looked at me. "What's she talkin' 'bout?"

I shook my head. "Forget it," I mouthed.

She led us to a different section of the room than she'd taken me and my mother to yesterday. "This is our genealogy section," she said. "Now, there's not a *lot* of information here. And it's pretty much confined to Alvin and the immediate outlying areas. We really don't go much farther out than Satsuma just because we don't have the room to store all the information. So, anybody in your family history who was born anywhere else might not show up. What's your last name?"

"Teal," I said. "T-E-A-L"

She wrote that down on a piece of paper.

"And what's your momma's maiden name?"

"You mean her name 'fore she married my pa?" I asked.

"Yes."

I had to think hard to remember. Finally, it came to me when I thought of Uncle Henry. His name was actually Henry Fowler, which was the name of my mother's dad. "Fowler."

"Okay. So far, so good. And your name is?"

"Abe," I said.

"And your ma's name?"

"Leah. L. E. A. H."

"And your pa's name?"

"Billy." I stumbled a bit. "He . . . died when I was two."

"Oh, I'm so sorry," she said. Then with her pen over her paper, she thought for a second. "I'll use William. He's probably in the archives as William. If nothin' comes up, we'll search for Bill or Billy. Okay, do you know your grandpa's name?"

Her questions kept going like this until I couldn't answer them anymore, which didn't take long. I knew my mom's dad was called Joe, but I couldn't remember the name of her ma. And I didn't know the name of my other grandparents on my pa's side of the family. Heck, I hadn't even met them yet. I told her about Uncle Henry, who was actually my *mother's* uncle, and Aunt Addison, but she didn't seem too concerned with uncles and aunts.

"Okay, that probably gives me enough to go on," she said. Pulling a large book from one of the shelves, she started turning pages. I watched from the side. Dewey tried to edge his way in and watch too, but I figured since we were looking up my family stuff, I should be the one who got to see what was going on. She kept flipping pages until she came to the F section and then found *Fowler*. Running her finger down the page, she came to the list of Joes. There were a lot of Joe Fowlers listed in that book.

"Do you know if your momma's pa was born in Alvin?" she asked me.

I shrugged. "I dunno."

She sighed. "Let's try Teal. We'll probably have better luck there. *You* were born here, right?"

"I was born in Satsuma."

"Okay, close enough. *You* should be in here." She pushed the volume she had out back onto the shelf and pulled out another one, this time opening it to the T section. "Oh, this is good," she said. "Teal is a much less common name than Fowler. Let's see. Oh, this is probably you right here, three from the top. There's only one Abraham on the list." Beside my name (if it really was me) were some reference numbers.

"What do those mean?" I asked.

"They tell us what book to go to next to get the real information from. These books are just sort of gigantic indexes."

"Wow," Dewey said.

She turned to the wall of shelves behind her and started studying the spines of those books. "Nope, not on this one." Then she walked around to the other side. Me and Dewey just stayed where we were beside the small table where the index book still lay opened to the T section.

"Found it!" she called out through the wall of books. She came around carrying a large binder with a blue cover. "Okay, according to this," she said, once more referring to the index, "your information is on page 125-A3."

She plopped the binder open on the table and began tossing pages, slowing as she got close to the right one. She ended up going a couple too far and had to turn back two. "Here we are: Abraham Teal. Let's see if this is you. Is your birthday March twenty-sixth, 1976?"

Suddenly, I got excited. "Yes! That *is* me! What else does it say?"

"Your momma's name is Leah Marie Fowler. Your

pa's name is William Robert Teal. Your grandma on your ma's side is Josephine Adeline Fowler." She looked at me. "There, see? Now you know."

"I guess my sister was named after her. My sister is called Caroline Josephine."

"You're probably right! Your grandpa on your ma's side as you know is Joseph Fowler, no middle name. Your grandma on your pa's side is Sara Lynn Teal, and your grandpa on your pa's side is Jeremiah Teal, no middle name."

Wow, did I ever feel important. I knew information about my family that my mother didn't even know yet. For once, it was *me* knowing stuff instead of everyone else.

"Does it say anythin' else? Does it talk 'bout what they did or anythin'?" Dewey asked.

"No, I'm afraid there isn't a lot of genealogy information kept."

"Can I write to Mobile for more, like my mom did?"

She frowned. "They don't keep much either. You'll probably get even less than we have. In fact, we've got more than most towns simply on account of Alvin bein' so small."

I frowned. This wasn't what I wanted to hear.

"I'm sorry," she said.

"That's okay." I examined my shoes.

Then she snapped her fingers. I looked up and she was beaming. "You know what you need?" And before I could answer she told me. "You need a historian. And I think I know *just* the person."

She walked quickly back to her desk and I followed behind her with Dewey on my tail, feeling the excitement rise like a trumpet blast in my chest. I wasn't certain what a historian was, but it sure sounded important. I supposed a historian was an expert on history. That made sense.

"I have a friend down in Chickasaw," she said, "who has been researching the genealogy of Alabama for years, but she especially knows *this* area. Let me give her a call for you."

I smiled. "Thanks!"

She dialed a number and waited for her friend to answer. Finally, she did.

"Hi, Dixie," the clerk said. "It's Mary Sue here. Yes, I know. Too long. Oh, you know. Yeah, still in Alvin. Still at the records office. Yeah . . ." I thought they were going to keep on chitchatting for days until finally Mary Sue, the apparent name of the clerk, interrupted. "Listen, Dixie, this is actually a business call of sorts. I have a young boy in my office. His mother is the detective of Alvin. Mmm-hmm. Anyway, he's trying to research his family history, and I showed him what we had, which was barely nothin', an' then I thought of you."

There was a long pause before Mary Sue spoke again. "Yes, he was born in Satsuma. I have some information about his daddy. He's passed away." She sort of whispered the words *passed away* as though saying them the same volume as the rest might have offended me. "Yes, I can give you the date of his birth and of his death."

She relayed all the pertinent information, including my grandparents and everything else, getting all of it from the book she'd pulled out. Then she asked me for my address, so I told it to her. "All right, I'll tell him to look forward to it. Thank you very much, Dixie. And I hope to see you soon."

She hung up the phone. "My, my, that woman can talk your ear off."

"Is she gettin' me information 'bout my family?" I asked with a big grin I couldn't hold back.

"She certainly is. She said to give her a couple days to compile it and then she'd put it in the mail for you. Her name is Dixie Spinner. You can watch for her package in your mailbox." Then she leaned over and whispered, "And you may want to write her a quick thank-you card after you get everything. She'd like that."

I thought that was a good idea, too.

I looked at Dewey. "This is great. I'm gonna finally learn 'bout my family."

"If there's anything to find out, she'll be the one to know 'bout it," Miss Mary Sue said. "And I can't guarantee she'll find any more information than we have here, but sometimes you get *real* lucky and she'll dig you up things like family crests and stuff like that."

"What's a family crest?" I asked.

"It's an insignia your family used way back to designate them from other families. It would appear on shields and flags and things."

That sounded pretty neat. I hoped I would get a copy of my family crest.

"Oh," she said, "and she won't find any real facts other than names, birthdays, cause of death, and that type of stuff 'bout anyone unless that person did something extraordinary or unusual. For instance, she told me she once dug up family history for this one feller who found out one of his grandfathers from way back was once wanted for seven train robberies. He turned out to be mighty proud of that."

I thought that sounded like a strange thing to be

proud of. I wondered if maybe the "feller" she was talking about was Preacher Eli.

I thanked her again, a little concerned about my mother's reaction to the mail coming from this Miss Dixie in Chickasaw being delivered straight to my house. I wondered if this was something my mother would mind me doing. Oh, well, I'd have to make sure I was the one who checked the mail throughout the coming weeks.

"I think she was overanxious to help us on account of she knew your mother worked for the police," Dewey said on our way out.

"You know, it is possible she's just nice," I said.

"It's possible, I guess. But I think my theory's more likely."

CHAPTER 17

Over the following days, thoughts about the Brown and Carson land dispute circled inside Leah's head like hungry vultures over a cattle carcass. Likely, Leah thought, it was all spawned by what Abe had said at the records office. *"Wouldn't Miss Sylvie own it? I thought kids got whatever their folks had when their folks died."* At the time, Leah had told Abe that Sylvie couldn't have afforded the ranch, but was that so true? The ranch could've stayed in her name and been run without her. Besides, even if the ranch had been sold as part of Tom Carson's estate, the difference in value between what he originally paid for it in 1963 and what it was worth at the time of his death was well over a hundred thousand dollars. Even if it went for a rock-bottom price at auction, there would still be a substantial amount of equity left for Sylvie, one would think.

Leah received the financial statements and tax information she'd requested for Tom Carson. They arrived together at the station just as Leah was leaving for the day and she brought them home with her. Sitting on the sofa in the living room, she eagerly went through them, trying to discover the reason why Sylvie hadn't appeared to have gotten anything from the deal.

She examined Tom Carson's bank information first. There was a lot to it. It covered nine years of his life, and told an interesting story. That nine-thousand-dollar initial investment he had made slowly went wrong for some reason, and it was all laid out before Leah in black and white. Tom had taken out a line of credit with the Alvin First National Bank against the ranch almost immediately following the death of his son. At first, the line of credit only used a third of the equity he held in his ranch, but as time went by, he increased the amount of the LOC at higher and higher rates. The only thing that kept him afloat was the fact that the market grew as fast, if not faster, than the rate of his expanding line of credit.

One thing was for certain, though. Tom Carson got in way over his head financially due to *something* very early on. And even when the value of his ranch started to reach upward of a hundred thousand dollars, so did what he owed on it. Not only that, but according to the tax sheets Leah had requested, many years the ranch ran at a loss. That didn't help his situation one bit. But the losses in no way compensated for the amount of money actually being spent. Wherever that money went, there was no record of it.

It made no sense. From what she knew about the Carsons, they didn't go on lavish vacations or anything like that.

"What were you doin' with all your money, Tom?" Leah asked, continuing from page to page.

Because of the booming market, Tom was able to get away with defaulting payments on his LOC. Compound interest simply kept piling up higher and higher. It never got to the point where the bank threatened to foreclose, but if things hadn't turned around soon, Leah could tell that point was coming fast.

By the time of his death in 1980, Tom Carson owed the bank just under eighty-eight thousand dollars, an amount he could never pay back. Tom Carson must've known this—a fact that struck a nerve with Leah. *Could this have contributed to his suicide?*

There was indication that the bank called in the line of credit upon Tom Carson's death, which probably preceded the auctioning off of the property. Leah remembered quite distinctly that no will had turned up after his death, so an auction of the property was the most likely outcome. Still, even if the ranch *were* sold at auction, there was a good chance it would've gone for enough money to pay the bank debt and still have some left over as a nest egg for Sylvie. But Leah had no records of the land being sold. All she really had was the property survey map with the words *Owner: Unlisted,* and the original deed with Tom Carson's name on it in her daddy's police folder.

Could it be possible that the bank *hadn't* auctioned the ranch and that Sylvie Carson's name was the one that belonged on that title? Maybe all she needed to do to claim ownership was fill out some forms or make a court appearance.

The market had continued to boom since 1981, and Leah suspected the appraised value of one hundred and twenty thousand dollars they showed at the public records office was probably now at least double that. Surely, with the ranch not running and Tom Carson not spending his money on whatever it was he had been spending it on, there would be value in that ranch today. Maybe a *lot* of value.

The one thing that niggled at the back of her brain was the date on the survey map. It had been updated March 2, 1981, a date that, in Leah's eyes, seemed entirely too coincidental. It was fewer than four months after the "supposed" suicidal death of Tom Carson.

When had she started putting the word "supposed" in front of suicide with quotation marks around it when it came to Tom Carson? Leah wasn't sure. She knew these sorts of thoughts were exactly the kind Ethan Montgomery had warned her against having. He'd be mighty upset to learn she was doing such a thing now. Leah decided to wait for the title search she'd sent away to Mobile for before she decided how she would refer to Tom Carson's death to herself.

All of this also had Leah thinking about Sylvie Carson's present state of mind and whether or not her delusions were quite as delusional as people thought. Maybe she really was in danger. Maybe she always had been. If that land had even fifty thousand dollars in equity and Sylvie was the one entitled to it, her life suddenly did have reason to be threatened. A very good reason, in fact. In Leah's experience, money was always a good motive for any criminal act.

After an hour or so of being unable to set her worried mind at ease, Leah decided to go pay Sylvie an unscheduled visit. This would likely alarm the girl, as she wasn't used to the police showing up without her calling them first. On the other hand, maybe it would help ease her fears, knowing that Leah really did care about her and wasn't just coming because of her irrational phone calls.

This time Leah was going for selfish reasons: to clear her own mind. She had some questions she wanted to ask Sylvie, although she wasn't quite sure how to bring them up. There was a very good chance they were the types of questions that might set Sylvie off—questions about the past. Leah always avoided treading where memories lay when it came to Sylvie.

But today Leah was going to take Sylvie on a little trip down memory lane. Not because she wanted to, but because the detective inside her *had* to.

It was the first day of rain Alvin had seen in almost three weeks and even though it wasn't a hard rain, it came with a strong wind that made the raindrops fall at a slant. Grabbing her Crimson Tide sweatshirt, Leah pulled the hood up over her head and ran to her car, doing her best not to get soaked along the way. She drove through the bleak streets to Sylvie's house, trying to piece together how she would phrase her questions. It was important she did it right.

Above her, the sky was the color of asphalt and the clouds hung low and heavy. The rain started coming down harder as she turned up Old Mill Road, splattering off the hood of her car and the street. It was a miserable day.

By the time Leah pulled into Sylvie's, the dirt driveway had become a layer of mud. Leah's shoes became caked with it as she jogged to the front porch, her clothes getting drenched along the way. The raindrops were heavy and the wind hadn't let up. Her blond bangs hung limp in front of her face. She tucked them up out of the way.

Rapping on the door, she called out, "Sylvie! Sylvie, it's Detective Teal! Alvin Police!"

Nobody answered.

She knocked again, louder. She called out again, louder.

Still no answer.

Her heart sank. Where would Sylvie be on a day like today? Around the yard, rain bounced and drizzled off everything in sight. If Sylvie was out with the baby and caught in all this it would be terrible. She didn't own a car. She would be on foot.

Leah tried knocking again, as hard as she could. This time she nearly screamed her name out. "Sylvie! It's Detective Teal! Open up!"

At last, she heard the dead bolts shoot, the chain slide. The door opened two inches. The blue eye of Sylvie Carson, usually wild and crazy, appeared welcoming and warm.

"Hey," Leah said, slightly out of breath from hollering. "It's me. I need to talk to you. Can I come in?"

Sylvie nodded through the crack. The door closed, the chain slid, the door opened, and Leah entered.

The house was warm and felt good. A sweet smell hung in the air. Sylvie had been cooking. "Are those cookies?" Leah asked, taking an exaggerated whiff.

Sylvie frowned. "A pie. It didn't turn out. Pecan. I make terrible pecan pie. I accidentally only put in a quarter the amount of sugar the recipe called for."

"Sure smells good."

Leah started taking off her shoes. "Leave 'em on," Sylvie said. "They're fine."

"No they're not," Leah said. "They're full of mud from your driveway." Finishing taking them off, she followed Sylvie into the living room. "Where's the baby?" Leah asked.

"In my room," Sylvie said. "Asleep. All she does is sleep."

"Be careful what you wish for. Things could be worse."

"I dunno. Sometimes I think she sleeps too much."

"It's healthy for her. It means she's growing . . ." A fruit fly buzzed around Leah's face. She clapped her hands at it, trying to squash it. ". . . And content."

"So *why* are you here?" Sylvie asked. Then she said timidly, "Sorry, that came out wrong. I don't mind you dropping by, I was just wonderin', is all."

"I need to ask you some questions. Can we sit somewhere?"

Sylvie nodded. "The kitchen? There's more light." Leah had to agree. The living room with its single yellow lamp looked particularly gloomy on this rainy afternoon.

They both sat at the kitchen table. "Are you sure that pie didn't turn out?" Leah asked. "It sure smells good."

"Oh, I'm sure. It's in my garbage."

Two more fruit flies buzzed around Leah. She killed them with one try. "You have a fruit fly problem, I see."

"Probably the pie."

"When did you make it?"

"An hour ago. Wasn't even cooled 'fore I threw it in the trash."

"Then I doubt it's the source of your fruit flies." The shotgun still hadn't moved from its place by the door. Four more fruit flies flew across the table.

Leah stood. "Where are they comin' from?" She checked the garbage under the sink. Sure enough, there was the pecan pie, not looking half bad. A little charred, but if it only had a quarter the sugar in it, it probably didn't taste near on as good as it looked. But there were no fruit flies around it. "It ain't the pie."

She checked the rest of the kitchen. "There's some here around the sink, but most seem to be comin' from your vents."

"Where do these vents go?" Sylvie asked.

"Outside." Leah opened the back door. The day had grown darker than ever. Her hand automatically went to the light switch. The outside light didn't come on. "I thought you was gonna replace this bulb."

"I did," Sylvie said, suddenly alarmed. "I replaced it a week ago."

"Well, it ain't workin' now." Leah tried the switch four or five times.

"It should be."

Standing up on her tippy-toes, Leah's fingertips touched the bottom of the bulb and slowly screwed it into the socket. After about two turns, it came right on. "It wasn't screwed in." Hesitantly, she looked at Sylvie.

Sylvie's eyes were wide. "I screwed it in. Believe me. I screwed it in all the way. Somebody unscrewed it!"

"I believe you."

"No you don't."

"Actually, I do."

Sylvie fell quiet. "Who would unscrew my light-bulb?"

"I don't know." A swarm of fruit flies were gathered around the back porch. "I also have no idea where these flies are comin' from, but you have a ton of 'em."

Obviously shaken up because of the bulb, Sylvie said, "Why don't you forget about the flies for now and come sit down and ask me whatever you want to ask me?"

"Okay."

Taking one last look at the bulb, Leah locked the door and turned off the light. She returned to her chair.

"Would you like a coffee?" Sylvie asked.

"No, I'm fine."

A moment went by while Leah gathered her thoughts.

"Well . . . ?" Sylvie asked.

"I don't know how to ask you these questions without potentially bringing up bad memories for you."

Sylvie looked at her. "Don't worry about my memories. They're always there and they're always bad."

"How do you deal with that?"

"I just *have* to. If not for me, then for the baby. Go ahead. Please? Especially if you think it will help figure out who's been in my backyard."

Leah took a deep breath and slowly let it out. "Okay. Here goes then. I need you to talk to me 'bout your pa. What do you remember 'bout him?"

The fingers of Sylvie's left hand began rubbing the fingers of her right. "You mean in general?"

"To start, sure."

"He was a good man. He made sure we had food and stuff. He loved my ma."

"What 'bout you? Did he love you?"

Something flashed in Sylvie's eyes. "Of course! What kind of question is that?"

"I'm only askin' cuz you left yourself out just now when you answered. And Caleb? He loved Caleb of course, too?"

Leah watched Sylvie's reaction and thought mentioning Caleb so early on may have been a bad idea.

She thought Sylvie was about to break down, but somehow she managed to hold it together after a bit. "He took Caleb's death the worst. I think he would've rather seen anyone else go but his little boy." Her eyes refused to meet Leah's gaze.

"I don't think that's true," Leah said.

"What part?"

"All of it. First, I think *you* took your brother's death the worst. Look how it's still affectin' you. And second, I don't think he'd want to see any of his family die."

Finally, Sylvie looked up at Leah. "He killed himself because of what happened over Caleb. I didn't do that. I *couldn't* do that. I'd be too . . . scared."

Leah reached out and touched Sylvie's hand. "That's not fear, Sylvie. That's strength. Don't confuse the two."

"And he was the one always askin' me if I was okay. Kept askin' if I needed to talk to somebody about it."

"Talk to somebody? You mean like—"

"Like a professional. Like a shrink or somethin'. He told me that could really help."

"It probably could've," Leah said. "It probably *still* could."

"Well, I don't know about that. When he'd say it back then, I'd just get mad and ask him what the hell he knew about what helps with anythin' cuz all I hear at night is him cryin' himself to sleep cuz he lost his little boy." Her eyes grew wet.

"Have you ever *tried* talkin' to anybody?"

Sylvie hesitated. "Not really."

"Not really? Or not at all?"

"Well, I saw this psychologist for a while right before I met Orwin. I only saw him three or four times. I was goin' through a rough patch at school. He didn't help. He thought all my problems were cuz of Caleb when they were all cuz of school. All he wanted to talk 'bout was Caleb. I went to talk 'bout school."

Leah pulled out her pad. "Can you give me the name of the psychologist?"

"I can't remember. He was provided through assistance. Langwood or Langdon or somethin' like that. I was just comin' outta foster care at the time."

Leah wrote these names on her pad.

"You ain't gonna talk to him, are you?"

"Would it be okay if I did?"

Sylvie thought about it a moment then shrugged. "I guess. We didn't really talk 'bout nothin'."

"And he was here in Alvin?"

"No, Satsuma."

"Okay, thanks." Leah put her pad back in her pocket.

A silence fell over the table for a few moments, finally broken by Sylvie. Leah noticed she'd become more and more open with her. Probably, Leah thought, because she had grown to trust her. "You know, there were many times I wished it was me instead of Caleb that Preacher Eli shot that evenin'."

"I think that's normal."

"Sure didn't *feel* normal.

"Anyway," Sylvie said, "now that Pa's gone, I feel so bad 'bout all those mean things I said. I wish I had the chance to take 'em all back."

Leah locked fingers with Sylvie. "Oh, honey, I'm sure he understood. He was goin' through the same things you were."

Sylvie went quiet for a long while. When she spoke

again, she said, "I guess in the end he proved I was right: He really didn't know how to make things easier. If he did, maybe he'd still be here."

"You can't think that way. You'll eat yourself up with the maybes and the guesses. Things are as they are. Everythin' happens for a reason."

"I don't believe that." Sylvie had let go of Leah's hand and was now looking at her fingers while they drummed on the table. "If you believe that, you have to believe God has a sick sense of humor. I want to believe God didn't play any part in what happened to my family. That He somehow managed to stay out of it, and I'll still find them one day when I leave this place and everything will make sense. But it's so hard to keep any faith sometimes."

"Do you go to church?"

Sylvie laughed. "Haven't done so in a long while."

"You should come with us sometime. We try to attend regularly." Truth be told, Leah's "regular" church attendance was more sporadic than she liked to admit. But she considered herself a God-fearing Christian woman just the same.

Sylvie laughed some more.

"I'm serious. Why are you laughing?"

"I have a baby. What would I do with her while I was in church?"

"Babies are allowed in church. There's lots of them there."

"Well, we'll have to see."

Leah gave her a warm smile. "Think 'bout it."

Sylvie looked into her lap and fell silent.

"Do you mind if I keep askin' questions?" Leah asked.

Sylvie shook her head silently.

"Did your pa ever do anythin' or act in any way that was unusual?"

Yet another laugh escaped Sylvie's lips. "He was the opposite of unusual. His world ran by his habits. He kept them up all the time. Out in the fields by six, Mother had breakfast on the table for him at eight; she had lunch ready at noon sharp. Twice a week he'd drive down to Mobile for supplies and things like that." She'd left out supper from her list of meals, and Leah figured, despite what she'd said about memories, there were some she really wanted to keep suppressed. Suppers were probably high on that list.

"Sounds like a good life."

"I don't know if he'd agree," Sylvie said. "Like I told you, he wasn't happy. He lost a lot. Then he finally gave up on it all, including me."

Leah sighed. She had no idea how to respond to something like that. There were some wounds that would just never heal, and nothing she could say was going to alter that.

She decided to change the subject. "Did he ever . . . *buy* things? For you and your family? Expensive things? Jewelry, maybe? Did you go on vacations? Anything like that?" Leah actually felt dumb even asking this question.

Sylvie laughed again. The girl could change her demeanor in a heartbeat. "Are you serious? Miss Teal, we lived a very simple life. We was farmers. We didn't ever go *nowhere*. I ain't never been on no vacation in all my life. I don't think I ever owned a piece of jewelry. No, my pa was a very sensible and practical man."

Leah knew in the back of her mind that there was some question to just how sensible he was. He had spent a lot of money on *something*, she just didn't know what, yet. From Sylvie's bedroom down the hall, she heard the baby wake up and start crying.

Sylvie looked at her. "I gotta go see to her."

"Okay, last question. Then I'll let you be. Do you know if your pa had a will?"

Sylvie mulled this over. "To be right honest, I never thought 'bout it. There never seemed to be any point in pursuin' somethin' like that and I'da thought if there had been one, someone woulda said somethin'. Ain't like we had nothin' anyway." Sylvie said most of this sentence as she walked away from Leah, leaving the kitchen and heading down the hall toward the cries of the baby.

Leah made a mental note to do a search for a will left by Tom Carson.

Sylvie returned with the baby on her breast, happily suckling away. Once again, Leah was impressed with how much of a good mother she'd become, given all the weaknesses she'd been handed in life. "You had a ranch, Sylvie," Leah said. "That was worth somethin'."

"Now what would I do with a ranch?"

She had a point, Leah guessed. "Listen, Sylvie. I want to thank you for takin' the time to talk to me."

Sylvie looked at her expectantly. "Will this help with anythin'?"

"I dunno yet. But I'm not givin' up until things make sense to *me*. So we're on the same team. Remember that, okay?"

"Okay."

Leah headed back out into the rain and got into her car. She drove toward home, both happy and frustrated. Happy that Sylvie was able to answer her questions without it causing her much undue duress, and frustrated because her answers hadn't seemed to answer anything. By Sylvie's account, Tom Carson was an ordinary man who had extraordinary things happen to him. If this turned out to be true, based on Leah's detective background, this would make him the exception to a very rigid rule.

CHAPTER 18

The property report Leah requested from the Mobile public records office finally arrived. Strangely, Abe had gotten the mail that day and had it sitting waiting for her on the kitchen table when she got home from work. For the past few days, Abe had been getting the mail every day. She was surprised at this new interest for him. Until now, he'd never paid much attention to the mail. Leah found his sudden concern over it weird, given that he didn't get any mail himself.

Oh, well, she thought, opening the manila envelope. *Kids go through phases. Be happy it's just mail he's interested in, Leah, and not something like setting fire to the house.*

She pulled the report from the envelope. There wasn't much there, just seven photocopied pages. One was a recent property assessment notice. The next five pages matched the survey maps she found in the Alvin records office exactly, right down to having "Unlisted" as the owner. She was starting to get very frustrated until she came to the final sheet.

This one was different. It wasn't a map. It was a

page of information and history about the property, showing all the buying, selling, and any liens that were against it over the past thirty years.

Thirty years ago, the property was listed as vacant, which, the clerk at the records office had told Leah, is the usual way of saying it simply belonged to the county. "So there goes your poppa's claim 'bout ownin' it, Eli," Leah said quietly.

Then on July 8, 1963, the property was sold to Tom Carson for nine thousand dollars, which exactly matched what both Eli Brown and Tom Carson had reported to the police during their interviews after Caleb was killed.

For all Tom Carson's financial problems, the report showed no liens against the property the entire time it was in his possession. In fact, the report was strangely quiet until January 25, 1981. The ranch was then sold at auction by the Alvin First National Bank and purchased by a Mr. Argo Atkinson for $34,000 even.

Leah flipped back to the survey maps and checked the little box in the lower right corner. "Not a bad price for a ranch that would be assessed at one hundred and twenty thousand dollars barely a month later, Mr. Atkinson," she said. "Whoever you are."

How did he manage to buy it so low? Had nobody else been interested in it? Maybe the two strange back-to-back deaths of Sylvie's folks had everyone spooked about the place. People could be weird that way. Leah bet the bank was a bit peeved. They wouldn't have gotten back near the money Tom Carson had owed them from that sale.

She'd never heard the name Atkinson before, but a question still hung in Leah's mind. Why had he bought the place? Was it as an investment? Had he just planned to sit on it? He was paying tax every year on that land—at the *appraised* cost—and yet it just sat there. Nothing had been done to it in the eight years since Tom Carson died. Other than the ravages of time and storms, everything was exactly as it had been that day. Or at least it was last time Leah checked.

Surely this Argo Atkinson had some plan for the property when he initially bought it. Could his plans have somehow gone wrong?

She found the last value that the property was appraised at:

> 405 Bogpine Way, Alvin, AL 36573
> $240,000.00
> 320 Acre Property (Cattle Ranch)
> Owner: Mr. Argo Atkinson.
> Mon. 4 Jan. 1988 08:00:00

It was the same parcel of land. Three hundred and twenty acres. It hadn't been broken up at all. And Argo Atkinson had made near on a quarter of a million dollars on his investment in eight years. That wasn't too bad, in Leah's eyes. So maybe it *was* just an investment.

But it had been a while since she'd been out to the ranch, so maybe things had changed since she was there last. Perhaps it was time for Leah to make another visit to 405 Bogpine Way. In the meantime, she was going to have Chris try to figure out who this Atkinson fellow was. She decided she'd radio him on her way out, and ask him to search the Alvin directory for anyone with that name. She doubted an outsider would be much interested in a ranch here in a small town like Alvin. Especially one, as her son had so eloquently put it, so close to a bog full o' stinky old toads.

* * *

The Carson Cattle Ranch (as it used to be known) was pretty much exactly as Leah expected to find it. At least it appeared that way from where she parked on the dirt drive leading up to the old farmhouse. Wildflowers and grass had taken over all of it that they could, but otherwise the place was just the way Tom Carson left it.

The steel gate at the street that ran between two wooden fence posts had broken from its hasp, so it was easy enough to swing out of the way so she could drive inside. The gate was flaked with dark red rust and squeaked as she pushed it open. Leah drove inside and parked at the end of the drive, staying close to Bogpine Way.

It had continued raining the past two days, although not nearly as hard as it had on that first day after the period of all the sunshine. Today there was a slight drizzle in the air and the cloud layer floated high in the sky, giving everything above the horizon a gunmetal-gray backdrop. The wind Leah had trudged through the other day when she drove out to Sylvie's was gone. Now it just felt wet and muggy with a slight mist that hung along the sloping ground.

Getting out of the car, Leah pulled the hood of her sweatshirt up and walked to the farmhouse.

The first thing she noticed was the smell. It was wafting down from Beemer's Bog like sulfuric acid. It was the sort of thing she doubted she could ever get used to. The second thing she noticed was the sounds of the toads. It wasn't even late spring when you expected a lot of toads. Beemer's Bog had to be a quarter mile from where she was and still all she could hear was them toads croaking. She couldn't imagine what the stench and sounds must be like if you went to the end of the property line where it came right up against the edge of the bog itself.

She was starting to see why there might not have been a lot of interest in purchasing this place at auction way back when this Argo Atkinson fellow basically stole it.

The farmhouse was built from timber that had weathered over time. It was gray, but then it had been gray even in Tom Carson's time—it had never been painted. She tried the front door and found it unlocked.

Stepping inside, she pulled off her hood as she came in through the living room, the same way Eli Brown must've entered on that fateful evening when everything changed for the Carson family. Leah could only imagine what it must've felt like sitting up at that kitchen table (which had long since been replaced by a new one, now covered with a layer of dust) while that old man trudged across the floor in his muddy boots with that gun in his hand.

Leah came up the short bank of stairs to the kitchen. Even though there was no blood left in that room, the shadows of death still remained. They ran through the cracks in the floorboards like Caleb's blood had that day Eli Brown had come. In Leah's head, his gunshot rang out, echoing through the kitchen, filling the darkened halls and winding its way up the stairs to the lonely bedrooms.

She saw the chair—not the same chair, mind you— but a chair in the same place Tom Carson had sat with his son in his lap when that bullet had left Eli's gun. She knew the scene by heart. She knew Sylvie had been seated to Tom's right, facing the doorway. She knew that Mother had been across the table from her husband, unable to do anything but look on in horror as her baby was taken away from her much too early.

Too many people knew about what had happened and, once again, Leah was beginning to see why Mr. Argo Atkinson got such a deal on this place. Who would buy a property with a farmhouse still full of the stench of death and its wicked memory? It lay everywhere she looked even though there were no physical signs of it at all. You could just *feel* it somehow. Something about the place wasn't right.

She suddenly wasn't sure she wanted to meet this Mr. Atkinson after all. She also wasn't sure she wanted to continue on through the rest of this house.

Strengthening her resolve, Leah stayed inside and began exploring the different rooms. The dust that had covered the kitchen table and countertops continued on, covering everything. She could taste it in the air. Corners were tangled with cobwebs. The farmhouse now belonged to nature and to its own past. It didn't feel like it had any place in time anymore.

At the top of a narrow staircase that led to the upper floor, Leah discovered Sylvie's room. It was exactly as Sylvie had left it when they'd found her pa hanged from the oak and put her into foster care. Most of Sylvie's things were still here. Her closet even had clothes hanging in it, unused for years. Little girls' clothes. Sundresses and pink and yellow things that were never to be worn again.

Leah found it all very sad. Something about the room just cried out loneliness. It was as though it was lost in its own shadows and engulfed in its own memories. Leah couldn't stay any longer in it and moved on through the house.

Next, she came upon the Carsons' bedroom and found it very stark and cold. It was a room that didn't feel like it could contain any love. She wondered if it ever had.

Caleb's room was a different story altogether. Like Sylvie's it still contained pieces of a childhood lost. There were toys in a toy box that would never again be played with. There were clothes in a chest that would never again be worn. But Caleb had died nine years before Tom Carson hanged himself.

So what did that mean?

This room had been kept as a living memory to a son the Carsons could never get back. They hadn't been able to let Caleb go, and now Leah wondered how much of this room was currently taking up Sylvie Carson's mind. Surely it couldn't have been easy living with this constant reminder of what had happened right beside where she slept every night. It had to take its toll. Sometimes, the best of intentions turn out to do the most damage. This was something Leah was learning all too well.

On top of the chest of drawers were dusty old photos of little Caleb in frames. Some of him playing with Sylvie, some of him out on the farm. In each one, he had a great big smile on his face.

Leah had noticed no such pictures in either of the other two bedrooms.

After seeing Caleb's room, Leah decided she'd been through enough of the farmhouse and went back outside. Deciding the rain had pretty much gone away, she opted to leave the hood of her sweatshirt down. The air still felt wet and, along with the scent of the bog, the gentle wind carried the smell of the woods.

She walked to the barn. She knew this area well. She had been called in when Tom Carson's wife was found dead in a horse stall. The stalls still looked the same to Leah as they had that day, only now there were no flies. There was nothing. Just a stillness. The hay still lay scattered across the wooden slatted floor. The white boards of the stalls still stood with marks where the horses' tack had run ridges into them. But no horses had been here for eight years.

She left the barn and walked out through the fields. First the horse field then on into the cattle field. Both fields and the entire property were surrounded by a white wooden fence made from three horizontal boards running between fence posts. The fence still stood, but much of it had fallen. Eight years of being ravaged by storms had taken its toll. In places, just individual boards were missing. In other places, entire sections had blown down, leaving gaps like missing teeth. Leah took advantage of these spaces to avoid any climbing. She kept going until she came to the woods on the other side of the cattle field.

And soon, there it was. The oak tree Tom Carson was found hanging from.

She remembered coming to the crime scene that day not really knowing what to expect and nearly getting sick at the sight of what awaited her. She could still see marks around the bough where the rope had been looped overtop. *Some marks never go away.*

The clouds overhead broke apart, revealing a watery afternoon sun. Leah stared at that oak for some time, not knowing what compelled her to keep looking at it. But it wasn't until the sun began dropping that she started back for her car. The whole time she'd been standing at that tree, she'd been lost in thoughts of things that hadn't crossed her mind for some time. Thoughts of her dead husband, Billy. Thoughts of her children. Thoughts of Sylvie and the baby. Thoughts of her own pa.

And strangely, while she had stood there, she had forgotten all about the terrible smell of the bog and hadn't heard the incessant croaking of toads.

Getting back into her car, she pulled out onto Bog-pine Way and headed home. The road obviously got its name from the bog and the fact that tall, spindly pines lined either side of it. It was a curvy road that ran right up and out of Alvin if one kept going north past the Carson Cattle Ranch. But now she was headed south, back down toward town. Back toward life.

Her radio crackled. It was Chris. He was reporting back about his attempts to find this Argo Atkinson.

"Hey, Chris," Leah said. "Give me some good news."

"Afraid I can't. There's no Argo Atkinson living in Alvin or no Atkinson of any variety that I can find."

"What about other cities nearby? Can you try them?"

"Already have. Satsuma's a bust, and so is Atmore. I checked all the smaller directories. They came up blank. Conecuh County, though, they got Atkinsons, let me tell you. Got a Thelma Atkinson out in Castle-berry, but I called her and she doesn't have any recol-lection of bein' related to nobody by the name of Argo. Same goes for Gus Atkinson in Evergreen. Ditto for Art Atkinson in McKenzie and Daisy Luanne Atkin-son in Repton. No Argos. No relatives named Argo. Same story with Cliff—"

"Okay, Chris, I get your point."

"Ah, good. So, yeah, nothing on Argo Atkinson."

"All right, thanks for tryin' at least."

Leah hung up her radio wondering what her next move should be. Could someone be using the name Argo Atkinson as a pseudonym? Argo was a very uncommon name. You'd think somebody trying to disguise themselves would go for a more everyday-type name. The question she really should be asking herself was: Who would *want* the land? The obvious choice was a conclusion she didn't want to jump to, because it was too easy—and that was Preacher Eli.

Leah didn't want to automatically assume the worst of the man. Yet, Sylvie Carson thought Eli Brown was doing something sneaky and even Leah's own son thought the man was up to no good. Could Leah's gut feeling be wrong this time? Eli Brown had been in prison when Tom Carson died and the ranch was auctioned. Was it possible for the finger of someone like Eli Brown, who once had the power of an entire congregation on his side, to reach beyond the bars of his cell?

Leah Teal was starting to do something she didn't like much at all: She was starting to second guess herself and mistrust her gut.

One thing was certain: This wasn't a good sign.

CHAPTER 19

Leah had just pulled into her driveway back home when her radio went off again. Of course, it was Chris. He was the only one who ever called her on her radio, other than Police Chief Montgomery the odd time.

"Yeah, Chris? What is it? Please tell me you've uncovered Argo Atkinson."

"Nope. But I got another call from Sylvie Carson. This one actually sounded serious."

This got Leah's attention. Outside the car window on her way home, dark, pregnant clouds had rolled in beneath the high ones. The sunset apparently brought them along with it. Dusk looked foreboding, as though the sky was preparing for thundershowers. "What? What did she say?"

"That someone's been in her house."

"*Inside* it?" Sylvie asked. "Are you sure she said *inside*?"

Chris chuckled, but it was a grave chuckle. "Oh, I'm sure, all right. She must've said it ten times in the two-minute phone call. Said somethin' 'bout a shotgun bein' monkeyed with or somethin'. As usual, she was too frantic for me to catch most of it."

The shotgun. The last thing Leah wanted to hear about was that shotgun. She pictured it in her mind, leaning up against the back door, loaded and ready to shoot.

"Okay, I'm on my way," she said.

Leah considered using the siren this time, but traffic wasn't bad at all so there was really no point. Even so, she broke most of the posted speed limits and made it to Sylvie's in what was probably record time. When she pulled up in front she got out of her car and looked up at the sky. The clouds were literally roiling right above her. Black, thick clouds that looked like harbingers of evil.

She hoped they didn't portend that anything horrible was going to be found inside Sylvie's house. Leah still had no idea really what was going on. Just that it had to do with the shotgun and somebody being inside. "Oh dear God," she said quietly. "Please don't let her have shot someone."

The first flash of lightning lit up the western sky somewhere over the ranches on the other side of Alvin just as Leah reached the porch steps. Leah knocked on Sylvie's door. "Sylvie!" she called out. "It's me! Leah! Open up!"

She hadn't bothered with all the formalities this time. She hadn't even thought to bother with them. She was too concerned about that shotgun and what might've happened. And she was concerned about that baby. Obviously, Sylvie was okay. Or, okay enough to make the call into the station, at least.

The door swung open without Sylvie checking through the latch first. "That was quick," she said. Her face had a forced-calm yet panicked look to it that Leah hadn't quite seen before.

"What's happened?" Leah asked. Just as she did, the low rumble of thunder swept across the sky. It sounded quite a ways off.

Lightning flashed across the sky three times.

"Gonna be a helluva storm," Sylvie said, her voice matching her face.

"Sylvie?" Leah asked. "What happened? You told Chris someone's been inside your house."

She nodded. "Someone has been. Come in."

Leah came in. She went to take off her shoes but Sylvie stopped her. "Don't. I don't care 'bout a little mud. This is too important. You have to see this while it's still here."

What did she mean by that? *While it's still here?* "Okay . . ." Leah said. She followed Sylvie into the kitchen where the shotgun still leaned against the door like it always did. Leah was just about to ask her what the hell she was supposed to be looking at, when she saw it: five 12-gauge shotgun shells lined up in a straight row along the top of the kitchen table.

Leah's eyes quickly went straight to Sylvie's. "Where did they come from?"

"They was in the shotgun."

"Who took 'em out?"

"Whoever was in my house."

Sylvie's eyes were still locked on Leah's. If the girl had blinked, Leah missed it.

"Okay, you need to tell me more. What the hell's goin' on?"

"Me and the baby were out shoppin'. We just went down to Finnegan's at Finley's."

Finnegan's at Finley's was Finnegan's Five and Dime. It was located at Finley's Crossing about a half mile from where Sylvie lived, so it got the nickname Finnegan's at Finley's. "You walk down?" Leah asked.

"Yeah, I ain't got no car."

"You carry the baby?"

"No, I brought the stroller."

"Didn't know you had one."

"I got one. Salvation Army donated it. It ain't the greatest, but it works well enough."

"Okay, so you walked to Finnegan's. Then what? Wait, did you lock the door before you left?"

Frustration flickered in Sylvie's eyes. "Of course I locked the door 'fore I left. I always lock my door. And my windows. I checked every one an' they was all locked. An' when I got home, they was *still* all locked. Every door and every window."

Concern fell over Leah. "Okay, so you walked to Finnegan's. Continue your story."

"I bought some milk and some juice and some eggs. Then we walked back."

A pocket of silence followed. "And then . . . ?" Leah asked.

"And then I came home and found the shells sittin' here just like this. I was careful not to touch nothin'. I called the police station right away."

"You *sure* you didn't touch anything?"

"I searched the goddamn house and made sure nobody was still here. That's what I did as soon as I hung up. I'm not stayin' in no house with my baby that might have some killer in it!"

Leah held up her hand. "Good," she said calmly. "That's good. You did the right thing. Now I want you to think back. Are you absolutely *sure* you didn't touch any of these shells or the gun or the table or nothin'?"

"Yeah," Sylvie said. "Of course I'm sure. Why? You think I did this and I'm lyin' 'bout it?"

"No, Sylvie. Not at all. I think we might be able to get prints off the shells."

"Oh." Sylvie finally broke her stare and looked away. "As long as you don't think I'm lyin'."

"Where *is* the baby?" Leah asked.

"Still in the stroller. She's in the bedroom. I checked the window. It's locked with a stick in it. Nobody is comin' in there. She was up all mornin'. Just fell asleep on the way home. She needs to nap."

"Go check on her."

"Why?" Sylvie asked, suddenly losing any trace of calmness from her face.

"Just to make me happy."

While she was gone, Leah took the opportunity to look around the rest of the house, making sure that Sylvie was right, and if anyone had been inside they weren't here any longer. She checked the pantry in the kitchen and the closet in the hall. Everything looked deserted. The rooms were all empty. The back door was locked.

Sylvie came back a few minutes later. "She's still sleepin'. You had me scared outta my wits."

"Sorry. Just my mother's instinct kickin' in. I have to go out to my car and radio Chris to come with the fingerprintin' kit. You okay here by yourself a few minutes?"

"Yeah. Don't you think I am?"

"I think you are. I just did a search of the premises. There ain't nobody here no more."

"I know. I already told you, I checked."

Outside, the storm had grown. Fork lightning cracked open the sky above Leah's head just as her foot hit the top step leading down the porch. It was followed quickly by the clap of thunder before she even made it to the car. Then the sky opened up and rain began washing down in one big wave. She pulled the hood of her sweatshirt up tight, but it was already too late. She could feel how wet her hair was underneath.

Inside her car, she radioed Chris back at the station and told him what she'd found at the scene.

"Are you serious?" Chris asked. "Is there any chance Sylvie did this and just doesn't remember?"

"Chris, she's never done things and not remembered before. I think we have to take this seriously. I want you to bring the printing kit. She says she hasn't touched anything. We might be able to lift somethin' from those shells."

"All right. Have you looked outside? It's crazy."

"I'm out in it now."

"All hell's breaking loose."

"Don't I know it."

CHAPTER 20

Back in the house, Leah did remove her shoes this time. They were completely covered in mud dredged up from all the rain splatter. Lightning spiked so brightly, Leah would catch it out of the corner of her eye, illuminating things in an iridescent glow. Thunder continued booming, at times so loud it felt like the house would shake apart.

Sylvie's hands trembled. She was pacing. Leah hoped this incident wasn't going to set her back years of development. She wondered how fragile the girl really was. Sometimes she seemed as breakable as a ceramic doll.

"You okay?" Leah asked her.

Sylvie nodded, and then said quietly, "It's just the storm. I've never liked lightning storms ever since what happened."

"I understand," Leah said. She could imagine that each time that thunder boomed it echoed in Sylvie's mind the way that gunshot had rung out in her kitchen right before supper that evening. Leah needed to take

Sylvie's mind off the storm. Luckily, she still had some questions that needed answering.

"So, how did they get in?" Leah asked.

"Who?"

"Whoever emptied the shotgun."

"I'm assumin' through the door."

"You said you locked it when you left."

"I always lock my doors. And my windows. But there were no windows busted when I got home, so I assume they somehow got in through a door."

"Was the door still locked when you came back?"

"Yeah. I already told you that, too."

Leah thought about this. "Get your locks changed tomorrow. If you need some money, I can lend it to you." But her thoughts continued lingering on who could get into a locked building. Picking locks seemed like the sort of skill you might learn after seventeen-odd years in prison.

"How's that gonna help if they didn't need keys this time?"

"I dunno," Leah said honestly, "but it certainly won't hurt."

"I don't feel safe," Sylvie said. Her eyes had widened. Leah could now see that fear had replaced most of the panic.

Leah gave Sylvie a hug. "Listen. So far, it's all been harassment. If they can get into the house, then they could've already hurt you if they wanted to, so obviously they don't want to. Someone's just out to scare you."

"Well, they're doin' a fine job o' it."

Sylvie began to quietly sob into Leah's shoulder. Leah considered what she had just told her and wondered how true it was. The harassment (if it all *had* been harassment) was ramping up. Was she *really* not in any danger? Leah didn't honestly know. "Is there . . . do you have anywhere you and the baby could go? A friend's place, maybe? The home of a relative? Just until things simmer down a bit for you?"

Panic rose in Sylvie's eyes. "You really think I'm in danger."

"No, I'm just tryin' to err on the side of caution, is all," Leah lied.

Sylvie scanned the floor. "I ain't got no place to go. All my relatives are dead, and I ain't got no friends."

Once again, Sylvie had managed to break Leah's heart. It seemed to happen more often than not lately. And as much as Leah hated to admit it, her gut feeling was starting to shift. Things were beginning to feel more and more like Eli Brown might be behind something after all.

Chris showed up at the door carrying the fingerprinting kit and looking like a drowned rat. His eyes were glued skyward when Sylvie opened the door. Thunder rattled the house as he came inside. Leah showed him the shells lined up on the kitchen table.

"That's so weird," he said.

"Wanna hear somethin' weirder?" Leah asked. "No sign of forcible entry. No broken windows. Doors were locked when Miss Sylvie left and they was still locked when she returned."

He looked at her. "So the lock was picked?"

"That's what I'm thinkin'."

"Who would go to all the trouble of pickin' her lock

just to empty her shotgun and leave the shells all tidy like this on the table?"

Leah let out a big sigh. "When we get back to the station I want you to get as much information on Preacher Eli Brown as you can. If that man so much as took an unscheduled crap in the woods while he was in prison, I want to know 'bout it."

Lightning lit up the backyard as, right behind it, another thunderous roar shook the world.

"Shouldn't we try to lift any prints before jumpin' to conclusions like that?" Chris asked.

"You're right. Get the prints. But I have serious doubts anything's gonna show up."

Turned out Officer Chris Jackson was able to lift a set of prints from the shells on Sylvie Carson's table. Each shell had one and only one set of prints on it and the same ones were on each shell—and they all belonged to Miss Sylvie.

"Figured as much," Leah said. Her and Chris were back at the station. "Anyone knowin' enough to get in and out of that house without showin' any sign of physical entry ain't 'bout to leave behind stupid evidence like fingerprints."

"Guess you were right," Chris said. "I suppose it's time for plan B?"

"If plan B involves seeing how Eli Brown fits into all this, then you're absolutely right in tune with my way of thinking," Leah said.

CHAPTER 21

I had been checking the mail before my mother could get to it every single day since me and Dewey went to the records office on our own and the lady made the call to her friend for more information about my family's history records. Mainly I was doing it on account of I didn't know how my mother would react to me going there behind her back. Her temper could be a mite unpredictable at times.

It wasn't always easy getting to the mail first. There were days the mail lady practically drove up and handed the mail right to my mother because my mother happened to be outside in the driveway. In fact, on two occasions when that happened I just braced myself and prayed that those weren't the days my information decided to arrive.

I got lucky. They weren't.

When my records finally did come, they turned up on a day my mother was at work. This made everything really simple and allowed me lots of time. As soon as I saw it, I knew the big yellow envelope was for me. Stuffed in our mailbox, it didn't even fit without the mail lady having to nearly bend it in half to get it in.

Sure enough, when I pulled it out, there was my name right on the front: *Abe Teal*. And, in the top left corner, was the name and address of the historian lady: *Miss Dixie Spinner* with an address in Chickasaw, Alabama. Excited, I rushed inside, happy my mother would be at work at least another four hours. This gave me a *ton* of time to go through all the information without even having to be sneaky about it.

I carefully opened the envelope using the silver letter opener my mother got as a gift from my uncle Henry one year for Christmas. She rarely used it, but I wanted to be sure not to rip any of the papers inside.

I pulled out a bundle of pages. There were some loose sheets on top and then some stapled together. I looked at the top one. On a small card, paper-clipped to the corner, was a note:

> *Dear Abe,*
>
> *I hope you find this information useful.*
> *It's nice to know young people are taking*
> *an interest in their family histories.*
> *If there's anything else I can do for you,*
> *please give me a call.*
>
> *Miss Dixie Spinner*

She even gave me her phone number. I couldn't believe how nice some people could be. Historians seemed especially nice to me.

Unclipping the card, I set it aside and started looking through the top sheets that were not stapled together. They had been put in separate. There were quite a few. At least a half a dozen.

I got really excited then. I wondered what kind of information I was about to find out. Obviously, there was a lot more here than just the names and birthdays of my parents and my grandparents like they had at the records office downtown.

The first page was more or less all about me. It said *Vital Statistics* at the top and listed things like my birthday and exactly where I was born and even had the time of my birth. I wondered if my *mother* even remembered that. I thought it was pretty neat that I now knew exactly when I was born right down to the minute.

Farther on, it showed that I'd lived in Alvin in this same house all my life and it showed the address. I began to realize that if they showed this much information for everyone, there might not be any more people listed in this package other than my parents and grandparents on all these pages after all.

Then it displayed my immediate family. Unlike the records office on Main Street, it had Carry (along with her birth date) included, and my mother and my pa. It not only showed my pa's birthday, but also said *Deceased* after his name and had the date he died and a small explanation: *Death due to motor vehicle accident.*

Then, at the bottom of the page, it said: *Teal and Fowler references supplied under separate cover.*

I didn't quite know what that meant, but I put down the first page and was surprised by the second. It was a listing of all the Teals, going back about one hundred and fifty years. And each one had extra information, like children and birthdays and how they died, and anything else pertinent. Right at the top of the list was me!

Teal, Abe
>   Born: March 26, 1976
>   Sister: Caroline Josephine
>   Mother: Leah Marie Fowler

Teal, William Robert
>   Born: May 7, 1955
>   Sister: Addison May
>   Mother: Sara Lynn Harris
>   Deceased: July 3, 1978
>   *Death due to motor vehicle accident.*

Teal, Jeremiah
>   Born: September 1, 1936
>   Son: William Robert (Deceased)
>   Mother: Rebekah Davis (Deceased.
>   *Heart failure*)

Teal, John Owen
>   Born: February 24, 1912
>   Son: Jeremiah
>   Daughter: Francine (Deceased)
>   Brother(s):   Mark Lee (Deceased)
>   Paul Adam (Deceased)
>   Sister: Lily Jude (Deceased)
>   Mother: Lily Anne Kendricks
>   (Deceased)

And so the list went on, going back to 1842. Everyone from John Owen Teal down was dead. Some had up to nine brothers and sisters, and some had none. I read them all, fascinated to find out I was related to so many people I had known nothing about.

And this was just on my daddy's side.

I came to the last one, right at the bottom:

Teal, Isaac Jacob Lee
    Born: June 12, 1842
    Son: Jacob Lee (Deceased)
    Brother: Joseph Matthew Isaiah
                       (Deceased)
    Mother: Martha Christina Franklin
                       (Deceased)

Then it had two words beneath that, before several paragraphs of stuff. And those two words were:

Historical Significance.

It turns out I was related to somebody really important after all! My great-great-great-great-great-grandpa won a major Medal of Honor for freeing a bunch of slaves during the Civil War.

I had to call Dewey and tell him.

"What did he do?" Dewey asked after answering the phone. He only seemed half interested, which bothered the heck out of me.

"He freed *slaves,* Dewey. There ain't much that's more important than that. Remember all that stuff my mom told us about racism? My great-great-great-great-great-grandpa fought against racism a hundred an' fifty years ago."

"What'd he do?"

"Well, accordin' to this paper in front of me he did lots. There's so much information 'bout it that it runs onto the next page. You want me to read it to you?"

"Can you just give me the general idea?"

"Well, it happened up in Georgia, right after the Union navy took over some port."

"Which port?"

"Doesn't say, but some port close to Fort Pulaski."

"What's that?"

"A fort, Dewey. What do you think it is?"

"What kind of fort?"

"The kind you fight from. This was during the Civil War."

"Oh, you didn't tell me that part."

"I reckoned you could figure that out for yourself. Anyway, I guess Fort Pulaski was an important target, but the Union hadn't hit it yet; they'd only taken the port. That's when my great-great-great-great-great-"— I was running out of breath sayin' all them greats— "grandpa walked right up to the door of one of those old plantations. He was carryin' nothin' but a couple of pistols and, I suppose, he just let himself in."

"You mean the door was unlocked?"

"I don't rightly know, Dewey. It don't actually say. Maybe he knocked. I dunno. Whatever happened, he demanded that the owner free all the black folk he'd been keepin' as slaves."

"What did the owner say?" Now Dewey sounded more interested.

"He said he didn't like people tellin' him what to do, is my guess," I said. "All it says here is that a gunfight broke out inside that plantation between my grandpa from a hundred fifty years back and a half dozen other folk who either owned the plantation or worked for the guy who did."

"So your however many greats grandpa was a Union soldier?"

"No, that's just it. He was a Confederate. I suppose he just didn't agree with slavery. That's the part that makes him a hero."

"Did he die?"

"No. In the end, it says, and I'm reading it straight off the paper now, Isaac Jacob Lee Teal won his battle and walked out the front door of that big white house with one hundred and ten black men jumpin' up and down around and behind him, all hootin' and a-hollerin'." I actually embellished that a little for Dewey's sake.

"That's what it says in the records you got?"

"Well," I admitted, "not quite. I made it more dramatic."

"So what happened next?"

"The next day the same Union navy that took the port attacked Fort Pulaski. They had more soldiers and better guns and the fort surrendered within a day. But word 'bout my ancestral grandpa must've spread because he came marching toward the captured fort, over the hills and through the trees with all the black men still following him."

"Why was they still followin' him?"

"Guess they didn't know where else to go. Will you quit interruptin'?"

"Okay."

"Anyway, the Union navy captain didn't arrest my great-great-great-great-great-grandpa. Instead they allowed him on board their ships and made him an honorary Union soldier. He was even given a medal for what he done and everythin'."

There was a bit of a pause, then Dewey said, "So your great-great-great-great-great-grandpa was a bit of a traitor, you're sayin'."

I got real mad. "No, Dewey. He was a good man who believed everyone should be free."

Dewey laughed. "I'm just kiddin'. I think that's a neat story."

"Me too. I'm real happy I got these records. I can't wait to meet my new grandparents now."

After hanging up the phone, I leafed through the rest of the document. There were other pages listing the line of daughters for the Teals, then these were followed by similar pages for the Fowler lines. All of them went back approximately the same number of years as the first one I had examined.

There were also cross-reference pages showing who married who and things like that, and even a tree structure that kind of explained how all my uncles and aunts and great-uncles and -aunts all connected. A lot of it I couldn't understand very well, but I still found it all very interesting and exciting.

But absolutely none of it compared to the story I'd found about my great-great-great-great-great-grandpa Isaac Jacob Lee Teal.

That man was a true hero.

That's when my sister, Carry, walked into the house, carrying a small plastic shopping bag. I guessed she'd been down at the mall with her friends where she usually hung out. I was about to tell her about Grandpa Isaac Jacob Lee (who was *her* ancestral grandfather, too), but she spoke before I had a chance.

"Come on, ass face, follow me."

"Mom *told* you not to call me that!" I said.

"Whatever." She walked into the living room and turned on the television.

I sat there, thinking I should really go see what she wanted, but then part of me thought I should just stay put, her being so rude and all.

"I told you to come here!" she demanded from the other room.

"Why should I do anything you tell me?" I shouted from the kitchen.

I had forgotten that there actually *was* a reason. The devil pact I'd signed with my sister the day we made the swords had somehow completely slipped my mind. Now it was about to come back and bite me in places it turned out I really didn't like being bitten in.

"Because we have a deal, remember? When we made the swords? Time to pay up."

Curious, I wandered into the living room.

Carry was sitting on the sofa with her socks off and one foot up on the coffee table. In her hand she had a bottle of brand-new purple nail polish. "Today," she said, "you learn how to paint toenails! Aren't you the lucky boy?"

"Uh-uh." I shook my head, slowly backing out of the room.

"Yep. You said *anythin'*. And this falls under any-thin'. Now get over here and pay up."

It was horrible, demeaning work, painting Carry's cheesy toes. I kept asking myself: *What would Dewey think if he could see me now?* Every time I tried to speed up the process, she'd slow me down and tell me to make sure I did a good job. When I was finally done with both feet, it was like someone had stopped stick-ing me with a hot poker. I was so glad to be finished.

I quickly bottled up the polish and handed it to her.

She twisted her foot in the sunlight falling in through the window behind her, looking at her toes gleaming purple in the afternoon light. I had to admit, they didn't look half bad.

"You did all right," she said.

"I'm just happy I'm done."

Then she said something that froze me to my core: "For now."

"What do you mean?" My eyes went wide. My hand trembled.

"You're doin' this every week for the rest of the summer."

"Am not."

"Am too."

"You can't make me."

"You gave me your word. What's Abe Teal's word worth?"

She had me there. My mother had drilled it into my head that you're only as good as your word. I consoled myself with the fact that she'd at least cut the job off at the end of summer.

With a hung head, I slunk back into the kitchen, leaving the smell of fresh nail polish and the sound of canned laughter from the television set in the living room behind me.

CHAPTER 22

The next day, Chris was holding out a report in his hand as Leah took her seat at her desk. "Ask and thou shalt receive," he said.

She looked at him. "Eli?"

He nodded. "Yup."

"Anythin' incriminatin'?"

He gave a little shrug. "I dunno. It just came in 'bout ten minutes ago. I skimmed it. Nothin' stood out at me as bein' particularly nasty. Other than shootin' a three-year-old, but we already knew 'bout that one."

Leah scanned the first page of the report. There were notes from all Eli's parole board hearings. They spilled on to the second and third sheets. "No wonder he got out early," she said. "He was like teacher's pet in prison. I've never seen such nice things said about anyone in one of these things."

Chris had his elbow on his desk with his hand supporting his head. "Maybe our preacher man really done gone an' changed his ways."

Leah flickered her eyes at him above the page she

was reading. "Nobody's this nice in prison. Eli was up to somethin'. That's what it tells me."

"Why, Detective Teal, ain't we a mite cynical?"

"No, I'd say I'm a mite realistic. This ain't my first bull ride." She quoted from the page: " 'A strong influence on his peer group with an attitude that's a welcome diversion from the normal dreary and contemptuous one that seems to infiltrate this establishment.' " She laughed. "Of course they're dreary and contemptuous! They're in goddamn prison! What the hell do they expect?"

"Apparently, what they like is someone who is a welcome diversion from that," Chris said. "Someone like Eli Brown."

"I've been to his house. The man was pretty contemptuous to me."

"Actually, he wasn't far off of contemptuous with me, either. Hmm."

"I think we definitely have a suspect," Leah said. She turned the stapled page over and found a page full of basic background information, including priors, education, family records, basic stuff.

She quickly looked it over. Other than the murder of Caleb Carson, it contained nothing unusual, but then she hadn't expected it to. She already knew Eli Brown had no prior run-ins with the law, and the rest of the information was basically useless to her.

Then something caught her eye.

"Whoa, Nelly," she said. "I think we just got ourselves a *Bingo*!"

Chris pulled his chair in close and looked at the page from the side. "What's that?"

"Look under family records," she said. "Check out the name of his deceased wife."

Chris found the part on the page she was referring to and gave a low whistle. "Well, I'll be damned."

There it was, typed right there in black and white:

Wife: Catherine Anna Brown nee Atkinson
(Deceased).
Died 1984 of stroke.

"I think we just found our link between Sylvie and Eli Brown," Leah said. "I mean other than through little Caleb."

It took one call to the Alvin public records office to find out that Argo Atkinson was the father of Catherine Atkinson and another call to the Mobile public records office to discover that he was alive and well and living up in Tuscaloosa.

"So, Eli Brown's father-in-law purchased the property as quickly as he could snatch it up after Tom Carson hanged himself," Leah said to Chris after putting down the phone. "It all seems a little too convenient to me."

"Definitely something fishy goin' on."

"I think the reason we haven't seen no development on it is on account of Eli's been in prison up until now. I think he plans to go ahead with that little 'project' of his."

"Could be."

"And you said his grandson was down from Alabaster? I bet that ain't no coincidence either. Did he seem like the business type to you?"

"Hard to tell. He was just wearin' a T-shirt and jeans, but he could be. Probably just got out of college or might still be in college, I dunno."

"I bet he's here to help Eli throw this thing together."

There was a silent spell between them. Outside the window, two yellowhammers dipped in and out of sight.

"Still doesn't tell us why this would amount to Sylvie bein' harassed," Leah finally said.

"That's what I was thinkin'."

"Unless . . ."

"What?"

"Unless they was worried she still had claim to the land."

"That would be impossible. You said the bank put it up for auction. And that was eight *years* ago," Chris said.

"Maybe Eli thinks different."

"Still, what's the point in harassin' her?"

Leah thought this over and shrugged. "Well, if he could get her to the point that she went off the deep end and actually became hospitalized she'd be much less of a threat to anyone. You gotta reckon, if what we's sayin's true, she's gonna have some kinda reaction when he starts buildin' on her daddy's plot of land."

"You reckon?"

"I reckon so. She hates Eli Brown more than anyone. And she probably has every right in the world to."

"So . . ." Chris said. "What do we do next?"

"That's a good question." Leah drummed her fingers on the desk. Outside a monarch butterfly fluttered among the tops of the hydrangea bushes that barely came up to the bottom of the window. "I suppose we have another talk with our favorite old preacher."

"I was afraid you'd say that. You or me?"

She smiled with a bit of a wicked grin. "Oh, you ain't gettin' this one."

CHAPTER 23

Me and Dewey rode our bikes down Hunter Road and over to Church Street where the Full Gospel Church was. Full Gospel was Alvin's black church, and we'd been there before. I knew Reverend Starks quite well and he always seemed happy to see us when me and Dewey dropped by. Today being a Thursday, I didn't know whether or not he'd be around. Church services were normally held on Wednesdays and Sundays, but I thought Reverend Starks lived in the church so I suspected we might catch him there if we were lucky.

My mother had told me she had asked Sylvie Carson to come to church with us next time we went on account of all the troubles she'd been going through lately. My mother thought it might bring her some comfort. Well, last time I was at Full Gospel, it was during the end of one of their services, and there was so much singing and happiness I couldn't imagine a place more comfortable than that. Certainly not Clover Creek First Baptist where we usually went. I had nothing against Reverend Matthew, but his sermons could put a gerbil with a sugar rush to sleep.

So, even though it was a black church, I was going to ask Reverend Starks if it was okay for us to come. Especially given what my great-great-great-great-great-granddaddy did for him and his people.

I hadn't mentioned any of this to my mother yet. I figured I'd wait and see if I could get permission from Reverend Starks first and then surprise her with it. This didn't seem like the sort of surprise that I'd get reprimanded for. Although, when I thought it through now, I realized if I included the part about my ancestry it was going to cause some complications to the story.

The church was an old wooden building painted white and had square stained-glass windows. It looked similar to Clover Creek First Baptist where we normally went, only Full Gospel was an older building and wasn't taken care of as well as Clover Creek. I don't think it was because anyone purposely neglected it, I think it was more on account of they didn't have the money to paint it as often or to put in as many gardens around it, and stuff like that. The paint on the boards was starting to come off. It definitely could use a new coat.

The church door was closed as me and Dewey rode our bikes into the churchyard and up to the entrance.

"So what do we do?" Dewey asked. "Knock? Or just see if it's unlocked and go inside?"

"I dunno," I said. I had no idea of the etiquette of what to do at church when it wasn't in service. "I suppose knocking can't hurt."

We set our bikes down on the ground and, with swords at our sides, climbed the steps to the church doors and knocked on them. Because they were made of thick, heavy wood, our knocks were not very loud.

We waited for a while, but nobody answered.

"I don't think he heard us. Try the door," Dewey said.

"You try it," I said.

Slowly, he reached out his hand and grabbed the handle and pulled. Nothing happened. I saw him let out a breath he'd been holding. "They're locked." He sounded relieved.

We tried knocking again, but again our knocks weren't very loud and again nobody came.

"We could try kicking it," Dewey suggested.

I stared at him. "We ain't gonna boot the church door."

"Why not?"

"It's a place of God, Dewey."

"Oh."

He didn't mention kicking it again, so I suppose that was explanation enough.

We stood there another minute until finally I came up with an idea. "You know, if Reverend Starks lives here, he doesn't live in the actual main part of the church. I mean, where would he sleep? In the pews? I bet there's another door in the back. One that goes into the part he lives in."

"That makes sense," Dewey said.

We walked around the church to where four large willows grew, their long branches draping like huge umbrellas with tiny flowers that shook gently in the breeze. One of the willows was close enough that it touched the side of the church.

I'd never noticed before, but the church was actually shaped in an ell. You couldn't really tell from the other side, but another building came off the main one. This building didn't have the stained-glass windows or any of the decorative religious look that the other did. It was just a normal houselike building, with small windows and a small porch. It was white, like the rest of the church, only the trim back here was all done in forest green. If this was where Reverend Starks lived, he had a very small house.

We walked up the two steps to the porch and knocked on the door. This time our knocks sounded like real knocks.

"Coming!" a deep voice called out from somewhere on the other side of the door.

"I hope it's him," Dewey said nervously.

"Who else could it be?" I asked.

A half moment later, Reverend Starks answered the door. Only, he wasn't dressed the way I was accustomed to seeing him. He was dressed like a normal person in dark green pants and a striped shirt. I nearly didn't recognize him until he smiled and I saw his gold-capped tooth. Then I knew it was him. There was no mistaking Reverend Starks's smile or that tooth.

"Abe! What a delightful surprise!" He took my hand in both of his and shook it. "And Dewey . . . right?"

"Yes, sir!" Dewey said, shaking his hand, too.

"What brings you boys round these parts? Been a while since I've seen you."

"I wanted to talk to you 'bout somethin'," I said.

"And he wants to ask you somethin', too," Dewey added.

I glared at him.

"Is that right?" Reverend Starks said. His voice was deep and full. "Well, why don't y'all come inside?" He looked around the yard. The sun glittered off his eyeglasses. "Nice to see the rain's stopped again."

"Yeah," I said.

"Let's hope we get back to that sunny spell we had a week ago," the reverend said. "I was quite enjoyin' that."

"So was we," Dewey said.

Reverend Starks led us through a small kitchen that was very neat and tidy, down a narrow hallway, and into a small parlor that contained a little divan with a floral pattern and two chairs, both upholstered in burgundy, situated around a low cherry table.

"Go ahead, sit wherever you like," Reverend Starks said.

Dewey and I sat beside each other on the divan. "Can I get you boys anything?" the reverend asked from the entranceway into the parlor.

"I'll have some sweet tea," Dewey said.

I glared at him again.

"What 'bout you, Abe?"

"I guess," I said. "Since you're gettin' some anyway."

Reverend Starks went back to the kitchen.

"Why are you askin' him for stuff?" I whispered harshly to Dewey.

"Because he offered."

"He was just bein' polite."

"I really want some tea."

"He didn't *really* want to get you some."

"Actually, I wouldn't have offered if I didn't want to get it," the reverend said, coming back into the room with two glasses of tea. Each had a slice of lemon floating in it. He set them on the table in front of us.

"Thanks," we both said, almost in unison.

Reverend Starks took a seat in the burgundy chair closest to me. "So, what is it exactly you wished to speak with me 'bout, Abe?"

I hesitated. Now that I was here, I wasn't sure how to begin.

"Well . . ." I stumbled. "I . . . um . . ."

"Abe's grandfather from way back freed a bunch of black slaves and he wants to tell you 'bout it," Dewey said after taking a gulp of tea. Then he quickly followed with, "This tea's really good. You make it yourself?"

The reverend laughed. "Yes, I did. So, what's this about your grandfather?"

"Well," I started again after glaring at Dewey for the third time, "my great-great-great-great-great-grandfather was a Confederate soldier who I suppose was actually *against* slavery. And one day after the Union navy took over a port up in Georgia, he marched into a plantation with just two pistols and, after winning a gunfight against six men who I reckon must've owned the plantation, he walked out with a hundred and ten slaves that he'd set free. He brought them to a fort that the Union navy had moved on and defeated and the Yanks made him an honorary Union soldier and even gave him a medal."

Reverend Starks sat back in his chair and interlaced his fingers. "How do you know all this?"

"I went to the records office here in Alvin and they connected me with this historian woman from Chickasaw who got information on my family history for me."

"Well now," the reverend said. "That's pretty inter-estin'. Sounds like you've got some pretty great blood in you."

I smiled. I knew, of all people, Reverend Starks would be impressed. "I reckon he was a hero," I said.

"Sounds like a hero to me." The reverend glanced down at the sword at my waist. "Is that what you're tryin' to become carryin' that sword?"

I felt my cheeks redden with embarrassment. "Oh. These are just pretend."

"I see."

Dewey was looking around the room. "How come you ain't got no TV?"

I couldn't believe how rude he was being.

Reverend Starks laughed. "Because the Lord keeps me busy enough without me needin' no television, that's for sure."

"I think it's weird not having a TV," Dewey said.

"Dewey!" I said, through gritted teeth.

The reverend leaned forward. "Abe, there was something you wanted to ask me?"

"Yeah. I was wonderin' . . . I mean, I know your church is for black folks and all . . . but—"

"Full Gospel is for everyone, Abe," he said, cutting me off.

I brightened. "So then it might be okay if some white folks attended? Just one time?"

"Abe, as I said, all folk are welcome in this house of the Lord. And not just one time but any time and all times. Why are you askin' me this?"

"On account of I wanted to know if it would be all right—that is, if my mom agrees—if we could come along one day to your services."

"I would absolutely love it if you did!" The reverend slapped his knees.

I hesitated. "Would it be okay if we brought Miss Sylvie? She's this girl—well, she's sort of a lady, I guess. She's older than me—my mom works with her and she's got quite a few problems and my mom promised to take her to church next time we went cuz her spirits need upliftin'. And I think her spirits would get way more uplifted here than at Clover Creek First Baptist where we usually attend. Not that I don't appreciate Reverend Matthew . . . it's just that . . . well . . . anyway . . . so, would it be okay if she came along?"

Reverend Starks just looked at me a long minute. "You're not listenin' to me, boy. All folks are welcome, all the time. You don't need to ask permission. And it sounds like she needs the Lord's help as much as anyone, maybe even more so. And I reckon my congregation would just love to see some new faces." The reverend's face lit up with a creased smile.

I didn't rightly know what my mother would say about attending church at Full Gospel, but I knew I was going to ask her first chance I got. From what I knew about God, He viewed all people the same, black or white. It was my mother who had spent a good deal of time teaching me that, so she should not be disagreeable to the idea. I didn't mind church at Clover Creek where we regularly attended (not that we attended quite so regularly), but I thought we could use a change for once. And I definitely thought bringing Miss Sylvie along was a good idea given all she was going through.

I told Reverend Starks I would do my best to see him next Sunday.

"That would be grand, Abe." He held out his hand for me to shake it. His brown fingers were huge with pink fingertips. They wrapped right around mine as we shook.

"Oh, and I want to say sorry," I said.

"Sorry? For what?"

"For the swords. I forgot we was wearin' them."

"Why are you sorry?"

"On account of I doubt Jesus would be very appreciative of swords, especially in the house of the Lord."

"Well, this isn't the church, this is my house. And Jesus doesn't have a problem with swords, Abe. In Matthew 10:34, Jesus says, 'Think not that I am come to send peace on earth: I came not to send peace, but a sword.' "

I couldn't *believe* he knew all this stuff by heart.

"So Jesus wanted people to fight?" Dewey asked. I was kind of wondering the same thing.

"Jesus was a warrior," Reverend Starks answered. "The word of God is represented by a sword. If we take two passages a little further on, it might make more sense to you. Matthew 10:38 and 10:39 where Jesus says, 'And he that taketh not his cross, and followeth after me, is not worth of me. He that findeth his life shall lose it: and he that loseth his life for my sake shall find it.' "

"I still don't get it," Dewey said. "And how come you don't have a cross on any of your walls?"

I could not believe how rude he was being.

"We don't need crosses to be reminded of Jesus, Dewey. Remembering the Word is enough." He shifted in his chair. "And I *do* have a cross. A very simple one. It hangs in my bedroom."

"And you have a cross in your church," Dewey said.

"Two of 'em. They're small ones, though. Compared to Clover Creek, at least."

"Dewey!" I hissed. He was completely out of line.

"What? I'm just tryin' to figure things out."

"Dewey," Reverend Starks said, "big crosses isn't what the Lord Jesus is about. This—" He tapped his chest where his heart was. "*This* is what the Lord Jesus is all about. Keeping Him in your heart and keeping your faith strong."

"So is *that* why He's sayin' we should follow him with our own cross or else we will lose our life or whatever it was you said?"

Reverend Starks pushed his lips together into a thin line, looking away in thought for a second or two. "Dewey, Jesus is sayin' that to be a warrior one must be brave, and if you are not brave enough to face your own fears, you do not deserve his love. And if you discover a way to live without his love, you shall lose all that is dear to you. It is only by being brave enough to give up everything you have that you will really find what's important, and it will all come through the love of the Lord Jesus." Reverend Starks turned his head and stared straight into my eyes. "This is the true strength of the warrior, Abe. The true test of the sword. Although, always remember the true test of a warrior is not *raising* that sword—it's knowing that even though you have the power to take a life, you also have the power to spare it; and there's always more power in mercy than in dealin' out death." The reverend's eyes drifted back to Dewey. "Is that clearer now?"

Dewey didn't answer right away, so I took advantage of the silent spot and jumped in. "I think so," I said. "My great-great-great-great-great-granddaddy was brave like that. He risked everythin' he had in order to free them slaves. I bet he didn't like shootin' those people at that plantation, but he probably reckoned he had to in order to get them people free. I'd hope that if I were in his shoes, I might do the same."

A smile came to Reverend Starks's face. "Abe," he said, "I reckon you just might have the heart of a warrior."

CHAPTER 24

Leah didn't like the expression on Eli Brown's face when he opened his door to find her on the porch. "I thought I made it clear that I was to be left alone," he told her in a commanding yet still somehow brittle voice.

"That ain't yours to command, I'm afraid," Leah said. "I'm here on police business."

"I ain't got no business with no police."

"That again ain't your call to make."

A young man dressed in a button-down white shirt tucked into a pair of dress pants came into the room behind Eli. "Is it the police again?" he asked.

"Never you mind, Leland," Eli said. "I'll take care of this."

"No," the boy—Leland (who couldn't have been much older than twenty)—said. "Let me." He came up beside Eli and told Leah, "My grandfather is old. Can't you see he's been through enough? Why do you people insist on botherin' him? He's done his time. Far as I know, that makes him a free man. Surely you have better things to do than bother old men who are re-pentin' their deeds 'fore the Lord."

Leah nearly laughed. Judging by the way the boy was dressed, which was much different from how Chris had described finding him that day he came out, she thought her guess that he was involved was probably on target. "First off," she said, her voice growing loud and stern, "you make your granddaddy sound like some decrepit ancient hermit. He ain't much a day over sixty. Secondly, I have reason to believe he might be involved in some illegal activity that requires my attention. In fact, the only reason I'm *telling* you this instead of telling you to go out and play is because I think you may be involved, too." She shifted her gaze to Eli. "Now we have a choice. We can do this here, or we can do it at the station. Personally, I'd prefer the station. I'm more prepared to back up everythin' I have to tell you with documentation down there. But I don't think we'll need those documents, on account of I don't think you'll be tellin' me I'm wrong."

Eli looked her up and down as though trying to decide how seriously he should take her. "What's this 'bout?"

"The Carson Cattle Ranch."

"And what of it?"

"And its connection to Argo Atkinson." Her eyes locked on Leland. His own eyes suddenly widened.

Eli looked around the yard, as if checking the weather. It had grown windy and a few clouds had gathered overhead since Leah left the station. "All right," he said. "You may as well come in. I don't relish a trip to your police station." His voice no longer held the commanding tone of the preacher part of him it had a few minutes ago.

"Fair enough," Leah said, and followed him inside.

Ahead of her she heard the boy whisper to Eli, "Are you sure this is a good idea?"

"It was gonna come out sooner or later," Eli replied to him. "It's just happenin' a bit sooner than we expected."

Eli led them to a little room just past the door where a settee stood along with a chair and an oval coffee table. None of the furniture matched in color. The settee was a dark green, the chair was made of oak, and the table pine. The floor of the room was rough-hewn knotty pine. A small, shiny cross hung on one wall. The rest of the walls were bare.

Pulling her notepad from her pocket, Leah took a chair as Eli and his grandson took a seat beside each other on the settee. They had to move a couple of blankets out of the way to do so; this was obviously where the boy had been sleeping.

"Before we start," Leah said to the grandson. "Your name's Leland? Leland . . . Brown?"

He just nodded.

"You have to say 'yes' or 'no,' son," Leah said.

"Yes," he said angrily.

"And you live in Alabaster?"

His face snapped to Eli's. "How . . . ?" He looked back to Leah. "How did you know that?"

Eli's hand came down on Leland's knee. "Because I told her," he said. "Now relax. You're actin' guilty. You haven't *done* anythin'."

"Why are you here, Leland?" Leah asked.

Eli interrupted. "I thought you wanted to question *me*."

"I'll get round to you, don't you worry 'bout that." Her gaze fell back on Leland. "Why are you here?"

Leland glanced across to Eli and back to Leah.

"Just . . . vistin' my grandpa. Haven't seen him in so long." He grinned, but Leah could tell it was a fake smile even if she'd been standin' five acres away. This kid may have been the worst liar in the history of scam artists.

"That all? Nothin' else?"

He shook his head. "Nope."

"Eli," Leah said. "Who is Argo Atkinson?"

"My father-in-law."

"And are you aware that his name is on the title of the Carson Cattle Ranch property?"

"Yes." The boy kept looking from Leah to Eli and back to Leah like he was watching a tennis game.

"Can I ask why you hadn't told me this before?"

"Lots of reasons," Eli said. "The main one bein' I don't see how it's any of your damn business. Another bein' that I was never asked."

"I came here and inquired specifically 'bout Sylvie Carson."

"And I told you the truth, that I ain't been near her property or her. Nor do I have any plans to be. That has got nothing to do with land purchased by my father-in-law. In fact, the land really isn't my business at all. It's his. Perhaps he's the one you should be questionin'."

Leah wrote down everything they said. Taking statements was something she'd had lots of practice at. And interviewing Argo Atkinson was something she had already planned on doing. Only, Eli came first because she had a sneaking suspicion that Argo hadn't bought the land for himself.

"Do you know what Mr. Atkinson plans to do with the ranch?"

There was a brief hesitation, during which Leland looked to Eli expectantly for an answer. Finally, Eli broke the silence. "I think," he said slowly, "that he plans on developing on it."

"What sort of development?"

"A religious educational institution."

"Grandpa . . ." Leland whispered, loud enough for Leah to hear.

Again Eli's hand came down on his grandson's knee. Eli turned to the boy and said, "It can't be kept a secret, Leland. Once the tractors start diggin', folks are gonna know what's goin' on. Better to get this out in the open now. It ain't like we're doin' anythin' wrong."

"So," Leah said, "Argo bought this land for you, on account of you was in prison?"

"Argo made an *investment,*" Eli said. "Do you have any idea how much he's already gained on that property since buyin' it? It turned out to be a very shrewd investment."

Leah knew exactly how much he'd already gained. She even had the paperwork to back it up. She looked to the kid. "I have a hunch, Leland," she said.

He just stared back, like a goldfish in one of them round glass bowls.

"Call it a gut feelin'," she said, "but it's definitely there."

"What's that?" he asked.

"That you's lyin' to me."

He shook his head. "No I ain't."

"I think you are. I think your granddaddy might be tellin' mostly the truth, but I think you lied to me earlier."

"No, ma'am, I did not." She could see his back coming up while simultaneously fear rose in his eyes.

"I think you are down here to help your grandpa Eli start workin' on his institution. In fact, I bet if I ran a check on you, I'd discover that you're either in college or just graduated with some sort of degree in business management."

She saw him swallow. She definitely wasn't far from the mark.

"Did you know I can arrest you for lying to a police officer?"

"Give the kid a break," Eli said. "He's not used to havin' questions fired at him. He's only twenty-two, damn it."

Twenty-two? Damn, he looked young for his age. "I'll tell you what," Leah said. "I'll give you another chance, Leland. Tell me again: Why are you down here?"

He looked at Eli. Eli nodded slightly.

When Leland spoke again, his voice was shaky. "I'm here to help find investors for Grandpa Eli's institution and help reorganize his congregation. We need to get his church back up and runnin' 'fore anythin' else can proceed. Then we need money."

"Surely the property has enough equity to move ahead with your project?"

Eli answered that one. "My father-in-law don't wanna risk his investment any more than he has to. He didn't buy the property *for* me. It will remain his, at least until he dies. If we have to mortgage the property for some of the funding, then I suppose that's a route we'll have to take. But he won't mortgage more than half of it. He's already made that clear. And building this facility is gonna cost more than that."

"We're eager to move ahead as quick as possible," Leland said. "Now that Grandpa Eli's back home."

"Hmm," Leah said. "I see a few complications in your plans."

"What's that?" Leland asked.

"I reckon that even though the sale went through eight years ago, there's still a chance Sylvie Carson might be able to have it overturned given the state she was in at the time of the sale and the matters surroundin' it. We need to follow that up with the courts. This is especially true with the new evidence I'll be presentin' on account of I'm reopenin' the case files for the deaths of Tom Carson and his wife. Something 'bout it all don't sit right with me. I'm startin' to think Tom Carson's hangin' wasn't suicide at all. I've been thinkin' maybe more people than just James Richard Cobbler were possibly responsible for Tom's wife's death."

"This could stall the project," Eli said, his voice rising. "You could hold up the question of land title for the property in the courts for years."

Leah shrugged.

"Listen," Eli said, trying to remain calm. "We've done nothin' wrong. We waited 'til the property was available, then bought it at auction. We was lucky enough to get it at a low price. There ain't no funny business happenin' in anythin' we're doin' despite what you may reckon. It's all fair an' square."

"I don't reckon it either way, Mr. Brown. Like I said, those deaths just don't sit well with me. And I want Sylvie to have a chance at gettin' a piece of any inheritance she might have comin' to her if she deserves one. That's all. There ain't no 'funny business happenin' in anythin' *I'm* doin' either. It's all fair an' square." She did say that last bit a mite sarcastically, she had to admit, but she wasn't prepared for the reaction that followed.

Leland lowered his eyes at her and, in a menacing voice no longer filled with any sort of shakiness, said, "You'd better stay out of our way, or I reckon I wouldn't

want to be in those shoes of yours." Eli's hand once
again fell onto Leland's knee. This time with an obvious squeeze.

"Is that a threat, Leland?" Leah asked.

"Take it any way you want to."

"You don't want me to take it as a threat. Trust me."

"You accuse us of all sorts of things, and then tell
me what I can and cannot do? In my granddaddy's
house, no less. I reckon you should leave now." Leah
started wondering if the whole "shaken up from talking to the policewoman" thing was an act. This young
man didn't seem to really be too shaken up at all. He
appeared completely in command. And a little scary.

One thing was for certain, though: They'd gone for
her bluff. That made her happy.

"Yes, it's 'bout that time," she said, standing and
tucking her notebook away. "Oh, just one last thing. If
I catch either of you anywhere *near* Sylvie Carson, I
won't be askin' no more questions. I'll be shootin'
first. And I'm a better shot than even you are, Preacher
Eli." As soon as she said that, even Leah thought she'd
overstepped the boundary of good taste.

"Get out!" Eli Brown roared.

CHAPTER 25

"I don't know 'bout this, Abe," my mother said as she pulled off Church Street and into the Full Gospel parking lot. She was watching all the black folks driving in and getting out of their cars. A whole bunch of them was walking up to the church's door where Reverend Starks was greeting each one of them.

"What don't you know?" I asked. "We was invited."

"We don't really . . . fit in."

"I thought you said there ain't no difference between black and white, especially in the eyes of the Lord."

She sighed. "I did say that, didn't I?" Pulling the car to a stop, she threw it into PARK. "Okay, I guess we're really doin' this."

I was sitting in the backseat with Miss Sylvie and the baby. The baby had been crying something awful when we picked her up. That crying continued through the first half of the drive. Then I suppose the car ride put her to sleep because she wasn't crying anymore. I was glad about that. Crying babies weren't something I much liked listening to.

"Seriously, Mom?" Carry asked from the front seat. Neither my mother nor my sister had taken off their seat belts yet. Me and Miss Sylvie had. My mother and Carry just kept watching the people funneling to the front door of the church. There wasn't a single white folk in the bunch. I thought it was exciting. "This is ridiculous," Carry said to my mother. "It's bad enough you make me go to *normal* church."

My mother shot Carry a look. "Just for that, I'm glad we're here. You need to learn more tolerance, both for religion and for differences in people. Now, I promised Abe we'd come here and try it one time, and so here we are. We was invited. It ain't like we're showin' up unexpected." Then, hesitantly, as though she weren't quite sure I actually told her the truth about being invited, she asked me, "Is it, Abe?"

"It most certainly is not," I said.

"How do you feel about it, Miss Sylvie?" my mother asked.

"It's fine," Miss Sylvie said. Her voice was soft and quiet, as though she didn't really care what we did. I don't think she really wanted to be here or anywhere. I wondered if Miss Sylvie ever got excited about anything.

"Okay," my mother said, taking a deep breath. "Let's go." She finally undid her seat belt.

The church's open front door where Reverend Starks was standing was at the top of three large concrete steps that were cracked. There was a hand railing running up the side of the stairs, but it was busted near the top and so it didn't look very safe.

I tried not to look at everyone else as we approached

the door, but I couldn't help but get the feeling that people were looking at us. I was happy when Reverend Starks spotted us and a wide grin immediately spread across his face. "Abe!" he said, after finishing up welcoming the couple entering in front of us. "I see you decided to take me up on my offer! What a great surprise!"

He squatted down and shook my hand. When he stood back up again, his knees popped. He shook his head. "Indications of gettin' old," he said, turning his attention to my mother.

The morning sunlight reflected off his eyeglasses and he pushed them up on his nose. "Ms. Teal," he said, taking her hand in both of his. "It's been a long time. How have you been?" His voice was low and soothing and full of what sounded to me like genuine concern.

"Good . . ."

He smiled. "You've done such an amazing job raising two wonderful children." Still holding my mother's hand, his gaze swept to Carry. "Caroline, right? I haven't seen you since you were about a foot or two shorter than you are now." He laughed. "You're still as pretty as I remember."

Carry blushed and said thank you.

Reverend Starks let go of my mother's hand and turned his attention to Miss Sylvie. "And you must be Miss Sylvie," he said. I couldn't believe he remembered her name just from the discussion me and him had the other day. "It is a pleasure to meet you." He lowered his voice while talking to Miss Sylvie, obviously in an effort not to wake the baby she had on her shoulder. He shook her hand.

"Pleasure," Miss Sylvie said. "I'm Sylvie Carson."

"It's a *genuine* pleasure, Miss Sylvie Carson." The reverend looked the baby over. "And who do we have here?" he asked in a whisper. "Someone who obviously enjoys a good nap, I see. We have somethin' in common." He smiled at Miss Sylvie. I saw the light reflect off the gold of his capped tooth.

Miss Sylvie looked awkwardly to my mother. "Um," she stammered, "she's my daughter. She . . . she doesn't have a name yet."

Reverend Starks's smile never flinched. "I see. Well, the Lord loves all babies, whether they be called by names or be nameless."

Relief flooded across Miss Sylvie's face and, for the first time since we'd picked her up, she actually smiled. It wasn't that big, but at least it was a smile.

"I'm so sorry to hear you're suffering through some hard times right now," the reverend told her. "Just keep your faith in the Lord Jesus. Remember that God is light and in Him there can be no darkness."

Miss Sylvie seemed a bit taken aback, but she just nodded. "Th . . . thank you," she said shakily. She probably wondered how Reverend Starks knew so much about her.

"Would it be all right if I ask my congregation to offer a special prayer for you today?" Reverend Starks asked her.

Once again Miss Sylvie looked to my mother, who didn't seem to have any response for her. "I guess so." Miss Sylvie's voice still quivered.

That big smile once again spread across Reverend Starks's face. "That's fine, then. Welcome to my church." He held out his arm in a gesture for us to enter.

It had been a long while since I'd been in the Full Gospel, and I'd forgotten how it looked. Inside, the church wasn't a lot different from Clover Creek. From the outside, I could have sworn it was a smaller building, but now that I was inside it actually felt larger. Or maybe it was just that the pews were closer together and there were more of them. Like Clover Creek, everything was made of wood (probably pine), although the wood here at Full Gospel didn't shine the way it did at Clover Creek. There were holes where knots had fallen out and gouges in some of the boards.

We were about three quarters from the front where the pulpit stood, which was as close as we could get. I wondered if the church would fill up completely. If so, that would be a lot of people, probably more than the congregation we usually had at Clover Creek. Considerably more.

The walls left and right of the pulpit were angled and each had a large stained-glass window set in the top. There were four other stained-glass windows along the main side walls. On the angled wall right of the pulpit stood a choir of twenty-six people. I counted them twice, so I knew. They formed three rows, each row standing on a higher bench. The back row stood above the rest. I think they were all teenagers. Mostly, they were girls, but six of them were boys. A white cross hung above them, just below the stained-glass window.

We didn't have a choir at Clover Creek. We did a lot of singing, but just by ourselves.

I knew services always ran longer here at Full Gospel than at Clover Creek on account of all the extra singing they did. They were really big on singing and the singing was the part I was most excited about.

The light shining through that window above the choir cast down on the pulpit, lighting it in an array of reds and yellows. It gave it an unearthly glow. Behind the pulpit was another cross, bigger than the one by the choir and very similar to the one that hung behind Reverend Matthew. Only this cross wasn't nearly as big as the one at Clover Creek.

Spaced along the main side walls every few feet were candles that weren't lit. I guessed they were used for special occasions. The sunlight coming through the stained glass was the only light inside the church, making everything feel as though I was in a dream.

Miss Sylvie shuffled in first, the baby still on her left shoulder, asleep. I went in next, followed by my mother and then Carry, who I could still hear complaining under her breath.

My mother kept shushing her.

The pews weren't padded like the ones at Clover Creek, they were just wooden, but they weren't that uncomfortable. They were old and the row we sat on wasn't attached to the floor very well. It rocked back and forth a bit as we took our seats.

About fifteen or twenty minutes later, Reverend Starks closed the front door and the light from the colored glass in the windows suddenly really made everything magical. I looked back over my shoulder, amazed to find every pew full. There were even some people standing behind the last one. I didn't know exactly how many people had shown up for church today, but it was a lot more than we ever got at Clover Creek.

And every single one of them except us was black.

Reverend Starks walked slowly up the center aisle and stepped up to his pulpit.

"First," he said, in his low voice that now grew as he used it to preach. "I would like you all to welcome some guests today. Y'all may have seen them as you came in. They are sittin' there." He pointed us out. "They are the Teals, Ms. Leah Teal, from the Alvin Police Department; her son, Abe Teal; her daughter, Caroline Teal; and their friend Miss Sylvie Carson."

All around us people began to clap. In front of me, people looked over their shoulders and smiled. A woman wearing a pink lacy hat gave me a little wave. I felt a mite embarrassed, but I did feel welcomed just the same.

"Now, Miss Sylvie is goin' through some tough times right now, so I promised her we'd all give a little prayer for her. So before I get started with our regular service, I'd like to do just that."

And he went right into his prayer for Miss Sylvie, asking the Lord Jesus to please help her find her way. He called her one of His flock and said she had lost her way and needed guidance and a road map. I was pretty amazed he was able to give such a detailed prayer about Miss Sylvie based on what little I'd said about her. He even made mention of the baby, who I hadn't even talked about and he'd only just met outside for the first time.

The fact that he had even remembered her name had been a miracle in my eyes. Then I remembered him quoting those Bible passages to me and Dewey off the top of his head. He was really something.

As he spoke each line, everyone in the congregation (who were sitting holding hands with their heads bowed and their eyes closed) repeated the line. When he was finished, he said, "Amen." And everyone followed with one loud "Amen" in unison.

Miss Sylvie looked as though she had no idea what

to make of everything or how she was supposed to react. The baby continued sleeping. To me, that was yet another miracle.

After that, Reverend Starks started the service with three songs from the hymnal. The choir led the way, bellowing out the words so loud and fine it sent a shiver through me. Everyone sang along, including me. At least I tried to, following with the hymnbook I found in the back of the pew in front of me. After the three hymns, Reverend Starks went into a pretty standard sermon, much like Reverend Matthew would give at Clover Creek First Baptist. Like I usually did, I tried to keep up but couldn't quite understand everything he was saying. Normally, it didn't bother me so much, but today I was trying extra hard to stay on top of things. I really wanted to know what Reverend Starks was talking about.

He went on for probably thirty minutes until finally coming to what sounded like the conclusion. Usually the conclusion was when you got the real important stuff.

"I would like you to recall Psalm Thirty-four, verses sixteen through nineteen," he said. " 'The face of the Lord is against them that do evil, to cut off the remembrance of them from the earth. The righteous cry, and the Lord heareth, and delivereth them out of all their troubles.' " Reverend Stark shifted his hands on the pulpit as he read the next verse. I couldn't see it, but I assumed he had an open Bible in front of him. I didn't think he could possibly have *all* this Bible stuff memorized. " 'The Lord is nigh unto them that are of a broken heart; and saveth such as be of a contrite spirit. And many are the afflictions of the righteous; but the Lord delivereth him out of them all.' "

He looked up and scanned the congregation in silence. I got the feeling this was the end of his sermon and, as I said, usually the end was pretty important so I really wanted to figure this part out.

I didn't rightly know if I understood completely what he had said, but it sounded to me like Lord Jesus was going to protect everyone who was good from evil and that even good people had problems and cried and stuff. I whispered to my mother if that was what he meant by what he said.

She shushed me.

"I'm only tryin' to understand church," I said quietly. "You should be happy." I never really took that much of an interest in church usually. I mean, I always listened to what Reverend Matthew said at Clover Creek First Baptist, but I didn't much understand what he went on about most of the time and didn't bother following up like this. Today I felt like I should really try to clarify things. I'm not sure why, but for some reason, today church felt kind of special. Maybe just because we were at Full Gospel. Maybe I didn't want to let Reverend Starks down by not being able to figure out what he was preaching about.

My mother whispered back, "He's sayin' God is close to the broken hearted."

Miss Sylvie sat there with the baby on her shoulder. If ever anyone looked broken hearted, she certainly did. I suddenly felt a whole lot better for her. I wondered if Reverend Starks had written this sermon special just for Miss Sylvie, but then I remembered he didn't know for sure that we were coming today or not.

There actually was more to the sermon after that, but the rest didn't last too long. Unlike at Clover Creek, the sermon ended early so that a lot of the time could be spent doing more singing, which really did turn out to be the best part. This was different singing from the hymns we sang at the beginning of the service. It was much more powerful. It seemed to hit me right in the heart.

The choir led every song and the singers had incredibly loud voices. Actually, so did the congregation. It seemed as though everyone attending Full Gospel knew how to carry a tune better than anyone I ever met in my life.

Their voices were beautiful and they rose up until they filled that entire building, which suddenly didn't seem very big at all. It felt so small, in fact, it seemed like the voices were going to shatter the stained glass. Then, the choir grew even louder and it felt like the whole church might burst with the joyousness of song.

I tried to sing along following the words in the hymnal, but I wasn't a very good singer. My mother also mouthed words, but she didn't seem to be actually singing anything. It didn't matter. There were more than enough people singing already. I was downright amazed how loud that group of people and that choir could sing. I was sure most people up and down Main Street could hear them right now.

And then it felt as though the song somehow did break through the small building and lifted it up into the sky where it shone in the heavens like a bright star.

Miss Sylvie held the baby tightly against her chest. Amazingly, the baby still appeared to be asleep. Miss Sylvie had her head tucked against the baby's cheek and tears spilled from her eyes. At first, I couldn't figure out why she was so upset. Then I realized she was overwhelmed by all the singing. I came to this conclusion on account of I felt the very same way, only not quite to the point of tears. But there was something very emotional about it all.

The tall black woman wearing a yellow summer dress standing in the pew behind her leaned ahead and put her lips close to Miss Sylvie's ear. The woman had black curly hair and wore glasses. Raising her voice loud enough for Miss Sylvie (and me) to hear her over the singing, she said, "Go ahead, child, it's okay. Cry. Cry, and let the blessed sing for you."

That moment felt almost magical to me. Time seemed to stop as something caught in my throat, and for an instant I did feel something like tears stinging the back of my eyes.

I thought later that maybe God really had been there in that church that day with all of us. At least in that moment He was.

CHAPTER 26

Me and Dewey were out in my backyard again, thrusting and parrying and swinging and blocking with our swords. We were sure getting a lot of fun from these wooden toys me and Carry had so simply constructed. I was so glad I had come up with the idea to make them now. And Dewey's invention for holding them around our waists had turned out to be brilliant. We virtually took them with us everywhere we went. Folks around town were getting used to seeing us with swords dangling from our hips. It was like we were real knights.

Today was particularly fun. The day was sunny, but not too hot, and there was a sweet smell in the air; I think it was the neighbor's magnolias from next door. The scent just made everything that much more perfect. And Dewey had yet to whine even once about me hurting his hand or anything.

Truth was, he had gotten so much better with his sword that I didn't hit his hand anymore. He had a good block and was able to see my moves coming and counter them or step out of their way before they could do any damage. It made me wonder how good we'd be with real swords. I hoped one day in the future, when I had money of my own, I might go back to Disney World so I could buy myself one of them real swords. Then I wouldn't need to go through my mother at all. Lots of things would be much easier when I got older.

Dewey had just come at me with a series of slashes and swings that had forced me almost all the way across the yard when Carry stepped out the back door and stopped us mid-play. I didn't realize right away what was about to happen, but when I did, a darkness passed over my heart. For I suddenly recognized what she had in her outstretched hand. She wiggled it at me from the porch: a brand-new bottle of bright pink nail polish that glistened even brighter and looked even sharper than it should have under all this sunlight.

"Oh, Abe," she sang out with chimes in her voice. "It's time to come inside for a bit."

I stared at her, my heart jackhammering like the foot of a rabbit thumping the ground. Then I looked at Dewey. I didn't know what to do. This was the last position I wanted to be stuck in. Dewey could *not* find out what terrible fate had befallen me. He would never let me forget this as long as we both were still alive.

"Abe," she sang out again. "Remember your word? It's been a week . . ."

I let out a deep breath. "Dewey . . . I have to go inside for a while." I wanted to get in the house before Carry said too much. I jogged over to the porch where she stood and carefully placed my sword up against the outside wall of the house.

"What's goin' on?" Dewey asked from the backyard, his sword pointing at the ground, his hand shielding his eyes from the sun. "You paintin' your sister's nails, Abe?"

There was a question I wasn't about to answer straight out. "I just have to go inside."

"But why?"

"To do something . . . chores."

"What kind of chores?"

"Not very fun ones."

"How long will you be? Should I just wait out here?"

I took off my shoes and followed my sister into the house.

"Yes," I called out over my shoulder. "Wait for me. I'll only be fifteen minutes!"

"More like twenty-five!" Carry shouted from the living room. "He's doin' a *proper* job!"

I felt my face cycle through ten shades of red. I wished Carry would just shut up. She'd already done enough damage. There was no way I would ever live this down. My only hope was that somehow Dewey was simple enough that I could cover up the truth. But if Carry kept on talking, that would be near on impossible.

CHAPTER 27

Leah sat at her desk making phone call after phone call to different psychologist offices in and around Satsuma, looking for anybody who knew anything about a psychologist with the last name of Langdon or Langwood or anything sounding like it. She wasn't having much luck. She was beginning to wonder if Sylvie had made the name up.

Truth was, she didn't rightly know what help some psychologist Sylvie saw while still back in school might be to her anyway, especially given that Sylvie said she'd only seen the man three or four times over a handful of months. Leah wished she was seeing somebody now. Somebody a lot more often than just three or four times in as many months. The girl needed someone to help her, someone who knew what he was doing.

Obviously, Tom Carson had known that too, despite Sylvie not taking him seriously on account of what he did to himself.

Leah started pondering that. From what she'd heard about Tom Carson he was a very proud man. It would've taken a lot for him to admit his daughter was in so much trouble she might need professional help. And professional help would require money. There was no way, being a cattle farmer and all, that Tom Carson had a medical plan. So, him telling Sylvie she should go see someone meant he must've had plans to further mortgage the farm just to pay for her expenses. Takes a mighty strong man to do something like that.

Or someone who could directly identify with her situation.

The thought struck Leah like lightning hitting an oak tree. What if *that* was where Tom Carson's money had been going? What if all that time since his son had been killed, Tom Carson had been seeing some sort of therapist and paying the bills by mortgaging the property?

It made sense. And it was easy to find out.

She made a quick call down to the station in Mobile. Officer Mindy Wright answered the phone.

"Hi, Mindy, it's Leah Teal, up here in Alvin." Leah had met Mindy quite a few times. The Mobile department often threw summer functions and invited all the officers from the small outlying towns to bring their families down and participate. It was a highlight of Abe's summer. The last one had only been just over a month or so ago, around the end of June. "I need medical records for a Mr. Tom Carson. Used to live up here. He passed away in 1980. Owned the Carson Cattle Ranch."

Mindy said she'd have to get them from the public records office, but it shouldn't take more than a phone call.

"That's why I'm callin' you." Leah laughed. "I have to write letters and jump through hoops for anythin' out of there. Then I gotta wait a week."

"That's crazy," Mindy said. "I can have 'em for you probably within the hour. I'll just fax 'em on up to you."

"Thanks. Oh, but . . . we don't have a fax right now. We *had* one, but it kinda broke. So can you just call me with the information? I only want a few items."

"Sure. What's your number?"

Leah gave her the number.

She hung up the phone and started remembering exactly what it was that Sylvie told her that her pa had said:

He was the one always askin' me if I was okay. Kept askin' if I needed to talk to somebody about it. Like a professional. Like a shrink or somethin'. He told me that could really help.

Now that she played it back in her mind, Leah thought it was an odd thing for Tom Carson to say unless he *knew* from his own experience how much it could help. No, the more she thought about it, the more this made sense. It fit with the money being spent. Medical bills weren't cheap, especially if medication was involved.

It had been just forty minutes since Leah called down to the station in Mobile when her phone rang. It was Mindy Wright with Tom Carson's medical records.

"Okay, what do you want to know?" she asked.

"Did the man ever go see a psychologist or a therapist of any kind on a regular basis?"

"Leah, he saw the same doctor every Tuesday and Thursday week in and week out from the fall of seventy-one right up until he died. It doesn't look here like he missed too many days at all."

"Where was that doctor?"

"It was a Dr. Lisa May Turner. She was right down here, in Mobile."

"Does the report show if he was on any medication?"

"Yep. She prescribed an assortment of different things, none of which I can pronounce. Looks like she changed it up every six months or so at the beginning and then every few years later on."

"I don't suppose you got an address for this Dr. Turner?"

"One sec, let me see if she's still doin' business here in Mobile." Leah could hear Mindy typing on her computer. They had a much bigger database then the Alvin department. It was controlled by something called a mainframe. "She is. Dr. Lisa May Turner, psychiatrist. You got a pen handy? I got a phone number and an address for you."

"Yep, shoot." Leah jotted down the information as Mindy relayed it. When she was done, Leah said, "Thanks a million. I owe you one."

"You owe me a sack race next year. You bowed out this time round."

"That was on account of my daughter and them boys, remember?"

"Oh, I remember," Mindy said. "Have a great day, Leah."

Leah lifted the phone and dialed the number she'd written down on the paper in front of her. A young woman answered. "Dr. Turner's office."

"Hi, this is Detective Leah Teal. I'm with the police force up here in Alvin. I was wonderin' if it would be possible to speak with Dr. Turner."

"I'm afraid she's with a patient right now. Can I get her to call you back?"

Leah left three numbers before hanging up: her office number, her home number, and her car phone number.

Hopefully, she'd be able to convince the doctor she was who she said she was over the phone, otherwise she would have to drive down and show her badge to get any information due to doctor/patient privileges. She figured worst case she could always just get Mindy to go question the doctor for her. She'd actually pretty near got all the information she really wanted to know anyway, other than the actual cost of each of Tom Carson's visits and the price of his medication.

The only other thing Dr. Turner would be able to tell her about the man was that he suffered from depression, but Leah had already figured that out in 1980 when she found his dead body swinging from the bough of that oak tree in his back ninety. After all, despite her recent suspicions, they *had* ruled it a suicide.

CHAPTER 28

Leah didn't hear back from the psychiatrist until after she got home from work that night. It was a pleasant enough evening. The sky was still a nice dark blue, just beginning to get a touch of color in the gloaming, and the weather was pleasant.

Caroline was out with friends, but due home sometime in the next hour. Leah's daughter had been much better lately about coming home when she said she would. This made Leah happy. Leah's plan was to fix her kids a decent meal tonight—something they didn't get nearly often enough. On the menu was chicken-fried steak, potato salad, and greens, a favorite of both Abe and Caroline.

Abe and Dewey were out in the front yard playing with their swords, making all sorts of racket. Leah closed the door when the phone rang.

"Hi, this is Dr. Lisa Turner," the woman said. She didn't sound as Southern as most folk down in Mobile. "I'm looking for Detective Teal."

"This is Leah Teal. Thank you for takin' the time to call me back."

"Absolutely no problem at all. What can I do for you, Detective?"

"I'm hopin' you can give me information on a patient you had from late 1971 until 1980. A man by the name of Tom Carson."

"Tom Carson. Let me think. You're asking me to remember a long way back. Let me check my files; can you hold on a sec?"

"Certainly."

She came back on the line momentarily. "Oh, yes. Mr. Carson. I remember now. What, exactly, did you want to know?"

"Can you tell me what you were treatin' him for?"

There was a silence on the other end. "Normally, Detective Teal, this would fall under privileged information. But—am I to assume this is a criminal investigation?"

"Yes, it is."

"And the man *did* commit suicide."

"Yes, he did. I handled the case."

"Then I think I can make an exception. I treated him for depression. He was actually diagnosed in 1973 with major depressive disorder."

"What medications was he taking?"

"Oh, let's see. A number of things. We kept trying different combinations of tricyclic antidepressants and MAO inhibitors. There's always a lot of guesswork with psychotropic drugs until you find things that work for patients. Generally, it's not one single drug but a combination that does the trick. Once Prozac came on to the market, he went straight on to that."

The medications didn't mean much to Leah. She only wanted to know one thing about them. "Were they expensive?"

"I'm a doctor, Detective, not a pharmacist. But I can't imagine they were cheap, especially not back in those days."

"So . . . around twenty-five dollars a month?"

The psychiatrist laughed. "Probably closer to two hundred. And like everything else they would've gone up in price as time went by."

"Can I ask you how much your rates were back when Mr. Carson started seeing you?"

"Um, let me check if I have that on file. Yes, it's right here. Two hundred and fifty dollars an hour."

"And he saw you an hour every Tuesday and an hour every Thursday?" Leah was astounded by the amount of money they were talking about.

"No, he came for two-hour sessions on each of those days."

"And, like everything else, did your rates also go up in price?"

"That's very likely."

"I see. Thank you, Dr. Turner, I think that's all the information I need."

Leah hung up the phone thinking, *Become a doctor, Abe. Jeez. Did I ever go into the wrong field.*

Me and Dewey were outside in my front yard, battling away with our swords as we usually were these days. The evening was getting on, and I figured in a few more hours there'd be swarms of lightning bugs out here flying between the bushes that were planted around my bedroom window. They always seemed to gather there on nights like tonight—nights when the sky had those red streaks through it, like it was beginning to get now.

"I'm gonna slice your hand off," Dewey said, stepping and swiping at me with his blade.

Normally, I'd have stepped back, but lately I'd gotten better at blocking his blows. Both of us were getting mighty good with our swords. Pretty soon we'd be as good as real knights, we were sure.

The big floppy flowers from the neighbor's magnolias next door filled the evening air with their sugary aroma. They always smelled stronger at night, but tonight they seemed unusually strong, for some reason. Bits of fluff from the cottonwood trees floated in the sky around us as we parried. It was certainly a good thing I didn't have hay fever like Luke Dempsey at school. Luke couldn't go out of doors from most of the late spring months right through to October on account of all the cotton in the air.

Just then, a beat-up old station wagon turned off the road and into my drive. I turned to look at it just as Dewey came in with another swing. Because I wasn't looking, he got me on the back of the hand.

"Ow, Dewey! For cripes' sake! I wasn't even lookin'!"

"Sorry," he said.

I held my hand up over my eyes and squinted into the windshield of the station wagon where the low sun was reflecting off the glass. My heart nearly leaped out of my body. "Do you know who that is?" I whispered to Dewey.

He came up beside me, lowering his sword. "No, who?"

"Preacher Eli!"

"Are you absolutely certain?"

We waited, watching as the car door opened and, sure enough, out stepped Preacher Eli in his cowboy boots.

"It is!" Dewey whispered.

I shushed him.

Preacher Eli was wearing a white dress shirt with a vest over the top and had his hair combed nice and neat. It looked like he'd just shaved his face. Walking right past, he gave us barely a glance before heading up the porch steps to the door and knocking.

My mother opened it. From the look on her face, she was obviously just as surprised as we were to see Preacher Eli show up at our house. I didn't even like knowing that he knew where I lived, him being a killer and all. My mother didn't look like she wanted to invite him in, but he seemed determined. Finally, she did. To me, she looked frightened.

"See?" I said to Dewey after the door was closed. "My mom's startin' to see things my way. I knew she would. I *told* her that man was up to no good. Did you see her face? She don't trust him."

Dewey shrugged. "Looked to me like she just invited him into your house. I don't think she looked untrusting."

"You don't know my mom."

He didn't have a reply to that.

After a while of staring at the house, we went back to our sword fighting.

Leah brought Eli Brown into the kitchen; looking at the steak sitting on a plate waiting to hit the frying pan, she wondered how late her dinner was going to wind up being. "So, Mr. Brown," she said after showing him to one of the kitchen chairs and taking the one beside it. "Where's that grandson of yours? What's his name? Leland?"

"That's right," Eli said. "He drove back to Alabaster to his daddy's for a while. Ain't nothin' more for him to do on the project 'til we get the permit to start workin' on the church."

"You're talkin' 'bout your old church? Beside the Carson property?"

"Beside my father-in-law's property," Eli corrected. "That's right. The town had it condemned. We want to fix it up so it's usable once more. Need to start up my congregation again."

"So you can raise money."

"That's right," Eli said again. "Nothin' illegal 'bout that, is there?"

"No, Mr. Brown, there isn't."

"Leland'll be coming back in a couple weeks. 'Sides, I wouldn't have brought him here anyway. That boy ain't levelheaded enough for adult conversation like the type we need to have. He's fine for business stuff. Just not . . ." He trailed off.

"Emotional stuff?"

"Yeah, I guess," he said. "Goes in like a bull moose. I tell him that's not the way to approach things. You want to soothe a bear, it takes honey. It certainly don't take no shotgun."

Interesting choice of words, Leah thought.

"To be right honest, the boy's just got a lot of passion." He laughed. "And you certainly bring the passion out in him, Miss Teal."

"I'd prefer if you called me *Detective* Teal," Leah said. "And to be right honest, I reckon I bring the bull-shit out in him. No offense."

"None taken, ma'am."

"So why don't you tell me why you're here, Mr. Brown?"

"I came here on friendly terms, hopin' we can work things out like civilized folk."

"I already see a problem with that, Mr. Brown. So far, there don't seem nothin' civilized 'bout the way you conduct yourself."

"Now hold on there just a sec, Miss—*Detective Teal,* that sounds like an accusation."

"No, I'm just statin' a fact."

"I ain't done nothin' wrong since goin' off to prison seventeen years ago."

"Your wife's daddy bought the Carson Cattle Ranch."

"Fair and square."

Their voices were rising. Both of them were getting their backs up, but Leah wasn't about to be the one to lower hers down.

"Just seems a mite suspicious to me," she said. "And he got it at such a low price. Now, how did he swing that?"

Eli Brown stood from his chair. "I don't see how my wife's daddy's business deals are any business of yours. The bank accepted the deal. The deed is in his name. Everythin' 'bout it is legitimate!"

"That's somethin' we'll have to see 'bout."

"Well, I don't need you stickin' your nose in my business and tryin' to mess things up for me. I finally have a shot at doin' somethin' good!" They were practically hollering now. There was no question Abe and Dewey could hear them from the front yard outside.

"Somethin' good?" Leah asked, her voice still loud. "Somethin' like tormentin' a poor girl after killin' her baby brother?"

Eli stamped his foot. "I told you! I don't even know where the girl lives, goddamn it!"

Leah cut him off. "Now that don't sound too preacher-like to me, using the Lord's name in vain. I'm startin' to think just maybe you had somethin' to do with what happened to Sylvie's folks so your wife's daddy could buy their land."

Something appeared in Eli Brown's eyes then. It passed by quickly, but it was dark and evil. It scared Leah. It must've been the same thing Tom Carson saw that afternoon, right before the man's finger pulled the trigger of that gun and forever changed the lives of his innocent family. The volume of Eli Brown's voice lowered and so did the tone. When he spoke, the words came out one at a time, very precise and methodical. "If you're gonna go round makin' accusations like that, you better have an arrest warrant backin' them up, you hear me? Or else—" He stopped himself.

"Or else what, preacher man?"

"Just watch yourself."

They both stared at each other in silence, the hatred in Eli Brown's eyes palpable.

Then the telephone rang and Leah nearly leaped onto the kitchen ceiling.

Breaking their stare, she answered it. It was Miss Sylvie. Once again, she was in turmoil.

"Slow down, girl," Leah said. "Tell me again."

"It's the backyard," Sylvie said on the other end. "Someone's been out there again."

"And you know this how?"

"The cellar door's open again."

"Same one?" Leah started suspecting there was something wrong with the latch after all.

But what Sylvie said blew that theory right out of the sky. "*Both* of 'em. And there ain't no wind, Officer Teal." Leah eyed Eli Brown, wondering if he could pick up who she was talking to. "Go outside and check. And there hasn't been any wind in the last thirty minutes, and this happened in the last thirty minutes."

She was talking so fast, Leah could barely understand her.

"Just calm down, Sylvie, please? I'm trying to keep up."

"There ain't no goddamn wind!"

"How do you know it happened in the past thirty minutes?"

"On account of I was outside sittin' with the baby in the sun, watching it go down. Then I got tired of breast-feedin' and went inside to fix her a bottle of milk that I'd pumped so I could put her down. When I came back out to get her blanket and stuff I found the doors open."

"Are you sure they weren't open when you were outside earlier, and you just didn't notice?" Leah asked.

Sylvie practically screamed into the phone. "They weren't goddamn open!"

Leah had to move the receiver away from her ear. She was getting tired of people yelling. "Okay, okay," she said calmly.

"Whoever done it must've been watchin' me. I'm afraid, Miss Leah!"

"Okay, Sylvie? It's all okay. You're fine, right?"

She heard Sylvie breathing hard on the other end.

"Y—yeah."

"Whoever did it is gone now. You're fine and your baby's fine, right?"

"Yeah, she's here with me."

"Good. I'll be there as soon as I can. Try to remain calm, okay?"

"Okay."

Leah hung up the phone and stared at it a few seconds. This basically just exonerated Eli Brown. He couldn't have been at Sylvie's in the past thirty minutes on account of he'd been here at her place during that time. "Your grandson really up in Alabaster?" she asked Eli, her eyes still glued to the phone.

"Yeah," Eli Brown said calmly. "No reason to lie 'bout that. You can check it out with his pa if you want. Let me give you the number."

He gave her the number.

"Sorry," Eli said, "but I couldn't help but overhear some of that. Miss Sylvie, I presume?"

Leah nodded.

"And she's had troubles in the past thirty minutes?"

Another nod.

"So you know it's not me doin' it, now?"

"Looks like on the surface that would be the case."

Eli rubbed his chin. "How 'bout we just say I accept your apology and move on? I came here tryin' to repair broken bridges, not blow 'em all to hell and high water."

Leah kept staring at the phone. If it weren't Eli, then she had no suspects.

"And I trust," Eli said, "that your little threat 'bout Sylvie disputin' the land deal was just a ruse?"

When Leah didn't react, Eli continued: "Yeah, I didn't think she had any argument for it. I just didn't want things held up." With a laugh, he shook his head. "You certainly put Leland in a panic, though. Think 'bout it, Detective. I'm tryin' to build a *school*. Why would I be harassin' and, hell, *murderin'* folk to do somethin' that, in the eyes of the Lord, will be such a blessing to this community? It don't make no sense."

He pushed his chair in, getting ready to leave. He laughed and shook his head again. Leah met the preacher man's eyes. The corners of his mouth creased into a small smile as he held out his hand. "Can we at least *try* to exist in the same town without tearin' each other's throats out?"

"I—I guess we can try," Leah stammered and actually, to her own surprise, shook his hand.

"I'd appreciate that."

One thing she could say about Eli Brown. Whatever charisma he had had as a preacher all them years ago still lurked underneath his scruffy demeanor. She had no doubt he'd be successful at raising the money he needed to build his school. That charm was all just hidden away a bit beneath years of being worn through from spending so much time in the state prison system. Being on the inside can change a man. Leah knew that. She'd seen it happen on many occasions. Usually, the changes weren't good. They manifested at the worst times, and in the worst ways.

She wondered what sorts of things she'd see manifesting from Eli Brown.

"I've gotta go get supper on," he said, heading through

her kitchen for the living room. "And I suspect you've gotta go pay Miss Sylvie a visit. Thank you for your time, Detective."

Ever since we heard my mother hollering, me and Dewey had stopped playing with our swords and had come as close as we dared to the picture window at the front of the house and tried to listen to what was going on inside.

"You *still* think she trusts him?" I asked.

"I have to admit," Dewey said, "that's a lot of yellin'. I reckon you might be right."

"Of course I'm right. I'm a good judge of character."

The yelling calmed down and then we heard the telephone. My mother was quiet while she talked on the phone, so we couldn't hear any of her conversation through the front window. We were also at least a room away on account of we couldn't see anyone in the living room, which meant my mother and Preacher Eli had probably gone into the kitchen.

I pointed this fact out to Dewey.

"She sure must've been yellin' awfully loud, then."

I smiled. "See? Told you."

A little bit later we did see my mother and Preacher Eli come around the corner into the living room and we quickly ducked down and crab-walked back to our places in the front yard where we'd been sword fighting. Assuming our positions, we went back to battling, although our attention was really on the front porch where the door was being opened. My mother said good-bye to Preacher Eli.

"I'll get to the bottom of this," she told him.

"I reckon you will," Preacher Eli said. "And I hope you do, soon. Have a fine evenin', Miss Teal." He caught himself. "Sorry. I mean *Detective Teal.*"

"You too, Mr. Brown."

Once again, Preacher Eli gave us the slightest of acknowledgments as he trudged past and got into his car. Me and Dewey had stopped fighting completely as he backed out and headed down the street toward Hunter Road, probably bound for his little shotgun shack sitting up in Blackberry Springs like a command post.

Back at the door my mother had slipped on her shoes and was coming outside, too. "So, I s'pose I was right after all," I said, pushing my chest out slightly.

" 'Bout what?" she asked.

"Preacher Eli. I told you he is not to be trusted. He already done and killed once. You can't trust killers. I bet you feel a bit silly now for getting so mad about me and Dewey having our stakeout."

My mother came down the steps staring at me. Something flashed across her face. "That man ain't up to nothin'."

"What do you mean?" I felt my own face begin to get warm. I was tired of having to explain the same things over and over when I was always right and everyone else seemed to always be wrong.

"Eli Brown's innocent."

I wondered if my face was getting red. It was definitely growing hot. "But—" I stammered. "We heard you yellin'."

"You should mind your business," she said, pointing at me.

That did it. Now I got really upset. I was tired of minding my business. I was tired of not being taken seriously. "I'm so sick of you not listenin' to me!" I snapped, my voice rising in volume and speed. "Preacher Eli is guilty!"

"Abe! Calm down right now!"

But I didn't calm down, and Dewey's face grew ashen and his eyes looked like saucers as he watched. They filled up with fear.

"Preacher Eli is the one who's been upsetting Miss Sylvie! You just refuse to listen on account of it's me tellin' you! If it were anyone else, you'd listen! You never listen to me!" My voice had grown to hollering. Tears stung the back of my eyes. "You didn't listen to me 'bout my aunt Addison and you ain't listenin' to me 'bout this!"

"Abe!" my mother yelled back. "Drop your tone, right now!"

"I will not! I'm so sick of bein' ignored! So sick of mindin' my own business! So sick of—" My face felt like it was on fire. As I screamed, I waved my sword in the air. With a frustrated wail, I held it out horizontally in front of me and lifted my knee. With one hard yank, I brought it down and with a loud *crack!* I split it in two, practically breaking it right at the hilt.

Dewey hadn't moved. His expression hadn't changed.

I felt a tear run down the cheek of my burning face.

"Dewey," my mother said calmly, "go home."

"Yes, ma'am." His voice trembled.

"Abe, go to your room. I have to go see Miss Sylvie. You'll stay in your room until I get back home, understood?"

Not another word was spoken as Dewey picked up his bike and rode off down Cottonwood Lane beneath that red-streaked sky, and I slowly stumbled up the front steps of my house, crying. Cotton floated in the air behind me as I went inside, kicked off my shoes, and went to my room.

Collapsing on my bed, I let the tears run from my eyes, over the bridge of my nose, and on to my pillow, unsure of what had come over me.

CHAPTER 29

On the ride over to Sylvie's, Leah forgot all about Abe's outburst, and began to unwind all the theories that had been building up in her head. She had done exactly what Ethan Montgomery warned her not to: She'd let her imagination run amok. Preacher Eli wasn't guilty of harassing Sylvie Carson. Why would the man get out on parole and then risk that freedom just to barnstorm the sister of the boy he'd accidentally killed? When she thought of it now, it so obviously made no sense; she chided herself for falling so easily into believing it. She had *wanted* to believe it.

Then there were the "mysterious" deaths of Sylvie's parents, which weren't so mysterious at all. Sylvie's mother's death had been a mystery for a few weeks when it happened all them years ago. Then Leah and those experts from Mobile had pieced together a perfectly fine working plot and followed a few leads that brought them straight to a suspect. One of Eli Brown's parishioners had gone out on his own and done the deed, thinking he was working in the name of God. Eli Brown tended to attract the extremists, and nobody was as extreme as James Richard Cobbler. Even on his way to the chair (known as Yellow Mama in these parts), the man still held that he'd done nothing wrong. He'd been working in the name of the Lord. Well, that was a Lord Leah was happy not to call her own, thank you very much.

Despite how torn up he'd been about losing his wife, even Tom Carson had seemed satisfied with how justice had prevailed once the actual sentence was carried out. The case had been solved, damn it. Shame on Leah for dredging up old memories that were in no need of dredging up.

And Tom Carson's case had never been anything but a suicide. Leah had no idea what made her suddenly decide to turn it into something else. The man had been so depressed he'd spent his life savings on a therapist. He'd even waited until Sylvie wasn't home to kill himself and made sure she wouldn't be the one who found his body; that responsibility fell to a farmhand.

No, so far, all Leah's theories had been mirages. In some ways, she was worse than Sylvie. She'd been jumping at shadows.

She was thinking about all this as she pulled into Sylvie's drive to discover, just as Sylvie had said she would, both cellar doors wide open around the back of the house. And just as Sylvie said, there wasn't any wind, or at least not enough to make that a credible excuse. Besides, last time she was here, Leah felt the way that clasp had tightened. There wasn't any way those doors were blowing open unless Alvin was hit by a twister.

So that meant someone really was coming into Miss Sylvie's backyard. This was hardly any surprise given that the last time Leah was called out someone had obviously been inside her actual house. Leah still found it disquieting how they'd somehow left the place completely locked up behind them. The strange part was the complete lack of any evidence of potential danger. Well, she supposed that mucking around with Sylvie's shotgun showed some disturbing signs—but whoever it was had *dis*armed it. They had made the place safer, not more hazardous.

This time it really seemed as though someone was trying to make Sylvie look like (or think that) she was going crazier than everyone thought she was. Because, if she really did only go inside for a half hour, this whole incident was set up to make it look like she was paranoid and delusional. And, possibly, to make people think she was doing these incidents to herself (which, of course, *had* crossed Leah's mind).

Like before, Leah got down on her hands and knees, and this time she forced back her fears and went partially into the crawl space with her flashlight. The dirt ground was uneven, but there was nothing and nobody down there. Just a bunch of dirt. Again she saw marks in the dirt, but she couldn't tell if they were any different than they had been before. Just like last time, Leah felt a little ashamed for not searching the crawl space properly, but she couldn't bring herself to go in any farther. As it was, her pulse was up. Besides, there didn't appear to be anything down here but probably some spiders stuck in this tight, dark space.

"Well, we've definitely found the source of your fruit-fly problem," Leah said to Sylvie. "They're all comin' from down here in your crawl space." There were flies everywhere beneath the house.

"Why would there be fruit flies in my crawl space if

there ain't no fruit down there?" Sylvie asked. She'd calmed down considerably since Leah had arrived. Leah got the feeling both of them were getting a little too used to this same routine.

Sylvie's question was one Leah couldn't answer. "I don't know, but there ain't no fruit that I can see. Not even a dead possum or anythin' like that. Could be a stray banana peel or somethin' tucked away in one of the corners, maybe."

Just like every other time she showed up at Sylvie's, Leah pulled out her pad and took down an official statement from Sylvie. And just like every other time, Sylvie added in her own editorial comment, this time using Preacher Eli's name in place of "the suspect" or "whoever did it."

"I wasn't gone for not even thirty minutes," Sylvie said. "And Preacher Eli came and opened these doors. God only knows what else the man did."

Leah didn't bother trying to explain that Eli Brown had been with her. Instead, she calmly said, "You don't know for sure *who* is responsible for this, Sylvie. Just remember that. Everyone is innocent until proven guilty."

"I know it's Preacher Eli. *You* might not, but I do." Sylvie was holding the baby, who was sucking on a soother.

Leah let out a breath. "I'm leavin' that out of the statement."

With a shrug, Sylvie said, "Suit yourself."

After she'd taken the report, Leah stood back and examined the doors one more time, wondering who really did it.

The baby started getting fussy and Sylvie said, "I have to go inside and give her the rest of her bottle. I spent all night pumpin' it, so she's gonna drink it. Is that okay? Or do you still need me?"

"No, go ahead. I'm just going to have a look around."

As Sylvie walked back inside, Leah started thinking about all of the different times she'd been called out to Sylvie's lately. First it was for the flowerpots. That one she wrote off as paranoia. Even if it turned out to be someone messing with Sylvie, it was so benign, it wasn't worth putting on the list. But then there were the big ones: the single cellar door being opened; the shotgun being unloaded, and the shells being lined up on the table; the dead cat on the porch; and now both cellar doors being opened.

She squatted back down and swept the cellar again with her flashlight. *Was* there something down here she wasn't seeing? And if there was, why would some-one draw attention to it by leaving the doors open, un-less they *wanted* it found? That made no sense. What *did* make sense was using the doors to make Sylvie *think* she was going nuts.

But who would want to do that?

Part of Leah was disappointed Eli Brown was no longer on the suspect list. He'd fit so well, in so many different ways. Maybe it could still be him. She had called Leland's dad in Alabaster from her car phone on the way over and he had been able to put Leland on the line, so Eli's story about his grandson going home checked out. Could there be a *third* partner?

What about the shotgun? How had they gotten into the house and back out again without any evidence of breaking and entering? There was no way in Leah's mind that she could see Sylvie accidentally leaving a door or a window unlocked, or not noticing if a door was not locked when she got back home. The girl was far too paranoid.

It had to be someone good at picking dead bolts. But in a town of fewer than two thousand people, how many potential suspects do you actually *have*? Again, that's why Eli Brown had been such a great suspect. It was a skill he could've picked up in prison during the past seventeen years.

Unless . . .

Unless it was someone who didn't have to use a door or a window.

Leah stepped back and took in the back of the house. How else could somebody get in?

There were ducts, but they were much too small to crawl in through. There was no fireplace and, besides, was she seriously considering someone coming down the chimney?

No, it had to be a door or a window.

And then it came to her.

And when it did, she had no idea why it had taken this long before she thought of it.

What if the person who broke in had used the door but didn't need to know how to pick locks?

Because, what if the person breaking in *already had a key*?

Now the question was: How many people might have keys to Sylvie Carson's house?

Leah walked in the back door where Sylvie was breast-feeding the baby. "Sylvie?" she asked. "Who has keys to your house?"

"Nobody," Sylvie answered. "I just changed the locks."

"I mean before that."

"Nobody."

"Are you sure?"

"Positive. Why would I give out any keys?"

"What about Orwin?"

There was a long silence while Sylvie considered this. "Actually, I don't know what happened to his key. I doubt he still has it."

Leah had her pad out again and was back to taking notes. "Can I ask you some questions about your relationship? With Orwin?"

Sylvie shrugged, rubbing the back of the baby's neck. "Sure."

"How would you describe it?"

"It was fine. I mean it wasn't perfect, but whose is, right? We had our good days and our bad days."

"Describe a bad day."

"He'd come home from work in a mood or it would be a day when he couldn't find work."

"And . . . ?"

"And he'd usually get drunk and loud. You know."

"Pretend I don't."

"Well, he'd call me names and stuff."

"So he'd get verbally abusive?" Leah asked.

"I guess. Not sure if I'd call it abusive."

"Did he ever get physical with you?"

"What do you mean?"

"Did he ever *hit* you?"

Sylvie looked away.

"I'll take that as a yes."

Sylvie looked back at Leah. "Not very often. And it was usually on account of me doin' somethin' dumb."

"And I'll ignore that completely." Leah jotted down a few more notes on her pad. "Do you know where Orwin is now?"

Sylvie shook her head.

"No idea at all?"

"None."

"Do you know anyone who *might* know? Close friends? Relatives?"

Sylvie looked at the ceiling while she moved the baby higher onto her shoulder so she could burp her. "Well, Orwin does have this aunt he was close to. She lives somewhere in . . . oh, I can't remember."

"He's close to her?"

"Yeah."

"How close?"

"Well, we were short money once and needed rent and he called her and she drove all the way down to lend it to us. She lives, like, four hundred miles away. Somewhere in Arkansas, I think."

"Wow, that's a long way to come to lend someone money. Do you remember her name?"

"His aunt . . . um . . . Jolayne. That's it. Jolayne."

"Did you pay the money back?"

Sylvie finished burping the baby and put her back into cradle position. "What?"

"The money Jolayne lent you. Did you ever pay it back?"

"Yeah. About three weeks later. Orwin drove it back to her."

"You didn't go?"

"No, I stayed here."

"How come?"

Sylvie shrugged. "I dunno. He just told me I didn't have to come and that he'd be fine goin' alone."

Leah put her pad back in her pocket. "Okay, thanks."

"Why are you askin' 'bout Orwin? You gonna try and find him?"

"I might."

"Think you can?"

"Shouldn't be too hard," Leah said. "After all, he still has your car, doesn't he?"

On her way home, Leah's thoughts wandered away from Orwin Thomas and Sylvie Carson and back to her son probably still lying in his bed back home. Leah wasn't mad about his outburst, but she was concerned. She was pretty sure she knew what had driven him to it, and, the truth was, she was going through a similar emotional conflict herself.

It was this whole new family popping up in their lives that was digging up memories of Billy. For Leah, those memories came mixed with anger, guilt, and blame.

He'd been gone ten years, but it'd only been very recently she'd realized she still hadn't gotten over his death. When he died, she took down all his pictures and put them away along with anything else that reminded her of him. Just thinking about him was too painful to bear, so she hid those thoughts away as best she could.

One of the best hiding spots turned out to be behind a big heap of blame. She blamed him for leaving her alone. Blamed him for dying. And that made her angry.

In the first couple years, she had gone to grief counseling, so she knew the drill: five steps of grieving and you have to go through it before you're out of it. Only she couldn't stand to get through the first step. So she stopped the cycle before it even had a chance to start.

It turns out there's a funny thing about grief. It won't be stopped. The cycle will keep going all by itself if you try to keep it bottled up too long.

And the part she hadn't realized was that by hiding Billy's death away from herself, she had taken a daddy away from her children. Especially from Abe. She saw that now, and it was that realization that allowed her to come to terms with needing to resolve Billy's death in her own mind.

Funny, but the therapist said first comes denial, then anger, then bargaining, then depression, and finally acceptance. Somehow that therapist had missed the one thing Leah needed to work out the most. And, in her mind, that was forgiveness. She needed to forgive her husband for dying on her.

But tonight, she had a little boy at home who needed her to push all of this aside and be there for him as his mother and, even if it killed her on the inside, to show him that she accepted his pa's death.

Because her boy wanted nothing more than to know about his pa. And he had every right in the world to get his wish.

CHAPTER 30

By the time my mother returned from Miss Sylvie's, I had stopped crying. I still didn't know why I had flipped out in my front yard. I was starting to think I might have some emotional problems or something like people on TV were always talking about. The worst part was I knew I was in for it the minute I heard her car pull in the driveway. Normally, I couldn't even give my mother the slightest "tone" (a word she used a lot that I didn't rightly understand), and this time, I out-right screamed at her for five whole minutes. I didn't know what was going to happen, but I had never wished I was Dewey so bad in all my life.

I heard every detail as she walked into the house. I listened to her take off her shoes and put away her keys. Then she checked the fridge. She was supposed to make chicken-fried steak and potato salad tonight, but I didn't think she still would. It was getting on quite dark and when I heard Carry come home at least an hour or two ago, I was sure I heard her fixing something to eat before she headed to the living room to watch television.

She never once wondered where I was or, if she knew, why I was in my room. My sister didn't really pay much attention to my life. We got along okay. We still did things together, like the day we made the swords, but I had found that more and more it required a lot of begging on my part to get her to be an active participant.

Or I wound up having to paint her toenails once a week for an entire month. Things like that.

Finally, after what sounded like my mother going through the mail, she left the kitchen and came down the hall. She didn't come right to my room; she went to her own first. I started thinking that maybe she'd forgotten what had happened.

But then I realized nobody could forget all that.

And she hadn't. She was in her room about ten minutes before she came in and sat on the edge of my bed. I was facing away from her, toward the wall with my window. I didn't turn around.

"Abe?" she asked. "You awake?"

Her voice was very calm, which can sometimes be even worse than when she sounds upset, so I've learned not to trust it. I've also learned never to lie to her, so I said, "Yes."

"Will you turn around?"

I turned over in my bed, leaving my head on my pillow. I could feel the stains from my tears still on my face even though it had been at least an hour since I stopped crying.

I expected to see her looking full of anger.

Only she wasn't.

"Are you okay now?" she asked.

Her question confused me. "I—" I started, then answered with, "Yeah."

"Do you know what happened outside?"

I just shook my head. It was the truth.

"I think I do. I think you got a little overwhelmed by everything that's been going on lately."

I hesitated. Was I not going to get in trouble? "What do you mean?"

"Well, first, I think I made a mistake taking you to Eli Brown's that day. Second, this whole thing with your new grandparents and that woman who's your aunt—I reckon it's got you thinkin' 'bout your pa and that's drummed up a bunch of feelin's you just don't know how to handle. And I've been very selfish, not tellin' you things 'bout him. So that's gonna stop. Right here. Right now."

There was something on the bed beside her. She'd brought it in with her. It was something I'd seen before, but not for many years: the shoe box from her closet that I "stole" the picture of my pa from, the one I kept in the drawer beside my bed and carried around in my pocket for good luck.

Seeing it now made my heart start hammering against my chest. What was she going to do?

Slowly, she lifted the top off the box. It was exactly as I remembered it: full of scattered photos of different sizes.

"I want to go through some of these with you, and tell you 'bout them. Tell you how old your pa was when they was taken and where we was and stuff we were doin'. That is, if you want to hear 'bout it?"

I gave her a big smile. "Boy, do I!" Then my throat went dry and felt too tight to get any more words out.

"And then I want you to have them."

I blinked, stunned. "Have what?" I managed to ask.

"The pictures."

"All of them?"

"Yes. As long as you'll take good care of them."

"Yes. I will." I couldn't believe it.

So we went through the pictures one at a time. Some we skipped on account of them being similar to others, but she told me stories about how my pa used to play football with his friends in the afternoons and how they used to go camping and hiking and then after Carry came along how they would take her down to the beach in Mobile and then they'd take me after I came along and how much I loved the waves and the sand. I listened to every word as though it were coming from the Gospels.

Then she reached into the box and stopped talking.

Her face fell sort of flat of emotion. She looked like somebody had just told her some very bad news.

"What is it?"

"Just—I forgot this was here," she said, pulling out a gold ring.

"What is it?"

"My wedding ring. I put it in here when I put the pictures away."

I watched her face, waiting to see if she was going to get angry the way she used to when I would bring up my pa. Or maybe she'd start crying, the way I remembered her doing a long time ago when things would remind her of him.

But she didn't do either. Instead, she just put the ring in her shirt pocket.

"What are you gonna do with it?" I asked.

"I'm not certain," she said. "But you certainly don't need it."

I laughed. "No. I'm happy with the pictures."

"I'm sure I'll find some use for it." Her voice sounded very far away.

"Mom?" I asked after a moment of silence.

She sort of jerked back to my room. "Yeah?"

"You okay?"

She reached down and hugged me. "Yes, I'm fine."

"Mom, when am I gonna meet my new grandma and granddaddy? You said we was going."

Sitting up, she replied, "Whenever I can get time away from work to drive to Georgia. We'll need a whole day. Right now Miss Sylvie's takin' all my time."

I frowned. "Does she have to call the station constantly?"

"Hey!" my mother snapped. "Sometimes people really *do* need the police to help them."

"Does Miss Sylvie?"

She thought that over. "Let's just say I don't think Miss Sylvie's as crazy as other people do." From the way she said it, it was obvious the topic was to be left at that.

It didn't matter; I was more interested in getting back to the photographs, anyway.

We continued going through pictures another thirty minutes or so. Then she asked me if I felt like eating anything. I told her I hadn't had any supper on account of she told me to go straight to my room and stay here until she got back from Miss Sylvie's.

"Well, I have potato salad already made," she said. "Let me quickly fry you up some steak Then I think it's bedtime."

"Okay," I said and got out of bed and followed her to the kitchen with the shoe box full of photos underneath my arm.

While she cooked, I kept looking through the pictures, feeling closer and closer to my pa. I was happy my mother was able to talk about him without getting angry or sad. It seemed to me that must be a definite improvement in the way she was handling him being gone. But then, I was just a kid, so what the heck did I know?

Well, I knew I loved chicken-fried steak and potato salad, which I had two helpings of before putting the pictures safely away in my own bedroom closet and going to bed for the night.

Not much later, Leah decided to go to bed early. During the summer she always went to bed before her daughter, Caroline, who didn't really have a bedtime through the summer break. But tonight Leah retired even earlier than usual.

It was around ten when she walked into her bedroom and turned on the lamp beside her bed. She began undressing so she could get into her pajamas when she remembered the wedding ring she'd put into her pocket earlier on.

Pulling it out now, she stared at it a long while under the soft glow of her bedroom lamp. It brought up strange emotions. A year ago, she wouldn't have been able to hold it in her hands without throwing it. Now, she just felt oddly empty looking at the big O it made.

When Billy died, she could very well have pawned it out. She threw out a lot of things with his memory attached to them, but something had made her keep this ring. There must've been a reason. She had hidden it away, but she'd kept it nonetheless.

Now the ring more intrigued her than upset her.

She had no idea what to do with it now that she'd given the shoe box to Abe. So, gingerly, she placed it on the table beside her bed right beneath her lamp, where it continued to sparkle in the warmth of the golden glow.

By the time she woke up the next day, she'd forgotten it was even there.

CHAPTER 31

The first thing Leah did after getting back to work was call directory assistance up in Arkansas and ask for all the numbers they had matching any Jolayne Thomases. She was given five.

She dialed the first one and nobody answered.

She called the second, asked to speak to Orwin, and was told, "I don't know no Orwin."

On the third try, she got lucky.

"He's out of town," the woman on the other end said. Her voice was deep and gruff. "Who is this, anyway? If you one of his ex-girlfriends you ain't got no business callin' here. How'd you get this number?"

Leah just hung up. "Yeah, he's not in town," she said to herself, "on account of him bein' here in Alvin."

"You say somethin'?" Chris asked from the desk beside her. He was doing the crossword in the newspaper.

"Nothin' important."

Using her computer, she looked up the area code of the telephone number she'd just called and discovered it was in Pine Bluff. That was another good use for the computer; it could do reverse phone numbers for most telephone listings in and around Alabama and had information for every area code in the country. Putting in another call to the Pine Bluff sheriff's office, she told them who she was, gave them her badge and station number, and asked if she could acquire information on Jolayne Thomas.

"You got more than just a name for us to go on?" the officer at the other end asked. He sounded a bit put out by her request.

"I got her telephone number." She gave it to him.

"So, what sorta stuff you lookin' for?"

Leah had learned from what happened with Tom Carson. *Don't overlook anything.* "Everything," she said. "Financial records, medical records, a background check, the works."

"You wanna know what size of panties she wears?"

Leah didn't laugh. "I'd really appreciate the favor if you could do this for me."

"This information *that* important to you?"

"Yes," she said. "I think it may be."

She heard him sigh. "All right. Let me see what I can do. What's your fax number?"

Luckily, Ethan had gone out and replaced the busted fax machine last week so she had a number to give him that would work.

"Some of this stuff is gonna take some time," the officer said. "I'm gonna have to make some calls. It's gonna take a while. You want me to send everythin' at once after I get it all, or would you rather have it in bits and drabs as it comes in?"

"I'll take it as it comes, if that's all right with you."

Another sigh. "Doesn't matter to me either way."

Leah thanked him again for his time and hung up, hoping the officer would actually do what he said he was going to do.

After the call into the sheriff's office, Leah wasted no time in getting on to her next task: running a background check on Orwin Thomas. Opening the cabinet containing the five hundred or so gray five-and-a-quarter-inch floppy discs that made up their station's computer database, she found the one listed in the T section between Ta and Tm. If they had any data on the computer for Orwin Thomas, this would be where she'd uncover it.

Returning to her desk, she slipped the disk into the drive and waited while the computer read it. It chunked and whirred like it always did. Pulling up data on the computers wasn't fast, but it was a helluva lot faster than going through drawers of file folders. She only hoped someone had entered the information from the file folder onto the disc.

While she waited, she chided herself for not considering Orwin a suspect immediately.

The goddamn house was still locked when Sylvie came home, Leah, she thought. *Why didn't you think of him right away? Why did it take so long to consider it might just be someone with a key?*

She knew the answer. It was because she had Eli Brown on the brain. And Sylvie was partially to blame for that, and so was Leah's son. But that was no excuse. *It shouldn't have mattered; you're a goddamn detective. Do your job.*

Eli Brown was an innocent man in all this whose father-in-law managed to finagle a ranch at such low cost there wasn't any chance of even a dime being left over for anything even remotely resembling an inheritance for Sylvie. The bank wouldn't even have got half of what was owed to them on the place.

When the background check finally loaded, it was full of surprises and yet, at the same time, none of them really surprised Leah at all.

The first surprise was how much information on Orwin Thomas was available on the computer. Someone (likely Chris) had gone through all his files and entered everything into the system. That made things a lot easier. As an adult, Orwin Thomas's record was absolutely clean, but his record as an adolescent was another story. It showed three counts of theft, one with aggravated assault, one count of possession, and "a noted history of fighting."

Unfortunately, because he was a minor, it was a juvenile record, and it was frustratingly vague.

"Chris?" Leah asked.

"Yeah." Chris had just returned from using the "facilities" and swung around in his chair so he was facing her. He had back-straddled it.

"I need you to work some magic for me."

"What kind?"

"That thing you can do with juvey records?"

"You mean get all the dirt?"

"Yeah, I need you to do that."

"Just give me a name," he said.

"Orwin Thomas."

"Orwin Thomas? Star tight end? Torn ACL?"

"That'd be the one."

"You suspect the superstar might not be so shiny?"

"Well, his adult record looks like it's been Turtle Waxed it's so clean, but from what I can see, there are hints that his juvey one might show a different picture."

"I'm on it." Chris grabbed a handful of floppy discs from the database cabinet and began inserting them into his computer one after another while madly typing away. Soon, he began making telephone calls, receiving calls, and receiving faxes. This was something the man truly had a gift for. Leah had no idea how he did it. He must have connections in all the right places because, literally, less than an hour later, he put a compiled report in Leah's hands.

"Okay," she said. "Sometimes you really do astound me."

"Oh, I bet you say that to all the boys."

"Warn me now, anything I'm not gonna like in here?"

"Depends on whether you're lookin' to nail him to the wall or to a cross."

"Okay . . . that sounds interesting. I'll leave it as a surprise."

The reports outlined everything and more.

Orwin Thomas got caught twice stealing from Applesmart's Grocery, and he once walked into Fast Gas with a tire iron and asked the person behind the register to empty it into a bag. He also got caught for possession. It was just a small amount of marijuana, but it was enough to almost get him tried in adult court (he'd been seventeen years old at the time).

There were also five separate incidents of fighting where police were called to the scene, although no arrests were made. Still, the report definitely showed a notable history of violence in his teen years. And these were only the fights where the police showed up. Leah was certain there were probably many more that went unreported.

The first happened when Orwin was fourteen and

the last was when he was eighteen. Even at eighteen, no legal action had been taken against him.

Twice when he was brought in on the other charges he was evaluated by a psychologist, a different doctor each time. The first one said Orwin showed violent outbreaks throughout their discussion and acted angrily toward some of the questions being asked. The report said the doctor found this pattern "disturbing" and that Orwin displayed an inherent distrust of authority figures.

The second psychologist suggested that Orwin showed signs of mental illness and even went so far as to say, at times, his behavior was borderline psychopathic in nature. The report stated, if left untended, Orwin's mental condition could grow into a potential risk to himself or others.

Orwin had been seventeen when that second assessment had been made. He'd managed to stay out of trouble ever since.

This fact did little to comfort the empty hollow expanding inside Leah's gut as she read.

She paged down to a list of Orwin's known associates and saw the usual suspects. Even for being a small town, Alvin had its share of troubled teens, just like everywhere else. And they tended to flock together like black sheep.

Then her eyes settled on one name in particular: Darius "Dee Bee" Baylor. Leah wasn't sure what it was, but something about that name was setting off alarm bells in her head.

"Chris?"

"Mmm?"

"Where have I heard the name Darius Baylor 'fore?"

"Dee Bee? He was part of that takedown I made.

Remember? *The Biggest Bust in Dixie?* I think that's what the *Alerter* called it." He smiled smugly.

"Oh, right. Now I remember."

Leaning back in his chair, Chris interlaced his fingers, pushed out his arms, and cracked his knuckles. "Yep," he said. "Four of *them. One* of me. *Incredible* odds."

"So I heard," Leah said, as disinterestedly as possible. "Like I said, you're a superhero."

The fax machine began slowly rolling out a thin sheet of paper. Chris got up out of his chair and, with an arrogant sashay to his step that made Leah wish she'd never asked about Darius Baylor, he strutted over and patiently watched each page crawl out and curl onto the gray carpet.

Picking up the cover sheet, he said, "Financial records for someone named Jolayne Thomas livin' in Pine Bluff, Arkansas? This for you?"

"That was quick," she said. "And you were sittin' right here beside me just over an hour ago when I made the call askin' for the records. Didn't you hear me?"

He shrugged. "Guess I wasn't listenin'."

Chris continued watching as each separate page crept from the machine and curled up onto the floor.

"You know watchin' it don't make it go any faster," Leah said.

"I know. I just find technology fascinatin' is all."

Finally, when it was all finished, Chris brought all the sheets to Leah's desk and handed them to her. She scanned them and quickly concluded things weren't exactly right with Jolayne Thomas.

At one time, near on a year ago, the woman had a

fair amount of money in the bank—just over a hundred grand.

But since then, she had drawn almost all of it out. And it came out in just three lump sums. The first happened pretty near ten months ago and was for the curious round number of seventy-five thousand dollars. The other two were for amounts around fifteen thousand dollars each, and both happened in the past six months.

There was another interesting tidbit of information inside these pages. Jolayne Thomas had two credit cards, but they were both attached to the same account. One was in her own name, and the other was in the name of Orwin James Thomas.

"Well, that answers *that* question," Leah said.

"What question?" Chris asked. He was back at his desk, more interested in what Leah was doing than his crossword.

Instead of answering him, Leah focused on that seventy-five-thousand-dollar withdrawal. She jotted down the date and did a quick calculation in her head. Despite what she'd wanted to tell Chris, she remembered his coke bust well. She knew exactly when it had happened. And this withdrawal took place within a week before that time. *And* now that she thought about it (and again, this was something she couldn't believe she was only thinking of now), Orwin Thomas had disappeared from Sylvie's life the day after Chris brought in those four guys and all them drugs.

Her brain quickly put two and two together. Orwin Thomas had once been a pretty big high school football superstar. He'd have connections. She was willing to bet one of those connections offered him an investment he couldn't turn down. Buy low, sell high. Easy money for Orwin, who was in need of some easy money. He just needed to find the funding for the deal.

That would be where Miss Jolayne came into the picture.

"When you, you know," she asked Chris, "single-handedly caught them guys with those drugs, you found money on them too, right?"

"Sure did," he said. "About sixty-three thousand dollars. Them DEA guys that come up from Mobile figured they musta sold some of that coke 'fore I managed to nail 'em."

"Hmm."

"Hmm, what?" Chris asked.

She searched his eyes. "What would you say if I told you I think I know who bought it?"

Chris gave a little laugh. "I'd say I wish you woulda known that ten months ago so I coulda caught him with it and put him away, too."

Leah mulled this over. Orwin was back in Alvin, and there had to be a reason he was back, and it wasn't just to get Sylvie all riled up. No, that part was a distraction, Leah figured. Orwin probably thought that if Sylvie called the police enough times with false alarms that the police would stop coming out and that would make her place a lot safer to get in and out of.

Leah turned her attention back to Chris. "I think he still has them. The drugs, I mean."

Chris gave another little laugh. "Now you're just teasin'."

"I reckon it was Orwin Thomas who bought 'em and when you made them arrests he got scared that one of them guys you put behind bars was gonna go on and tell you who they sold it to, so he hid the stuff and left town. And now, I think he's come back to get 'em."

"Why now?"

That was a good question. Leah considered it. "I don't rightly know. Maybe enough time has gone by that he no longer feels afraid that someone's gonna squeal on him." The dwindling balance left on the financial records sitting in front of her popped off the page. "Maybe he needs the money, so he needs to sell 'em."

"Okay, so where did he hide them?"

This one didn't take much thought. Orwin had come and checked to make sure his stash was still there once and not closed the crawl space door properly behind him. That's why the wind had blown it open.

"Under Sylvie's house. In the cellar," she said. Then she remembered the last time Sylvie had called her out to show her both doors thrown wide open. That hadn't been because of Orwin checking anything and not closing something properly. "Only," she said, "I think we're too late. I think he's already got them."

"Because he left those cellar doors open?" Chris asked.

"Mmm-hmm."

"Why wouldn't he close them on his way out?"

"Two reasons, I reckon," Leah answered. "One, he didn't need to. He got what he was after. But the second is more disturbin' to me. For one reason or another, Orwin Thomas is tryin' to make Sylvie Carson look crazier than she is. Or make her more paranoid than she is." And the scariest part about that to Leah was that the man knew she had a loaded shotgun leaning up beside her back door.

Chris was already halfway out of his chair, grabbing

his keys and heading for the door by the time Leah finished her sentence. "Well, we're damn well gonna check and make sure those drugs ain't still there," he said. "Come on. You can come with me in the cruiser."

It was midmorning when they arrived at Sylvie's. They found her home, running around like a dog chasing its own tail. For once, the baby wasn't sleeping. In fact, it was downright cranky, and didn't seem to want to eat, or be burped, or be held, or be put down. Or nothing. Even Leah gave it a try.

"Well, I don't know what she wants," Leah said, handing her back to Sylvie.

"Let's go check that cellar," Chris said, walking past.

Leah followed him outside. Sylvie trailed behind, baby wailing in her arms.

"So, which of us is goin' under?" Leah asked nervously.

Chris gave a small chuckle as he opened the cellar doors and shined his flashlight inside. "It's just dirt. Doesn't even look wet. It does look like someone's been under here recently, though. What are you 'fraid of, spiders?"

"I ain't afraid of nothin'," Leah said, not wanting to admit he'd hit half the equation directly on the bull's-eye. "I just don't relish the thought of bein' squashed up in that two-foot-high space while I wiggle round like a snake searchin' out the area."

"That's okay, I wanna go anyway. If the coke *is* down here, this is still part of my bust."

Leah let that one go by. Far as she could tell, she'd done all the work.

"It's all yours," she said.

Chris started to go in stomach first. He made it in about as far as his feet, then turned around and came back out.

"What's wrong?" Sylvie asked from the porch.

"Nothin'. I think it would be better to go in on my back."

He went at it again, on his back this time. It did seem to give him more leverage with his feet. Soon he was out of sight. Leah squatted down and watched through the doors, but all she could make out was the occasional sweep of his flashlight. Then, from beneath the house came a loud, "Eww!"

"What is it?" Leah called out, a little worried.

"Found the cat puke!"

More time passed while his light went from one side of the house to the next. After about fifteen minutes, he finally yelled, "I found something!"

"What?"

"Looks like . . . bags of coffee. Twelve of 'em. All stuffed around in a circle. The middle of the circle is empty, but it looks like it used to have somethin' in it. I'm guessing that's where the coke was. There's a white powder sprinkled all around the outside of the ring of coffee bags."

"Is it coke?"

A pause and then, "No. I think it's brodifacoum. Orwin was probably worried about rats getting into his drugs. It was a good thing to be worried 'bout too, on account of it looks like they got into at least two of the sacks of coffee. There's fruit flies everywhere."

"Well, that explains why they're under your house," Leah said to Sylvie.

"I think that's it," Chris said. "There ain't nothing else under here."

"Okay," Leah said, "You may as well come out then."

"I don't understand," Sylvie said. "Why is there sacks of coffee in my cellar?"

"Because your ex-boyfriend is a dumb shit," said Chris, pulling himself through the crawl space doors. Standing up, he brushed dirt off his uniform. He turned and let Leah get the dirt off the back. Most of it cleared away, but there was some that would stay until his uniform was properly washed. "Sometimes drug traffickers pack cocaine in coffee to throw drug dogs off the scent in airports."

"Does that work?"

"Hell if I know. But I have no idea why he thought using coffee under your house was a good idea. I guess he suspected we might come round with some airport drug dogs and send them into your cellar lookin' for coke. Unfortunately, the closest thing to that happening was your cat goin' in when that door was left open and eatin' some of that brodifacoum."

Sylvie looked about ready to cry. "That bastard killed my cat. He killed my goddamn cat."

Leah came up and gave her a hug. "Hey, at least you don't have to worry 'bout him comin' round here no more. He'll be gettin' outta Dodge as quick as a cat with its tail on fire. If he even suspects we're onto him, he won't hang round Alvin a minute longer than he has to, and I got a hunch Orwin's a pretty suspicious guy. When we made all them arrests last year, he was gone before the sun came up." She looked Sylvie straight in the eyes. "You're safe now. This is the last place he'll turn up again."

"Yeah," Chris said. "If he's smart, he'll stay as far away from Alvin as he can possibly get." He thought for a moment, and then turned to Leah. "Which reminds me. I better call the DEA in Arkansas and give them a heads-up on what's goin' on. He probably won't be stupid enough to keep the stuff at his house, but I bet they'll put him under surveillance and, sooner or later, catch him tryin' to push it."

"What 'bout the guys you arrested?" Leah asked. "Can't you get one of them to swear to selling it to him? Might be enough to take him in on. Then I've got Jolayne's financial records . . ."

"Maybe. They'd want a deal, though. I'd have to talk to the DA. Right now, we need all the states between here and Arkansas to issue an APB on the plates to Sylvie's Skylark he's driving."

"I'll get that done," Leah said. "Although, he took the stuff out of here. He's gone. No question 'bout it."

CHAPTER 32

Leah decided to take the kids out for supper at Vera's Old West Grill at the west end of Main Street. It had been a while since they'd been out together as a family. Two days ago, all the stress of the Orwin Thomas case she'd been working on had come to a rather unsatisfying end. Sure, the law would probably eventually catch up to Orwin Thomas, but Leah wanted it to happen here and she wanted to be part of it. She wanted to show Sylvie that the bad guys don't always get away. She thought it might help with the girl's paranoia. At any rate, Leah thought the next best thing was to spend some quality family time and just get out of the house for a nice meal and unwind a bit.

The weather was horrible. Rain washed through the town, and black clouds hung so low and heavy in the sky they seemed like they might almost touch the tops of some buildings.

At dinner, the kids appeared to enjoy themselves. At least they weren't arguing—not *really* arguing, anyway—which was a welcome change. They did banter back and forth a lot, but that was something they always did, whether they were happy or not.

Abe had ordered a hamburger and fries, and Caroline had gotten barbecued ribs with coleslaw and white bread. Leah ordered a sirloin steak, medium well.

"So are you kids enjoyin' your summer?"

"I was," Abe said.

"Not anymore?" Leah asked.

"Not so much. I ain't got my sword."

"That's cuz you broke it," Caroline said. She had barbecue sauce all around her lips. Her fingers were covered in it, too.

"How do *you* know I broke it?" Abe asked her.

"Dewey told me. He was outside in our backyard having a sword fight by himself and I asked him where the heck you were, and he said he didn't know and that it didn't matter anyway on account of you broke your sword over your knee cuz you threw a little fit."

"It wasn't a fit."

"What was it then? Dewey said it was a fit. He called you a girl."

I was surprised my sister didn't consider that a sexist remark. "Dewey says lotsa stuff that ain't true. You know, he thinks he's a genius." Abe took such a big bite of his burger, Leah was worried he might choke on it.

"Maybe he is," Caroline said. "Ever thought of that?"

Abe laughed. "You've *met* Dewey, right? He tried to get satellite TV by using up all our aluminum foil."

"At least he *tries* stuff. He's smart for tryin'. Don't you think so, Mother?" Caroline put a rib in her mouth and pulled out a clean bone and set it upon her plate.

"Leave me out of this."

"Mom don't like Dewey," Abe said. "She thinks he's weird."

"I never said that."

"You have too. Lotsa times."

Leah cut off a piece of steak and had it ready on her fork to go into her mouth. "Well, he's a bit *different* at times," she said. "But I've never said I don't like him." She put the steak in her mouth.

"Well, I *like* Dewey," Caroline said. "I find him quite interestin' and entertainin'."

"I like Dewey well enough," Abe said. "If I didn't, why would I hang round with him?"

"On account of you only have one friend?" Caroline laughed.

"That's not true."

"It's not? Name two more."

"I can name lots more. I just don't wanna."

"You're so full of shit your eyes are brown."

"Hey!" Leah snapped. "Language."

" 'Sides," Abe said, "my eyes are blue. Just like my pa's were, ain't that right, Mom?" He took another bite of burger. He was definitely starting to grow up. There was a time not so long ago when Leah could remember Abe not being able to get through half a Vera's Texas Burger. Now tonight it looked like he might finish this one entirely.

"That's right," Leah said.

Caroline studied Leah as if her hair had turned into rattlesnakes. "You're talking 'bout Pa now?"

Leah smiled. "We're testin' the waters."

"Huh," Caroline said. "That's new. It's a nice change. I miss him sometimes."

"I do too, honey," Leah said sadly.

"I wish I could," Abe said. "You guys are lucky to have known him good enough to miss him."

Leah's heart almost broke then. "I'm sorry."

On that note, they all went back to finishing up their food.

The rain was coming down like marbles being poured out of a bucket from somewhere in heaven when they walked outside of the restaurant. Luckily, they weren't parked far away, or they'd all have been soaked by the time Leah quickly unlocked the car doors and everyone piled inside. As usual, Caroline got the front seat and Abe got in the back.

"Boy, am I full," he said, lying across the cushions as if the entire backseat were a sofa.

But Leah shushed him. As soon as she opened her door, she immediately heard Chris on her radio trying to reach her. Quickly, she picked it up and answered it. "Chris. It's me. What's up?"

"Leah! I've been trying to reach you for half an hour."

"Sorry, I was out for dinner with the kids. What's up?"

"Well, it was one thing, then it became two things, and now it's three things."

"Uh-oh. Sounds like a disaster. Go ahead." Leah didn't start the car, she just sat there, parked, talking on the radio. The rain continued pelting the windshield. It made a ruckus, splattering on the roof of the car.

"First, we got a credit card transaction flag for Orwin Thomas for a purchase he made *yesterday*."

"Okay."

"Ask me where he made it."

"Where?"

"Fast Gas. In *Alvin*."

"In *Alvin*? Why the hell is he still *here*?"

"Well, we don't know if he's *still* here. It looks like he filled his tank, so he may have been heading back to Pine Bluff. But he was here yesterday."

"Why would he have hung round all this time? He got them drugs *days* ago."

"I can't answer that."

Leah's mind raced. It made no sense. He should have left town immediately upon getting what he came for. It was the only logical thing to do. *And people always do the most logical thing, unless there are other variables at play you don't know about.* Now *that* was the detective in her thinking.

"What's the second thing?"

"About fifteen or twenty minutes ago Miss Sylvie called."

"What did she want?" *This is new,* Leah thought. *Chris calling her* Miss *Sylvie.*

"She said she reckoned she saw the shadow of someone outside her house lookin' in her window."

"Was she panicky?"

"She sounded a little upset."

"Did you go check it out?"

"Er—" Chris stumbled. "No."

"Did Ethan go?"

"No."

"Why didn't anyone go? If you can't get hold of me, it's your responsibility to go."

"I just, um, figured since you've always gone before that you'd want to be the one to go this time." He sounded fumbly and embarrassed and Leah was glad. He deserved to be embarrassed.

"Okay, I'll stop in there on my way home. Now, what's the third thing? Your things are gettin' me progressively more and more irked, by the way."

"Not my intention."

"I know."

"Third thing is you got another fax. This one is the medical records for Jolayne Thomas in Pine Bluff, Arkansas."

"Do you mind givin' me the highlights? Go from most recent events first and head backward please."

"That's easy. This year there's only two things of note, really, an' they're both the same thing."

"What's that?"

"She had two visits to some place in Little Rock called Forever Fertility. The last one was just shy of two months ago and the time before that was around four months ago."

"Sounds like a fertility clinic. That explains the two fifteen-thousand-dollar withdrawals from her account. So Miss Jolayne's tryin' to have herself a baby."

"Yeah, but by the looks of this, it don't seem like she's havin' much success." Chris laughed.

A thought suddenly struck Leah like a brick bein' dropped on her from a fourth-story window. "Oh dear God," she said.

"What is it?"

"Chris, I gotta go. I'll radio back when I can."

"Um . . . okay."

Cutting off their conversation, Leah clipped the radio back into its holder and started the car. "Buckle up, kids."

"Aw," Abe complained from the backseat. "But I'm so full."

Reaching down beneath her console, Leah pulled

out her blue-and-red light and plunked it on the dash. It lit up the street around them. The falling rain reflected the light like colored sheets. She hit the siren. "I don't care," she told Abe. "This might be a bumpy ride."

"You ain't takin' us to a crime scene, are you?" Caroline asked from beside her, quickly clipping her seat belt on while Leah peeled out off the curb and did a U-turn right in the middle of the street.

"I dunno yet," Leah said. "I just might be."

"Do you really think that's a good idea?"

"Oh, trust me," Abe said. "After a while, you get used to it."

Leah picked up the big telephone that sat in the console of her vehicle and dialed Sylvie Carson's home number. "Please don't let me be too late," she said under her breath as she heard it ring on the other end. "Please, God, don't let me be too late."

Leah had realized during her talk with Chris that Orwin had indeed come back for his drugs, but he'd also come back for something else. There was a reason he'd been trying to make Sylvie look insane. He'd been trying to make her look like an unfit mother, but it hadn't happened fast enough for him. He'd tried pushing her over the edge, but what he hadn't realized was that Sylvie was already so far over the edge there wasn't much farther for her to go. She was used to living over the edge, if that was even possible. So used to it, Orwin Thomas had failed to make her any crazier.

But now, Leah knew, with a full tank of gas, Orwin was ready to finish the job he'd come down from Arkansas for and then truly get out of town. And the real job hadn't just been to get his drugs. That had been *half* of it. The other half was to get something else. Something much more precious than seventy-five-thousand-dollars' worth of cocaine. Something Joylane wanted for her very own but couldn't have, and so Orwin Thomas was going to provide her with one.

And that thing was Sylvie's three-month-old baby girl.

CHAPTER 33

Thank the Lord Jesus Sylvie Carson not only had a telephone in her bedroom, but she answered it. As soon as she did, Leah heard more panic in the girl's voice than she ever had before. Sylvie was scared practically to the brink of her last breath of life.

"Sylvie, it's Leah. Listen to me, now. I think you and the baby are in danger." Leah was driving as fast as she could. Her siren wailed and her red and blue lights danced in the darkness. Still, it was a treacherous night to be driving fast and she had to be careful. The last thing she needed was to get into a crash. That would only guarantee she didn't make it to Sylvie's on time. Plus she had her kids in the car with her.

"Leah!" Sylvie said, nearly screaming into the phone. Her voice was quivering. The baby wailed in the background. "I—I've been trying to call the station, but I—I left the phone number in the kitchen . . . I—I'm locked in my bedroom. It's . . . it's Preacher Eli! He's at the door! He's—" Her words cut off. She was too panicked to talk.

Goddamn it, Leah was too late.

"What's goin' on, Sylvie?" Leah asked. "Talk to me. Slow down."

"He's tryin' to get in! He's comin' at it with an ax or somethin'!" Sylvie yelled. "The door. My goddamn front door!"

Shit. Leah had seen that door enough times. *That door ain't gonna stand up to an ax very long.*

"Listen to me, Sylvie. I might not get there in time. It's not Eli. It's Orwin. He's come for your baby." Rain pounded the windshield of Leah's car, making it hard to see and forcing her to drive more slowly than she wanted to. Everything outside was awash in rain and went by in streaks.

"Orwin? He's come back?" Suddenly, Sylvie's entire demeanor changed. This wasn't good. Leah needed her to stay scared.

"Yes," Leah said. "But he's come back to hurt you and take your baby. Sylvie! Listen to me. You say you're in your bedroom?"

"Y—yes." Good. At least the panic was back.

"With the door locked?"

"Of . . . of course."

"You have the baby?"

"Yes."

"And . . . Sylvie?" Leah asked. "Do you have your shotgun?"

A hesitation. Then, "Yes. Do you think Orwin has a gun?"

"I don't know," Leah said. She was about to say that if Orwin had a gun he'd probably have already used it to shoot the lock out of the door, but she decided not to. Thank God Sylvie had had her locks changed.

Leah passed a road marker, her dashboard flasher lighting it up blue and red on this horrible night. She remembered the kids in the car and cursed under her breath. She still had near on two miles to go. She wasn't going to make it in time at this rate. But it was going to be close.

Leah decided she had to tell Sylvie something important, just in case. Something she actually couldn't believe she was about to say. "Listen to me carefully, Sylvie," Leah said. "I may not make it there in time. Do you understand?"

"Oh God . . ." Sylvie said.

"Sylvie, listen. If I don't get there, it's up to you. You've *got* to protect that baby, understand? You have to save your child, and her mother. *At whatever cost it takes.*"

"I don't know if I can." Sylvie's voice cracked in a loud whisper. "My hands are shaking something fierce. I can hear him pounding on the outside door. It ain't gonna stand up much longer."

Damn it.

"You *have* to," Leah said. In the darkness, trees whipped past both sides of the car. The heavy dark clouds made everything nearly impossible to see on this dark rain-soaked night; all Leah made out was just what reflected back in red and blue. Occasionally, a streetlamp roared by, its light blurred because of the rainwater on the car's windows. There wasn't a lot of other traffic on the roads. For that, Leah was thankful.

"I don't know *how,*" Sylvie said. "I keep thinkin' about what happened to Caleb."

"What happened to your brother is *why* you have to do this."

Silence. And then, "I'm scared."

"I know you are," Leah said. "So am I. I'm coming as fast as I can."

Leah knew she had to take a break from this call and contact the station for backup, but she didn't know how to do it without causing Sylvie to completely break down. "Listen, Sylvie? I need to radio the station. I'm not gonna hang up, but I need you to just sit tight one minute. Can you do that?"

"No! Don't go!"

"Okay, okay." Leah thought hard. Then she said to her daughter, "Caroline, pick up the radio and get Chris on the line. Tell him I need backup at Sylvie's house. Him *and* Ethan. Tell him it's a ten thirty-five."

"What?"

"Just do it!"

"Okay." Caroline picked up the radio. As Leah continued to fumble through her pep talk with Sylvie she heard her daughter convince Chris she was who she said she was and that she wasn't kidding around. Part of Leah became very proud of her in that moment.

"I hear him," Sylvie said. "Now he's bootin' the door."

"Sylvie?" Leah asked. She could tell the girl was on the verge of breaking down.

There was no response.

"Sylvie!"

"Yeah," she finally answered. She was out of breath. The night around Leah's car seemed to close in and grow even darker as she approached the edge of town.

"You can do this."

"I can do this."

Leah was coming up fast on the end of Main Street where the railroad tracks were, right before the turnoff to Old Mill Road, which was only a few minutes from Sylvie's house. But a train was coming. In fact, it was almost at the road.

Leah's brain scrambled to make a decision. The rain streaming down made it look like Leah had more clearance than she actually did, and she slammed her foot heavy on the gas pedal.

For a moment, all she saw was Caroline silhouetted in the train engine's white light. "Mom!" Caroline screamed.

Leah's heart felt like a wet bag trying to beat its way free from her rib cage. With barely a foot to spare, the car bolted over the tracks as the train rumbled past behind them. She'd made it, but the train would definitely slow down Chris and Ethan. They would be at least five to ten minutes behind her.

Cranking the wheel sharply to the left, Leah fishtailed onto Old Mill Road and flew up the curvy, wet street. Leah's pulse slowed a touch as she tried to catch her breath.

"Oh my God!" Caroline said, breathing hard. "That was crazily close."

Abe just sat in the backseat. If he'd noticed the train at all, he didn't let on.

"Sylvie?" Leah said, the phone still to her ear. "You can save your baby. Your brother would want you to."

Leah heard a loud *crack!* Sylvie cried, "He's broken down the front door!"

Now all that was left between Sylvie and her baby and Sylvie's psychopathic ex was a locked bedroom door not nearly as thick as the one he'd just made it through.

And still the rain continued to hammer Leah's car. Her headlights barely lit up the road ten feet in front of her. The rest was showered away into darkness by the deluge of rain.

"Oh my God!" Sylvie shrieked. "He's coming!" Her fear flooded through the line as Leah heard Sylvie's phone drop to the floor. Leah listened hard. She heard Sylvie say Orwin's name, but after that, all she heard was the sound of Orwin yelling. It crackled in her car phone's speaker and didn't stop until . . .

One gunshot.

Then . . .

Then there was nothing else.

Just silence.

The phone went dead.

CHAPTER 34

Leah's car bounced into Sylvie's driveway, her red-and-blue light giving the house and surrounding trees a surrealistic glow. She'd passed Sylvie's old Skylark that Orwin had taken off in parked about a half mile down the road, positioned discreetly off to the side—barely visible in this torrent of rain. She already had her seat belt undone and her door partially open as she threw her vehicle into PARK and raced to the front door of the house, pulling out her gun along the way. "You kids stay down on the floor of the car!" she shouted back. "You hear me? I'm talking specifically to *you,* Abe. And in the name of *Jesus,* do not get out of that car!"

The rain had turned the dirt drive to muck. From somewhere inside the house came the wailing of the baby, nearly screaming at the top of its lungs. Leah so rarely heard that baby cry that she immediately took it as a bad sign.

This was not a time to wait for backup. She was going in alone.

The front door of the house was swung partially open. In its center was a huge hole full of wooden splinters where Orwin obviously came through with the ax. On the side of the porch, there was just enough room for Leah to stand with her back against the siding along the edge of the door without being in the doorway. She stood there, feet at shoulder width apart, with her gun pointed down at a forty-five-degree angle, ready to be raised and fired.

"Alvin Police!" she called out as loudly and commandingly as she possibly could. "Whoever's inside, identify yourself!" Then, for good measure, she added, "The house is surrounded."

She didn't expect an answer. What she expected was a gunfight, but she knew Orwin was young and probably working alone. She was experienced and a pretty good shot. She liked the odds.

There was no answer, just like she figured. Just the continued screaming of the baby. At least *she* was okay and sounded as though she was still in the back bedroom. Leah decided to give Orwin one more chance before she turned and started shooting into the house. "Alvin Police!" she hollered again. "This is your last chance!"

Then she heard it. And it wasn't what she expected at all. It was the gentle sobbing of a girl. Leah could barely make it out over the noise of the baby shrieking. From the sobs, she heard Sylvie's voice nervously call out, "I—it's me, Miss Leah. Sylvie. I—I'm in the bedroom."

"Where's Orwin?" Leah yelled back.

"Lyin' beside me. I—I shot him. I think he's dead."

"Where's his gun?"

"I—I don't know. I never saw no gun. J—just the ax."

"Where's the ax?"

"Lyin' beside him."

"Throw the ax down the hall toward the living room," Leah called back.

There was a pause and some stumbling then a loud clump. It didn't sound like Sylvie had managed to toss the ax very far.

"Was there anyone with Orwin?"

"I—I don't think so."

"Okay. Sylvie? I'm comin' in." In the distance, over the cries of the baby, Leah heard Chris's and Ethan's sirens getting closer.

Leah turned into the open doorway and braced to take a shot. With her left arm, she gently pushed the door open so she could see more of the living room. She took a step into the house, making a circle with her gun ready. The living room was clear.

She got to the kitchen and did the same. The kitchen was clear.

She saw the ax laying a third of the way down the hall from Sylvie's bedroom. Slowly making her way toward it, Leah got to the ax and lifted it up. She tossed it the rest of the way to the living room. It landed with a very loud *thunk!*

Unlike the front door, Sylvie's bedroom door looked like it only took one or two swings of the ax to get through. It had popped open at the latch. Leah gently pushed it all the way open, keeping her gun ready in case she was looking at a hostage situation, and Sylvie had just been answering what Orwin had been wanting her to answer.

But that wasn't the case.

Leah found Sylvie crouching in the corner, the crying baby held tightly in her arms. Lying on the floor about six feet from her, at the foot of the bed, was Orwin's body, faceup, his arms outstretched between the bed and the wall, a hole in his chest where the shot from the shotgun entered his body.

Squatting beside him, Leah felt for a pulse, even though from the looks of the body there was no need. She could see the carpet of Sylvie's bedroom floor through the hole the shell left behind. Nobody could look like that and be alive.

"Is he dead?" Sylvie asked softly, still cowering in the corner.

Leah nodded. "Very." She went over and knelt beside Sylvie and the baby. "How are you? Are you okay?"

Sylvie nodded.

"And the baby?" The baby was still crying.

"She's okay." Sylvie was cradling her, rocking her gently. The baby's crying slowed down and she grew quieter.

Sylvie stared at Orwin's body, wide-eyed and terrified.

Leah wrapped her arms around Sylvie and the baby, rocking them both together. "It's okay, honey. It's over. He can't hurt you now."

"I know."

Leah pulled away and looked in Sylvie's speckled blue eyes. "You *sure* you're okay?"

She just nodded quickly, biting her lower lip.

"Absolutely sure?"

"I *will* be."

Leah's lips formed a thin smile. "You *will* be." It was the most positive thing she'd ever heard the girl say.

"So it wasn't Preacher Eli after all? All this time?" Sylvie asked.

Leah shook her head. They were pressed up against the white heating radiator that stood along the bedroom wall. "No, hon. That man wants only one thing," she said. "Forgiveness."

Sylvie's voice quivered. "I—I can't give him that. I don't think I'll ever be able to."

Leah began rocking her again. "That's okay, honey," she said. "It's not *you* he wants it from."

Sylvia stayed quiet a moment then said, "Guess what?"

"What?" For a moment, Leah thought the girl's face was bleeding, but when she touched the spot where the blood was, she found it wasn't Sylvie's blood. It was Orwin's, just smeared on Sylvie's body. Probably from when Sylvie crawled across the floor to get the ax.

Sylvie smiled sadly. "I picked out a name for the baby."

Leah brightened. Outside, she heard two police cruisers pull into Sylvie's yard. "You did? Well, it's about time. This baby deserves a name." They spoke almost in a whisper. The baby had stopped crying completely. "What're you gonna call her?"

Sylvie gazed down at the tiny girl cradled in her arms. "Hope," she said, and gave Leah a great big smile. "I think it fits. How 'bout you?"

Leah returned the smile. "I reckon it's near on perfect."

CHAPTER 35

Two days after my mother solved the Sylvie Carson incident, Ethan Montgomery gave her a week off work. She decided we would use the first day of this time off to finally make the trip up to Georgia to meet my new grandparents. In the end, my mother didn't have to worry: Carry was just as excited about meeting them as I was.

At least at *first* she appeared to be. Then the long drive got to Carry and, about an hour and a half in, she started complaining about her legs being cramped and having to go to the bathroom. We must've stopped four times on account of things wrong with Carry, but eventually we got to Columbus.

My new grandparents lived in a pretty, one-level house with a nice lawn and well-kept gardens. The windows all had boxes full of flowers. Everything was blossoming or full bloom, making it not only look like the kind of house you see in fairy tales, but it also made the air sweet, too.

It was late afternoon when we arrived and the sun was slamming down like a hammer striking an anvil. I don't know that I ever felt the sun as hot as I did that day. It reflected so brightly off the yellow siding of my grandparents' house that it looked like they lived on the sun.

Their door was white, and under the afternoon sky, it was the brightest white I could ever imagine. The grass was trimmed perfectly and felt lush and green beneath my new sneakers as we walked to the door. I couldn't believe how excited I was to be meeting blood relatives I didn't know I even had barely a month and a half ago. Especially relatives on my pa's side.

My mother opened the screen door and knocked on the white wooden one behind it. I examined the house, wondering how often they painted it, on account of everything looking so brand-new. A few seconds later, a tall man with thinning white hair and black-rimmed glasses answered.

The minute he saw us, a big, toothy smile came to his mouth. "Why, I know you. You're Abe! And you're Carry! I'd know you two anywhere!" he said. And then to my mother, he held out his hand. "And you must be Miss Leah. It's a pleasure to meet you and I sincerely want to thank you for taking the time to make the trip out." The sun glittered in his glasses.

My mother shook his hand. She smiled back, but not with nearly as big a smile as my granddaddy was beaming at her. I wished hers was bigger.

"Come in! Come in! Sure is nice outside, though. But the air is so dry. It's drier today than happy hour at the Betty Ford Clinic."

I looked at my mom to see what he meant.

"Just go inside," she whispered.

We piled into the house and began taking off our shoes when he stopped us. "Leave 'em on. Everybody does round here. Come on, your grandma's anxious to meet you!" He took us through the living room and down a hallway into a smaller room that reminded me of the parlor at Reverend Starks's house, only this room was bigger and had a television. A woman sat in a rocking chair in the corner knitting. The minute we walked in she beamed at all of us. Then she stood and gave us all hugs. "Oh, I'm so glad you came! Little Abe! And Carry! And Miss Leah!"

She took a step back. "Well, let me take a look at you."

Awkwardly, me and Carry stood there, not certain what we were supposed to do. I felt like maybe I should do a twirl for her or something. Then she said, "I'm your grandma Sara. That there is your grandpa Jeremiah." She shook her head at me. "Oh, boy, do you ever look like your daddy. Don't you think he looks like his daddy, Jer?"

I gave a broad smile back. Nobody'd ever told me I looked like my pa before. That made me very happy. "Have a seat," my grandma Sara said, gesturing to the davenport and chairs around the room. She sat back in her rocker. "Grandpa Jer will put on a pot of coffee."

Looking to my mother, I got the slightest of nods from her. I was allowed to drink coffee, but only on special occasions. I guessed this must've counted as one of those special occasions.

Me and Carry sat on the davenport. My mother appeared very uncomfortable, looking at all the pictures in the room. "Are you hungry?" Grandma Sara asked us. When she spoke, she did so louder than she should've, almost like she was yelling everything at us.

"No," I said back. "Carry made us stop for lunch." I paused and added, "Almost twice." Then, after another pause, I said, "And two more times so she could go to the toilet."

Grandma Sara laughed and slapped her knee. Carry just glared at me. She was keeping remarkably quiet.

Grandpa Jeremiah came back in and told us the coffee'd be ready soon. "The pot's on the blink," he said. "You gotta work with it. I had to go round my elbow to get to my thumb."

I had no idea what he was talking about. I looked at Carry, but she just looked back blankly.

"We were so surprised when Addison told us you'd talked to her," Grandpa Jeremiah told my mother. "We had no idea she had planned to come down and set this up. It was one of the nicest things she's ever done for us."

"Can I ask you somethin'?" my mother asked him.

"Certainly."

"Well, you two were at Billy's funeral—that's where you apparently met my pa—how come Addison never came to the funeral?"

I saw Grandpa Jeremiah cast a nervous glance at Grandma Sara. "Well . . . that's a bit of a story."

"We have time," my mother said, which I thought was quite rude of her. He obviously didn't want to talk about it.

"She was up in Boston."

"I know. That was gonna be my next question: How come she lives in Boston and y'all is way down here in Georgia?"

Grandpa Jeremiah's gaze dropped to the floor. "We sent her to Boston when she was seventeen on account of she got involved with a bad group of kids. Got hooked on all kinds of things. You know—drugs and that. So, when Billy passed away, she was up there in one of them rehabilitation clinics. We was too worried if we let her out for the funeral she might have one of them relapses."

My mother was clearly taken aback by this news. "Oh, I'm so sorry. I shouldn't have pried."

"No, it's fine. It's probably best that you know."

"Is she still . . . ?"

"No, she's been clean now goin' on . . . well, Abe's what? Eleven?"

"I'm twelve," I said.

"Oh, I'm sorry. Of course, you are twelve. And you was two when Billy died. So she's been clean near on eleven years."

"That's fantastic!" my mother said. "Good for her. You must be very proud. She stays up in Boston because she likes it up there, then?"

"She's built herself a life up there. She's got friends and a husband. She's workin' on startin' a family of her own. She comes down to see us often enough, I suppose. Calls at least twice a week."

"I see." My mother fell silent again. She still hadn't sat down. She seemed captivated by some pictures they had displayed in frames, sitting on top of the cabinet that held the television. I looked harder and realized they were pictures of me and Carry. "You got these from my pa?" she asked.

Grandpa Jeremiah gave Grandma Sara another quick glance before answering. "That's right. Your pa was a good man. He sent us lots of pictures so we could see our grandchildren grow. Sure missed him when he went."

My mother picked up a picture of a young man in a T-shirt. He had blond hair and did sort of look a bit like me, so I figured it must be my pa. "Yeah," she said, sounding very far away. "Me too."

Grandpa Jeremiah came up behind her. He looked over the top of his glasses at the photograph. "Billy'd have been 'bout, oh, fifteen or so when that was taken, I reckon," he said. "Always wanted to be a rock star."

Grandma Sara laughed. "A singer!" she said. "Can you believe it? That boy couldn't carry a tune if he had it in a bucket with a lid on it! But oh, he tried."

"Did he ever sing for you, Mom?" Carry asked.

"He tried."

I wished I could have heard him sing.

My mother picked up another picture of my pa. This time it was one of him and a girl. The girl didn't look like my mother. Grandpa Jeremiah lifted his glasses above his eyes and got a better look at it. "Oh, I remember her. Girl was a few crayons short of a complete rainbow, if you ask me." He laughed. When he laughed his voice broke up and he sounded much older than when he spoke.

"Better go check on the coffee, dear," Grandma Sara said.

Grandpa Jeremiah left and she added, "Good thing that man has me. He couldn't find his own ass with both hands stuck inside his pockets." Her eyes cut to me and she quickly covered her mouth. "Oh, I'm sorry. I guess I should've said rear end."

"It's okay," I said. "I know the word *ass*."

"Hey," my mother said. "Language."

"I was just pointin' somethin' out."

"I don't care."

Grandpa Jeremiah returned with the coffee. By the time he'd poured five mugs and we'd started drinking it, everyone seemed much more relaxed, even my mother. She'd stopped curiously looking at pictures and taken a seat in one of the chairs. I discovered my grandpa Jeremiah had a fondness for talking about his son, and, in the next hour, I learned more about my pa then I ever knew the entire time I'd been alive. I was even getting used to the funny way both my grandparents talked.

We found out that my pa used to like to sneak out and then make up stories to cover his tracks, but my grandpa always found out the truth. "I'd tell him, 'That dog don't hunt,' " he said. "But he'd try it again and again, thinkin' each time he could pull the wool down over my eyes." He turned to me. "Back then his elevator was stuck on the second floor."

"Yeah," my grandmother said, "but he had a knack for fallin' into a barrel full of crap and comin' out smellin' just like a rose."

"That's only on account of you let him get away with so much."

"I most certainly did not," my grandma said. "He would get into one of his angry moods and I'd tell him, 'Well, you can just go and get glad the same way you got mad or you can just die.' "

When she said that, the room went silent. She brought her hand to her mouth. "Oh, I'm sorry . . ." she said, trailing off. "I didn't mean . . ."

Everyone looked at my mother, who seemed to not even notice what had been said. Then she realized everyone was looking at her. "Oh, hey, it's fine. Seriously." She laughed. "It's just a figure of speech, right?"

My grandpa pointed at her. "See? This is why I've always liked you. You were always best for my Billy. You kept him out of trouble. You were the one who'd say, 'My cow died last night, mister, so I don't need your bull.' "

There was a pocket of silence, finally broken by my mother.

"How do you know what I would say?"

"What's that?" Grandpa Jeremiah asked.

"How do you know what I would say? Billy never saw you after him and me started goin' out."

Grandma Sara laughed. "Of course he did. He kept dropping by right up until a few weeks before your weddin'. Then Jeremiah and him had that fight. We should've seen it comin'. After Billy met you, it was like he was a new man. He used to fight with us constantly. Wasn't a week went by that Billy and his daddy didn't almost come to fisticuffs. I think once they actually did, but Jeremiah refuses to tell me the truth."

"I've told you the truth," Jeremiah mumbled. "You just refuse to believe it."

"But then you came along and everythin' seemed to change." She paused and then asked my mother quietly, "Didn't you know this?"

My mother shook her head. "Until Addison met my boy in the street, I didn't really know y'all existed. Billy hardly ever talked 'bout you."

Both my new grandparents just shook their heads slowly and sipped their coffee. "Ain't that just like Billy," my grandpa Jeremiah finally said.

"What do you mean?" my mother asked.

"Ain't nobody gonna mess all over him and call it apple butter," my grandma answered.

"I—I don't understand."

"Billy blamed me," my grandpa said. "For the way he was. On account of he could get violent. In fact, it's amazing he never had no run-ins with the police, but he got lucky."

"I never knew Billy to be violent," my mother said.

"That's probably why you never heard 'bout his family. In Billy's mind, his family was the cause of his violent tendencies. If he don't tell you 'bout them and leaves 'em out of your relationship, the violence stays away, too."

My mother looked like she was a deer caught in a trucker's headlamps. "But—if that's true . . . then . . . it worked."

"The mind is a funny thing," my grandpa said.

"And a tragic one," my grandma added. She kept studying me and Carry sitting on the davenport. I realized Carry hadn't spoken much at all, even though I hadn't really either. "And we've missed so much."

"Thank the Lord Jesus we met your daddy," Grandpa Jeremiah said to my mother.

There was more conversation, most of it filled with funny phrases from my new grandparents, and there was a lot of laughs. Even my mother laughed. It had been a long time since I'd heard her laugh, and I was happy to witness it again. We wound up staying for homemade jambalaya that was really good and for dessert Grandma Sara pulled a freshly baked pecan pie out of the oven. Nothing ever tasted as good as that pie.

When we finally said good night and headed home, it was nearly nighttime. The first stars had begun to peek out of the sky around a full moon that was rising low in the east.

"We're awfully glad you came out to see us," Grandpa Jeremiah said at the porch, after hugging each of us and shaking my hand.

Grandma Sara hugged us all, too. "Please come by anytime. Or maybe we can make the trip out your way.

We'll see you again, good Lord willin', and the creek don't rise."

"We'll have to see, dear," my grandpa said, and a stillness fell over everyone that I didn't rightly understand. I caught my mother sharing a knowing look with my grandpa Jeremiah.

After our good-byes, we got into our car. Of course, Carry took the front seat and I was relegated to the back. It wasn't so bad; at least I had it all to myself.

On the way home, Carry wasn't nearly as annoying as she had been on the way there. She only made us stop twice and both times were for her to use a restroom. One of those times my mother was stopping for gas anyway, so it wasn't a wasted stop.

We talked about my new grandparents during the drive home, each of us agreeing we had a very enjoyable time and that they were good people. "It was a nice visit," my mother said.

"It certainly was," I agreed. "I just wish we'd have done it a lot sooner."

To this, there was no reply, and my mother seemed to get lost in her thoughts for a long while. In fact, she pretty near stayed silent all the way back to Alvin.

When we hit the city limits, I decided it was time that silence was broken. "I guess my pa came from good blood."

"I guess he did," my mother agreed.

"I'm happy that I look like him."

"You *do* look a *lot* like him sometimes."

"How come you never tell me that?"

"I will. From now on. I'll make a point of it."

I beamed a great big smile in the darkness.

"They sure talk funny," Carry said. "Half the time, I

was still tryin' to figure out what they'd just said while they went on to sayin' the next thing."

When she said this, we all laughed and laughed as the last of the stars popped out of the night sky. Above us, the moon, big, full, and round, shone brightly, reflecting off the hood of our car, and lighting the road for the rest of our way home.

CHAPTER 36

It was late by the time Leah and the kids arrived back home in Alvin.

Leah saw the kids quickly to bed and had a feeling Abe was asleep before she even left his room after tucking him in. The purple light of early evening had darkened to an almost-black through his thick curtains, and his bedroom was cast in shadows.

In Caroline's room, Leah's daughter had some odd points to make about meeting her grandparents earlier. Leah didn't normally see Caroline to bed. Usually (especially during the summer months) Caroline stayed up well past Leah's bedtime. But tonight she'd headed straight to her room, something unprecedented. So Leah had just sort of popped in to say good night before going to bed herself.

It had been a long day, undoubtedly for everyone.

"Mom?" Caroline asked, getting under the covers. She'd already slipped on her pajamas and brushed her teeth while Leah was tucking Abe in.

"Yes?"

"Am I ever as bad as Grandpa Jeremiah and Grandma Sara said Pa was when they were talkin' 'bout him bein' so disobedient and all?"

Leah let out a small laugh. "You have your moments."

Frowning, Caroline said, "I don't mean to be, you know."

"I know. And I also know you'll grow up into a fine young woman." She paused and said, "You *have* been makin' your brother paint your toes every week, though. I'd say that classifies as bein' a tiny bit mean."

"Did *he* tell you that?"

Leah shook her head.

"Then how do you know?"

"Honey, I *am* a police detective *and* a mother. We have our ways. Not much gets past us. I reckoned by now you'd have figured that out."

Caroline turned and looked out her window. Leah followed her gaze. The drapes were open and a few stars twinkled around the full moon hanging outside.

"Think maybe it's time you let him off the hook?" Leah asked.

Caroline pulled her covers up to her chin. The moon and stars lit up her face as though it had a spotlight on it. "Yeah, I s'pose. Gonna miss havin' such nice toes, though. He really did do a good job."

"That's your brother. He don't do nothin' without puttin' his heart into it. But you're doin' the right thing for lettin' him off the hook. And as far as me and you go, you're just a bit tricky when it comes to my part in it all."

"How so?"

"Well . . ." Leah sighed. "I'm realizin' I need to start spendin' more time with you. And, as your grandparents would probably say, 'Sometimes I find myself busier than a cat tryin' to cover its crap on a marble floor.' "

Caroline laughed.

Leah kissed her daughter's forehead.

"Go to sleep," Leah said. "Don't worry 'bout the way you are. You're perfect. You an' Abe both are. I wouldn't change an ounce of you even if I was able to. You're my perfect daughter."

Leah got up and left Caroline's bedroom, pulling her door closed behind her. She went into her own room and collapsed onto the bed. It had been a long day with a lot of driving, and a lot of emotions had been tossed up inside her from meeting Billy's parents.

She couldn't believe what they'd said about Billy having anger and violence issues. She'd never seen it. Not once. Not even an indication of it.

Could someone really change that much?

The lamp on the table beside Leah's bed was still on and its light caught the edge of something gold on the doily beneath it. It was the wedding band she'd placed there just over a week ago. Leah picked it up.

Lying on her back with her head against her pillow, she held it up toward the ceiling, examining it in her fingers—a circular band of gold; an unbreakable symbol that went around and around, without a beginning and without an end. A symbol of eternity.

Only, there had been a beginning, and there had been an end.

A very abrupt end.

Billy had been taken from her one morning when Abe was just two years old and Caroline five, and Leah had been left all by herself to raise both their children. And for that, until now, she had never been able to forgive him. And she'd felt guilty about that selfishness ever since. She's hated herself for hating him. Even when she had pulled this ring out of the shoe box before giving the rest of the contents to Abe, she wasn't sure why she had done it. The ring only reminded her of what had happened, and that had always made her angry.

Except tonight, there was no anger. No guilt.

Nothing but acceptance and relief.

For the first time since she could remember, she knew her kids were going to be okay.

She knew *she* was going to be okay.

Sometime between placing this ring on her nightstand and this moment right now, something inside Leah had changed, and she'd found something that had been hidden from her for ten long years.

Forgiveness.

She wasn't even sure who, exactly, or even what, she had forgiven.

But that didn't matter.

The important part was that she'd found what she'd been unable to find all these years.

Slipping the ring onto her finger, she reached up and switched off the lamp. Turning over, she pulled her blankets up over her body, wrapping her hands around them. A tired heaviness sank her deeper into her pillow.

A soft smile came to her lips. She felt it in the starlit

darkness as she closed her eyes and gently fell into a quiet sleep. And, for the first time in ten years, she happily dreamed of being Mrs. Billy Bob Teal once again.

Tomorrow would be another day.

Tomorrow, there'd still be lots more time to play detective.

*In Michael Hiebert's haunting and powerful novel,
a long-ago tragedy echoes through small-town
Alabama as one woman tries to track down a
serial killer.*

Detective Leah Teal is privy to most of the secrets
in her hometown of Alvin, but there are always surprises to be had. Like the day she agrees to take her
daughter, Caroline, to see a psychic for a reading. The
psychic homes in on Leah instead, hinting at a string of
gruesome killings and insisting that she intervene to
prevent more deaths.

When you go looking for trouble, you never know
how much you'll find. Sure enough, the psychic's scant
clues lead Leah to a cold case from six years ago, when
a young woman was found shot to death, her eyelids
sewn shut. As Leah digs deeper into old files, a second
unsolved case surfaces with the same grisly pattern.
While her shrewd young son, Abe, observes from the

sidelines, Leah races to prevent another horrific murder, unaware of just how deep the roots of evil can go.

Taut, suspenseful, and rich in Southern atmosphere, *A Thorn Among the Lilies* is a mesmerizing novel of loss and vengeance, and the lengths some will go to out of loyalty and love.

Please read on for an exciting sneak peek of Michael Hiebert's third Alvin, Alabama, novel

A THORN AMONG THE LILIES

now on sale wherever print and e-books are sold!

PROLOGUE

Alvin, Alabama—1976

The moon hangs in the sky above Alvin like a sickle surrounded by a field of stars. It's a pretty night, but it's cold, being barely two months since Christmas. Susan Lee Robertson is on her way home from the five-and-dime after buying a quart of milk for her baby, who is at home with her twelve-year-old son. The milk sits on the passenger seat beside her.

Rain had been pouring all day, but it finally let up and a westerly wind quickly blew out all the clouds. But the dampness is still in the air, making the store-fronts on either side of her look slick, like oil paintings. She hits a pothole and the car bounces in a splash of rainwater, nearly hydroplaning into the oncoming lane. She's driving east up Main Street when she comes to the intersection of Sweetwater Drive. It's a one-way intersection, with no stop signs for Main Street, so Susan Lee continues through with the streetlights reflecting brightly from the hood of her car.

That may explain why, when it happens, she never sees it coming.

A blue Buick with out-of-state plates screams through the stop sign on Sweetwater Drive from Susan Lee's left. The driver, Anna Marsh, is coming back early from a bachelorette party for one of her friends after having a fight with the maid of honor. The party was at the Rabbit Room, a place normally reserved for male patrons and female strippers who take off their tops for ten-dollar bills. But, somehow, the fourteen girls in the wedding party managed to come up with enough money and a good enough argument to convince the owner of the Rabbit Room, Gus Snow, into letting them have a girls-only night with male strippers. And, of course, cocktails. Lots of cocktails.

Anna Marsh never did well when it came to lots of cocktails.

She doesn't hesitate at the stop sign. Without touching her brakes, she T-bones Susan Lee's silver Honda, hitting it near the rear of the car, causing it to spin, and caving in the driver's side, breaking both of Susan Lee's arms—one when the door collides with it, the other when it's slammed against the console. The top of her spinal column is partially severed on impact. The windshield of the Honda explodes in a shower of glass as Susan Lee Robertson's body (which was not secured by a seatbelt) gets tossed through it in a sideways motion. The glass rains into her eyes, blinding her for life.

She lands headfirst on the asphalt in front of her car after bouncing off the hood and is still lying there unconscious when the authorities show up. "I reckon she's lucky to be alive," one of the EMTs says to another.

"I don't know if you'd call this lucky, Jerrod." They try to ascertain where her head is bleeding from. A pool of blood has formed beneath it, with tiny rivers that run along the road.

Carefully, they lift her onto a gurney and place her in the back of an ambulance. She's taken to Providence Hospital in Mobile, where she'll remain in a coma on life support.

With Susan Lee still alive, Anna Marsh is arrested for first-offense DWI. Her blood alcohol level is measured at just over 0.12. Her license is revoked.

Despite her Buick looking like an accordion, Anna's wounds are superficial. She actually gets out of the car and can walk. She doesn't look any worse than if she'd fallen down a few stairs.

Authorities take a slurred statement from her. Turns out she lives in Clarksdale, Mississippi, and, along with her other thirteen friends, came down to Alvin specifically for the bachelorette party. Her friends had arranged a limo back to their hotel, but after her fight with the maid of honor, Anna decided to drive herself home.

Probably not the best decision she ever made.

Twelve years later, when doctors take Susan Lee off life support and pronounce her dead, a jury at a circuit court changes Anna Marsh's sentence, giving her five years for reckless vehicular manslaughter, the maximum sentence in Alabama. Her appeal is turned down.

But before that, for twelve years of her life, Susan Lee Robertson lies in that hospital bed unconscious while the world continues to go round without her.

Twelve long years.

For her, it's just a blink.

But for those who love her, it's an eternity. . . .

CHAPTER 1

Almost Thirteen Years Later

It was a clear winter day when the Christmas parade wound its way down Alvin's Main Street. Which, of course, meant it was cold. Dewey said it smelled like snow, but I told him he was crazy. First off, it ain't never snowed in Alvin far as I know, and second, it wasn't *that* cold. I guessed it to be probably in the midforties somewhere. Still, I was glad I had my heavy jacket on. I wasn't used to this sort of weather.

We were all standing together as close as we could, which was extremely strange for my sister, Carry. Normally, Carry liked to be as far away from everyone else as she could get, but I guess huddling to keep warm took precedence over trying to look cool. Other than me, Dewey, and Carry, there was my uncle Henry, who had come down to spend the holidays with us.

Christmas was barely two weeks away, and boy you could sure feel the excitement in the air. I loved Christmas. It was the best day of the year as far as I was rightly concerned. My mother always played Elvis songs at

Christmastime and he had this one that was called something like "If Every Day Was Christmas." I found myself thinking that same question all the time. Of course, then it probably wouldn't be so special. Which sounded just like something my mother would say.

More and more, I found myself saying stuff that sounded like it should be coming out of her mouth instead of mine.

Carry was extra lucky. She not only got Christmas to celebrate, but four days later, she got her birthday, too. If she had been born just four days earlier, she'd have the same birthday as baby Jesus. I'm glad she didn't. That would be just too weird.

"Here they come!" Uncle Henry said. "Can you see all right, Abe?" he asked me.

"I certainly can!" I said.

Down the street, the float my mother was on turned the corner and came into view. There was a tall riser up front where Hubert James Robertson, the mayor of Alvin, stood waving to people on both sides of the street. Beside him, on much lower risers, stood my mother on his left and Officer Chris Jackson on his right. Both my mother and Chris worked for the Alvin Police Department. Chris was just a regular officer, but my mother was a detective, which meant she didn't have to drive around in a special car or wear a special uniform. She could go out looking any way she wanted. Although, sometimes, she worked as a normal officer, too. They were the only two police officers in Alvin other than Police Chief Ethan Montgomery, who ran things at the station.

"Where's Chief Montgomery?" I asked, blinking into the sun as I looked up at Uncle Henry. A cold breeze hit my pant legs, sending a chill up my body.

Uncle Henry shielded his eyes with his hand, almost looking like he was saluting someone. "I don't know. You'd reckon he'd be on there, too."

There were all sorts of floats. The one my mother was on didn't seem to "be" anything in particular, but the one coming up behind it was a pirate ship advertising the Alvin First National Bank. It was big and it blocked out most of the stores on the other side of the street. It had a huge Union Jack flag that flapped and snapped in the winter wind.

"Isn't that a weird float for a bank?" I asked.

"What do you mean?" Dewey asked back.

"I mean, didn't pirates *steal* money? It's like they're sayin' they're gonna steal your money."

"You think too much, Abe," Uncle Henry said.

"Maybe they're sayin' that they'll steal money *for* you and put it into your account," Dewey offered.

"Maybe it's *just* a friggin' pirate ship," Carry said.

She could be very unsociable at times.

Someone in a giant kangaroo suit came bounding down the side of the road and stopped right in front of us, waving.

I waved back, but the kangaroo didn't move on. It just kept waving. I felt very awkward and uncomfortable, waving from the sidewalk with the kangaroo two feet from me, waving from the street. Finally, the kangaroo reached up and took off its giant head. It was Police Chief Montgomery. "You guys all havin' fun?"

"Um, yeah. It's dandy," Dewey said.

"It's okay," I said.

"My feet are killin' me," Carry whined. "How much longer is this thing anyway?"

"They're all having a terrific time," Uncle Henry said, swatting the back of Carry's head.

Chief Montgomery leaned in, and whispered to Carry, "At least you don't have to hop around in a stupid kangaroo suit. My legs feel like Jell-O. I can't *wait* until this is over. I reckon there's only three or four more floats until the big guy comes round and finishes it."

"The big guy?" Dewey asked.

"You know," Chief Montgomery said. "Mr. C? Ho ho ho? St. Nick?"

"Santa Claus!" A huge smile beamed from Dewey's face.

Oh my God, he didn't really still believe in Santa, did he? Me and Dewey were practically exactly the same age. Our birthdays were within days of each other, which meant he would be thirteen in March. Someone had to put an end to this.

"Dewey," I said, "you do know there is no real Santa, right?"

I got instant glares from three people. Even Carry joined into the Glare Group.

"What?" I asked. "He's almost thirteen, for cryin' out loud. Do you want him to go into the workforce believin' in the tooth fairy?"

"Wait," Dewey said, sounding dejected. "There's no Santa *and* no tooth fairy?"

"Dewey, you have no baby teeth left. Why do you even care 'bout the tooth fairy?"

"She was nice to me. She gave me money."

"He's got a point, ass face," Carry said. Uncle Henry swatted the back of her head again.

"Language," he said. To me, he didn't sound too much like he meant it.

"Are you serious about Santa?" Dewey asked.

I took a deep breath and let it go, looking at all the heads shaking behind Dewey's back. I smiled. It was a terribly faked smile. "No, Dewey, I'm just pullin' your leg. Of course there's a Santa Claus. Who else would be eatin' those carrots and drinkin' that milk you put out?"

His face immediately transformed. The wonder was back. It sort of peeved me off because he was living in a world much more spectacular than the one I was.

"And just so you know," he said, "I *am* aware there is no Easter bunny."

I squinted at him. "Why do you reckon there's no Easter bunny, yet you believe in Santa?"

"Duh. Why the heck would rabbits be givin' out eggs? It makes absolutely no sense."

"He's got a point," Uncle Henry said.

Everyone fell silent and I realized the Existence of Santa Claus and Other Miscellaneous Childhood Lies discussion had come to an end. The silence was finally broken by Uncle Henry asking Carry: "So, what does my little sugarplum want for her birthday this year?"

Carry smiled. "It's super cool."

"What is it?"

"I want you and my mom"—she hesitated and examined me and Dewey—"and I guess you two little rug rats too if you want, to come with me to a psychic while I get my fortune told."

"What a neat idea," Uncle Henry said. "But if you want me there, you're gonna have to do it earlier than your birthday. I'm only stayin' until the mornin' after Christmas and then I have to go."

"Okay, I'll talk to Mom. Maybe we can book an appointment this week. I reckon it'll be so cool."

"Just remember, sugarplum, a lot of those so-called psychics are frauds. They only tell you what you wanna hear. Or they're gypsies. Gypsies give me the willies."

"I'm not gonna *tell* her what I wanna hear. I'm not gonna answer any questions. I wanna see what she can figure out without me sayin' a word."

"Well, that sure should be interestin' to watch."

"Maybe I'll find out that one day I'll be rich," Carry said.

"Or that you'll die an early death in a house fire before you're twenty," Dewey said.

We all looked at him. "What?" he asked.

"Oh, nothin'," I said. "There's just somethin' wrong with you, is all."

CHAPTER 2

Me and Dewey were playing tag in the backyard. Tag was one of those games we didn't play for very long, on account of there being just the two of us and it getting a mite boring. You really need more than two people to play tag properly. Mainly, it was just fun being outside this close to Christmas. Me and my mother had spent the last weekend hanging lights up around the eaves of the house. Now it looked really Christmassy. I just couldn't wait for Christmas to come.

One game we used to play a lot of I would call "balancing rocks on sticks." It consisted of taking a stick and a rock and trying to see how long you could go with the rock on the end of the stick before it fell off. Now this was more of a sport for two people. In fact, you could just as easily do it with one person. It was the perfect multiplayer game.

Truth be told, there just wasn't much to do outside in the afternoon in winter in Alvin. Tag or otherwise. We were too used to the heat to stay outside too long in the cold, and some days it would rain something fierce and it felt like God was throwing ice at you. My backyard wasn't the most fun place on the planet to hang out on those days. Sometimes we'd just run around to stay warm.

Even the trees looked like they hated it outside. We had two cherry trees in the backyard and neither had any leaves left. All the leaves had fallen off and died. I was starting to feel like them leaves, as Dewey touched me, and yelled, "You're It!"

I decided I couldn't be It for one more round. "Let's stop playin'," I said.

"How come, Abe?" Dewey asked.

"Well, for one, I'm outta breath. For two, it's too damn cold out here. I'm dyin', Dewey."

"What's for three?"

"Um . . ." I knew for three had to be the clincher. "For three, I think we can probably go inside and get my mom to make us some hot cocoa."

"That sounds great!"

Dewey never gave up a chance for free food, no matter what it was. It was his weakness, the way Superman couldn't go near kryptonite. Everyone has a weakness, I think, and Dewey's was rustling up free food. We could be having the time of our lives and I could stop, and tell him, "Hey, old Newt Parker just called and invited us over for raccoon, wanna go?" And Dewey would be on his bike in a flash, ready to make the trip.

Newt Parker was no longer with the living souls of this world, but when he was here, many folk thought he ate barbecued roadkill. Myself, I have no convictions either way as to whether or not the rumors were true or false. I do know this, though. I had enough belief that the rumors *could* be true that I would never go for a barbecue at Newt Parker's house. Dewey, on the other hand, would go in a flash, if for no other reason than to be able to tell people he ate barbecued road-killed raccoon with Newt Parker. That's just how Dewey was.

So, compared to the dead raccoon, my offer of hot cocoa was a quick way to get me out of the stark cold of the backyard and into the warmth of the house.

We got inside and pulled off our boots. It took Dewey at least twice as long as me to get his off his feet on account of I think he outgrew his last year or something. Do twelve-year-old feet even still grow? I had no idea. Maybe his ma just bought them too small. Dewey's ma wasn't the sharpest crayon in the box. Of course, I never told that to Dewey.

My own mother was in the kitchen on the phone. Carry kneeled on a chair beside her, anxiously watching while my mother made some phone calls. I figured out pretty quick what they were doing—they were trying to book a psychic to see Carry for her birthday present. By the sounds of things, they weren't having much luck.

"No," my mother said, "it needs to be *between* now and Christmas. Sometime this week would be best . . . okay, thank you for your time." She hung up and looked at Carry. "That's eight I've called. They're all not working through the holidays."

Carry frowned. "Stupid psychics. Don't they know that's when they'd get their most business?"

"Maybe it's just as well," my mother said.

"Don't give up now!" Carry said. "There's still some you haven't tried."

"I know, and I will, I just don't want you to get your hopes up too high."

"If they're all psychic and stuff," Dewey said, "why do you have to call them? Shouldn't they just know you're comin'?"

I looked at Dewey. "You're an idiot."

My mother said, "I reckon he has a very good point."

Carry didn't hear the exchange at all. She had her head in the phone book. "Try this one. Madame Crystalle—True Psychic Medium from Persia. One hundred percent satisfaction or your money returned in full."

"Wow," my mother said, "that's going out on a limb. And she's not a gypsy if she's from Persia. I'm a little leery of gypsies. Okay, what's the number?"

Carry told her as my mother dialed. "Hello, I'd like to book an appointment with Madame Crystalle. . . . Oh, that's *you*. Well, hi. My name's Leah and I'm the detective here in Alvin, and my daughter, Caroline, would like to see you and get her fortune read for her birthday. . . . It would have to be sometime this week. I know, it's sort of last minute." My mother always told everyone she was the detective here. I think she thought it brought her some kind of respect or something that she wouldn't get otherwise.

She stopped talking, held the phone away, and said to Carry, "She's gone to get her schedule."

Placing the handset back to her mouth, she said, "Yes, I'm still here . . . *tomorrow*? Yes, tomorrow works *fine*. What time? Two o'clock. Perfect. Oh, and is it okay to bring along her family to watch? Okay, that's great. Thank you."

My mother hung up and smiled at Carry. "You're goin' tomorrow at two!"

Carry beamed back. "This is goin' to be so awesome! Thank you, Mother!"

"What if she tells you somethin' bad?" Dewey asked.

"Why are you being so negative?" my mother asked back.

"Because *most* things are bad. Read a newspaper or watch the news. You never see happy stuff."

"I'm sure Carry's stuff will all be nice and happy."

"Yeah, but what if it isn't? What if she says, 'Your mother's gonna get shot next Wednesday while on duty'?"

"Dewey!" my mother snapped. Even I looked at him like this was out of line.

"I'm just sayin' she could, so you should be prepared for somethin' like that."

"I reckon maybe it's time for you to go home," my mother told him.

"Actually," I said, "we was hopin' for some hot cocoa."

My mother took another look at Dewey and exhaled slowly. "All right, but no more talk about 'bad stuff,' you hear?"

"Yes, ma'am," Dewey said.

He fell quiet. I just looked at him, and whispered, "You're an idiot."

CHAPTER 3

The psychic's shop turned out to be a very small building that me and Dewey had ridden by on our bikes many times and had not noticed. The shop couldn't have been more than ten feet tall with a sign in the window that read:

> ### *Madame Crystalle*
> ### *True* **Psychic Medium**
> #### *100% satisfaction*
> #### *Or your money returned in full.*

The pink blinds behind the sign were pulled closed, so you couldn't see inside. A large shrub hid most of one side of the building. The rest of the building was painted black, which was obviously the reason me and Dewey never saw it. You don't normally look for small black buildings while out on bike rides.

The only really strange thing on the outside of the place was this statue right beside the door. It stood between the sidewalk and the steps leading up to the door, facing down toward the hustle and bustle of town. It was a frog standing on his hind legs. It stared wall-eyed down Main Street at all the other shops. In its hands it held a top hat, and its mouth was wide open with a bright red tongue. It seemed so out of place it took a minute for my brain to even figure out what I was looking at. Me and Dewey must've missed it because it was set back a bit, and you had to look right at the building to see it.

"Why is there a frog standin' here starin' off down the street?" I asked my mother. "It looks kind of creepy."

"I don't rightly know, Abe, but I think maybe we should all go inside before we freeze to death," my mother said.

"Reminds me of that frog from that cartoon," Dewey said. "The one that will only dance and sing for one guy. Only this one wouldn't fit in a shoebox."

"I agree with Abe for once," Carry said. "It's really creepy. No wonder she was available for a readin'. She probably scares off most customers with this frog."

"Now, don't go writin' her off just because of some crazy statue outside her shop," Uncle Henry said. "Look at her sign. It says, '*True* Psychic Medium.' Not only that, she'll refund your money if you ain't satisfied. I'd say that's pretty darn good. I also agree with your mom. We should go inside before we freeze."

"I guess," my sister said.

Uncle Henry looked up at the roof; then his eyes fell to the door. "So what do we do? Just knock?"

"I dunno," my mother said. "Maybe try the door."

Of course, before anyone could say another word, Dewey's hand was on that doorknob. He turned it and the door opened. A bell on the top of the door rang out, announcing our arrival.

We shuffled into a small room that was more like a landing for the top of a narrow stairway. A beaded curtain hung at the entrance to the stairway. The small room we found ourselves in smelled funny, and the walls and ceiling were all colored red, matching near on exactly the tongue of the frog statue outside. The floor was white with repeating red diamonds. Nobody seemed to hear the bell that rang because we stood there, all crammed together on that small landing for a good five minutes and nobody came to see us.

"What's that smell?" I asked.

"Incense," my mother said.

"What's that?"

"It's supposed to have mystical powers, I reckon," Uncle Henry said. He sneezed. "I think I might be allergic to it."

"It has mystical stink," Dewey said.

"What do we do now?" my mother asked.

"Hello?" Uncle Henry called out. "Anybody home?"

From downstairs, behind the beaded curtain, a heavily accented woman's voice called up. "Come downstairs!"

We pushed our way through the curtain. The beads were all glass and very beautiful. Green, red, blue, yellow, with the light reflecting inside of them. They made a loud swishing that sounded almost like water as we went through them. The stairway wound down in two tight circles. I was behind Uncle Henry. It was too narrow to go any way but single file.

About halfway down, Uncle Henry bumped his head. At that exact moment, from the bottom of the stairs, in a much quieter and lower voice than she had used before, we heard the woman say, "Be careful of head. If you are tall, those stairs are like plague."

"You'd think, bein' psychic and all, she'd have told me that *before* I hit my head," Uncle Henry whispered before letting go with a big sneeze.

"I heard that," the woman replied.

When we made it to the bottom, there was another beaded curtain to go through that exactly matched the one at the top. Again, it sounded like a waterfall as we all pushed through it and came to our final destination. I felt my eyes grow as big as paper plates. We had descended into the weirdest room I'd ever seen in my entire life.

Everything was a deep golden yellow. The room was maybe twice the size of the small landing we managed to squeeze onto at the top of the stairs. On one side were rows of shelves holding candles of all different types. Every one was lit, and that was the only light in the room, so it cast an eerie, flickering glow on the yellow walls, yellow curtains (which hung on some walls and were obviously just for show as we were underground), and yellow tablecloth that covered the round table on the other side of the room. The cloth came right down to the floor, which was a deep pile carpet, also in golden yellow.

On the other side of the table sat who I assumed to be Madame Crystalle. I had no idea how she got in to sit on that chair. From where I stood, it looked like she would have to spend the rest of her life seated there, as there was no way in or out.

She wore a leather headband with gemstones set along it, and had long strands of beads in her curly, deep auburn hair. It hung down past her shoulders. Her lips were very red, and her eyes were very blue and they sparkled in the candlelight. I immediately liked her because of her smile. It was one of the warmest, friendliest, and reddest smiles I'd ever seen.

The first thing she did was look straight at Carry. "You must be Caroline," she said, and extended her hand without standing. I didn't think it was possible for her to stand from where she sat.

"I am," Carry said happily.

"I understand it's your birthday," Madame Crystalle said.

"Well, not for another week or so, but we wanted my uncle to come along and he's leavin' the mornin' after Christmas."

"Ah! Early birthday present. So nice!"

"You talk funny," Dewey said.

"Shut up!" I snapped in a whisper to him.

But Madame Crystalle just laughed. "I am from Persia. Everyone talk like this in Persia."

"And I bet she speaks better English than you speak Persian," Carry said to Dewey. Uncle Henry sneezed again.

"I always thought Persians were cats," Dewey said.

Once again, I told Dewey to shut up, but Madame Crystalle laughed very loudly at what he said. "We are people, too. Oh, and also carpet. Or, how you say? Rug. Persian rug."

"How come you ain't got no crystal ball?" Dewey asked.

I wished he'd stop asking questions.

"Oh, crystal balls don't work," Madame Crystalle said. "They're all just hocus-pocus, fluff stuff. You either real medium or you're not. If real, you don't need crystal ball to tell you anything."

"Oh," Dewey said.

"I'm Leah," my mother said, extending her hand with a smile. She did it quickly, before Dewey could say anything else.

Smiling, Madame Crystalle went to shake my mother's hand, but as soon as their hands locked Madame Crystalle's face changed immediately.

"What's goin' on?" Dewey asked.

"Please," Madame Crystalle said. "Sit in chair." Her face was very serious as she gestured to the chair across the table from her.

"No, this is for Caroline," my mother said. "I'm just here to watch."

"There will be no charge. There are things you must know. Sit. Now. Before I lose them."

Reluctantly, my mother sat in the chair. I could tell Carry felt a little put out just by the expression on her face.

"You . . . you work in justice, no?"

"Yes, I told you that on the phone. I'm the detective for the Alvin Police Department." I figured my mother had just caught the psychic in a trap. She was using information she gained ahead of time from the phone call my mother made to set up Carry's appointment.

Madame Crystalle closed her eyes and held both my mother's hands. "I see something almost indescribable. It is someone . . . a sort of, how you say? Maniac. A tailor. Deprives those of their sight. Very dangerous."

"Who are you talkin' 'bout?" my mother asked. I could tell she had grown a bit anxious.

"Just listen, before it goes away," Madame Crystalle said. "I see a body in darkness, waiting. I see writing. Writing on the body."

"What does the writing say?" my mother asked, but Madame Crystalle shushed her.

"I can't see enough to read it, just to know it's there. But remember the number seventy-eight. It is important. Remember the maniac tailor. Knowing this can save many lives over the coming times. I . . . I see a name on a sign. . . . 'Welcome to . . . to . . . Gray . . .'" She paused again. "'Gray . . . Gray . . .'" Then she stopped.

She let go of my mother's hands. "Sorry, it's gone."

"What *was* it?" my mother asked, her voice shaky.

"Did it not mean something to you?"

"No, can you give me some more information?"

Madame Crystalle shook her head. "No, I can't tell you what it was I just saw. I don't remember details, the visions come like that. I just knew I had message and it was for you. If not useful now, I am sure you will find useful soon. It was a very powerful message the way it came through."

"That freaked me out a little," I said.

"Me too," Dewey said.

Uncle Henry sneezed.

"You still up to doin' yours?" Uncle Henry asked Carry.

"Yeah," Carry said as though he'd just asked the stupidest question ever. "Mine better not be in code like Mom's was, though. I want to actually understand it."

"I will try to do better for you," Madame Crystalle said. "Please, take seat."

My mother got out of the chair and let Carry take her place. I noticed my mother was shaking, especially her hands. I think she was more freaked out than anyone. It was pretty spooky.

Madame Crystalle took a deck of cards from somewhere beside her and handed them across the table to

Carry. She had them with the backs up and the backs were pretty neat. They were black with a silver ring painted on the center. Inside the ring was a red dragon curled up with its wings hanging down over the bottom of the ring. The deck looked thicker than a normal deck of cards.

"Shuffle these," Madame Crystalle said. "Use overhand shuffle, though. I don't want my cards bent."

Carry did as she was told. "When do I stop?" she asked.

"Go for as long as feels good to you. You are imprinting your future onto the cards."

Carry shuffled some more, then came to a stop. She looked like she was about to set down the deck, then she started shuffling again for another minute or so. "I just felt compelled to," she said.

Madame Crystalle smiled. "This is good. It means you go with your instincts."

Finally, Carry actually did stop. "Okay, what do I do now?"

"Hold the deck in your left hand and make three piles of cards on the table from left to right."

Carry did and then Madame Crystalle leaned over and picked up the piles from left to right with *her* left hand. I couldn't figure out what was so important about everything being done using lefts.

She laid out seven cards in all and in the end they formed a T shape. First she laid out five cards in a straight row and then two cards beneath the center card in the row. Some were upside down from me and others weren't. I wondered if that mattered. And boy, if I thought the backs of the cards were neat, the fronts were even better.

Each one was different. The first looked like an old scraggly tree with a green gem tangled in its root. It read "Ace of Pentacles" on the bottom.

The second was the Five of Cups and showed a dwarf drinking something out of a bottle with his back against a tree and five cups in the grass around him. The dwarf looked drunk to me.

The third one was The Lovers and showed two dragons looking like they were about to kiss. That one sort of disturbed me. Dragons don't kiss. They go and burn down castles and collect treasure.

The fourth one was the Four of Cups and showed a lady with very long ponytails standing at a table where four little lizards were playing with four golden cups. Two of the cups were on their side, the other two were standing.

The fifth one (which was the last one along the top row) was the Queen of Wands and showed an older lady with a beautiful dress made from purple and gold silk. She was seated on a tall wooden throne with a blue dragon sleeping at her feet.

The remaining two came down from The Lovers card. The first one was the Knight of Wands, which showed a younger-looking man riding a dragon in the moonlight. This one was pretty awesome. I would love to ride a dragon. Especially at night.

The final card, at the very bottom of the *T*, was the Two of Cups, and it showed a young man and woman holding hands in a garden with a huge moon over their heads and the face of a dragon inside the moon. It almost looked like they were getting married or something.

"What do they mean?" Carry asked, anxiously, just

as Uncle Henry sneezed for what seemed like the hundredth time.

"Well, let's see," Madame Crystalle said. "I see you are smart in school. This is good. I also see you know it. This, not so good. You would have more friendships if you didn't always act so sarcastic."

Carry's face reddened. She hated getting lectured the best of times. Now she was being lectured by a psychic whom she got as a birthday present.

Madame Crystalle noticed Carry's reaction and quickly covered. "It's okay, though, you have good heart. See these cup cards? Cups represent love and compassion. You have many. So your heart is in right place. But . . ."

"But what?" Carry asked.

"You get very lonely at times," Madame Crystalle said.

"No, I don't," Carry said back snarkily.

"You cover it with your sarcasm or your quick wit. But you wish you had more friends. You also long for a boyfriend."

We all sort of giggled at that and Carry's face went completely purple. This was turning out to be the best birthday present ever. I started thinking for my birthday I'd get Carry a psychic reading.

"Well, I have good news for you," Madame Crystalle said. "I see a boy in the immediate future. Someone more than just a friend."

"He won't be nineteen and drivin' a red Pontiac Firebird, will he?" my mother asked, referring to a boy we once caught with Carry in the backseat of a car. "Actually, he'd be twenty now."

"No, but he will be older than you, Caroline. And

he'll probably have dark hair. Brown, black, maybe a dark red. And don't worry about your mother. See this card here?" She tapped the Queen of Wands. "This is your mother and she's sitting right beside one of your cup cards. Which means she will be approving of your love choices from now on. So this new boy for sure your mother will be accepting of him. But, I see at first you won't trust her to be, and you will try to hide your relationship. Rest assured this is unneeded. Your mother will not try and sabotage anything."

There was a little more after that, but that was the main part. That was the part that made Carry happiest (and most embarrassed). I thought it must be weird, living her life now, just waiting for this boy to drop into it who is going to become her new boyfriend.

By the time we left Madame Crystalle, I noticed a change in every one of us. Carry was in deep thought, probably about this new boy. My mother was in deep thought, probably about the stuff she was told that made absolutely no sense to anyone. Uncle Henry had changed because he found out he was allergic to incense. I was quietly cursing myself because I forgot to ask Madame Crystalle about the frog standing outside her shop, and Dewey had changed because he found out that, along with rugs and cats, there were also Persian people.

CHAPTER 4

That night, Leah lay in bed unable to sleep. Her encounter with the psychic kept rolling around in her mind. What happened earlier had affected her more than she had thought. She didn't really believe in psychics or the ability to "see the future" at all; in fact, she normally referred to it as "hocus-pocus gobbledy-gook." But her ad hoc session with Madame Crystalle had been so intense, Leah couldn't help but be touched by it.

The problem was, the woman didn't make any sense. Leah was a logical person, and there was no logic in what she'd been told. It was just a bunch of sketchy details without any definition. And to top it off, Leah kept going back to the fact that she had *told* Madame Crystalle on the phone she was a detective. That part made it a little too convenient for Leah's liking.

Leah remembered every word the psychic told her. She'd gone over the words at least fifty times in her head, and there was nothing there she could do anything with. None of it made any sense. Some of it was downright ridiculous and funny. A maniac tailor who deprives people of their sight. Now *there's* an image that's really hard to conjure up in your imagination. Something about finding a body in darkness with writing on it. The psychic had been unable to say anything about the writing at all.

Yet, writing on a body found in darkness is pretty specific. They aren't just things you pull out of your sleeves. So this was where Leah was torn into possibly believing the woman and attempting to follow up on the clues. But really, what clues did she have? She didn't even have a name or place for a victim. Or any kind of context to put this into.

It was the last piece of evidence Madame Crystalle had given Leah that made Leah consider trying to follow the sparse path of clues; it was the one thing that was tangible and possible to get something out of. The words on the sign: WELCOME TO GRAY . . .

It was a partial on a road sign. *That* should be traceable.

This road sign was something Leah might be able to find. But so what if she did? She still had no idea what it meant.

Did she even *want* to know what it meant? And sweet Jesus, if Police Chief Ethan Montgomery ever found out she was hunting around on a case with the sparse evidence she had been given from a psychic, he'd have a heyday with it.

It would probably be the day before Leah had to start looking for a new job.

"I guess you ain't goin' to get much sleep tonight," she said to herself, deciding her best course of action at this point was to get up and go fix herself a mug of warm milk.

Sliding her feet into her slippers, she stood from her bed and slowly padded her way down the hardwood floors into the kitchen. Opening the fridge, she pulled out a carton of milk. She closed the fridge door and immediately her pulse went up twenty notches and she nearly jumped right out of her slippers. Hank had moved beside the opened door while she was peering in the fridge.

"God, Hank, you tryin' to give me a coronary?"

"Sorry. I guess I'm a little sneaky in my old age. I just heard you walkin' round and thought I'd come check on you, make certain you were all right."

"Oh," she said, almost in a sigh. "I'm okay. It's just that psychic has me in a bit of a tizzy."

"I can imagine. The woman was pretty intense. *I* was almost left in a tizzy, and it wasn't even me she was talkin' to!"

Leah pulled a pot from one of the cupboards and put it on the stove. She turned on the burner and poured in some milk. "Would you like some warm milk, too?" she asked Hank.

"Hmm. Actually, that sounds like it might just hit the spot. Thank you."

Leah poured more milk into the pot and returned the milk carton to the fridge. Then she came back and started stirring the milk with a spoon as it simmered on the burner. "So," she asked, "seriously. Why *are* you up?"

"Oh, you know me," he said. "I don't sleep at the best of times. And your sofa is comfortable and all, but it ain't no bed in no five-star hotel room." He laughed.

"I'm sorry," Leah said. "I wish we had somewhere else to put you."

Hank raised his hand. "No, no, I'm not really complainin', I'm just bein' funny. I don't mind the sofa at all. So, about that psychic lady—you gonna act on anythin' she said?"

"Well, that's just it. Even if I wanted to do somethin' based on what she told me, she didn't actually *say* anythin' I could possibly use to do anythin'."

"Well, she told you folk are in danger. She told you someone is blindin' them and that he's actin' like some maniac tailor, which could mean lots of disgustin' things when I think it over."

Leah set two mugs on the counter, took the pot of milk off the burner, and carefully tipped it to fill them with the now-warm milk. "Is that what *you* heard?" she asked Hank. "Because that's not what *I* heard. I just heard a bunch of half-baked facts all rolled together." She handed one of the mugs to Hank.

"Thank you," he said. "That's because you chose not to try and form the bits and pieces of information she gave you into somethin' real. You're too analytical. Sometimes you need to fill in the blanks yourself so that you can create—or at least finish—the story. Your story might not always be the right one—fact is, most of the time it probably isn't—but it gives you a place to start. And as you go you can change your story as circumstances change and you gather more facts."

Leah took a sip of her warm milk. It felt good going down her throat. "Ethan would kill me if he knew I was even considerin' doin' this."

"Yeah, well, Ethan owes you a lot. He knows that. Hell, half this town knows that. Take chances, Leah. It's the only way in life to push yourself to your full potential, and if we don't all reach our full potential, what's the point in being here?" He took a sip of his milk. "This is really good milk, by the way."

"It's just milk warmed up in a pot, Hank."

"Still really good."

"Thanks."

A silence followed while Leah thought about what the psychic had told her. "So, say I *do* try and follow this up, Hank. Where the hell do I start? The only thing she gave that's even slightly possible to research is a partial on a road sign."

"Then that's where you start. The road sign. Then at least you'll know what town she's talkin' 'bout."

Every bone in Leah's body was telling her not to do this, telling her that following the scattered advice given to her from a Main Street psychic was a dumb idea. And yet, she knew, deep down in the pit of her gut, that was exactly what she was going to do. So she may as well stop fighting it and just give in and get it over with.

"What made you so smart, anyway?" she asked Hank.

"Watchin' you grow up," he replied.

"We both know what I'm gonna do," she said.

"Yep, you've decided already," Hank said.

Leah sighed. "I guess I have. Sometimes I hate my gut instincts."

"Your gut instincts are what make you good at your job."

Turned out, this time, she didn't have to listen to any instincts.

A case from the past sparks a nightmare for Detective Leah Teal in Michael Hiebert's masterful new novel of suspense.

Fifteen years ago, a serial killer tagged by the media as The Stickman spread terror throughout Alabama and became Alvin police officer Joe Fowler's obsession. After six months and at least fifteen victims, Harry Stork was identified as the Stickman and Fowler shot him dead. The killings stopped. For a while.

Now, more bodies are turning up, each staked through the chest with a stick-figure drawing in the killer's signature style. Detective Leah Teal—Joe Fowler's daughter and Alvin's sole detective—receives a letter before each victim is found, just like her late father did. The only people who knew about the letters were the cops on the task force back then—and the killer himself. Did Joe shoot the wrong man, or was one of the detectives he handpicked involved all along? As a single mother, Leah tries to balance an increasingly disturbing case and a new relationship with caring for her children—bright, perceptive Abe, and teenaged Caroline, who's in the first flush of young love. But with each menacing communication, each gruesome discovery, Leah realizes just how personal, and how devastating, the truth may be.

Weaving lyrical prose and emotional richness into a taut, gripping mystery, Michael Hiebert creates a fascinating novel of life, love, and death in a small Southern town.

Please read on for an exciting sneak peek of Michael Hiebert's fourth Alvin, Alabama, novel

STICKS AND STONES

Now on sale wherever print and e-books are sold!

PROLOGUE

Alvin, Alabama, 1974

The Stickman.

Harry Stork.

A year and a half of Detective Joe Fowler's life.

Joe Fowler: one of the two main officers working the Alvin Police Department, and the only detective. The other cop is a tall, lanky man with a bad combover whose name is Strident. Officer Peter Strident. Strident has the eyes of an arctic wolf—that crisp morning sky blue—and when he looks at you, it feels like he sees right *through* you. Nobody interrogates a suspect like Strident.

What Fowler lacks in his eyes, he makes up for in gumption.

A year ago February, the first evidence that Harry Stork would eventually come onto Detective Fowler's radar appeared when Stork's first victim turned up beneath the tracks at Finley's Crossing. A black male, mid-thirties, turned out to be one Waylon Ferris. Ferris's body was found shirtless. His hands and feet hog-tied behind him, putting him in an almost reverse-fetal position. A thirty-eight-caliber bullet hole entering the back of the skull, a big exit hole in the front.

Even more horrific, a wooden stave was hammered through Ferris's chest, staking him into the ground. On a piece of paper affixed to the stave, a drawing of a stickman made in black permanent marker.

Lack of blood and brain matter at the crime scene and evidence from the ligature marks on his wrists and ankles suggested Ferris was shot somewhere else, somewhere he had spent a day, maybe two, before his killer put the bullet through his brain.

For the press release, Fowler held back the stake and the paper attached to it.

Waylon Ferris was victim number one.

A succession of killings followed, all inside or circling the small town of Alvin, each with the same MO: shirtless victims inversely hog-tied with a .38 Special-caliber slug entering the back of the skull. Victims ranged in age from mid-twenties to early forties, men and women, black and white. Each one staked to the ground with the picture of a stick figure. The female stick figures had circles for breasts, hair rising to tips on either side of the head.

Every killing brought more cops into the mix. Fowler created a task force and managed to continue holding back the staked paper with the stickmen from the press. Until the information leaked out after victim six. Someone on the task force talked. Someone obviously needed cash.

Almost immediately, the killer was tagged the Stickman by the media. Fowler hated the name. Thought it trivialized everything, almost turning it into a game.

The case was long and arduous. Too many victims. Too many pieces of paper with bloody stickmen.

Nine in total, that is, *if* Fowler knows about all of them.

Nine bodies, almost a year and a half away from his daughter—Leah—and his wife, Josephine. Because Fowler is *like* that. Even when he's home, if he's on a case, he's *still* on the case. He lets them get to him. They pick away at his bones, eating him up until he solves them. They take their toll on his family, especially on his daughter, Leah. He worries about her and how she's affected by his stress. It's the part of the police game he hates most.

Harry Stork.

The Stickman.

It took Fowler too long to figure out they were the same man. When he did, Stork disappeared.

That was almost a month ago.

But tonight, Fowler and four other officers surround an abandoned shotgun shack with Stork inside. He'll be taken either alive or dead. It's all up to him now, how he plays it.

The dilapidated shack is set back in the woods, flanked by tall oaks, their boughs heavy with Spanish moss. Fowler's positioned at the shack's rear door. Fog and a light mist cover the ground, making the dense forest ghostlike. If not for the band of stars and the silvery gold of the moon overhead, Joe Fowler wouldn't even be able to see his own hands.

The rest of the officers are broken into two teams of two, waiting at the shack's front for Fowler's instructions. Team A will batter down the door, Team B will rush in and clear the front room. Team A will move on to clear the rest of the place.

Joe Fowler is Team C, protecting the only other exit, other than a window. Stork won't have time for windows.

Pushing his fingers through his short, graying hair, Fowler feels sweat pop onto his forehead. He brings the blow horn to his lips. "Come out, Harry!" he yells into it. "You're surrounded. Come out or we're coming in! And if we come in, it could go bad." He rubs his chin, feeling three days' worth of stubble. He wonders if maybe Stork wants it to go bad, wants to go out in a blaze of glory.

A fitting end to the Stickman? Maybe.

From the windows, the occasional flashlight beam dances erratically into the night, the only indication Stork's still alive. He silently moves from room to room.

Fowler counts to five. Stork stays quiet. Stays inside.

"All right," Fowler says. He tosses the blow horn onto the loamy ground, lifts his walkie-talkie. "Team A, go! Team B, ready! Team C is ready!"

Dropping into a crouch, Fowler pulls his weapon, readying himself in case Stork's stupid enough to come out shooting.

There's a *boom!* as Fowler hears the front door go down. "Front clear!" Someone shouts.

"He's running!" Someone else.

It all happens in a blur. The back door bursts open, and Harry Stork appears, silhouetted by the flashlights from the cops in the hall behind him. Fowler sees the gun in Stork's hand, tightens his grip on his own weapon—a snub-nosed Colt Cobra revolver—and readjusts his crouch, balancing his weight on the balls of his feet.

"Drop your weapon!" Fowler screams. "Drop your weapon or I will shoot!"

Stork hesitates while his eyes adjust to the darkness. He must've dropped his flashlight in the scramble. He sweeps his gun blindly in front of him. Fowler sees the barrel tremble. "Don't kill me!" Stork yells, panicked. "I was set up! I'm a fuckin' patsy!"

"Then drop it, Harry!" Fowler calls out. He notices a slight shake in his own hand. Arthritis. Doc gave him the news six months ago. He readjusts his grip and the shake goes away, replaced by a tingling pain shooting up his right arm. Fowler knows too well what it means: He's getting too old for this game.

He pushes the thought away, focuses on Stork. Everything becomes a tunnel around the man. Stork hasn't dropped his weapon. "Drop your gun!" Fowler shouts again.

But Stork doesn't. Instead, no longer blinded by the night, Stork levels the barrel straight at Fowler. There's little choice left. In that split second, Fowler reacts on instinct, pulling off a .38 Special round destined straight for Harry Stork's heart.

Fowler wanted to hit the man's gun arm, but overcompensated, too afraid he might miss. Too afraid Stork wouldn't. Fowler's shot clips the edge of Stork's lower left ventricle, the kind of shot there's no coming back from.

The gun barrel goes limp in Stork's hand before falling and rattling on the broken wooden porch at Stork's feet. Stork falls right behind it.

And that's how it happened the night the Stickman went down and Joe Fowler gave his life back to his wife, Josephine, and his daughter, Leah. The daughter who would one day follow in her pa's footsteps.

CHAPTER 1

Fifteen Years Later

Summer came to Alabama the way it always did, like a twister out of the east. The heat from the early morning sun pounded down on the red maple and black gum trees out along Cottonwood Lane. Officer Leah Teal drove by these trees every day on her way to work, but this was the first day she could remember in a long time it being so hot at only half past seven.

Everything was alive in vivid colors. Alvin looked like a picture book filled with images of white clusters of berries bursting on the mayhaw, and yellow, green, and orange flowers popping out of the tulip trees, late bloomers. Even with her window rolled down, the air lay in the car like a dead animal, making the heat even more intolerable. As she came to her turn, the smell of sweet bay magnolias trying their best to bloom wafted inside. Drifts of cottonwood fluff fell like snow onto the brown hood of her Bonneville as she turned down the hill.

As she drove, Leah hummed a tune, unsure of what it was. She was in good spirits lately—ever since Christmastime, really, because of a man she was rapidly falling for: a detective out of Birmingham whom she'd met on her last big case, a case that started with a psychic—of all things—and ended with a serial killer.

Things were never dull for long around Alvin.

The detective's name was Dan Truitt and he was different from any man Leah had ever met. She hadn't dated a lot of men in her life. In fact, Dan was the first in over a dozen years since her husband, Billy, died in an automobile accident.

For too long she had let that accident spin her life out of her control. Now she felt like she was finally taking her life back. And Dan Truitt was helping her do it. No, more than that, he was making her *want* to do it. She was starting to admit to herself she was falling in love.

Pulling her sedan to a stop at the curb outside the Alvin Police Station, Leah exited the vehicle and was immediately overwhelmed again by the melting, stagnant heat. Honeybees buzzed around the red buds on the sweetshrubs planted in front of the station's windows.

She picked up the *Alvin Examiner* from in front of the station door on her way inside. The station was locked, which meant she'd beaten Officer Chris Jackson to work. Officer Jackson was the only other cop at the Alvin Police Station apart from the chief, Ethan Montgomery. Jackson was also black, which caused quite a stir in this little community when he first came on the force, but that quickly faded. Now he was respected as much as Leah or Ethan.

After putting on a pot of coffee, Leah took the

newspaper she had tucked beneath her arm, pulled the elastic off it, and unrolled it.

She read the front page and her happy demeanor immediately changed.

The headline read: *15 Years Later, Stickman Strikes Again*.

The photograph beneath the headline could've been a lot more gruesome than it was. It was taken some distance from the crime scene, which left out a lot of the details described in the article. It didn't matter; Leah knew immediately what the actual scene would've looked like. The victim, unnamed in the paper, would've been shirtless with her ankles and wrists bound together behind her back. Her body would be staked to the ground, through the chest, and attached to that stake would be a piece of paper with a stickwoman drawn on it. But that's not what would've killed her. A gunshot wound to the back of the skull would've done that job. Leah didn't have to see it all in a picture; she could imagine it pretty well. She'd lived it.

Scanning the photo, Leah made out strangler fig and cypress trees. The dirt looked soft. She guessed the body was found near water. Indeed, the article confirmed it had turned up on the bank of Leeland Swamp, an area surrounded by forest just outside of the ranch lands in the northwestern corner of Alvin.

And then the rest of the train caught up with her thoughts and she realized what this really meant. It made her breath catch and her heart tumble into her stomach.

She had lived the case vicariously through her pa, Joe Fowler, fifteen years ago when he spent a year and a half hunting down a serial killer. But—

Her pulse quickened.

Heat rose to her face.

This, all because there was one thing Leah knew with absolute dead fact: *But . . . what I'm looking at, it's . . . it's impossible.*

Her pa killed Harry Stork, the man who earned the nickname "Stickman" in papers from one side of Alabama to another. Shot him through the heart. The *Birmingham News* had called it "The Shot Heard 'Round the World." It made the front page. Suddenly everyone knew about Alvin, a town with a population of just over six thousand people almost nobody in Alabama had ever heard of.

She glanced up to the newspaper's date, hoping for some bizarre reason to find the paperboy had accidentally delivered a paper from 1974, but today's date stared back at her under the black script headlining the *Alvin Examiner*. She hadn't *really* expected to see anything else.

But how . . . ? The more she thought of it, the more impossible it was.

The door opened and she jumped. It was Chris. He took one look at her sitting on the edge of her desk, paper in one hand, forgotten coffee mug steaming in the other, and closed the door quietly behind him. "How you doing?" he asked in his low-timbered voice. Chris spoke slowly, and with near on perfect enunciation. It made him sound as though he was a man who chose his words carefully and said them with reverence. "I see you got the coffee started." He smiled, wiping his brow with his uniform sleeve. "Man, is it hot."

Leah said nothing back, and he realized she was reading the paper.

"Oh," he said, with a big sigh. His smile faded quickly as he plunked into his chair. "So you know." He ran his dark fingers through his cropped black hair. Sweat, even at this early hour, popped over his hand. He looked like he wished he would've called in sick.

Leah snapped the front page of the paper toward him. "This can't be the Stickman," she said. "The Stickman was Harry Stork and my pa *killed* Harry Stork fifteen years ago."

"Yeah, I know," Chris said, "but he shows every sign of having come back to life."

Leah bit her lower lip. It couldn't be Harry Stork. She remembered her pa on that case like it was yesterday. He would come home physically exhausted most nights, but mentally he stayed on the job twenty-four/seven. His brain never stopped trying to solve it. It took him near on a year and a half to finally do it, and, near the end of it all, Leah and her ma both thought he would be needing intense therapy. It all tied up because of a lucky break, an anonymous tip called in to the station—although he would never use the word *lucky*. Leah could hear him in her mind. "No," he'd say, "lucky would've been catching him 'fore anybody had to die. This ain't luck, Leah, after all this time, this is God throwing down justice." Back then, he had told her she was too young to understand, but one day it would all make sense.

He lived long enough to get her on the force after he left, but not long enough to find out exactly how much sense his words would one day make.

She was more like her pa than she ever cared to admit, but Police Chief Ethan Montgomery constantly reminded her. Like her pa, she took full responsibility for everything that happened during any of her cases. Any blood spilled was spilled on her own hands. She took everything personally, same way he had. And, like him, it wore on her. She wondered how much of the stress contributed to the cancer that finally took him.

Leah's son, Abe, had been six when his grandpa died. Leah always consoled herself with the fact that he at least got to know his grandpa those half-dozen years. Not like Abe's own pa, Leah's husband, Billy, who died in an early morning head-on collision that took him out of not only her life, but Abe's, and her daughter, Caroline's, life, too. Billy left them all far too early. Leah doubted, if not for the shoe box full of photos she had given him, that her little Abe even remembered what his pa looked like. He was only two when Billy passed.

Now Abe was thirteen and Caroline turned sixteen this past Christmas, and Leah wondered how different things would be for them if they hadn't lost their pa twelve years ago—if Billy hadn't decided to pass that eighteen-wheeler in front of him.

But there was no point in thinking about it; some mistakes you just can't come back from. Billy's decision to pass that truck that fatal morning was one of those mistakes.

She still missed Billy and her pa, but her pa was different. Somehow, she still felt him with her some days. She even found herself talking to him during those times when she could badly use his sage advice. Of course, he never answered, but it still usually helped to ask the questions.

Ethan Montgomery had hired Leah's pa and he'd also agreed to bring Leah on when her pa suggested it. And after all this time, he was still working at the station, although every year he seemed to come in later and later. These days, he rarely arrived before eleven.

Leah expected he would just keep being later until there was no time left in the day and that would be when he retired. Until then, he spent most of his time behind a ridiculously large desk in a squeaky chair watching the Crimson Tide stop the Auburn Tigers from making any yardage.

Because of the connection her pa had to Ethan, Leah knew she was treated differently than Chris. She was made "detective" not just to walk in her pa's footsteps, but also to allow Ethan to pay her a higher wage. She and her two kids needed all the help they could get. This was something Ethan and her pa arranged without her even knowing, but now it was pretty much common knowledge. At least Chris didn't seem to hold any animosity toward her because of it. She wondered sometimes, though. Especially on those days when Chris sat at his desk doing nothing but crossword puzzles his entire shift. Even if the phone rang, there were days he'd wait for her to take the call.

She didn't mind so much. Chris was more of a desk cop anyway. That's how he was cut. According to Ethan, Leah was different. Chris did have some special talents, though, like his uncanny ability to unearth the details of juvenile records.

"I see your mind moving," Chris said to her. His regulation boots were up on his desk and the coffee he'd fetched for himself was sitting beside his hat. Leaning back in his chair, he put his arms behind his head. "What I don't see are the details moving around. Care to let me in?" He spoke tentatively, almost like he was scared.

Leah looked back at the paper. "This is impossible."

Chris just shrugged.

"It's a copycat. It's gotta be. But why would some-one copycat a case they had to dredge up from fifteen years—"

Chris cut her off. "I know what you're thinking, but it's not a copycat. It can't be."

"Yes, it can, Chris. Remember, the holdback about the stakes with the drawings was leaked. That's how Harry Stork *became* the Stickman."

"I know," he said. "But the staked stickman page wasn't the only holdback. There was another. A *big* one. And it wasn't leaked."

A thought suddenly came to Leah, one that probably should've come long before now. "Wait a minute. Why am I just reading about this now? Which police department was on the scene last night? Last time I checked, Leeland Swamp was in *Alvin*."

"Yeah," Chris stumbled. "That . . . I . . . we . . ." He glanced at the door to Ethan Montgomery's office. It was mainly glass, like the walls, but brown blinds hung down that Leah couldn't remember ever seeing open. She could only imagine how much dust was collecting inside them. Of course, now the door would be locked. Leah glanced at the white clock hanging in front of her desk on the wall between the door and the window. It was twenty past eight. They wouldn't see Ethan for an-other two or three hours.

"What time did you get the call?" Leah asked. She remembered Chris was still at his desk when she left. She doubted he would have stayed much longer than fifteen more minutes, and she had gotten home just after five.

"What call?"

"Whoever found the body. I'm guessing it must've been around five?"

Chris scratched the back of his head. "Ethan called me at home," he said.

Leah tried to process this. "Ethan was still here when it came in? That's"—*a miracle*—"unusual."

"Yeah, um, the body hadn't turned up yet."

Narrowing her eyes, Leah asked, "What do you mean? Wait, if this holdback you're talking about was so secret, how come you know about it?"

"Ethan told me about it yesterday. What matters is, it wasn't a copycat kill. It's more than that. Ethan was pretty clear."

Leah felt the heat rise in her skin. A trickle of sweat ran down the back of her blouse, tracing a line from the bottom of her bra strap, along her vertebrae, and right into her brown pants.

"Sure is hot out there," Chris said, looking out the window.

Leah snapped the paper at him. "What aren't you telling me? What do you mean 'the body hadn't turned up yet'? What's this super-secret holdback and why did Ethan tell *you*?"

Chris took a deep breath. "Leah, it was a long night. We searched that swamp for three hours before finding the body."

"What are you talking about?" The hair rose on the back of her neck. "I wasn't called in on any search last night."

"That's on account of we didn't know how you'd react to it. With what happened with your pa and the Stickman fifteen years ago and all . . ."

Leah's stomach roiled. Anger swooped in like a hungry vulture. She did her best to hold it back, but heard the edge it put on her words when she spoke. "If you hadn't found a body, how would you know . . . ? Wait, I am missing something here. What made you even know to *look* for a body? What aren't you telling me?"

Chris said nothing, just shifted uncomfortably in his seat.

"Someone had to call someone," Leah said. "I don't . . ." No matter how much she tried to make sense of things, nothing worked.

Chris let out a big sigh. "Man, it's hot."

Leah's anger swelled. "I am getting mighty pissed off about talking about the goddamn weather, Chris. If there's something you're not tellin' me, you'd best be making your mouth start going sooner rather than later." Both Chris and Ethan knew Leah had a temper. Neither of them ever wanted to push the envelope and find out how bad it really was.

When she looked back at Chris, he had seemed to take a sudden interest in the floor.

"Okay, first things first," she said. "Tell me about the stuff."

"What stuff?"

"The super-secret stuff that actually *was* held back from the press throughout the Stickman murders."

Chris sighed again and took a big drink of coffee. He was running out of stall tactics. "Well, for every victim, this station—well, your pa—was given a letter."

Leah cocked her head. "Letter? How was it given? Who gave it?"

Chris shrugged. "Apparently it came from the Stickman. It would be left in an envelope with no postmark or address, simply your pa's name written across the front. Inside there was always a single piece of paper folded three times. It had a drawing of a stickman, a time, and a location."

"A time and location of the killing?"

"Yeah."

"Sounds weird. Why didn't my pa just show up and arrest the Stickman then?"

"The locations were general. Like the one last night simply said *Leeland Swamp, 8:30 P.M.* That's a large area to search in two and a half hours. Not counting travel time. And we had to assume it could also mean somewhere in the surrounding forest."

"So the time in the letter designates when the body will be dumped at the secondary crime scene?"

"According to Ethan it's more like the maximum time in a range. So, when the letter comes in they knew they had from whenever it was opened until the time it said before the body was staked."

Leah thought this over. "If the staked drawings were leaked, this letter thing could easily have been, too."

Chris held up his palm. "I know what you're thinking, but listen. Not every cop on the task force knew about the letters. In fact, Ethan said other than him and your pa, there were a half-dozen or so other detectives in the loop, each handpicked by Joe. After the first leak, he wasn't about to take any chances."

"And forensics said all the letters were written by the same person?" Leah asked.

"All except the last one. They had a weird slant to the left."

"And what was different with the last one?"

"The last one was the one that came the night your pa shot Stork. Mobile said the handwriting didn't match the rest. It could be the same person, but if so, he wanted it to seem like someone else."

"The night my pa shot Stork? There was no victim that night."

Chris put his feet back up on his desk. "No, the letter was for Stork. It had the address of the shotgun shack. The actual address. There was no time. Harry was holed up there. He was there when your pa and Strident arrived with the other officers. And there was one more difference."

"What was that?"

"The letter had the initials *H.S.* written on it."

"Harry Stork?"

Chris nodded. "One would gather, yes."

"I thought Stork's whereabouts came from an anonymous call?"

With a shake of his head, Chris said, "That's the story your pa made up. He didn't want to release the holdout."

"Why not, if Stork was dead? The Stickman case was solved."

Chris shrugged. "That, I don't know. I asked Ethan that exact question and he didn't seem to know, either. He just said your pa asked the other four cops to keep the letters secret. Said your pa always said the case felt 'unfinished.'"

Leah considered this. He did always go back to the case. Even years later, she remembered him bringing home Stickman files and staying up late some nights poring over them. She hated those nights. "No wonder my pa got so wrapped up in that case. I always thought he seemed to take it particularly personal. Now I understand. It *was* personal. He was getting letters addressed directly to him."

Chris nodded. "Can't get much more personal than that. Plus, Joe was the one being quoted in the papers and being interviewed on the news. He was the face of the Stickman task force."

It was Leah's turn to sigh as her eyes went to the clock. "I don't suppose we're goin' to see Ethan anytime soon. You'd think he'd want to tell me all this himself," she said, trying to keep her anger and frustration out of her voice. Truth was, she also felt a bit betrayed by her pa not confiding in her about the letters all those years.

"So," Leah said, "the letter came last night after I left?"

"It came after I left, too," Chris said. "Ethan found it on his way out jammed halfway under the door. He called me right after I got home. Said he almost didn't open it. Figured it was probably another thank-you card from the Ladies Auxiliary for your helping out with their Mother's Day parade."

Leah gave her coffee mug a half turn where it stood on her desk. "Mother's Day was at least a month and a half ago. Besides, this one didn't come to me. It came to you and Ethan. Or . . . ? Who was it addressed to?"

Chris took a deep breath and blew it out slowly. Sweat was dotting his forehead. She didn't bother following his gaze when it shifted to the window.

"Well, you know . . . that doesn't really matter." Chris stood from his chair, walked over to the coffeemaker, and poured two new mugs full. To one he added three teaspoons of sugar and some cream. He left the other black and handed it to Leah, nodding to her half-filled one. "I think that's probably getting cold," he said and sat back down.

Without saying thanks, Leah took the mug. She stood there silently, holding it and slowly shaking her head.

"What?" Chris asked.

Her emotions rose to the surface. "The letter wasn't goddamn addressed to you *or* Ethan, was it? Christ, no wonder he's not here yet. Chickenshit."

Chris scratched the back of his head again. "It was just like all the other times," he said. "The information was delivered to us. The police."

"Last time it all came to my pa. Exactly *who* was this new letter addressed to?"

Chris didn't answer. He sat in his chair and ran his fingers once more through his hair.

"Who was it addressed to, Chris?" Leah said, louder.

"You," Chris said, almost too quiet to hear.

"Who? Say again?"

He swung his chair toward her. "You. Okay? The letter came addressed to *Leah Fowler*, so obviously whoever is behind this doesn't know you were married."

"Or he wants to drive home a point," Leah said in a clipped tone before falling silent. When she spoke again, it was quiet and pensive. "Otherwise, did Ethan say it was exactly like the other ones?"

"Yes. Exactly." Chris took a swig of coffee and turned back toward the window. Leah was pretty sure *he* couldn't wait for Ethan to get in to the office, either.

"And you didn't call me in?" she asked. "You and Ethan decided to just handle this alone like a couple of cowboys?"

"We thought you might freak out," Chris said. "You have in the past."

"You could have *used* me," Leah said, growing louder again. "You needed as many cops as you could get. I should have been called, goddammit!"

"Well, Ethan said not to."

"Well, Ethan and I are goin' to have some discussion when he gets in." She looked at the clock again. That big black minute hand was inching its way closer and closer to twelve. "That is, *if* he ever gets in."

Chris took a big, calming breath. "Don't you find it hot today?"

"Show me the letter," Leah said, trying to remain calm. "Surely you thought to make a copy of it."

"Of course, but it will only make things worse."

"Show me the goddamn letter!"

"All right." Chris reached into a file folder on his desk and pulled out a piece of paper. Leah could tell it was a photocopy because it had no fold creases.

"Mobile has the original?"

"Yeah. Their forensic experts are goin' to see what they can get off it. Maybe a fingerprint—I don't know. There won't be nothin' on it. We all know that. This guy's smart." He stopped mid-sentence and corrected himself. "*Was* smart."

"Yes, *was*, because this guy is *not* the Stickman, Chris! Are you not hearing me? The Stickman was Harry Stork and Harry Stork is dead. The dead don't come back."

"Well, this time, maybe one did," Chris said.

The time and place on the paper was 8:30 P.M. Leeland Swamp. The stick-figure drawing had breasts and hair. It was female.

"What time did you get to the swamp?" Leah asked.

"Around ten after six."

"So you had under two and a half hours to try to save this woman's life." She looked once again at the photo on the front page of the *Examiner*, her brain automatically filling in the missing details. A hideous sight. "Does she have a name? Our victim? Or do you just want me to keep referring to her as 'she'?"

Chris wiped his forehead with his right hand. He was starting to sweat in his uniform, even though Leah hadn't noticed an increase in temperature. "Abilene Williams. Married with two kids. She went missing around eight-forty-five after dropping her son off at school."

"So one of you at least went to her house and told her husband what happened?" It actually surprised Leah that they didn't leave that fun bit to her.

"Of course. Here." He handed the rest of the file folder to Leah. She flipped through it quickly. Copies of photos and sketches made at the scene. Reports. "It's all in here. Her husband was pretty frantic when we got to their house."

"That surprises you?" Leah knew what it was like to lose a spouse. Frantic didn't even come close to describing it. "Two and a half hours isn't nearly enough time to search that swampland, especially not for two people," she snapped. "You would've had a lot better chance with me helping. I should've been called."

"In retrospect, I agree."

"In retrospect, you and Ethan are assholes. What you two did last night is wrong on so many levels. The letter came to me, I should've been called *then*. And if not, once you opened it and you saw what it was, there should've been no question."

"I didn't open it, Ethan did."

Leah bit her tongue. "I know."

"We don't always make good decisions, Leah. We aren't perfect."

She let out a fake laugh. "No, you definitely aren't goddamn perfect. Don't worry, I know you wasn't the one making the orders. It's Montgomery who's goin' to get a piece of me. *If* he ever comes in."

Chris smiled. "He's probably 'fraid to."

"Don't smile. There ain't nothin' funny. A woman is dead, possibly because of dumb decisions made by this department."

Chris sipped his coffee. "Sure is hot outside," he said absently.

Leah just slinked down in her chair. "I should've been goddamn called."

CHAPTER 2

It wasn't long after Leah stopped being angry at Chris that the phone started going crazy.

Leah took the first call, from a woman who said she lived in Cloverdale and wanted to know if she should lock herself and her family in her house until the Stickman was caught. Leah did her best to console her, but the call kind of blindsided her. In hindsight, she should have expected it. And the twenty-five or so other ones that had come through since. Alvin was a small town. The Stickman was big news fifteen years ago. Folks were panicked then, and Leah certainly should have realized they'd panic now.

"No, I don't think there is any reason to be too concerned," she told the woman. "But yeah, I understand how you feel. No, right now we only have an isolated instance. We don't know for sure what we're looking at yet. No, I don't reckon it's the same Stickman. Yes, I am well aware that Harry Stork is dead. Well aware."

Two phone lines came into the station, and there were times when Leah and Chris had them both on hold while they tried to settle down. Near on every call went almost exactly the same way. That was until around twenty after nine. Then the real calls started coming in. Calls from the newspapers, radio stations, and the television news programs. Some from as far north as Huntsville. Everybody wanted an official statement about last night's murder. *Is this really the return of the Stickman? Did Joe Fowler—my very own Pa . . . could he possibly have killed the wrong guy?*

"That's it," Leah said to Chris after fumbling through a conversation with Nick Danger, a newsman from WAFF News, channel forty-eight out of Huntsville. Danger asked a lot of the same questions Leah had been asking herself. *Why have the murders started up again? Why a fifteen-year absence? Who really is the Stickman?* Of course, Leah had no answers. Her official statement was that she'd "release an official statement soon."

"Soon, as in hours? Days? Weeks?" Danger asked.

"I don't know right now."

"Well, people want to know what's happening."

"I realize that," Leah said. "We're being inundated with calls. Right now, we really don't know much more than you people do from reading the paper."

"Folks aren't goin' to find that very comforting."

"I'm afraid that's the way it is. I'm sorry, there's really nothing I can do other than tell you what you already know."

Danger eventually got off the phone. Reluctantly.

"What's it?" Chris asked. Both HOLD buttons were flashing.

"I can't do this anymore, Chris. You've gotta handle the calls. I need to read over the file you gave me from the murder last night. I need—I just have to stop talkin' to people. I'm goin' to lose it."

"So you expect *me* to take all the calls?"

"You know, it's kind of a little like justice after what you guys pulled last night."

"I thought we were past that," Chris said.

"Handle the calls and you'll be headin' a long way to getting there."

Chris's shoulders heaved while he let out a big sigh. "Fine."

Leah took the folder he'd given her and rolled her chair over to the coffee table. It probably wasn't as comfortable as sitting at her desk, but it was a few feet farther away from the phone. That counted for a lot.

She started going through the folder's contents, first looking at the sketches Chris had made of the scene and comparing them to the Polaroids. She could see where Abilene Williams's body had been found, staked into the soft dirt beneath a particularly large cypress tree about six feet from the edge of Leland Swamp. Unlike in the *Examiner,* these photos showed all the gory details. Leah's stomach clenched. The phones continued to ring as Chris answered one line, only to have to put it on hold to answer another. She tried to block him out, but between the telephones ringing and the gruesome photos and the nagging thought that her pa might've killed the wrong guy, Leah was having a hard time holding things together.

The Polaroids felt familiar after having listened to her pa talk about the crime scenes for so long. Many times, she listened from her room as he and Peter Strident spoke either in person or over the phone. Her pa always kept his voice low, almost in a whisper, but Leah had good ears and heard pretty near every word.

So she wasn't surprised at the grotesque way Abilene's body was wrenched backward and held up with the wooden stave. The top of the stake was mushroomed. Even in the soft earth of the swampy edge, whoever killed her used something heavy to hammer it in. Maybe a rock. Maybe a sledgehammer. Leah looked closer at the Polaroid. The stake hadn't been driven into the dirt at all. The ground was probably too soft to hold the body up. Instead, the killer had hammered it into one of the gnarled roots of the cypress tree.

No wonder its top had been so mushroomed.

Just like the murders from fifteen years ago, there wasn't near on enough blood for the body to have been killed at the scene. She was shot somewhere else, a primary crime scene. What her pa used to refer to as "the slaughterhouse." It was the one piece of evidence he had so wanted to find and the one that wound up eluding him. According to his notes, finding the primary scene was the key to unlocking everything.

Leah wondered if that was still true and, if it was, how would she be able to find it when even her pa failed to? This part of the Stickman case reminded Leah of her last big case—one involving another serial killer. Only that one came to be known as the Maniac Tailor case on account of the way the killer stitched up the victim's eyes.

A shiver pulsed through her veins, like the feeling you got when you touched an electric fence. She was glad the Tailor case was behind her. Only, did anything ever really get left behind? For some reason, she could never put anything fully into the past. There were always parts dragged along behind her, like a heavy chain that only grew heavier and longer as new cases came up.

That chain added an intensity and a focus to her work that became sharper as time went by.

She went back to the report.

Chris noted that along with the blood, pieces of her skull and other internal parts were missing, as well. Leah remembered what he said about her dropping her son off at school. That's when she'd gone missing, eight-thirty in the morning. The killer had lots of time to hog-tie and shoot her before bringing Abilene to that swamp.

In some ways, that made Leah feel a mite better about last night. Odds were, nobody could have found her alive, because she probably hadn't been alive when the letter was left at the door. But they still would've had a better chance of catching the son of a bitch.

Leah wondered how the killer had brought Abilene's body into the swamp area. It was surrounded by twisted cypress and strangler fig that fell hard against a dark and dense wood of birch and poplar. There was no way to drive in. The body would've had to have been carried, or brought in on a dolly or something like that.

She found more of Chris's notes explaining that there was a trail that opened near where they'd found the body. He'd figured that was the way the killer came in. The trail ran for five country blocks until finally leading out to one of the old logging roads still accessing parts of the forest. Chris walked the trail back to the road. Near the site, for about a block or so, it was narrow and he guessed the killer had carried Abilene through that part. But after that, it widened and Chris found a fresh wheel track running along it. In the photos it looked almost sunk into the moist, brown ground that was littered with pebbles and bits of broken stumps. Immediately, Leah suspected the same thing Chris had: The killer threw Abilene in a wheelbarrow after taking her out of his vehicle and wheeled her until the path became too narrow, then carried her the rest of the way, leaving the wheelbarrow behind to be fetched on his way back.

Chris and Ethan hadn't made out any tire tracks on the side of the logging road. The gravel and dirt had been too hard-packed, so there was no guess as to what sort of vehicle the killer drove. Of course, depending on the size of the wheelbarrow, it could even be tossed into a trunk if the trunk was left open and tied down with bungees.

They did find boot prints. Not on the trail, but in the mud around Abilene's body. To Leah, the sole cast looked like some kind of hiking boot or maybe even a combat boot. They certainly weren't galoshes or anything like that.

Chris hung up the phone. For once, it had stopped ringing. "Oh my God!" he said. "Do you hear that? It's the sound of silence." He smiled.

Leah looked back at the photocopy of the Polaroid. "You got Mobile working on these boot prints?" she asked him.

"Yep. That's why you don't have the original Polaroid. It went down with all the other evidence we found. Not that there was much."

Leah found another Xerox of a Polaroid. "This a fingerprint?" she asked, squinting at it. The fact that it was a black-and-white copy made it hard to tell.

"We're not really sure. It looked like it might be, so we thought we'd give it a shot. If it is, it's only a partial."

"Better than nothin'."

The phones rang again. Leah gave Chris a sympathetic smile. "Just think how much character this is building," she said.

"Yeah, I could do without character." He picked up the phone. "Alvin Police. This is Officer Chris Jackson."

Leah rolled her chair back to her desk so she could get her empty coffee cup. She was just about to roll it back to where she'd set up camp when Chris held the receiver away from his mouth and said, "Hey, it's Jacqueline Powers from the *Examiner*. She wants to speak to you."

Biting her lower lip, Leah looked past Chris to the framed newspaper page hanging on the wall. It was the front page of section two, where the *Alvin Examiner* always ran their "Spotlight on Success" article on Sundays. Each week, they picked some resident of Alvin and did an interview with them. The people were typically blue-collar workers and their stories usually revolved around what they did for work. A week and a half ago, Jacqueline Powers interviewed Leah, and Ethan had been so proud he immediately framed it. Ironically, much of the article was Leah talking about her pa. She'd even mentioned his success at finally solving the Stickman case. Ms. Powers thought that must have been his crowning achievement. Thinking about that now brought Leah a sigh. She hoped it would turn out to be a crown and not a jester hat.

Most of the article consisted of anecdotal bits. Jacqueline asked Leah how she managed to juggle the busy life of a cop with raising kids, to which Leah had responded that most of her time wasn't spent solving cases but going through files and doing data entry. Jacqueline laughed at this. But the reality was, in a small town like Alvin, there was a lot of downtime.

Then Ms. Powers asked about holidays, saying she knew at least one officer had to be assigned to work during things like the upcoming Fourth of July celebration.

Leah responded the truth, that usually those jobs fell to her, which meant for a long day spent without her family. She usually checked in to the station around eight and found herself back there after the festivities had mostly wound down, twelve to fourteen hours later.

It made for a very long workday.

As she responded, Leah felt a flip in her stomach because she knew her kids didn't *like* her being gone on special days. She hoped like heck Chris would actually be slotted for the Fourth. For once, she'd like to spend a holiday actually relaxing. Of course, she said none of that to Jacqueline Powers. Instead, Leah told her about how supportive and great her children were.

After that, thankfully, Powers's questions went back to things like police procedure and different cases Leah had worked on. Of course, she asked about the Cornstalk Killer and the more recent Maniac Tailor case. Like her pa before her, Leah *hated* the names the press liked to paste on things without thinking. The "case of the Maniac Tailor" bordered on ridiculousness.

But in the end, the published article not only put Leah and her pa in a very nice light, but it also did a good job of showcasing the entire Alvin Police Department. Now Leah felt like she owed Jacqueline Powers and felt obligated to talk to her.

"I'll take it," Leah said, resignedly. Lifting her phone's receiver, she took the call off of HOLD. "Hi, Jacqueline. It's Leah. How are you today? What do you think of this weather? Hot, hey? I've noticed a wind's picked up, though."

Right away, Leah knew Powers had no intention of talking about the weather. She got straight to the point. "Leah, I need you to answer some questions about last night's murder. Turns out the article we ran this morning scooped everybody else and now my phone's ringing off the hook for more details. I don't know what to tell anyone—"

Leah cut her off. "*Your* phones are ringing? You ain't heard ringing till you've come down here. It's nuts."

"Well, I guess my first question is, when will we get an official statement from your department?"

Leah let out a breath. "I really don't know. When we've got somethin' to state. Right now, we don't know any more than you do."

"I see. Do you think this is the same Stickman that was killin' folk fifteen years ago?"

Leah's head was shaking even though Powers couldn't see it. "I don't—no, I don't think it is. But it *could* be. I can't really give you an opinion on that at the moment. Again, we really don't—"

"Leah?" Powers asked, cutting her off this time.

"Yeah."

"Can we talk, like, off the record?"

"Um, sure. What's up?"

"You guys have to give the public something, or you're goin' to have hysteria on your hands. Everybody's thinking the worst. Like it's goin' to be a streak of killin's like before."

"There is no evidence to support that."

"The public doesn't care about evidence. They care

about you telling them that they're goin' to be safe. If you can't, things will get out of control. Even if you have to lie, tell folk they're goin' to be safe. Do you understand what I'm sayin' here?"

"Yeah, I think I do. Point taken. I'll try to put a statement together."

"Good. In the meantime, do you honestly think this is *not* the same Stickman as before? Still off the record, of course."

Leah thought this over while her eyes scanned her "Spotlight on Success" article. She got to the part where Powers referred to the case as her pa's "crowning achievement," and she knew the answer to the question. "Yes," she said. "I honestly think this is *not* the same man. Harry Stork was the Stickman, and Harry Stork is dead. My pa killed the boogeyman. I'll issue a statement before the end of the day."

Jacqueline Powers thanked her and Leah hung up the phone. *Even if you have to lie, tell folk they're goin' to be safe.* The words still rang in her ears.

Ethan finally decided to show up. He came in quietly (which wasn't hard with all the telephones ringing), opening the door slowly. Not that it mattered; Leah's desk sat eight feet from the door. She'd spotted Ethan through the window as he walked past on the sidewalk. At least he was earlier than his usual 11 A.M.: The clock had just clicked past nine-twenty-five.

Without so much as a "good morning" or even a "hello," Ethan marched straight past Leah and Chris and unlocked his office door. Leah thought she'd never seen a man move so fast while still give the semblance of walking. His office door *clicked* quietly closed behind him before she heard the strain of his desk chair and the annoying and unique squeak it made as he sat back in it, probably letting go of a deep breath he hadn't known he'd been holding.

Leah realized Chris was probably right: Ethan really was scared about what she was going to do. And well he should be, she thought. Ethan was in a bit of a tight squeeze. He couldn't very well fire her, not because she wasn't in the right for what she was about to do (she knew she was on pretty firm ground with this one), and not just because she was one of the only three people in all of Alvin trained to be a police officer. The big reason she felt so secure in her job was on account of Ethan and Leah's daddy being such good friends while her pa was alive. So close, they were almost like blood. You don't fire blood. You get mighty pissed off at it sometimes, and may say things you later regret, but blood is blood. At the end of the day, you go home happy, and you've always managed to say your piece and clear your chest.

Leah's anger about what happened last night had all but dissipated while she had been performing the job of inputting data, but seeing Ethan strut right past her without saying a word brought the irritation right back like a wet slap in the face. Pulling one of her blond bangs down over her face, she let go and felt it spring back into place. Her time to act had come. She had a piece or two to say and some chest clearing to do.

But first things first. She stood and brought her empty mug to the coffee machine, which Chris had so nicely just brewed. Since this morning, he'd been on his best behavior, even doing data entry alongside her instead of crossword puzzles. In fact, since they finished their talk, both his boots had remained on the floor instead of up on his desk.

Carrying her mug of fresh coffee with her, Leah started for Ethan's door.

Chris hung up the phone. "Oh, I'm about to hear some cussing and screaming, aren't I?" he asked.

Leah stopped and looked back. "No, you're about to hear someone get blamed for somethin' they did wrong. I realize people make mistakes all the time, but some mistakes you can't come back from. Like this one. We have a dead woman on our hands who very well might still be alive if that one little mistake hadn't been made."